W9-BXQ-414

100 Ghastly Little Ghost Stories

100 Ghastly Little Ghost Stories

Edited by
Stefan R. Dziemianowicz,
Robert A. Weinberg
& Martin H. Greenberg

BARNES
&NOBLE
BOOKS
NEW YORK

The edition published by Barnes & Noble, Inc.,
by arrangement with Martin H. Greenberg.

1993 Barnes & Noble Books

ISBN 1-56619-106-8

Printed and bound in the United States of America

M 9   8   7   6

Acknowledgments

"The Night Wire" by H. F. Arnold; "Drowned Argosies" by J. Wilmer Benjamin; "The Piper from Bhutan" by David Bernard; "Dust" by Edna Goit Brintnall; "A Visitor from Far Away" by Loretta M. Burrough; "Behind the Screen" by Dale Clark; "Highwaymen" by W. Benson Dooling; "McGill's Appointment" by Elsie Ellis; "Concert to Death" by Paul Ernst; "The Woman in Gray" by Walker G. Everett; "Rendezvous" by Richard H. Hart; "Ghosts of the Air" by J. M. Hiatt and Moye W. Stephens; "The Splendid Lie" by S. B. H. Hurst; "Date in the City Room" by Talbot Johns; "The Honor of Don Pedro" by Wallace J. Knapp; "He Walked by Day" by Julius Long; "Black Gold" by Thorp McClusky; "The Garret of Madame Lemoyne" by Kirk W. Mashburn, Jr.; "Mordecai's Pipe" by A. V. Milyer; "Mandolin" by Will Charles Oursler; "The Return" by G. G. Pendarves; "The Tree-Man Ghost" by Percy B. Prior; "Guarded" by Mearle Prout; "Edge of the Cliff" by Dorothy Quick; "Under the Eaves" by Helen M. Reid; "The Ghost Farm" by Susan Andrews Rice; "The Phantom Express" by H. Thompson Rich; "Shadows Cast Behind" by Otto E. A. Schmidt; "The Sixth Tree" by Edith Lichty Stewart; "The Light Was Green" by John Rawson Speer; "The Ghosts at Haddon-le-Green" by Alfred I. Tooke; "The Closed Door" by Harold Ward; "Attorney for the Damned" by Renier Wyers; "The Considerate Hosts" and "Dark Mummery" by Thorp McClusky.

All of the above are copyright © 1924–1938 by Popular Fiction Publishing Co.; copyright © 1938–1951 by Weird Tales. Reprinted by permission of Weird Tales Ltd.

"Away" by Barry N. Malzberg—Copyright © 1985 by Barry N. Malzberg. First published in A TREASURY OF AMERICAN HORROR STORIES. Reprinted by permission of the author. "Clocks" by Darrell Schweitzer—Copyright © 1989 by Phantasm Press. First published in THE HORROR SHOW, Spring 1989. Reprinted by permission of the author. "Coming Home" by Nina Kiriki Hoffman—Copyright © 1990 by Nina Kiriki Hoffman. First appeared in AUTHOR'S CHOICE MONTHLY #14. Reprinted by permission of the author. "Daddy" by Steve Rasnic Tem—Copyright © 1986 by Steve Rasnic

Contents

Introduction

The ghost story is the oldest type of supernatural tale, and thus the one closest to the European oral storytelling tradition. Initially, it was meant to be brief, the better to deliver its thrills to captivated listeners before the tenuous air of suspense had time to dissipate.

Although contemporary ghost fiction sometimes run to novel length, the short-short ghost story continues to entertain readers around the world. The proof can be found in *100 Ghastly Little Ghost Stories*, which brings together more than one-and-a-half centuries of compact ghost stories.

A sampling of the contents shows just how widespread the short-short ghost story's appeal is. The earliest (although by no means the first published), Joseph Sheridan Le Fanu's "The Ghost and the Bone-Setter," dates from 1838, and the most recent, Donald R. Burleson's "The Pedicab," was written especially for this volume. Although most of these stories were published originally in Great Britain or the United States, Guy Boothby's "A Strange Goldfield" first appeared in Australia, while Stefan Grabinski's "The Grey Room" (originally published in Poland) and Lafcadio Hearn's "A Dead Secret" (written by an American expatriate living in Japan) suggest the familiarity of the form in non-English-speaking countries. Writers who attempted the short-short ghost story include those whose names are synonymous with supernatural fiction (M. R. James, Ramsey Campbell), renowned figures in the literary mainstream (O. Henry, Oscar Wilde), and even authors who professed disdain for the traditional frights of supernatural horror fiction (H. P. Lovecraft).

Part of the reason for this popularity is the great amount of latitude possible within the short-short ghost story's narrow confines. Writers have used the form to explore a variety of human emotions and behaviors: avarice (Renier Wyers's "Attorney for the Damned," August Derleth's "Pacific 421"), revenge (Thorp McClusky's "Black Gold," H. P. Lovecraft's "The Terrible Old Man"), jealousy (Steve Rasnic Tem's "Daddy," constancy of character (Fred Chappell's "Miss Prue," Louisa Baldwin's "How He Left the Hotel"), obligation to duty (H. F. Arnold's "Night Wire"), honor (Ambrose Bierce's "The Stranger," Edith Nesbit's "John Charrington's Wedding"), love

(H. Warner Munn's "A Sprig of Rosemary," Darrell Schweitzer's "Clocks"), infidelity (Mary E. Braddon's "The Cold Embrace"), and family relationships (Al Sarrantonio's "Two").

The short-short ghost story has been used both to deliver reassurance of an afterlife (S. B. Hurst's "The Splendid Lie," Will Charles Oursler's "Mandolin") and to frighten with the horrors beyond the grave (Jessica Amanda Salmonson's "Harmless Ghosts"). The ghosts themselves can appear in a variety of forms, ranging from figments of memory (Nina Kiriki Hoffman's "Coming Home," Robert Sampson's "Relationships"), to inanimate objects imbued with personality (O. Henry's "The Furnished Room," A. V. Milyer's "Mordecai's Pipe"), fragments (W. C. Morrow's "The Haunted Burglar"), premonitions (Vincent O'Sullivan's "The Burned House," Arthur Gray's "The True History of Anthony Ffryar"), unfulfilled opportunities and expectations (Bernard Capes's "A Ghost-Child"), and projections of the haunted's personality (Clark Ashton Smith's "Thirteen Phantasms"). They can also be put to a variety of uses: comedy (Saki's "The Soul of Laploshka"), social satire (Barry Malzberg's "Away"), moral instruction (Richard Middleton's "On the Brighton Road"), and subjects for both stream of consciousness narrative (Alan Brennert's "Ghost Story") and prose poems (Alfred I. Tooke's "The Ghosts at Haddon-le-Green").

As far as readers are concerned, though, probably the most attractive quality of the short-short ghost story is that it uses a minimum of elements to evoke a powerful response. Just as it is possible to be scared by what you *don't* see, so is it possible to be haunted long after by this briefest of encounters with the supernatural. Fear comes in all shapes and sizes, and although these ghosts are small, they will loom large in your memory.

Stefan Dziemianowicz
New York, 1993

Across the Moors

by William Fryer Harvey

It really was most unfortunate.

Peggy had a temperature of nearly a hundred, and a pain in her side, and Mrs. Workington Bancroft knew that it was appendicitis. But there was no one whom she could send for the doctor.

James had gone with the jaunting-car to meet her husband who had at last managed to get away for a week's shooting.

Adolph, she had sent to the Evershams, only half an hour before, with a note for Lady Eva.

The cook could not manage to walk, even if dinner could be served without her.

Kate, as usual, was not to be trusted.

There remained Miss Craig.

"Of course, you must see that Peggy is really ill," said she, as the governess came into the room, in answer to her summons. "The difficulty is, that there is absolutely no one whom I can send for the doctor." Mrs. Workington Bancroft paused; she was always willing that those beneath her should have the privilege of offering the services which it was her right to command.

"So, perhaps, Miss Craig," she went on, "you would not mind walking over to Tebbits' Farm. I hear there is a Liverpool doctor staying there. Of course I know nothing about him, but we must take the risk, and I expect he'll be only too glad to be earning something during his holiday. It's nearly four miles, I know, and I'd never dream of asking you if it was not that I dread appendicitis so."

"Very well," said Miss Craig, "I suppose I must go; but I don't know the way."

"Oh you can't miss it," said Mrs. Workington Bancroft, in her anxiety temporarily forgiving the obvious unwillingness of her governess' consent.

"You follow the road across the moor for two miles, until you come to Redman's Cross. You turn to the left there, and follow a rough path that leads through a larch plantation. And Tebbits' farm lies just below you in the valley."

"And take Pontiff with you," she added, as the girl left the room.

"There's absolutely nothing to be afraid of, but I expect you'll feel happier with the dog."

"Well, miss," said the cook, when Miss Craig went into the kitchen to get her boots, which had been drying by the fire; "of course she knows best, but I don't think it's right after all that's happened for the mistress to send you across the moors on a night like this. It's not as if the doctor could do anything for Miss Margaret if you do bring him. Every child is like that once in a while. He'll only say put her to bed, and she's there already."

"I don't see what there is to be afraid of, cook," said Miss Craig as she laced her boots, "unless you believe in ghosts."

"I'm not so sure about that. Anyhow I don't like sleeping in a bed where the sheets are too short for you to pull them over your head. But don't you be frightened, miss. It's my belief that their bark is worse than their bite."

But though Miss Craig amused herself for some minutes by trying to imagine the bark of a ghost (a thing altogether different from the classical ghostly bark), she did not feel entirely at her ease.

She was naturally nervous, and living as she did in the hinterland of the servants' hall, she had heard vague details of true stories that were only myths in the drawing-room.

The very name of Redman's Cross sent a shiver through her; it must have been the place where that horrid murder was committed. She had forgotten the tale, though she remembered the name.

Her first disaster came soon enough.

Pontiff, who was naturally slow-witted, took more than five minutes to find out that it was only the governess he was escorting, but once the discovery had been made, he promptly turned tail, paying not the slightest heed to Miss Craig's feeble whistle. And then, to add to her discomfort, the rain came, not in heavy drops, but driving in sheets of thin spray that blotted out what few landmarks there were upon the moor.

They were very kind at Tebbits' farm. The doctor had gone back to Liverpool the day before, but Mrs. Tebbit gave her hot milk and turf cakes, and offered her reluctant son to show Miss Craig a shorter path on to the moor, that avoided the larch wood.

He was a monosyllabic youth, but his presence was cheering, and she felt the night doubly black when he left her at the last gate.

She trudged on wearily. Her thoughts had already gone back to the almost exhausted theme of the bark of ghosts, when she heard steps on the road behind her that were at least material. Next minute the figure of a man appeared: Miss Craig was relieved to see that the stranger was a clergyman. He raised his hat. "I believe we are both going in the same direction," he said. "Perhaps I may have the pleasure of escorting you." She thanked him. "It is rather weird at night," she went on, "and what with all the tales of ghosts and bogies that one hears from the country people, I've ended by being half afraid myself."

"I can understand your nervousness," he said, "especially on a night like this. I used at one time to feel the same, for my work often meant lonely walks across the moor to farms which were only reached by rough tracks difficult enough to find even in the daytime."

"And you never saw anything to frighten you—nothing immaterial I mean?"

"I can't really say that I did, but I had an experience eleven years ago which served as the turning point in my life, and since you seem to be now in much the same state of mind as I was then in, I will tell it you.

"The time of year was late September. I had been over to Westondale to see an old woman who was dying, and then, just as I was about to start on my way home, word came to me of another of my parishioners who had been suddenly taken ill only that morning. It was after seven when at last I started. A farmer saw me on my way, turning back when I reached the moor road.

"The sunset the previous evening had been one of the most lovely I ever remember seeing. The whole vault of heaven had been scattered with flakes of white cloud, tipped with rosy pink like the strewn petals of a full-blown rose.

"But that night all was changed. The sky was an absolutely dull slate colour, except in one corner of the west where a thin rift showed the last saffron tint of the sullen sunset. As I walked, stiff and footsore, my spirits sank. It must have been the marked contrast between the two evenings, the one so lovely, so full of promise (the corn was still out in the fields spoiling for fine weather), the other so gloomy, so sad with all the dead weight of autumn and winter days to come. And then added to this sense of heavy depression came another different feeling which I surprised myself by recognising as fear.

"I did not know why I was afraid.

"The moors lay on either side of me, unbroken except for a straggling line of turf shooting butts, that stood within a stone's-throw of the road.

"The only sound I had heard for the last half hour was the cry of the startled grouse—Go back, go back, go back. But yet the feeling of fear was there, affecting a low centre of my brain through some little used physical channel.

3

"I buttoned my coat closer, and tried to divert my thoughts by thinking of next Sunday's sermon.

"I had chosen to preach on Job. There is much in the old-fashioned notion of the book, apart from all the subtleties of the higher criticism, that appeals to country people; the loss of herds and crops, the break up of the family. I would not have dared to speak, had not I too been a farmer; my own glebe land had been flooded three weeks before, and I suppose I stood to lose as much as any man in the parish. As I walked along the road repeating to myself the first chapter of the book, I stopped at the twelfth verse.

" 'And the Lord said unto Satan: Behold all that he hath is in thy power' . . .

"The thought of the bad harvest (and that is an awful thought in these valleys) vanished. I seemed to gaze into an ocean of infinite darkness.

"I had often used, with the Sunday glibness of the tired priest, whose duty it is to preach three sermons in one day, the old simile of the chess board. God and the Devil were the players: and we were helping one side or the other. But until that night I had not thought of the possibility of my being only a pawn in the game, that God might throw away that the game might be won.

"I had reached the place where we are now, I remember it by that rough stone water-trough, when a man suddenly jumped up from the roadside. He had been seated on a heap of broken road metal.

" 'Which way are you going, guv'ner?' he said.

"I knew from the way he spoke that the man was a stranger. There are many at this time of the year who come up from the south, tramping northwards with the ripening corn. I told him my destination.

" 'We'll go along together,' he replied.

"It was too dark to see much of the man's face, but what little I made out was coarse and brutal.

"Then he began the half-menacing whine I knew so well—he had tramped miles that day, he had had no food since breakfast, and that was only a crust.

" 'Give us a copper,' he said, 'it's only for a night's lodging.'

"He was whittling away with a big clasp knife at an ash stake he had taken from some hedge."

The clergyman broke off.

"Are those the lights of your house?" he said. "We are nearer than I expected, but I shall have time to finish my story. I think I will, for you can run home in a couple of minutes, and I don't want you to be frightened when you are out on the moors again.

"As the man talked he seemed to have stepped out of the very background of my thoughts, his sordid tale, with the sad lies that hid a far sadder truth.

"He asked me the time.

"It was five minutes to nine. As I replaced my watch I glanced at his face. His teeth were clenched, and there was something in the gleam of his eyes that told me at once his purpose.

"Have you ever known how long a second is? For a third of a second I stood there facing him, filled with an overwhelming pity for myself and him; and then without a word of warning he was upon me. I felt nothing. A flash of lightning ran down my spine, I heard the dull crash of the ash stake, and then a very gentle patter like the sound of a far-distant stream. For a minute I lay in perfect happiness watching the lights of the house as they increased in number until the whole heaven shone with twinkling lamps.

"I could not have had a more painless death."

Miss Craig looked up. The man was gone; she was alone on the moor.

She ran to the house, her teeth chattering, ran to the solid shadow that crossed and recrossed the kitchen blind.

As she entered the hall, the clock on the stairs struck the hour.

It was nine o'clock.

Attorney
for the Damned

by Renier Wyers

Camberton knew, by the muffled ring, which of his two telephones to pick up. Yet, he hesitated. Who could be calling him at this late hour, on this secret, unlisted wire?

Only six of his underworld clients knew the number. Two of these gentlemen of doubtful integrity had just gone out the door; two were in Europe, and one in prison. The sixth was Burke Hawtin. But—Burke Hawtin was dead!

The muffled bell rang again. Camberton's pudgy hand closed on the cradled instrument and lifted it to his ear. He said nothing. He never spoke first on this line. Whoever knew the number of it was expected to know also the code word which had to be uttered before Camberton would respond.

Presently the word came: "Reference-room." It was spoken in low, unfamiliar tones.

"Who are you?" rasped Camberton. His round, pasty face was an expressionless mask, save for the glint of suspicion in his beady, fat-encircled eyes.

"A friend of Hawtin's," the unknown whispered. "He gave me this number. Said for me to call it when—when I'm in a jam."

"What's your name?"

"Smith. John Smi—"

"Very unusual," sneered Camberton. "I've never heard it before. I don't know you."

"Wait. You'll know me when you see me."

"Why should I see you?"

"Because I've got plenty of money for legal advice. Are you alone?"

"Yes, I am," drawled Camberton in a bored tone which was belied by the greed in his piggish eyes. "Do you know how to get here?"

"I know everything about you that Hawtin knew. I'll come up the back way—like—like *he* always did. I'll be there in ten minutes."

Horace L. Camberton, criminal lawyer, any way you say it, put down the telephone, leaned back in his chair and looked again at the newspaper item which he had been reading before the interruption. Early that morning, according to the item, Burke Hawtin and two confederates were shot to death while looting the First Industrial Bank of Willow Ridge, a southwestern suburb of Chicago. Hawtin's corpse was identified by the police. The other two had apparently been crime recruits. Their names were as yet unknown.

Camberton's only pang of regret, on reading the item, was in his purse. Hawtin had been a well-paying client; and, although he had not required legal counsel during the past year, he would have, sooner or later, had he not been mowed down.

Perhaps, reflected the attorney, this stranger who had just telephoned would take the place of the dear departed as a source of revenue. However, one couldn't be too sure. It was best to prepare for any kind of a comer.

From his library table, Camberton transferred a loaded revolver to his right-hand coat-pocket. Then he went into the bedchamber and opened the top drawer of his bureau. From this he took another loaded pistol which he dropped into his left-hand pocket.

He waddled impatiently back and forth in the two rooms which comprised his suite in the Avon Arms Hotel, a receivership skyscraper towering in Diversey Parkway, east of Clark Street. It was a nest of shysters, racketeers, and elegantly clad hoodlums. Ordinarily he felt perfectly at home in this environment, in the shadow of the double-cross, but tonight he was uneasy. Never before had he been so apprehensive of impending trouble as he was now, while awaiting his nocturnal visitor.

Rather than be called upon to open the door and find himself only several inches from his guest, he released the latch, backed across the room and sat down on a straight-backed chair, facing the entrance. Each of his clammy hands was plunged into a pocket, gripping a gun.

"Now," he thought, "if I don't like your looks, Mr. Smith, or whoever, or whatever you are, I'll make you back right out again. Nobody's going to pull a fast one on little Horace."

The knocking he presently heard was stealthy, almost inaudible. But loud and blustering was his response to it.

"Come in!" he shouted.

The door opened silently. A man whose broad shoulders and muscular arms bulged visibly under his tightly draped jacket stepped in and closed the door behind him. His right hand remained in his pocket, as though he, too, was grasping a weapon. With his other hand he tilted the dip-brimmed, summer-felt hat back from his forehead.

"Dernac!" exclaimed Camberton, jumping to his feet. There was no mistaking the name of this visitor. His face was pictured almost daily in the newspapers. He was Anton ("Tony") Dernac, widely publicized as America's Public Enemy Number One.

"So you do know me, after all," the stranger grunted, defiantly jutting out his jaw. "And you know there's a reward of twenty-five grand on my hide. But"—his pocketed hand lifted the coat slightly— "don't think you'll collect it. Besides, I can more than double the ante —if you'll work on my side."

Camberton's fat, greedy face broke into an oily grimace which he believed was a cordial smile. "Let's be friends," he said, extending a welcoming hand.

Dernac grinned out of the side of his mouth as he grasped the lawyer's flabby fingers in his own ham-like fist. "Okay. Now you're my mouthpiece and you'd better be a good one. That's what I need."

"You need a drink, too, my boy."

The two men sat down facing each other and talked; that is to say, Dernac talked. Camberton merely listened and watched his guest down one drink after another from the whisky bottle which the lawyer had placed on a convenient magazine table. Camberton, at the same time, simulated just the proper degree of sympathetic understanding. He was adept at it. It was in this way that he came to know so many things which necessitated such under-cover equipment as the secret telephone.

Dernac, the hunted, seemed eager to unburden himself to the attorney. For all his bulk and reputation as a hard hombre, he was plainly frightened. He had achieved too much notoriety for his peace of mind. Having lived by the gun he apparently feared death by the gun. Every man's hand was against him. He poured himself yet another drink and said:

"I met Hawtin in Minneapolis, about six months ago. He joined my gang and we did several jobs, payroll raids in St. Louis. The last one there wasn't so good. Three of my boys were killed."

"I remember reading about that," remarked Camberton, "but I didn't know that Hawtin was there—or you either."

"Nobody knows it, now. Hawtin and the other two were killed this morning." The bandit licked his lips. "I almost went along—but I had a hunch. Besides, why should I take any chances when I've got more than a hundred grand salted away? Part of it was Hawtin's. But he's dead and the rest of the mob that ain't dead is in jail. So there's nobody left to split with—exceptin' you. How much will it cost me to get out of the country?"

Camberton's porcine eyes narrowed as he looked at his visitor. Was it really possible for such a hulking lout to retain so much loot? Would he give up half, three-quarters of it to save his skin? The attorney was confident that both questions could be answered in the affirmative.

"It'll be a hard job," he said. "Your picture, given to the police by that dame you ditched, is being printed so often, nowadays, that your face is as well known as Babe Ruth's. Your mug and description are posted in every police chief's office, in every detective bureau and agency in the country—and in every post-office."

"That's just it. Even people who only look like me are getting arrested and shot at!" cried Dernac. "What chance have I got?"

"A good chance," said Camberton, watching his client closely. "But, as I said, it'll be a hard job—and expensive. There will be certain preliminary costs. First of all, I'd have to hire someone to do a little plastic surgery on that well-known face of yours. Then, too, I'd have to pay for 'fixing' aids along the route you're to take and—"

"Hell!" exclaimed Dernac; "if you're worried about my bein' able to pay—here's twenty-five grand for a starter." He reached into his breast pocket and tossed a packet of greenbacks into the attorney's lap. "And remember, there's more than a hundred grand where that came from. It's all safe and snug under the floor of the Ideal Shoe Repair Shop, just a few blocks from here." He hiccupped. Then, loosening his tongue with another drink of whisky, he rambled on: "Yeah, I own the Ideal Shoe Repair Shop. The old shoemaker who's supposed to own it is just a stooge for me. He learned cobbling in the penitentiary."

"Does he know the money's there?"

"Ha, ha! Not much! Old Fred Miller's too dumb to ever know anything important. All he knows is that I sometimes used the joint for business meetings with Hawtin and the boys. I always sent Miller out with enough money to get drunk on. Other times he sleeps there. I chased him out tonight, figgerin' that me and you might take a walk over there after a while and settle our deal."

Mere slits now, the criminal lawyer's greedy eyes flashed from the money to Dernac. Camberton thought fast. How much money would it be worth to risk disbarment, perhaps prison, if anything went wrong in smuggling his client out of the United States? The problem caused a frown to crease his round bland face.

Like a flash an easy solution suggested itself. He leered sinisterly at Dernac. Startled, the fugitive reached for his gun, but the lawyer, with a speed surprizing in one so fat and flabby, whipped out his own pistol and fired before the other could take aim.

Public Enemy Number One toppled from the chair, a bullet in his head.

With a deep breath of satisfaction, inhaling a whiff of gunpowder smoke, Camberton noted that his victim's lifeless hand still held a revolver. It would make the story of self-defense more dramatic. He arose, hurriedly put the packet of greenbacks in the wall-safe, leaving the door open, cleared away the whisky and glasses, and then picked up the telephone—the one connected with the hotel switchboard.

"Send for the police," he said calmly. "I've just shot a burglar. He looks like Tony Dernac."

Police officers, reporters, and hotel employees crowding into the suite a few moments later heard his thrilling narrative of how, upon returning from a stroll, he had caught Dernac in the act of ransacking the wall-safe.

"He rushed at me, his gun leveled at my heart. But I was quicker on the trigger."

"Ever see him before?" asked a police sergeant.

"Never. My guess as to his identity was based on press pictures I've seen."

"Gosh, Mr. Camberton," blurted one of the reporters. "You'll get the twenty-five thousand dollar reward!"

"That's so. I hadn't thought of it. I was merely trying to protect my life and property. I'll agree that perhaps I do deserve some reward for having rid society of a dangerous killer."

Highly pleased with himself, the lawyer then posed for innumerable newspaper photographs. He posed pointing his gun at the camera, pointing his finger at the wall-safe, shaking hands with the sergeant, shaking hands with the hotel manager, with bellhops, with chambermaids, with almost everyone excepting his dead victim. He obliged the cameramen willingly—refusing only the request of one who wanted him to stand with one foot resting on the corpse, in the manner of a big-game hunter. This, the attorney declared, would be beneath his dignity.

Not until the dark hour just before the dawn was he left alone. Excitedly he turned the leaves of his telephone directory, seeking the address of the Ideal Shoe Repair Shop. Here it was, "692 Elwell Court." Less than four blocks away! He patted the revolvers in his pockets, took an electric torch from his bureau, put on his hat and went out, leaving the building by a rear stairway.

Although only a few blocks from the brightly lighted corner of Clark and Broadway, Elwell Court was a shabby little side-street of dismal, frame shanties. Bleakest of these was number 692 with "Shoe Repairing" crudely lettered on the glass of the front door. It was hardly a place you would suspect of being the depository of a hundred thousand dollars in cash. Camberton, however, was confident that he would find this sum. He knew his crooks and had correctly judged Dernac as the simpleton that he was. The fool hadn't even put a modern lock on the door. Camberton's skeleton key opened it easily.

Inside, he observed that the weakened rays of a distant street lamp penetrated the grimy front windows just enough to cast a dim and eery light, blocked out here and there by machinery and furnishings which cast grotesque and misleading shadows. Feeling his way, he stepped forward. His shin encountered something in the dark—something that sprang through the air with a hissing spitting sound. Two yellow eyes glared balefully at him. He flashed his torch at it and cursed under his breath at the cat that arched its back in the glare. He threw the beam around the room to get his bearings.

There was a door at the rear of the shop. Camberton regarded it apprehensively as he put out the light. What if old Miller, who, according to Dernac, sometimes slept in the rear of the shop, had returned? The lawyer decided to look into that back room before searching for the loot.

Tiptoeing forward, he placed his hand on the door-knob. As he turned it, slowly and silently, a strange fear gripped him. It was unusual; for, though he was not the bravest man in the world, he was certainly not one to be frightened by darkness and the angrily gleaming eyes of a cat. The touch of terror was caused by something else, he knew not what. It angered him.

Forgetting his caution, he jerked the door open. An icy draft swept round him, enveloping him so completely that he shivered with intense cold. There was something wrong about this, too, this chill on a warm, July night. It required all his will-power to stop the quivering of his fatty flesh as he stared into the room: it was better lighted than the other. The illumination which streamed through the window came from the rear porch light of a house next door.

Camberton's nervous scrutiny sweeping the room was halted and held by an object in the darkest corner. It seemed to be the figure of a man lying on a cot. So! That old cobbler, Miller, had come back to sleep off his drunkenness here! But the odor that assailed Camberton's nostrils was not of alcohol. It was of something equally familiar, something that did not belong here. Sniffing to clear his nostrils and at the same time firmly grasping his revolver, Camberton started to slink toward the recumbent form, then stood stock-still, wide-eyed with fright.

The figure on the cot was sitting up—and it wasn't the figure of an old man. It was the husky, broad-shouldered figure of Tony Dernac, America's Public Enemy Number One! Tony Dernac, whose corpse at this moment should be stretched on a slab in the county morgue, was sitting up. The face of the figure seemed to gleam with a greenish phosphorescent light, making more horrible the vilipending leer that was directed at the horrified attorney. In the forehead of the face was a bullet hole. And the odor that was creeping into Camberton's brain was the odor of burnt gunpowder!

His round countenance paled to sickly white. His eyes almost popped out of their thick, fleshy pouches. He moved his lips but could not utter a sound.

11

"You!" he managed to croak at last, "you—why, damn you, Dernac, I killed you once and I'll kill you again."

He aimed his pistol at the apparition. The shanty seemed to shake as the gun roared again and again. The spurts of gunfire seemed to pierce right through the figure which rose slowly from the cot and moved relentlessly toward Camberton, step by step. The lawyer backed away from it, firing desperately. Try as he might, he could not turn and run. The eyes staring into his with a hypnotic fixedness seemed to fasten his own with invisible bands, permitting him to step back only as far as the other had stepped forward, no farther.

Sobbing wildly, Camberton pulled out his other gun and emptied its contents at the wraith. Automatically his twitching fingers jerked at the triggers of the emptied weapons, clicking them futilely.

That was the way the police squad-car crew found him, idiotically clicking the triggers of two empty guns. The shooting had aroused the neighborhood and brought the prowl car to number 692 within three minutes of the first crack of the first gun.

The lifeless body of old Fred Miller, riddled with the bullets from the attorney's pistols, lay on the cot. That was all that the police saw—that and the drooling madman who had once been Horace G. Camberton, well-known criminal attorney, pressing the revolver triggers like an automaton.

It is hardly likely that he will ever be tried for the murder of the aged shoemaker because he does not seem able to comprehend what he's done. In an asylum for the criminal insane, he crouches in his cell, insisting that he and Dernac were the only occupants of the back room at number 692.

Few people are permitted to visit the broken attorney. Fewer care to do so, since, as the authorities explain it, the mad terror which creeps over his face at intervals is of such awfulness that the most hardened observers shudder at the sight of it. The intervals are becoming more and more frequent. And, should the apparent suffering he experiences in these intervals become a permanent mental condition, it will not be necessary to punish Horace L. Camberton further for his crimes.

Away

by Barry N. Malzberg

My name is Josiah Bushnell Grinnell. In 1853, responding to the invocation of the famous Horace Greeley, publisher of the New York Tribune, I take myself to the new state of Iowa and thereupon establish both a town and a college. "Go west, young man, go west and grow with the country," Greeley has said, and solemn young fellow that I am, I take him seriously. What a surprise, what a disappointment to learn only after I am established where the tall corn grows that Greeley stole this from an obscure Indiana newspaperman named Soule and has appropriated the statement as his own. If I had known this, I might have gone to Indiana.

Instead, here I am in Iowa. What an unusually solemn man I am! I have always taken the invocations of my elders seriously, which is why the college I establish, the town to be named after me, the entire state itself takes on a somewhat sectarian whiff. A century later it is impossible for citizens to enter upon our interstates without murmuring prayers. In 1857, Sioux Indians massacre men, women, and children at Spirit Lake, the last massacre by Indians in the midwest and the released souls, the violated spirits add their pain and terror to the general chatter. On a hot May afternoon, the dead sun sprawling low in the panels of sky, the sounds of the cattle rising toward the dusk, it is possible to imagine oneself if one were a small man lying in a field, gazing, that one had entered upon the outer regions of the landscape painted by the honorable John Calvin. It is a difficult state, a difficult time.

I, Josiah Bushnell Grinnell, know this; know of all the interstices and difficulties of the sovereign state of Iowa. Cleaved from the Wisconsin territory, admitted to statehood on December 28, 1846, Iowa sprawls, flatland, on the way to the west. There are ways around it— there are ways around everything the good Lord knows—but once on the interstate, it is hard to find the way.

Here it is. It is 1954. I have been deceased for many decades, however, my spirit—no less than those massacred at Spirit Lake—lives on. Iowa is the possessor of its inhabitants, no one who has ever lived in this state has known true release. We hang around. This may seem an unlikely statement, a remarkable condition, but wait your turn, enjoy the common passage before you act in judgment. Here in 1954 the senior senator from this great state, the honorable, if that is quite the term I am seeking, Bourke B. Hickenlooper is inveighing against the Communists at a Fourth of July picnic. Hickenlooper, with McCarthy, with Jenner, is the pride of what may be called the conservative wing. To Hickenlooper it is an insult when the first Negro set the first Negro foot on the Negro shores of the first Negro city in this country, uttering incoherent Negro chants. It is not that Hickenlooper is a racist, you understand. It is merely that he is still linked to Spirit Lake by ancestry and blood, still sees the frame of the assassin arched against the moonlight. "We must expel the Communists from our shores," Hickenlooper says. He is on a podium, at some remove from the crowd, screaming without benefit of microphone. Fourth of July picnics are still important in the Iowa of this time. Politicians are expected to make speeches, to invoke Americana. Hickenlooper is merely doing his duty. Of his true thoughts of the matter we know not. He may or may not have an interior. Most politicians do not. "McCarran Act!" Hickenlooper screams. "Joseph McCarthy! Millard Tydings! Eighty-seven hundred card-carrying Communists!" And so on. The crowd reacts stiffly. It is very hot. A band plays in the distance, raucous parade ground arias of the kind soon enough to be popularized by Meredith Willson (born in Mason City) in *The Music Man*. "Who promoted Peress?" Hickenlooper asks. The crowd mutters. Their mood is not hostile but they are tired.

My name is Josiah Bushnell Grinnell. It is hard to explain exactly what I am doing at this picnic or what I expect to come of it. We Iowans (or transplanted Iowans) as I have said, our spirits live on. Even after death. Relegated to some limbo we come in and out, reincarnates or observers, bound to some flatland of the spirit, replicating our history, moving in and out of time. Screams of the settlers at Spirit Lake. Bullshit of Greeley. Moving ever west. From this limbo I emerge at odd times, strange moments, find myself at Iowa State Events. Such seems to be the case now. I am jammed in with this crowd, listening to Bourke B. Hickenlooper. To my left and right are Iowans of various sexes and ages, most of them young, in a burst of color, standing at parade rest, listening to the rantings of the honorable senator. Now and then a baby yowls or a young woman faints, her parasol preceding her on a graceless slide to the ground. Men leap to the rescue of the women, the babies are pacified in other ways. The huge bowl of the sky presses. It is indecently hot, even for a spirit, even for the gullible sectarian spirit of a man who would listen to Horace Greeley (at least I

14

never knew of Horatio Alger; it is impossible to say to what state he might have sent me.) "Hickenlooper!" I shout. "Hey, Hickenlooper!"

The crowd stares at me. Sometimes I can be heard and sometimes not; sometimes I am visible and at other times invisible. Reincarnation, like life itself, is a chancy business. At this time it would appear that I can be seen. Yards down range the senator stares at me, his stride momentarily broken. "Hey, Senator!" I shout. Hickenlooper removes his enormous hat, peers at me. I stride forward, closing the ground between us.

"You're all wrong, don't you know that?" I say. "Listen to me!" I say, turning around, gesturing at the farmers, their wives, the beaus and beauxettes in their holiday undress who look at me incuriously. "This man is not telling the truth. We lived to open frontiers, he is closing them!"

I am stared at incomprehendingly. One could, after all, envision no other possibility. Politics may be entertainment but metaphysics is unendurable in the Hawkeye State. "He speaketh with forked tongue!" I point out.

There are a forest of shrugs around me. I turn back toward the podium, find Hickenlooper in brisk conference with several aides who have jumped to the sides of the platform. He cups an ear, listens intently. They gesture at me. "Answer the charge!" I yell. "Don't hide behind the others, explain yourself. Tell why you are breeding fear, why you are seeking to close off that which will be opened."

Hickenlooper points at me. The hand is commanding, enormous. At my side, suddenly, are two earnest, honest Iowa state police; they seize me by the elbows. "If you will, sir," one says, "if you'll just come along."

"Don't arrest me," I say, struggling in their grasp, "arrest that man. That man is the assassin. I am Josiah Bushnell Grinnell, the founder of Grinnell College. I am a man of substance—"

"Card-carrying!" I hear Hickenlooper shout and then, this is the truth, I hear no more; speedily, forcibly, forcefully, I am carried from the grounds. Beaus and beauxettes, farmers and their daughters, little towheaded children and Iowa cattle, they all look at me mournfully. The troopers are insistent. "Don't you understand?" I say to them. "This isn't the end, this is just the passage, it's going to happen again, again and *again*—"

"Stay calm, sir," one says, "everything will be all right. Just don't struggle, understand the situation—"

I close my eyes. Again and again and it is too late. In the sudden, cool rushing darkness ninety-seven years are taken from me as if by death itself and I am at Spirit Lake once more, oh God, I am at Spirit Lake and in the sudden, clinging, rushing, tumultuous darkness, I hear the sound of the Sioux closing in around us; one high wail coming then, concentrating them, poised—

I scream then, try once more to give the alarm. But I cannot; my throat is dry, my lungs are cut out, my fate is darkness; in the night, eleven years after union, three years before the Civil War, they are coming, they are coming and the stain will leach outward, ever outward—

Go west, young man, go west—

I listened, I came. I propagated, and I could not save them. And in the face of the Hickenloopers, through to dissolution itself, I never, never will. Until by something that is, at last, beyond me, I too will be cut off.

𝕭𝔢𝔥𝔦𝔫𝔡 𝔱𝔥𝔢 𝔖𝔠𝔯𝔢𝔢𝔫

by Dale Clark

Sight of the police officer at the corner roused Catlin from his delirious frenzy like a spray of cold water. He stopped short; he gasped, almost expelling the cigarette from his mouth. The lifting red haze of anger and dismay left him sober and shivering, and a little stunned. He stared stupidly up the dingy Chinatown street into which the first rays of the morning were stealing. He had run many blocks, perhaps miles, to reach the heart of this dismal and unsavory quarter. But why? He could not say. Somnambulistic fumes clouded his mind; he could remember only plunging on madly and blindly without having noticed either his direction or the breaking of day overhead. It was as if some invisible power had guided his flight. Aroused now, Catlin found his situation inexpressibly terrifying. And after a glance at the slit trouser leg, where the recently shaved flesh showed a bald and chalky white, he shrank into the doorway under the sign of Lung Wei.

To Catlin's surprize, the latch yielded under his fumbling hand. Inside, he stood stock-still, puffing hard at the cigarette and staring warily about the shop. A melancholy light leaking through the small, dust-coated window quickly melted and died in the pervading murky gloom. But a faint and nebulous glow spread from an Oriental screen stretched across the rear of the long, narrow, low room. The screen was of some translucent and gauzy stuff; it had the color of silver, and shimmered with a rosy iridescence as minute ripples stirred the gossamer surface.

Behind the screen, a single candle burned with a wan and discouraged flame; its dim glimmer fell in crepuscular half-tones upon a robed figure slumbering in a cane chair. That, too, was behind the gauzy curtain.

Catlin wet his lips nervously. An uneasy sensation overpowered him: it was that he had been here before. But that, of course, could not be. His mind was playing tricks again. . . . Then he smiled harshly.

It was the odor he had recognized. There was in the shop a smell of dead incense, dry and musty and blended with the peculiar trail of opium. The musky taste in the air resembled that which he had often detected in his wife's room—she was a narcotic addict.

It was only the odor; it could be nothing more.

On tiptoe, without making a sound, he advanced into the shadows and inspected the squat show-cases and counters ranged along the low walls. He saw tiny figurines of wood and jade, vases and jars of porcelain, cabinets, sandals, and embroidered cloths. But there was nothing he could convert into money without much difficulty.

He glided toward the screen. (He had become marvelously adept in muffling his footfalls, these past few hours.)

Nevertheless, the figure in the chair behind the screen stirred, and looked around, and arose. He was Chinese, and very old. He came close to the diaphanous gauze, smiling a strange and enigmatic smile.

"Ah, here you are!" he said. "At last!"

This Lung Wei wore a black skull-cap, and had gathered about his thin shoulders a stiff, richly brocaded crimson robe. Above the robe, his thin, wrinkled, clean-shaven face had in its expression the delicacy of ancient and yellowed lace. It was, in fact, an expression too delicate, too indefinable, for analysis; it was bland, inscrutable, and mystic as well.

Staring, Catlin forgot that he had been about to hurl himself through the screen. It struck him that there was something dimly familiar in that countenance; he might have glimpsed Lung Wei in a crowd once, or it might have been only in a dream.

"Yes," he faltered, confused.

"I knew you'd come," the Oriental said. He spoke without any accent, with the merest sibilant slurring of syllables. "You see, I have waited so patiently!"

Catlin reflected. Concealed as he stood in the shadows—and seen through the screen, too—he decided that the Chinaman had mistaken him for someone else.

"Well, here I am!" he parried gruffly. It could be no harm, this little game.

Lung Wei arched his eyebrows. "You are not afraid, young sir?" he asked softly.

Catlin puffed his cigarette. "No," he said with a laugh. "Not at all. Of course not."

"That is well." The Oriental removed his hands from the sleeves of the robe, extending them in a curious gesture of—was it appeal? Or perhaps invitation. The outspread fingers looked quite as tenuous and pale as the gossamer screen itself. "You must believe this," he said, "that I want only to help you."

Catlin did not say anything, but his heart began to beat with a furious, groping hope. Decidedly, this became interesting!

Lung Wei regarded him steadily through the shimmering curtain. "That is why I waited so long. I thought that I might be of some service to you." The delicate, unknowable smile played upon his worn and yellowed face. "Do you find that hard to understand? You—you are so very young! That was what impressed me at the first—your so-blind youth. I wonder what you thought of me. Perhaps that I was so very old, eh? Or perhaps you did not think at all?"

The musing voice dripped away into placid silence. Catlin leaned watchfully against a show-case, filling his lungs with the cigarette smoke and letting it drift from his nostrils. He said nothing. There was nothing to say.

"You do not understand, do you?" the Oriental murmured.

Catlin watched the candle brighten, watched a ripple of ruby cross the screen.

"No," he said at last.

"But that is natural." Lung Wei bobbed his head sagely. "It is confusing. One is not exactly prepared. And then, you left in such haste. You have had no time to think."

Cold perspiration cropped forth on Catlin's face at these soft, sibilant words. Some divining sixth sense warned him of an inexplicable peril.

"No!" he exclaimed roughly. "I—that is, you—both of us—why,

it's all a mistake! I'm not the man, whoever he is, you were waiting for; I came in to"—he hesitated—"to the wrong shop!"

But with his enigmatic and relentless smile, the old Chinaman said: "In that case, you had better go back. If you think I can help you when you have returned to the prison—"

With a strangled cry, Catlin started toward the screen. He raised his clenched fist.

"So you know!" he panted.

Then, and at the moment he was about to dash aside the shimmering veil, a dazzling light burst within his disordered mind; he stopped short, and the fist dropped numbly to his side.

"But then," he faltered, "if you knew—what you said about helping me—?"

He peered at the face of Lung Wei, serene and bland behind the gauze.

"It's a trick!" he said hoarsely. "A Chinese trick!"

Lung Wei laughed musically. It was not a laugh of amusement or of scorn; there was perhaps a note of pity in it.

"You do not understand, young sir," the liquid voice said.

"No," Catlin muttered.

He felt strangely dizzy. That was the sheen of the candlelight flickering on the glistening gossamer; that, and the smell of the dead incense crawling into his lungs and into his very blood.

He began to walk to and fro in front of the curtain. Presently he said slowly, "There is one solution. This man I killed—you knew him, is that it? He might have been your enemy. Let us say, he belonged to a rival Tong. That is why you offer me your help?"

He stared interrogatively at the veil. But the face of the Chinaman remained impassive, like a sheet of parchment wrinkled into indecipherable lines.

Catlin made an apologetic gesture, an opening and falling of his hands. "I do not expect you to commit yourself," he said hurriedly. "It does not matter. The thing is, I must get away. I need money. Clothes." He looked despairingly at the slit trouser leg. "I can't go far, like this."

"It is not that," Lung Wei said. "You will have to tell me exactly what happened. Otherwise—I am sorry. There would be nothing I could do."

Catlin took a long pull at the cigarette.

"I know what you mean," he muttered. "You are afraid. You needn't be. They can't trace me here. No one has seen me since I escaped. No one at all."

"We are talking at cross-purposes," Lung Wei said. "If you will tell me exactly how it was—then, it may be, I can help."

"I am at your mercy," Catlin muttered. "I will try to remember. It is not very clear—there are things I can recall perfectly, and other parts of it that are quite gone."

Lung Wei made again that gesture of appeal—of sympathy, it might have been—with his hands outspread, the fingers like pale smoke, the palms dark shadows. "It is for your good, young sir."

Catlin shivered. "The worst was when the priest put the oil, the peculiar oil, over my eyes. And on my fingers. That happened, you understand, in the cell. It was because I could not stand any more! I rolled the cigarette. And when I licked it, at the same time I dropped onto my tongue the wad of cigarette papers."

He looked through the screen into the Oriental's face.

"The pellet tasted bitter. In your country, you know about that. You may have saturated paper, or a cloth with a drug? That is the way Blossom—my wife—smuggled this stuff to me."

He stood silent, thinking, watching the smoke drift upward from his lips into the dry, dead-scented air.

"I did not intend to kill that man," he said at last. "I am a respectable man, a chemist. And I could not earn money enough for her—for Blossom—to buy that stuff. That was how she met Trent, Billy Trent, met him in one of those dens where they smoke it. They put their heads together and told me how I could get it for them. It was Trent's gun I used. They waited outside in his automobile and I went in; they sent me in because the dealer would not know me. But I did not intend to kill him."

He resumed his pacing in front of the screen.

"The police were continually after me, continually asking me who had been in the car. They even promised to commute the sentence to life imprisonment if I'd tell where I got the gun. That was why Blossom brought me the cigarette papers—so at the last I wouldn't lose my nerve and confess. Being doped, you see, I could go to the chair without any fear. I swallowed the wad, the whole pellet, all that she had brought me.

"I could feel it burning in my stomach. I wasn't used to that sort of thing, and for a while I was afraid it wouldn't take hold soon enough. The warden had come in. I tried to put him off, asking for a match to light the cigarette. He didn't have one. Perhaps he saw through me. I had been sitting on the edge of the bunk; I got up and went over to the wash-stand to the candles, those candles the priest was burning.

"I remember he said something horrified. Then it happened. As I straightened up from the candles, with the first puff I became all at once sick. The dose must have been a big one. I staggered. I could feel and hear the bones in my head grinding and crunching upon themselves. When I opened my eyes, I was lying on the floor. I sat up and looked around. The priest was kneeling there in front of his candles, praying. His robe made it look like he was kneeling in a pool of black water, the robe spilled around his knees. The warden was gone."

Catlin flung back his head and laughed, filling the shop with the reverberations of his laughter.

"I suppose he had run to get the prison doctor, making sure I shouldn't cheat the chair, after all!"

He lowered his voice.

"You won't believe it," he said, "but he had left the cell door open. I crept there, on my hands and knees, so as not to disturb the priest. And the corridor was empty. I closed my eyes and opened them again to make sure.

"So I went out. I walked down the corridor, and down the stair, and so into the prison yard. You understand, all this was in the dark, before sunrise. I waited there beside the death-house wall. After a while they opened the gate to let in a car—newspaper men coming to cover the execution—and I ran out through the open gate. No one saw me."

He looked fixedly at the man behind the screen of gauze.

"It was as simple as that," he said insistently. "It was as easy as coming in here, coming into your shop."

"Of course," said Lung Wei. "Proceed."

"I went straight home," Catlin muttered. "I thought that the three of us—Blossom, and Trent, and I—could think of some safe place for me. I remember fancying how, afterward, we'd all laugh about the way that drug fooled the warden. I was quite happy about it."

The Chinaman gave him a curious glance. "Did you walk?" he asked.

Catlin became confused. "I don't know," he stammered. "I can't remember—the drug, you see—I suppose I took a street-car. It is quite a long way. I suppose that is what I did. I am perfectly sure no one noticed me, however it was."

The Oriental said, "But it is important, young sir. Can't you think?"

"I got there, anyway," Catlin told him. "I rang the bell—rang it again and again. And Blossom didn't answer. I waited there on the porch, smoking, and trying to think what to do next. And then a car—

Trent's car—stopped out in front, and those two came up onto the porch together."

His voice trembled.

"They were in evening clothes. They had been to some club or other. On the night I was to die, you see, it had been that way with them. They had been dancing and drinking. I smelled the liquor on them when I went up and spoke to her."

The eyes of the Oriental burned with a strange eagerness. "So, young sir—?"

"She did not even hear me!" Catlin declared. He avoided the gaze of Lung Wei, and continued wearily:

"They had eyes and ears only for each other. Without noticing me, they fell into each other's arms."

He began to laugh shakily. "Perhaps I should have killed them both! On the contrary, I was glad to escape. I was like an animal crawling away to lick its hurt in silence. Besides, would they have helped me? They would only have notified the police!" Then he added, almost calmly, "But, as they did not see me, there is no danger from that source."

"That is true," said Lung Wei. He appeared to reflect; his pointed yellow chin rested upon the gathered collar of the brocade robe, and his eyes were lowered.

"Your cigarette," he said at last.

"What did you say?" Catlin asked.

He stared at the screen, which had grown suddenly brighter, with a myriad of little colored glints flashing upon its shining surface. The candle in the background burned no better than before. . . . The gossamer seemed to quiver and glow with a luminous life of its own.

He looked down at the cigarette. The steady white wisp rose in a spiral from its end, from the little molten tip; and he had been smoking it for so long, for hours perhaps.

"Did I roll another?" he asked in bewilderment. "I don't remember that."

"If you will observe its odor," said the liquid Oriental voice of Lung Wei. "That is not a drug, young sir. I, who am used to such things, recognize the presence of a poison—"

"*Poison!*" cried Catlin in a dry sob. "Then she—then that is why—but *that* would mean—"

The words stumbled and blurred into a groan as Catlin reeled back from the thought. He stared blankly into that shimmering veil of gauze. And now it blazed up in pitiless molten brilliance; it extended to titanic proportions; it became a scroll of fire. His confused eyes beheld incandescent suns wheeling in its argent depths. He cowered in a funnel of searing light. His flesh seemed to shrivel in that glare, his breath clotted in his throat, and a fierce whining, crackling sound thrashed and gibbered about his ears. The suns rushed past him, the curtain enfolded him and drew him into a weird spaceland where the myriad lights receded to pin-points. This sudden darkness was more terrible than the intolerable light had been. With a cry of despair he plunged ahead, striking madly with both fists.

Then he realized that he was fighting the little gauze screen. The gossamer was cool, like a stream of water passing over his hands. It tore with a strange tinkling sound, a patter of distant bells.

It lay in a cloud of crumpled silver at his feet. The little jeweled particles in the fabric winked in the candle-light.

Catlin raised his eyes to the face of Lung Wei.

A chill seized him; the next moment, a fever came stinging through his veins. Without the screen to veil it, the face was—

"I remember you, now," he said. "You are the man I killed."

The Oriental smiled his enigmatic, mystic smile.

"That is so," replied the imperturbable yellow man. "You understand, then. Are you ready?"

"Ready?" Catlin faltered.

"To go," said Lung Wei.

Catlin nodded. Lung Wei blew out the candle, and walked out of the shop, and the younger man followed.

There was a long moment in which Lung Wei locked the door of his establishment, and in which Catlin stood gazing into the street. The sun was well up, now, and a thin trickle of traffic stirred upon the pavement. A milk-wagon clattered over the street-car rails. A fruit peddler went by, his legs scissoring between the shafts of his cart. Away off in the city a factory whistle blew.

Catlin touched the brocaded sleeve of Lung Wei.

"Which way?" he asked.

Black Gold

by Thorp McClusky

Henry Cabot Wade stood in the small main cabin of the schooner *Marianne,* his patrician forefinger pointing out a small black cross that enigmatically marked the faded chart beneath his hands. Henry Cabot Wade's thin shoulders were stooped, for the cabin, although comfortably appointed, was low-ceiled. The last of the Wades was not as rich as his forefathers had been; as the family fortunes had shrunk so had their sailing craft.

"I think that this is the spot, Captain Manly." Wade's voice was thin, New Englandish, like the bite of frosty air.

Jeremiah Manly nodded. He spoke in a slow, twangy drawl.

"Yes. These are without doubt the two islands indicated on the chart. The strait between is the proper width, and our soundings indicate six fathoms of water."

Wade smiled bleakly.

"I suppose it is too late to begin the search today."

"Yes. The sunlight is fading. We'll remain at this anchorage for the night, and begin work around ten in the morning."

Wade's precise smile broadened.

"That glass-bottomed boat should get results in quick time. This isn't a wide channel." For a moment he squinted at the chart. "I wonder what we'll find? Black gold! What a secretive way for my revered ancestor to put it down on paper! Ten tons of black gold! And he hid this chart away in the bottom of his personal chest, so carefully. What *is* black gold?"

Both men stared down at the chart.

It *was* enigmatic—that black cross marked at the mouth of a narrow strait that ran between two small islands. But more enigmatic than the aged chart was the incoherent message written in irregular, angular letters across its face:

Here lie, six fathoms down, ten tons of black gold. And I know now that for this crime I am accursed. May God have mercy on my soul!

Captain Manly cleared his throat in embarrassment.

"You know how your ancestor Ebenezer Wade got his wealth, I assume?"

The owner's lips curled in a thin smile.

"Oh, yes, Captain," he assented, not at all apologetically. "He ran slaves. He bought them on the west coast of Africa and sold them in Savannah and New Orleans. There was money in it. We Wades, until the stock market up and busted us, always made money. Buying furs from the Indians, running loan banks, plunging in stocks—we were always exploiters, we Wades. Don't worry, Captain Manly; I know the bourgeois opinion of our family. But, as man to man it's the only way to get along."

Captain Manly did not lift his eyes from the chart.

"Perhaps," he said then, dryly. "A great many people seem to agree with you. But all this is beside the point. Mr. Wade, did you ever hear the old story that your great-grandfather dumped a shipload of niggers overboard—one time a curious frigate chased him? That he never went to sea afterward?"

Wade laughed sardonically.

"No Wade would have been that soft."

Captain Manly stroked his grizzled chin. He kept his eyes focused on the chart as he replied:

"This is a narrow, shallow channel, Mr. Wade. A light vessel, if chased, would very likely put in here, where a square-rigged frigate might be expected to have trouble, especially with a quartering wind. It would give a man time to unload his cargo. Nigger smell isn't real evidence, Mr. Wade."

For an instant the small cabin was still. Then Wade smiled, a trifle thinly.

"You're trying to tell me that one of my ancestors was fool enough to draw a chart showing where he'd dumped overboard a shipload of niggers?" he snapped. "You don't know the Wades."

Captain Manly's eyes lifted to the owner's finely chiseled face.

"No person can say with certainty what another human being might do," he said quietly.

Wade laughed harshly.

"We Wades *aren't* human beings—or so a great many people have said. I'll go on deck now and join Evelyn."

Slowly, as the owner stooped through the companionway, Captain Manly rolled up the chart.

"Thank heaven, Aunt Leona's gone to bed at last."

Evelyn Phelps' clear, faintly metallic voice tinkled the words. With an appreciative laugh her fiancé hunched his deck chair closer to her own and slipped his wiry right arm possessively about her shoulders. Behind their backs the foremast, a naked black finger, reared up toward the stars. The tropic breeze, balmy from the near-by Gulf Stream, fragrant with the scent of near-by land, whispered in their faces; the islands to port and starboard were low-lying, palm-fringed masses edged with gleaming white. The moon climbing over the bowsprit was bigger than an orange.

Henry Cabot Wade chuckled.

"A chaperone can be a nuisance on a night like this."

The girl sighed. "Isn't it lovely? Boston seems so far away—and money so unimportant."

For an instant, while the thought of their desiccated family fortunes swept between them, they were silent. No one knew better than they that if this search for black gold proved a failure she must marry someone else.

Restlessly, Henry Cabot Wade stirred.

"We'll get it up," he promised her, the words hard, "if we have to search every inch of this damned channel. We've brought the best diver money could buy, dynamite enough to blow up a city—"

She turned toward him and kissed his cheek, the fringe of his eyelashes, his thin, cruel lips. She admired his profile, sensitive, aquiline, somehow like that of a great predatory bird. . . .

They made love, while the moon crept from above the bowsprit to the foremast. . . .

Suddenly he stiffened, sat erect.

"Look there," he said sharply, pointing forward. Then he shook his head bewilderedly. "It's gone. Did you see it?"

She was touching her disheveled hair into place.

"See what?" she asked, her voice sleepy and warm. "I didn't see anything."

Puzzledly he muttered, "I thought I saw a—a head appear momentarily above the rail, and then vanish. It was just a—sort of dark blob. Optical illusion, I guess." He shrugged, took her, unresisting, in his arms. For long minutes they loved.

Then, abruptly, he loosed her, turned his head to peer forward. He had heard, distinctly, a soft, naked shuffling behind him!

And in that instant a strangled, high-pitched scream burst from his lips, and he was stumbling, scrambling to his feet, his face ashen, his mouth and eyes hideous with terror.

"Run, Evelyn, run!" He was flailing out with his fists in the moonlight, flailing out into—emptiness!

Swiftly she rose, took one step toward him. But he motioned her back. "Run! run! Get Captain Manly—I'll hold them off as long as I can!"

She found her voice, then. "Henry Cabot Wade," she said sharply, "have you gone suddenly crazy? Or is this your idea of humor?"

He did not seem to hear. And suddenly her flesh crawled.

His right fist, lashing out frenziedly, had jolted to an abrupt stop, as though it had struck something she could not see. And slowly, step by step, he was backing, backing toward the rail.

She could see his face now, half turned toward her. And she could see that this was no play-acting, that whatever was happening was, to him at least, horribly real. And still his fists lashed out, until suddenly his left arm lashed out no more, but remained close to his side, tugging, struggling weirdly, as though pinioned to his body by invisible hands.

And through his screams came nightmarish words:

"Run, Evelyn, run! For God's sake, get help! They're swarming over the rail; they're too many for me. Big black niggers, in rusty chains—ahh!"

The words ended in a bubbling moan. His right hand clawed frantically at his throat.

Like a puppet dangling at the end of invisible strings, he rose up and over the rail, *backward*, and vanished from sight. There was a hollow splash. . . .

Evelyn heard her own voice, babbling incoherently. Intermittent, chill waves of terror swept over her, waves of terror and of horror. For she knew that no man could have leaped like that—over the rail. And the deck was moon-bathed, serene in its utter desertedness. . . .

𝔍𝔍𝔍

Captain Jeremiah Manly stood at the *Marianne*'s rail, ear-phones clamped to his head, looking down into the gray, gently heaving channel. His face, in the early dawn, was pale, and there was an odd quaver in his voice as he talked, in low tones, with the diver thirty feet below.

Except for the rhythmic soughing of the pump and the murmur of his own words there was no sound on the *Marianne*'s deck. Evelyn Phelps was below, asleep; her aunt had given her morphine. The three members of the crew who were on deck did not speak.

The diver's mechanical speech came through the ear-phones.

"All right. Haul away. Then bring me up. I'm gettin' the jitters."

Half a minute later Henry Cabot Wade's body, the end of a half-inch rope knotted beneath the armpits, came over the rail. The sailors put the dripping corpse down gingerly on the deck and covered it with a tarpaulin.

The diver came up next, bulbous and cumbersome in his heavy suit and helmet. While the sailors stripped him of his helmet Captain Manly took the ear-phones from his own head and put them down with a sigh of relief. The soughing of the pump had ceased.

The diver climbed out of his suit, left it lying in a dripping heap on the deck. He looked at Captain Manly, and Captain Manly saw that the pupils of his eyes were enormous. Suddenly he began to tremble. He was afraid, now that he was safe on deck.

When he spoke, his voice was a croak.

"They were down there, dozens of them—skeletons picked clean by barracuda and shark—all linked together by one endless chain with half a ton of ballast on the end."

Captain Manly's lips moved. But no distinguishable words came forth. The diver sat down weakly beside the pump. He did not look toward the tarpaulin-shrouded form.

"Wade was tangled up in them—there were twenty or more of them piled *on top of him!* They broke all apart when I touched them.

"And one of them, right on the bottom of the pile, had him by the throat. I had to pick the fingerbones out of his neck. And the strangler wore this—this thing."

He extended a peculiar-looking ornament toward Captain Manly. Both men stared silently at the object.

It was a necklace of enormous *teeth*, curiously carved, and bound together by a thin golden wire.

Captain Manly cleared his throat. His mouth felt oddly dry.

"God!" he said, then, slowly. "He must've been a witch-doctor, a *shaman*. I've read about such things in the National Geographic Magazine. He must've put a curse on the Wades."

Bone to His Bone

by E. G. Swain

William Whitehead, Fellow of Emmanuel College, in the University of Cambridge, became Vicar of Stoneground in the year 1731. The annals of his incumbency were doubtless short and simple: they have not survived. In his day were no newspapers to collect gossip, no Parish Magazines to record the simple events of parochial life. One event, however, of greater moment then than now, is recorded in two places. Vicar Whitehead failed in health after 23 years of work, and journeyed to Bath in what his monument calls 'the vain hope of being restored'. The duration of his visit is unknown; it is reasonable to suppose that he made his journey in the summer, it is certain that by the month of November his physician told him to lay aside all hope of recovery.

Then it was that the thoughts of the patient turned to the comfortable straggling vicarage he had left at Stoneground, in which he had hoped to end his days. He prayed that his successor might be as happy there as he had been himself. Setting his affairs in order, as became one who had but a short time to live, he executed a will, bequeathing to the Vicars of Stoneground, for ever, the close of ground he had recently purchased because it lay next the vicarage garden. And by a codicil, he added to the bequest his library of books. Within a few days, William Whitehead was gathered to his fathers.

A mural tablet in the north aisle of the church, records, in Latin, his services and his bequests, his two marriages, and his fruitless journey to Bath. The house he loved, but never again saw, was taken down 40 years later, and re-built by Vicar James Devie. The garden, with Vicar Whitehead's 'close of ground' and other adjacent lands, was opened out and planted, somewhat before 1850, by Vicar Robert Towerson. The aspect of everything has changed. But in a convenient chamber on the first floor of the present vicarage the library of Vicar Whitehead stands very much as he used it and loved it, and as he bequeathed it to his successors 'for ever'.

The books there are arranged as he arranged and ticketed them. Little slips of paper, sometimes bearing interesting fragments of writing, still mark his places. His marginal comments still give life to pages from which all other interest has faded, and he would have but a dull

29

imagination who could sit in the chamber amidst these books without ever being carried back 180 years into the past, to the time when the newest of them left the printer's hands.

Of those into whose possession the books have come, some have doubtless loved them more, and some less; some, perhaps, have left them severely alone. But neither those who loved them, nor those who loved them not, have lost them, and they passed, some century and a half after William Whitehead's death, into the hands of Mr Batchel, who loved them as a father loves his children. He lived alone, and had few domestic cares to distract his mind. He was able, therefore, to enjoy to the full what Vicar Whitehead had enjoyed so long before him. During many a long summer evening would he sit poring over long-forgotten books; and since the chamber, otherwise called the library, faced the south, he could also spend sunny winter mornings there without discomfort. Writing at a small table, or reading as he stood at a tall desk, he would browse amongst the books like an ox in a pleasant pasture.

There were other times also, at which Mr Batchel would use the books. Not being a sound sleeper (for book-loving men seldom are), he elected to use as a bedroom one of the two chambers which opened at either side into the library. The arrangement enabled him to beguile many a sleepless hour amongst the books, and in view of these nocturnal visits he kept a candle standing in a sconce above the desk, and matches always ready to his hand.

There was one disadvantage in this close proximity of his bed to the library. Owing, apparently, to some defect in the fittings of the room, which, having no mechanical tastes, Mr Batchel had never investigated, there could be heard, in the stillness of the night, exactly such sounds as might arise from a person moving about amongst the books. Visitors using the other adjacent room would often remark at breakfast, that they had heard their host in the library at one or two o'clock in the morning, when, in fact, he had not left his bed. Invariably Mr Batchel allowed them to suppose that he had been where they thought him. He disliked idle controversy, and was unwilling to afford an opening for supernatural talk. Knowing well enough the sounds by which his guests had been deceived, he wanted no other explanation of them than his own, though it was of too vague a character to count as an explanation. He conjectured that the window-sashes, or the doors, or 'something', were defective, and was too phlegmatic and too unpractical to make any investigation. The matter gave him no concern.

Persons whose sleep is uncertain are apt to have their worst nights when they would like their best. The consciousness of a special need for rest seems to bring enough mental disturbance to forbid it. So on Christmas Eve, in the year 1907, Mr Batchel, who would have liked to sleep well, in view of the labours of Christmas Day, lay hopelessly wide awake. He exhausted all the known devices for courting sleep, and, at the end, found himself wider awake than ever. A brilliant moon shone into his room, for he hated window-blinds. There was a light wind blowing, and the sounds in the library were more than usually suggestive of a person moving about. He almost determined to have the sashes 'seen to', although he could seldom be induced to have anything 'seen to'. He disliked changes, even for the better, and would submit to great inconvenience rather than have things altered with which he had become familiar.

As he revolved these matters in his mind, he heard the clocks strike the hour of midnight, and having now lost all hope of falling asleep, he rose from his bed, got into a large dressing gown which hung in readiness for such occasions, and passed into the library, with the intention of reading himself sleepy, if he could.

The moon, by this time, had passed out of the south, and the library seemed all the darker by contrast with the moonlit chamber he had left. He could see nothing but two blue-grey rectangles formed by the windows against the sky, the furniture of the room being altogether invisible. Groping along to where the table stood, Mr Batchel felt over its surface for the matches which usually lay there; he found, however, that the table was cleared of everything. He raised his right hand, therefore, in order to feel his way to a shelf where the matches were sometimes mislaid, and at that moment, whilst his hand was in mid-air, the matchbox was gently put into it!

Such an incident could hardly fail to disturb even a phlegmatic person, and Mr Batchel cried 'Who's this?' somewhat nervously. There was no answer. He struck a match, looked hastily round the room, and found it empty, as usual. There was everything, that is to say, that he was accustomed to see, but no other person than himself.

It is not quite accurate, however, to say that everything was in its usual state. Upon the tall desk lay a quarto volume that he had certainly not placed there. It was his quite invariable practice to replace his books upon the shelves after using them, and what we may call his library habits were precise and methodical. A book out of place like this, was not only an offence against good order, but a sign that his privacy had been intruded upon. With some surprise, therefore, he lit the candle standing ready in the sconce, and proceeded to examine the book, not sorry, in the disturbed condition in which he was, to have an occupation found for him.

The book proved to be one with which he was unfamiliar, and this made it certain that some other hand than his had removed it from its place. Its title was 'The Compleat Gard'ner' of M. de la Quintinye made English by John Evelyn Esquire. It was not a work in which Mr Batchel felt any great interest. It consisted of divers reflections on various parts of husbandry, doubtless entertaining enough, but too deliberate and discursive for practical purposes. He had certainly never used the book, and growing restless now in mind, said to himself that some boy having the freedom of the house, had taken it down from its place in the hope of finding pictures.

But even whilst he made this explanation he felt its weakness. To begin with, the desk was too high for a boy. The improbability that any boy would place a book there was equalled by the improbability that he would leave it there. To discover its uninviting character would be the work only of a moment, and no boy would have brought it so far from its shelf.

Mr Batchel had, however, come to read, and habit was too strong with him to be wholly set aside. Leaving 'The Compleat Gard'ner' on the desk, he turned round to the shelves to find some more congenial reading.

Hardly had he done this when he was startled by a sharp rap upon the desk behind him, followed by a rustling of paper. He turned quickly about and saw the quarto lying open. In obedience to the instinct of the moment, he at once sought a natural cause for what he saw. Only a wind, and that of the strongest, could have opened the book, and laid back its heavy cover; and though he accepted, for a brief moment, that explanation, he was too candid to retain it longer. The wind out of doors was very light. The window sash was closed and latched, and, to decide the matter finally, the book had its back, and not its edges, turned towards the only quarter from which a wind could strike.

Mr Batchel approached the desk again and stood over the book. With increasing perturbation of mind (for he still thought of the matchbox) he looked upon the open page. Without much reason beyond that he felt constrained to do something, he read the words of the half completed sentence at the turn of the page—

'at dead of night he left the house and passed into the solitude of the garden.'

But he read no more, nor did he give himself the trouble of discovering whose midnight wandering was being described, although the habit was singularly like one of his own. He was in no condition for reading, and turning his back upon the volume he slowly paced the length of the chamber, 'wondering at that which had come to pass.'

He reached the opposite end of the chamber and was in the act of turning, when again he heard the rustling of paper, and by the time he had faced round, saw the leaves of the book again turning over. In a moment the volume lay at rest, open in another place, and there was no further movement as he approached it. To make sure that he had not been deceived, he read again the words as they entered the page. The author was following a not uncommon practice of the time, and throwing common speech into forms suggested by Holy Writ: 'So dig,' it said, 'that ye may obtain.'

This passage, which to Mr Batchel seemed reprehensible in its levity, excited at once his interest and his disapproval. He was prepared to read more, but this time was not allowed. Before his eye could pass beyond the passage already cited, the leaves of the book slowly turned again, and presented but a termination of five words and a colophon.

The words were, 'to the North, an Ilex.' These three passages, in which he saw no meaning and no connection, began to entangle themselves together in Mr Batchel's mind. He found himself repeating them in different orders, now beginning with one, and now with another. Any further attempt at reading he felt to be impossible, and he was in no mind for any more experiences of the unaccountable. Sleep was, of course, further from him than ever, if that were conceivable. What he did, therefore, was to blow out the candle, to return to his moonlit bedroom, and put on more clothing, and then to pass downstairs with the object of going out of doors.

It was not unusual with Mr Batchel to walk about his garden at nighttime. This form of exercise had often, after a wakeful hour, sent him back to his bed refreshed and ready for sleep. The convenient access to the garden at such times lay through his study, whose French windows opened on to a short flight of steps, and upon these he now paused for a moment to admire the snow-like appearance of the lawns, bathed as they were in the moonlight. As he paused, he heard the city clocks strike the half-hour after midnight, and he could not forbear repeating aloud

'At dead of night he left the house, and passed into the solitude of the garden.'

It was solitary enough. At intervals the screech of an owl, and now and then the noise of a train, seemed to emphasise the solitude by drawing attention to it and then leaving it in possession of the night. Mr Batchel found himself wondering and conjecturing what Vicar Whitehead, who had acquired the close of land to secure quiet and privacy for a garden, would have thought of the railways to the west and north. He turned his face northwards, whence a whistle had just sounded, and saw a tree beautifully outlined against the sky. His breath caught at the sight. Not because the tree was unfamiliar. Mr Batchel knew all his trees. But what he had seen was 'to the north, an Ilex.'

Mr Batchel knew not what to make of it all. He had walked into the garden hundreds of times and as often seen the Ilex, but the words out of 'The Compleat Gard'ner' seemed to be pursuing him in a way that made him almost afraid. His temperament, however, as has been said already, was phlegmatic. It was commonly said, and Mr Batchel approved the verdict, whilst he condemned its inexactness, that 'his nerves were made of fiddle-string', so he braced himself afresh and set upon his walk round the silent garden, which he was accustomed to begin in a northerly direction, and was now too proud to change. He usually passed the Ilex at the beginning of his perambulation, and so would pass it now.

He did not pass it. A small discovery, as he reached it, annoyed and disturbed him. His gardener, as careful and punctilious as himself, never failed to house all his tools at the end of a day's work. Yet there, under the Ilex, standing upright in moonlight brilliant enough to cast a shadow of it, was a spade.

Mr Batchel's second thought was one of relief. After his extraordinary experiences in the library (he hardly knew now whether they had been real or not) something quite commonplace would act sedatively, and he determined to carry the spade to the tool-house.

The soil was quite dry, and the surface even a little frozen, so Mr Batchel left the path, walked up to the spade, and would have drawn it towards him. But it was as if he had made the attempt upon the trunk of the Ilex itself. The spade would not be moved. Then, first with one hand, and then with both, he tried to raise it, and still it stood firm. Mr Batchel, of course, attributed this to the frost, slight as it was. Wondering at the spade's being there, and annoyed at its being frozen, he was about to leave it and continue his walk, when the remaining works of 'The Compleat Gard'ner' seemed rather to utter themselves, than to await his will—

'So dig, that ye may obtain.'

Mr Batchel's power of independent action now deserted him. He took the spade, which no longer resisted, and began to dig. 'Five spadefuls and no more,' he said aloud. 'This is all foolishness.'

Four spadefuls of earth he then raised and spread out before him in the moonlight. There was nothing unusual to be seen. Nor did Mr Batchel decide what he would look for, whether coins, jewels, documents in canisters, or weapons. In point of fact, he dug against what he deemed his better judgement, and expected nothing. He spread before him the fifth and last spadeful of earth, not quite without result, but with no result that was at all sensational. The earth contained a bone. Mr Batchel's knowledge of anatomy was sufficient to show him that it was a human bone. He identified it, even by moonlight, as the *radius*, a bone of the forearm, as he removed the earth from it, with his thumb.

Such a discovery might be thought worthy of more than the very ordinary interest Mr Batchel showed. As a matter of fact, the presence of a human bone was easily to be accounted for. Recent excavations within the church had caused the upturning of numberless bones, which had been collected and reverently buried. But an earth-stained bone is also easily overlooked, and this *radius* had obviously found its way into the garden with some of the earth brought out of the church.

Mr Batchel was glad, rather than regretful at this termination to his adventure. He was once more provided with something to do. The reinterment of such bones as this had been his constant care, and he decided at once to restore the bone to consecrated earth. The time seemed opportune. The eyes of the curious were closed in sleep, he himself was still alert and wakeful. The spade remained by his side and the bone in his hand. So he betook himself, there and then, to the churchyard. By the still generous light of the moon, he found a place where the earth yielded to his spade, and within a few minutes the bone was laid decently to earth, some 18 inches deep.

The city clocks struck one as he finished. The whole world seemed asleep, and Mr Batchel slowly returned to the garden with his spade. As he hung it in its accustomed place he felt stealing over him the welcome desire to sleep. He walked quietly on to the house and ascended to his room. It was now dark: the moon had passed on and left the room in shadow. He lit a candle, and before undressing passed into the library. He had an irresistible curiosity to see the passages in John Evelyn's book which had so strangely adapted themselves to the events of the past hour.

In the library a last surprise awaited him. The desk upon which the book had lain was empty. 'The Compleat Gard'ner' stood in its place on the shelf. And then Mr Batchel knew that he had handled a bone of William Whitehead, and that in response to his own entreaty.

The Burned House

by Vincent O'Sullivan

One night at the end of dinner, the last time I crossed the Atlantic, somebody in our group remarked that we were just passing over the spot where the *Lusitania* had gone down. Whether this were the case or not, the thought of it was enough to make us rather grave, and we dropped into some more or less serious discussion about the emotions of men and women who see all hope gone, and realise that they are going to sink with the vessel.

From that the talk wandered to the fate of the drowned. Was not theirs, after all, a fortunate end? Somebody related details from the narratives of those who had been all-but drowned in the accident of the war. A Scotch lady inquired fancifully if the ghosts of those who are lost at sea ever appear above the waters and come aboard ships. Would there be danger of seeing one when the light was turned out in her cabin? This put an end to all seriousness, and most of us laughed. But a little, tight-faced man, bleak and iron-grey, who had been listening attentively, did not laugh. The lady noticed his decorum, and appealed to him for support.

"You are like me—you believe in ghosts!" she asked lightly.

He hesitated, thinking it over.

"In ghosts?" he repeated slowly. "N-no, I don't know as I do. I've never had any personal experience that way. I've never seen the ghost of anyone I knew. Has anybody here?"

No one replied. Instead, most of us laughed again—a little uneasily, perhaps.

"All the same, strange enough things happen in life," resumed the man, "even if you leave out ghosts, that you can't clear up by laughing. You laugh till you've had some experience big enough to shock you, and then you don't laugh any more. It's like being thrown out of a car—"

At this moment there was a blast on the whistle, and everybody rushed up on deck. As it turned out, we had only entered into a belt of fog. On the upper deck I fell in again with the little man, smoking a cigar and walking up and down. We took a few turns together, and he referred to the conversation at dinner. Our laughter evidently rankled in his mind.

"So many strange things happen in life that you can't account for," he protested. "You go on laughing at faith-healing, and at dreams, and this and that, and then something comes along that you just can't explain. You have got to throw up your hands and allow that it doesn't answer to any tests our experience has provided us with. Now, I'm as matter-of-fact a man as any of those folks down there; but once I had an experience which I had to conclude was out of the ordinary. Whether other people believe it or not, or whether they think they can explain it, don't matter. It happened to me, and I could no more doubt it than I could doubt having had a tooth pulled after the dentist had done it. If you will sit down here with me in this corner, out of the wind, I'll tell you how it was.

"Some years ago I had to be for several months in the North of England. I was before the courts; it does not signify now what for, and it is all forgotten by this time. But it was a long and worrying case, and it aged me by twenty years. Well, sir, all through the trial, in that grimy Manchester court-room, I kept thinking and thinking of a fresh little place I knew in the Lake district, and I helped to get through the hours by thinking that if things went well with me I'd go there at once. And so it was that on the very next morning after I was acquitted I boarded the north-bound train.

"It was the early autumn; the days were closing in, and it was night and cold when I arrived. The village was very dark and deserted; they don't go out much after dark in those parts, anyhow, and the keen mountain wind was enough to quell any lingering desire. The hotel was not one of those modern places which are equipped and uphol-stered like the great city hotels. It was one of the real old-fashioned taverns, about as uncomfortable places as there are on earth, where the idea is to show the traveller that travelling is a penitential state, and that, morally and physically, the best place for him is home. The land-lord brought me a kind of supper, with his hat on and a pipe in his mouth. The room was chilly, but when I asked for a fire, he said he guessed he couldn't go out to the woodshed till morning. There was nothing else to do, when I had eaten my supper, but to go outside, both to get the smell of the lamp out of my nose and to warm myself by a short walk.

"As I did not know the country well, I did not mean to go far. But although it was an overcast night, with a high north-east wind and an occasional flurry of rain, the moon was up, and, even concealed by clouds as it was, it yet lit the night with a kind of twilight grey—not vivid, like the open moonlight, but good enough to see some distance. On account of this, I prolonged my stroll, and kept walking on and on till I was a considerable way from the village, and in a region as lonely as anywhere in the country. Great trees and shrubs bordered the road, and many feet below was a mountain stream. What with the passion of the wind pouring through the high trees and the shout of the water racing among the boulders, it seemed to me sometimes like the noise of a crowd of people. Sometimes the branches of the trees became so thick that I was walking as if in a black pit, unable to see my hand close to my face. Then, coming out from the tunnel of branches, I would step once more into a grey clearness which opened the road and surrounding country a good way on all sides.

"I suppose it might be some three-quarters of an hour I had been walking when I came to a fork of the road. One branch ran downward, getting almost on a level with the bed of the torrent; the other mounted in a steep hill, and this, after a little idle debating, I decided to follow. After I had climbed for more than half a mile, thinking that if I should happen to lose track of one of the landmarks I should be very badly lost, the path—for it was now no more than that—curved, and I came out on a broad plateau. There, to my astonishment, I saw a house. It was a good-sized house, three storeys high, with a verandah round two sides of it, and from the elevation on which it stood it commanded a far stretch of country.

"There were a few great trees at a little distance from the house, and behind it, a stone's-throw away, was a clump of bushes. Still, it looked lonely and stark, offering its four sides unprotected to the winds. For all that, I was very glad to see it. 'It does not matter now,' I thought, 'whether I have lost my way or not. The people in the house will set me right.'

"But when I came up to it I found that it was, to all appearance, uninhabited. The shutters were closed on all the windows; there was not a spark of light anywhere. There was something about it, something sinister and barren, that gave me the kind of shiver you have at the door of a room where you know that a dead man lies inside, or if you get thinking hard about dropping over the rail into that black waste of waters out there. This feeling, you know, isn't altogether unpleasant; you relish all the better your present security. It was the same with me standing before that house. I was not *really* frightened. I was alone up there, miles from any kind of help, at the mercy of whoever might be lurking behind the shutters of that sullen house; but I felt that by all the chances I was perfectly alone and safe. My sensation of the uncanny was due to the effect on the nerves produced by wild scenery and the unexpected sight of a house in such a very lonely situation. Thus I reasoned, and, instead of following the road farther, I walked over the grass till I came to a stone wall, perhaps two hundred and fifty yards in front of the house, and rested my arms on it, looking forth at the scene.

"On the crests of the hills far away a strange light lingered, like the first touch of dawn in the sky on a rainy morning or the last glimpse of twilight before night comes. Between me and the hills was a wide stretch of open country. On my right hand was an apple orchard, and I observed that a stile had been made in the wall of piled stones to enable the house people to go back and forth.

"Now, after I had been there leaning on the wall some considerable time, I saw a man coming towards me through the orchard. He was walking with a good, free stride, and as he drew nearer I could see that he was a tall, sinewy fellow between twenty-five and thirty, with a shaven face, wearing a slouch hat, a dark woollen shirt, and gaiters. When he reached the stile and began climbing over it I bade him goodnight in neighbourly fashion. He made no reply, but he looked me straight in the face, and the look gave me a qualm. Not that it was an evil face, mind you—it was a handsome, serious face—but it was ravaged by some terrible passion: stealth was on it, ruthlessness, and a deadly resolution, and at the same time such a look as a man driven by some uncontrollable power might throw on surrounding things, asking for comprehension and mercy. It was impossible for me to resent his churlishness, his thoughts were so certainly elsewhere. I doubt if he even saw me.

"He could not have gone by more than a quarter of a minute when I turned to look after him. He had disappeared. The plateau lay bare before me, and it seemed impossible that, even if he had sprinted like an athlete, he could have got inside the house in so little time. But I have always made it a rule to attribute what I cannot understand to natural causes that I have failed to observe. I said to myself that no doubt the man had gone back into the orchard by some other opening in the wall lower down, or there might be some flaw in my vision owing to the uncertain and distorting light.

"But even as I continued to look towards the house, leaning my back now against the wall, I noticed that there were lights springing up in the windows behind the shutters. They were flickering lights, now bright—now dim, and had a ruddy glow like firelight. Before I had looked long I became convinced that it was indeed firelight—the house was on fire. Black smoke began to pour from the roof; the red sparks flew in the wind. Then at a window above the roof of the verandah the shutters were thrown open, and I heard a woman shriek. I ran towards the house as hard as I could, and when I drew near I could see her plainly.

"She was a young woman; her hair fell in disorder over her white nightgown. She stretched out her bare arms, screaming. I saw a man come behind and seize her. But they were caught in a trap. The flames were licking round the windows, and the smoke was killing them. Even now the part of the house where they stood was caving in.

"Appalled by this horrible tragedy which had thus suddenly risen before me, I made my way still nearer the house, thinking that if the two could struggle to the side of the house not bounded by the verandah they might jump, and I might break the fall. I was shouting this at them; I was right up close to the fire; and then I was struck by—I noticed for the first time an astonishing thing—the flames had no heat in them!

"I was standing near enough to the fire to be singed by it, and yet I felt no heat. The sparks were flying about my head; some fell on my hands, and they did not burn. And now I perceived that, although the smoke was rolling in columns, I was not choked by the smoke, and that there had been no smell of smoke since the fire broke out. Neither was there any glare against the sky.

"As I stood there stupefied, wondering how these things could be, the whole house was swept by a very tornado of flame, and crashed down in a red ruin.

"Stricken to the heart by this abominable catastrophe, I made my way uncertainly down the hill, shouting for help. As I came to a little wooden bridge spanning the torrent, just beyond where the roads forked, I saw what appeared to be a rope in loose coils lying there. I saw that part of it was fastened to the railing of the bridge and hung outside, and I looked over. There was a man's body swinging by the neck between the road and the stream. I leaned over still farther, and then I recognised him as the man I had seen coming out of the orchard. His hat had fallen off, and the toes of his boots just touched the water.

"It seemed hardly possible, and yet it was certain. That was the man, and he was hanging there. I scrambled down at the side of the bridge, and put out my hand to seize the body, so that I might lift it up and relieve the weight on the rope. I succeeded in clutching hold of his loose shirt, and for a second I thought that it had come away in my hand. Then I found that my hand had closed on nothing, I had clutched nothing but air. And yet the figure swung by the neck before my eyes!

40

"I was suffocated with such horror that I feared for a moment I must lose consciousness. The next minute I was running and stumbling along that dark road in mortal anxiety, my one idea being to rouse the town, and bring men to the bridge. That, I say, was my intention; but the fact is that when I came at last in sight of the village I slowed down instinctively and began to reflect. After all, I was unknown there; I had just gone through a disagreeable trial in Manchester, and rural people were notoriously given to groundless suspicion. I had had enough of the law, and of arrests without sufficient evidence. The wisest thing would be to drop a hint or two before the landlord, and judge by his demeanour whether to proceed.

"I found him sitting where I had left him, smoking, in his shirt-sleeves, with his hat on.

" 'Well,' he said slowly, 'I didn't know where you had got to.'

"I told him I had been taking a walk. I went on to mention casually the fork in the road, the hill, and the plateau.

" 'And who lives in that house?' I asked with a good show of indifference, 'on top of the hill?'

"He stared.

" 'House? There ain't no house up there,' he said positively. 'Old Joe Snedeker, who owns the land, says he's going to build a house up there for his son to live in when he gets married; but he ain't begun yet, and some folks reckon he never will.'

" 'I feel sure I *saw* a house,' I protested feebly. But I was thinking— no heat in the fire, no substance in the body. I had not the courage to dispute.

"The landlord looked at me not unkindly. 'You seem sort of done up,' he remarked. 'What you want is to go to bed.' "

The man who was telling me the story paused, and for a moment we sat silent, listening to the pant of the machinery, the thrumming of the wind in the wire stays, and the lash of the sea. Some voices were singing on the deck below. I considered him with the shade of contemptuous superiority we feel, as a rule, towards those who tell us their dreams or what some fortune-teller has predicted.

"Hallucinations," I said at last, with reassuring indulgence. "Trick of the vision, toxic opthalmia. After the long strain of your trial your nerves were shattered."

"That's what I thought myself," he replied shortly, "especially after I had been out to the plateau the next morning, and saw no sign that a house had ever stood there."

"And no corpse at the bridge?" I said; and laughed.

"And no corpse at the bridge."

He tried to get a light for another cigar. This took him some little time, and when at last he managed it, he got out of his chair and stood looking down at me.

"Now listen. I told you that the thing happened several years ago. I'd got almost to forget it; if you can only persuade yourself that a thing is a freak of imagination, it pretty soon gets dim inside your head. Delusions have no staying power once it is realised that they are delusions. Whenever it did come back to me, I used to think how near I had once been to going out of my mind. That was all.

"Well, last year, being up north, I went up to that village again. I went to the same hotel, and found the same landlord. He remembered me at once as 'the feller who stayed with him and thought he saw a house,' 'I believe you had the jim-jams,' he said.

"We laughed, and the landlord went on:

" 'There's been a house there since, though.'

" 'Has there?'

" 'Yes; an' it ha' been as well if there never had been. Old Snedeker built it for his son, a fine big house with a verandah on two sides. The son, young Joe, got courting Mabel Elting from Windermere. She'd gone down to work in a shop somewhere in Liverpool. Well, sir, she used to get carrying on with another young feller 'bout here, Jim Travers, and Jim was wild about her; used to save up his wages to go down to see her. But she chucked him in the end, and married Joe; I suppose because Joe had the house, and the old man's money to expect. Well, poor Jim must ha' gone quite mad. What do you think he did? The very first night the new-wed pair spent in that house he burned it down. Burned the two of them in their bed, and he was as nice and quiet a feller as you want to see. He may ha' been full of whisky at the time.'

" 'No, he wasn't,' I said.

" 'The landlord looked surprised.

" 'You've heard about it?'

" 'No; go on.'

" 'Yes, sir, he burned them in their bed. And then what do you think he did? He hung himself at the little bridge half a mile below. Do you remember where the road divides? Well, it was there. I saw his body hanging there myself the next morning. The toes of his boots were just touching the water.' "

Clocks

by Darrell Schweitzer

He returned to the house again on an evening in November. He had been away a year, but nothing had changed. The house stood pale and dark among the trees as the twilight deepened, as the walls, trees, ground and sky all faded into that particular autumn grey which is almost blue. He stood in the cold, listening to the rain hiss faintly on the fallen leaves, wishing he could stand there forever, that time would cease its motion and this moment would never pass.

But, inevitably, as he did every year, he made his way along the leaf-covered path to the front porch. Again he stood procrastinating, fumbling with his keys until his fingers, by themselves, found the key he needed and his hand had turned it in the lock before he was even aware. Then he stepped into the dark house, the door sweeping aside a year's worth of junk mail he had never been able to cancel.

Behind him, the rain whispered, and when he closed the door there was another sound, a faint ticking. He stooped to gather the junk mail into a basket, and noticed the clock on the mail stand, a few inches from his face. It was a cheap, plastic thing, decorated with figures of shepherd girls, like characters out of *Heidi*.

It was one of his wife's clocks. As long as her clocks were here, she was too, in a way. All her life, Edith had collected clocks.

He wound it, and it seemed to tick louder. Then he stood up and wound a row of little golden alarm clocks that stood along the top of a bookcase to his left. They had stopped, and now they added to the faint, rhythmical ticking. He didn't set the time on any of them. That wasn't the point.

It was only after he had completed this task that he turned on the lights, surveyed the hallway, and stepped to his right, into the living room. The ticking followed him, until it was lost in the deeper sound of the grandfather clock that waited in the shadows by the fireplace. He remembered how they had found that grandfather clock in an antique shop once, long, long ago, how Edith had raved over it, begging him to buy it in her joking-but-earnest way, until he relented (even though they *couldn't* afford it). There had been weekends spent polishing, repairing, finishing. In the end, when they were ready, when

43

the thing stood dark and gleaming in the living room, it had been like a birth. Or that was how he remembered it now.

He flicked on one small light, and saw in the semi-darkness another clock humped on the mantelpiece. There was a story about that one, too, and as he wound the clock, once more the memory came to him.

Then he sat down by the empty fireplace, exhausted and sad. He put his feet up on a little stool and stared into the fireplace for a while, listening to the clocks. The house was stirring, the soft tick-tick-ticking like the breathing of a great beast turning in its sleep.

He dozed off, and when he awoke it was dark outside. He heard sounds from the kitchen, dishes touching gently, a cabinet door closing, but he remained where he was, listening to those sounds and to the clocks. The grandfather clock chimed softly.

A few minutes later he did get up, his joints aching. He realized that he was still wearing his hat and coat. He left them on the chair and walked through a narrow hall, past the dark basement stairway, into the kitchen.

There was a steaming cup of tea on the counter by the sink, and two slices of warm toast on a plate, both buttered, one with jam, one without, the way she had always fixed them for him when he worked late at night. He turned and stretched to wind the clock on top of the spice cabinet. It was a smiling metal Buddha with the clock face in its belly, a ridiculous thing (again, full of memories), but she had put it there once, long, long ago, and there it remained, gazing down at him serenely as he ate his toast and drank his tea.

He was almost crying then, but he held back his tears as he went from room to room, winding clocks, until their sound was like that of a million tiny birds outside the windows, gently, very patiently pecking to get in.

Upstairs, a door closed.

In the library he found a brush with long, blonde hairs in it, discarded on a desktop.

He used a key to wind an intricately carven wooden castle of a clock, where armored knights appeared on the battlements at the ringing of every hour.

The ticking was still gentle, but more insistent, unyielding, like the sound of surf on a quiet night.

When he had made a circuit of the first floor, he came to the front door again, but turned away from it and slowly climbed the front stairs. He was sobbing by then. The sounds from behind him seemed to rise, to propel him up the stairs.

He found his wife's furry slippers at the top, neatly together by the bathroom door where she often left them. He wept, and leaned his head against the wall, pounding softly with his fist.

More than anything else, he wanted just to leave, but then he heard the singing from behind the bedroom door, and he knew that, of course, he could not go away. The song was one he had taught Edith before they were married, long, long ago.

He entered the bedroom and she was there, and she was young and beautiful. She helped him undress and pulled him into the bed, whispering softly as she did, then silent, and for a while he was completely happy, suspended in a single moment of time.

A clock ticked on the nightstand.

When he awoke it was morning and she was gone. The empty-half of the bed was cold, the covers thrown back. He wept again, bitterly, deeply, cursing himself for having continued the cruel, miraculous farce, for torturing himself one more time, for doing this, somehow, to her, once again. He held up his hands before his face, and he saw how wrinkled the backs of them were, how age-spotted. He touched the top of his head, running his fingers through his thinning hair.

She had still been twenty-six and beautiful. She would always be twenty-six and beautiful.

And the memories came flooding back with horrible vividness, until he was living them again: the rainy night, the screeching tires, the car on its side by the road's edge, Edith in his arms while one set of headlights after another flared by and nobody stopped for what seemed like hours.

He turned over in the bed and pressed his face into the pillow, crying like a small child, and hoping, absurdly, that he would eventually run out of tears.

He tried to tell himself that he wouldn't come again next year, that this would finally cease, but he knew better. When he got up to dress and found a note stuck onto the telephone by the bed, it was only a confirmation.

The note said: I LOVE YOU. —EDITH.

He was still crying, but softly, as he went down the front stairs, around and into the kitchen, and from there down the dark, creaking stairway into the basement. At the bottom he stood once more, wishing he could stand there motionless forever, that he didn't have to go forward, but, again, he knew better. He flicked on the lights, revealing the thousands upon thousands of clocks that filled the basement, crowded on shelves, standing against the walls, spread across the floor, and holding in their midst by a fantastic spiderweb of wires a closed coffin that seemed to float a few inches above the rug. It was as if the clocks had grown there, proliferating. He had long since give up wondering if there were more of them now than there had once been.

His mind could supply no explanation, but he knew that somehow, if even one clock in the whole house remained running—and somehow, in defiance of all reason, one or more would always keep running for a whole year, awaiting his return—on this one night in November time would stop, or perhaps slide backwards, and Edith would be as she had been the night before her death, loving him, never aware of any future, forever young while he continued to age. He didn't know if it was real or not. There no longer seemed to be such things as real and unreal.

But he could never, never bring himself to put an end to it, and he wept as he made his way gingerly among the clocks, winding each one. Their voices grew louder and louder, resonating in the cramped basement, while he wept and trembled and worked with furious, desperate care, and in the end the sound of them was like screaming.

The Closed Door

by Harold Ward

Dying, Obie Marsh cursed his wife as he had cursed her every day of their wedded life.

"You've poisoned me!" he gasped, writhing in agony. "Yes, you've poisoned me, you she-devil!"

Lucinda, his wife, nodded dully.

"Yes, I poisoned you," she answered without emotion. "You are going to die, anyway; the doctor said so. It's just a matter of time— maybe years, maybe months. And I can't stand this fightin' any longer. Fifteen years of it! Fifteen years of hell!"

"Damn you!" Marsh snarled through his clenched teeth, his bearded face twitching as a spasm of pain shot through his vitals.

"We should have never got married," the woman went on quietly.

46

"I never loved you and you never loved me. 'T was a case of your folks and my folks stickin' in between us and the ones we loved. You've always hated me 'cause of Lizzie Roper, an' God knows I wanted t' marry Al Sides. Just 'cause they wanted the farms joined, they made us get married, me an' you. Now we can't get a divorce 'cause of the church and I've just got sick of it all, Obie—sick of it all."

"You hellion!" he gasped, his body twitching spasmodically.

"I got the idee of poisoning you when you first took sick," she went on in the same even tone. "Old Doc Plummer said that you might linger along for years. And I just couldn't stand it, Obie—I just couldn't stand it any longer, your constant bullyin' an' runnin' over me."

"You'll hang for it," Marsh said huskily. "I hope they torture you in hell—"

"Probably they will," Lucinda Marsh answered without emotion. "But it's worth it t' have a little peace here on earth. It hasn't been any heaven livin' with you."

Marsh twisted convulsively, his gnarled fingers closing and unclosing, his thick lips drooling. He pulled himself together with a mighty effort. He was a hard man and strong; hard men are difficult to kill.

"I'll come back . . . from th' grave, you hussy!" he gasped.

" 'T would be like you," his wife answered.

". . . Waitin' for . . . you—" he went on, trying to shake his fist in the woman's face.

The effort was too great. He dropped back upon the pillow again, the sweat standing out on his forehead in beads, his body shaking with spasms.

"God, it hurts!" he whispered. "Just like a . . . knife."

The woman suddenly lifted her head. She was listening.

"Somebody coming," she muttered, moving swiftly to the window. A roadster was entering the lane.

"It's old Doc Plummer," she said, half to herself, half to the dying man. "Th' old fool's earlier'n usual. An' you c'n still talk."

The man on the bed quivered. His fists clenched and his muscles tensed as he tried to drag himself back from the yawning pit that awaited him.

". . . Getting . . . dark—"

"Doc's liable to rec'nize th' symptoms," the woman went on as she heard the car come to a stop in the front yard. A sheet had been thrown carelessly across the foot of the bed. Seizing it, she wadded it into a bundle and pressed it against the face of the dying man. He fought against the stoppage of his breath with a feeble effort. She threw her whole strength against him. Suddenly his limbs straightened jerkily. She knew that he was dead. She sat up with a sigh of relief.

The outside screen door slammed shut. Leaping to her feet, she threw the sheet across the back of a chair and turned to meet the doctor.

"He just passed away in one of those spells," she said without emotion. "Come on him all of a sudden. Both th' kids are at school and I didn't have nobody to send for you. 'Tain't no use to say I'm sorry, for I'm not. I'm glad he's dead."

The physician shook his head sympathetically. Like all country practitioners, he was conversant with the family affairs of his patients. For a moment he stood looking down at the still form of Obie Marsh. Then he pulled a sheet over it and turned to the woman.

"Better sit down and take things easy, Mrs. Marsh," he said, following her into the other room. "I'll notify the undertaker and stop at the school and have the teacher send Mary and Jimmy home. Anybody else you want?"

She shook her head negatively.

"Tell Bill Reynolds to come prepared t' take th' body back with him," she said slowly. "This is my house, now—mine. That's th' way my pap and his pap fixed up th' deeds. An' the quicker I get him outen my sight, th' better it'll suit me. I never want t' see him again 'till th' day of th' funeral, an' I wouldn't 'tend that if it wasn't that people'd talk.

"He made life hell for me," she went on bitterly. "I've hated him from th' day I married him. It's my house now and I'm goin' t' lock that room as soon's they take him away. I never want t' see th' inside of it again. There's too many mem'ries hovering around it. I'd burn it to th' ground if it wasn't for burnin' th' rest of th' house."

She dropped into a rocking-chair and gazed at the doctor, her gaunt body quivering with unshed tears. The physician patted her on the shoulder sympathetically.

"You're overwrought, Lucinda," he said kindly, "overwrought and nervous. I'll fix up a tonic and bring it over tonight."

"I don't need no tonic," she responded. "Knowin' he's dead'll be tonic enough for me."

The physician wagged his head solemnly.

"Let's not speak ill of the dead," he said. "Everybody knows how he treated you. If there's nothing else I can do, I'll be getting along."

In due time the undertaker and his assistant came with their narrow wicker basket. Lucinda Marsh stood beside the door and waited for them as they carried their burden out. They looked at her queerly as she turned the key in the lock, then, removing it, placed it in her pocket.

"I hope t' God I never see th' inside of that room till my dyin' day," she said.

Bill Reynolds, the undertaker, shook his head in agreement. He, too, knew the life that she had led with Obie Marsh.

The passing years brought little change in the outward appearance of Lucinda Marsh. Gaunt, hard-featured, tight-lipped and unemotional, she moved about the farm as of yore, doing a man's work in the field, adding to the dollars that were already in the bank, conducting her business along the lines to which she had been trained. She had never had friends; Obie Marsh had seen to that. She made none now.

Her children grew to manhood and womanhood. Little Mary married and moved to the adjoining township. Lucinda made no complaint and no comment. Jimmy took the place of the hired man, lifting a bit of the burden of labor from his mother's shoulders. But she still held the reins of management. Then he, too, married and brought his wife to the big, gloomy old house at the end of the lane. Children came, six in quick succession. If their happy laughter wrought any change in the heart of the grim, silent old woman, she never showed it. Emma, Jimmy's wife, busy rearing her brood, was content to remain in the background; Lucinda Marsh was still mistress of the house.

Through all the years that one room just off from the parlor—Father's room, they called it—remained closed, the key hidden away in Lucinda's bureau drawer. It was never mentioned in the family circle. The children knew that there was something—some horrible taboo—that kept it from being talked about. Their childish imaginations did the rest. They passed it with baited breath; when darkness fell and shadows hovered outside the circle made by the big kerosene lamp on the center table, they always played on the other side of the room, casting furtive glances toward the dark panels behind which lurked they knew not what.

Then, with the passing of the years, came the hard times. First the grasshoppers destroyed the crops. Then came the drought. Prices went up; wages dropped. Factories closed.

Mary was the first to feel the blow. The bank foreclosed on her husband's farm. Then came illness and another baby. Finally she was forced to come home with her sick husband and her little brood. Lucinda Marsh, as unemotional as ever, made room for them. Jimmy's wife's brother lost his place in the city. Destitute, he appealed to his sister. She told her troubles to Lucinda Marsh.

"Four more won't make no difference at th' table," the old woman said grimly. "Write an' tell 'em we'll make room for 'em somehow. Goodness knows, though, where we'll sleep 'em."

They were sitting at the supper table when this conversation took place. It was Mary who, with a quick glance at her brother, ventured to speak that which was in all of their minds.

"Father's room," she said timidly. "Couldn't we open that up and air it before they come and let 'em sleep in there?"

For a moment there was an awed silence. Lucinda Marsh turned her sunken eyes on her daughter, then glanced at the faces of the others.

"I vowed that I'd never set foot in that room 'till my dyin' day," she said finally.

"But they—they wouldn't be you, Mother," Mary argued. "And we're cramped for room right now. Where else can we sleep 'em?"

Lucinda Marsh quietly laid down her knife and fork, her thin lips set in a straight, grim line.

"If anybody sleeps in that room, 't will be me," she said finally. "I lived with your father for fifteen years, hatin' him every day more'n more. And he hated me worse'n I hated him—if such a thing is possible. The room's filled with our hatred—it's locked up in there smolderin' an' ready t' be fanned into flame again."

"But, Mother—"

Lucinda Marsh straightened her bent old shoulders with a gesture of finality.

"I'll move into it," she said grimly.

"I wish that I hadn't mentioned it," Mary said regretfully. "I knew that there was some sort of sentiment attached to it, but—"

The old woman cut her off.

"Sentiment! Hate, you mean," she snapped. "But maybe it's for th' best. I'm an old woman—'way past seventy. I'm about due to die, anyway."

She stopped, her aged eyes taking on a far-away look.

"Maybe it's foreordained," she said, half to herself. "He said that he'd be . . . waitin' for me. Maybe he is. Who knows?"

She rose from the table and took a step toward the door.

"I'll open it up in the mornin' and let it air out," she said.

She moved up the stairway to the upper floor, her lips straight and tight.

* * *

50

For a long time Lucinda Marsh sat in the straight-backed chair beside her bed, her weary eyes gazing into vacancy while the panorama of the years unfolded itself. To her had come a great urge, a desire which she had kept in leash for close to half a century—the longing that comes to all murderers—a yearning to visit the scene of her crime.

A thousand times before, the same desire had swept over her and she had always fought it off. Now, however, with the fulfilment of her wish only a few hours away there had come to her a seeming need for haste. The closed room was calling to her. Within her brain a voice was shrieking: *"Now! Now!"* To her aged mind it was the voice of the man she hated—the man she had killed.

Getting up, she went to the bureau and, opening the drawer, found the key where she had hidden it so many years before. She held it in her gnarled fingers, fondling it, crooning over it.

Her room was at the head of the stairs. One by one, she heard the members of the household go to their rooms. Finally the gloomy old house was filled with an indescribable quietness.

Rising, she opened the door a tiny crack and peered out into the dark hallway. Satisfied that all were asleep, she picked up the small hand-lamp and tiptoed furtively down the creaking stairs.

A storm was in the air. She could hear the wind rising and shrieking through the branches of the trees. There was something reminiscent about the mournful wail. She stopped a moment, her head bent forward. Then remembrance swept over her.

" 'T was like this th' night before—before he died," she muttered to herself.

Her heart was beating a trifle faster as she reached the dark, grim door. She hesitated an instant. Then, transferring the lamp to her left hand, she inserted the key in the lock. It turned hard, as if reluctant to reveal the mysteries it hid. Then the tumbler shot back. For a moment she waited, her fingers on the knob. She was trembling now—shaking with an emotion she did not understand.

"He said that . . . he'd be . . . waitin' for me," she murmured. "I wonder . . . if he is."

She turned the knob and pushed against the panel. The aged hinges squeaked protestingly. Then the door swung open. A wave of malignancy and hatred surged over her.

She stepped inside, her lips closed in a tight, grim line. Just inside the door she waited, the lamp held high above her head, her eyes taking in every detail. There was the bed, unmade, where he had died. The thought came to her that Bill Reynolds, the undertaker, the last person to step foot in the room, was gone, too. At the head of the bed was the little stand; on top of it was the glass in which she had administered the poison. Beside it was a bottle of medicine, half empty; the label, covered with old Doc Plummer's crabbed hieroglyphics, was yellow and faded. Doc Plummer . . . he, too, had been festering in his grave for years. There was the pillow where Obie's head had rested when he died; one corner was twisted where he had held it when the last spasm of agony had knifed its way through his vitals. Nothing was changed.

"He said that he'd . . . be waitin' for me," she said again.

The room was musty and mildewed, the dust of years over everything. She closed the door and set the lamp upon the little stand. Going to the window, she pushed it up to its full length. The wind swept in, howling and shrieking.

The lamp sputtered, causing queer, grotesque shadows to dance in the distant corners. Across the back of the chair where she had thrown it years before was the yellowed sheet with which she had smothered the dying breath out of her husband. There was a darker spot upon its mildewed surface; she knew it for the spittle that had drooled from his mouth.

She moved to the center of the room, still peering furtively into the shadows.

"He said that he'd come . . . back from th' grave an' be . . . waitin' for me," she said again and again.

A fresh gust of wind howled through the window. The lamp sputtered, smoked, flared up, then went out.

With the sudden darkness came a feeling of dread. For the first time in her life Lucinda Marsh was afraid.

Out of the darkness came a thing—a shapeless thing of white. For a moment it hung suspended in midair. It hovered over her, its long, shapeless arms reaching out for her. The wind shrieked with merry gusto.

". . . said that he'd be waitin'—" she murmured.

It swept over her, holding her in its folds, twisting about her, smothering her. . . .

"God!" she shrieked, clawing at the enveloping tentacles. "He kept his word! He was . . . waitin'—"

In the morning they found her. Twisted about her head and throat was a yellowed sheet—the sheet with which she had smothered her husband.

The Coat

by A. E. D. Smith

I am quite aware that the other fellows in the office regard me as something of an oddity—as being rather a 'queer bird', in fact. Well, of course, a man who happens to be of a studious disposition, who dislikes noise and prefers his own company to that of empty-headed companions, and who, moreover, is compelled by defective vision to wear thick glasses, is always liable to be thus misjudged by inferior minds; and ordinarily, I treat the opinion of my colleagues with the contempt it deserves. But at this particular moment I was beginning to think that perhaps, after all, there might be something to be said for their view. For, though I might still repudiate the 'queer bird' part of the business, undoubtedly I was an ass—a first-class chump; otherwise I should have been spending my holidays in a nice comfortable way with the rest of the normal world, listening to the Pierrots or winking at the girls on the promenade of some seaside resort at home, instead of having elected to set out alone on this idiotic push-bike tour of a little-known part of France. Drenched, hungry and lost; a stranger in a strange land; dispiritedly pushing before me a heavily-laden bicycle with a gashed tyre—such was the present result of my asinine choice.

The storm had overtaken me miles from anywhere, on a wild road over a spur of the Vosges, and for nearly two hours I had trudged through the pelting rain without encountering a living soul or the least sign of human habitation.

And then, at long last, rounding a bend, I glimpsed just ahead of me the chimney-pots and gables of a fair-sized house. It was a lonely, desolate-looking place standing amid a clump of trees a little way back from the road, and somehow, even at a distance, did not convey a very inviting impression. Nevertheless, in that wilderness, it was a welcome enough sight, and in the hope of finding temporary shelter and possibly a little badly-needed refreshment, I quickened my pace towards it. Two hundred yards brought me to the entrance gates, and here I suffered a grievous disappointment; for the roofless porter's lodge, the dilapidated old gates hanging askew on their hinges, and the overgrown drive beyond, plainly indicated that the place was no longer inhabited.

I speedily comforted myself, however, with the reflection that in the circumstances even a deserted house was not to be despised as a refuge. Once under cover of some kind, I might make shift to wring out my drenched clothing and repair my damaged mount; and without further ado I pushed my bicycle up the long-neglected drive and reached the terrace in front of the house itself. It proved to be an old château, half smothered in creepers and vines that had long gone wild, and, judging by the carved stone coat-of-arms over the main entrance, had once been occupied by a person of some quality. Mounted on a pedestal on either side of the iron-studded front door stood a rusty carronade—trophies, probably, of some long-forgotten war in which the former occupier had played a part. Most of the windows had been boarded up, and it was evident that the place had stood empty for many years.

I tried the front door. To my surprise it was unfastened, and a thrust of my shoulder sent it creaking grudgingly back on its hinges. My nostrils, as I stepped into the dim, wide hall, were at once assailed by the stale, disagreeable odour of rotting woodwork and mouldy hangings and carpets. For a moment or two I stood peering uncertainly about me, with the slight feeling of eeriness that one usually experiences when entering an old, empty house. Facing me was a broad staircase, with a long, stained-glass window, almost opaque with dirt and cobwebs, at its head. I mounted the stairs, and throwing open the first door at hand, found myself looking into a spacious, handsomely furnished room that had evidently once been the chief apartment of the house, though long neglect and disuse had now reduced it to a sorry state. The ornate cornice hung here and there in strips, and in one corner the plaster of the ceiling had come down altogether. Green mould covered the eighteenth-century furniture; curtains and draperies hung in tatters; and one half of the beautiful old Persian carpet, from a point near the door right across to the fireplace, was overspread by an evil-smelling, bright orange fungus.

The fireplace gave me an idea. Could I but find fuel I might light a fire, make myself a hot drink, and get my clothes properly dried.

A little searching in the outbuildings discovered a sufficient quantity of old sticks to serve my purpose, and with a bundle of them under my coat I re-entered the house and briskly made my way upstairs again. But on the threshold of the big room, without quite knowing why, I suddenly checked. It was as though my legs, of their own volition, had all at once become reluctant to carry me farther into the apartment— as if something quite outside of me were urging me to turn about and retreat. I laid the sticks down at my feet, and for a moment or two stood there uncertainly in the doorway. I was beginning to sense some subtle suggestion of danger in the atmosphere of the place. Everything was apparently just as I had left it; yet I had an uneasy sort of feeling that during my brief absence something evil had entered that room and left it again.

I am neither a nervous nor a superstitious person; yet I found myself, a moment later, rather shamefacedly picking up my sticks and moving back towards the head of the stairs. Actually, it was not so much fear as a vague, precautionary sense of uneasiness that prompted me. It had occurred to me that perhaps I might feel more comfortable if I remained nearer to the front door, and made my fire in one of the rooms on the ground floor. If—it was an idiotic fancy, I know—but . . . well, if anything—er—queer DID happen, and I had to make a sudden bolt for it, I could get out quicker that way.

It was on this second descent of the stairs, as I faced the light from the open front door, that I suddenly noticed something that pulled me up with a decided start. Running up the centre of the staircase, and quite fresh in the thick dust, was a broad, broken sort of track, exactly as though someone had recently trailed up an empty sack or something of that nature.

From the foot of the staircase I traced this track across the hall to a spot immediately below an old, moth-eaten coat that hung from one of a row of coat-pegs on the opposite wall. And then I saw that similar tracks traversed the hall in various directions, some terminating before the doors on either side, others leading past the foot of the stairs to the rear regions of the house, but all seeming to radiate from the same point below the coat-pegs. And the queerest thing about it all was that of footprints, other than my own, there was not a sign.

Uneasiness once more assailed me. The house appeared to be uninhabited, and yet, plainly someone, or something, had recently been in the place. Who, or what, was the restless, questing creature that had made those strange tracks to and from the old coat? Was it some half-witted vagrant—a woman possibly—whose trailing draperies obliterated her own footprints?

I had a closer look at the old garment. It was a military greatcoat of ancient pattern with one or two tarnished silver buttons still attached to it, and had evidently seen much service. Turning it round on its peg with a gingerly finger and thumb, I discovered that just below the left shoulder there was a round hole as big as a penny, surrounded by an area of scorched and stained cloth, as though a heavy pistol had been fired into it at point-blank range. If a pistol bullet had indeed made that hole, then obviously, the old coat at one period of its existence had clothed a dead man.

A sudden repugnance for the thing overcame me, and with a slight shudder I let go of it. It may have been fancy or not, but all at once it seemed to me that there was more than an odour of mould and rotting cloth emanating from the thing—that there was a taint of putrefying flesh and bone. . . .

A taint of animal corruption—faint but unmistakable—I could sniff it in the air; and with it, something less definable but no less real—a sort of sixth-sense feeling that the whole atmosphere of the place was slowly becoming charged with evil emanations from a black and shameful past.

With an effort I pulled myself together. After all, what was there to be scared about? I had no need to fear human marauders, for in my hip pocket I carried a small but serviceable automatic; and as for ghosts, well, if such existed, they didn't usually 'walk' in the daytime. The place certainly felt creepy, and I shouldn't have cared to spend the night there; but it would be ridiculous to allow mere idle fancies to drive me out again into that beastly rain before I'd made myself that badly needed hot drink and mended my bicycle.

I therefore opened the door nearest to me, and entered a smallish room that apparently had once been used as a study. The fireplace was on the side opposite to the door, and the wide, ancient grate was still choked with the ashes of the last log consumed there. I picked up the poker—a cumbersome old thing with a knob as big as an orange—raked out the ashes, and laid my sticks in approved Boy Scout fashion. But the wood was damp, and after I had used up half my matches, refused to do more than smoulder, whilst a back-draught from the chimney filled the room with smoke. In desperation I went down on my hands and knees and tried to rouse the embers into flame by blowing on them. And in the middle of this irksome operation I was startled by a sound of movement in the hall—a single soft 'flop', as though some one had flung down a garment.

I was on my feet in a flash, listening with every nerve a-taut. No further sound came, and, automatic in hand, I tiptoed to the door. There was nothing in the hall; nothing to be heard at all save the steady swish of the rain outside. But from a spot on the floor directly below the old coat the dust was rising in a little eddying cloud, as though it had just been disturbed.

'Pah! A rat,' I told myself, and went back to my task.

More vigorous blowing on the embers, more raking and poking, more striking of matches—and, in the midst of it, again came that curious noise—not very loud, but plain and unmistakable.

Once more I went into the hall, and once more, except for another little cloud of dust rising from precisely the same spot as before, there was nothing to be seen. But that sixth-sense warning of imminent danger was becoming more insistent. I had the feeling now that I was no longer alone in the old, empty hall—that some unclean, invisible presence was lurking there, tainting the very air with its foulness.

'It's no use,' I said to myself. 'I may be a nervous fool, but I can't stand any more of this. I'll collect my traps and clear out whilst the going's good.'

With this, I went back into the room, and keeping a nervous eye cocked on the door, began with rather panicky haste to re-pack my haversack. And just as I was in the act of tightening the last strap there came from the hall a low, evil chuckle, followed by the sound of stealthy movement. I whipped out my weapon and stood where I was in the middle of the floor, facing the door, with my blood turning to ice. Through the chink between the door hinges I saw a shadow pass; then the door creaked a little, slowly began to open, and round it there came—the COAT.

It stood there upright in the doorway, as God is above me—swaying a little as though uncertain of its balance—collar and shoulders extended as though by an invisible wearer—the old, musty coat I had seen hanging in the hall.

For a space that seemed an eternity I stood like a man of stone, facing the Thing as it seemed to pause on the threshold. A dreadful sort of hypnotism held me rooted to the spot on which I stood—a hypnotism that completely paralysed my body, and caused the pistol to slip from my nervless fingers, and yet left my brain clear. Mingled with my frozen terror was a feeling of deadly nausea. I knew that I was in the presence of ultimate Evil—that the very aura of the Hell-engendered Thing reared there in the doorway was contamination—that its actual touch would mean not only the instant destruction of my body, but the everlasting damnation of my soul.

And now It was coming into the room—with an indescribable bobbing sort of motion, the empty sleeves jerking grotesquely at its sides, the skirts flopping and trailing in the dust, was slowly coming towards me; and step by step, with my bulging eyes riveted in awful fascination on the Thing, I was recoiling before it. Step by step, with the rigid, unconscious movement of an automaton, I drew back until I was brought up with my back pressed into the fireplace and could retreat no farther. And still, with deadly malevolent purpose, the Thing crept towards me. The empty sleeves were rising and shakily reaching out towards my throat. In another moment they would touch me, and then I knew with the most dreadful certainty that my reason would snap. A coherent thought somehow came into my burning brain— something that I had read or heard of long ago . . . the power . . . of the . . . holy sign . . . against . . . the forces of evil. With a last desperate effort of will I stretched out a palsied finger and made the sign of the Cross. . . . And in that instant, my other hand, scrabbling frenziedly at the wall behind me, came into contact with something cold and hard and round. It was the knob of the old, heavy poker.

The touch of the cold iron seemed to give me instant re-possession of my faculties. With lightning swiftness I swung up the heavy poker and struck with all my force at the nightmare Horror before me. And lo! on the instant, the Thing collapsed, and became an old coat— nothing more—lying there in a heap at my feet. Yet, on my oath, as I cleared the hellish thing in a flying leap, and fled from the room, I saw it, out of the tail of my eye, gathering itself together and making shape, as it were, to scramble after me.

Once outside that accursed house I ran as never man ran before, and I remember nothing more until I found myself, half fainting, be-fore the door of a little inn.

'Bring wine, in the name of God!' I cried, staggering inside.

Wine was brought, and a little wondering group stood round me while I drank.

I tried to explain to them in my bad French. They continued to regard me with puzzled looks. At length a look of understanding came into the landlord's face.

'Mon dieu!' he gasped. 'Is it possible that Monsieur has been in *that place!* Quick, Juliette! Monsieur will need another bottle of wine.'

Later, I got something of the story from the landlord, though he was by no means eager to tell it. The deserted house had once been occupied by a retired officer of the first Napoleon's army—a semi-madman with a strain of African blood in him. Judging from the land-lord's story, he must have been one of the worst men that God ever allowed to walk the earth. 'Most certainly, monsieur, he was a bad man —that one,' concluded my host. 'He killed his wife and tortured every living thing he could lay hands on—even, it is said, his own daughters. In the end, one of them shot him in the back. The old château has an evil name. If you offered a million francs, you would not get one of our country-folks to go near the place.'

* * *

As I said at the beginning, I know that the other fellows in the office are inclined, as it is, to regard me as being a bit queer; so I haven't told any of them this story. Nevertheless, it's perfectly true.

My brand-new bicycle and touring traps are probably still lying where I left them in the hall of that devil-ridden château. Anybody who cares to collect them may keep them.

The Cold Embrace

by Mary E. Braddon

He was an artist—such things as happened to him happen sometimes to artists.

He was a German—such things as happened to him happen sometimes to Germans.

He was young, handsome, studious, enthusiastic, metaphysical, reckless, unbelieving, heartless.

And being young, handsome and eloquent, he was beloved.

He was an orphan, under the guardianship of his dead father's brother, his uncle Wilhelm, in whose house he had been brought up from a little child; and she who loved him was his cousin—his cousin Gertrude, whom he swore he loved in return.

Did he love her? Yes, when he first swore it. It soon wore out, this passionate love; how threadbare and wretched a sentiment it became at last in the selfish heart of the student! But in its first golden dawn, when he was only nineteen, and had just returned from his apprenticeship to a great painter at Antwerp, and they wandered together in the most romantic outskirts of the city at rosy sunset, by holy moonlight, or bright and joyous morning, how beautiful a dream!

They keep it a secret from Wilhelm, as he has the father's ambition of a wealthy suitor for his only child—a cold and dreary vision beside the lover's dream.

So they are betrothed; and standing side by side when the dying sun and the pale rising moon divide the heavens, he puts the betrothal ring upon her finger, the white and taper finger whose slender shape he knows so well. This ring is a peculiar one, a massive golden serpent, its tail in its mouth, the symbol of eternity; it had been his mother's, and he would know it amongst a thousand. If he were to become blind tomorrow, he could select it from amongst a thousand by the touch alone.

He places it on her finger, and they swear to be true to each other for ever and ever—through trouble and danger—sorrow and change—in wealth or poverty. Her father must needs be won to consent to their union by-and-by, for they were now betrothed, and death alone could part them.

But the young student, the scoffer at revelation, yet the enthusiastic adorer of the mystical asks:

'Can death part us? I would return to you from the grave, Gertrude. My soul would come back to be near my love. And you—you, if you died before me—the cold earth would not hold you from me; if you loved me, you would return, and again these fair arms would be clasped round my neck as they are now.'

But she told him, with a holier light in her deep-blue eyes than had ever shone in his—she told him that the dead who die at peace with God are happy in heaven, and cannot return to the troubled earth; and that it is only the suicide—the lost wretch on whom sorrowful angels shut the door of Paradise—whose unholy spirit haunts the footsteps of the living.

The first year of their betrothal is passed, and she is alone, for he has gone to Italy, on a commission for some rich man, to copy Raphaels, Titians, Guidos, in a gallery at Florence. He has gone to win fame, perhaps; but it is not the less bitter—he is gone!

Of course her father misses his young nephew, who has been as a son to him; and he thinks his daughter's sadness no more than a cousin should feel for a cousin's absence.

In the meantime, the weeks and months pass. The lover writes—often at first, then seldom—at last, not at all.

How many excuses she invents for him! How many times she goes to the distant little post-office, to which he is to address his letters! How many times she hopes, only to be disappointed! How many times she despairs, only to hope again!

But real despair comes at last, and will not be put off any more. The rich suitor appears on the scene, and her father is determined. She is to marry at once. The wedding-day is fixed—the fifteenth of June.

The date seems burnt into her brain.

The date, written in fire, dances for ever before her eyes.

The date, shrieked by the Furies, sounds continually in her ears.

But there is time yet—it is the middle of May—there is time for a letter to reach him at Florence; there is time for him to come to Brunswick, to take her away and marry her, in spite of her father—in spite of the whole world.

But the days and weeks fly by, and he does not write—he does not come. This is indeed despair which usurps her heart, and will not be put away.

It is the fourteenth of June. For the last time she goes to the little post-office; for the last time she asks the old question, and they give her for the last time the dreary answer, 'No; no letter.'

For the last time—for tomorrow is the day appointed for her bridal. Her father will hear no entreaties; her rich suitor will not listen to her prayers. They will not be put off a day—an hour; tonight alone is hers —this night, which she may employ as she will.

She takes another path than that which leads home; she hurries through some by-streets of the city, out on to a lonely bridge, where he and she had stood so often in the sunset, watching the rose-coloured light glow, fade, and die upon the river.

He returns from Florence. He had received her letter. That letter, blotted with tears, entreating, despairing—he had received it, but he loved her no longer. A young Florentine, who has sat to him for a model, had bewitched his fancy—that fancy which with him stood in place of a heart—and Gertrude had been half-forgotten. If she had a rich suitor, good; let her marry him; better for her, better far for himself. He had no wish to fetter himself with a wife. Had he not his art always?—his eternal bride, his unchanging mistress.

Thus he thought it wiser to delay his journey to Brunswick, so that he should arrive when the wedding was over—arrive in time to salute the bride.

And the vows—the mystical fancies—the belief in his return, even after death, to the embrace of his beloved? O, gone out of his life; melted away for ever, those foolish dreams of his boyhood.

So on the fifteenth of June he enters Brunswick, by that very bridge on which she stood, the stars looking down on her, the night before. He strolls across the bridge and down by the water's edge, a great rough dog at his heels, and the smoke from his short meerschaum-pipe curling in blue wreaths fantastically in the pure morning air. He has his sketch-book under his arm, and attracted now and then by some object that catches his artist's eye, stops to draw: a few weeds and pebbles on the river's brink—a crag on the opposite shore—a group of pollard

61

willows in the distance. When he has done, he admires his drawing, shuts his sketch-book, empties the ashes from his pipe, refills from his tobacco-pouch, sings the refrain of a gay drinking-song, calls to his dog, smokes again, and walks on. Suddenly he opens his sketch-book again; this time that which attracts him is a group of figures: but what is it?

It is not a funeral, for there are no mourners.

It is not a funeral, but a corpse lying on a rough bier, covered with an old sail, carried between two bearers.

It is not a funeral, for the bearers are fishermen—fishermen in their everyday garb.

About a hundred yards from him they rest their burden on a bank—one stands at the head of the bier, the other throws himself down at the foot of it.

And thus they form a perfect group; he walks back two or three paces, selects his point of sight, and begins to sketch a hurried outline. He has finished it before they move; he hears their voices, though he cannot hear their words, and wonders what they can be talking of. Presently he walks on and joins them.

'You have a corpse there, my friends?' he says.

'Yes; a corpse washed ashore an hour ago.'

'Drowned?'

'Yes, drowned. A young girl, very handsome.'

'Suicides are always handsome,' says the painter; and then he stands for a little while idly smoking and meditating, looking at the sharp outline of the corpse and the stiff folds of the rough canvas covering.

Life is such a golden holiday for him—young, ambitious, clever—that it seems as though sorrow and death could have no part in his destiny.

At last he says that, as this poor suicide is so handsome, he should like to make a sketch of her.

He gives the fishermen some money, and they offer to remove the sailcloth that covers her features.

No; he will do it himself. He lifts the rough, coarse, wet canvas from her face. What face?

The face that shone on the dreams of his foolish boyhood; the face which once was the light of his uncle's home. His cousin Gertrude—his betrothed!

He sees, as in one glance, while he draws one breath, the rigid features—the marble arms—the hands crossed on the cold bosom; and, on the third finger of the left hand, the ring which had been his

62

mother's—the golden serpent; the ring which, if he were to become blind, he could select from a thousand others by the touch alone.

But he is a genius and a metaphysician—grief, true grief, is not for such as he. His first thought is flight—flight anywhere out of that accursed city—anywhere far from the brink of that hideous river—anywhere away from remorse—anywhere to forget.

He is miles on the road that leads away from Brunswick before he knows that he has walked a step.

It is only when his dog lies down panting at his feet than he feels how exhausted he is himself, and sits down upon a bank to rest. How the landscape spins round and round before his dazzled eyes, while his morning's sketch of the two fishermen and the canvas-covered bier glares redly at him out of the twilight!

At last, after sitting a long time by the roadside, idly playing with his dog, idly smoking, idly lounging, looking as any idle, light-hearted travelling student might look, yet all the while acting over that morning's scene in his burning brain a hundred times a minute; at last he grows a little more composed, and tries presently to think of himself as he is, apart from his cousin's suicide. Apart from that, he was no worse off than he was yesterday. His genius was not gone; the money he had earned at Florence still lined his pocket-book; he was his own master, free to go whither he would.

And while he sits on the roadside, trying to separate himself from the scene of that morning—trying to put away the image of the corpse covered with the damp canvas sail—trying to think of what he should do next, where he should go, to be farthest away from Brunswick and remorse, the old diligence comes rumbling and jingling along. He remembers it; it goes from Brunswick to Aix-la-Chapelle.

He whistles to his dog, shouts to the postillion to stop, and springs into the *coupé*.

During the whole evening, through the long night, though he does not once close his eyes, he never speaks a word; but when morning dawns, and the other passengers awake and begin to talk to each other, he joins in the conversation. He tells them that he is an artist, that he is going to Cologne and to Antwerp to copy Rubenses, and the great picture by Quentin Matsys, in the museum. He remembered afterwards that he talked and laughed boisterously, and that when he was talking and laughing loudest, a passenger, older and graver than the rest, opened the window near him, and told him to put his head out. He remembered the fresh air blowing in his face, the singing of the birds in his ears, and the flat fields and roadside reeling before his eyes.

He remembered this, and then falling in a lifeless heap on the floor of the diligence.

It is a fever that keeps him for six long weeks on a bed at a hotel in Aix-la-Chapelle.

He gets well, and, accompanied by his dog, starts on foot for Cologne. By this time he is his former self once more. Again the blue smoke from his short meerschaum curls upwards in the morning air—again he sings some old university drinking-song—again stops here and there, meditating and sketching.

He is happy, and has forgotten his cousin—and so on to Cologne.

It is by the great cathedral he is standing, with his dog at his side. It is night, the bells have just chimed the hour, and the clocks are striking eleven; the moonlight shines full upon the magnificent pile, over which the artist's eye wanders, absorbed in the beauty of form.

He is not thinking of his drowned cousin, for he has forgotten her and is happy.

Suddenly some one, something from behind him, puts two cold arms round his neck, and clasps its hands on his breast.

And yet there is no one behind him, for on the flags bathed in the broad moonlight there are only two shadows, his own and his dog's. He turns quickly round—there is no one—nothing to be seen in the broad square but himself and his dog; and though he feels, he cannot see the cold arms clasped round his neck.

It is not ghostly, this embrace, for it is palpable to the touch—it cannot be real, for it is invisible.

He tries to throw off the cold caress. He clasps the hands in his own to tear them asunder, and to cast them off his neck. He can feel the long delicate fingers cold and wet beneath his touch, and on the third finger of the left hand he can feel the ring which was his mother's—the golden serpent—the ring which he has always said he would know among a thousand by the touch alone. He knows it now!

His dead cousin's cold arms are round his neck—his dead cousin's wet hands are clasped upon his breast. He asks himself if he is mad. 'Up, Leo!' he shouts. 'Up, up, boy!' and the Newfoundland leaps to his shoulders—the dog's paws are on the dead hands, and the animal utters a terrific howl, and springs away from his master.

The student stands in the moonlight, the dead arms around his neck, and the dog at a little distance moaning piteously.

Presently a watchman, alarmed by the howling of the dog, comes into the square to see what is wrong.

In a breath the cold arms are gone.

He takes the watchman home to the hotel with him and gives him money; in his gratitude he could have given that man half his little fortune.

Will it ever come to him again, this embrace of the dead?

He tries never to be alone; he makes a hundred acquaintances, and shares the chamber of another student. He starts up if he is left by himself in the public room at the inn where he is staying, and runs into the street. People notice his strange actions, and begin to think that he is mad.

But, in spite of all, he is alone once more; for one night the public room being empty for a moment, when on some idle pretence he strolls into the street, the street is empty too, and for the second time he feels the cold arms round his neck, and for the second time, when he calls his dog, the animal slinks away from him with a piteous howl.

After this he leaves Cologne, still travelling on foot—of necessity now, for his money is getting low. He joins travelling hawkers, he walks side by side with labourers, he talks to every foot-passenger he falls in with, and tries from morning till night to get company on the road.

At night he sleeps by the fire in the kitchen of the inn at which he stops; but do what he will, he is often alone, and it is now a common thing for him to feel the cold arms around his neck.

Many months have passed since his cousin's death—autumn, winter, early spring. His money is nearly gone, his health is utterly broken, he is the shadow of his former self, and he is getting near to Paris. He will reach that city at the time of the Carnival. To this he looks forward. In Paris, in Carnival time, he need never, surely, be alone, never feel that deadly caress; he may even recover his lost gaiety, his lost health, once more resume his profession, once more earn fame and money by his art.

How hard he tries to get over the distance that divides him from Paris, while day by day he grows weaker, and his step slower and more heavy!

But there is an end at last; the long dreary roads are passed. This is Paris, which he enters for the first time—Paris, of which he has dreamed so much—Paris, whose million voices are to exorcise his phantom.

To him tonight Paris seems one vast chaos of lights, music, and confusion—lights which dance before his eyes and will not be still—music that rings in his ears and deafens him—confusion which makes his head whirl round and round.

But, in spite of all, he finds the opera-house, where there is a masked ball. He has enough money left to buy a ticket of admission, and to hire a domino to throw over his shabby dress. It seems only a moment after his entering the gates of Paris that he is in the very midst of all the wild gaiety of the opera-house ball.

No more darkness, no more loneliness, but a mad crowd, shouting and dancing, and a lovely Débardeuse hanging on his arm.

The boisterous gaiety he feels surely is his old light-heartedness come back. He hears the people round him talking of the outrageous conduct of some drunken student, and it is to him they point when they say this—to him, who has not moistened his lips since yesterday at noon, for even now he will not drink; though his lips are parched, and his throat burning, he cannot drink. His voice is thick and hoarse, and his utterance indistinct; but still this must be his old light-heartedness come back that makes him so wildly gay.

The little Débardeuse is wearied out—her arm rests on his shoulder heavier than lead—the other dancers one by one drop off.

The lights in the chandeliers one by one die out.

The decorations look pale and shadowy in that dim light which is neither night nor day.

A faint glimmer from the dying lamps, a pale streak of cold grey light from the new-born day, creeping in through half-opened shutters.

And by this light the bright-eyed Débardeuse fades sadly. He looks her in the face. How the brightness of her eyes dies out! Again he looks her in the face. How white that face has grown! Again—and now it is the shadow of a face alone that looks in his.

Again—and they are gone—the bright eyes, the face, the shadow of the face. He is alone; alone in that vast saloon.

Alone, and, in the terrible silence, he hears the echoes of his own footsteps in that dismal dance which has no music.

No music but the beating of his breast. For the cold arms are round his neck—they whirl him round, they will not be flung off, or cast away; he can no more escape from their icy grasp than he can escape from death. He looks behind him—there is nothing but himself in the great empty *salle;* but he can feel—cold, deathlike, but O, how palpable!—the long slender fingers, and the ring which was his mother's.

He tries to shout, but he has no power in his burning throat. The silence of the place is only broken by the echoes of his own footsteps in the dance from which he cannot extricate himself. Who says he has no partner? The cold hands are clasped on his breast, and now he does not shun their caress. No! One more polka, if he drops down dead.

The lights are all out, and, half an hour after, the *gendarmes* come in with a lantern to see that the house is empty; they are followed by a great dog that they have found seated howling on the steps of the theatre. Near the principal entrance they stumble over—

The body of a student, who has died from want of food, exhaustion, and the breaking of a blood-vessel.

Coming Home

by Nina Kiriki Hoffman

I love this house. Except that one closet. I don't think I'll ever, ever leave this house, no matter what happens or who lives here, even though I don't like the closet and it's so close to my room I hate to leave my room because then I have to go past it. I know what happened in that closet, but I don't think about it, or where my brother Matt is. He's been dead longer than I have. I'm still not sure if he's here in the house or not.

My room is the big room at the sunrise side of the upstairs. There's a great big picture window I can see the mountains from, and I love looking at them when the moon slips up behind them, because that's when I'm strongest, in the cool moonlight, not like the mornings when the sun flames across the sky. The sun makes me feel pale. I think that's funny because it used to turn me brown every summer.

This house is like a white wedding cake with a piece cut out in front. The upstairs is smaller and sits on top of the downstairs, and a giant came and cut a piece out of the middle of the downstairs. I think it might have been the piece with the biggest rose. The house is frosted white as a wedding, and upstairs, doors lead out onto the roof so I can pretend to be the bride on top of the cake. Mama called this house adobe. I think it's like living inside a cake with windows.

My best friend Robin, ten, a year older than me, used to live next door in the flat, ordinary house I can see from one of my windows. She liked to come visit, especially after I told her about the cake. She wanted to be a scientist. She said, "Livvie, if I had your brain, I'd put it in a glass bowl and ask it questions all the time."

She didn't say that after Matt was in the closet. Nobody said anything nice to me for a long time after that. We moved away and I never saw Robin again.

After twenty-five years, I was going back to the house I couldn't ever remember calling home, though I lived there with four brothers and my parents the first nine years I was alive. When my husband Scott turned the van onto the private lane that led to the house, I felt as though a lump of ice formed in my chest, as though I were all alone, even with Scott in the driver's seat beside me and the eight kids yelling all around us. Sarah was in my lap and she was as squirmy as a puppy. Dion kept tugging on my braid and saying, "Are we there yet, Mommy? Can I have my own room?" Sterling said he was the oldest and deserved a room of his own if anybody did. Carol said who said Sterling was the oldest? He didn't know his real birthday, did he? Maybe she was older. They had this argument every year when it got too close to June 20th, when we celebrated their birthdays together. The adoption agency had told us they had no birth certificate for Sterling.

Nick yelled for everybody to shut up. He had a deep little voice that reminded me of a frog's croak. He said this was a special moment and Maria wanted it to be nice so shut up. He always spoke up for Maria; she was our newest, only with us seven months, and still shy and quiet. Sometimes I wondered if she really said any of the things Nick credited her with, but it didn't matter; she clung to him and he cared for her, and that was enough. Later, when she settled in, I would ask her how she felt about things.

Prudence said, "Is this it, Mommy? Is this where you lived when you were little?"

I said, "It must be." I felt cold, even though sunlight splashed down on the lush greenery of gardens on both sides of the car. "It must be, but I don't really remember. Except—" I saw a patch of pampas grass in somebody's front yard, and a drive bordered with fuchsia bushes. I felt a shiver ripple up my back. None of this was new. Yet, when I reached for memories, I found only gray fog. My life began at my grandmother's house in San Francisco, almost ten years after I was born.

I thought that was what it was like for our kids. They had lives behind them, mostly in institutions, where they waited for someone to want them; then we adopted them, and their lives really started. I remembered the first time I handed Sterling, our first child, a rolling pin and invited him to flatten out some gingerbread dough so we could cut cookies. He was six, and very solemn. I didn't know how to talk to him; children seemed like another species to me, a fascinating species I wanted to study, but I didn't know how to approach them. When I handed Sterling the rolling pin, his eyes brightened. When I gave him the raisins for the gingerbread boys' eyes, I remembered my grandmother reaching out to drop precious raisins in my small hand—almost my first-ever memory.

That first contact with Sterling had warmed me, kindling my desire to learn about and love children the way Scott did. Scott spend a lot of his work time doing custody determinations; he was always concerned that the children he worked with stay with the best parent for them.

"What's that?" Artie asked, leaning forward to point past my shoulder, nearly hitting Sarah on the head as he did it.

"A stone pine tree," I said. And how did I know?

It was like a bonsai left by a giant, an enormous twisted tree, standing in the center of the driveway in an elevated circle of ground ringed by stones. There was the big turnaround in front of the houses at the end of the drive. I stared at the white one, a piece of the old Southwest transplanted to this Southern California town, blocky white adobe with vigas poking out here and there, its unlikeliest features its huge windows—in real adobe buildings, the windows were small, the thick walls conserving heat in the winter and cool in the summer. I had studied the Indian cultures of the Southwest in my anthropology courses. The vanished cultures interested me the most.

Scott pulled the van to a stop in front of the white adobe house. The lawn that separated it from the suburban house on the left looked weedy and overgrown. "Who wants to mow the lawn?" Scott asked in his best cheery voice.

"I do!" yelled Nick. Dion chimed in. Sterling laughed. He knows a trick when he hears one.

"Okay, Nick, you and Dion can help me, just as soon as the moving van gets here."

"Honey. Let's get the furniture set up first, okay?" I said. I had never suspected Scott had a passion for yard work. In the rambling house on the edge of town we'd been living in until this house came open, he left the yard to me, and concentrated on keeping the furniture in good repair and the plumbing healthy. I planted the tulip bulbs and coaxed Prudence and Carol into helping me weed. I had wanted to stay there, but Scott kept griping. "Via, you *own* that enormous house, for heaven's sake. How easy is it going to be to find renters? Why don't we just move in? We're one of the few families I know of who could actually use all that space."

I couldn't explain my reluctance. There was something about that house. . . . Ever since my father's will had been read three years earlier and he left the house to me, I had felt something in some tucked-away corner of my mind. After hearing the clause that left me title to the house, I had looked at my three brothers, strangers to me, angry strangers, who stared back.

Douglas, the oldest, had smiled a terrible smile at me.

Karl's eyes had gone wide. Then he turned his face away from me.

Mark said, "No. He can't mean that." He slumped down, a slender insubstantial thirty-year-old who had never grown up.

"I don't need it," I said. "I'll deed it over to you."

"No, Olivia," said Douglas. "That house belongs to you. Keep it."

Karl shook his head, but he didn't say anything.

Since the house came to me I had let Scott take care of all the maintenance and yard work. I let him deal with the renters. I didn't even want to see the house, and I couldn't tell him why. He accepted it, the same way he accepted my blank-slate childhood: with a kiss, and a "That's all right, Via. I don't have to understand."

"Come on, troops," Scott said now, hopping down out of the van and going around to sling open the sliding door.

"Mommy, I want out," said Sarah, reaching for the door handle. I let her out, then descended to the gravelly drive myself and stood staring at the blank white façade of the house. The children trooped up the brick walkway toward the front courtyard, a cobblestone patio between the wings of the lower story.

"Open it, open it," Carol cried, tugging at the front door.

Scott fished keys out of his pocket and opened the front door. The children pushed past him into the house. My throat closed. I felt dizzy. "Scott, don't let them out of your sight."

"What?" He glanced after them. They went whooping through the house, scattering. "Via. Calm down. I've been through this place with the termite people and there isn't an unsound board in the whole house. It's great."

"Scott," I said, and gripped his arm. "Scott."

He put his arm around me. "What is it, honey?"

"There's a—" I took two staggering steps and I was over the threshold and into the house, Scott supporting me. "Doesn't it smell bad in here?"

"Lysol, maybe. I had professional cleaners in. The last tenants left a mess, but they left a big cleaning deposit too."

"Not that," I said. I eased out of his embrace and strode down the front hallway, toward the western wing.

"The master bedroom's through here," Scott said, pointing down a little hall.

I turned away from him and mounted the stairs. "Nick!" I called. I heard his voice, arguing with Sterling's, above us. "Nick? Where's Artie?"

Carol came to the top of the stairs. "Mom! Guess what? There's a closet up here big enough to be a bedroom!"

I ran up the stairs. "Get out of there!"

I don't like that closet. It's the one place in the house I don't like. I haven't for a long time. Even before it turned into Matt's closet. Before Matt was in the closet, I was in the closet. He locked me in all the time. He was only one year older than me but he was lots bigger. When he was really feeling mean he'd hide the key so the others couldn't let me out, except Doug would hear me screaming in the closet and go get Mama and she had a key that worked too. She always said, "I must get Daddy to take the lock off that door!" but she never did.

I spent a lot of time in that closet. It had all kinds of great games and puzzles and things in it because it was the upstairs playroom closet, and crayons and poster paints and sketch pads. But Matt locked me in and left the light off—the light switch was outside—so I couldn't do anything about it. Once I found crayons and marked all over the walls in the dark because I was just so mad and nobody was home to let me out. Mama gave me Windex and a razor blade and some scrubbing things and made me clean everything off. I cut myself. There were some marks back behind the costumes for dress-up I never did get off, but she didn't look very close.

Matt and I were always fighting. He was mad because I got the big bedroom with its own bathroom. He said that wasn't fair, when he had to share a room with Doug, and Karl and Mark had to share a room too. Mama said it was because I was a girl. Matt said that wasn't fair either. Daddy said nobody ever promised anybody life would be fair.

After Matt was in the closet, nobody would talk to me. It took Daddy and Mama a long time to find a new house. They tried to sell our house but no one would buy it. So we stayed here.

I *do* love this house.

One night I ran down the stairs past Matt's closet and went to Daddy's study. At dinners and at breakfasts everybody looked at me and looked away. Nobody talked. I took a sack lunch to school and ate outside because nobody there would talk to me either. I went to

Daddy and said, "Tell me you love me, Daddy. Please please. Just tell me you love me. Just once."

And he cried, and he said, "Livvie, I know you can't understand this, baby. We're doing the best we can."

Scott held me and said, "What's wrong? What's wrong?"

I said, "Don't let the children go into that closet! Not until you take the door off, Scott. Promise me."

Sterling looked sideways at me. Maria came and hugged my waist. I picked her up and hugged her, burying my face in her clean black hair. "Oh, baby," I whispered, "I love you, I love you."

Scott said, "You kids, you heard your mother. Nobody goes in that closet, all right? I mean it, now."

"But Daddy," said Carol, "there's nothing in there. It's just empty. Except there's some marks on the wall."

I went to the threshold and stared in. Way on the back wall, some faint scribbles in purple crayon—a child's stick figure drawing of a person with a big frown on its face. And lower down, in green, three words: "help help help."

Somebody's been sleeping in my bed.

It's not really my bed. I mean, I can sit on my bed. Most of the time I just walk through all the furniture new people bring into the house, and I can walk through the new people, too. But now there are two girls sleeping in my room, on a bed that's in the same place my bed is. I can see and hear them better than I usually do.

And one of them is having a nightmare.

"Mommy! Mami!"

I heard two voices. Scott stirred in the bed beside me. "Go back to sleep," I murmured, "it's probably just first-night-in-a-new-place jitters."

He mumbled something about first-day jitters and how many jitters could the world possibly hold. I kissed him and got my robe and went upstairs.

Carol and Maria got the big room at the east end of the upstairs. The voices were theirs. I ran up the stairs, looked at the playroom closet—which Scott had nailed shut for me, after I checked it three times to be absolutely certain none of the children was inside—and went to the girls' room.

"Mommy, Maria's having a nightmare," Carol said, sitting up in her white nightgown. Maria had a grip on Carol's hand, and her eyes were wide and frightened. "She wouldn't let me go get you."

"Mami! A spirit, a spirit!"

"What? What is it, baby?" I sat on the bed beside her and hugged her.

"Is my sister," she whispered. "The little one, oh, pobrecito."

"Maria," I whispered. "You have a sister?"

"Nick said she had a little sister but she died," said Carol.

"The agency didn't tell us. Oh, baby. I'm so sorry." And I thought, no, I was wrong. Their lives don't start when they join our family. Scott talks to them about their pasts. Whenever something like that comes up I turn it over to Scott. He remembers being a child. He knows what it is like to have a past, and how to live with one. "Would you like some warm milk with honey in it?" I asked Maria.

"Mami!" she cried, and pointed past my shoulder.

I looked, and saw a little girl shimmering there, in front of the closet door. Cold terror touched my heart. I hugged Maria tightly, more for my comfort than hers. Carol climbed onto the bed behind me, putting her arms around my shoulders. "Daddy!" she screamed.

"Shh," I said, "shh." And then a song woke in me, a lullaby, not one of Grandma's, though. I sang.

> Evening's come, and day is done,
> Gone are sing and shout
> Time to rest in blanket nest
> And blow the candles out.
>
> Down the road to dreams you'll go
> There to stay and play
> Nothing here but sleeping self
> Come to the end of day.
>
> Know I love you when you go
> Wherever you may roam
> I'll be here to welcome you
> When you come back home.

I heard my voice, and thought it wasn't really my voice. It was my mother's voice. I couldn't even remember my mother speaking to me, let alone singing to me. The little shimmering girl crept closer to us. I felt Carol's fingers tighten like talons on my shoulders. "Mama," said the little girl. Her voice sounded like someone talking underwater.

Maria let out a wail and buried her face against my breast.

"Mama," said the little girl. She reached out and touched my face——The little girl vanished.

The three of us sat on the bed and wailed and wailed, clutching at each other. And I remembered. . . .

I colored in my coloring book so carefully, staying inside the lines. Matt took a black crayon and marked across my three favorite pictures. I wanted to put them on my bulletin board. But he wrecked them.

I locked him in the closet.

Matt was in sailing camp with Robin's brother Tommy and he didn't want to leave the neighborhood. He was supposed to stay with Robin and Tommy while the rest of us went to visit Gramma in San Francisco. She was sick. I locked Matt in the closet right before we left.

And I forgot.

Matt was supposed to feed our cats while we were gone, even my cat, Little Explorer. They were outside cats and when they didn't get fed they all ran away.

When we came back from two weeks at Gramma's there was a smell in the house.

Tommy's and Robin's mother saw our big station wagon pull in and she came running across the lawn. "Isn't Matt with you?" she said. "I tried to call you and ask but I couldn't remember your mother's name." And she looked in the car and Doug and Karl and Mark and I looked back. I thought maybe Matt ran away. He used to talk about running away. So did I. Sometimes at night we snuck out on the roof together and talked about running away. Matt wanted to go to Mexico. He wanted to find an iguana and tame it for a pet. For a minute I thought maybe Matt went to Mexico, but then I remembered . . .

Carol's face was hot and wet, pressed into the back of my neck. I could feel Maria's hot tears soaking through my robe and nightgown. I felt a chill in me that even the heat of tears could not banish, as the nine-year-old child inside me began to speak.

Concert to Death

by Paul Ernst

The stage was illuminated brightly, rawly. Every ridge on the ugly steel fire-curtain stood out in the ghostly white radiance.

On the stage were a concert grand piano and a battered piano stool. The top of the piano was down, shutting in the sounding-board. A black drape was thrown over it. A vase of yellow roses was set on the closed, draped lid.

All was in readiness for Lucchesi to enter from the wings, to bow and smile as he walked to the piano, as he had done so many times in his life. Everything was as the master pianist liked it: his favorite, battered old piano stool; piano set in the right-center of a perfectly bare stage; nothing but the raw steel fire-curtain for a backdrop; harsh, uncompromising light.

Only the piano itself was different. For it is not usual for the lid of a concert grand to be down during a performance, nor for the case to be draped and to support a vase of flowers or anything else that might muffle pure clarity of tone.

In the orchestra pit sat the orchestra, instruments tuned and ready, musical scores opened on the racks before each member, tiny lights glimmering like glow-worms over the racks. The orchestra conductor stood before them with arms poised like the wings of a bird about to take off, and with his head back to nod for the opening crash of harmony.

Behind him, in the great auditorium with its thousands of seats, a breathless hush prevailed. In the hush the gradual dimming of the indirect lights overhead had been like a silent dusk over an unrippled lake. In the vast silence just one sound was heard, for an instant—a woman's sobbing.

The conductor's arms swooped down. The opening bar of Lucchesi's *Minuet in G* flooded the huge hall with quivering melody. Every instrument was adding to the tide of music—but the piano. Every musician was playing—but the great Lucchesi himself.

The sobbing sounded again, instantly stifled.

The piece, a short one, drew to its conclusion and silence again held the house. The conductor turned from his rack and faced the thousands of seats. He raised his baton as though to still thunderous applause; which was odd, because there was no applause.

"We will now play Lucchesi's *Dance of the Sprites,*" the conductor said. And his voice rang in the auditorium with the hollow boom of a voice in an empty cavern. Rightly so! For there was no one in the vast hall.

The thousands of seats were empty. The boxes, galleries and balconies were empty. On the bare stage was Lucchesi's piano. Yes, but there was no Lucchesi there to play it. There never would be again.

Lucchesi was dead.

"Kind of gets you, doesn't it?" whispered one of the three men in the left wing.

The three were Howard Kent, star reporter for the *Globe,* who was here on sufferance and not for publicity purposes; Milnor Roberts, music critic on the same newspaper; and Isaac Loewenbohn, owner of the auditorium. It was Kent who had spoken.

"Kind of gets you," he repeated, looking across the length of bare stage between the footlights and the fire-curtain.

In the other wing a woman stood alone: a woman dressed in mourning, with a white face standing out against the black like a dainty white cameo. The woman's red underlip was caught between her teeth and her body shook with suppressed sobs.

"It's certainly a unique idea," Kent whispered on. He was afraid that if he didn't talk he would get sloppy, which is no way for a hard-boiled reporter to get. "Staging a Lucchesi concert when Lucchesi is food for worms. Eccentric idea."

"A nice idea, I t'ink," said Loewenbohn, scowling at the reporter. "Today, one year from the day Lucchesi has died, his friends and fellow musicians hold an all-Lucchesi concert in memoriam. That is a nice tribute."

Roberts, the music critic, nodded abstractedly. His mind was full of the piece the orchestra was now playing. *Dance of the Sprites* had been written for a piano lead. There were three long interludes in it when only the piano played—and the piano on the stage had no player before its keyboard!

"Wonder how they'll treat the piano interludes," he whispered to Loewenbohn as the first one drew near. "Will they fill in?"

The auditorium owner shrugged. There was a piano in the pit. Perhaps the orchestra pianist would play Lucchesi's interludes.

But the conductor was more subtle than that.

The three men leaned forward a little as the composition reached the first interlude and died away in a shower of flute notes. Now it was time for the piano to pick up the thread. Now it was time for Lucchesi to crash in. . . .

Only there was no Lucchesi.

There was silence, while the conductor faced the piano on the stage, with his baton at rest by his side. Silence. The tense, oppressive silence that comes when music is interrupted, but when you know the piece is not yet finished.

In that silence conductor and orchestra stared at the piano on the stage; stared and held their instruments in readiness to play again. There was an eery matter-of-factness about orchestra and conductor. It was as though of course Lucchesi was seated on the stool; of course he was playing his piano. Death? They were wordlessly refusing it its power. Particularly the conductor. . . .

"Look at him!" muttered the reporter, running his forefinger around under his collar. "Look at him!"

The orchestra leader's body was swaying very slightly. His eyes were wide, mystic, as he stared at the piano—and at the empty stool.

"You'd think Lucchesi really was there, playing!"

The other two paid no attention to him. The critic softly hummed the interlude Lucchesi would be playing if he were alive. Loewenbohn's heavy face seemed less florid than usual.

The critic stopped humming. Even as he did so, the conductor raised his baton and the orchestra went on with the composition, softly, for the piano notes were supposed to sound over the other instruments for a few more bars.

Kent moistened his lips and stared at the keyboard. Curious. For just an instant it had seemed to him that the keys were being rhythmically depressed, as though at the touch of unseen fingers. But that, of course, was imagination.

The piano standing on the bare stage in lonely majesty; the funereal drape over the closed case, and the scent of the yellow roses; the somber dignity with which the orchestra played to an empty auditorium—these things tended to make you see what did not exist.

"Marvelous stuff, that music," Kent said, resolutely keeping the shiver out of his voice.

Roberts nodded. "Lucchesi had supreme genius. It was tragic that he had to die."

"Yeah. And only forty-one. A guy that could turn out stuff like this!"

Roberts smiled.

"Yes, this is superb. But it's not as fine as Lucchesi's last composition—one he finished just before he died last year. That piece was greatest of all."

Loewenbohn's heavy eyebrows went up.

"I don't t'ink I ever heard of that piece," he said.

"Few have," replied Roberts. "And no one ever heard it played. It's lost."

"Huh?" said Kent. "But if nobody ever heard it, how do you know it was so great?"

The critic shrugged.

"Lucchesi said it was," he said simply. "He worked on it for nearly a year, in secret, as he always composed. He finished it. He told me and one or two other close friends about it. He died—and no one has ever been able to find the score."

Kent shook his head. "That's tough. And Mrs. Lucchesi is flat broke, too. I did a story on her six months ago. Living with her sister —lost the insurance money—even Lucchesi's piano in storage. By the way, the piano on the stage is really Lucchesi's own, isn't it?"

Roberts looked at the shrouded piano and nodded.

"We got it out of storage for the occasion. Tomorrow"—he looked across at Lucchesi's widow—"it is to be sold at auction. She has to have money."

"If only she could find the song!" sympathized Kent.

"It would mean a lot to her," responded Roberts. "There's no real wealth in genius. But the song would bring several thousand dollars. And it would bring Lucchesi tremendous posthumous fame."

He stopped talking. The second piano interlude was near.

The orchestral notes slowed. The conductor and each musician in the pit gazed at the draped piano.

Instinctively the three men in the left wing stared at it too. And in the right wing Lucchesi's widow swayed forward a little, with her arms going out and her lips parting.

The orchestra stopped playing. Everything was in readiness. All was waiting on Lucchesi, who would play no more. . . .

But as the thick stillness of the interlude continued, Kent, watching the keyboard of Lucchesi's piano with eyes that were less cynical than usual, began to have an insane idea that perhaps the great composer *was* here at the concert held in his memory.

Surely there was a tall, shadowy figure seated on the old stool. Surely long, steely fingers were flying over the keyboard. Surely a shower of notes was sounding from the instrument that had known for so long the touch of those fingers.

78

The conductor was again swaying, as though to a cascade of harmony. But now his eyes were wide, almost frightened-looking; and his mouth was a little open and his head was bent as though he dimly heard something not quite audible to others there. The musicians, too, in this second, almost ghastly silence, were not quite the same as they had been in the first interlude. They were rigid in the pit, the lights over their racks reflecting on the whites of their staring eyes and on points of moisture on their tense faces.

Kent drew a deep breath, and glanced at Roberts and Loewenbohn quickly to see if they had heard how shaky his sigh was.

The atmosphere of this memorial concert—this concert to death— had changed. A new element had entered it, somehow. A sort of electricity charged the air. Kent could feel it. He knew the others felt it. He found himself holding his breath, waiting, waiting . . . for what? He did not know.

Once more he tore his eyes from the keyboard of Lucchesi's piano. The keys were *not* moving! How could they, with no fingers to move them?

He saw Lucchesi's widow stagger a little, and started impulsively toward her. She raised her slim hand and waved him back.

The conductor raised his baton. Sweat was glistening on his forehead. He waved his arms, and the musicians, with an obvious effort, swung into the *Dance.*

Kent gulped with relief as the hushed stillness was broken. The strain was lifted a little now; and he took refuge from his inexplicable nervousness by telling himself that this whole thing was a silly farce: getting Loewenbohn to donate the place this afternoon, scraping up an orchestra, dragging Lucchesi's piano from the warehouse—and then acting as though the dead man were here and playing before an accustomed audience! Crazy!

And it was ripping Lucchesi's widow to pieces. He stared across at her and was alarmed by her pallor. They simply shouldn't have permitted this.

She must be terribly broke—forced to put Lucchesi's piano in storage because she had no home of her own to put it in. And it must be the devil for her to have to sell it. It would bring a good price, though. Lucchesi's own piano. . . .

"You say they looked everywhere for that last composition of his?" he whispered to Roberts under cover of the music.

The critic nodded. "Of course. All his effects were gone over." His voice was like Kent's: not quite steady, a little strained. And his eyes, like Kent's, were continually turning toward the keyboard of the funereally draped piano. "I helped in the search myself. But he'd hidden it too well."

"Hidden it?" repeated Kent. "Why did he hide it?"

"He thought somebody was trying to steal it. At the very last, he was not a well man. He had delusions. But there were no delusions about his composition. That must have been grand."

The music welling from the musicians in the pit was sublime. No man there had ever played so well before. They were inspired, playing beyond themselves, as though they themselves were but instruments manipulated by a master hand.

The third, and last, piano interlude in *Dance of the Sprites* drew near. The orchestral notes began fading as the piano was supposed to pick up the thread of the composition. Kent scowled.

"I wish they wouldn't *do* this! It's . . . it's . . . damn it, it's ghostly!"

"Shut up," whispered Roberts, his voice thin and brittle.

The last note died away. The great, empty hall swam again in silence. Live, electric silence. Every gaze was riveted on the black-draped piano on the bare stage.

Again the illusion came to Kent, terrifically, that there was a figure on the stool, that long fingers raced over the keyboard in the climactic crash of the interlude. Surely, surely . . .

Roberts started, and stared first at the piano on the stage and then at the piano in the pit. His mouth hung open and his face paled. The great vein in his throat pulsed jerkily.

Kent avoided looking at him. The reporter didn't want to see in the critic's eyes confirmation of something he was telling himself wildly had *not* happened. For he, too, had thought to hear the thing that had sent the blood from Roberts' face: a low, dim note sounding from Lucchesi's piano.

It did not help any to gaze at Loewenbohn and discover that the auditorium owner's face had gone a sickly gray; nor to look from there to the orchestra pit and see that the conductor had dropped his baton and was pressing his fists against the sides of his head while he stared as though in a trance at the piano on the stage.

The interlude was ending. On the score a fountain of notes in upward crescendo culminated in a single note, loud and clear, sustained a moment; then a crescendo to the bass.

Kent gazed at the keyboard of Lucchesi's piano. He didn't want to look at it; he willed his eyes to turn away; but he couldn't look in any other direction. He stared at it, and he saw the keys ripple in an upward sweep. Up and up. A trick of the light! he told himself wildly. A trick of the light!

In the throbbing silence of the empty auditorium a piano note sounded loud and clear.

The three men stared at each other and then, like sleep-walkers, at Lucchesi's piano.

The note faded in the immense stillness . . . faded and was lost.

Lucchesi's widow screamed. She stumbled onto the stage toward the piano, fell, got up again, went on. She collapsed over the piano, cheek to the sable drape, hands clutching at its funereal folds.

"He's *here!*" she screamed. "That note . . . you all heard . . . he's *here!*"

Kent's nails bit into the palms of his hands. Then he caught Roberts' shoulder in a convulsive grip.

"The piano in the pit!" he stuttered. "It was the piano in the pit! Someone in the orchestra sounded it!"

Roberts only wrenched his shoulder free and turned to the woman sobbing over the piano. There was no one near the piano in the pit.

"Here—with us!" cried Lucchesi's widow brokenly. "He came to our anniversary concert! Carlo . . . Carlo! . . ."

"I won't be a fool!" Kent heard his own voice sound out, high and flat. "I won't believe this! I won't!"

But no one paid attention. His voice died away. But the ghostly vibration of the clear high note still seemed to stir the air of the empty hall.

Lucchesi's widow stood erect beside the piano, with her arms spread in supplication toward the empty piano stool.

"Carlo, you are here! You are! Carlo . . . tell me . . . where is the missing score? Where is your last masterpiece?"

The silence hurt the ears as she faced the battered, empty stool, as she called to a man a year dead. Loewenbohn's thick lips were moving soundlessly. The musicians in the pit seemed figures of stone. Roberts and Kent rigidly faced the piano.

"Carlo, tell me," entreated Lucchesi's widow. "Tell me! Please, please, where is the score? Not for me—for you. Your greatest piece. Tell me where it is."

The myriad seats in the auditorium seemed occupied by a vast audience turning ghostly faces toward the stage, uniting with the living folk in wings and pit in staring at the keyboard of Lucchesi's piano.

And the keys—the keys! . . .

They were rippling in a downward sweep, a downward crescendo toward the bass.

"Carlo!" called Lucchesi's widow.

A bass note sounded from Lucchesi's piano—that piano which had no player that mortal eyes could see. A single note, loud and clear. . . .

No, not clear! Loud, it was; but it was cracked, tinny, as if invisible hands were laid on the strings in the closed ebony case.

A thick exclamation tore from Roberts' lips. He stared at the orchestra leader, who stared back at him while comprehension dawned in the eyes of both. Then the music critic started running along the strip of stage to the piano.

Lucchesi's widow was gazing pitifully, tragically, at the battered piano stool.

"Here!" she faltered. "He was here. And he would not answer me . . . would not tell me!"

"But he *has* answered you," Roberts said gently. "He *has*. With that last note. You heard how it sounded. How stupid for no one of us to think to look there before!"

With a trembling hand he took the vase of yellow roses from the top of the concert grand and set it on the floor. He swept the black drape aside and opened the lid—the first time the top had been opened since Lucchesi's death a year ago.

There, on the bass strings where Lucchesi had hastily thrust them, were penciled sheets of music.

The priceless score, Lucchesi's missing masterpiece!

The Considerate Hosts

by Thorp McClusky

Midnight.

It was raining, abysmally. Not the kind of rain in which people sometimes fondly say they like to walk, but rain that was heavy and pitiless, like the rain that fell in France during the war. The road, unrolling slowly beneath Marvin's headlights, glistened like the flank of a great blacksnake; almost Marvin expected it to writhe out from beneath the wheels of his car. Marvin's small coupé was the only man-made thing that moved through the seething night.

Within the car, however, it was like a snug little cave. Marvin might almost have been in a theater, unconcernedly watching some somber drama in which he could revel without really being touched. His sensation was almost one of creepiness; it was incredible that he could be so close to the rain and still so warm and dry. He hoped devoutly that he would not have a flat tire on a night like this!

Ahead a tiny red pinpoint appeared at the side of the road, grew swiftly, then faded in the car's glare to the bull's-eye of a lantern, swinging in the gloved fist of a big man in a streaming rubber coat. Marvin automatically braked the car and rolled the right-hand window down a little way as he saw the big man come splashing toward him.

"Bridge's washed away," the big man said. "Where you going, Mister?"

"Felders, damn it!"

"You'll have to go around by Little Rock Falls. Take your left up that road. It's a county road, but it's passable. Take your right after you cross Little Rock Falls bridge. It'll bring you into Felders."

Marvin swore. The trooper's face, black behind the ribbons of water dripping from his hat, laughed.

"It's a bad night, Mister."

"Gosh, yes! Isn't it!"

Well, if he must detour, he must detour. What a night to crawl for miles along a rutty back road!

Rutty was no word for it. Every few feet Marvin's car plunged into water-filled holes, gouged out from beneath by the settling of the light roadbed. The sharp, cutting sound of loose stone against the tires was audible even above the hiss of the rain.

Four miles, and Marvin's motor began to sputter and cough. Another mile, and it surrendered entirely. The ignition was soaked; the car would not budge.

Marvin peered through the moisture-streaked windows, and, vaguely, like blacker masses beyond the road, he sensed the presence of thickly clustered trees. The car had stopped in the middle of a little patch of woods. "Judas!" Marvin thought disgustedly. "What a swell place to get stalled!" He switched off the lights to save the battery.

He saw the glimmer then, through the intervening trees, indistinct in the depths of rain.

Where there was a light there was certainly a house, and perhaps a telephone. Marvin pulled his hat tightly down upon his head, clasped his coat collar up around his ears, got out of the car, pushed the small coupé over on the shoulder of the road, and ran for the light.

The house stood perhaps twenty feet back from the road, and the light shone from a front-room window. As he plowed through the muddy yard—there was no sidewalk—Marvin noticed a second stalled car—a big sedan—standing black and deserted a little way down the road.

The rain was beating him, soaking him to the skin; he pounded on the house door like an impatient sheriff. Almost instantly the door swung open, and Marvin saw a man and a woman standing just inside, in a little hallway that led directly into a well-lighted living-room.

The hallway itself was quite dark. And the man and woman were standing close together, almost as though they might be endeavoring to hide something behind them. But Marvin, wholly preoccupied with his own plight, failed to observe how unusual it must be for these two rural people to be up and about, fully dressed, long after midnight.

Partly shielded from the rain by the little overhang above the door, Marvin took off his dripping hat and urgently explained his plight.

"My car. Won't go. Wires wet, I guess. I wonder if you'd let me use your phone? I might be able to get somebody to come out from Little Rock Falls. I'm sorry that I had to—"

"That's all right," the man said. "Come inside. When you knocked at the door you startled us. We—we really hadn't—well, you know how it is, in the middle of the night and all. But come in."

"We'll have to think this out differently, John," the woman said suddenly.

Think what out differently? thought Marvin absently.

Marvin muttered something about you never can be too careful about strangers, what with so many hold-ups and all. And, oddly, he sensed that in the half darkness the man and woman smiled briefly at each other, as though they shared some secret that made any conception of physical danger to themselves quietly, mildly amusing.

"We weren't thinking of you in that way," the man reassured Marvin. "Come into the living-room."

The living room of that house was—just ordinary. Two overstuffed chairs, a davenport, a bookcase. Nothing particularly modern about the room. Not elaborate, but adequate.

In the brighter light Marvin looked at his hosts. The man was around forty years of age, the woman considerably younger, twenty-eight, or perhaps thirty. And there was something definitely attractive

84

about them. It was not their appearance so much, for in appearance they were merely ordinary people; the woman was almost painfully plain. But they moved and talked with a curious singleness of purpose. They reminded Marvin of a pair of gray doves.

Marvin looked around the room until he saw the telephone in a corner, and he noticed with some surprise that it was one of the old-style, coffee-grinder affairs. The man was watching him with peculiar intentness.

"We haven't tried to use the telephone tonight," he told Marvin abruptly, "but I'm afraid it won't work."

"I don't see how it *can* work," the woman added.

Marvin took the receiver off the hook and rotated the little crank. No answer from Central. He tried again, several times, but the line remained dead.

The man nodded his head slowly. "I didn't think it would work," he said, then.

"Wires down or something, I suppose," Marvin hazarded. "Funny thing, I haven't seen one of those old-style phones in years. Didn't think they used 'em any more."

"You're out in the sticks now," the man laughed. He glanced from the window at the almost opaque sheets of rain falling outside.

"You might as well stay here a little while. While you're with us you'll have the illusion, at least, that you're in a comfortable house."

What on earth is he talking about? Marvin asked himself. Is he just a little bit off, maybe? That last sounded like nonsense.

Suddenly the woman spoke.

"He'd better go, John. He can't stay here too long, you know. It would be horrible if someone took his license number and people—jumped to conclusions afterward. No one should know that he stopped here."

The man looked thoughtfully at Marvin.

"Yes, dear, you're right. I hadn't thought that far ahead. I'm afraid, sir, that you'll have to leave," he told Marvin. "Something extremely strange—"

Marvin bristled angrily, and buttoned his coat with an air of affronted dignity.

"I'll go," he said shortly. "I realize perfectly that I'm an intruder. You should not have let me in. After you let me in I began to expect ordinary human courtesy from you. I was mistaken. Good night."

The man stopped him. He seemed very much distressed.

"Just a moment. Don't go until we explain. We have never been considered discourteous before. But tonight—tonight . . .

"I must introduce myself. I am John Reed, and this is my wife, Grace."

He paused significantly, as though that explained everything, but Marvin merely shook his head. "My name's Marvin Phelps, but that's nothing to you. All this talk seems pretty needless."

The man coughed nervously. "Please understand. We're only asking you to go for your own good."

"Oh, sure," Marvin said. "Sure. I understand perfectly. Good night."

The man hesitated. "You see," he said slowly, "things aren't as they seem. We're really ghosts."

"You don't say!"

"My husband is quite right," the woman said loyally. "We've been dead twenty-one years."

"Twenty-two years next October," the man added, after a moment's calculation. "It's a long time."

"Well, I never heard such hooey!" Marvin babbled. "Kindly step away from that door, Mister, and let me out of here before I swing from the heels."

"I know it sounds odd," the man admitted, without moving, "and I hope that you will realize that it's from no choosing of mine that I have to explain. Nevertheless, I was electrocuted, twenty-one years ago, for the murder of the Chairman of the School Board, over in Little Rock Falls. Notice how my head is shaved, and my split trouser-leg? The fact is, that whenever we materialize we have to appear exactly as we were in our last moment of life. It's a restriction on us."

Screwy, certainly screwy. And yet Marvin hazily remembered that School Board affair. Yes, the murderer *had* been a fellow named Reed. The wife had committed suicide a few days after burial of her husband's body.

It was such an odd insanity. Why, they *both* believed it. They even dressed the part. That odd dress the woman was wearing. 'Way out of date. And the man's slit trouser-leg. The screwy cluck had even shaved a little patch on his head, too, and his shirt was open at the throat.

They didn't look dangerous, but you never can tell. Better humor them, and get out of here as quick as I can.

Marvin cleared his throat.

"If I were you—why, say, I'd have lots of fun materializing. I'd be at it every night. Build up a reputation for myself."

The man looked disgusted. "I should kick you out of doors," he remarked bitterly. "I'm trying to give you a decent explanation, and you keep making fun of me."

"Don't bother with him, John," the wife exclaimed. "It's getting late."

"Mr. Phelps," the self-styled ghost doggedly persisted, ignoring the woman's interruption, "perhaps you noticed a car stalled on the side of the road as you came into our yard. Well, that car, Mr. Phelps, belongs to Lieutenant-Governor Lyons, of Felders, who prosecuted me for that murder and won a conviction, although he knew that I was innocent. Of course he wasn't Lieutenant-Governor then; he was only County Prosecutor. . . .

"That was a political murder, and Lyons knew it. But at that time he still had his way to make in the world—and circumstances pointed toward me. For example, the body of the slain man was found in the ditch just beyond my house. The body had been robbed. The murderer had thrown the victim's pocketbook and watch under our front steps. Lyons said that I had *hidden* them there—though obviously I'd never have done a suicidal thing like that, had I really been the murderer. Lyons knew that, too—but he had to burn somebody.

"What really convicted me was the fact that my contract to teach had not been renewed that spring. It gave Lyons a ready-made motive to pin on me.

"So he framed me. They tried, sentenced, and electrocuted me, all very neatly and legally. Three days after I was buried, my wife committed suicide."

Though Marvin was a trifle afraid, he was nevertheless beginning to enjoy himself. Boy, what a story to tell the gang! If only they'd believe him!

"I can't understand," he pointed out slyly, "how you can be so free with this house if, as you say, you've been dead twenty-one years or so. Don't the present owners or occupants object? If I lived here I certainly wouldn't turn the place over to a couple of ghosts—especially on a night like this!"

The man answered readily, "I told you that things are not as they seem. This house has not been lived in since Grace died. It's not a very modern house, anyway—and people have natural prejudices. At this very moment you are standing in an empty room. Those windows are broken. The wallpaper has peeled away, and half the plaster has fallen off the walls. There is really no light in the house. If things appeared to you as they really are you could not see your hand in front of your face."

Marvin felt in his pocket for his cigarettes. "Well," he said, "you seem to know all the answers. Have a cigarette. Or don't ghosts smoke?"

The man extended his hand. "Thanks," he replied. "This is an unexpected pleasure. You'll notice that although there are ash-trays about the room there are no cigarettes or tobacco. Grace never smoked, and when they took me to jail she brought all my tobacco there to me. Of course, as I pointed out before, you see this room exactly as it was at the time she killed herself. She's wearing the same dress, for example. There's a certain form about these things, you know."

Marvin lit the cigarettes. "Well!" he exclaimed. "Brother, you certainly seem to think of everything! Though I can't understand, even yet, why you want me to get out of here. I should think that after you've gone to all this trouble, arranging your effects and so on, you'd want somebody to haunt."

The woman laughed dryly.

"Oh, you're not the man we want to haunt, Mr. Phelps. You came along quite by accident; we hadn't counted on you at all. No, Mr. Lyons is the man we're interested in."

"He's out in the hall now," the man said suddenly. He jerked his head toward the door through which Marvin had come. And all at once all this didn't seem half so funny to Marvin as it had seemed a moment before.

"You see," the woman went on quickly, "this house of ours is on a back road. Nobody ever travels this way. We've been trying for years to —to haunt Mr. Lyons, but we've had very little success. He lives in Felders, and we're pitifully weak when we go to Felders. We're strongest when we're in this house, perhaps because we lived here so long.

"But tonight, when the bridge went out, we knew that our opportunity had arrived. We knew that Mr. Lyons was not in Felders, and we knew that he would have to take this detour in order to get home.

"We felt very strongly that Mr. Lyons would be unable to pass this house tonight.

"It turned out as we had hoped. Mr. Lyons had trouble with his car, exactly as you did, and he came straight to this house to ask if he might use the telephone. Perhaps he had forgotten us, years ago— twenty-one years is a long time. Perhaps he was confused by the rain, and didn't know exactly where he was.

"He fainted, Mr. Phelps, the instant he recognized us. We have known for a long time that his heart is weak, and we had hoped that seeing us would frighten him to death, but he is still alive. Of course while he is unconscious we can do nothing more. Actually, we're almost impalpable. If you weren't so convinced that we are real you could pass your hand right through us.

"We decided to wait until Mr. Lyons regained consciousness and then to frighten him again. We even discussed beating him to death with one of those non-existent chairs you think you see. You understand, his body would be unmarked; he would really die of terror. We were still discussing what to do when you came along.

"We realized at once how embarrassing it might prove for you if Mr. Lyons' body were found in this house tomorrow and the police learned that you were also in the house. That's why we want you to go."

"Well," Marvin said bluntly, "I don't see how I can get my car away from here. It won't run, and if I walk to Little Rock Falls and get somebody to come back here with me the damage'll be done."

"Yes," the man admitted thoughtfully. "It's a problem."

For several minutes they stood like a tableau, without speaking. Marvin was uneasily wondering: Did these people really have old Lyons tied up in the hallway; were they really planning to murder the man? The big car standing out beside the road belonged to *somebody*. . . .

Marvin coughed discreetly.

"Well, it seems to me, my dear shades," he said, "that unless you are perfectly willing to put me into what might turn out to be a very unpleasant position you'll have to let your vengeance ride, for tonight, anyway."

"There'll never be another opportunity like this," the man pointed out. "That bridge won't go again in ten lifetimes."

"We don't want the young man to suffer though, John."

"It seems to me," Marvin suggested, "as though this revenge idea of yours is overdone, anyway. Murdering Lyons won't really do you any good, you know."

"It's the customary thing when a wrong has been done," the man protested.

"Well, maybe," Marvin argued, and all the time he was wondering whether he were really facing a madman who might be dangerous or whether he were at home dreaming in bed; "but I'm not so sure about that. Hauntings are pretty infrequent, you must admit. I'd say that shows that a lot of ghosts really don't care much about the vengeance angle, despite all you say. I think that if you check on it carefully you'll find that a great many ghosts realize that revenge isn't so much. It's really the thinking about revenge, and the planning it, that's all the fun. Now, for the sake of argument, what good would it do you to put old Lyons away? Why, you'd hardly have any incentive to be ghosts any more. But if you let him go, why, say, any time you wanted to, you could start to scheme up a good scare for him, and begin to calculate how it would work, and time would fly like everything. And on top of all that, if anything happened to me on account of tonight, it would be just too bad for you. *You'd* be haunted, really. It's a bad rule that doesn't work two ways."

The woman looked at her husband. "He's right, John," she said tremulously. "We'd better let Lyons go."

The man nodded. He looked worried.

He spoke very stiffly to Marvin. "I don't agree entirely with all you've said," he pointed out, "but I admit that in order to protect you we'll have to let Lyons go. If you'll give me a hand we'll carry him out and put him in his car."

"Actually, I suppose, I'll be doing all the work."

"Yes," the man agreed, "you will."

They went into the little hall, and there, to Marvin's complete astonishment, crumpled on the floor lay old Lyons. Marvin recognized him easily from the newspaper photographs he had seen.

"Hard-looking duffer, isn't he?" Marvin said, trying to stifle a tremor in his voice.

The man nodded without speaking.

Together, Marvin watching the man narrowly, they carried the lax body out through the rain and put it into the big sedan. When the job was done the man stood silently for a moment, looking up into the black invisible clouds.

"It's clearing," he said matter-of-factly. "In an hour it'll be over."

"My wife'll kill me when I get home," Marvin said.

The man made a little clucking sound. "Maybe if you wiped your ignition now your car'd start. It's had a chance to dry a little."

"I'll try it," Marvin said. He opened the hood and wiped the distributor cap and points and around the spark plugs with his handkerchief. He got in the car and stepped on the starter, and the motor caught almost immediately.

The man stepped toward the door, and Marvin doubled his right fist, ready for anything. But then the man stopped.

"Well, I suppose you'd better be going along," he said. "Good night."

"Good night," Marvin said. "And thanks. I'll stop by one of these days and say hello."

"You wouldn't find us in," the man said simply.

By Heaven, he *is* nuts, Marvin thought. "Listen, brother," he said earnestly, "you aren't going to do anything funny to old Lyons after I'm gone?"

The other shook his head. "No. Don't worry."

Marvin let in the clutch and stepped on the gas. He wanted to get out of there as quickly as possible.

In Little Rock Falls he went into an all-night lunch and telephoned the police that there was an unconscious man sitting in a car three or four miles back on the detour. Then he drove home.

Early the next morning, on his way to work, he drove back over the detour.

He kept watching for the little house, and when it came in sight he recognized it easily from the contour of the rooms and the spacing of the windows and the little overhang above the door.

But as he came closer he saw that it was deserted. The windows were out, the steps had fallen in. The clapboards were gray and weather-beaten, and naked rafters showed through holes in the roof.

Marvin stopped his car and sat there beside the road for a little while, his face oddly pale. Finally he got out of the car and walked over to the house and went inside.

There was not one single stick of furniture in the rooms. Jagged scars showed in the ceilings where the electric fixtures had been torn away. The house had been wrecked years before by vandals, by neglect, by the merciless wearing of the sun and the rain.

In shape alone were the hallway and living-room as Marvin remembered them. *"There,"* he thought, "is where the bookcases were. The table was *there*—the davenport *there.*"

Suddenly he stooped, and stared at the dusty boards and underfoot.

On the naked floor lay the butt of a cigarette. And, a half-dozen feet away, lay another cigarette that had not been smoked—that had not even been lighted!

Marvin turned around blindly, and, like an automaton, walked out of that house.

Three days later he read in the newspapers that Lieutenant-Governor Lyons was dead. The Lieutenant-Governor had collapsed, the item continued, while driving his own car home from the state capital the night the Felders bridge was washed out. The death was attributed to heart disease. . . .

After all, Lyons was not a young man.

So Marvin Phelps knew that, even though his considerate ghostly hosts had voluntarily relinquished their vengeance, blind, impartial nature had meted out justice. And, in a strange way, he felt glad that that was so, glad that Grace and John Reed had left to Fate the punishment they had planned to impose with their own ghostly hands. . . .

Daddy

by Steve Rasnic Tem

Daddy will never let me go.

Daddy said he would come for me; he said Mother couldn't keep me away from him forever. He would be back, with candy and toys, and the two of us would go away to where the forest grew all along the seashore, and there were animals there that talked, and all the lumberjacks smiled at you because they were so happy you wanted to live there too.

I don't understand why Daddy and Mother don't like each other anymore. But they haven't liked each other for a long time. I must have been very small when they liked each other, because they haven't been friends for as long as I can remember. I heard Daddy say one time that Mother hated him, and when I asked him if he hated her too he said he couldn't say. That must mean he does. I wonder sometimes how they could like me, when they hate each other so much.

Daddy's face used to go funny when I asked him about that. But he still didn't answer me.

My Daddy is a woodworker; he makes cabinets and chairs and other wood things, and sometimes wooden toys. Ducks and dogs and chickens you push; their wheels go round and a metal piece on the wheels makes a funny noise. He's given me lots of those. Painted in bright colors: red and blue and yellow and green. Smell so nice. Like pine trees.

Mother told me Daddy wouldn't let her go places, do things and have any fun. He wanted her to stay home with us and do family things all the time. She says a family is important, but you have to have your own life too.

I don't really understand what she means, but she's real serious when she says it.

One day Daddy caught her about to drive away when he told her she couldn't go. He took his gun and shot the front of the car; the radiator made a funny noise. He said now nobody would go anywhere.

A few days after that I heard them yelling at each other and Daddy must have slapped her. That's what it sounded like, and she was crying. Daddy shouldn't do things like that. I stayed in my room and pretended not to hear. And played with my push toys, making the metal squeak as loud as I could.

About a year ago Mother left. A friend picked her up. And then the policeman came out and told Daddy he had to leave Mother alone.

Daddy laughed at the policeman. I never understood why; I didn't hear any joke.

And then Mother and the policeman came out a little while after and got me. I didn't want to go, and Daddy didn't want me to go, but the policeman said I had to. He had a *order*. That means he has to do something.

That's when Daddy said he would come back for me. That Mother couldn't keep me away from him for long. He would never let me go. And he made them take a lot of nice wooden things he had made for me along—a toy chest, a wooden duck and a crow and a rabbit, and a big shiny wood cabinet. They're real pretty, and smell like pine trees.

Mother didn't want to take them at first; but I begged her, and so I got to take them.

I haven't liked it very much with Mother. I don't like her new friend at all. I don't think he's very nice.

Sometimes I dream about Daddy taking me away from here, to live with the lumberjacks in the forest. That would be fun.

I've been in the new house, her friend's house, a long time now.

Mother keeps saying something real bad happened to Daddy. I didn't understand for a very long time what she was saying. She says Daddy had a gun and was pointing it at her friend. And the policeman had to come. Then I know what she means.

She says that my Daddy's dead.

I was sad for a real long time, until I knew that Mother had lied to me. She just didn't want me to see Daddy anymore. But Daddy and me, we're too smart for her and her friend.

See, Daddy visits me sometimes.

Sometimes he doesn't come inside . . . he just looks in my bedroom window to make sure I'm okay. His face is all silvery cause of the moon and the dark and I think it's pretty.

Sometimes when I open my cabinet he's hiding in there, all crumpled up like a pile of clothes, but then he pulls his head out and it's real funny looking so I laugh.

Sometimes he's inside the wooden crow when I push it, and I can hear him laughing over the metal squeaking.

Sometimes he jumps out at me from the toy chest. It scares me at first, but then he hugs me.

He smells so good, just like a pine tree.

And sometimes he whispers to me from my cabinet at night, right after Mother has put me to bed. That's the nicest time. He sounds just like a small wind in the trees, the leaves moving back and forth, but there's words in it.

Mother talks about moving away sometimes, but I know it will never happen. Daddy will never let me go away.

At first those were the only places I saw Daddy: at my window and in the things he gave me. But then I started seeing him everywhere.

In the living room clock, when it strikes six at dinnertime, my Daddy's eyes in the numbers.

In the linen Mother brings back from the laundryroom, piled up in the big red basket. Sometimes I see Daddy's white hands there.

In the bottom of a plate of beets: Daddy's long tongue. In the bushes by the porch: Daddy's head.

A few days ago Mother and her friend decided we were going to move. I knew Daddy wouldn't let them take me away.

Mother and her friend went down into the basement to get some boxes for their things. Then I heard them screaming. Daddy was down there. And they never came back up.

Sometimes I wonder why we haven't gone to live with the lumberjacks, Daddy and me. It would be nice there. But maybe Daddy can't do that now.

Everything smells like pine trees, just like the forest.

Sometimes I wish I could go out and play. But I can't get the door or the windows open. Daddy won't let me. And I haven't eaten in a long time. With all the windows shut the pine tree smell is so strong I feel sick.

I guess Daddy is afraid something might happen to me. So he's decided to watch me real close, take care of me. I see my Daddy's dark eyes and silvery face all over the house: in the wallpaper, in the dark blue rug, crawling across the ceiling. I smell him everywhere. Daddy loves me very much.

Daddy will never let me go.

Dark Mummery

by Thorp McClusky

Until the early spring of 1939 I had never entered a reputedly "haunted" house, nor had I ever met anyone who had done so.

It all came about in rather a rambling sort of way, starting off with twelve or fifteen of us driving down to Phipps' Cove on a Saturday afternoon to spend the weekend with the Bradley Merrills. How long ago that seems now!

I looked forward to a truly delightful weekend; I already knew, or at least was acquainted with, several of the guests—Bob Mansfield, who paints for art's sake but designs fanciful and expensive apartments for the very wealthy for a living; Rebikoff, who has a marionette show; Gladys Sugden, the caustic, hoydenish novelist; and three or four others. Merrill, by the way, was and still is an illustrator.

The afternoon was very casual and delightful; we played a sort of haphazard tennis on the lawn, swam—those of us with Polar Bear instincts—in the freezing surf, and just talked and wandered about. Dinner was at seven, in a high-ceilinged, creamy-white room with a huge black marble fireplace at one end in which a driftwood fire snapped, showering multicolored sparks against the heavy screen. The meal was leisurely; it was already dark outside as we finally assembled in the big, gracious living room for brandies and highballs.

As usual, Bradley and Elsa had prepared no set routine for the evening; Vladimir Lessoff started things off by wandering over to the Chickering and treating us to an impromptu concert. Then Clevedore put on some of his magic, and following Clevedore we danced.

The evening passed swiftly; it was with incredulous surprise that I saw Bradley glance at the tall walnut clock in the hall and dramatically raise his hand.

"In ten seconds, my pious friends and I hope not-too-drunken companions, it will be exactly midnight, Eastern Standard Time."

He had hardly finished speaking when the old clock whirred and rasped, and bonged out twelve slow strokes. We all listened gravely, and immediately the brazen clangor had ceased Gladys Sugden made the inevitable suggestion.

"Ghost story! Who'll tell a ghost story?"

Drily, Bob Mansfield applied the sophisticated squelch. "Why, Gladys! You of all people! We don't have to do anything as tame as that. Not when there's a haunted house right here at the Cove!"

I had heard of that house. A few miles distant along the shore road, it had stood empty for a half century or more. It was popularly supposed to have been built by Jeremiah Phipps, one of New England's more successful privateersmen, or, too frequently, pirates.

Gladys, with just a trifle too much eagerness—so it seemed to me—fell in with the idea. "Perfect! What could be better for Saturday night high jinks? I've always had a sneaking longing to go inside that house. Let's snoop over there tonight. There's a lovely moon . . . !"

Well, we took a vote. The "Ayes" won, of course, overwhelmingly.

I think I suspected trickery from the very start. As a matter of fact, I learned afterward that I was right, and who the ringleaders were—Bradley, Bob Mansfield, and a meek-looking little cartoonist named Gregory. Gladys was in it, too.

My certainty that we were in for some ghostly amateur theatricals was clinched when I noticed, as we were getting ready to leave the house, that Mansfield and Gregory had unobtrusively disappeared. I suspected that they were to be the ghosts of the evening.

We piled into three or four cars and drove the six or seven miles to the Phipps mansion. In the moonlight it looked even more ancient, more forbidding than in daylight, with its gaunt exterior chimneys and its deeply-recessed, many-paned windows. As we swarmed toward its black pile I looked in the shadows cast by the house, by the trees, for Mansfield's car, but there were a hundred pools of inky shadow where a car could be hidden.

Bradley did not have to unlock or force the door; it was unlocked and opened easily. That seemed significant to me. I was surer than ever that some one had gone ahead and was already hidden inside.

When we were all in the hallway, Bradley closed the door behind us with a creaking of ponderous hinges, a rusty click of the wrought iron latch, and turned on a flashlight. He led the way, with an assurance that led me to believe he had been there before, into a large room at the front of the house. I glimpsed briefly a long staircase leading up into the darkness at the end of the hallway; I sensed rather than saw the ornate mouldings surmounting cold, vaultlike spaces, a shrouding of heavy fine dust over everything. But I noticed too that Bradley had been careful to keep the beam of his flashlight turned upward until we were all inside that huge parlor, and I felt sure he had done that to keep us from noticing the fresh footprints of Mansfield and Gregory in the dust underfoot.

Except for the light from the flashlight, the parlor was almost totally dark. Heavy wooden shutters over the windows permitted no moonlight to enter, except through two or three narrow cracks in the warped panels. The light was too faint to reveal more than the presence and position of the people in the room; certainly it was not strong enough to permit us to identify each other.

"Well, Brad, we're here," Gladys Sugden chirped perkily. "Bring on your ghosts. Or shall we go looking for them? Who's afraid of the big bad ghosts, anyway?"

Bradley parried that one. "This is supposed to be a haunted house, isn't it, Gladys? Can't a ghost appear in this room as well as upstairs or in the cellar? I for one am for staying here and waiting for whatever happens. I don't want any rotten floors collapsing under me. This place isn't any Palace of Mirth."

I suspected he was afraid that we might stumble onto his ghosts before they had a chance to get into their phosphorous paint.

He won his point; he turned off the flashlight—to make it seem more realistic, he said—and we waited.

I don't know just what I expected to happen. I admit the uncertainty of waiting made me feel creepy, and it must have affected the others who did not suspect any funny business much more powerfully. There was unreality in the whole adventure, there was unreality in the shadowy vagueness of our figures, there was unreality in the cold stillness of the long-shuttered room. I caught myself wondering how a bunch of supposedly intelligent adults could act so downright foolish.

Then I began to notice the light. At first, it was just the faintest, vaguest glow, hardly more than a lessening of the total blackness beyond the open hallway door. I seemed to feel the outlines of the hallway growing into visibility without actually seeing them as yet, limned in a sort of purplish absence of complete darkness. That strange light was so vague that it might almost have been imagined.

But the sudden creeping shriveling down my spine was real enough! The others felt it too; I could sense that they were shrinking away from the doorway.

The faint light grew stronger, and tension gripped me with the certainty that something was creeping silently down that staircase into the hall, invisible to me as yet from where I stood.

I acknowledged unwillingly, then, that Bradley was putting on his show with utter artistry. No hollow groans or clanking chains, none of those too-theatrical effects that defeat their own purpose. It was the very absence of effect that left our imaginations unhampered and built up an eerie apprehension in us. I wondered how Bradley would produce his ghosts without spoiling the effect. Perhaps he didn't intend to actually produce them at all, perhaps he intended to get his effect in some other, less obvious way.

I don't know how long we stood there in that empty room—it may have been several minutes, while no person spoke or changed position, while we strained our eyes trying to see in the light that was hardly less than blackness—the light, I told myself with admiration of my own cleverness, that must be made by the slow uncovering of a stained glass window, letting the moonlight in. Once or twice I heard someone's breathing sharply indrawn, then released in a half-gasp.

Then I saw the figures, standing in the unearthly, purplish gloom.

Again a queer flash of unwilling approbation swept me. Those figures were not skeletoned in phosphorous paint, or anything as crude as that; they were merely vague blotches in human shape, standing silently in the almost non-existent visibility in the hallway.

I have wondered, since, just how few of us did not, at that moment, really believe that they were ghosts!

Gradually, then, in much the same manner as indirect lighting is controlled, the purplish glow began to brighten. With the increase in illumination, I began to feel sure that I recognized those two motionless figures.

The one on the right, tall, slightly stooped, was certainly Mansfield. The dark blotch hiding the lower part of his face was a false beard, those baggy trousers, that hinting of a cutlass at the waist, were all parts of the pirate costume Bradley had considered most appropriate for the occasion. The other fellow, standing to the left and slightly behind Mansfield was Gregory, all right. He'd put a great daub of paint on his breast to simulate blood; he kept his hands folded over it.

The figures neither moved nor spoke. The light was too dim for me to distinguish details of their features, and as it became slightly stronger something of a nervous shock swept over me as I sensed, rather than saw, that their lips were moving, as though they were trying to speak, that their hands were outthrust toward us, as though warning us back. It was an effect, undeniably; Bradley was putting his show over well, after all!

Splitting the silence, a woman screamed, a high-pitched, keening note. In an instant the hypnotic tension that had gripped us all was broken. Bradley cursed and flipped on the flashlight; with a quick rushing of anxious footsteps Gladys Sugden was at the side of the girl, who was sobbing violently. Bradley's voice boomed out reassuringly, "That's all, that's enough. It's just been a joke, folks. For God's sake, make her understand that it's just a joke, Gladys! A joke that wasn't in very good taste. I'm sorry."

He swung the light on the two figures standing in the doorway.

"All right, Bob, Gregory. Fun's fun, a joke's a joke, enough's enough. Come on in. Break it up."

But the two figures did not move. They still stood there, holding their hands outstretched toward us, their lips moving.

Then Bradley swore, viciously, horribly, without mirth. "You pig-headed fools! Can't you see that you're scaring one of the girls half to death? Get in here and take off that junk!"

Still the figures stood there motionless, tableauesque. I think that we were all beginning to be afraid that they had entered so fully into the spirit of the deception that they were temporarily crazed; even Bradley had no knowledge of what they might do next; what further macabre jest they might have planned was as unknown to him as to us. Curiously, though I was watching them with single-minded attention, I noticed other things too; I noticed with a sort of detached interest that there really was, as I had suspected, a stained glass window high above the staircase, a window which dispelled that unearthly glow over the hallway, now stronger, now weaker as the moon was bright or obscured by clouds.

Almost stealthily, Bradley kept edging forward. He was within six feet of Mansfield, his torch shining blindingly in Mansfield's face. I was only a pace or two behind, and I could see Mansfield's face clearly. There was an uncanny fixity in his gaze that gave me, despite myself, a feeling of discomfort that was very close to horror. The thought came to me abruptly, "Is this damned place really haunted, after all? Have these fellows seen something that drove them out of their minds?"

Bradley cursed again, sharply. The unexpected, brutal sound jarred against my eardrums with the force of an explosion. With the curse Bradley leaped forward. His right hand, furiously outstretched, clutched at Mansfield.

Mansfield and Bradley glided, yes, *glided,* back, swiftly, yet effort-lessly. The sudden, relatively violent motion of all three reminded me bizarrely of the quick shifting of scenes thrown on a screen by an old-fashioned magic lantern. Then the tableau was resumed, but now Bradley was standing in the center of the hallway, holding his right hand out before him, looking at it with a strange intentness. Mansfield and Gregory had halted at the foot of the staircase, their hands still outthrust, thrusting us back.

Bradley spoke like a drunken person.

"Bob? Bob?"

His shoulders hunched, he shuffled doggedly, unsteadily forward, and as he approached Mansfield and Gregory turned and leaped up the staircase, the light from the flashlight shining full on them, on the staircase and the wall above and behind them.

Then that thing happened which is beyond normal human experience. Instantaneously, suddenly as a bolt of lightning, two strangers were also there at the top of the staircase, two sun-swarthed, lithe-muscled men, men with flashing teeth beneath heavy mustaches, with the glint of gold in their ears and the glitter of cutlasses in their hands.

It was like a silent motion picture, running at top speed. There was no sound, only an utter violence of motion. There should have been the thudding of bare feet on the staircase, but I heard no such sound; there should have been the heavy panting of those men and the harsh burst of their curses, but I heard only silence.

Mansfield and Gregory plunged upward to the head of the staircase. Mansfield was slightly in the lead; his right arm swung up in a chopping blow that seemed to go through one of the men as through a mirage; his body, tensed to meet resistance that was not there, spun crazily around and plunged over the low balustrade; I listened for the crash of his fall and heard no sound. I saw Gregory catapult against the other stranger, hurtle through that man in the instant a cutlass flashed, and disappear beyond my range of vision on the staircase landing.

Abruptly, no one was there, no one at all. The head of the staircase gaped down at us, blank, barren, deserted!

I heard Gladys Sugden screaming. She was trying to call Mansfield's name, but the sounds that came from her lips were unrecognizable. My body was trembling violently, and spasms of hot and cold swept over me. I think that horror gripped us all then like a mighty fist, squeezed us until we were incapable of thought, until we could only stand there and feel it engulfing us in beating waves. . . .

I knew then that those two strangers were the ghosts—the true ghosts of old Jeremiah Phipps' mansion!

What, in the Name of the Almighty, had we just seen re-enacted? The experience through which Mansfield and Gregory had passed early in the evening—an experience so mind-shattering that it had driven them mad?

Where were they?

"Bradley!" My voice was a whispered rattle. "Where are they? Mansfield and Gregory? Where are they?"

Bradley looked at me, his eyes enormous, his lips trembling.

"Where are they?" he repeated slowly. He moved his hands in an odd, uncontrolled way, helplessly.

While he stared at me, I took the flashlight from him. Somehow, I started up the staircase, and Bradley followed.

At the top, on the landing where, like uplifted arms, narrower flights continued upward into the gloom, we halted.

There, beneath the stained glass window, huddled far back against the wall and hidden from view from below by the pitch of the staircase, lay the twisted body of a man, fallen as if death had come as he had catapulted across the landing from the staircase below.

Bradley moaned, and I felt the balustrade shudder as he sagged heavily against it. I was trembling, uncontrollably.

The body was the body of Gregory!

Somehow we found the courage, after a moment, to look down. With photographic clarity our eyes saw, and our numbed minds recorded automatically, the staring horror in Gregory's wide-open, glazing eyes, the smear of crimson paint over his heart.

Without speaking, we turned away and staggered down that staircase. As though urged by a Fate beyond human capacity to resist, I turned the flashlight beam into the dark recess behind the staircase, beneath the balustrade across which Mansfield had seemed to plunge.

Without surprise I saw that Mansfield's body was there, spreadeagled as though he had put out his arms to break the fall, crushed against the naked floor, his neck broken.

I remember little of what else happened that night. I do not know if among us there were hysterical outbursts or a more terrible, controlled silence. I do not remember how or when we left that house. Memory grows clearer with the next day, with the beginnings of the grinding police investigation, the certainty with which the police believed that we had trumped up a fantastic story to cover a double murder in our "fast set," the newspaper headlines.

It was a long time before that night in the old Phipps house was forgotten by the public. But it was forgotten at last, and for years it remained as no more than an area of nightmare in the recesses of my memory, until last summer, when the old house was finally torn down, to save taxes, somebody told me.

About that time I chanced to meet Bradley in town one day. He looked more distinguished than ever, with his prematurely white hair, and he looked at my graying temples with wry understanding.

"They're either too young or too old." He softly sang a phrase from the hit song and made a quick, angry gesture with his right hand. "We're too old, and that's that. How about lunch?"

In the quiet, around the corner off the Avenue restaurant to which he took me, he told me those things which drew all the threads together, wrote "Finis" to the story of Phipps' mansion.

"I couldn't stay away—after they started to raze that house," he said slowly, quietly. "I went down there almost every day; I knew that they would find something—call it premonition, intuition, what you will. . . .

"I knew that they would find something, some explanation, in that staircase. I watched them take up the flooring on that landing, rip up the rubble, the stone and mortar, beneath. . . .

"That house was built to endure. Old Phipps, when he built it, was ready to settle down, all right.

"But first he had to get rid of his past. He must have had a couple of his men who wanted to stay on shore with him, even though he'd split his bloody plunder with them, with his crew. But old Phipps knew that those two fellows we saw at the top of that staircase weren't the kind he wanted around him in his respectability.

"This must have been what happened. When the masons had just about finished filling in that staircase, old Phipps just bashed in the heads of those two sailors of his and dumped the bodies in the mortar and covered them up. They found the skeletons just the other day, you know."

I picked up my coffee, put it down again.

"I read in the paper about the gold earrings and the cutlasses they dug up with those skeletons," I said.

Bradley looked at me thoughtfully. "Funny about those cutlasses. Remember that Gregory's body was unmarked, and that he died of heart failure?"

I picked up my cup again; once again I put it down.

"Gregory—Mansfield," I whispered. "What a horrible way to die! Think of it; they went up that staircase the second time, after they had already seen the ghosts! That was a re-enactment, wasn't it, Bradley? We could have saved them then; they were crazy with fear, but not crazy enough not to try to yarn us. We should have knocked them down, tied them up—anything—only we should have saved them, somehow."

Slowly Bradley shook his head. A curious, faraway look—the look of one who gazed into the depths of the infinite—came into his eyes.

"No, my friend. We couldn't have saved them. It was too late for that. For they were already dead when we saw them in that—yes, it *was* a re-enactment. They were dead before we entered the house. We saw, not two, but *four* ghosts that night. When I tried to grasp Mansfield, there in that hallway, my hand went through him as though through a nothingness—a nothingness that was cold and empty and terrible as the black dead space beyond the farthest stars!"

Date in the City Room

by Talbot Johns

He stood on the door-sill of the old Globe city room and looked around. The place seemed about the same, though after a year's absence he seemed to see it differently—sort of all at once instead of item by item. There was a new and shiny teletype clicking monotonously in the corner, but the faded yellow bulbs with their green metal shades hanging from the ceiling still cut triangles through a perpetual haze of blue smoke. Cigarette-charred desks, crumpled wads of yellow copy-paper and the old crack in the ceiling that the owners had never fixed because the plaster had fallen on Bart Davis' head and he'd been killed the next day on a fire story—the old-looking boy in the doorway took them all in with a glance and turned to Clem, sitting at the night desk.

"Hello, Reggie," said Clem.

"It's been a long time," said Reggie.

"It has, at that," said Clem.

That was all, for a minute. It was enough, Reggie thought. Things would begin to iron themselves out in a while. No use trying to rush them.

The smoke from his cigarette curled under a lampshade and shot out in a little swirl as it hit the hot bulb. Red Mackenzie, of the twelve-to-eight shift, slouched into the city room, cursing softly because he was a couple of minutes late.

He almost collided with Reggie, but didn't give him a glance. I suppose that's what happens, thought Reggie, when you've been away as long as I have. He didn't have to look right through me, though.

"It's just a year to the day, isn't it?" said Clem, drumming noiselessly on the night desk with his big knuckles.

"That's right," said Reggie, "just a year."

"I was wondering if you'd come," said Clem.

"You knew very well I would," said Reggie. "I told you, didn't I?"

Funny thing, but it was getting colder. Red was on the phone now, getting a stick from AP on some wedding in Baltimore, and had his coat off, despite the chill. Reggie wanted to speak to Red, but decided not to. Red was a good enough guy, but probably wouldn't understand. Clem—good old fat Clem, with his thinning gray hair and his forty-year jowls—was leaning back in his chair, staring at Bart Davis' hole in the ceiling, his thumbs linked in the arm-holes of his vest as Reggie had seen them for years when he worked on the night staff. "One of Clem's boys," they used to call Reggie in the old days. One of the boys who would go through a herd of wildcats and a hundred cops to get any story that Clem wanted—until a year ago.

"We were fools, Reggie," said Clem.

"I'll say," replied Reggie.

"We should never have let her jam our lives up that way," said Clem.

"Women are poison to good newspapermen," said Reggie.

Now it was coming out, and he was glad of it. He'd worried about this for a year, and here it was, staring him right in the face. Three hundred and sixty-five nights of thinking about Clem, to whom he should have been loyal—of the girl, who knew no loyalty to anything, and of himself, too. All added up, they made this moment, right now, face to face with Clem and the whole thing ready to blow off.

All Clem said was, "We should have found some other way out of it."

"You know I felt that way, too, at the last minute," said Reggie, "when it was too late."

"Yes," said Clem, "I know."

Reggie had known that Clem would be like this, because Clem always understood. His heart warmed up in spite of his chill. He was glad he'd come—glad he'd kept this crazy date, made a year ago when neither of them thought it could be kept. No matter how hard it was, these things ought to be talked out, he thought. No matter what

104

happened or what they'd done a year ago, he and Clem were still as close as any two men could be. Sometimes, during the past year, he'd wondered if they *would* be men when they met tonight. People can stand just so much and no more. Clem seemed the same, though. Probably he did, too.

Time seemed to race through his brain as he stood there, six feet of curly-topped reporter, gray slouch hat on the back of his head. Time was a funny thing. For a year it had dragged until he almost went insane, waiting to come and see Clem as they'd planned it. Now, here he was and there was no time, really—just he and Clem, and Red on the phone, still getting the paragraph from Baltimore and paying no attention to either of them. No minutes or seconds in this moment— just he, Reggie, waiting for Clem, his friend, to say something.

"It wasn't really your fault, Reggie," said Clem. "She was a wild one and I was sort of a fool. None like an old one, they tell me." He laughed, and startled Reggie, because it wasn't like one of Clem's old rollicking bellows that used to clear the wires as far as Chicago. It was just a little, thin, sardonic laugh, like the wind whispering in a tenement fire-escape.

"Don't blame her too much," said Reggie. "A couple of years before she met you she and I were pretty thick. Came a time when I couldn't forget it, and neither could she."

His words seemed to come to his ears from very far away, and sounded short and clipped. How else should they sound? he wondered. He was tired. The constant clacking of the teletype got on his nerves, and he seemed unable to hold his thoughts together as well as he used to. He wandered over to the teletype to see what all the racket was about, and pulled a yard of paper out of the basket. "Famous Movie Actress Gets Fourth Divorce; Senator Promises Lower Taxes If; Orange, N. J., Bride and Groom Killed in Triple Crash. . . ." A dream world, he thought—he and Clem had the only reality—he and Clem and their problem.

". . . And I was too old, anyway. Must have been crazy." Reggie realized that Clem was still talking. Funny—they must have gotten out of tune for a minute. "You two kids—I loved you both. Should have just backed out of the whole thing. But I had to go and marry her, and try to set up housekeeping. Me, Clem Roberts, whose home is right behind this desk and always has been! Thank the Lord there were no kids. What's she doing now, Reggie?"

"I don't know," said Reggie. What did he care what she was doing?

"Don't care, either, hey kid?" Clem was more like himself now, but a little pale still. "Neither do I. It's you and me from now on!"

There it was. That was what Reggie had been waiting for. Now that he had it, now that he knew that he and Clem were as they always had been, what of it? What was left for them now? He felt tired again. Let Clem figure it out.

"You figure it out, Clem," he said. "Where do we go from here?"

"Now you're talking sense, boy," said Clem. "I don't see any reason why we can't go on as usual, and pick up right where we left off. Things are going to be different—don't kid yourself on that—because we're different. We have to be, after"—he made a funny, quick motion with his hand—"all that. But we're still pals, we've got more sense than we used to have, and that's that."

They used to call him, the boys that didn't like him—and there were plenty who didn't, though they slaved for him—"That's That" Roberts.

Clem pulled his big antique watch out of his vest pocket, looked at it and started to pull on his coat. Then he reached for the phone.

"Shoot me up a morning final!" he barked in a voice that didn't sound like his at all. Red Mackenzie, batting out the Baltimore story on his typewriter, looked around suddenly as if he'd heard Clem for the first time, and then turned back to his pecking with a puzzled look on his face.

A boy brought the paper in, tossed it on the desk, and ran out again without saying a word. Reggie leaned over with his fists on the desk top, and watched Clem turn to page three.

"You didn't make front page, Reggie," said Clem. "Bad luck to the end."

"O. K. with me," said Reggie. He leaned over further to see the half-column story, and his coat sleeve slipped up on his arm.

"Bad burn you have there," said Clem.

"Doesn't hurt now," said Reggie, and they read the story together.

PAYS WITH LIFE FOR CRIME ON MURDER ANNIVERSARY

Ossining, N. Y., July 26: At two minutes past midnight tonight Reginald J. Fallon, New York Globe reporter, went calmly to the electric chair for the murder by shooting a year ago today of his city editor, Clement J. Roberts of White Plains, N. Y. Witnesses marveled at the composure of the condemned man, who seemed to welcome . . .

"That's that," said Clem. "Let's go."

They walked out of the city room arm in arm, and the clock said quarter after twelve.

A Dead Secret

by Lafcadio Hearn

A long time ago, in the province of Tamba, there lived a rich merchant named Inamuraya Gensuké. He had a daughter called O-Sono. As she was very clever and pretty, he thought it would be a pity to let her grow up with only such teaching as the country-teachers could give her: so he sent her, in care of some trusty attendants, to Kyōto, that she might be trained in the polite accomplishments taught to the ladies of the capital. After she had thus been educated, she was married to a friend of her father's family—a merchant named Nagaraya—and she lived happily with him for nearly four years. They had one child—a boy. But O-Sono fell ill and died in the fourth year after her marriage.

On the night after the funeral of O-Sono, her little son said that his mamma had come back, and was in the room upstairs. She had smiled at him, but would not talk to him: so he became afraid, and ran away. Then some of the family went upstairs to the room which had been O-Sono's; and they were startled to see, by the light of a small lamp which had been kindled before a shrine in that room, the figure of the dead mother. She appeared as if standing in front of a *tansu*, or chest of drawers, that still contained her ornaments and her wearing-apparel. Her head and shoulders could be very distinctly seen; but from the waist downward the figure thinned into invisibility—and it was like an imperfect reflection of her, and transparent as a shadow on water.

Then the folk were afraid, and left the room. Below they consulted together; and the mother of O-Sono's husband said: "A woman is fond of her small things; and O-Sono was much attached to her belongings. Perhaps she has come back to look at them. Many dead persons will do that—unless the things be given to the parish-temple.

107

If we present O-Sono's robes and girdles to the temple, her spirit will probably find rest."

It was agreed that this should be done as soon as possible. So on the following morning the drawers were emptied; and all of O-Sono's ornaments and dresses were taken to the temple. But she came back the next night, and looked at the *tansu* as before. And she came back also on the night following, and the night after that, and every night— and the house became a house of fear.

The mother of O-Sono's husband then went to the parish-temple, and told the chief priest all that had happened, and asked for ghostly counsel. The temple was a Zen temple; and the head-priest was a learned old man, known as Daigen Oshō. He said: "There must be something about which she is anxious, in or near that *tansu*." "But we emptied all the drawers," replied the old woman; "there is nothing in the *tansu*." "Well," said Daigen Oshō, "to-night I shall go to your house, and keep watch in that room, and see what can be done. You must give orders that no person shall enter the room while I am watching, unless I call."

After sundown, Daigen-Oshō went to the house, and found the room made ready for him. He remained there alone, reading the sû-tras; and nothing appeared until after the Hour of the Rat. Then the figure of O-Sono outlined itself in front of the *tansu*. Her face had a wistful look; and she kept her eyes fixed upon the *tansu*.

The priest uttered the holy formula prescribed in such cases, and then, addressing the figure by the *kaimyo* of O-Sono, said: "I have come here in order to help you. Perhaps in that *tansu* there is something about which you have reason to feel anxious. Shall I try to find it for you?" The shadow appeared to give assent by a slight motion of the head; and the priest, rising, opened the top drawer. It was empty. Successively he opened the second, the third, and the fourth drawer; he searched carefully behind them and beneath them; he carefully examined the interior of the chest. He found nothing. But the figure remained gazing as wistfully as before. "What can she want?" thought the priest. Suddenly it occurred to him that there might be something hidden under the paper with which the drawers were lined. He removed the lining of the first drawer:—nothing! He removed the lining of the second and third drawers:—still nothing. But under the lining of the lowermost drawer he found—a letter. "Is this the thing about which you have been troubled?" he asked. The shadow of the woman turned toward him,—her faint gaze fixed upon the letter. "Shall I burn

108

it for you?" he asked. She bowed before him. "It shall be burned in the temple this very morning," he promised—"and no one shall read it, except myself." The figure smiled and vanished.

Dawn was breaking as the priest descended the stairs, to find the family waiting anxiously below. "Do not be anxious," he said to them: "she will not appear again." And she never did.

The letter was burned. It was a love-letter written to O-Sono in the time of her studies at Kyōto. But the priest alone knew what was in it; and the secret died with him.

The Door

by Henry S. Whitehead

Those in the motor car hardly felt the slight, though sickening impact. It was rather, indeed, because of the instinct for something-gone-wrong, than because of conviction that he had struck anything more important than a roll of tangled burlap from some passing moving van, that the driver brought his heavy car to a stop with a grinding of brakes strenuously applied, and went back to see what he had struck.

He had turned the corner almost incidentally; but when he alighted and went back, when the thin gleam of his flashlight revealed to him the heap of huddled pulp which lay there, the driver realized in the throes of a hideous nausea what it was his heavy machine had spurned and crushed . . .

Roger Phillips, intent upon the first really decent act of his whole life, hardly noticed what was forward. He had been crossing the street. He continued to be intent on his own concerns. Interrupted only by a kind of cold shudder to which he gave only passing thought as if with the very outer edge of his mind, he did not stop, but crossed the sidewalk, looking up as he had done many times before to reassure himself that the lights were out in the living-room of the apartment up there on the third floor of the apartment house.

They were out, as he had confidently anticipated, and, reassured, he quickly mounted the steps to the front entrance. Some one came out, hurriedly, and passed him as he entered, the rush taking him by surprize. He turned his head as quickly as he could, to avoid recognition. It was old Mr. Osler, his father's neighbor, who had rushed out. The elderly man was in his shirt sleeves, and appeared greatly agitated, so much so that young Phillips was certain he had not been recognized, hardly even noticed, indeed. He breathed an audible sigh of relief. He did not want old Osler to mention this chance meeting to his father the next time he should see him, and he knew Osler to be garrulous.

The young man mounted lightly and hurriedly the two flights of steps that led to the door of his father's apartment. He thrust his key into the patent lock of the apartment door confidently, almost without thought—a mechanical motion. As mechanically, he turned the key to the right. It was an old key, and it fitted the keyhole easily. He knew that his father and mother were at the symphony concert. They had not missed one for years during the season for symphony concerts, and this was their regular night. He had chosen this night for that reason. He knew the colored maid was out, too. He had seen her, not five minutes earlier, getting on a car for Boston. "The coast," as he phrased the thought to himself, somewhat melodramatically, "was clear!" He was certain of security from interruption. Only let him get safely into the apartment, do what he had to do, and as quietly and unobtrusively depart, and he would be satisfied, quite satisfied.

But the lock offered unexpected resistance. It was inexplicable, irritating. His overtensed nerves revolted abruptly at this check. The key had slipped into the slot, as always, without difficulty—but it would not turn! Furiously he twisted it this way and that. At last he removed it and stared at it curiously. There was nothing amiss with the key. Could his father have had the lock changed?

Anger and quick shame smote him, suddenly. He looked closely at the lock. No, it was unchanged. There were the numberless tiny scratchmarks of innumerable insertions. It was the same.

Gingerly, carefully, he inserted the key again. He turned it to the right. Of course it turned to the right; he remembered that clearly. He had so turned it countless times.

It would not move. He put out all his puny strength, and still it would not turn. Hot exasperation shook him.

As he swore under his breath in his irritation at this bar to the fulfillment of his purpose, he became for the first time conscious of a rising commotion in the street below, and he paused, irresolutely, and listened, his nerves suddenly strung taut. Many voices seemed to be mingled in the excited hum that came to his ears. Bits of phrases, even, could be distinguished. Something had happened down there, it seemed. As he listened, the commotion of spoken sound resolved itself into a tone which, upon his subconscious effort to analyze it, seemed to him to express horror and commiseration, with an overtone of fear. The fear communicated itself to him. He shook, as the voice of the growing throng, a blended, corporate voice, came up to him in sickening waves of apprehension.

What if this should mean an interruption? Impatiently wrenching himself away from his preoccupation and back to his more immediate concern with the door, he thrust the key into the lock a third time, this time aggressively, violently. Again he tried to snap the lock. Again it resisted him, unaccountably, devilishly, as it seemed to him.

Then, in his pause of desperation, he thought he heard his own name spoken. He could feel his face go white, the roots of his hair prickle. He listened, intently, crouching catlike there on the empty landing before the door of his father's apartment, and as he listened, every nerve intent, he heard the entrance-door below flung open, and the corporate voice of the throng outside, hitherto muffled and faint, came to him suddenly in a wave of sound, jumbled and obscure as a whole, but with certain strident voices strangely clear and distinct.

A shuffle of heavy feet came to his ears, as if several persons were entering the lower hallway, their footsteps falling heavily on the tiled flooring. They would be coming upstairs!

He shrank back against the door—that devilish door! If only he could get it open!

Something like this, he told himself, in a wave of self-pity that swept him—something like this, unexpected, unforeseen, unreasonable—something like this was always happening to him!

That door! It was an epitome of his futile, worthless life! That had happened to him, just the same kind of thing, a month ago when he had been turned out of his home. The events of the intervening weeks rushed, galloping, through his overtensed mind. And now, as ever since that debacle, there was present with him a kind of unforgettable vision of his mother—his poor mother, her face covered with the tears which she made no effort to wipe away—his poor mother, looking at him, stricken, through those tears which blurred her face: and there was his father, the kindly face set now in a stern mask, pale and with deep lines—his father telling him that this was the end. There would be no public prosecution. Was he not their son? But he must go now! His home would be no longer his home . . .

He recalled the dazed days that followed: the mechanical activities

111

of his daily employment; his search, half-hearted, for a furnished room. He recalled, shuddering, the several times when, moved by the mechanism of long-established usage, he had nearly taken an Allston car for "home," which was to be no longer his home . . .

He had not sent back the key. He could not tell why he had kept it. He had forgotten to hand it back to his father when he had left, and his father, doubtless unthinkingly, had not suggested its return. That was why he still had it, and here he stood, now, on the very threshold of that place which had been "home" to him for so many years, about to make the restitution that would do something to remove the saddest of all the blots on his conscience—and he could not get in!

The men, talking with hushed voices, had reached the first landing. Young Phillips, caught by a sudden gust of abject terror, shrank against the stubborn door, the door which, unaccountably, he could not open. Then, his mind readjusting itself, he remembered that he had no reason for concealment, for fear. Even though he might be seen here, even though these people should be coming all the way up the stairs, it could not matter. Let him be seen: what of it? He was supposed to live here, of course. It was only a short time since he had actually ceased to live here, and his father had said nothing. No public charge had been made against him. How one's conscience could make one a coward!

Under the invigorating stress of this reaction, he straightened himself, stood up boldly. Realizing that it might appear odd for him to be discovered standing here aimlessly on the landing, he started to go downstairs. But by now the narrow staircase was completely blocked by the ascending group. He stopped, halfway from that flight. The men were carrying something, something heavy, and of considerable bulk, it would seem. He could not see clearly in that dim light just what it was. He stopped, half-way down, but none of the men carrying the awkward bundle, covered with what looked like an automobile curtain, looked up, nor appeared to notice him. Neither did the straggling group of men, and a woman or two, who were following them.

Fascinated, he gazed at what they were carrying. As they approached and took the turn in the stairs, so that the electric light on the upper landing shone more directly upon it, he looked closer. It was the body of a man! It hung, limp and ungainly in their somewhat awkward grasp as they shouldered up toward him.

Something about it seemed vaguely familiar, the details presenting themselves to his fascinated gaze in rapid succession: the trouser-ends, the shoes . . .

*   *   *

112

The men turned the last corner in the winding stairway and came into full view. As they turned the corner, the leather curtain slipped and the face of the dead man was for a moment exposed to view. Roger Phillips looked at it, fascinated, horrified. Then one of the men, halting for an instant, drew the corner of the curtain over the face again, and he could no longer see it. The head rolled. The broken body had been grievously crushed.

Roger Phillips, utterly distraught, cowered, a limp heap, against the unyielding door of his father's apartment. He had looked for one horrific instant into his own distorted, dead face!

The men, breathing hard, reached the landing. One of them, gingerly shifting his portion of the burden upon the shoulder of another, stepped forward to ring the bell of the Phillips apartment. No one answered the ring, and the man rang again, impatiently, insistently. The bell trilled inside the empty apartment. The men stood, silently, shifting uneasily from one foot to another. Behind them, a thin mutter came from the waiting stragglers who had followed them, moved by an inordinate curiosity.

"Here's a key sticking in the door," said the man who had rung the bell. "Guess we'd be all right if we opened the door and took the young fellow in. There doesn't seem to be anyone home."

A murmur of assent came from the other men.

He turned the key to the left, then to the right, and the door opened. They carried the broken body inside and carefully laid it out on the sofa in the living-room.

Drowned Argosies

by Jay Wilmer Benjamin

The *Volcania* had gone down. This much Charteris knew. It was all he felt he could possibly lay claim to knowing. Drifting five days in an open boat in the Carribbean Sea is not conducive to sanity.

Not that Charteris was going mad. Far from it. But he couldn't understand the ghastly people who seemed to be trying to talk to him.

113

They were sailormen. He knew it. But what a peculiar crew! There were half-naked galley slaves with the great calluses still on their palms. There were old shellbacks, barefoot, and naked above the waist. There were men who had driven the great clipper ships from Canton to London in sixty days. And there were men like Charteris, who knew the intricacies of the great liners' guts.

They were trying to talk to him—then Charteris shook his head. "Dead men can't talk!"

The sun beat down. The brazen sea reflected it. Water—*water*—WATER! That was Charteris' sole thought.

Finally one old shellback, whose gaunt figure betokened great strength and greater endurance, beckoned him, and Charteris heard: "I say, maty—don't worry. Who do you want to sign on with?"

"What do you mean?" asked Charteris. "You can't—"

The old shellback laughed, and Charteris shuddered. It is odd to hear ghosts laugh, and Charteris knew these were ghosts. Where else could men have come from in all that dying sea?

"Think we're dead, don't you?" said the shellback. "Well, we ain't! Only time a sailor dies is when they plant him six feet under in a churchyard. There's men here who served in every kind of craft, from a bireme to a liner."

"Who are you?" asked Charteris.

"Me? Why, bless you, I sailed with Paul Jones on the *Ranger*. A good cap'n, that, only a bit of a driver."

"*Paul Jones*? Why, man, he's dead nearly two hundred years!"

"Not quite that," said the old shellback, and laughed.

"Ugh!" thought Charteris, "I *must* be going mad."

"Not quite that," said the old shellback again. "Now you take Petrus here"—and he waved a hand toward a squat hairy half-naked man—"he sailed with Quintus Maximum when they stripped the Mediterranean of the Carthaginian boats."

Petrus grinned and gabbled something. The old shellback translated. "He says it was a hell of a good fight, and you should have seen 'em scatter when the biremes came."

"What? Served under Quintus Maximus? Why, man, that's nineteen hundred years ago!"

"Nigher two thousand—but what's time, what's time?"

And he spat.

That, thought Charteris, was the ragged limit. He must be mad.

There was silence once more until Charteris leaned his head against a thwart and began to cry, in long, racking sobs. The shellback reached over, and Charteris shivered at the touch of his hand. It was icy cold, in

114

spite of the brazen sun still sending its red-hot rays to beat on Charteris' back.

"I felt that way when they left me to drift, too. You know, I was the man they lost from the *Ranger*. But hell—here's Hendrik Hudson. Want to talk to *him* about driftin'?"

"No," said Charteris, "no—no—no—no—no—no—no—"

A voice broke in, a deep voice vibrant with sympathy.

"Poor youngster! They all feel that way just before they sign on. Myself, I felt it too."

"Who are you?" Charteris asked wildly.

"Hendrik Hudson, cap'n of the *Half-Moon.*"

"What are you doing here?"

"I signed on to sail under Admiral Beresford. I command the *Saturnia*. Do you want to sign on with me?"

"What do you mean?"

"Young fool! Do you not know that we who sailed the seven seas still sail beneath her bosom? Look!"—and he stabbed a thick fat finger at the green waves.

Weakly Charteris crawled to the gunwale and looked. Down below he saw a tall clipper ship sailing serenely. Her sails were gone, and in their places were long streamers of kelp. From truck to keelson she was wreathed with flying seaweed, but about her decks moved sailormen going to and fro quite as if it were their normal life. Muffled by sixty fathoms of water, he heard the strokes of a ship's bell and a dim voice: *"Three bells! Relieve the wheel and lookout."*

"But I know nothing about sailing-ships, Cap'n. I'm an engineer."

"So? Nat!" And Hendrik Hudson turned to the old shellback. "Does Cap'n Lucks need an engineer?"

"Depends, Cap'n. I hear he needed a man with an extra first's certificate."

"Call him up, will you?"

And Charteris' eyes bulged as he saw the sailor, Nat, produce a bosun's whistle and blow an odd piping call.

The sea boiled, and up rose a man dressed even as Charteris' old captain. The four gold stripes of a master mariner shone as they had in the days when Captain Lucks had proudly trod the deck of the *Titania*.

"Hello. What's up?" he boomed.

And Charteris noticed that there was a slight hiss to the S's, as though the captain had false teeth.

"This man, Cap'n," said Nat, respectfully pulling his forelock, "is gonna sign on with you."

"Hmm. What can he do?"

"I'm an extra first, sir," said Charteris, convinced by now that all this was more than just a dream, that it was indeed actually life.

Dimly on the horizon rose a faint smudge of smoke as a long, lean coast-guard cutter drove its knife-like prow through the waters, searching for survivors of the *Volcania*. On the bridge a tense officer quartered the sea with terrible efficiency.

"God!" he thought. "To be left adrift here! Bos'n!"

His voice was sharp. He had picked up the white speck that was Charteris' boat.

"A quarter west! Call the cap'n. I see a boat!"

"Aye, aye, sir!"

The wheel spun. A messenger raced aft to get the captain.

The captain took his position on the bridge and whistled down the speaking-tube.

"Engine room," he said, "bridge speaking. Can you get a couple more knots outta this hooker?"

The funnels belched black smoke. The destroyer's frame quivered as her mighty engines thrust her forward with renewed speed.

She stood by Charteris' floating prison. A boat was lowered and able seamen lifted Charteris, trying weakly to salute someone they could not see, to its security.

"I'll be honored to sign on, sir," mumbled Charteris vaguely.

They had seen men adrift in open boats before. They knew what the sea and sun can do. So they looked at him sympathetically and went about the business of transferring him to the cutter.

Tenderly the hard seamen carried him below, still talking of things they did not understand, of drowned ships, and that ghastly whistle on the *Saturnia*.

Charteris gazed wildly about him. He seemed to be trying to place his surroundings. "My new quarters, Cap'n?" he asked hoarsely.

"Take it easy, son—you're all shipshape now," advised a grizzled bosun's mate.

Charteris looked at the speaker without comprehension. Suddenly he fell back and began to babble unintelligibly.

The old bosun's mate pursed his lips and spat thoughtfully. Then he bent forward.

His eyes widened. Swiftly he straightened and crossed himself reverently.

"Cripes!" said he in amazement; "how'd *this* guy know Lucks—*and know he had false teeth?*"

116

Dust

by Edna Goit Brintnall

At first, Nellie thought it was all only a dream. There had been no stinging summons from the rusty little alarm clock, no petulant call from her mother's room down the long flight of stairs. Yet she could hear her mother moving about in the kitchen and her father's low answers. Miraculously enough, they were not quarreling.

She lay very still and tried to readjust herself. She was very tired and it was pleasant, unbelievably pleasant, to just lie quietly and pretend she was asleep.

It was high time she was getting father's breakfast, and a rather pathetic breakfast it would be. Just the two of them always. Mother usually had a headache and Nellie took breakfast up to her on a tray. Not a tray with a rose clinging lovingly to the curl of a long crystal vase, but roses were expensive and not to be thought of even in midsummer. Mother usually ate her breakfast and turned over discontentedly and went back to sleep. Then Nellie hurried downstairs and dusted the living-room. Mother was most particular about the living-room. Beyond the living-room nothing much mattered.

Nellie sensed that she was lying on the couch in the alcove off the living-room. It was stuffy; she could smell the dust on the "porteers" and the heavy odor of the afghan couch cover. There were six strips to the couch cover, two tan, two rust-red and two faded blue, alternating and strung together loosely with coarse tan twine.

Sometimes she and Wilbur sat there at night and Wilbur held her hand and kissed her (she skipped over the thought hurriedly), but she had never before lain quietly on its spongy softness. Mother spoke of the alcove as the cozy corner.

It was nice.

Even the sheet was over her face, just as she always put it (even in her own hard little bed up under the roof) to keep off the wind that sucked down through the flue in the chimney.

She liked her room, though it had nothing in it besides a very old marble-top dresser shabbily painted white, and an old mirror of her grandmother's, that once had been resplendent with shining gold leaf. It was nothing much to look at now, after she had painted the clusters of grapes along the sides. Blobs of paint made pimples on the sides of the grapes, unpleasant even to think about. The bed was thin and white and iron. It was cold in winter—like the rest of the room, and hot in summer.

In the winter there was no heat. The tiny sheet-iron stove in the corner was not good to look at, but no one bothered to take it down. It was painfully inadequate against the winter winds that threw themselves off the lake and beat frantically against the eight tiny windows.

Only half of the woodwork was white. Nellie had intended it all to be white, but one can hardly judge the limits of a quart of paint. Even the white part was not all white—just a muddy gray where the deep brown of the old woodwork showed through—and now only two of the windows would open. The paint held them quite securely, making the room like a furnace during the hot summer nights.

Even at that Nellie liked the room.

There were eight more of such rooms strung along the row toward the street corner. Nellie often wondered what they looked like—if they were as warm and as cold as hers, and if the wallpapers were as pretty as hers. Nellie loved the wallpaper. She had selected it herself. It was pale green with broad silver trellises fairly bursting with pink roses, roses that hung over her bed in joyous profusion. So low was the ceiling that she could fancy herself lying in bed and merely reaching out one slim arm and gathering handfuls to her thin young breasts.

Looking at the flowers, she forgot the paint, and the lack of curtains at the windows didn't bother her any more. She had wanted Swiss curtains with pink dots and frilled tie-backs, but as her mother convinced her—curtains were not necessary up so high from the street. No one saw.

As the door opened softly, she lay very still. It was too nice for just a little longer.

She wondered why her father hadn't gone to work, wrenching himself into his coat, pulling his hat down viciously over his bespectacled eyes and slamming the door until the colored glass fairly rattled in its casing.

From the kitchen she could hear the mother's voice as a general directing his army.

"Be careful now, with that dust-rag. Wipe off the window-sills and the top of the piano and the rungs of the chairs!"

So Father was dusting!

She would have loved to peek out from under the sheet, just to have seen him, but it was all too delicious.

Mother getting breakfast! Father dusting!

Too delicious just to lie all warm and comfortable and let some one else do something.

Her mother came through the dining-room and stood in the doorway.

"We can put those roses in the green vase," she was saying to her father, "two whole dozen roses—from the Goodmans' around the corner!"

Two dozen roses—it was beyond comprehension!

Soon she would stir herself and get up and wash the vase—'way down at the bottom so that no brown line would show—but not now —no, not now!

She thought about the house—stiff with red, dark red brick and a jutting porch that went up stiffly as if making a long nose at the shabby cellar beneath. It had cutwork and balls and scrolls all painted red, dark red like the brick.

The living-room was nice. Mother always spoke of it that way. There was the onyx table with a bronze statue on it, by the front window—the bronze lamp with the big red shade on the glass-top table by the morris chair. There were green over-curtains—scant, very scant, it was true, and not quite covering the coarse lace edgings of the scrim curtains underneath, but Mother had made them in a hurry and her sense of measurement was not always accurate. Still they looked nice.

The piano was rosewood. Even Father was proud of the piano, though there had been weeks of wrangling and bitter biting argument over it, but Mother won. Mother always did.

Just as she had about the house. Father had wanted a house in the country. A house that stood by itself and didn't have to be propped up by seven others, all alike in a row like alphabet blocks. A house that had sides to it that one could see and not only just one stern high front. Windows that looked wide to the sun and not into a gray court that grew darker and darker as it neared the dining-room windows.

Perhaps that was why the dining-room was rarely dusted. No one could see dust in the dining-room, even in midday—that is, no one but Father. Father could see and sometimes he wrote the word *Dust* in a big scrawling hand across the shelf of the high golden-oak sideboard. It always made Mother angry—which he knew it would. Often Nellie saw it before Mother did, though she was not so tall; and that saved a row.

Nellie hated rows, but Father and Mother seemed to enjoy them.

Father always telling about his mother's housekeeping and Mother flinging back about never having a dime to call her own.

Often Nellie could hear them below her—tense bitter voices snarling at each other in the darkness.

But when callers came Mother and Father took on, in some mysterious fashion, the niceness of the living-room. Mother was proud of the Oriental rugs and Father even praised the piano.

Nellie didn't stir. She heard Mother's steps close beside her—very close beside her. She was speaking.

"I think the roses look nicest here, don't you? We can put the rest of the flowers here—but the roses *are* lovely!"

"She liked roses," said the father.

"I like roses too, but with never a dime—" She stopped, suddenly; her father said nothing.

"Her graduating-dress was a bit too small, but I split it down the back. Looks real nice against—" her mother continued.

"She has real pretty hair." Her father seemed very close to her. He was praising her. Tears flooded to her eyes, but she kept her lips closed tight. She wanted to hear more—just a very little more.

"I had real pretty hair, too, once—you used to say so yourself—but what with scrimping and washing and ironing and standing over a hot stove and raising a—" Her mother hesitated.

"She wasn't exactly thankless," her father said, slowly, as if supplying the word. "Maybe we shouldn't have said she had to marry Wilbur. Wilbur is a nice fellow, but maybe she didn't just fancy him—girls are sometimes that way. Maybe, if we hadn't just forced her too far, she woulda got used to the idea slow-like and not run out into the street like a wild thing and get runned over by a fire engine."

Nellie felt her mother's breath freeze against her lips.

"Don't you ever let me hear you say those words again—not to anybody, any time," she said firmly. "After all, she was running out to see where the fire was and that's how it all happened."

"I guess you're right," said the father.

"Well, I've got all the food ready and most of the flowers set up and you better go up and get a fresh collar on and your black gloves ready. The man ought to be here now any minute and you can help lift her."

Her mother came close to her and lifted the sheet. Nellie kept her eyes tightly closed and waited.

"She looks real nice," she said almost defiantly, "just like she was sleeping."

"Yes," said her father, "just like she was sleeping.

Her mother laid the sheet back over her face. They tiptoed away.

The heavy scent of roses came back to Nellie pleasantly. She wished the "porteers" didn't smell like dust.

So close the roses seemed, as if she could reach out one slender arm and gather them to her thin young bosom.

She was very tired. She wondered about the alarm clock. Perhaps there had never been any alarm clock. Perhaps she had only been dreaming.

It was nice of the Goodmans to send roses to her mother. They were nice people—even her mother and father were nice. A nice living-room it was. A nice couch, comfortable, restful. . . .

Even Wilbur was nice. . . .

She gave a thin, peaceful little sigh—the room was dusted—some-where Father was putting on a clean collar and some black gloves—somewhere Mother, well—it was just all—too—nice. . . .

Nellie slept.

Edge of the Cliff

by Dorothy Quick

The girl sat on the edge of a cliff and gazed down at the jagged rocks below her, watching the water beat relentlessly upon them. The last rose tints of the sunset gave the eddying waters a translucent loveliness, but she shuddered as she looked at them. She couldn't see the beauty, only that the rocks and water were terribly far away.

"I haven't the courage," she half whispered, her voice lost in the rushing waters. For a long while she sat quite still, staring blankly before her. From somewhere in the distance came the shriek of a whistle.

Automatically the girl raised her head, listened, and laughed—a laugh that had no mirth in it. Her thoughts, which had been a formless confusion, suddenly focused.

"The factory whistle. Jim will be home soon. How he'll rave when he doesn't find me. If I went back, he'd beat me. But I won't go! Dear God, help me to be brave."

With the force of her prayer she clasped her hands and moved convulsively. As she did so her pump slipped off and went down into the dimness. She strained her eyes to watch, but she could discern nothing in the darkness. So she listened, every nerve tense.

But she heard nothing—only the swishing snarl of the water beating on the rocks. Her slipper had gone—soon she would follow. She dully wondered if it would hurt. She saw herself lying crushed and mangled, perhaps not dead, and began to shake. Unsteadily she got to her feet. She was going away from the terror of the cliff, back to Jim— It would be horrible, but at least she knew what it was like.

"If I were only brave," she thought, "I wouldn't go back." She buried her face in her hands and sobbed hopelessly.

All at once she was conscious of someone near. She took her hands away to look. There was a stranger standing beside her.

"What is the matter?" he asked softly. There was no light and she could not see his face, but something in his voice swept her terror away.

Without an instant's hesitation she began, "I want to die." She pointed downward. "But I haven't the courage."

"Perhaps I can help you." There was deep understanding in his tones. "But first you must tell me why."

Strangely she didn't wonder that he made no attempt to preach or dissuade her from her project. Her soul went out to the sympathy and understanding she sensed in him. Her words came tumbling out jerkily, one sentence after another.

"I loved Bob—my family married me to Jim. Jim had money—a house. I was pretty and could cook. Jim didn't love me, but I was useful. I hated him!" She clenched her hands until the nails, digging into the soft flesh, brought drops of blood to the surface.

"Yes?" questioned the stranger. "So—" Monysyllables which left a gap to be filled.

She went on, "I tried hard to like Jim—I couldn't. He was a drunken beast. Bob kept on being sweet to me, brought me little things when Jim wasn't there. Once he found me crying, saw my arms all black and blue. Then he took me in his arms." She paused a second to savor fully the joys of the remembrance.

"We decided to go away together when Bob got enough money," the thread of her memory continued to unwind. "Jim came home early. I hid Bob but Jim was drunk. He began beating me. I tried to be brave, but God must have been asleep that night. I cried out. Bob came to help me—and Jim killed him!"

The stranger was silent.

She continued, "Jim got off—he was a wronged husband. The jury was on his side. It was worse than ever for me when he came back. I can't stand it anymore. I want to go to Bob, only—I'm not brave enough."

The stranger moved a little nearer.

"It only takes a minute," he whispered, but in his low tones there was a vibrancy. "One second and it is over."

Her slight figure swayed, "I can't!" she gasped.

The stranger took another step.

"You won't be alone. I will go too," he said slowly.

"But why?" she began, then suddenly reached her hand out toward him.

He ignored that and took a step toward the edge of the cliff. "Come."

She moved forward. All at once she was aware of the sound of the water striking the rocks below—those sharp, jagged rocks. She shrank back. "I'm afraid."

"Then return to him!" He flung the words at her.

"No, no!" cried the girl.

"You must choose between Jim and Bob," he said sternly, then added, "once you did not take so long to decide."

"Bob might not find me," she sobbed.

"It only takes a second," he pleaded, "and then there is—Eternity!"

The girl shivered again. "It is very dark!"

"At the bottom there is light."

"It will be very cold."

The stranger smiled. "My arms will be warm. Come!" he said softly, and this time held out his hand.

The girl tried to grasp it, but he was going down—down into the blackness. There was a strange luminous light about him. It didn't look quite so dark. The girl suddenly found courage.

"Wait!" she cried, "I am coming!"

From below the stranger was smiling at her with Bob's smile, and his arms were outstretched. He wasn't a stranger anymore—he was—Bob! Without one second's hesitation, she flung herself into his arms.

They went down and down, toward the bottom. Bob's lips were warm on hers. She did not even know when the waters enveloped her completely.

Faces

by Arthur J. Burks

People who know me say that I am insane. Many of them tell me so to my face. They do it jokingly, but in their eyes I read that they half believe it.

But who wouldn't be crazy after going through what I experienced during those dread hours when, huddled in the after cockpit of a wrecked airplane, in the very center of the dread Gran Estero, the pilot dead in the seat ahead of me with his brains dashed out, I sat the hours away with my eyes peering into the shadows of the great swamp?

Perhaps I did not see all the things memory brings to mind from that dread page of the past. For the silver plate in my head suggests many things, added to which there is a long blank in it somewhere during which I somehow won free of the mysterious region of rotting slime and bubbling ooze—a blank that I find myself glad I can not fill. For it must have contained terrible things.

We had taken off from the flying field at Santo Domingo City with plenty of time to spare ere we should be due at Santiago. It only takes a little over an hour, and it still lacked three hours of sundown when we lifted, in a series of climbing turns, into the sunny sky of the Dominican Republic.

But we had forgotten the fog which sometimes rises suddenly in the Pass through the Cordilleras.

We were half-way through when the fog was upon us, shutting us out from the ground below as effectually as though we both had suddenly gone blind, and were hurtling through a sea of mist at more than a hundred miles an hour—quite too fast to think of piling up on some unseen mountainside. I could scarcely see the pilot in the seat ahead. He looked back at me once and shook his head. Then he tried to see the ground below us, as did I. But whichever way we looked there was nothing but that sea of impenetrable white. Even the roaring of the engines was muffled by the density of the fog.

The pilot came back on his stick, and I knew by the way my back pressed against the cowling in rear that he was pointing her nose into the sky in the hope of climbing above the clouds.

Minutes that seemed like hours passed as we continued to climb, on

124

a slant just great enough to keep from stalling, but great enough that I knew we had already cleared the tops of the mountains on either hand. Yet the fog held steadily. It must have been miles high.

Then the aviator got confused. I don't blame him. Though I have never flown a plane I have ridden in planes many times, and know what it means to be caught in a fog or among heavy clouds which shut out the earth. Had he flown straight he might have ridden through the fog; but he did a turn or two in an attempt to find an opening, and lost us completely. Only by the slackness of the belt which held me in could I be sure that we were flying right-side up—which was all I did know!

The altimeter said 10,000 feet, with the needle crawling slowly toward the 11,000 mark! And still the fog.

Finally the flyer held her nose in one direction, at least he tried to, and plunged like a mad thing through the fog. Yet we didn't penetrate the mist wall.

Long after we should have reached Santiago we were still in the fog, still above 8,000 feet, and darkness was settling down upon us.

There was enough gas in the tanks when we left the field to keep us in the air for four hours. My wristwatch told me that we lacked but fifteen minutes of that time! In God's name, where were we? We might as easily have been far out over the Atlantic Ocean, the Caribbean Sea or Mona Passage.

I know now that we came down within five miles of Bahia de Escocesa, which is an arm of the Atlantic, and that, had our luck held for a few minutes more, we might have made a fairly safe landing on the broad shelving beach. Just a few minutes, as time is figured, and a life is lost—while another man lives to hear himself called a madman!

The engine spluttered and died. What a dread silence after the roaring of the motors!

The humming of the wind through the wires and braces told me that we were spiraling downward. We might be headed for a mountaintop or for the open sea and certain drowning—or might be heading directly into the field at Santiago, though only a fool would have hoped for such great good fortune. And still the fog about us held.

The pilot flung his helmet and goggles over the side and looked back at me, grinning widely.

"We're through, kid!" he said. "Ain't one chance in ten thousand of getting out of this with our hides. Let's hope that they find the remains sometime."

I am not ashamed to confess that I could not take it so light-heartedly as this; but then I am not made of the stuff of which flyers are constructed.

The aviator turned his eyes back to the instruments on the board before him, and our spiral continued to the tune of the wind in the struts, a tune that had a sinister meaning, a tune that sang of death uprushing to meet us. The altimeter said 1,500 feet now, with the needle fairly dancing down toward zero.

When we broke through the fog we were directly above a forest of nodding treetops, with scarcely a breathing space before the inevitable crash, which could have been avoided only did a miracle happen and the propeller start whirling again.

It seemed to me that we leveled and seemed to sink straight into the forest, though common sense told me that we must have struck at a speed of not less than ninety miles an hour. We hit the treetops and crashed through.

My head banged against the cowling when we hit, and I remember nothing afterward—until I opened my eyes in the shadows which hold sway in El Gran Estero, and found that the safety belt still held me in my seat. What was left of our right wing was above the dank waters of the vast swamp, while on my left I could see nothing but shadows, and the oozy slime of the dread quagmire. Only the main part of our ship had held together, and this was steadily sinking forward because of the dead weight of the motor.

The aviator was asprawl in the forward cockpit, his arms hanging over the side. I noted that blood dripped from the fingers of his right hand.

I unfastened my belt and leaned forward, swaying dizzily as a terrible feeling of vertigo seized me.

I shook the aviator roughly by the shoulder.

"McKenzie!" I shouted. "Are you bad hurt, boy?"

He was. For, as I shook him, pulling him around by the shoulder, I caught a glimpse of his face. It was not a face, but a bloody smear, with a gaping wound in the forehead. His body was still warm, proof that I had been unconscious but a short time. There was no mark of blood on the cowling before McKenzie's face, and I wondered what had dealt him that blow which had dashed out his brains. Leaning forward carefully I strove to peer down into the cockpit.

When I saw what had done it I all but collapsed. For the forward cockpit had fallen squarely upon the jagged stump of a tree and this had gone through the light fabric and penetrated McKenzie's body in a way that I find myself unable to mention in cold print. He had been dead even before that blood-stained stump had come on through to bash out his brains.

There was nothing I could do for him. And there seemed little chance of saving myself.

I knew that I was somewhere within mysterious Gran Estero, in a plane that was gradually sinking of its own weight—and that I was mighty fortunate to have lived even this long. Besides which I knew that I was badly hurt, how badly I could only guess—as you can do when I tell you that a goodly portion of my skull is silver at the present moment.

How to get out, and what direction to take? How to reach land solid enough to support my weight? In the daytime I knew I could have done it somehow—had I been in full possession of my faculties and my strength.

I studied the swamp around me, but as far as I could see in the darkness there was nothing but oozy morass, into which I should have disappeared within a few minutes at most. Ever the plane seemed to sink lower, as though a great mouth were relentlessly sucking it down.

My head was aching terribly, and oddly colored dots were dancing before my eyes. Any moment I expected to lose consciousness—and rather hoped that, did I do so, I would never regain it. Death would be easy, and would save me untold trouble and privation, to say nothing of unplumbed suffering.

"Well, why don't you climb out of there and find us a way out?"

I started as though someone had suddenly placed a hot iron against my quivering flesh. In my mind I heard the words, yet I swear that my ears had heard nothing at all. Just an impression that someone had spoken—an impression that had the force of actuality.

The hair at the back of my neck seemed to lift oddly as I whirled and stared into the gloom which was now so deep in Gran Estero that I could scarcely see my hand before my face.

Under a tree with many great branches, in the very midst of an area acrawl with the ooze of the vast quagmire, stood Lieutenant McKenzie, boyishly smiling as he had smiled before the crash! From his puttees to his helmet and goggles he was dressed for flying—save for that ghastly red weal across his forehead!

My eyes must have bulged from their sockets as I stared at him; for he smiled again and the smile froze on his lips, never again to leave them. This time when he spoke his voice sounded hollow, and as cold as a voice from the tomb.

"Well, get going! We must get out of here!"

Yet I couldn't move a muscle!

Will you understand why when I mention that the dead body of McKenzie still lolled motionless in the forward cockpit?

McKenzie was dead, killed in a manner that has many times since caused me to waken from horrible nightmares with screams on my lips; yet he couldn't be dead when I could see him, as plainly as you see this page, standing there beneath that tree in the midst of Gran Estero!

I screamed aloud when I found that I could look through that figure under the tree and see the bole of the tree itself. Still that frozen smile rested upon those white lips; still that red weal showed on the forehead beneath the helmet—a red weal that seemed to be steadily dripping, dripping, dripping.

Then I began to laugh, a horrible laugh, in which my body shook so convulsively that I all but fell out of the cockpit into the slime.

And as I laughed the phantom of McKenzie disappeared as though a breath had erased it, leaving me alone in the sinking plane with the dead body for company.

But my laughter was short-lived.

For, looking around again for some possible footing place, my eyes found something in the swamp which had at first escaped my notice—a pair of bare feet, with their water-whitened soles just above the surface of the ooze! By some weird necromancy I could look down through the mud to the body which hung upside-down below those feet—the skeleton of a native who had been lost in the swamp.

For some reason my eyes darted back to where I had seen the phantom of McKenzie, to see the figure of a ragged native in his place. This one looked at me out of sunken eyes, and slowly his arm upraised as he pointed to the bare feet, which were all that I could now see of the gruesome thing just outside the plane. A voice issued from the motionless lips of the native—a voice that spoke soft words in gentle Spanish.

"Si, Señor," said the voice, "it is I whom you see there!"

Wildly I laughed, and the phantom of the native vanished as the shade of McKenzie had done at the sound of my maniacal laughter.

Wildly, since I knew that my mind was going because of this weird horror, I searched the jungle wall with frightened eyes.

The night drew on apace, and I will not dwell on it unduly, for I know that in that direction lies madness—madness more mad, even, than is now mine.

For I discovered that El Gran Estero is the trysting place of countless shades!

Out of the shadows they came to stare at me—out of the shadows to stare, to smile coldly, and to vanish—while I laughed at each in turn.

It is strange that I laughed; but I could not help it, for my head ached abominably, and I laughed to ease the pain. Is that a good reason? To me at the time it seemed so; but perhaps I laughed at the faces.

The faces?

I lost count of their vast number, for assuredly there must have been many who have lost their lives in El Gran Estero—whose faces came up before me, for the lips to smile coldly, to smile coldly and to vanish, while others came to take their places.

As it grew cooler as the night drew on, will-o'-the-wisps came up from the ooze. Balls of weird flame, balls that had the shape of faces with smiling lips—all sorts of faces. Faces of negroes, men and women —yes, and children; faces of Dominicans, bronze-burnished by a smiling sun, with here and there the pale, staring faces of white men. Thank God there were but few of these! For I found myself unable to look into their staring eyes. It was as though the white men were brothers of mine, and that I had somehow failed them in the weary search for a way out of the vast quagmire. When they smiled coldly, reproachfully, and I could give them no aid, they would shake their heads sadly and disappear, only to show again down some vista through the tree-lanes, always looking back at me sadly before they disappeared for good.

The saddest of them all was a white woman with a babe in her arms. She stood for many minutes where McKenzie and the native had stood, and her eyes were sunken caverns ablaze with a vast reproach. Her eyes searched ceaselessly the wall of trees, seeking, seeking, seeking. At last she wandered down a lane through the trees, gliding softly atop the ooze. She looked back several times as she wandered aimlessly away, and once I fancied I could hear the subdued wailing of the babe in her arms. She must have heard it, too, for her head bent as though she soothed the phantom infant. She did not look up again, and, thus soothing the baby with which she must have died, she vanished into the vastness of the swamp. I wondered what man had been the cause of her going to her death in Gran Estero. For there was that in her eyes that told me a man was to blame.

Faces, faces, always the faces! And the dead blackness of El Gran Estero.

When all the shades I had seen, together with a host I had never seen before, some of the latter aborigines who must have gone to their death in the swamp during the regime of Columbus and his governors, came at last and gathered in the ooze about me, to smile coldly and sadly into my face, I must have gone clear out of my head, for that is the last dread happening which I remember.

The plane had sunk so low that slime was beginning to trickle into the cockpit in which I still sat huddled, when the army of shades gathered about me—silent and motionless as though they waited for something. Did they wait for me to lead them out of this never-ending thraldom of theirs? I do not know. I do not know anything about it.

I only know the next thing I remember is that I awoke in a cot in the hospital in Santiago, and that the colonel of the regiment occupying the city was sitting at my bedside. When I opened my eyes the colonel turned to the doctor.

"Can he talk now, Doctor?"

The doctor nodded.

I told the colonel all that had befallen me. As I talked I saw a queer light come into his eyes, and knew that he doubted my story, may perhaps even have blamed me a little for what happened. I wonder why. His questions took a queer trend at the last.

"Why didn't you go back into the swamp with McKenzie and help him salvage the engine of the plane?"

"But McKenzie is dead, sir! He was killed in the crash!"

Again that queer light in his eyes.

"But the natives who found you at the edge of the swamp swear that a man in uniform was with you—a man in helmet and goggles, a man answering in every detail the description of McKenzie. They say he led you out; but that as soon as he had attracted their attention and saw that you would be taken in charge, he turned back into the swamp before they could come close to him. You should have gone back in with him."

But assuredly the colonel must have been mistaken. Perhaps his limited Spanish caused him to misinterpret the reports of the natives. I *know*, in my heart, that McKenzie never left that forward cockpit after the crash into El Gran Estero.

But do I know? After all there is that blank to be accounted for, and often I waken in the middle of the night and lie awake until dawn, wondering.

130

Fancy That

by J. N. Williamson

"Fancy meeting you here!" A pleased resonance.

"Well, I like *that!* Who else would you expect to meet in your bedroom, mister?"

"It certainly isn't like the old days." Mock sigh. "Hold on, don't turn away. Please. I was only joking."

Mood shift. "I'm so glad you married me this morning." Genuine pause of concern. "It *was* this morning. Wasn't it?"

"—Was it? Feels like an eternity. Wait; that isn't a joke, honey. It really does seem like some while ago. Or, always. I'm confused about it."

"Darling, it doesn't matter when we got married. Only that we were. And are."

"Look, beautiful, let's meet this way every now and then. All right?"

A smile to be recognized, experienced, by other senses. "I'm not sure we even have a choice about it. But this is special; I *want* to be with you, this way . . . 'Night."

"Night."

"Fancy meeting you this way." The hint of a chuckle.

"I'm not here now because I wished to be! I know about *her*, and what you did."

"But I didn't . . . All right, you've got me. I can't lie, *this* way." With great earnestness, and again now: "But I only kissed her once or twice. Well—three or four times. That's all."

"At a time when I scarcely even felt like a woman!"

"That's why I—the *other* part of 'me'—did it." Anguished sigh. "Because, being pregnant, you don't feel pretty, don't feel like you. When you're *you*, you're always pretty to me. Always."

"Perhaps that's the truth. I don't think we can lie, this way. But don't do it again, darling. Please? We have made us as we're meant to be—but either of us can change that, can spoil it forever. I sense that—don't you?"

131

"I do. And I'm sorry." Awkward, tender pause. "Wish I could touch you now. Put my arm around you."

"Remember, tomorrow, that you want to." Urgency, stridently but sweetly. "And try not to let your pride get in the way."

"I will. And try not to forget that I love *all* of you, *all* you *are*. 'Night."

" 'Night."

"Fancy meeting you after all this . . . *whatever* it is."

"Darling, we must talk. This way." Concerned hum of need.

"You absolutely mustn't worry that, well, you *couldn't*. Last night, before sleep. You had a rough day. It wasn't your fault. You worry so much about Billy and that crowd of friends he runs with. They—"

"It isn't just that." Something quite like a sigh. "I'm not forty yet, but I'm—I'm over the hill."

"Not really. Just the *other* 'you'; just temporarily!" Merriment, reassuringly.

"Honey, that other part can be important, too. Look, I can't help how I feel."

Softly, seductively. "That's why I wanted us to meet *this* way once more."

"Come *on*." Rueful, unpleasant vibrations. "What can we do this way?"

Still more softly: "Everything else, I think. Reach each other more deeply than the other way. Try. *Try*, just remembering that you love . . . all I *am*."

Out-reaching, outpouring of private, unspoken emotions. Openness, and receiving. Contacting, mutually experienced; known; accepted. "I do love you, babe. Oh, I *do*."

"Wasn't that lovely?" Bubbling contentment. "Hm-m, you're something special!"

"But y'didn't say 'I love you, too.' *Do* you, still, after the years— after what a fool I am—after how many times I forget *this* us?"

"Always and always, I love you.—Better?"

"*So* much. 'Night."

" 'Night . . ."

"Fancy my wanting to meet you here. This way. You know why, don't you?"

Distance. No fast reply. A dark, small resistance, lies impossible. "You probably desire to bully me, about our son. —No; that's not it. You never bullied anyone. But—"

"Honey, Bill has a life of his own. What's happening to him is not your fault. Or mine."

"But he's so unhappy, so miserable. He's ruining *everything*."

"No. Not everything." Very firm. "Not—*us*. Unless you allow it to happen."

"You've never understood for an instant what it is to be a mother, to give birth, raise them, go *on* caring—"

"But Bill's path is *his*." Even more firmly, but gently. "Now he must find himself, and someone for him. On his own. There is nothing that you and I—or *we*, when we're that by day—can do to help him find himself, and her."

"I yearn to save him, darling, so badly. He's meant so *much*. I want him to—"

"To satisfy your hopes for him; mine; ours?" Noiseless, wry laughing vibration. "I wanted this, too, remember? Remember how I tried first to get him into Olympics-style sports—then when he grew up, I wanted him to become a—"

"You were so *silly* about Billy!" The return, mercifully, of laughter. "Yet tried, showed him you cared; you were there. After awhile, darling, that was all there was for you to do."

"Which is what I have been telling *you!* One more point: As long as we both want it to be that way, more than anything else, there will always be *us*. We cannot keep Bill part of us; he never truly was. But you have me, honey, and I have you—for ever." Sweet, snuggling sounds. "I love you. 'Night."

"Fancy this: I'm old. Not getting old. *Old.*"

"Well, I like *that!* What would I want with an old person in my bedroom, Mister!"

"Beats me. You haven't gotten old at all, beautiful."

Scornful but pleased amusement. "You look at me first, always, with your daylight eyes, my love. And sometimes I think you have never seen me clearly, at all."

"Oh, yes; I have." A shaky, wandering whisper. "Those times I've had to be away from you. And *these* times, when—when I can't quite see you at all. Yet I know you best, now."

"You see me precisely as I see you, these times." A pause. "As all the things we truly are, used to be, nearly became, and *will* be, for good." Low-pitched, laugh-like vibration. "Honestly, hon, don't you understand yet what we are doing, now, and exactly what we are?"

No quick answer. "Sometimes I believe we are one another's dreams. At other moments, I think we are—ghosts, somehow. Because we meet this way only in the dark, at midnight and beyond. Yet I awaken and there's daylight and I believe you arise, too. Or is *that* the dream?"

"No, no. But this—these precious moments—are the threshold of the *long* reality, the *important, enduring* reality."

Irascible masculine resonance: "I don't get it! I've tried, but I do *not* understand—*this*. All I know is that you are truly you and I am I. Not as we are by day, but . . . *more*, in an odd way. And another thing I know, beautiful: That when I awaken, I never consciously remember these nocturnal meetings."

"And yet, they influence you, and me, during the period of light." A contemplative moment, as if used to gather difficult thought. "You married me in the morning of my grownup life, and I'm still glad. But of course, you don't 'consciously' remember these times, silly. These are the moments when, in our sleep, our *unconscious selves* may talk, commune—always with honesty, forever to reaffirm our love and enable us to make the waking *us* go on."

"We're our *own* ghosts, then?" Wonder; understanding. "But how could you figure it out, how can you know?"

"Unlike you, a part of me has always remembered the night. And" —a loving, cautious pause—"the daylight time is drawing to a close."

"Should I fear it?" Wind, whispering softly across the sleeping, the aged forms, bony and brittle under the press of winter blankets. "Should I—fear—that real night that is coming?"

"Silly!" Two syllables like lips kissing. "Remember, you said that you loved '*all* of me there is?' Well, *that* is what lies ahead for you; and you are what lies ahead for me. Truly so, and for the first time: The *all* of love."

Hesitation. "I'm so tired." The slightest tremor. " 'Night."

" 'Night."

"Fancy meeting you—*here!*"

"Well, I like that! Who else would you expect to meet for eternity?"

"You're . . . lovely. And *this*—*this* is something special." Wonder; joy. "I see you, everything, *clearly* now! Good morning!"

"It is, isn't it?" Smiling satisfaction, an embrace, a loving kiss. "A very *good* morning . . . !"

Father Macclesfield's Tale

by R. H. Benson

Monsignor Maxwell announced next day at dinner that he had already arranged for the evening's entertainment. A priest, whose acquaintance he had made on the Palatine, was leaving for England the next morning; and it was our only chance therefore of hearing his story. That he had a story had come to the Canon's knowledge in the course of a conversation on the previous afternoon.

'He told me the outline of it,' he said. 'I think it very remarkable. But I had a great deal of difficulty in persuading him to repeat it to the company this evening. But he promised at last. I trust, gentlemen, you do not think I have presumed in begging him to do so.'

Father Macclesfield arrived at supper.

He was a little unimposing dry man, with a hooked nose and grey hair. He was rather silent at supper; but there was no trace of shyness in his manner as he took his seat upstairs, and without glancing round once, began in an even and dispassionate voice:

'I once knew a Catholic girl that married an old Protestant three times her own age. I entreated her not to do so; but it was useless. And when the disillusionment came she used to write to me piteous letters, telling me that her husband had in reality no religion at all. He was a convinced infidel; and scouted even the idea of the soul's immortality.

'After two years of married life the old man died. He was about sixty years old; but very hale and hearty till the end.

'Well, when he took to his bed, the wife sent for me; and I had half-a-dozen interviews with him; but it was useless. He told me plainly that he wanted to believe—in fact he said that the thought of annihilation was intolerable to him. If he had had a child he would not have hated death so much; if his flesh and blood in any manner survived him, he could have fancied that he had a sort of vicarious life left; but as it was there was no kith or kin of his alive; and he could not bear that.'

Father Macclesfield sniffed cynically, and folded his hands.

'I may say that his death-bed was extremely unpleasant. He was a coarse old fellow, with plenty of strength in him; and he used to make remarks about the churchyard—and—and in fact the worms, that used to send his poor child of a wife half fainting out of the room. He had lived an immoral life too, I gathered.

'Just at the last it was—well—disgusting. He had no consideration (God knows why she married him!). The agony was a very long one; he caught at the curtains round the bed; calling out; and all his words were about death, and the dark. It seemed to me that he caught hold of the curtains as if to hold himself into this world. And at the very end he raised himself clean up in bed, and stared horribly out of the window that was open just opposite.

'I must tell you that straight away beneath the window lay a long walk, between sheets of dead leaves with laurels on either side, and the branches meeting overhead, so that it was very dark there even in summer; and at the end of the walk away from the house was the churchyard gate.'

Father Macclesfield paused and blew his nose. Then he went on still without looking at us.

'Well, the old man died; and he was carried along this laurel path, and buried.

'His wife was in such a state that I simply dared not go away. She was frightened to death, and, indeed, the whole affair of her husband's dying was horrible. But she would not leave the house. She had a fancy that it would be cruel to him. She used to go down twice a day to pray at the grave; but she never went along the laurel walk. She would go round by the garden and in at a lower gate, and come back the same way, or by the upper garden.

'This went on for three or four days. The man had died on a Saturday, and was buried on Monday; it was in July; and he had died about eight o'clock.

'I made up my mind to go on the Saturday after the funeral. My curate had managed along very well for a few days; but I did not like to leave him for a second Sunday.

'Then on the Friday at lunch—her sister had come down, by the way, and was still in the house—on the Friday the widow said something about never daring to sleep in the room where the old man had died. I told her it was nonsense, and so on, but you must remember she was in a dreadful state of nerves, and she persisted. So I said I would sleep in the room myself. I had no patience with such ideas then.

'Of course she said all sorts of things, but I had my way; and my things were moved in on Friday evening.

'I went to my new room about a quarter before eight to put on my cassock for dinner. The room was very much as it had been—rather dark because of the trees at the end of the walk outside. There was the four-poster there with the damask curtains; the table and chairs, the cupboard where his clothes were kept, and so on.

'When I had put my cassock on, I went to the window to look out. To right and left were the gardens, with the sunlight just off them, but still very bright and gay, with the geraniums, and exactly opposite was the laurel walk, like a long green shady tunnel, dividing the upper and lower lawns.

'I could see straight down it to the churchyard gate, which was about a hundred yards away, I suppose. There were limes overhead, and laurels, as I said, on each side.

'Well—I saw some one coming up the walk; but it seemed to me at first that he was drunk. He staggered several times as I watched; I suppose he would be fifty yards away—and once I saw him catch hold of one of the trees and cling against it as if he were afraid of falling. Then he left it, and came on again slowly, going from side to side, with his hands out. He seemed desperately keen to get to the house.

'I could see his dress; and it astonished me that a man dressed so should be drunk; for he was quite plainly a gentleman. He wore a white top hat, and a grey cut-away coat, and grey trousers, and I could make out his white spats.

'Then it struck me he might be ill; and I looked harder than ever, wondering whether I ought to go down.

'When he was about twenty yards away he lifted his face; and it struck me as very odd, but it seemed to me he was extraordinarily like the old man we had buried on Monday; but it was darkish where he was, and the next moment he dropped his face, threw up his hands and fell flat on his back.

'Well, of course, I was startled at that, and I leaned out of the window and called out something. He was moving his hands I could see, as if he were in convulsions; and I could hear the dry leaves rustling.

'Well, then I turned and ran out and downstairs.'

Father Macclesfield stopped a moment.

'Gentlemen,' he said abruptly, 'when I got there, there was not a sign of the old man. I could see that the leaves had been disturbed, but that was all.'

There was an odd silence in the room as he paused; but before any of us had time to speak he went on.

'Of course I did not say a word of what I had seen. We dined as usual; I smoked for an hour or so by myself after prayers; and then I went up to bed. I cannot say I was perfectly comfortable, for I was not; but neither was I frightened.

'When I got to my room I lit all my candles, and then went to a big cupboard I had noticed, and pulled out some of the drawers. In the bottom of the third drawer I found a grey cut-away coat and grey trousers; I found several pairs of white spats in the top drawer; and a white hat on the shelf above. That is the first incident.'

'Did you sleep there, Father?' said a voice softly.

'I did,' said the priest, 'there was no reason why I should not. I did not fall asleep for two or three hours; but I was not disturbed in any way, and came to breakfast as usual.

'Well, I thought about it all a bit; and finally I sent a wire to my curate telling him I was detained. I did not like to leave the house just then.'

Father Macclesfield settled himself again in his chair and went on, in the same dry uninterested voice.

'On Sunday we drove over to the Catholic Church, six miles off, and I said Mass. Nothing more happened till the Monday evening.

'That evening I went to the window again about a quarter before eight, as I had done both on the Saturday and Sunday. Everything was perfectly quiet, till I heard the churchyard gate unlatch; and I saw a man come through.

'But I saw almost at once that it was not the same man I had seen before; it looked to me like a keeper, for he had a gun across his arm; then I saw him hold the gate open an instant, and a dog came through and began to trot up the path towards the house with his master following.

'When the dog was about fifty yards away he stopped dead and pointed.

'I saw the keeper throw his gun forward and come up softly; and as he came the dog began to slink backwards. I watched very closely, clean forgetting why I was there; and the next instant something—it was too shadowy under the trees to see exactly what it was—but something about the size of a hare burst out of the laurels and made straight up the path, dodging from side to side, but coming like the wind.

'The beast could not have been more than twenty yards from me when the keeper fired, and the creature went over and over in the dry leaves, and lay struggling and screaming. It was horrible! But what astonished me was that the dog did not come up. I heard the keeper snap out something, and then I saw the dog making off down the avenue in the direction of the churchyard as hard as he could go.

'The keeper was running now towards me; but the screaming of the hare, or of whatever it was, had stopped; and I was astonished to see the man come right up to where the beast was struggling and kicking, and then stop as if he was puzzled.

'I leaned out of the window and called to him.

' "Right in front of you, man," I said. "For God's sake kill the brute."

'He looked up at me, and then down again.

' "Where is it, sir?" he said. "I can't see it anywhere."

'And there lay the beast, clear before him all the while, not a yard away, still kicking.

'Well, I went out of the room and downstairs and out to the avenue.

'The man was standing there still, looking terribly puzzled, but the hare was gone. There was not a sign of it. Only the leaves were disturbed, and the wet earth showed beneath.

'The keeper said that it had been a great hare; he could have sworn to it; and that he had orders to kill all hares and rabbits in the garden enclosure. Then he looked rather odd.

' "Did you see it plainly, sir?" he asked.

'I told him, not very plainly; but I thought it a hare too.

' "Yes, sir," he said, "it was a hare, sure enough; but, do you know, sir, I thought it to be a kind of silver grey with white feet. I never saw one like that before!"

'The odd thing was that not a dog would come near, his own dog was gone; but I fetched the yard dog, a retriever, out of his kennel in the kitchen yard; and if ever I saw a frightened dog it was this one. When we dragged him up at last, all whining and pulling back, he began to snap at us so fiercely that we let go, and he went back like the wind to his kennel. It was the same with the terrier.

'Well, the bell had gone, and I had to go in and explain why I was late; but I didn't say anything about the colour of the hare. That was the second incident.'

Father Macclesfield stopped again, smiling reminiscently to himself. I was very much impressed by his quiet air and composure. I think it helped his story a good deal.

Again, before we had time to comment or question, he went on.

'The third incident was so slight that I should not have mentioned it, or thought anything of it, if it had not been for the others; but it seemed to me there was a kind of diminishing gradation of energy, which explained. Well, now you shall hear.

'On the other nights of that week I was at my window again; but nothing happened till the Friday. I had arranged to go for certain next day; the widow was much better and more reasonable, and even talked of going abroad herself in the following week.

'On that Friday evening I dressed a little earlier, and went down to the avenue this time, instead of staying at my window, at about twenty minutes to eight.

'It was rather a heavy depressing evening, without a breath of wind; and it was darker than it had been for some days.

'I walked slowly down the avenue to the gate and back again; and I suppose it was fancy, but I felt more uncomfortable than I had felt at all up to then. I was rather relieved to see the widow come out of the house and stand looking down the avenue. I came out myself then and went towards her. She started rather when she saw me and then smiled.

' "I thought it was some one else," she said. "Father, I have made up my mind to go. I shall go to town tomorrow, and start on Monday. My sister will come with me."

'I congratulated her; and then we turned and began to walk back to the lime avenue. She stopped at the entrance, and seemed unwilling to come any further.

' "Come down to the end," I said, "and back again. There will be time before dinner."

'She said nothing, but came with me; and we went straight down to the gate and then turned to come back.

'I don't think either of us spoke a word; I was very uncomfortable indeed by now; and yet I had to go on.

'We were half way back I suppose when I heard a sound like a gate rattling; and I whisked round in an instant, expecting to see someone at the gate. But there was no one.

'Then there came a rustling overhead in the leaves; it had been dead still before. Then I don't know why, but I took my friend suddenly by the arm and drew her to one side out of the path, so that we stood on the right hand, not a foot from the laurels.

'She said nothing, and I said nothing; but I think we were both looking this way and that, as if we expected to see something.

'The breeze died, and then sprang up again, but it was only a breath. I could hear the living leaves rustling overhead, and the dead leaves underfoot; and it was blowing gently from the churchyard.

'Then I saw a thing that one often sees; but I could not take my

140

eyes off it, nor could she. It was a little column of leaves, twisting and turning and dropping and picking up again in the wind, coming slowly up the path. It was a capricious sort of draught, for the little scurry of leaves went this way and that, to and fro across the path. It came up to us, and I could feel the breeze on my hands and face. One leaf struck me softly on the cheek, and I can only say that I shuddered as if it had been a toad. Then it passed on.

'You understand, gentlemen, it was pretty dark; but it seemed to me that the breeze died and the column of leaves—it was no more than a little twist of them—sank down at the end of the avenue.

We stood there perfectly still for a moment or two; and when I turned, she was staring straight at me, but neither of us said one word.

'We did not go up the avenue to the house. We pushed our way through the laurels, and came back by the upper garden.

'Nothing else happened; and the next morning we all went off by the eleven o'clock train.

'That is all, gentlemen.'

The Furnished Room

by O. Henry

Restless, shifting, fugacious as time itself is a certain vast bulk of the population of the red brick district of the lower West Side. Homeless, they have a hundred homes. They flit from furnished room to furnished room, transients forever—transients in abode, transients in heart and mind. They sing 'Home, Sweet Home' in ragtime; they carry their *lares et penates* in a bandbox; their vine is entwined about a picture hat; a rubber plant is their fig tree.

Hence the houses of this district, having had a thousand dwellers, should have a thousand tales to tell, mostly dull ones, no doubt; but it would be strange if there could not be found a ghost or two in the wake of all these vagrant guests.

One evening after dark a young man prowled among these crumbling red mansions, ringing their bells. At the twelfth he rested his lean hand-baggage upon the step and wiped the dust from his hat-band and forehead. The bell sounded faint and far away in some remote, hollow depths.

To the door of this, the twelfth house whose bell he had rung, came a housekeeper who made him think of an unwholesome, surfeited worm that had eaten its nut to a hollow shell and now sought to fill the vacancy with edible lodgers.

He asked if there was a room to let.

'Come in,' said the housekeeper. Her voice came from her throat; her throat seemed lined with fur. 'I have the third-floor back, vacant since a week back. Should you wish to look at it?'

The young man followed her up the stairs. A faint light from no particular source mitigated the shadows of the halls. They trod noise-lessly upon a stair carpet that its own loom would have forsworn. It seemed to have become vegetable, to have degenerated in that rank, sunless air to lush lichen or spreading moss that grew in patches to the staircase and was viscid under the foot like organic matter. At each turn of the stairs were vacant niches in the wall. Perhaps plants had once been set within them. If so they had died in that foul and tainted air. It may be that statues of the saints had stood there, but it was not diffi-cult to conceive that imps and devils had dragged them forth in the darkness and down to the unholy depths of some furnished pit below.

'This is the room,' said the housekeeper, from her furry throat. 'It's a nice room. It ain't often vacant. I had some most elegant people in it last summer—no trouble at all, and paid in advance to the minute. The water's at the end of the hall. Sprowls and Mooney kept it three months. They done a vaudeville sketch. Miss B'retta Sprowls—you may have heard of her—Oh, that was just the stage names—right there over the dresser is where the marriage certificate hung, framed. The gas is here, and you see there is plenty of closet room. It's a room everybody likes. It never stays idle long.'

'Do you have many theatrical people rooming here?' asked the young man.

'They comes and goes. A good proportion of my lodgers is con-nected with the theatres. Yes, sir, this is the theatrical district. Actor people never stays long anywhere. I get my share. Yes, they comes and they goes.'

He engaged the room, paying for a week in advance. He was tired, he said, and would take possession at once. He counted out the money. The room had been made ready, she said, even to towels and water. As the housekeeper moved away he put, for the thousandth time, the question that he carried at the end of his tongue.

142

'A young girl—Miss Vashner—Miss Eloise Vashner—do you remember such a one among your lodgers? She would be singing on the stage, most likely. A fair girl, of medium height, and slender, with reddish, gold hair and a dark mole near her left eyebrow.'

'No, I don't remember the name. Them stage people has names they change as often as their rooms. They comes and they goes. No, I don't call that one to mind.'

No. Always no. Five months of ceaseless interrogation and the inevitable negative. So much time spent by day in questioning managers, agents, schools and choruses; by night among the audiences of theatres from all-star casts down to music halls so low that he dreaded to find what he most hoped for. He who had loved her best had tried to find her. He was sure that since her disappearance from home this great, water-girt city held her somewhere, but it was like a monstrous quicksand, shifting its particles constantly, with no foundation, its upper granules of today buried tomorrow in ooze and slime.

The furnished room received its latest guest with a first glow of pseudo-hospitality, a hectic, haggard, perfunctory welcome like the specious smile of a demirep. The sophistical comfort came in reflected gleams from the decayed furniture, the ragged brocade upholstery of a couch and two chairs, a foot-wide cheap pier glass between the two windows, from one or two gilt picture frames and a brass bedstead in a corner.

The guest reclined, inert, upon a chair, while the room, confused in speech as though it were an apartment in Babel, tried to discourse to him of its divers tenantry.

A polychromatic rug like some brilliant-flowered rectangular, tropical islet lay surrounded by a billowy sea of soiled matting. Upon the gay-papered wall were those pictures that pursue the homeless one from house to house—*The Huguenot Lovers, The First Quarrel, The Wedding Breakfast, Psyche at the Fountain.* The mantel's chastely severe outline was ingloriously veiled behind some pert drapery drawn rakishly askew like the sashes of the Amazonian ballet. Upon it was some desolate flotsam cast aside by the room's marooned when a lucky sail had borne them to a fresh port—a trifling vase or two, pictures of actresses, a medicine bottle, some stray cards out of a deck.

One by one, as the characters of a cryptograph become explicit, the little signs left by the furnished room's procession of guests developed a significance. The threadbare space in the rug in front of the dresser told that lovely women had marched in the throng. Tiny finger prints on the wall spoke of little prisoners trying to feel their way to sun and air. A splattered stain, raying like a shadow of a bursting bomb, witnessed where a hurled glass or bottle had splintered with its contents against the wall. Across the pier glass had been scrawled with a diamond in staggering letters the name 'Marie'. It seemed that the succession of dwellers in the furnished room had turned in fury—perhaps tempted beyond forbearance by its garish coldness—and wreaked upon it their passions. The furniture was chipped and bruised; the couch, distorted by bursting springs, seemed a horrible monster that had been slain during the stress of some grotesque convulsion. Some more potent upheaval had cloven a great slice from the marble mantel. Each plank in the floor owned its particular cant and shriek as from a separate and individual agony. It seemed incredible that all this malice and injury had been wrought upon the room by those who had called it for a time their home; and yet it may have been the cheated home instinct surviving blindly, the resentful rage at false household gods that had kindled their wrath. A hut that is our own we can sweep and adorn and cherish.

The young tenant in the chair allowed these thoughts to file, softshod, through his mind, while there drifted into the room furnished sounds and furnished scents. He heard in one room a tittering and incontinent, slack laughter; in others the monologue of a scold, the rattling of dice, a lullaby, and one crying dully; above him a banjo tinkled with spirit. Doors banged somewhere, the elevated trains roared intermittently; a cat yowled miserably upon a back fence. And he breathed the breath of the house—a dank savour rather than a smell —a cold, musty effluvium as from underground vaults mingled with the reeking exhalations of linoleum and mildewed and rotten woodwork.

Then, suddenly, as he rested there, the room was filled with the strong, sweet odour of mignonette. It came as upon a single buffet of wind with such sureness and fragrance and emphasis that it almost seemed a living visitant. And the man cried aloud: 'What, dear?' as if he had been called, and sprang up and faced about. The rich odour clung to him and wrapped him around. He reached out his arms for it, all his senses for the time confused and commingled. How could one be peremptorily called by an odour? Surely it must have been a sound. But, was it not the sound that had touched, that had caressed him?

'She has been in this room,' he cried, and he sprang to wrest from it a token, for he knew he would recognize the smallest thing that had belonged to her or that she had touched. This enveloping scent of mignonette, the odour that she had loved and made her own—whence came it?

The room had been but carelessly set in order. Scattered upon the

144

flimsy dresser scarf were half a dozen hairpins—those discreet, indistinguishable friends of womankind, feminine of gender, infinite of mood and uncommunicative of tense. These he ignored, conscious of their triumphant lack of identity. Ransacking the drawers of the dresser he came upon a discarded, tiny, ragged handkerchief. He pressed it to his face. It was racy and insolent with heliotrope; he hurled it to the floor. In another drawer he found odd buttons, a theatre programme, a pawnbroker's card, two lost marshmallows, a book on the divination of dreams. In the last was a woman's black satin hair-bow, which halted him, poised between ice and fire. But the black satin hair-bow also is femininity's demure, impersonal, common ornament, and tells no tales.

And then he traversed the room like a hound on the scent, skimming the walls, considering the corners of the bulging matting on his hands and knees, rummaging mantel and tables, the curtains and hangings, the drunken cabinet in the corner, for a visible sign, unable to perceive that she was there beside, around, against, within, above him, clinging to him, wooing him, calling him so poignantly through the finer senses that even his grosser ones became cognisant of the call. Once again he answered loudly: 'Yes dear!' and turned, wild-eyed, to gaze on vacancy, for he could not yet discern form and colour and love and outstretched arms in the odour of mignonette. Oh, God! whence that odour, and since when have odours had a voice to call? Thus he groped.

He burrowed in crevices and corners, and found corks and cigarettes. These he passed in passive contempt. But once he found in a fold of the matting a half-smoked cigar, and this he ground beneath his heel with a green and trenchant oath. He sifted the room from end to end. He found dreary and ignoble small records of many a peripatetic tenant; but of her whom he sought, and who may have lodged there, and whose spirit seemed to hover there, he found no trace.

And then he thought of the housekeeper.

He ran from the haunted room downstairs and to a door that showed a crack of light. She came out to his knock. He smothered his excitement as best he could.

'Will you tell me, madam,' he besought her, 'who occupied the room I have before I came?'

'Yes, sir. I can tell you again. 'Twas Sprowls and Mooney, as I said. Miss B'retta Sprowls it was in the theatres, but Missis Mooney she was. My house is well known for respectability. The marriage certificate hung, framed, on a nail over—'

'What kind of a lady was Miss Sprowls—in looks, I mean?'

'Why, black-haired, sir, short, and stout, with a comical face. They left a week ago Tuesday.'

'And before they occupied it?'

'Why, there was a single gentleman connected with the draying business. He left owing me a week. Before him was Missis Crowder and her two children, they stayed four months; and back of them was old Mr Doyle, whose sons paid for him. He kept the room six months. That goes back a year, sir, and further I do not remember.'

He thanked her and crept back to his room. The room was dead. The essence that had vivified it was gone. The perfume of mignonette had departed. In its place was the old, stale odour of mouldy house furniture, of atmosphere in storage.

The ebbing of his hope drained his faith. He sat staring at the yellow, singing gaslight. Soon he walked to the bed and began to tear the sheets into strips. With the blade of his knife he drove them tightly into every crevice around windows and door. When all was snug and taut he turned out the light, turned the gas full on again and laid himself gratefully upon the bed.

It was Mrs McCool's night to go with the can for beer. So she fetched it and sat with Mrs Purdy in one of those subterranean retreats where housekeepers forgather and the worm dieth seldom.

'I rented out my third floor, back, this evening,' said Mrs Purdy, across a fine circle of foam. 'A young man took it. He went up to bed two hours ago.'

'Now, did ye, Missis Purdy, ma'am?' said Mrs McCool, with intense admiration. 'You do be a wonder for rentin' rooms of that kind. And did ye tell him, then?' she concluded in a husky whisper, laden with mystery.

'Rooms,' said Mrs Purdy, in her furriest tones, 'are furnished for to rent. I did not tell him, Mrs McCool.'

' 'Tis right ye are, ma'am; 'tis by renting rooms we kape alive. Ye have the rale sense for business, ma'am. There be many people will rayjict the rentin' of a room if they be tould a suicide has been after dyin' in the bed of it.'

'As you say, we has our living to be making,' remarked Mrs Purdy.

'Yis, ma'am, 'tis true. 'Tis just one wake ago this day I helped ye lay out the third floor, back. A pretty slip of a colleen she was to be killin' herself wid the gas—a swate little face she had, Mrs Purdy, ma'am.'

'She'd a-been called handsome, as you say,' said Mrs Purdy, assenting but critical, 'but for that mole she had a-growin' by her left eyebrow. Do fill up your glass again, Missis McCool.'

The Garret
of Madame Lemoyne

by W. K. Mashburn, Jr.

When Merriweather's idea took definite shape, Annette refused to have anything to do with it. A haunted house was a haunted house, as far as she was concerned. Yet she was really the cause of all that happened. The innocent cause, of course; but she suggested the thing to Merriweather.

Merriweather wanted to scare his wife, just for the sake of upsetting her poise. That wasn't really as cruel as it sounds, because Janice was a calm, blond Juno, whose eternal self-possession would at times have irked a more reasonable man than her husband. He had had some very vague idea when the pair of them first started for New Orleans to spend the carnival season with Walter and Annette Owen. There would be masks, an Old World atmosphere, and an altogether proper stage setting to make the possibility promising.

The Monday morning before the Mardi Gras Day, the quartet rode through the *Vieux Carré*—the "Old Quarter"—in Owen's car, visiting every spot that was likely to interest the Merriweathers. Annette made a perfect guide: she was of the Quarter herself, and she knew its every legend and historic spot as well as she knew the beads of her amber rosary. As all must do who tour the Quarter with competent guides, they came eventually to the "haunted" house.

Like so many of the old buildings of that section, the house had, of later years, seen mostly the seamy side of life. Just now, it was desolate and unoccupied. Somebody had recently bought it—a Sicilian, rumor had it—and there was much talk of raising a fund to preserve the place to its traditions, while the Vieux Carré Historical Society passed the usual resolution of protest against the desecration of an old landmark. That was all it amounted it, and it was not the fault of any of the protestants that the old house escaped the ignominious fate of becoming a spaghetti factory. Annette said, later, that the legend saved it. That may be so, too, but the Sicilian probably abandoned the place to the Historical Society because of the Merriweathers, and nobody associated them with the legend. Nobody, that is, except the Owens.

On this particular morning, there was an old crone, maybe one of the Sicilian's dependents, possibly just an opportunist, taking advantage of the influx of carnival visitors to charge an admittance fee of twenty-five cents to everyone who wanted a peek at Madame Lemoyne's garret. Annette led the way up, and told the story to the Merriweathers, standing there in the attic's legend-haunted gloom.

"Nearly a hundred years ago," she informed them, "this house was occupied by a Madame Lemoyne. There was a Monsieur Lemoyne, too, but he doesn't seem to have amounted to anything more than Madame's husband, so it is still known as Madame Lemoyne's house.

"This Madame Lemoyne was a Parisian of wealth and excellent family, so that her house became a gathering place for the élite of that day. Everyone agreed that Madame was a most charming woman, a brilliant hostess, and thoroughly worth cultivating. None suspected her of being the human fiend she was, nor dreamed of what her garret —*this* garret!—concealed, until one day her house burned.

"It didn't burn much, because the fire brigade arrived with unusual promptness. The blaze was in the attic, and that led to the discovery of the other things up there. At last Madame's secret was out! The horrified volunteer firemen—some of them blades of her very own circle— discovered seven black slaves in chains, all of them in various stages of mutilation.

"The charming *Parisienne* had maintained a private torture chamber, where she gratified her secret lust for cruelty upon the bodies of shackled and helpless negro slaves. All the details were never given out, but you can imagine them to have been horrible from the fact that one of the pitiful victims, a woman, somehow obtained the means to fire the garret, in the hope of ending, in the flames, her torment at Madame's beautiful white hands."

Annette paused to give her story dramatic effect, and Janice Merriweather made a slight grimace of distaste. Her husband, watching her, laughed at even so slight a ruffling of her calm; and Annette's climax fell rather flat as a result.

"What happened to the old girl herself?" Merriweather then wanted to know.

"Luckily for her, she was away from home when the fire broke out," Annette answered. "Very luckily," she continued, "for a mob soon formed and set about finding her, and Madame barely made her way aboard a French ship that was just then in the act of clearing port. She spent the rest of her life in Paris, and report had it that she became very noted for her piety and charity, and died at a ripe old age."

"So prosper the wicked," sententiously pronounced Merriweather. "But you have yet to tell us why the place is supposed to be haunted."

"Ah!" Annette enlightened. "The slaves. They are said still to haunt this old attic, hoping that Madame may some day come back."

"Hoping that she may come back?" echoed Merriweather, with a show of interest. "Then that means hoping for a chance for revenge?"

Annette nodded. "Surely. There was one horribly mutilated giant of a black, so the story goes, whose tongue had been torn out with pincers, and who refused to leave his torture-chamber after they had taken the chains off him. He made people understand that he wanted to wait for Madame's return; and, as his unshackled hands and arms were unmaimed, and of enormous size and strength, he resisted all efforts to move him so savagely that they left him there until he died, a few days later."

"I don't blame them," volunteered Walter Owen. "I've seen buck niggers working on the wharves with arms as big as my thighs, and knotted with muscles until they looked like the limbs of an oak."

"Well, I don't suppose ghost arms could do much harm, regardless of how tremendously they were thewed," was Janice's practical observation.

"Oh, but they could in this case," Annette quickly corrected. "You see, if they are able to stay on earth at all, spirits seeking vengeance on their murderers have the power to embody themselves momentarily, under the right circumstances, and on the scene of the crime. That's what the old mammies say, I mean."

Janice laughed a little, indulgently. "I'm almost inclined to suspect that you half believe all that, yourself," she gently scoffed.

Annette retorted, in a flash, "Would *you* come up here, alone, at midnight?"

"Oh, come," interrupted Owen. "None of us believe that part of it, of course. But it would be sort of creepy up here, at that time of night. Right now, it's just stuffy: let's get down to the car, and out into the sunshine."

With that, they went down to the street, but Annette decided, on the way, that she didn't wonder that Janice's calm superiority irritated her husband.

Merriweather was not content to let the subject drop. Next day he brought it up again. "You *wouldn't* go up alone into that haunted attic at midnight, would you?"

"Why not?" Janice coolly demanded.

"Would you?" insisted her husband.

"Certainly," replied Janice, "if there were any reason for it."

"I *dare* you—tonight!" challenged Merriweather.

Janice laughed, tolerantly. "Did you ever before see such persistence on a foolish subject?" she asked the Owens. Then, with the slightest of shrugs, she answered her husband. "Very well, since you are so set on it. After the ball, tonight."

"Bully for you!" Merriweather applauded. He seemed delighted with her decision.

"Oh!" Annette uneasily objected. "I wouldn't, if I were you."

"Why?"

"Oh, I don't know, but I just don't like it. You know, you're going to wear a costume that is just the sort of dress Madame Lemoyne might have worn in her day."

"Meaning—?" suggested Janice.

"Nothing!" decided Annette, rather flatly. "You-all go if you will, but I shall not." If Pontius Pilate had been a Louisiana Creole, he would have disavowed responsibility with just such a shrug of his shoulders as she used.

At a little after a quarter of midnight, Merriweather sought out Owen in the crowd of revelers at the Mardi Gras ball. Both were in costume, and masked, but each was, of course, acquainted with the other's disguise; so that finding him was no great matter. Owen, in fact, was also searching for Merriweather, and anticipated the latter's question when they met. "The ladies have already gone out to the car," he stated. "It's a couple of blocks down the street and, as I didn't know how long it would take to find you, I sent them on to save time."

"Good!" approved Merriweather. "So Annette decided to go, after all?"

Owen nodded. "Yes; Janice persuaded her that it was just a harmless lark."

"Good!" Merriweather said again. "Now listen: I'm not going with you. You tell 'em you couldn't find me and that I told you beforehand that I'd follow in a taxi, if you went off and left me. I want to beat you down there," he went on, in explanation, "and be in the garret when Janice climbs up. I'll scare her out of her calm, for once!"

Owen remonstrated, but Merriweather cut him short. "I know I wouldn't do for Annette—she'd have double hysterics, and so would any normal woman. Not Janice! I may hand her a jolt, but it won't be a very big one."

Merriweather had become detached from the others, earlier in the night, and it was evident to Owen that he had found a bootlegger in the interval, and, more or less, taken a doubtful advantage of his discovery. Owen realized, moreover, that Merriweather's determination to shatter his wife's irritatingly cool self-possession had become something of an obsession with the man, even without the whisky.

"Go ahead," urged Merriweather. "I *am* going in a taxi—I have one waiting. The door to the stairs will be open: I fixed it with that old hag this afternoon."

With that, he was off, and Owen went out to repeat his lame story to the women.

Janice smiled. "I know quite well what he plans," she remarked, "but I think he'll be disappointed."

Owen said nothing as he started the car toward the Old Quarter, but he, as Annette had already done, reached the decision that a woman so eternally poised was a phenomenon to set the nerves of any man on edge.

Arrived at Madame Lemoyne's house, Walter tried the stair door, and found it unlocked, as Merriweather had said it would be.

"Well," he said, consulting his watch, "let's go up; it doesn't lack a full minute of midnight."

"I am going alone," Janice reminded him. "That was the bargain."

Without more ado she slipped past, and climbed lightly and quickly up the first flight of stairs. Walter looked at Annette in some hesitation. "She didn't even take the flashlight," he remarked. "Hadn't we better follow her?"

"Let her go!" Annette had not forgotten her own contribution to Janice's amusement on their previous visit to the house, and so was inclined to be a bit catty. (She was not anxious to climb those stairs, anyway!) She swiftly became contrite, however, and as swiftly reversed her decision. "No, I didn't mean that! Let's go!"

They climbed the first flight of stairs, listening for Janice's footfall above them; but the house was as oppressively silent as a country churchyard. Acting upon some impulse, Annette grasped Walter's coat sleeve as they started up the second and final flight of stairs to the garret.

"Hurry!" she whispered.

At that instant, a clock somewhere commenced to strike the midnight hour. Instinctively, Walter paused upon the stairs, and Annette drew closer to him, while the twelve strokes rang out dolorously upon the still night. For no apparent reason they were holding their breaths when the last stroke died out. The quiet was more noticeable than ever, and it seemed that an electric tension had been added to the air. Then—

"Oh!" moaned Annette, clutching frantically at her husband. "I knew it! Oh-h!"

Heedless of her grasping hands, Owen sprang up the stairway, in answer to the agony-laden screams that had come from the garret— screams that had stopped short with a suddenness that was even more awful.

The impetus of his last upward leap carried Walter into the attic, or else he would have stopped short to fight off the fear, terrible and mastering, that gripped him at the top of the steps. He felt his scalp prickle, and sensed the presence of *something* in the farther darkness of that black and barren garret—something terrible, something huge, and black, and utterly malignant.

Dimly conscious of it, he could hear Annette wailing, upon the stairs below him. Ahead, in the thick, almost tangible darkness, there sounded a mouthy, incoherent babble, like unto the gibbering of a soul lost in the dismal wastes between worlds. That, and the *something*—

Suddenly Owen realized that he had, in his last headlong upward flight, instinctively snapped the switch of his powerful electric torch— snapped it *off*. Click! it went on again. Did he but imagine that a towering shape, blacker than mere darkness, shrank away and melted under the sudden powerful ray of light? A flood of relief and fresh assurance swept over Walter as the white beam leaped forward.

His relief was short-lived! In the light of the torch, Owen beheld a twisted and oddly terrifying heap upon the dusty boards of the attic. Janice! And bending over her, patting her face with hands that came away darkly stained, crouched a frantically gabbling figure, garbed in a harlequin suit.

"Merriweather!" croaked Owen; and the babbler clutched the figure from the floor to his breast, changing his awful mouthing to a whimpering snarl of defiance.

So ended Merriweather's jest. The law would have had his life, except that the police found him raving mad, when they came and forced his arms from their pitiful embrace. Gravely, those upon whom the responsibility for such things rests constructed a theory that satisfied them and the public. From Owen's testimony (they got nothing from Annette but shudders and sobs), they deduced that Merriweather's obsession to break the perpetual self-control of his wife had become almost monomania; poison whisky, and his rage when he supposedly failed to frighten Janice in the garret, had supplied the final leverage to unbalance his reason. Thus his intended joke became stark tragedy, and Merriweather strangled his wife. In this wise argued the law, and was complacently satisfied when press and public docilely accepted its theory.

As for Walter Owen and Annette his wife, they had their doubts. They kept them, wisely, to themselves, but they had them, none the less. For Owen had seen that huddled heap crumpled upon the floor of Madame Lemoyne's garret—garbed much as Madame might have been!—and had observed that the great marks upon her white neck were more, by nearly double, than Merriweather's small hands could compass. Neither did Walter believe that Merriweather's occasional irritation at his wife's disconcerting lack of feminine "temperament" had become anything like an obsession that finally snapped his reason. Instead, Owen remembered his own almost overpowering fear of the *something* in the attic, that he had only sensed. Suppose Merriweather *saw*—came to grips with—*It!*

One thing more—one detail the coroner, in all propriety, suppressed: *Janice Merriweather's tongue had been torn from her mouth by the roots!*

The Ghost and the Bone-Setter

by J. Sheridan Le Fanu

In looking over the papers of my late valued and respected friend, Francis Purcell, who for nearly fifty years discharged the arduous duties of a parish priest in the south of Ireland, I met with the following document. It is one of many such, for he was a curious and industrious collector of old local traditions—a commodity in which the quarter where he resided mightily abounded. The collection and arrangement of such legends was, as long as I can remember him, his *hobby;* but I had never learned that his love of the marvellous and whimsical had

carried him so far as to prompt him to commit the results of his enqui-
ries to writing, until, in the character of *residuary legatee,* his will put
me in possession of all his manuscript papers. To such as may think the
composing of such productions as these inconsistent with the character
and habits of a country priest, it is necessary to observe, that there did
exist a race of priests—those of the old school, a race now nearly
extinct—whose habits were from many causes more refined, and whose
tastes more literary than are those of the alumni of Maynooth.

It is perhaps necessary to add that the superstition illustrated by the
following story, namely, that the corpse last buried is obliged, during
his juniority of interment, to supply his brother tenants of the churchyard in which he lies, with fresh water to allay the burning thirst of
purgatory, is prevalent throughout the south of Ireland. The writer
can vouch for a case in which a respectable and wealthy farmer, on the
borders of Tipperary, in tenderness to the corns of his departed help-
mate, enclosed in her coffin two pair of brogues, a light and a heavy,
the one for dry, the other for sloppy weather; seeking thus to mitigate
the fatigues of her inevitable perambulations in procuring water, and
administering it to the thirsty souls of purgatory. Fierce and desperate
conflicts have ensued in the case of two funeral parties approaching the
same churchyard together, each endeavouring to secure to his own
dead priority of sepulture, and a consequent immunity from the tax
levied upon the pedestrian powers of the last comer. An instance not
long since occurred, in which one of two such parties, through fear of
losing to their deceased friend this inestimable advantage, made their
way to the churchyard by a *short cut,* and in violation of one of their
strongest prejudices, actually threw the coffin over the wall, lest time
should be lost in making their entrance through the gate. Innumerable
instances of the same kind might be quoted, all tending to shew how
strongly, among the peasantry of the south, this superstition is entertained. However, I shall not detain the reader further, by any prefatory
remarks, but shall proceed to lay before him the following:—

*Extract from the Ms. Papers of the Late
Rev. Francis Purcell, of Drumcoolagh*

"I tell the following particulars, as nearly as I can recollect them, in the
words of the narrator. It may be necessary to observe that he was what
is termed a *well-spoken* man, having for a considerable time instructed
the ingenious youth of his native parish in such of the liberal arts and
sciences as he found it convenient to profess—a circumstance which
may account for the occurrence of several big words, in the course of

this narrative, more distinguished for euphonious effect, than for cor-
rectness of application. I proceed then, without further preface, to lay
before you the wonderful adventures of Terry Neil."

"Why, thin, 'tis a quare story, an' as thrue as you're sittin' there;
and I'd make bould to say there isn't a boy in the seven parishes could
tell it better nor crickther than myself, for 'twas my father himself it
happened to, an' many's the time I heerd it out iv his own mouth; an'
I can say, an' I'm proud av that same, my father's word was as incredible as any squire's oath in the counthry; and so signs an' if a poor man
got into any unlucky throuble, he was the boy id go into the court an'
prove; but that dosen't signify—he was as honest and as sober a man,
barrin' he was a little bit too partial to the glass, as you'd find in a day's
walk; an' there wasn't the likes of him in the counthry round for nate
labourin' an' *baan* diggin'; and he was mighty handy entirely for
carpenther's work, and mendin' ould spudethrees, an' the likes i' that.
An' so he tuck up with bone-setting, as was most nathural, for none of
them could come up to him in mendin' the leg iv a stool or a table; an'
sure, there never was a bone-setter got so much custom—man an'
child, young an' ould—there never was such breakin' and mendin' of
bones known in the memory of man. Well, Terry Neil, for that was my
father's name, began to feel his heart growin' light and his purse heavy;
an' he took a bit iv a farm in Squire Phalim's ground, just undher the
ould castle, an' a pleasant little spot it was; an' day an' mornin', poor
crathurs not able to put a foot to the ground, with broken arms and
broken legs, id be comin' ramblin' in from all quarters to have their
bones spliced up. Well, yer honour, all this was as well as well could be;
but it was customary when Sir Phelim id go any where out iv the
country, for some iv the tinants to sit up to watch in the ould castle,
just for a kind of a compliment to the ould family—an' a mighty unpleasant compliment it was for the tinants, for there wasn't a man of
them but knew there was some thing quare about the ould castle. The
neighbours had it, that the squire's ould grandfather, as good a gintleman, God be with him, as I heer'd as ever stood in shoe leather,
used to keep walkin' about in the middle iv the night, ever sinst he
bursted a blood vessel pullin' out a cork out iv a bottle, as you or I
might be doin', and will too, plase God; but that dosen't signify. So, as
I was sayin', the ould squire used to come down out of the frame,
where his picthur was hung up, and to brake the bottles and glasses,
God be marciful to us all, an' dhrink all he could come at—an' small
blame to him for that same; and then if any of the family id be comin'
in, he id be up again in his place, looking as quite an' innocent as if he
didn't know any thing about it—the mischievous ould chap.

"Well, your honour, as I was sayin', one time the family up at the castle was stayin' in Dublin for a week or two; and so as usual, some of the tenants had to sit up in the castle, and the third night it kem to my father's turn. 'Oh, tare an ouns,' says he unto himself, 'an' must I sit up all night, and that ould vagabond of a sperit, glory be to God,' says he, 'serenading through the house, an' doin' all sorts iv mischief.' However, there was no gettin' aff, and so he put a bould face on it, an' he went up at night-fall with a bottle of pottieen, and another of holy wather.

"It was rainin' smart enough, an' the evenin' was darksome and gloomy, when my father got in, and the holy wather he sprinkled on himself, it wasn't long till he had to swallee a cup iv the pottieen, to keep the cowld out iv his heart. It was the ould steward, Lawrence Connor, that opened the door—and he an' my father wor always very great. So when he seen who it was, an' my father tould him how it was his turn to watch in the castle, he offered to sit up along with him; and you may be sure my father wasn't sorry for that same. So says Larry,

" 'We'll have a bit iv fire in the parlour,' says he.

" 'An' why not in the hall?' says my father, for he knew that the squire's picthur was hung in the parlour.

" 'No fire can be lit in the hall,' says Lawrence, 'for there's an ould jackdaw's nest in the chimney.'

" 'Oh thin,' says my father, 'let us stop in the kitchen, for it's very umproper for the likes iv me to be sittin' in the parlour,' says he.

" 'Oh, Terry, that can't be,' says Lawrence; 'if we keep up the ould custom at all, we may as well keep it up properly,' says he.

" 'Divil sweep the ould custom,' says my father—to himself, do ye mind, for he didn't like to let Lawrence see that he was more afeard himself.

" 'Oh, very well,' says he. 'I'm agreeable, Lawrence,' says he; and so down they both went to the kitchen, until the fire id be lit in the parlour—an' that same wasn't long doin'.

"Well, your honour, they soon wint up again, an' sat down mighty comfortable by the parlour fire, and they beginn'd to talk, an' to smoke, an' to dhrink a small taste iv the pottieen; and, moreover, they had a good rousing fire of bogwood and turf, to warm their shins over.

"Well, sir, as I was sayin' they kep convarsin' and smokin' together most agreeable, until Lawrence beginn'd to get sleepy, as was but nathural for him, for he was an ould sarvint man, and was used to a great dale iv sleep.

" 'Sure it's impossible,' says my father, 'it's gettin' sleepy you are?'

" 'Oh, divil a taste,' says Larry, 'I'm only shuttin' my eyes,' says he, 'to keep out the parfume of the tibacky smoke, that's makin' them wather,' says he. 'So don't you mind other people's business,' says he stiff enough (for he had a mighty high stomach av his own, rest his sowl), 'and go on,' says he, 'with your story, for I'm listenin',' says he, shuttin' down his eyes.

"Well, when my father seen spakin' was no use, he went on with his story. —By the same token, it was the story of Jim Soolivan and his ould goat he was tellin'—an' a pleasant story it is—an' there was so much divarsion in it, that it was enough to waken a dormouse, let alone to pervint a Christian goin' asleep. But, faix, the way my father tould it, I believe there never was the likes heerd sinst nor before for he bawled out every word av it, as if the life was fairly leavin' him thrying to keep ould Larry awake; but, faix, it was no use, for the hoorsness came an him, an' before he kem to the end of his story, Larry O'Connor beginned to snore like a bagpipes.

" 'Oh, blur an' agres,' says my father, 'isn't this a hard case,' says he, 'that ould villain, lettin' on to be my friend, and to go asleep this way, an' us both in the very room with a sperit,' says he. 'The crass o' Christ about us,' says he; and with that he was goin' to shake Lawrence to waken him, but he just remembered if he roused him, that he'd surely go off to his bed, an lave him completely alone, an' that id be by far worse.

" 'Oh thin,' says my father, 'I'll not disturb the poor boy. It id be neither friendly nor good-nathured,' says he, 'to tormint him while he is asleep,' says he; 'only I wish I was the same way myself,' says he.

'An' with that he beginned to walk up an' down, an' sayin' his prayers, until he worked himself into a sweat, savin' your presence. But it was all no good; so he dhrunk about a pint of sperits, to compose his mind.

" 'Oh,' says he, 'I wish to the Lord I was as asy in my mind as Larry there. Maybe,' says he, 'if I thried I could go asleep'; an' with that he pulled a big arm-chair close beside Lawrence, an' settled himself in it as well as he could.

"But there was one quare thing I forgot to tell you. He couldn't help, in spite av himself, lookin' now an' thin at the picthur, an' he immediately observed that the eyes av it was follyin' him about, an' starin' at him, an' winkin' at him, wherever he wint. 'Oh,' says he, when he seen that, 'it's a poor chance I have,' says he; 'an' bad luck was with me the day I kem into this unforthunate place,' says he; 'but any way there's no use in bein' freckened now,' says he; 'for if I am to die, I may as well parspire undaunted,' says he.

"Well, your honour, he thried to keep himself quite an' asy, an' he

157

thought two or three times he might have wint asleep, but for the way the storm was groanin' and creekin' through the great heavy branches outside, an' whistlin' through the ould chimnies iv the castle. Well, afther one great roarin' blast iv the wind, you'd think the walls iv the castle was just goin' to fall, quite an' clane, with the shakin' iv it. All av a suddint the storm stopt, as silent an' as quite as if it was a July evenin'. Well, your honour, it wasn't stopped blowin' for three min-nites, before he thought he hard a sort iv a noise over the chimney-piece; an' with that my father just opened his eyes the smallest taste in life, an' sure enough he seen the ould squire gettin' out iv the picthur, for all the world as if he was throwin' aff his ridin' coat, until he stept out clane an' complate, out av the chimly-piece, an' thrun himself down an the floor. Well, the slieveen ould chap—an' my father thought it was the dirtiest turn iv all—before he beginned to do any-thing out iv the way, he stopped, for a while, to listen wor they both asleep; an' as soon as he thought all was quite, he put out his hand, and tuck hould iv the whiskey bottle, an' dhrank at laste a pint iv it. Well, your honour, when he tuck his turn out iv it, he settled it back mighty cute intirely, in the very same spot it was in before. An' he beginn'd to walk up an' down the room, lookin' as sober an' as solid as if he never done the likes at all. An' whinever he went apast my father, he thought he felt a great scent of brimstone, an' it was that that freckened him entirely; for he knew it was brimstone that was burned in hell, savin' your presence. At any rate, he often heer'd it from Father Murphy, an' he had a right to know what belonged to it—he's dead since, God rest him. Well, your honour, my father was asy enough until the sperit kem past him; so close, God be marciful to us all, that the smell iv the sulphur tuck the breath clane out iv him; an' with that he tuck such a fit iv coughin', that it al-a-most shuck him out iv the chair he was sittin' in.

" 'Ho, ho!' says the squire, stoppin' short about two steps aff, and turnin' round facin' my father, 'is it you that's in it?—an' how's all with you, Terry Neil?'

" 'At your honour's sarvice,' says my father (as well as the fright id let him, for he was more dead than alive), 'an' it's proud I am to see your honour to-night,' says he.

" 'Terence,' says the squire, 'you're a respectable man (an' it was thrue for him), an industhrious, sober man, an' an example of inebriety to the whole parish,' says he.

" 'Thank your honour,' says my father, gettin' courage, 'you were always a civil spoken gintleman, God rest your honour.'

" 'Rest my honour,' says the sperit (fairly gettin' red in the face with the madness), 'Rest my honour?' says he. 'Why, you ignorant spalpeen,' says he, 'you mane, niggarly ignoramush,' says he, 'where did you lave your manners?' says he. 'If I *am* dead, it's no fault iv mine,' says he; 'an' it's not to be thrun in my teeth at every hand's turn, by the likes iv you,' says he, stampin' his foot an the flure, that you'd think the boords id smash undher him.

" 'Oh,' says my father, 'I'm only a foolish, ignorant, poor man,' says he.

" 'You're nothing else,' says the squire; 'but any way,' says he, 'it's not to be listenin' to your gosther, nor convarsin' with the likes iv you, that I came *up*—down I mane,' says he—(an' as little as the mistake was, my father tuck notice iv it). 'Listen to me now, Terence Neil,' says he, 'I was always a good masther to Pathrick Neil, your grandfather,' says he.

" 'Tis thrue for your honour,' says my father.

" 'And, moreover, I think I was always a sober, riglar gintleman,' says the squire.

" 'That's your name, sure enough,' says my father (though it was a big lie for him, but he could not help it).

" 'Well,' says the sperit, 'although I was as sober as most men—at laste as most gintlemen'—says he; 'an' though I was at different pariods a most extempory Christian, and most charitable and inhuman to the poor,' says he; 'for all that I'm not as asy where I am now,' says he, 'as I had a right to expect,' says he.

" 'An' more's the pity,' says my father; 'maybe your honour id wish to have a word with Father Murphy?'

" 'Hould your tongue, you misherable bliggard,' says the squire; 'it's not iv my sowl I'm thinkin'—an' I wondher you'd have the impitence to talk to a gintleman consarnin' his sowl;—and when I want *that* fixed,' says he, slappin' his thigh, 'I'll go to them that knows what belongs to the likes,' says he. 'It's not my sowl,' says he, sittin' down opposite my father; 'it's not my sowl that's annoyin' me most—I'm unasy on my right leg,' says he, 'that I bruck at Glenvarloch cover the day I killed black Barney.'

"(My father found out afther, it was a favourite horse that fell undher him, afther leapin' the big fince that runs along by the glen.)

" 'I hope,' says my father, 'your honour's not unasy about the killin' iv him?

" 'Hould your tongue, ye fool,' said the squire, 'an' I'll tell you why I'm anasy an my leg,' says he. 'In the place, where I spend most iv my time,' says he, 'except the little leisure I have for lookin' about me here,' says he, 'I have to walk a great dale more than I was ever used to,' says he, 'and by far more than is good for me either,' says he; 'for I must tell you,' says he, 'the people where I am is ancommonly fond iv could wather, for there is nothin' betther to be had; an', moreover, the weather is hotter than is altogether plisint,' says he; 'and I'm appinted,' says he, 'to assist in carryin' the wather, an' gets a mighty poor share iv it myself,' says he, 'an' a mighty throublesome, warin' job it is, I can tell you,' says he; 'for they're all iv them surprisingly dhry, an' dhrinks it as fast as my legs can carry it,' says he; 'but what kills me intirely,' says he, 'is the wakeness in my leg,' says he, 'an' I want you to give it a pull or two to bring it to shape,' says he, 'and that's the long an' the short iv it,' says he.

" 'Oh, plase your honour,' says my father (for he didn't like to handle the sperit at all), 'I wouldn't have the impitence to do the likes to your honour,' says he; 'it's only to poor crathurs like myself I'd do it to,' says he.

" 'None iv your blarney,' says the squire, 'here's my leg,' says he, cockin' it up to him, 'pull it for the bare life,' says he; 'an' if you don't, by the immortial powers I'll not lave a bone in your carcish I'll not powdher,' says he.

" 'When my father heerd that, he seen there was no use in purtendin', so he tuck hould iv the leg, an' he kept pullin' an' pullin', till the sweat, God bless us, beginned to pour down his face."

" 'Pull, you divil', says the squire.

" 'At your sarvice, your honour,' says my father.

" 'Pull harder,' says the squire.

"My father pulled like the divil.

" 'I'll take a little sup,' says the squire, rachin' over his hand to the bottle, 'to keep up my courage,' says he, lettin' an to be very wake in himself intirely. But, as cute as he was, he was out here, for he tuck the wrong one. 'Here's to your good health, Terence,' says he, 'an' now pull like the very divil,' 'an' with that he lifted the bottle of holy wather, but it was hardly to his mouth, whin he let a screech out, you'd think the room id fairly split with it, an' made one chuck that sent the leg clane aff his body in my father's hands; down wint the squire over the table, an' bang wint my father half way across the room on his back, upon the flure. Whin he kem to himself the cheerful mornin' sun was shinin' through the windy shutthers, an' he was lying flat an his back, with the leg iv one of the great ould chairs pulled clane out iv the socket an' tight in his hand, pintin' up to the ceilin', an' ould Larry fast asleep, an' snorin' as loud as ever. My father wint that mornin' to Father Murphy, an' from that to the day of his death, he never neglected confission nor mass, an' what he tould was betther believed that he spake av it but seldom. An', as for the squire, that is the sperit, whether it was that he did not like his liquor, or by rason iv the loss iv his leg, he was never known to walk again."

A Ghost-Child

by Bernard Capes

In making this confession public, I am aware that I am giving a butterfly to be broken on a wheel. There is so much of delicacy in its subject, that the mere resolve to handle it at all might seem to imply a lack of the sensitiveness necessary to its understanding; and it is certain that the more reverent the touch, the more irresistible will figure its opportunity to the common scepticism which is bondslave to its five senses. Moreover one cannot, in the reason of things, write to publish for Aristarchus alone; but the gauntlet of Grub Street must be run in any bid for truth and sincerity.

On the other hand, to withhold from evidence, in these days of what one may call a zetetic psychology, anything which may appear elucidatory, however exquisitely and rarely, of our spiritual relationships, must be pronounced, I think, a sin against the Holy Ghost.

All in all, therefore, I decide to give, with every passage to personal identification safeguarded, the story of a possession, or visitation, which is signified in the title to my narrative.

Tryphena was the sole orphaned representative of an obscure but gentle family which had lived for generations in the east of England. The spirit of the fens, of the long grey marshes, whose shores are the neutral ground of two elements, slumbered in her eyes. Looking into them, one seemed to see little beds of tiny green mosses luminous under water, or stirred by the movement of microscopic life in their midst. Secrets, one felt, were shadowed in their depths, too frail and sweet for understanding. The pretty love-fancy of babies seen in the eyes of maidens, was in hers to be interpreted into the very cosmic dust of sea-urchins, sparkling like chrysoberyls. Her soul looked out through them, as if they were the windows of a water-nursery.

161

She was always a child among children, in heart and knowledge most innocent, until Jason came and stood in her field of vision. Then, spirit of the neutral ground as she was, inclining to earth or water with the sway of the tides, she came wondering and dripping, as it were, to land, and took up her abode for final choice among the daughters of the earth. She knew her woman's estate, in fact, and the irresistible attraction of all completed perfections to the light that burns to destroy them.

Tryphena was not only an orphan, but an heiress. Her considerable estate was administered by her guardian, Jason's father, a widower, who was possessed of this single adored child. The fruits of parental infatuation had come early to ripen on the seedling. The boy was self-willed and perverse, the more so as he was naturally of a hot-hearted disposition. Violence and remorse would sway him in alternate moods, and be made, each in its turn, a self-indulgence. He took a delight in crossing his father's wishes, and no less in atoning for his gracelessness with moving demonstrations of affection.

Foremost of the old man's most cherished projects was, very naturally, a union between the two young people. He planned, manoeuvred, spoke for it with all his heart of love and eloquence. And, indeed, it seemed at last as if his hopes were to be crowned. Jason, returning from a lengthy voyage (for his enterprising spirit had early decided for the sea, and he was a naval officer), saw, and was struck amazed before, the transformed vision of his old child-play-fellow. She was an opened flower whom he had left a green bud—a thing so rare and flawless that it seemed a sacrilege for earthly passions to converse of her. Familiarity, however, and some sense of reciprocal attraction, quickly dethroned that eucharist. Tryphena could blush, could thrill, could solicit, in the sweet ways of innocent womanhood. She loved him dearly, wholly, it was plain—had found the realisation of her old formless dreams in this wondrous birth of a desire for one, in whose new-impassioned eyes she had known herself reflected hitherto only for the most patronised of small gossips. And, for her part, fearless as nature, she made no secret of her love. She was absorbed in, a captive to, Jason from that moment and for ever.

He responded. What man, however perverse, could have resisted, on first appeal, the attraction of such beauty, the flower of a radiant soul? The two were betrothed; the old man's cup of happiness was brimmed.

Then came clouds and a cold wind, chilling the garden of Hesperis. Jason was always one of those who, possessing classic noses, will cut them off, on easy provocation, to spite their faces. He was so proudly independent, to himself, that he resented the least assumption of proprietorship in him on the part of other people—even of those who had the best claim to his love and submission. This pride was an obsession. It stultified the real good in him, which was considerable. Apart from it, he was a good, warm-tempered fellow, hasty but affectionate. Under its dominion, he would have broken his own heart on an imaginary grievance.

He found one, it is to be supposed, in the privileges assumed by love; in its exacting claims upon him; perhaps in its little unreasoning jealousies. He distorted these into an implied conceit of authority over him on the part of an heiress who was condescending to his meaner fortunes. The suggestion was quite base and without warrant; but pride has no balance. No doubt, moreover, the rather childish self-depreciations of the old man, his father, in his attitude towards a match he had so fondly desired, helped to aggravate this feeling. The upshot was that, when within a few months of the date which was to make his union with Tryphena eternal, Jason broke away from a restraint which his pride pictured to him as intolerable, and went on a yachting expedition with a friend.

Then, at once, and with characteristic violence, came the reaction. He wrote, impetuously, frenziedly, from a distant port, claiming himself Tryphena's, and Tryphena his, for ever and ever and ever. They were man and wife before God. He had behaved like an insensate brute, and he was at that moment starting to speed to her side, to beg her forgiveness and the return of her love.

He had no need to play the suitor afresh. She had never doubted or questioned their mutual bondage, and would have died a maid for his sake. Something of sweet exultation only seemed to quicken and leap in her body, that her faith in her dear love was vindicated.

But the joy came near to upset the reason of the old man, already tottering to its dotage; and what followed destroyed it utterly.

The yacht, flying home, was lost at sea, and Jason was drowned.

I once saw Tryphena about this time. She lived with her near mindless charge, lonely, in an old grey house upon the borders of a salt mere, and had little but the unearthly cries of seabirds to answer to the questions of her widowed heart. She worked, sweet in charity, among the marsh folk, a beautiful unearthly presence; and was especially to be found where infants and the troubles of child-bearing women called for her help and sympathy. She was a wife herself, she would say quaintly; and some day perhaps, by grace of the good spirits of the sea, would be a mother. None thought to cross her statement, put with so sweet a sanity; and, indeed, I have often noticed that the neighbourhood of great waters breeds in souls a mysticism which is remote from the very understanding of land-dwellers.

How I saw her was thus:—

I was fishing, on a day of chill calm, in a dinghy off the flat coast. The stillness of the morning had tempted me some distance from the village where I was staying. Presently a sense of bad sport and healthy famine 'plumped' in me, so to speak, for luncheon, and I looked about for a spot picturesque enough to add a zest to sandwiches, whisky, and tobacco. Close by, a little creek or estuary ran up into a mere, between which and the sea lay a cluster of low sand-hills; and thither I pulled. The spot, when I reached it, was calm, chill desolation manifest— lifeless water and lifeless sand, with no traffic between them but the dead interchange of salt. Low sedges, at first, and behind them low woods were mirrored in the water at a distance, with an interval between me and them of sheeted glass; and right across this shining pool ran a dim, half-drowned causeway—the seapath, it appeared, to and from a lonely house which I could just distinguish squatting among trees. It was Tryphena's house.

Now, paddling dispiritedly, I turned a cold dune, and saw a mermaid before me. At least, that was my instant impression. The creature sat coiled on the strand, combing her hair—that was certain, for I saw the gold-green tresses of it whisked by her action into rainbow threads. It appeared as certain that her upper half was flesh and her lower fish; and it was only on my nearer approach that this latter resolved itself into a pale green skirt, roped, owing to her posture, about her limbs, and the hem fanned out at her feet into a tail fin. Thus also her bosom, which had appeared naked, became a bodice, as near to her flesh in colour and texture as a smock is to a lady's-smock, which some call a cuckoo-flower.

It was plain enough now; yet the illusion for the moment had quite startled me.

As I came near, she paused in her strange business to canvass me. It was Tryphena herself, as after-inquiry informed me. I have never seen so lovely a creature. Her eyes, as they regarded me passing, were something to haunt a dream: so great in tragedy—not fathomless, but all in motion near their surfaces, it seemed, with green and rooted sorrows. They were the eyes, I thought, of an Undine late-humanised, late awakened to the rapturous and troubled knowledge of the woman's burden. Her forehead was most fair, and the glistening thatch divided on it like a golden cloud revealing the face of a wondering angel.

I passed, and a sand-heap stole my vision foot by foot. The vision was gone when I returned. I have reason to believe it was vouchsafed me within a few months of the coming of the ghost-child.

On the morning succeeding the night of the day on which Jason and Tryphena were to have been married, the girl came down from her bedroom with an extraordinary expression of still rapture on her face. After breakfast she took the old man into her confidence. She was childish still; her manner quite youthfully thrilling; but now there was a newborn wonder in it that hovered on the pink of shame.

'Father! I have been under the deep waters and found him. He came to me last night in my dreams—so sobbing, so impassioned—to assure me that he had never really ceased to love me, though he had near broken his own heart pretending it. Poor boy! poor ghost! What could I do but take him to my arms? And all night he lay there, blest and forgiven, till in the morning he melted away with a sigh that woke me; and it seemed to me that I came up dripping from the sea.'

'My boy! He has come back!' chuckled the old man. 'What have you done with him, Tryphena?'

'I will hold him tighter the next time,' she said.

But the spirit of Jason visited her dreams no more.

That was in March. In the Christmas following, when the mere was locked in stillness, and the wan reflection of snow mingled on the ceiling with the red dance of firelight, one morning the old man came hurrying and panting to Tryphena's door.

'Tryphena! Come down quickly! My boy, my Jason, has come back! It was a lie that they told us about his being lost at sea!'

Her heart leapt like a candle-flame! What new delusion of the old man's was this? She hurried over her dressing and descended. A garrulous old voice mingled with a childish treble in the breakfast-room. Hardly breathing, she turned the handle of the door, and saw Jason before her.

But it was Jason, the prattling babe of her first knowledge; Jason, the flaxen-headed, apple-cheeked cherub of the nursery; Jason, the confiding, the merry, the loving, before pride had come to warp his innocence. She fell on her knees to the child, and with a burst of ecstasy caught him to her heart.

She asked no question of the old man as to when or whence this apparition had come, or why he was here. For some reason she dared not. She accepted him as some waif, whom an accidental likeness had made glorious to their hungering hearts. As for the father, he was utterly satisfied and content. He had heard a knock at the door, he said, and had opened it and found this. The child was naked, and his pink, wet body glazed with ice. Yet he seemed insensible to the killing

165

cold. It was Jason—that was enough. There is no date nor time for imbecility. Its phantoms spring from the clash of ancient memories. This was just as actually his child as—more so, in fact, than—the grown young figure which, for all its manhood, had dissolved into the mist of waters. He was more familiar with, more confident of it, after all. It had come back to be unquestioningly dependent on him; and that was likest the real Jason, flesh of his flesh.

'Who are you, darling?' said Tryphena.

'I am Jason,' answered the child.

She wept, and fondled him rapturously.

'And who am I?' she asked. "If you are Jason, you must know what to call me.'

'I know,' he said; 'but I mustn't, unless you ask me.'

'I won't,' she answered, with a burst of weeping. 'It is Christmas Day, dearest, when the miracle of a little child was wrought. I will ask you nothing but to stay and bless our desolate home.'

He nodded, laughing.

'I will stay, until you ask me.'

They found some little old robes of the baby Jason, put away in lavender, and dressed him in them. All day he laughed and prattled; yet it was strange that, talk as he might, he never once referred to matters familiar to the childhood of the lost sailor.

In the early afternoon he asked to be taken out—seawards, that was his wish. Tryphena clothed him warmly, and, taking his little hand, led him away. They left the old man sleeping peacefully. He was never to wake again.

As they crossed the narrow causeway, snow, thick and silent, began to fall. Tryphena was not afraid, for herself or the child. A rapture upheld her; a sense of some compelling happiness, which she knew before long must take shape on her lips.

They reached the seaward dunes—mere ghosts of foothold in that smoke of flakes. The lap of vast waters seemed all around them, hollow and mysterious. The sound flooded Tryphena's ears, drowning her senses. She cried out, and stopped.

'Before they go,' she screamed—'before they go, tell me what you were to call me!'

The child sprang a little distance, and stood facing her. Already his lower limbs seemed dissolving in the mists.

'I was to call you "mother"!' he cried, with a smile and toss of his hand.

Even as he spoke, his pretty features wavered and vanished. The snow broke into him, or he became part with it. Where he had been, a gleam of iridescent dust seemed to show one moment before it sank and was extinguished in the falling cloud. Then there was only the snow, heaping an eternal chaos with nothingness.

Tryphena made this confession, on a Christmas Eve night, to one who was a believer in dreams. The next morning she was seen to cross the causeway, and thereafter was never seen again. But she left the sweetest memory behind her, for human charity, and an elf-life gift of loveliness.

The Ghost Farm

by Susan Andrews Rice

When Steven was killed we did not know it until nearly thirty days afterward. He went overseas in April, and it was the last of June before we knew he went out with a party of engineers to repair the railroad track, and was blown to pieces by a German shell.

We could not tell Maidie the truth. She knew he was dead, but concerning the manner of his going she was ignorant. They were engaged. Her love for him amounted to adoration. She was an intense, emotional girl, bound to be unhappy because of her sensitive nature and strong feelings.

She was under my professional care for several weeks the latter part of the summer, suffering from a broken ankle.

"It is the silence, the awful blank wall between Steven and me, that drives me frantic," she burst out one day, when I was making her a visit. She had been reading a letter from Steven, and it lay in her lap. She had a little package of his letters always near her.

"I know," I returned, with a sigh. I, too, had lost my nearest and dearest.

"I wish I could consult a medium," she said, lowering her voice. "How wonderful it would be to receive a message from him! I could hardly bear it, I'm afraid."

"Don't do it, Maidie," I said. "Better leave such people alone."

"The ouija board, then? It seems rather like a silly game, but—"
I shook my head.
" 'That way madness lies'," I quoted. "I wouldn't, Maidie. Steven lives in your heart, in your memories of him."
She smiled that pathetic little smile she had worn when she wished to appear cheerful.
"You are right," she answered, and changed the subject.
In spite of what she had said I discovered she was reading everything she could find about spirit communication, although I never heard of her making any attempt to reach Steven in that way.
I was very busy that fall with influenza cases, and Maidie went into Red Cross work, and when the epidemic was over I heard she had gone to California. She returned early the following summer looking haggard and ill. I prescribed for her, but could find nothing really wrong with her. She took long walks, and, her mother told me, she always went alone and resented any offer of companionship. She thought it queer, and said she feared Maidie was drifting into melancholia.

Maidie came into my office one afternoon, and I was struck with the change in her expression: she looked happy and young; the strained misery had vanished from her face. I was puzzled. Could she have fallen in love? I ran over in my mind a list of her young men acquaintances, but none of them could I see as Maidie's lover.
Her mother had informed me her walks were always in one direction. Thinking of that, I asked, "Why do you always walk along the river road, Maidie?"
She turned a vivid pink.
"You won't understand, I know, but I'm going to tell you," she replied, twisting her gloves in her hands. "In the first place, you must know Steven and I used to plan that when we were married we would own a little farm. Just a little summer place, you know. He used to say every man wanted to have a farm. Doctor, when I go up the river road, just past the school house, on the bank, where the road turns into the woods, I see a little farm. The fields are neat and cultivated. The house is painted white with green blinds and the door is open into the hall, as if people lived there. Hollyhocks are growing around the kitchen door. On a table milk-pans are turned up to dry in the sun. There are some dish-towels drying on a line. And at any moment I expect to see Steven come around the corner of the house. I feel he is there, out of my sight. I wait, and listen. He hasn't come yet, but he will, some day, and when he comes, I shall go with him."

168

Her face was luminous with joy. What could I say? What ought I to say?

"Do you think I could see the farm if I were with you?" I asked, speaking slowly.

"I'm afraid you couldn't," she replied. "No one knows it is there but Steven and me."

"Then, my dear Maidie, it exists only in your imagination," I told her, gently.

She smiled, as one smiles at a child who doubts one's word, and she went away.

I studied her case carefully. A good psychanalyst might have helped her, but I was not skilful in that method of treatment. I see now that we did wrong in circumventing her. In accordance with my advice her friends attempted to divert her attention from her daily walk. She was taken on automobile excursions; visitors came at that hour of the day; she was invited to go to moving pictures; duties were crowded upon her, in the hope of altering the fixed idea in her mind of Steven's waiting at the ghost farm. She was very sweet about acceding to the demands and requests, though sometimes she would obstinately refuse to listen to them.

August brought hot weather. The extreme heat wore upon our nerves; everybody relaxed. Released from vigilant watchfulness, Maidie left the house, unnoticed.

A terrific thunder storm came up, and Maidie's mother was beside herself. She had been lying down taking a nap when Maidie slipped away. She telephoned to me when the shower was over, as Maidie was not missed until then.

I got out of my car and started up the river road, a sense of foreboding in the back of my mind. I had not proceeded far when a tire blew out. Impatiently I left the machine and hurried on foot past the weather-beaten old schoolhouse a short distance. Suddenly I stopped in my tracks. The sun had come out, and I saw the ghost farm. It was exactly as Maidie had described it: a stretch of green fields; a small white house with green blinds; hollyhocks growing by the kitchen door; milk-pans glistening in the sun, drying on a table; towels fluttering on a line. I was struck dumb, and stood motionless, hardly able to draw my breath at the strangeness of the scene.

In a few minutes the vision, or mirage, vanished. Then I perceived a tall oak tree split in half by a bolt of lightning. At the foot of the tree lay Maidie, on the wet ground, a smile of rapture on her upturned face.

169

I knelt beside her and examined heart and pulse. Nothing could be done, her spirit had left its earthly body. She had gone to be with Steven.

Ghost Story

by Alan Brennert

Dusk-devils come spinning up from behind the swollen horizon, all blood and scabs in the sunset glow, pinwheeling into the gray shadows at our feet. We catch them down there, tugging-scratching-kicking themselves into our path, trying to make us trip and fall. And they hide. In the ground, in the rocks, in the new dust and the old. Nuisances, nothing more than that; scratchy scrawny annoyances that chatter and chuckle at our feet. Dusk-devils.

Dusk deepens to night and the devils drop away, scurry back to meet the sinking sun. Then the real devils start in, then the Skyghosts flicker and dance on the cloudless black. They're tall, wider than the sun; the moon could be one of their balls turned white and free-swung. And they're covered. All *over:* dim reds, faded greens, colors worn to a whisper by the sky. Only their hands and faces are pasted naked against the night, even some of their eyes framed by glass and metal. The same six or seven of them, feet cut off at the horizon, staring down at us, moving their mouths but damn it if nothing ever comes out. I watch their lips sometimes, try to read the words, but they're speaking in a distant tongue; I turn away and to hell with it, they're only ghosts.

Skyghosts. Knew a man once looked a lot like them, close enough to be a brother; same type of face, you know, same kind of build; he was like a ghost himself, but didn't fade with the day; we had to kill him . . .

You get through the night all right—Skyghosts above you staring and speaking, you're cold and huddling in groupfucks to keep 'em away—and then there's a sort of almost-dawn, gray enough for the dusk-devils to come back and scuttle round at naked thighs and cold, flat bottoms. Day comes quicker than night, though, and they run back to the edge of the world to wait out the sun. They've got time.

Time. Wondered how it worked, once; one moment you're here and the next you're *there,* what happened to *here?* is it gone or what?; tried to stand still between seconds but I couldn't, I just kept moving . . .

Everything's moving. Morning's the hunt for food, the scrambling that puts the devils to shame. Morning's the rush for shrubs and pissholes; if you don't do it private, there's a stink on the land nobody wants. Morning's the first moment of day and the start of the long slow slide down to night. Morning's moving.

Moving's something to do while you die.

It's the laughter, mind you; it's the giggling and cackling you hear from beneath the earth, that's what hurts. Beneath the earth, that's where they're buried, those dead ones who do the job the ghosts and devils do, but do it best.

Fine day, they'll say. *Look at the sky!*

A buried chuckle.

Look at that sky.

Goes on like that, laughter in the earth. Our parents' laughter, damn them. Laughing at us for being so stupid. So we move. We run over the parched desert through the ruins of a yestertown, we search for food and try not to hear the laughter. Some of us, we run fast enough, we die from the effort; we're not all that strong. That calls for a celebration, then, that calls for running and yelling and dayfucking, that calls for a lot.

Goes like this:

Someone falls, usually he's been chasing something across the plains, he keels over and lies flat on the ground. Where he's lying there's no laughter for a while, as if the dead ones don't know what to make of this yet. Then suddenly it starts up again, weaker: they've lost another victim, but they've got to keep laughing.

We'll gather round and stare at the body a few seconds, and then somebody'll start laughing right in with those bastards down *there* and it's started. The food of the morning is wolfed down, and then we try some games before the body's got too stiff to stand a good prick, and then we'll start some stories going, maybe about the dead man, maybe not.

Stories are my specialty. You know that, listening. I make a few up, hear secondhand of some, pass others along.

Once I told how I visited a cave in the bleeding valley, near the horizon where the Skyghosts stand; saw metal inside, dabbed red by the sun; heard the clack of the dead ones' metal soles on the hard iron floor of the earth's belly. Apart from the machines, the cave is hollow; some say that's where the Skyghosts go during the day. Maybe so. Maybe that's why some call the ghosts by other names: like *hollow-grams*. Maybe so.

Stories help fill the days when most of the time there's nothing to do but shrug off the heat or the cold and sit on the torn ground while the dead ones poke and point at the sky. They always did that, even when they weren't dead: *The sky. Look at the sky. We used to touch it* . . .

I'll tell you something and I don't care who hears it, I'm sick of the sky and I hate it and I say fuck it, fuck the whole bluewhitehotcold sky!

Fine day . . .

One of my stories never caught on is the one about people who used to make things in their heads, waking dreams they tried to build and sometimes did. Most everyone laughs at that, says, "No one can build, it isn't done." Then I say that these people didn't always build *right,* sometimes they made nightmares for themselves because they couldn't dream anything else, and then they built those too—only they weren't real, just dreams that only they could see. Everyone turns away at this and won't speak to me for the longest while and I'm sorry I said it and please don't you turn away, no!

Something else. Something else:

Afternoons are playtimes, times you go exploring, walk three steps past where you walked yesterday, or hurl a rock over a hill and wait to hear a noise. It's getting harder to play every day, though; the rocks bite and the ground turns to mud as you walk. Getting harder to do anything more than sweat or shiver.

Knew a woman once got it into her head that the dead flew over the burnt hills to another world; damned if she didn't go trotting over there after her dead brother; she never came back, but at least she *went.* I loved her for that.

No one goes over the hill anymore.

The sun's got too old to light our way, I guess. Times it looks as dead as the rest of us. That's what the dead ones told us before they were dead: it's the color of blood because it's bleeding, and one day soon the last drop will be drawn and we'll all of us die . . .

The sky!

Then there's the story that boils up off the dried earth every night as the dusk-devils scamper and scream around us and the Skyghosts flicker into life above. The words come scattered from every voice,

172

from childhood tales and wandering travelers, words torn and brittle with time.

About what the Skyghosts are saying. Nothing that ever makes any sense: *You're men,* someone remembers their grandfather telling them as a child; *Your minds,* whispers a woman who'd once lain with an old man and watched him die in her, her eyes are glassy with the memory ever since; *Think, please think,* begs a beggar, the plea handed down from beggar-father to beggar-son. Other words, other pleas: Sun. Die. Leaveyou. Sorry. Star. Sky.

No one knows how long they've been up there; every generation's seen them and there's never any argument over particulars, never anyone who claims they're *not* there, not like with the dusk-devils. Everyone sees the same thing, clear as the night they're hung on.

Someone says: They're tombstones.

Someone asks: For who?

Leaveyou. Die. *Your minds!* Star—

—ship . . .

We get hot and tired of the words: tired of trying to remember, trying to think. They all want us to think and it's getting so god damned *hard*. Maybe we aren't as smart as our fathers, or their fathers before them. Maybe we aren't . . . *right*. But we *try*.

I start to tell a story then to break up the sadness, to bring everyone into better spirits and start the laughing and singing and fucking. I start talking and my voice is sky-cool and very quiet, and before I know it I'm telling them about the people who make things up in their minds and live their nightmares and can't ever break out, and as I brush away a dusk-devil I see they're all turning and frowning and staring at the sky—just like you, damn it, just like *you* . . .

The Ghosts at Haddon-le-Green

by Alfred I. Tooke

The Bishop was poking the library fire. His wife had gone out for a walk, when the Vicar dropped in, and expressed a desire to have a most serious talk. It seemed that a story was floating about, that the church-yard was haunted at night. The Vicar had heard it from Absalom Prout, who'd had a most terrible fright, and swore he had seen, by the light of the moon, some specters cavorting around; while old Mrs. Mortimer-Bryce in a swoon by the gate of the churchyard was found, and later declared she was sure she had seen some ghosts at their midnightly revels; though several people of Haddon-le-Green quite loudly averred they were devils.

The Bishop was shocked as the story he heard, absorbing it *cum grano salis;* then muttered: "Ghosts? Devils? The thing is absurd! Some crank giving vent to his malice, or else some preposterous prank it must be, or somebody's idea of humor. Let's go to the churchyard. Perhaps we shall see what caused this ridiculous rumor!" And so, through the darkness, the two of them strolled, discussing the Curate —a new one; a rather frail chap, who by someone was told he should have a mustache—so he grew one! Thus talking, their way to the churchyard they sought, and opened the gate and went in, and sat on a blanket the Bishop had brought, discussing original sin.

The Bishop, orating, his mission forgot, and glibly expounded his views. The Vicar picked out a less bumpier spot, and gently fell into a snooze, till the Bishop's long discourse ran suddenly dry. The Vicar awoke, and felt queer. The Bishop leaped up, with a muttered: "Oh, my!" The Vicar responded: "Dear, dear!" For up from behind a new tombstone there loomed a shape that made both of them cower; and just at that instant above them there boomed twelve strokes from the clock in the tower.

Right over the tombstone the visitant hopped, and in the dim light they observed a piece of a shroud that about it still flopped, and both were extremely unnerved. The Bishop was portly; the Bishop was stout, with a wobble in both of his knees. The Vicar was prone to attacks of the gout—yet each ran with remarkable ease. They didn't go round by the gate, but, instead, they climbed o'er the wall, which was quicker. The Vicar fell hard on his nose, and it bled. The Bishop, he fell on the Vicar, and murmured: "Forgive me! The night is so dark!", then was up and away with a bound. The Vicar replied with a scathing remark which by mud was most luckily drowned. Then after the Bishop he hurriedly fled, till the vicarage safely received them. The Vicar's wife gasped; then she put them to bed, and with hot-water bottles relieved them.

The Vicar soon sent her the Curate to wake. Returning, she said with alarm: "He isn't in yet! No, I made no mistake! I hope he has come to no harm!" But just at that moment the Curate came in. They heard his light step on the stair. The Bishop, he muttered: "Original sin!" The Vicar called out: "Are you there?" The Curate, he entered with guilt on his face at this unexpected detection. A butterfly net he revealed to their gaze, and in a large jar, a collection of moths he had caught. "Pardon me!" he explained, as he gazed at the bottle enraptured. "My hobby, you know! I was somewhat detained by a splendid new species I captured."

The Bishop, he stared at the Vicar aghast. The Vicar collapsed with a moan. "Where were you tonight?" asked the Bishop at last, with a hint of relief in his tone.

"Where the finest of trophies my efforts reward. In the church-yard!" the Curate explained. "I hope you don't think it improper, my lord?"

The Bishop's expression was pained, but he choked back the words that he wanted to use, and murmured: "I'd rather you'd not. Perhaps some more suitable place you could choose, or some—er—less fre-quented spot?"

The Curate declared he would take the advice, and said he'd be going, and bowed, while behind him there fluttered the butterfly net that looked like a piece of a shroud.

My story is finished. There's no more to write, except that "ghosts" no more are seen cavorting around in the churchyard at night, by the good folk of Haddon-le-Green.

Ghosts
of the Air

by J. M. Hiatt & Moye W. Stephens

Man long ago peopled the dark with specters that stalked the earth or flitted along close to the ground. And, when he took to the seas, he saw phantom ships and "Flying Dutchmen" and heard the souls of long-drowned sailors crying from the deep. Now that he has mastered the air, is he to have ghosts of the air? Civilization has advanced too far, perhaps. Yet there is a rumor in Europe of skeleton aviators piloting their broken planes far up in the silent heights above the battlefields of France. And there is a wood in Maine, they say, where on stormy nights a cloudy airplane falls and splinters noiselessly among the somber trees.

Easley appeared, none of us ever knew whence, in response to an advertisement for a stunt man to perform in a flying circus at Garland's aviation field. I was employed at the field as a mechanic, but it chanced that I was in the office when the wing-walker arrived. He entered with a slow, heavy tread, like a man half in a dream, and, at the manager's question, started as if roused from some guilty revery. In a few terse, almost sullen words he explained his mission.

The manager looked him up and down. The applicant's clothes were shabby and hung loosely, even on his huge, gorillalike frame. A thick, dirty stubble fringed his jowls, and his dark, greasy hair was tousled and uncut. His broad face, immobile and almost vacant in its expression, was not improved by a pair of broken teeth and by small eyes that glittered occasionally, but were, for the most part, dull.

"So you're a stunt man, eh?" said the manager, rolling his cigar in his mouth. "What can you do?"

"Why not find out?" answered Easley.

Something in the rasping voice suggestive of a sneer angered the employer. He glared and seemed about to order the fellow out, then threw away his cigar, and barked, "Well, we'll try you out right now. You'll have to sign this waiver, absolving us from liability, and I'll have a plane ready for you right away."

The muscles on the other's face did not move, but I would have sworn that he snarled. Currents of antagonism seemed to flow from the man. Seizing the pen, he scratched a hideous scrawl, "K. Easley," on the dotted line, at the same time smearing the paper with several blots.

Within a quarter of an hour the plane was warmed up and ready. Bert Cottrell, the pilot who had been assigned to take up the prospective stunt man, was curtly introduced to him by the manager, but smilingly extended his hand. Bert was a big blond man of thirty, an old flyer, liked by all at the field. In his easy, domineering way he seemed to have arrived at intimate terms with everybody. Bert laughed uproariously at his own stories and those of others, though it might be said that he was somewhat partial to his own.

Easley shook hands stolidly and peeled off his coat, preparatory to going up. Someone offered him goggles and a leather jacket, the last of which he refused. It was often remarked that he seemed impervious to the elements.

The plane took off, and, in a few minutes, Easley had proved himself a stunt man of rare caliber. He worked his way to the end of the wing, walking along the forward wing-beam outside the wires, hung by his knees from the wing-skid, and stood on the end of the top wing, bracing himself with his knees against the cabane. Then, beginning the unusual and really dangerous part of his repertory, he cautiously traversed the top wing, leaning far over to brace himself against the wind, till he reached the center section. Thence lowering himself on to the fusilage, he got into a position straddling the turtleback in the rear of the pilot's cockpit, and worked himself back to the tail section. After hanging a few minutes from the tailskid, he returned to the cockpit.

When the plane landed, Easley leaped down with a "Well, how's that?" However unprepossessing the fellow's personality, his abilities and the company's need of them had to be recognized. He was placed on the pay-roll forthwith.

After the flying circus, in which the stunt man acquitted himself well, Garland's kept him to give exhibitions to the Sunday crowds and do some motion picture work for which they had contracts.

But the passing weeks did not improve his standing with the boys at the field. Despite his daredevil courage, which they had to admire, his contemptuous reticence—together with something brutish and, I may say, sinister in the atmosphere of the man—shut him out from their sympathies. Bert, in what he believed his genius for parody, transformed "Easley" into "Beastly." He thus referred to the performer—in the absence of that aerial Hercules.

Indeed, it was big, formerly easy-going Bert who took the greatest antipathy to Easley. He flew the ship in all the wing-walker's performances, and any mention of the stunt man unloosed his anathemas. Pleasant-tempered the pilot could scarcely be termed now, for he, too, had become moody, snappish, and sullen.

"By God, I can't stand him!" he burst out one day. "When he looks at me out of those little pig eyes, I come near to committing murder."

One evening not long after, Bert returned from the studios in a fury. He did not leave us long in ignorance of the cause. First came a crackle of oaths and ejaculations, followed by, "The damn fool! On the way back from Marburg's he climbed out and started doing his stuff over the city. It's all right for a guy to risk his neck when there's an audience and money in sight, but nobody but Beastly would think of it on a cross-country flight. He deserves to pile up in a heap. If he tries it again, and don't bust his pants—nobody'd cry if he did—I'll bust them for him myself with my shoe."

"Did you say anything to him about it?" asked Shorty Wiggin, one of the mechanics.

"Did I say anything to him about it! I said enough to him, just now when we landed, but all he did was grunt. I was so mad I could have spun the ship and pitched him off."

Realizing, perhaps, the ugliness of his last words, the pilot suddenly fell silent and walked away.

Time went by, and Bert and Easley made frequent trips to one of the studios, where they were working on a Garland contract. On two or three of the return trips the wing-walker, it seems, was taken with the mood to "do his stuff," well-nigh driving Bert into a frenzy. Their clashing natures seemed to have seized upon this point for a bone of contention. Though none of the pilot's threats, made in our hearing, were executed, the relations of the pair seemed nearing a dangerous place.

At length Bert asked the manager to change him to other work.

"No, Cottrell," was the answer. "I haven't a seasoned pilot I can spare for Easley just now. Besides, all the other boys feel just about the way you do toward him, and, since you've flown for him all along, I guess you can put up with it a little longer. After this carnival at Moylesburg next Sunday, I mean to let Easley go. I've already notified him that we won't need him after that."

"All right," said Bert, and walked away muttering.

Though at a tension, things went smoothly until the following Sunday. Shorty Wiggin and I were warming up the ship for Bert and Easley, preparatory to their taking off for Moylesburg, a town some fifty miles distant. The stunt man was on the program of some carnival, scheduled there that afternoon.

"Now listen," Bert addressed the wing-walker suddenly and sharply. "Don't pull any of this cross-country stuff on this trip. It gets on my nerves."

"Aw, go to hell," was the reply, and Easley turned his back.

Bert's pent-up wrath burst forth. Striding rapidly forward, he grasped the other's shoulder and spun him around.

"Keep your paws off me," snapped Easley, striking away the hand.

Then, before anyone could intervene, there was a shower of savage blows from both men, which ended in Bert's going down in a heap under the plane.

"I'll stunt when I please," said Easley.

Bert sat up wildly, wiping the blood from his lips. "So will I!" he shouted.

He was pulled to his feet in chill silence. His last words really amounted to a threat of murder.

A horrible laugh came from the wing-walker, the upcurled lip exposing the broken teeth.

Here Shorty and I broke in with hurried interjections, patting both men on the back and urging them to forget it. They bundled into the plane and took off. We felt uneasy about letting them go, but there was nothing we could do about it. No one else had seen the incident.

The plane came back late that afternoon, and, with a sickly feeling, we saw it land with but one passenger. Bert climbed out and walked shakily toward us. His face was gray, and the muscles of his cheeks were twitching.

"Where's Easley?" someone asked in a hollow voice.

"Easley started his walking over Pennington Woods on the way home and fell off. I couldn't land to look for him on account of the trees."

Pennington Woods covers a good many square miles, and, though the locality where the pilot said Easley fell was searched pretty thoroughly, the body was not found.

Some of us had ugly suspicions, but we did not air them. Even should Bert be guilty, where was proof?

Cottrell, himself, was a badly shaken man. Obtaining a leave of absence, he went back to his folks in Michigan. Six months later he returned, red-cheeked and smiling, quite his old self. The affair of the wing-walker had largely blown over, and, though for my part I often thought of it, Easley's death was rarely mentioned.

One day Shorty Wiggin and I were overhauling an engine in the shop, when Bert walked in. "Say, Shorty," he said, "something's wrong with my motor. She rev's up all right on the ground, but in the air she doesn't seem to turn up at all. Now I've got to fly over to Moylesburg on an errand for the boss. I'd like to have you come along and listen to her. I'd take Pink Eye here"—wiggling a finger at me—"but he gave me the razz on my brand-new joke this morning. The boss says it will be all right."

"Deedle dee do," said Shorty, thumbing his nose by way of leave-taking, and departed.

It began to grow late in the afternoon, and Bert and Shorty had not returned. Somebody phoned to Moylesburg and learned that they had not been there. Accordingly, a plane was sent to fly over the route and look for signs of them.

Darkness halted the search until the next morning, when Bert's wrecked machine was discovered in Pennington Woods. In it was Shorty, not badly hurt, but suffering from exposure and shock. Bert was not to be found. His safety-belt was noted to be broken, but he should not have been hurled far.

In the hospital Shorty was able to throw light on the mystery. He informed us that Bert fell or leaped from the plane some distance from where it plunged to earth. "As soon as they let me out of here," declared the injured machinist, "I think I can lead you to the spot."

Mechanics are a hardy breed, and Shorty was back in a few days.

While the party was getting ready to start for the woods, Shorty led me aside. He had a hesitating, troubled look.

"Say," he said, "I haven't told all I know about this, for fear they might think I'm off my head. Maybe I dreamed this that night I was with the plane in the woods. Maybe I didn't. But I've got to get it off my chest."

"About Bert?" I asked.

"Yes. About Bert's fall. We were over Pennington Woods; I had been listening to the motor, and looked up to signal Bert to throttle her down. Just then he shouted something and pointed toward the end of the wing. I looked, but saw nothing wrong. Bert was in the rear cockpit, of course, and I screwed my head around again just in time to see him tear off his helmet and goggles, evidently for the purpose of rubbing his eyes. The fearful wind took him full in the face, of course, making his long, sleek hair fly in every direction. With one hand over his eyes, he fumbled with his goggles, replaced them, and again screamed and pointed. Horror seemed to have seized the man—horror and frantic fear. After about as long as it might take a wing-walker to get from the end of a wing to the fusilage, I felt a cold, sluggish breath of air pass slowly by me toward the rear. That is, if such a breath of air is possible at seventy miles an hour. It isn't, of course. Maybe it was fear. Fear of Bert's going crazy and killing us both. He began to strike and struggle as if he were fighting madly. In some way his safety-belt became unfastened—"

"It broke," I put in.

"Well, then, it broke, and Bert jumped out of the plane. I saw him waving his legs and arms and turning slowly over and over. Then he dropped from sight.

"I had my own hands full, for here I was, in an unpiloted ship. She had controls in the front seat, thank God, and I've had some flying instruction. But before long the machine began banking over sharply; she went into a side-slip and then into a spin. I remembered enough to shove forward on the stick and straighten up on the rudder-bar, bringing her out of the spin. But by that time I had fallen so close to the ground that I crashed among the trees."

Despite Shorty's directing, we had searched fruitlessly for many hours. Trees and bushes formed a dense entanglement. Nettles and other weeds came knee-high and we stumbled through a thick carpet of plants, leaves, and fallen branches. The dank, thick odor of vegetation pervaded the gloomy shade.

Suddenly a sharp shout at a distance split the chilly silence. I and those with me hastened toward it. There was Shorty, already the center of an excited group.

"My God!" he cried to me; "look at that! Look—what did I tell you?"

I looked. There lay the twisted corpse of an aviator, featureless and bloody—Bert Cottrell. But what was that entangled with the body? Whose splintered bones were those impaled in the bloated flesh? That shock of dark hair still adhering to the stove in skull, those broken teeth now blackened by decay betrayed K. Easley! And the skeleton of Easley was *on top!*

Shorty and I faced each other with an unspoken question.

Before long a fellow who had been staring up into the tree above spoke. "Look, Easley's skeleton must have been hanging in that big tree up there. Cottrell struck it in his fall and fell with it to the ground.

Cottrell's body was, of course, the heavier, and naturally went undermost. See, the branches are all broken."

His guess, they judged, was right. There were the broken branches to support it. But I—well, I often wonder.

Gibbler's Ghost

by William F. Nolan

Plippity-plop.

A girl a night.

Rainbow chicks: blonde on Monday, brunette on Tuesday, redhead on Wednesday. Falling like soft, ripe plums into Des Cahill's bed. Des shook the tree, and down they came.

Plippity-plop.

Ole Des, the Makeout King. Cahill the Cool. Mr. Codpiece. Remember how it was? Every young stud in the country envied him—walked like Des in his Gucci buckle-clips, wore his hair with the same cruel curl over one eye, thumb-crushed his cigs after three quick puffs the same savage way Des did.

Sure. Who could forget?

But now he's gone. No more movies or TV specials or Broadway guest shots in the nude. Women (and a lot of men) paid scalpers up to a hundred bucks to get a front-row peek at Cahill's equipment, and they were never disappointed.

So what happened? How come, at the top of the ladder, he walks, does the big fade, and is seen no more? I can tell you. I figure his public deserves to have the real rap laid down on Des Cahill.

I was his best friend—if he ever had one. My name is Albert. I took care of his income tax problems and lent him my shoulder. For crying on. And believe me, Des had plenty to cry about.

It begins with a ghost.

Des liked to swing high. His pad was in Benedict Canyon. Rafters, crackling fire, mile-deep rugs, a bear's head on the wall. Cozy. I was working in the back of the house, late one night, on a capital gains tax dodge for Des—my first time over to his place—when I hear this ago-nized female shriek of fear from the master bedroom. As I rush toward the room, out the door comes this pneumatic blonde wearing Mid-night Hush eye makeup and a really terrified expression. She snake-shakes into her clothes, looking great doing it, and does a quick exit. Then she misses three gears on her MG going down the hill.

Des is standing by the bed, wearing a rumpled pair of Tiger's Eye shorts and looking bereft. That's the only word for how he looked. Bereft.

"It was him again," he says softly.

"Who's him?"

"The frigging ghost. Who the hell else would I have in there?"

Right away, I take his word.

"Then you've seen this spook before?"

At my question, Des chuckles. He laughs. He throws back his head and howls. He falls down on the rug, breaking up. Then he stops and looks at me.

"Albert," he says. "I am going to tell you something I have never told anybody else in this living world. I'm twenty-five, loaded with bread, up to my ass in fame, with maybe ten thousand cuddly little numbers ready to make the sex scene any time I lift a pinky—and you know what?"

"What?"

"Albert, I am a virgin."

We have a drink. Two drinks. We're on our third (vodka martinis with hair on their chests) when Des lays it out for me.

"First time I tried to make it all the way with a chick, I was fifteen—and that's when I saw him. The ghost. In broad daylight, at the beach on a Saturday afternoon. An old geezer dressed in full armor, looming right above us with this horse over his head."

I stop Des there and he tells me that whenever the ghost appears, he is always holding up a horse—holding it in the air.

"Like he's about to throw it at you," says Des. "Anyhow, the chick fainted and I was very disturbed. It happened again the following Fri-day, with me and the mayor's daughter. And that's the way it's been ever since. I get a chick into the hay and we are at the absolute mo-ment of truth, you know . . ."

"I know."

". . . and *that's* when the ghost comes on with the horse. Natu-rally, it scares the shit out of my date."

"Naturally."

"No matter where I am, it happens. On location down in Pennsylvania last summer for the coal mine flick, I had every precious young available female in town panting at my motel door. So I took 'em on, one per night, and always got up to the grand moment, you know . . ."

"I know."

". . . when out he pops with his goddamn overhead horse, and the scene is blown. Thirty-six days on location, thirty-six chicks, thirty-six blowups." He knuckles his eyes, rolls his head. "Albert, I cannot go on. I've got the hottest sex rep in show biz, and I haven't made it once." He sobs—a broken, terrible sound. "Not *once!*"

That's when I give him my shoulder.

To cry on.

Later, I give him advice. Hire a class ghost-breaker, who knows his spooks, and go after the bastard with the horse.

This he does. The ghost-breaker is a nervous, kinky little guy, but he guarantees his work. There will no longer be a ghost when he is through. This we can bank on.

He goes the full route. With powders that flash and explode. With chalked circles around the bed and invocations and curses and lots of arm-waving. With incense that really stinks and hand-clapping and plenty of yelling.

But each time, just as Des and the particular lady of his choice reach the ultimate moment, WHAP! the ghost is there. Naturally, all the stinking incense and exploding powders and yelling and hand-clapping don't exactly delight the young thing who happens to be sharing the sheets with Des, and she always demands to know just what the hell is going on with this creepy guy hopping nervously around their bed. But Des is able to calm her down, and she's usually okay until the ghost shows. At which point she bolts, like they all bolt—straight out of the room, shrieking.

This goes on for three weeks, with Des getting thinner and more bereft-looking by the week. Finally, I ask him if he'd mind if I joined the group—to kind of size up the ghost for myself and maybe come in with some fresh ideas. Sure, he says, and that night there's Des and the uneasy ghost-breaker and a redhead with an immense heaving bosom and me, all of us in the master bedroom.

Sex, under these conditions, is never good—but Des manages to thrash himself into a damned remarkable performance until, ZAMBO! there's the ghost, right on the ole button.

I give him the careful once-over. A seedy old gink, scowling inside a cheapsie suit of backlot armor, with a crazy-eyed palomino above his head. I concentrate on the face. Suddenly, I let out a whoop.

184

"I *know* the bum! That's Joey Gibbler. It's Gibbler, I tell you!"

The ghost looks startled and vanishes, but, by then, the girl is shrieking and the nervous ghost-breaker is exploding more powders and Des is in no real condition to listen to me.

After, when things are more settled, I spell it out.

"Gibbler was an extra back in the days of the silents," I tell Des. "I remember reading about how he and this palomino horse both broke their necks doing a battle sequence for *The Queen's Cute Question,* one of those slapstick historicals they used to grind out at Monarch."

Des shoots up an eyebrow. "Dad directed that one—I know he did. It was his last picture."

"Exactly! And he died of a stroke the following week. Which explains everything."

"Not to me, it doesn't."

"Joey was sore over getting his neck broke, and he blamed your pop for it. But he didn't have time to haunt him. The stroke beat him out. So Gibbler decides to haunt *you* instead. He waits until you're old enough to taste the sweet fruits of life and then he cunningly denies them to you. And he'll keep on until we placate him."

"But how? How do you placate a sore spook?"

"The key is Joey Gibbler, Jr. The kid must be about thirty by now. Not bad-looking, I've seen his name in the trades."

"An extra trying to make it as an actor?"

"Right. So set it up for him. Throw around some weight at the studio and get him into a picture. Junior clicks, and his old man stops haunting you out of sheer gratitude. You can do it."

"Albert," he says, "I can do it."

He does it. Joey winds up with a fat part in *The Big Bottom* and overnight, the way it can happen, Joey Gibbler, Jr. is a star.

And, overnight, Des makes it all the way through the moment of truth. No ghost. Ole Des Cahill is devirginized.

He hugs me, dances me around the room, thrusts signed checks at me, insists that I accept his mother's wedding ring. It is a tearful, joyous occasion.

The next night, I get a jingle at my place. Des on the horn. Sounding terribly bereft.

"What's wrong?" I ask.

"A new one showed," he says.

"Another ghost?"

"Albert, it can't be—but it is. It's Joey Jr."

I buzz over to Benedict Canyon in my Porsche. Des meets me at the door, crazy-eyed like the palomino.

We get it all on the eleven o'clock news: "Actor dies in freak set accident. Rising star Joey Gibbler, Jr. suffers a broken neck when a delicatessen set falls on him during a Jewish film sequence." Wow.

Des sighs. "That accounts for the white butcher's apron he's wearing and what he holds above his head."

"Which is?"

"A display case full of, mostly, bagels and cream cheese."

I'm sorry to tell you, but this story had no happy ending. Des, who swears he'll never resign himself to celibacy, has quit the acting game and is on the move. Last I heard, he'd covered most of Europe, Asia, and the Middle East, and was in the Australian back country.

What he's looking for is a very brave chick, well-stacked, eighteen to twenty-five, who isn't afraid of seeing, each night, a scowling spook in a butcher's apron with a display case full of, mostly, bagels and cream cheese above his head.

And they just don't hardly *make* that kind anymore.

A Grammatical Ghost

by Elia W. Peattie

There was only one possible objection to the drawing-room, and that was the occasional presence of Miss Carew; and only one possible objection to Miss Carew. And that was, that she was dead.

She had been dead twenty years, as a matter of fact and record, and to the last of her life sacredly preserved the treasures and traditions of her family, a family bound up—as it is quite unnecessary to explain to any one in good society—with all that is most venerable and heroic in the history of the Republic. Miss Carew never relaxed the proverbial hospitality of her house, even when she remained its sole representative. She continued to preside at her table with dignity and state, and to set an example of excessive modesty and gentle decorum to a generation of restless young women.

It is not likely that having lived a life of such irreproachable gentility as this, Miss Carew would have the bad taste to die in any way not pleasant to mention in fastidious society. She could be trusted to the last, not to outrage those friends who quoted her as an exemplar of propriety. She died very unobtrusively of an affection of the heart, one June morning, while trimming her rose trellis, and her lavender-colored print was not even rumpled when she fell, nor were more than the tips of her little bronze slippers visible.

"Isn't it dreadful," said the Philadelphians, "that the property should go to a very, very distant cousin in Iowa or somewhere else on the frontier, about whom nobody knows anything at all?"

The Carew treasures were packed in boxes and sent away into the Iowa wilderness; the Carew traditions were preserved by the Historical Society; the Carew property, standing in one of the most umbrageous and aristocratic suburbs of Philadelphia, was rented to all manner of folk—anybody who had money enough to pay the rental—and society entered its doors no more.

But at last, after twenty years, and when all save the oldest Philadelphians had forgotten Miss Lydia Carew, the very, very distant cousin appeared. He was quite in the prime of life, and so agreeable and unassuming that nothing could be urged against him save his patronymic, which, being Boggs, did not commend itself to the euphemists. With him were two maiden sisters, ladies of excellent taste and manners, who restored the Carew china to its ancient cabinets, and replaced the Carew pictures upon the walls, with additions not out of keeping with the elegance of these heirlooms. Society, with a magnanimity almost dramatic, overlooked the name of Boggs—and called.

All was well. At least, to an outsider all seemed to be well. But, in truth, there was a certain distress in the old mansion, and in the hearts of the well-behaved Misses Boggs. It came about most unexpectedly. The sisters had been sitting upstairs, looking out at the beautiful grounds of the old place, and marvelling at the violets, which lifted their heads from every possible cranny about the house, and talking over the cordiality which they had been receiving by those upon whom they had no claim, and they were filled with amiable satisfaction. Life looked attractive. They had often been grateful to Miss Lydia Carew for leaving their brother her fortune. Now they felt even more grateful to her. She had left them a Social Position—one, which even after twenty years of desuetude, was fit for use.

They descended the stairs together, with arms clasped about each other's waists, and as they did so presented a placid and pleasing sight. They entered their drawing room with the intention of brewing a cup of tea, and drinking it in calm sociability in the twilight. But as they entered the room they became aware of the presence of a lady, who was already seated at their tea-table, regarding their old Wedgwood with the air of a connoisseur.

There were a number of peculiarities about this intruder. To begin with, she was hatless, quite as if she were a habitué of the house, and was costumed in a prim lilac-colored lawn of the style of two decades past. But a greater peculiarity was the resemblance this lady bore to a faded Daguerrotype. If looked at one way, she was perfectly discernible; if looked at another, she went out in a sort of blur. Notwithstanding this comparative invisibility, she exhaled a delicate perfume of sweet lavender, very pleasing to the nostrils of the Misses Boggs, who stood looking at her in gentle and unprotesting surprise.

"I beg your pardon," began Miss Prudence, the younger of the Misses Boggs, "but—"

But at this moment the Daguerrotype became a blur, and Miss Prudence found herself addressing space. The Misses Boggs were irritated. They had never encountered any mysteries in Iowa. They began an impatient search behind doors and portières, and even under sofas, though it was quite absurd to suppose that a lady recognizing the merits of the Carew Wedgwood would so far forget herself as to crawl under a sofa.

When they had given up all hope of discovering the intruder, they saw her standing at the far end of the drawing-room critically examining a water-color marine. The elder Miss Boggs started toward her with stern decision, but the little Daguerrotype turned with a shadowy smile, became a blur and an imperceptibility.

Miss Boggs looked at Miss Prudence Boggs.

"If there were ghosts," she said, "this would be one."

"If there were ghosts," said Miss Prudence Boggs, "this would be the ghost of Lydia Carew."

The twilight was settling into blackness, and Miss Boggs nervously lit the gas while Miss Prudence ran for other tea-cups, preferring, for reasons superfluous to mention, not to drink out of the Carew china that evening.

The next day, on taking up her embroidery frame, Miss Boggs found a number of old-fashioned cross-stitches added to her Kensington. Prudence, she knew, would never have degraded herself by taking a cross-stitch, and the parlor-maid was above taking such a liberty. Miss Boggs mentioned the incident that night at a dinner given by an ancient friend of the Carews.

"Oh, that's the work of Lydia Carew, without a doubt!" cried the hostess. "She visits every new family that moves to the house, but she never remains more than a week or two with any one."

"It must be that she disapproves of them," suggested Miss Boggs.

"I think that's it," said the hostess. "She doesn't like their china, or their fiction."

"I hope she'll disapprove of us," added Miss Prudence.

The hostess belonged to a very old Philadelphian family, and she shook her head.

"I should say it was a compliment for even the ghost of Miss Lydia Carew to approve of one," she said severely.

The next morning, when the sisters entered their drawing-room there were numerous evidences of an occupant during their absence. The sofa pillows had been rearranged so that the effect of their grouping was less bizarre than that favored by the Western women; a horrid little Buddhist idol with its eyes fixed on its abdomen, had been chastely hidden behind a Dresden shepherdess, as unfit for the scrutiny of polite eyes; and on the table where Miss Prudence did work in water colors, after the fashion of the impressionists, lay a prim and impossible composition representing a moss-rose and a number of heartsease, colored with that caution which modest spinster artists instinctively exercise.

"Oh, there's no doubt it's the work of Miss Lydia Carew," said Miss Prudence, contemptuously. "There's no mistaking the drawing of that rigid little rose. Don't you remember those wreaths and bouquets framed, among the pictures we got when the Carew pictures were sent to us? I gave some of them to an orphan asylum and burned up the rest."

"Hush!" cried Miss Boggs, involuntarily. "If she heard you, it would hurt her feelings terribly. Of course, I mean—" and she blushed. "It might hurt her feelings—but how perfectly ridiculous! It's impossible!"

Miss Prudence held up the sketch of the moss-rose.

"That may be impossible in an artistic sense, but it is a palpable thing."

"Bosh!" cried Miss Boggs.

"But," protested Miss Prudence, "how do you explain it?"

"I don't," said Miss Boggs, and left the room.

That evening the sisters made a point of being in the drawing-room before the dusk came on, and of lighting the gas at the first hint of twilight. They didn't believe in Miss Lydia Carew—but still they meant to be beforehand with her. They talked with unwonted vivacity and in a louder tone than was their custom. But as they drank their tea even their utmost verbosity could not make them oblivious to the fact that the perfume of sweet lavender was stealing insidiously through the room. They tacitly refused to recognize this odor and all that it indicated, when suddenly, with a sharp crash, one of the old Carew teacups fell from the tea-table to the floor and was broken. The disaster was followed by what sounded like a sigh of pain and dismay.

"I didn't suppose Miss Lydia Carew would ever be as awkward as that," cried the younger Miss Boggs, petulantly.

"Prudence," said her sister with a stern accent, "please try not to be a fool. You brushed the cup off with the sleeve of your dress."

"Your theory wouldn't be so bad," said Miss Prudence, half laughing and half crying, "if there were any sleeves to my dress, but, as you see, there aren't," and then Miss Prudence had something as near hysterics as a healthy young woman from the West can have.

"I wouldn't think such a perfect lady as Lydia Carew," she ejaculated between her sobs, "would make herself so disagreeable! You may talk about good-breeding all you please, but I call such intrusion exceedingly bad taste. I have a horrible idea that she likes us and means to stay with us. She left those other people because she did not approve of their habits or their grammar. It would be just our luck to please her."

"Well, I like your egotism," said Miss Boggs.

However, the view Miss Prudence took of the case appeared to be the right one. Time went by and Miss Lydia Carew still remained. When the ladies entered their drawing-room they would see the little lady-like Daguerrotype revolving itself into a blur before one of the family portraits. Or they noticed that the yellow sofa cushion, toward which she appeared to feel a peculiar antipathy, had been dropped behind the sofa upon the floor; or that one of Jane Austen's novels, which none of the family ever read, had been removed from the book shelves and left open upon the table.

"I cannot become reconciled to it," complained Miss Boggs to Miss Prudence. "I wish we had remained in Iowa where we belong. Of course I don't believe in the thing! No sensible person would. But still I cannot become reconciled."

But their liberation was to come, and in a most unexpected manner.

A relative by marriage visited them from the West. He was a friendly man and had much to say, so he talked all through dinner, and afterward followed the ladies to the drawing-room to finish his gossip. The gas in the room was turned very low, and as they entered Miss Prudence caught sight of Miss Carew, in company attire, sitting in upright propriety in a stiff-backed chair at the extremity of the apartment.

Miss Prudence had a sudden idea.

"We will not turn up the gas," she said, with an emphasis intended to convey private information to her sister. "It will be more agreeable to sit here and talk in this soft light."

Neither her brother nor the man from the West made any objection. Miss Boggs and Miss Prudence, clasping each other's hands, divided their attention between their corporeal and their incorporeal guests. Miss Boggs was confident that her sister had an idea, and was willing to await its development. As the guest from Iowa spoke, Miss Carew bent a politely attentive ear to what he said.

"Ever since Richards took sick that time," he said briskly, "it seemed like he shed all responsibility." (The Misses Boggs saw the Daguerrotype put up her shadowy head with a movement of doubt and apprehension.) "The fact of the matter was, Richards didn't seem to scarcely get on the way he might have been expected to." (At this conscienceless split to the infinitive and misplacing of the preposition, Miss Carew arose trembling perceptibly.) "I saw it wasn't no use for him to count on a quick recovery—"

The Misses Boggs lost the rest of the sentence, for at the utterance of the double negative Miss Lydia Carew had flashed out, not in a blur, but with mortal haste, as when life goes out at a pistol shot!

The man from the West wondered why Miss Prudence should have cried at so pathetic a part of his story:

"Thank Goodness!"

And their brother was amazed to see Miss Boggs kiss Miss Prudence with passion and energy.

It was the end. Miss Carew returned no more.

The Grey Room

by Stefan Grabinski
Translated by Miroslaw Lipinski

My prior apartment also didn't please me. At first it seemed that what I had escaped from was definitely not present here and that I would be safe from that intangible element which had forced me to leave my previous residence. But a few days spent in this newly-rented room convinced me that this place was even worse than the last, as certain disturbing features which had estranged me from the other one began to exhibit themselves here in a sharper, more emphatic form. After a week at my new locale, I came to the sad conclusion that I had fallen into a trap a hundred times more intricate than the previous one. The unpleasant mood that had driven me away from my former home was now repeating itself, and in a considerably intensified form.

Becoming aware of this dismal outlook for the future, I initially tried to find the cause in myself. Maybe the habitat had nothing to do with it? Maybe I myself had dragged this sad tone along with me, and not fully realizing its immanent character, I was blaming my surroundings in a dishonest attempt at masking my own weakness?

But this conjecture was contradicted by the complete state of happiness I found myself in at the time and by my exceptional good health. Before long I arrived at another hypothesis, which soon became a certainty when confirmed by daily experience.

Armed with this knowledge, I sought information about the tenant who had formerly occupied this room. Imagine my surprise when Chainem's name was mentioned. This was the same person after whom I had rented my previous room. Some strange coincidence had twice made me his successor. Nothing connected us besides this; I didn't know who he was or what he looked like.

I couldn't find out anything more about him other than his name was Benjamin Chainem and that he had lived here a couple of months. When I inquired of the janitor about the date of his departure and his new address, he muttered some vague answer, apparently not having the least willingness to plunge into any specific explanation. Judging by the expression on his face, I suspected he could tell me a lot about my predecessor, yet he preferred to be silent either on his own initiative or because of the dictate of the landlord; maybe there was a good reason for his silence, or maybe information about tenants was not readily given out.

Only much later did I understand this careful tactic; indeed, from the landlord's point of view there was just one concern: it wouldn't do to frighten away potential boarders. The affair clarified itself, however, after my own experiences shed light on the former tenant and his real fate, which had been intentionally concealed from me.

At any rate, the similarity in mood at both places and the identity of their previous tenant gave much food for thought.

Gradually I came to the belief that the spirit, as it were, of both apartments had become imbued with Chainem.

I have no doubt that something of the sort is possible. On the contrary, I believe that an expression like "leaving behind a bit of yourself" should not be taken merely as a figure of speech. Our daily co-existence with a given place, a longer stay in certain surroundings, even if it is limited to the organic world without any human connection, or even if it is confined to the sphere of so-called "inanimate objects," has to elicit after a certain time a reciprocal effect and mutual influence. Slowly an imperceptible symbiosis develops whose traces repeatedly consolidate themselves over a long period and after a break of direct contact. Some psychic energy remains after us and clings to the places and things it became accustomed to. These inventories, subtle remnants of the previous associations, linger for years—who knows, maybe even for entire centuries—imperceptible to the insensitive, but no less real, and sometimes they're made manifest in a more distinctive form. This is why people have a strange fear of and concurrent respect for old castles, dilapidated houses, and revered relics of the past. Nothing disappears and nothing goes out in vain. Along empty walls and desolate halls stubbornly wander the echoes of bygone years . . .

In my case, however, one important detail had to be accounted for from the outset. As the janitor maintained, Chainem had lived in this building for a couple of months, before moving somewhere else. Consequently, the time in which he could exert an influence on my room and infuse it with his mood was considerably shorter than the time he had spent before me in the previous room. Nevertheless, his imprint was more strongly pronounced here than in the prior locale, where he had the opportunity to effect the environment for upwards of two years. Apparently the strength of his radiance had increased and achieved results considerably more prominent in a disproportionately shorter length of time.

The question then became: To what could one attribute this increase in the capacity to pass oneself on to the environment?

Judging by the mood which permeated my present room, the cause of this phenomenon didn't lie in an intensification of the life force of its previous tenant. On the contrary. Based on various signs, I concluded that some inner dissolution, some breakdown of the spirit, was at work here—and a strong one at that—which had contaminated the surrounding atmosphere. Therefore, Chainem was most probably a sick man.

This was verified by the fundamental tone of the apartment. There was in it a silent, hopeless melancholia. It exuded from the grey wallpaper, the steel-hued velvet armchairs; it emanated from the silver-frames of pictures. One could feel it in the air in a thousand, elusive

193

atoms; it almost rubbed off against the slender, delicate spider-threads being spun inside. A sad, depressing room. . . .

Even the potted flowers by the windows, and also the larger flowers in a couple of vases on the shelves, seemed to have adopted to the prevalent style by leaning sorrowfully in torpid pensiveness. Even one's voice subsided in fright somewhere among nooks and crannies, like an intruder scared by his own boldness, though the room was large and sparsely furnished. The sound of my footsteps died away without an echo. I walked about like a shadow.

One instinctively wanted to sit in a corner, on a comfortable plush armchair, and, lighting a cigarette, while away hours in reveries, as one aimlessly pursued with one's eyes little clouds of smoke, following their spiralling turns, their framed rings, their trailing ribbons under the ceiling. . . . Something drew one to the palisander piano to play gentle melodies in tones hushed and sad like the sobs of autumn. . . .

Against this grey, sickly background the embroidery of a strange dream began to reveal itself after the first week of my stay. From then on, I dreamt every night.

The content of my dreams was more or less always the same. The dreams appeared to be of a fixed subject matter undergoing only slight modification or minor diversity: they were various drafts of the same story.

The setting of this monotonous action was my apartment. At some point during the night my grey room, with its dormant furnishings, its melancholic, studied boredom, showed up on my dream screen. By the window sat a man with a pale, oval face, his head propped up by his hand, and he was looking sadly to the street outside. At times, this scene lasted for many hours. Then he would stand up and pace the room with a slow, mechanical step, his gaze fixed obstinately on the parquet floor, as if engrossed with some singular thought. Once in a while he would put his hand to his forehead and rub it, and in the process raise his bright, large eyes infused with silent melancholy. When his walking tired him, he would sit down again, but this time usually by a desk against the left wall, and once more would spend some time in a motionless position, his face hidden in his palms. Periodically he would write something in small, nervous lettering. Finishing this, he would roughly throw aside his pen, straighten up his frail figure, and resume his pacing. Apparently he wanted to make the most of the space he had, for he walked about the room in a circular line which the furniture arrangement didn't obstruct. I noticed, however, that the line was broken unevenly in the area to the right of the door, where stood a wardrobe; here the curve, which he described, changed from the convex to the concave: it seemed as if he wanted to avoid this corner.

At this point, my dream ended. After several hours of his monotonous tramping, interrupted by a long or short rest at the window, the desk, or in one of the armchairs—this sad person, and with him the picture of the room, vanished into a sleepy limbo, and I usually awoke at daybreak. This entire sequence repeated itself every night.

The persistence of these recurring images and their most symptomatic style soon led me to the firm conclusion that the actor playing out these pantomimes was no one else but Chainem. These dreams, full of melancholic monotony, were, so to speak, a formative realization of the spirit of the apartment that I felt so depressingly, day after day; they were a materialization of things too subtle for the conscious state.

I assumed that the same event was constantly occurring throughout the day, but wandering thoughts and a vain intellect, too clever for its own good, prevented any clear perception; indeed, stars also exist in the day, but dimmed by the turbulence of the sun's overpowering rays they can only be seen after the setting of the sun.

Initially, I became preoccupied in observing these dreams and searching out the proper connections between them and the mood of the room. But I gradually noticed that I was succumbing to the harmful influences of my surroundings, and that the visions seen in my dreams and the room I dwelled in during the day had a negative effect, poisoning me with hidden venom.

I decided to defend myself. One had to engage in a determined fight with my invisible predecessor, obliterate him, and oust his traces, which permeated everything here.

Above all, one had to remove and replace the pieces of furniture found in this room. For, as I correctly presumed, they were one of the points of attraction for the menacing residue of his psyche. After their elimination from the apartment, I hoped to dry up several fundamental sources of allurement, cut several important, and dangerous, ties of sympathy.

I carried out the affair systematically, almost experimentally, through small, barely perceptible changes. So, at first, I had the hefty plush armchair by the window removed, replacing it with a simple chair. Already this minor modification in furniture reflected itself in a clear change in my dream, which underwent something of a simplification; namely, one of its moments was missing: the picture of Chainem in a sitting position by the window. Throughout the entire night, this melancholic did not once occupy the new chair.

The next day I removed the desk, and in its place I put a small, neat card table, not omitting, besides this, to change the writing implements. That night Chainem did, in fact, sit down in this area on an old, not yet removed, chair, but he didn't lean on a writing desk anymore, he didn't touch the pen lying nearby, and generally appeared to avoid any contact with the new furniture.

When, the following day, I exchanged this chair for an elegant, recently acquired taboret, he didn't even come close to the table. This side of the room became for him, as it were, a terrain foreign and unfriendly, one he shunned.

Thus I threw out, step by step, furniture after furniture, bringing in completely new furnishings in glaring discrepancy with the old—furnishings of lively-colored upholstery and full of intentional brightness. After two weeks the only remaining previous items were the aforementioned wardrobe and a nearby hanging mirror. These two pieces I had no intention of changing for the obvious reason that such action seemed superfluous: nothing appeared to connect Chainem to this corner of the room, and he ostentatiously avoided it. Therefore, why invite unnecessary trouble?

But this time I was mistaken. The reason for Chainem's avoidance of this part of the room was not indifference but a horrible memory. Not realizing this, however, I didn't touch that area.

The instituted changes elicited a beneficial influence on my daily surroundings: the room cheered up, the oppressive mood of the interior weakened, giving way to a more sunny atmosphere. Concurrently, my dreams changed to a new phase. As the metamorphosis of my home progressed, the ground was being cut out from under Chainem. At first I blocked him from the window, then removed him from that part of the room where once stood the writing desk, and next limited him to a few armchairs. Finally, after clearing these away, just a narrow space remained for him among the new pieces of furniture. Evidently the altered atmosphere began to depress him, for I noticed in his previously well-defined figure a certain dissipation: with each succeeding night this person became more subtle and started to evaporate; I saw him as through a mist. Eventually, he stopped pacing among the chairs and moved like a shadow along the walls. Sometimes his entire figure broke up, and I only saw fragments of arms, legs, or an outline of his face. There was not the slightest doubt—Chainem, beaten down, was withdrawing. Delighted with already certain victory, I wrung my hands with joy and set about to deal him the final blow. I had the grey wallpaper torn down and the room re-papered in red.

196

The result wasn't disappointing: the shadow of my stubborn opponent ceased to loiter about the walls.

Yet I still felt his presence in the air; elusive, exceedingly diluted, but despite this, it was still there. I had to make the atmosphere completely loathsome to him.

Toward this end, I arranged a wild orgy in my place for two successive nights. I encouraged the disorderliness of my inebriated guests, I inflamed their youthful appetites and passions. We went crazy. After these two riotous, sleepless nights, which caused me great unpleasantness from my co-tenants, I finally threw myself down on my bed in my clothes, totally exhausted, and immediately fell asleep.

At first my weariness prevented anything from happening, and I slept without visions. But after several restful hours my room once again emerged from the mist of sleep. I looked at it calmly, smiling in triumph through the dream: there was no one in the room, absolutely no one.

Trying to strengthen this conviction in myself, I began to victoriously pass my eyes over every inch of the apartment, starting at the window. Thus I traversed three-quarters of the room, inspecting closely the armchairs, scrutinizing the ceiling and the walls—nowhere a sign of that culprit, nowhere even the slightest trace. Suddenly, casting my glance casually to the dark corner by the door, that one part of the room he had always so neatly avoided—I saw him. He stood in a full, distinct figure, typically a little bent, his back toward me.

Just then he extended his hand to the wardrobe and, turning the key, opened it. He paused, apparently fixing his eyes on the empty interior with its rows of plain wooden pegs. Slowly, with calm reflection, he drew out from his pocket a type of belt or leather strap, and tied it to one of the pegs; he turned a loop and made a circle at the dangling end. Before I could figure out what was happening, he was already hanging. His body squirmed in its death throes, turned to the side, and was reflected in the mirror on the adjoining wall. In its depths I clearly saw the face of the hanging man: his mouth was twisted into a sneering grin; his eyes were looking directly at me. . . .

Uttering a cry, I jumped out of bed and, shaking with feverish chills, leaped through the window onto the sidewalk. Not looking back, I ran through empty streets, until I came upon some inn. I was soon surrounded by the shady company of suburban hoodlums. Their gaiety revived me; they were necessary for me at that moment. They dragged me along to another, more squalid tavern; I went. Then I went to a third one, a fourth, and so on—I accompanied them everywhere until the very end, until bright morning. Then, staggering on my legs, I finally tucked myself into some hotel and fell into a dead sleep.

The following day I rented a cheerful, sunny little room at the outskirts of the city. I never returned to my old apartment.

Guarded

by Mearle Prout

The sound of a shot suddenly broke the stillness of the May morning, and echoed back from across the valley. A puff of blue smoke arose from a clump of green-briars and drifted away downwind. Out in the road, Abner Simmons dropped the bag of grain he was carrying and, with a look of dumb surprize, sank in a quivering heap to the ground. Half his side had been shot away.

The green-briars parted with a sudden life and Jed Tolliver emerged, straightening his long form as he shambled toward the road. As he walked he broke his double-barreled shotgun, flicked out the empty cartridge and blew through the barrel, sending a thin stream of acrid smoke out of the chamber. He stooped over his fallen enemy.

"Said I'd get you," he reminded the other brutally. He inserted a fresh cartridge and closed the gun with a snap.

The man in the road rolled over with a convulsive movement and stared up at him.

"That kid brother of yours is next—and last," Jed continued. "Then I'll be through with the lot of you."

Abner grinned. It is an awful thing to see a dying man grin. Jed shuddered in spite of himself.

"You can't, Jed—not Ezekiel—"

It was not a pleading. Rather, it was calm, assured, as though the other were stating a known fact. Jed shuddered again, before he felt quick anger rising.

"I got you, didn't I?" he said, ejecting a thick stream of tobacco juice. "What makes you think I won't get Ezekiel the same way?"

"You won't, Jed—you can't—because—I won't let you!"

He was fast weakening from the frightful flow of blood. Overcome from the effort of speaking, Abner closed his eyes and lay still. A second later a sudden convulsive movement shook his body, and his eyes opened again. This time they were fixed and staring.

With a grunt of satisfaction Jed shouldered his gun and started back up the mountain, moving with the long effortless stride of the Tennessee mountaineer. He did not fear punishment for his crime. Here in the Tennessee mountains the long arm of the law seldom reached. The only thing to fear in a case of this kind was the dead man's relatives, and now there was only one—Ezekiel, a slim lad of twenty, who could not even shoot expertly.

Yes, Jed reflected as his long strides carried him through the sparse growth of cedar and blackjack, this part of Tennessee would soon again be a decent, God-fearing community. . . . Foreigners, the Simmonses had been, from somewhere back East—Carolina, or Virginia, maybe. They hadn't been like the mountain-folk. . . .

And what was that crazy talk Abner had made? He'd stop Jed from getting Ezekiel? How could he, if he was dead? Jed chuckled to himself. Here in Tennessee, folk didn't believe. . . .

More than a week passed before Jed again took his well-oiled shotgun from its place on the wall and started over the mountain. He was in no great hurry about Ezekiel—instead, he rather enjoyed waiting. Ezekiel was the last of the three Simmons brothers, and knowing that the foreigner was over there, and that he was going to kill him, gave life a curious sort of zest. . . . Likely the kid didn't even know who shot his brother. Jed laughed silently at the thought, adding to himself that the boy probably wouldn't do anything about it if he did know. He wasn't like the mountain people. . . .

But this morning all of Jed's impatience had returned. The sun shone hotly on the Tennessee hills, and raised an almost visible veil of vapor from the tiny branch which flowed through the hollow. Well, he'd waited long enough. With a grimace of distaste at the three-mile traipse across two mountains, Jed swung his gun over his shoulder and started down the slope.

When, an hour and a half later, he arrived at the small clearing which was the Simmons place, he was not as tired as he had expected to be. The nervous exhilaration of the man-hunt buoyed him up, made him tensely aware of things around him. He paused only a moment at the fringe of scrub oak that bordered the clearing; then, bending almost double, he sprinted a hundred feet to the grape-arbor.

Safe inside the leafy bower, Jed leaned his gun against a supporting post and looked about. Here the vines had been trained over a rude wooden lattice so that a thick wall and roof of leaves now effectively hid him from anyone outside.

Jed parted the leaves carefully and peered out. A hundred feet behind him was the low wall of forest he had just left; two hundred feet in front of him was the house—a rude two-room shack; two hundred feet beyond that the wall of the forest began again. Jed looked at the house more closely. There was no sign of movement, but the thin line of smoke which curled from the chimney told him that Ezekiel was inside, probably preparing his midday meal. With a sigh of contentment he sat down and leaned back closer to his gun, idly listening to the chatter of birds in the forest, and the rustling of the leaves in the arbor.

How long Jed sat there he did not know. He was suddenly aroused from a semi-stupor by the sound of a banging door. Startled into instant activity, he swung around to peer through the leaves. Ezekiel was leaving the house, swinging in his hand an empty water-bucket. Going to the spring, Jed reckoned. If so, his path would take him within fifty feet of the arbor. Jed gloated.

With hands suddenly unsteady, the man in the arbor laid his gun on the ground, the muzzle barely extending through the leaves. Why take a chance? He would wait—at fifty feet he couldn't miss.

Unmindful of his danger, Ezekiel came slowly down the path, bearing diagonally nearer to the arbor. . . . Jed suddenly wondered why he no longer heard the aimless chatter of birds in the forest, why the light wind no longer stirred the broad leaves above him. It was uncanny, this noonday quiet. Impatiently, he shook off the feeling.

"So I can't do it, Abner?" he whispered to the empty air, but somehow the words clutched at his throat, and he wished he hadn't said it. No matter, a few seconds now—

Jed cursed the trembling of his hands as he aimed. What was the matter with him? He could see Ezekiel's slender form now above the barrel of his gun; he nerved himself to pull the trigger. The top of his head suddenly gone cold, Jed dropped the gun and looked quickly around him. No, the day was bright as ever—yet he could have sworn. . . . Half-heartedly now, he picked up the gun to sight at the form which had already passed the nearest point. He had not been wrong! A black nebulous cloud hovered over the barrel of his gun and created the illusion of darkest night!

Shrieking a curse, Jed Tolliver leapt upright and pointed, not aimed, the gun at where Ezekiel should be. He snapped both triggers simultaneously, but as he fired something clutched at his arm, and the hot lead sizzled harmlessly through the air.

Shaking as with a chill, blind rage within him struggling with black fear, the mountaineer stood irresolutely within his leafy ambush. He was quickly aroused to activity by a loud report and the crash of lead against the wooden lattice. A sharp pain burned his left arm where one of the pellets had found its mark. Ezekiel had fled to the house and opened fire.

Without waiting to reload his gun, Jed crashed through the side of the bower and fled to the safety of the trees. As he entered, buckshot spattered harmlessly around him.

Safe within the sheltering growth, Jed halted to reload his gun.

"Damn you, Abner!" he shouted to the stunted oaks. "I'll get him yet!"

As he turned to go he thought he heard a low mocking laugh, but reasoned later that it was only a squirrel chattering a protest at the sound of his voice.

Jed reached home in a blue funk. The long tramp across the mountains in the early summer heat had melted away most of his fears, but his nerves were still badly shaken. Now that he could look at the incident in a sober light, he refused to credit his senses. As the distance between himself and the scene increased, he had come more and more to believe the occurrence an hallucination, brought on by the long walk through the heat. After all, he recalled, he had almost fallen asleep in the arbor while waiting for Ezekiel to appear. Perhaps he had dreamed part of it? . . .

However logical Jed believed his explanation, he did not again go near the Simmons place. Weeks passed. Always he promised himself that he would soon finish the task so ingloriously begun, but day by day he waited, until nearly three months had gone. At first he had feared Ezekiel had recognized him in those few seconds it had taken to sprint from the grape-arbor to the cover of the woods. Later, as he heard nothing of it, he decided he was safe from that side. The end came in an unexpected manner. One afternoon early in August Jed had walked to the village. He stayed longer than he had intended, and shadows were already growing long when he started home. Not wishing to be out later than necessary, he took a short-cut through the woods which would take him within a half-mile of the Simmons place.

The sun was setting as he entered the Simmons hollow, a half-mile below the house. He felt vaguely uneasy. Though he told himself he was not frightened, he found himself wishing for the protection of his gun. Nervously, his hand strayed to the hunting-knife stuck in his belt, and tested the keen edge.

Walking diagonally across the hollow, which was largely devoid of trees, he turned aside to go around a cluster of young cedars which was directly in his path. Suddenly he drew back sharply. Again his hand tested the keen edge of that knife, but not this time from nervousness. Jed was not thinking now of defense.

Two hundred feet beyond the cedars, on the smooth unbroken grass floor of the hollow, was a man milking. His back was turned to the cedars, but Jed thought he recognized that slim youthful form. He believed it was Ezekiel.

Stepping lightly, one hand on his belt where he could immediately grasp the knife, Jed moved into the open. Halfway across the level space, his hand moved yet closer to the knife, while the ghost of a grin curved his lips. Without a doubt it was Ezekiel Simmons. The man milking did not look up. The milk jetted into the half-filled bucket with a low murmur, just loud enough to mask Jed's guarded footsteps.

Step by step Jed advanced. If only Ezekiel did not see him! If only the cow did not sense his presence and turn unexpectedly! Step by step further—Jed was tense with excitement. There was no midday sun this time to blind his eyes and fill his soul with a nameless fear. Nor would he be unnerved by the twilight stillness; it was always still at sunset, here in these mountains. . . .

Ten feet now. The milk still swished into the pail uninterruptedly, the steady grinding of the cow's molars never ceased.

Suddenly Jed tugged at his belt and leapt forward.

"Got you!" he shouted aloud.

But the exultant cry died suddenly into a moan of horror. The arm bearing the knife poised high for the blow, Jed felt something like an electric shock course through its length. Instead of swinging forward to strike the man in front of him, the knife turned in his hand, his wrist and elbow bent at a crazy angle, and the razor-edge steel ripped through the cords of his neck.

Staggered more by his realization of the awful consequences than by present pain, Jed sank to the grass, while gouts of blood spurted from a torn jugular. His first mad terror past, he became aware that Ezekiel was standing over him, scorn darkening his features.

"So it *was* you, Tolliver. Abner warned me—about you."

"I'd have got you too—only Abner—"

"Abner was a good brother. He told me—weeks before he died—that if anything happened, he'd—guard me."

Jed felt himself weaker. His head was strangely without weight, and objects around swam lazily in the pale twilight. He lay back on the grass.

"Should have got you, Ezekiel—shouldn't have—missed," he murmured sleepily as the shadows gathered.

He raised his head slightly to listen. Was that a light mocking laugh he heard in the grass beside him? He listened again, before the darkness came down. No—he could not be sure. . . .

Harmless Ghosts

by Jessica Amanda Salmonson

"Truth be told, my dear Penelope, I *do* believe in ghosts. Yet you will forgive me for saying I have my doubts about some of the stories chronicled in your various books and articles."

I must say I was stunned by Jerome's confession. I had known him for years and thought him an utter skeptic. He loved to cast aspersions on what I, whether eccentrically or not, consider my life's work. And I've never demanded that all my friends support me in endeavors they find peculiar. But here I was finding out that Jerome had never been a skeptic in the least. The many times he 'pshawed' my chronicles of supernatural events, he was really doubting my personal integrity!

"Jerome," I ventured, "do you realize what you have just said to me?"

"Yes, that I don't believe any of those silly stories you have written down for that antiquary's journal in England, much less those big books you've done about modern hauntings."

"Yet you do believe in ghosts."

"Yes I do. I have an acquaintance, a relative I might say, who lived in a haunted apartment building. I had something to do with resolving that particular mystery. The resolution was quite simply the identity of the ghost, who my relative could not possibly have known anything about. So I'm not a doubter as far as that goes, although I've never personally made the acquaintance of any such creature."

"Forgive me if I seem affronted," I said, sounding only half as annoyed as I felt inside. "So ghosts are real—it's *my* ghosts which are fabrications. Why have you chosen this moment to inform me that you consider one of your closest friends an outright fraud?"

Jerome's animated and much-creased expression went suddenly pale. "I meant no insult at all!" he exclaimed. "I thought we were good enough friends that I could tell you an honest feeling."

"Indeed we are," I allowed. "And I have never minded your treating me as though you thought me prematurely dotty and a superstitious eccentric. But your honest thought, it turns out, is that your good friend Penelope Pettiweather spits mistruths left and right."

"That wasn't my thought at all! I don't doubt you believe everything that you say you believe."

"Then, dear friend, you are calling me mad."

"A bit angry, I gather, but not mad," he said, trying feebly to inject a moment of amusement into our conversation. I did not feel ameliorated. He ventured further. "You say that you are sensitive to the occult world, and I believe you are. But isn't it possible that, once in the vicinity of such creatures as my very own relative witnessed, you become somewhat excitable on account of your sensitivity, and enlarge upon the experience in a manner calculated to heighten the effect?"

"Calculated, you say?"

"Only subconsciously, Penelope. I don't mean you're trying to fool people—only yourself."

I could not for the life of me tell what he was getting at. He didn't think me either mad or a liar. But he did think I made things up without realizing it. This was patently absurd to me, and I felt no less insulted. "I must say," I began, "you express yourself badly. You say I'm not a liar but have told tales which cannot be true. You say I'm not mad but have experienced things that could not have happened."

"Yes, that's right. You've got it." He was more satisfied than I with my rephrasing of his opinion. He continued. "You see, while ghosts surely exist for some reason or another, there's no reason to suppose them in any manner malicious. Yet the books and articles you have written, many about personal experiences, all have a foreboding tone to them, if not an absolutely menacing character. But this cannot be right. Why, I'm certain that ghosts are nothing but lingering aspects of our own selves. Even someone with a bad character can only be an insubstantial, utterly helpless shade. And shadows, my dear Penelope, do not bite!"

"I see," said I, thinking I was beginning to understand his belief. "Despite the fact that you have never seen me in a temper, or suffering the vapors, or getting excited in any untoward manner, yet you believe that I have an excessive and unjustifiable response to mere shadows."

"That's it. The shadows may indeed be *something*. But that something is harmless. Just as some people are instantly terrified and have an unreasoning sense of doom at the sight of an itty-bitty spider or some old tomcat, you, Penelope, have a phobia for ghosts, all the more tragic for your affinity or sensitivity to their existence."

"And you feel you have empirical evidence as to the harmlessness of supernatural events?"

"My friend's ghost, yes."

"Friend is it, or relative?" I asked. "You're a bit vague on that point, Jerome. I for one never draw sweeping conclusions without the specifics."

Now it was Jerome's turn to be embarrassed. He'd gone pale when he realized he'd insulted me. Now he became very red-faced because I'd tripped him up in, at least, a mild mistruth. "All right," he said. "I hate to carry tales about my own dear mother, rest her soul, and it has been my habit to tell the story as having happened to 'a friend' or 'a relative'. But yes, it was my own mother, though I entreat you not to think she was any kind of fool or madwoman to see a ghost."

"Since only fools and madwomen generally see them?" I said with a rueful expression.

"No, no! Not that! Oh, dear, I do offend you today, don't I? Well, let me tell it quickly, so you'll know what I mean. My mother and her second husband—my father had been dead for years, and I anything but a young man—moved into an old apartment building near Everett. This must have been, oh, twenty years ago. Bill—he was my stepfather, but as I was a grown man at the time I tended to just think of him as a friend and my mother's husband—was an antique wholesaler often traveling about making 'finds'. So my mother was often alone. She had been a widow long enough before her second marriage, she didn't mind the weeks Bill was gone. But the apartment bothered her for some reason and she frequently called to have me stay over. It was some while before she told me there was a ghost. Of course I laughed at that. I'd stayed with her numerous times and never seen a thing.

"She told me that the ghost sometimes turned on the bathtub tap in the middle of the night, opened doors, and now and then moved things about to suit herself. The ghost was an old woman. My mother claimed to have seen such things as the over-stuffed chair sink in, as though an invisible person had sat down. And on various occasions, the old woman would appear, especially in the kitchen. The odd thing was that the old woman would be floating about four inches above the floor, generally in front of the stove; and she would be making a stirring motion as though there were a pot of bubbling stew. It quite unnerved my mother.

"My mother's sense of honesty was so extreme that I often thought it was a fault rather than a virtue. If someone's hair looked awful though it had just been done, and that someone asked, 'How do you like my hair?' she was apt to say, 'It looks dreadful and your hairdresser should be stuffed.' No tact, my mother; but honesty was her obsession. So I believed she had seen what she said she'd seen. But without corroboration, I had to admit to her that I feared she was suffering from delusions. She was getting on in years herself and probably thinking so much about becoming a senior citizen that she had begun to imagine an even older woman in the apartment with her.

"Mother insisted it was no such thing. She added that on two occasions she had actually spoken with the ghost. 'This is my home and I want you to get out,' she told the ghost. And the translucent old woman drifting above the floor replied, 'It was my home first and you should leave.' My mother felt mildly threatened by this and started having me stay with her quite a lot, when Bill was away.

"I asked around about a tenant who might have worn black slacks and black sequin blouse, of a sort popular in the late 1940s; who was stout and had short, tightly curled white hair and rather too much make-up in the wrong places. This was as my mother described the ghost. Nobody had heard of such a woman having lived there. But the fellow who owned the apartment was a senile goat in a nursing home. His children managed the apartment house. I went to see him and it was hard going but I made him understand what I wanted to know.

"He said a lady named Eppy Sarton had died in that room in 1953, wearing her 'night out' clothes, including a black sequin blouse. As she was old and half blind, it was true she put on rather too much make-up in odd places. But she was otherwise pretty healthy and her death had been a surprise to everyone. An unexpected stroke.

"After that, I looked up the Everett Sartons, and found a greatniece of Eppy Sarton who had some pictures of her great-aunt. I borrowed one faded photograph to show my mother. It was exactly the woman my mother had been seeing. So, I knew I had the corroboration I needed, the evidence! I had to admit my mother was by no measure demented and that such a thing as a revenant does exist!"

When Jerome had finished telling me his mother's ghost story, he looked perfectly satisfied that I would no longer be miffed.

"But this does not explain," I said evenly, "why you confess such a wholehearted doubt of my own experience!"

206

"Why, don't you see . . ." he was getting animated again, ". . . the old woman's ghost was absolutely harmless! In fact, once my mother was able to call it Mrs Sarton, it stopped troubling her at all. Oh! There was one more thing. I looked at some blueprints kept by the city of Everett and established that the apartment house had been completely renovated in the late 1950s. The floors had been higher originally, the ceilings vaulted. That was all changed. The ceilings were lowered. An extra floor was gotten out of it. That's why the ghost of Mrs Sarton appeared to walk above the present floor. Fit very neatly, I thought! But every bit of it, harmless as can be. Yet have you ever seen a harmless ghost, my good friend Penelope?"

"Certainly," I said, still quite annoyed.

"Well, perhaps you have; but aren't most of them malevolent? I've read your books and they're always scary stories. Not like a real ghost at all."

"My dear Jerome," I said, my voice strained. "As well to say that since George Washington was a fine leader for his country, then surely there was nothing wrong with Hitler. But to be frank with you, ghosts are trouble wherever they appear, to one degree or another. And if your mother was never harmed in any manner, she was rather luckier than you may realize."

"See! Just as I thought! You always find a malevolence to things! Absolutely no reason for that, Penny! Except for the drama, of course. My mother's ghost would make a pretty boring chapter for one of your books, unless it had bitten off some of her fingers or something like that."

He was referring to the Maynard Ghost I had written about. It bit off some poor child's fingers before it could be gotten rid of. The smug look on Jerome's face was an extraordinary annoyance to me! Did he think young Jenny Maynard bit off her own fingers and spirited them away without trace before her parents got her out of that room? I shook my head in dismay and said to Jerome:

"Did your mother die peacefully?"

"Isn't that a change of topic?" he said.

"Only if she died peacefully. I seem to recollect your mentioning she died of a broken neck, poor old gal."

"Well she was getting feeble by then. Shouldn't have been in a second floor apartment, I suppose. I'm rather glad I didn't find her at the foot of the stairs. It was Bill found her, poor fellow. He really loved my mother. But what is this you're suggesting? That my mother was *pushed* by a ghost? I won't stand for that, Penelope! Getting morbid where my mother is concerned! You have absolutely no reason to presume such a thing!"

"You're right, and I would not venture to say it happened that way at all, Jerome. At least, not until I could correlate some dates and interview some neighbors."

"What an insidious seed to plant in my mind, Penny! It's not a coincidence that escaped my notice. I had found the exact date of Mrs Sarton's death. It was May 22, 1953. My mother slipped and fell down those stairs on a May 22, also. I do say, though, that this is exactly the kind of meaningless coincidence that you are capable of running wild with!"

"If you will read my books more carefully, you'll know that I only heed coincidences when they begin to pile up. For instance, what were the ages of Mrs Sarton and your mother the day of their deaths? Well, you don't know that one yourself. I venture you'll be checking the newspaper morgue tomorrow. Don't be too surprised by it. Your methods of detection in tracking down the ghost's identity were very impressive, Jerome, so you must have asked yourself some other questions later on: Had your mother been especially anxious during the days before the accident? Did she disagree with you that Mrs Sarton was a harmless spirit? Did you talk your mother into taking no precautions? Do you call me variously a fool, a liar, an imaginative hysteric, and so on, because it hides your own guilty feelings in having reassured your mother a ghost was only a harmless shadow?"

Jerome was awash with sweat. He stood quickly, fists clenched, though I wasn't afraid of him one bit. He stammered, "The dead can't hurt anyone! I tell you that!"

"Very well, Jerome. You may be right," I said, trying to calm him. I really hadn't meant to hit his sore spot so firmly. I wouldn't have said anything but that he'd piqued me with unintentional insults the whole afternoon. He sat down, removed a handkerchief from a pocket and mopped his brow. He said, "You won't write about this one, will you?"

"I should think not," I said. "I never investigated it. I don't write about hearsay—and it was your mother's adventure, not yours."

He sank into himself, looking unhappy. "I did tell her it would be silly to worry Bill or to trouble everyone by moving out. It *was* my fault, wasn't it, Penelope? I made an awful error. I always knew it! I practically killed her myself!"

"Don't excite yourself, Jerome," I said. "I wish I'd understood your mind a couple minutes sooner. I wouldn't have teased you as severely. Your mother was old, after all. If it hadn't been a quick death with a broken neck, it might have been a slow and awful one with strokes and a failing mind. Sometimes the only thing we can do is think of a tragedy as a blessing in disguise. Do that for me, Jerome. And if tales of evil spirits upset you, do you and me both a favor. Don't read my books from now on."

The Haunted Burglar

by W. C. Morrow

Anthony Ross doubtless had the oddest and most complex temperament that ever assured the success of burglary as a business. This fact is mentioned in order that those who choose may employ it as an explanation of the extraordinary ideas that entered his head and gave a strangely tragic character to his career.

Though ignorant, the man had an uncommonly fine mind in certain aspects. Thus it happened that, while lacking moral perception, he cherished an artistic pride in the smooth, elegant, and finished conduct of his work. Hence a blunder on his part invariably filled him with grief and humiliation; and it was the steadily increasing recurrence of these errors that finally impelled him to make a deliberate analysis of his case.

Among the stupid acts with which he charged himself was the murder of the banker Uriah Mattson, a feeble old man whom a simple choking or a sufficient tap on the skull would have rendered helpless. Instead of that, he had choked his victim to death in the most brutal and unnecessary manner, and in doing so had used the fingers of his left hand in a singularly sprawled and awkward fashion. The whole act was utterly unlike him; it appalled and horrified him, —not for the sin of taking human life, but because it was unnecessary, dangerous, subversive of the principles of skilled burglary, and monstrously inartistic.

A similar mishap had occurred in the case of Miss Jellison, a wealthy spinster, merely because she was in the act of waking, which meant an ensuing scream. In this case, as in the other, he was unspeakably shocked to discover that the fatal choking had been done by the left hand, with sprawled and awkward fingers, and with a savage ferocity entirely uncalled for by his peril.

In setting himself to analyze these incongruous and revolting things he dragged forth from his memory numerous other acts, unlike those two in detail, but similar to them in spirit. Thus, in a fit of passionate anger at the whimpering of an infant, he had flung it brutally against the wall. Another time he was nearly discovered through the needless torturing of a cat, whose cries set pursuers at his heels. These and other insane, inartistic, and ferocious acts he arrayed for serious analysis.

Finally the realization burst upon him that all his aberrations of conduct had proceeded from his left hand and arm. Search his recollection ever so diligently, he could not recall a single instance wherein his right hand had failed to proceed on perfectly fine, sure, and artistic lines. When he made this discovery he realized that he had brought himself face to face with a terrifying mystery; and its horrors were increased when he reflected that while his left hand had committed acts of stupid atrocity in the pursuit of his burglarious enterprises, on many occasions when he was not so engaged it had acted with a less harmful but none the less coarse, irrational, and inartistic purpose.

It was not difficult for such a man to arrive at strange conclusions. The explanation that promptly suggested itself, and that his coolest and shrewdest wisdom could not shake, was that his left arm was under the dominion of a perverse and malicious spirit, that it was an entity apart from his own spirit, and that it had fastened itself upon that part of his body to produce his ruin. It were useless, however inviting, to speculate upon the order of mind capable of arriving at such a conclusion; it is more to the point to narrate the terrible happenings to which it gave rise.

About a month after the burglar's mental struggle a strange-looking man applied for a situation at a saw-mill a hundred miles away. His appearance was exceedingly distressing. Either a grievous bodily illness or fearful mental anguish had made his face wan and haggard and filled his eyes with the light of a hard desperation that gave promise of dire results. There were no marks of a vagabond on his clothing or in his manner. He did not seem to be suffering for physical necessities. He held his head aloft and walked like a man, and an understanding glance would have seen that his look of determination meant something profounder and more far-reaching than the ordinary business concerns of life.

He gave the name of Hope. His manner was so engaging, yet withal so firm and abstracted, that he secured a position without difficulty; and so faithfully did he work, and so quick was his intelligence, that in good time his request to be given the management of a saw was granted. It might have been noticed that his face thereupon wore a deeper and more haggard look, but that its rigors were softened by a light of happy expectancy. As he cultivated no friendships among the men, he had no confidants; he went his dark way alone to the end.

He seemed to take more than the pleasure of an efficient workman in observing the products of his skill. He would stealthily hug the big brown logs as they approached the saw, and his eyes would blaze when the great tool went singing and roaring at its work. The foreman, mistaking this eagerness for carelessness, quietly cautioned him to beware; but when the next log was mounted for the saw the stranger appeared to slip and fall. He clasped the moving log in his arms, and the next moment the insatiable teeth had severed his left arm near the shoulder, and the stranger sank with a groan into the soft sawdust that filled the pit.

There was the usual commotion attending such accidents, for the faces of the workmen turn white when they see one of their number thus maimed for life. But Hope received good surgical care, and in due time was able to be abroad. Then the men observed that a remarkable change had come over him. His moroseness had disappeared, and in its stead was a hearty cheer of manner that amazed them. Was the losing of a precious arm a thing to make a wretched man happy? Hope was given light work in the office, and might have remained to the end of his days a competent and prosperous man; but one day he left, and was never seen thereabout again.

Then Anthony Ross, the burglar, reappeared upon the scenes of his former exploits. The police were dismayed to note the arrival of a man whom all their skill had been unable to convict of terrible crimes which they were certain he had committed, and they questioned him about the loss of his arm; but he laughed them away with the fine old *sang-froid* with which they were familiar, and soon his handiwork appeared in reports of daring burglaries.

A watch of extraordinary care and minuteness was set upon him, but that availed nothing until a singular thing occurred to baffle the officers beyond measure: Ross had suddenly become wildly reckless and walked red-handed into the mouth of the law. By evidence that seemed indisputable a burglary and atrocious murder were traced to him. Stranger than all else, he made no effort to escape, though leaving a hanging trail behind him. When the officers overhauled him, they found him in a state of utter dejection, wholly different from the light-hearted bearing that had characterized him ever since he had returned without his left arm. Neither admitting nor denying his guilt, he bore

211

himself with the hopelessness of a man already condemned to the gallows.

Even when he was brought before a jury and placed on trial, he made no fight for his life. Although possessed of abundant means, he refused to employ an attorney, and treated with scant courtesy the one assigned him by the judge. He betrayed irritation at the slow dragging of the case as the prosecution piled up its evidence against him. His whole manner indicated that he wished the trial to end as soon as possible and hoped for a verdict of guilty.

This incomprehensible behavior placed the young and ambitious attorney on his mettle. He realized that some inexplicable mystery lay behind the matter, and this sharpened his zeal to find it. He plied his client with all manner of questions, and tried in all ways to secure his confidence: Ross remained sullen, morose, and wholly given over to despairing resignation. The young lawyer had made a wonderful discovery, which he at first felt confident would clear the prisoner, but any mention of it to Ross would only throw him into a violent passion and cause him to tremble as with a palsy. His conduct on such occasions was terrible beyond measure. He seemed utterly beside himself, and thus his attorney had become convinced of the man's insanity. The trouble in proving it was that he dared not mention his discovery to others, and that Ross exhibited no signs of mania unless that one subject was broached.

The prosecution made out a case that looked impregnable, and this fact seemed to fill the prisoner with peace. The young lawyer for the defence had summoned a number of witnesses, but in the end he used only one. His opening statement to the jury was merely that it was a physical impossibility for the prisoner to have committed the murder, —which was done by choking. Ross made a frantic attempt to stop him from putting forth that defence, and from the dock wildly denounced it as a lie.

The young lawyer nevertheless proceeded with what he deemed his duty to his unwilling client. He called a photographer and had him produce a large picture of the murdered man's face and neck. He proved that the protrait was that of the person whom Ross was charged with having killed. As he approached the climax of the scene, Ross became entirely ungovernable in his frantic efforts to stop the introduction of the evidence, and so it became necessary to bind and gag him and strap him to the chair.

When quiet was restored, the lawyer handed the photograph to the jury and quietly remarked:

212

"You may see for yourselves that the choking was done with the left hand, and you have observed that my client has no such member."

He was unmistakably right. The imprint of the thumb and fingers, forced into the flesh in a singularly ferocious, sprawling, and awkward manner, was shown in the photograph with absolute clearness. The prosecution, taken wholly by surprise, blustered and made attempts to assail the evidence, but without success. The jury returned a verdict of not guilty.

Meanwhile the prisoner had fainted, and his gag and bonds had been removed; but he recovered at the moment when the verdict was announced. He staggered to his feet, and his eyes rolled; then with a thick tongue he exclaimed:

"It was the left arm that did it! This one"—holding his right arm as high as he could reach—"never made a mistake. It was always the left one. A spirit of mischief and murder was in it. I cut it off in a saw-mill, but the spirit stayed where the arm used to be, and it choked this man to death. I didn't want you to acquit me. I wanted you to hang me. I can't go through life having this thing haunting me and spoiling my business and making a murderer of me. It tries to choke me while I sleep. There it is! Can't you see it?" And he looked with wide-staring eyes at his left side.

"Mr. Sheriff," gravely said the judge, "take this man before the Commissioners of Lunacy tomorrow."

He Walked by Day

by Julius Long

Friedenburg, Ohio, sleeps between the muddy waters of the Miami River and the rusty track of a little-used spur of the Big Four. It suddenly became important to us because of its strategic position. It bisected a road which we were to surface with tar. The materials were to come by way of the spur and to be unloaded at the tiny yard.

We began work on a Monday morning. I was watching the tar distributer while it pumped tar from the car, when I felt a tap upon my back. I turned about, and when I beheld the individual who had tapped me, I actually jumped.

I have never, before or since, encountered such a singular figure. He was at least seven feet tall, and he seemed even taller than that because of the uncommon slenderness of his frame. He looked as if he had never been warmed by the rays of the sun, but confined all his life in a dank and dismal cellar. I concluded that he had been the prey of some insidious, etiolating disease. Certainly, I thought, nothing else could account for his ashen complexion. It seemed that not blood, but shadows passed through his veins.

"Do you want to see me?" I asked.

"Are you the road feller?"

"Yes."

"I want a job. My mother's sick. I have her to keep. Won't you please give me a job?"

We really didn't need another man, but I was interested in this pallid giant with his staring, gray eyes. I called to Juggy, my foreman.

"Do you think we can find a place for this fellow?" I asked.

Juggy stared incredulously. "He looks like he'd break in two."

"I'm stronger'n anyone," said the youth.

He looked about, and his eyes fell on the Mack, which had just been loaded with six tons of gravel. He walked over to it, reached down and seized the hub of a front wheel. To our utter amazement, the wheel was slowly lifted from the ground. When it was raised to a height of eight or nine inches, the youth looked inquiringly in our direction. We must have appeared sufficiently awed, for he dropped the wheel with an abruptness that evoked a yell from the driver, who thought his tire would blow out.

"We can certainly use this fellow," I said, and Juggy agreed.

"What's your name, Shadow?" he demanded.

"Karl Rand," said the boy, but "Shadow" stuck to him, as far as the crew was concerned.

We put him to work at once, and he slaved all morning, accomplishing tasks that we ordinarily assigned two or three men to do.

We were on the road at lunchtime, some miles from Friedenburg. I recalled that Shadow had not brought his lunch.

"You can take mine," I said. "I'll drive in to the village and eat."

"I never eat none," was Shadow's astonishing remark.

"You never eat!" The crew had heard his assertion, and there was an amused crowd about him at once. I fancied that he was pleased to have an audience.

"No, I never eat," he repeated. "You see"—he lowered his voice—"you see, I'm a ghost!"

We exchanged glances. So Shadow was psychopathic. We shrugged our shoulders.

"Whose ghost are you?" gibed Juggy. "Napoleon's?"

"Oh, no. I'm my own ghost. You see, I'm dead."

"Ah!" This was all Juggy could say. For once, the arch-kidder was nonplussed.

"That's why I'm so strong," added Shadow.

"How long have you been dead?" I asked.

"Six years. I was fifteen years old then."

"Tell us how it happened. Did you die a natural death, or were you killed trying to lift a fast freight off the track?" This question was asked by Juggy, who was slowly recovering.

"It was in the cave," answered Shadow solemnly. "I slipped and fell over a bank. I cracked my head on the floor. I've been a ghost ever since."

"Then why do you walk by day instead of by night?"

"I got to keep my mother."

Shadow looked so sincere, so pathetic when he made this answer, that we left off teasing him. I tried to make him eat my lunch, but he would have none of it. I expected to see him collapse that afternoon, but he worked steadily and showed no sign of tiring. We didn't know what to make of him. I confess that I was a little afraid in his presence. After all, a madman with almost superhuman strength is a dangerous character. But Shadow seemed perfectly harmless and docile.

When we had returned to our boarding-house that night, we plied our landlord with questions about Karl Rand. He drew himself up authoritatively, and lectured for some minutes upon Shadow's idiosyncrasies.

"The boy first started telling that story about six years ago," he said. "He never was right in his head, and nobody paid much attention to him at first. He said he'd fallen and busted his head in a cave, but everybody knows they ain't no caves hereabouts. I don't know what put that idea in his head. But Karl's stuck to it ever since, and I 'spect they's lots of folks round Friedenburg that's growed to believe him—more'n admits they do."

That evening, I patronized the village barber shop, and was careful to introduce Karl's name into the conversation. "All I can say is," said the barber solemnly, "that his hair ain't growed any in the last six years, and they was nary a whisker on his chin. No, sir, nary a whisker on his chin."

This did not strike me as so tremendously odd, for I had previously heard of cases of such arrested growth. However, I went to sleep that night thinking about Shadow.

The next morning, the strange youth appeared on time and rode with the crew to the job.

"Did you eat well?" Juggy asked him.

Shadow shook his head. "I never eat none."

The crew half believed him.

Early in the morning, Steve Bradshaw, the nozzle man on the tar distributer, burned his hand badly. I hurried him in to see the village doctor. When he had dressed Steve's hand, I took advantage of my opportunity and made inquiries about Shadow.

"Karl's got me stumped," said the country practitioner. "I confess I can't understand it. Of course, he won't let me get close enough to him to look at him, but it don't take an examination to tell there's something abnormal about him."

"I wonder what could have given him the idea that he's his own ghost," I said.

"I'm not sure, but I think what put it in his head was the things people used to say to him when he was a kid. He always looked like a ghost, and everybody kidded him about it. I kind of think that's what gave him the notion."

"Has he changed at all in the last six years?"

"Not a bit. He was as tall six years ago as he is today. I think that his abnormal growth might have had something to do with the stunting of his mind. But I don't know for sure."

I had to take Steve's place on the tar distributer during the next four days, and I watched Shadow pretty closely. He never ate any lunch, but he would sit with us while we devoured ours. Juggy could not resist the temptation to joke at his expense.

"There was a ghost back in my home town," Juggy once told him. "Mary Jenkens was an awful pretty woman when she was living, and when she was a girl, every fellow in town wanted to marry her. Jim Jenkens finally led her down the aisle, and we was all jealous—especially Joe Garver. He was broke up awful. Mary hadn't no more'n come back from the Falls when Joe was trying to make up to her. She wouldn't have nothing to do with him. Joe was hurt bad.

"A year after she was married, Mary took sick and died. Jim Jenkens was awful put out about it. He didn't act right from then on. He got to imagining things. He got suspicious of Joe.

" 'What you got to worry about?' people would ask him. 'Mary's dead. There can't no harm come to her now.'

"But Jim didn't feel that way. Joe heard about it, and he got to teasing Jim.

" 'I was out with Mary's ghost last night,' he would say. And Jim got to believing him. One night, he lays low for Joe and shoots him with both barrels. 'He was goin' to meet my wife!' Jim told the judge."

"Did they give him the chair?" I asked.

"No, they gave him life in the state hospital."

Shadow remained impervious to Juggy's yarns, which were told for his special benefit. During this time, I noticed something decidedly strange about the boy, but I kept my own counsel. After all, a contractor can not keep the respect of his men if he appears too credulous.

One day Juggy voiced my suspicions for me. "You know," he said, "I never saw that kid sweat. It's uncanny. It's ninety in the shade today, and Shadow ain't got a drop of perspiration on his face. Look at his shirt. Dry as if he'd just put it on."

Everyone in the crew noticed this. I think we all became uneasy in Shadow's presence.

One morning he didn't show up for work. We waited a few minutes and left without him. When the trucks came in with their second load of gravel, the drivers told us that Shadow's mother had died during the night. This news cast a gloom over the crew. We all sympathized with the youth.

"I wish I hadn't kidded him," said Juggy.

We all put in an appearance that evening at Shadow's little cottage, and I think he was tremendously gratified. "I won't be working no more," he told me. "There ain't no need for me now."

I couldn't afford to lay off the crew for the funeral, but I did go myself. I even accompanied Shadow to the cemetery.

We watched while the grave was being filled. There were many others there, for one of the chief delights in a rural community is to see how the mourners "take on" at a funeral. Moreover, their interest in Karl Rand was deeper. He had said he was going back to his cave, that he would never again walk by day. The villagers, as well as myself, wanted to see what would happen.

When the grave was filled, Shadow turned to me, eyed me pathetically a moment, then walked from the grave. Silently, we watched him set out across the field. Two mischievous boys disobeyed the entreaties of their parents, and set out after him.

They returned to the village an hour later with a strange and incredible story. They had seen Karl disappear into the ground. The earth had literally swallowed him up. The youngsters were terribly frightened. It was thought that Karl had done something to scare them, and their imaginations had got the better of them.

But the next day they were asked to lead a group of the more curious to the spot where Karl had vanished. He had not returned, and they were worried.

In a ravine two miles from the village, the party discovered a small but penetrable entrance to a cave. Its existence had never been dreamed of by the farmer who owned the land. (He has since then opened it up for tourists, and it is known as Ghost Cave.)

Someone in the party had thoughtfully brought an electric searchlight, and the party squeezed its way into the cave. Exploration revealed a labyrinth of caverns of exquisite beauty. But the explorers were oblivious to the esthetics of the cave; they thought only of Karl and his weird story.

After circuitous ramblings, they came to a sudden drop in the floor. At the base of this precipice they beheld a skeleton.

The coroner and the sheriff were duly summoned. The sheriff invited me to accompany him.

I regret that I can not describe the gruesome, awesome feeling that came over me as I made my way through those caverns. Within their chambers the human voice is given a peculiar, sepulchral sound. But perhaps it was the knowledge of Karl's bizarre story, his unaccountable disappearance that inspired me with such awe, such thoughts.

The skeleton gave me a shock, for it was a skeleton of a man *seven feet tall!* There was no mistake about this; the coroner was positive.

The skull had been fractured, apparently by a fall over the bank. It was I who discovered the hat near by. It was rotted with decay, but in the leather band were plainly discernible the crudely penned initials, "K. R."

I felt suddenly weak. The sheriff noticed my nervousness. "What's the matter, have you seen a ghost?"

I laughed nervously and affected nonchalance. With the best off-hand manner I could command, I told him of Karl Rand. He was not impressed.

"You don't—?" He did not wish to insult my intelligence by finishing his question.

At this moment, the coroner looked up and commented: "This skeleton has been here about six years, I'd say."

I was not courageous enough to acknowledge my suspicions, but the villagers were outspoken. The skeleton, they declared, was that of Karl Rand. The coroner and the sheriff were incredulous, but, politicians both, they displayed some sympathy with this view.

My friend, the sheriff, discussed the matter privately with me some days later. His theory was that Karl had discovered the cave, wandered inside and come upon the corpse of some unfortunate who had preceded him. He had been so excited by his discovery that his hat had fallen down beside the body. Later, aided by the remarks of the villagers about his ghostliness, he had fashioned his own legend.

This, of course, may be true. But the people of Friedenburg are not convinced by this explanation, and neither am I. For the identity of the skeleton has never been determined, and Karl Rand has never since been seen to walk by day.

Her New Parents

by Steve Rasnic Tem

At first, Barbara had been thrilled. The Winfields were everything parents should be. Mr. Winfield was an accountant, interested in antiques and bird-watching, and loved to spend hours telling Barbara about the days of his youth. His exuberant stories might be considered tedious by some, but he told them in such a comical way, interspersed with winks and nods and little affectionate pinches on his new daughter's arm, Barbara could not get enough of them. She could have sat listening at his feet for hours.

Mrs. Winfield gave a lot of parties and spent most of her days doing charity work. But she wasn't like other rich women Barbara had heard about—dabbling a little here and there before going shopping or out to lunch. Mrs. Winfield worked hard in her volunteer work, and came home exhausted most every day. But she still always seemed to have plenty of time for Barbara, no matter how tired she was.

"A movie, Barbara?" Mrs. Winfield sat up in her chair, suddenly alive with energy. Barbara stared at her, a bit startled. Only moments before Mrs. Winfield had been slumped down in the cushions, her shoes off, one gray hair dangling in the middle of her forehead.

"Well, yes. I'd really like that, Mother. You're sure you're not too tired?"

"Why, of course not! I'm never too tired to spend a little time with my favorite daughter!" Mrs. Winfield stood up, walked over, and gave Barbara a kiss on the cheek. "Now let's talk your daddy into going with us!"

They'd both strode into her new father's den, who looked up startled from the book he was reading. For a moment Barbara was afraid; after all, they'd just barged into his private study, interrupted his reading like two silly school girls.

But he grinned broadly and put his book away when her new mother told him of the plan. "Wonderful idea!" Before Barbara knew what was happening he'd ushered them both into the family car, and they were on their way.

It was a wonderful movie, and Barbara was aware of her new father and mother looking at her occasionally, just making sure she was having a good time. And that made it all the better. After the movie her new father took them all out to a nice restaurant and let them order whatever they wanted. They told jokes and stories—all of them, even Barbara—until quite late in the evening. They were the last to leave the restaurant and Mr. Winfield gave the waiter a big tip. Barbara could not remember ever having so much fun.

She first felt something odd about her new parents when her new father touched her on the left wrist. They'd been driving up into the Rockies, higher up than she'd ever been before, her new father driving and her new mother sitting in the back seat. Barbara herself was sitting in the front passenger seat, staring out the window peacefully.

Just before he had touched her, something had seemed odd about their arrangement in the car, and the way each member of the family gestured, spoke; and carried his or her body. Barbara had had the strange sensation of lost time, of a short-term amnesia. Suddenly she could not remember where she was, where they were going in this shiny new car, or even who these people were. Watching her new father driving, the way he held his burly hands on the steering wheel, and seeing the way her new mother held herself almost to the edge of the back seat, almost pensive in her expression, Barbara had a sense of overlapping time, and suddenly it was her old father Bob at the steering wheel, rolling down his window and screaming at a passing motorist, her old mother Eve sitting on the back seat, ready to throw up as they neared the beachfront drive.

He hadn't meant to hurt her; he'd just been trying to draw her attention to the deer up on the bank, and she hadn't been listening so he had to nudge her. But it felt as if she'd been shocked. She jerked her arm back and screamed. Rubbing her wrist nervously, Barbara thought at first it might have been broken.

"What's wrong, honey?" her new mother asked with obvious concern.

"I . . . I don't know. It's funny . . . I'm just weird I guess, but it felt as if . . . daddy had broken it . . ."

"Oh, Barbara," her new father said with even more obvious concern. "You know I wouldn't hurt you on purpose."

For some reason their voices didn't sound right to her. It was like a dream, almost. Like her new name: Barbara Winfield. It didn't seem to fit yet.

"I know . . . sure. It was funny, guess you just surprised me, sort of. I guess I'm pretty weird, huh?"

"Why, Barb! Don't say such things," her new mother said. "You're a smart, beautiful girl, and we're just thrilled to be your new parents."

"Certainly are," her new father said.

Barbara smiled. But it didn't seem right; nothing seemed right. Something was . . . strange.

She touched her arm. She imagined she could feel the break in the bone.

Barbara rubbed the back of her dresser chair nervously, periodically going to the mirror to check her hair, her dress. Would they think she dressed too liberally, or not stylishly enough? It was her first dinner party at the Winfields, and she wanted to make a good impression on all their friends.

She rubbed the sore spot on her wrist. It had really been broken; they'd had it X-rayed after she'd gone sleepless for a week. The doctor couldn't understand it.

And he'd found evidence of the old break. She knew the Winfields were pretty sure her birthfather Bob had done that, and they were right of course, but for some reason she couldn't bring herself to talk about it. She had insisted on pretending she knew nothing about it, even though it was obvious the Winfields didn't believe her. What must they think? Probably that she was some sort of crazy liar. She felt as if she might throw up any second.

But when she had first been up for adoption she'd had this continuing fantasy that if she mentioned her parents' names, wrote the words "Bob and Eve Baker," or even thought them, then her old parents would suddenly appear and kidnap her. She knew they'd never forgive her for letting the social workers take her away from them. They'd make her sorry she'd ever been born.

"Ungrateful little pig," Bob and Eve said from the mirror, Bob's fat ham of a left arm around Eve's scrawny shoulders, Eve's worried little mouse eyes suddenly gone fierce, Bob's alcoholic facial muscles slack and reddened. "All the money and aggravation we wasted on you . . ." Bob and Eve blurred out as Barbara began to cry.

Biff, the small black dog the Winfields had given her when she had moved in with them, began to growl at her old parents in the mirror, approaching the shiny surface, seemingly attempting to push his black nose through it. Barbara picked him up and petted him.

Her new mother had prepared the dining room wonderfully. The Winfields weren't really rich, Barbara had finally decided, but they did seem to always know the right way to do things. Her new mother had spent hours in preparation; the party came off like something from a magazine.

And Barbara had done well; she knew she had—said all the right things, made no mistakes at the dinner table, and seemed to know just when to smile or laugh to please people, even though she really didn't know what they were talking about most of the time. And everyone seemed to like her; that was the best part.

Even though it felt odd, as if she were some character the people at the party were watching, like they were watching a TV show, and she was a likable character in the program, so of course they just had to like her. But what if they turned the program off, would they see her as just an ordinary person then, and not like her? She chided herself for worrying so much.

Barbara walked over to her new mother as she was taking one of the dessert trays out of the refrigerator. She was going to thank her, tell her what a good time she'd had. She was going to tell her how much she liked living there.

But when her new mother turned and smiled it was with mouse eyes; it was with Eve's nervous, trembling lips.

"But Barbara, what's wrong, honey?" her new mother called through the door. Barbara hadn't been out of her room except for a few silent and uncomfortable meals for three days, ever since the dinner party. And because of what had happened after the dinner party. Biff had come into the kitchen where Barbara was closely, nervously scrutinizing her new mother, and the dog had started growling, as if he didn't recognize Mrs. Winfield. And the expression that had crossed Mrs. Winfield's face, ever so briefly, Barbara was sure it was hatred she had seen there.

"Barbara?" It was her new father now. "You've got to come out sometime; we need to talk about this thing. We're your parents now . . ."

Barbara waited anxiously for his voice to change. As it had every time he'd talked to her since the dinner party.

"You little bitch!" Bob shouted through the door. "Come out or I'll break the door down!" She could hear Eve shuffling nervously beside him. "Come out or I'll tan your hide good!"

What had she done? Why wouldn't they leave her alone?

"Barbara . . . Barbara, it's your mother," her new mother called again. But Barbara couldn't answer. She kept waiting for the voice to change.

Over the next few days Barbara tested her new parents, asking them little questions about favorite foods, frequent activities, and events from her life with Bob and Eve. But nothing seemed conclusive; she didn't really know her new parents well enough. Her new father had developed a craving for hot dogs, which was Bob's favorite food, but perhaps he had liked hot dogs all along. Her new mother suddenly seemed allergic to a particular brand of household cleanser, the same brand Eve had been sensitive to, but couldn't it just be coincidence? After all, her new parents were still nice to her, were interested in how she was feeling.

But Barbara still wondered if perhaps it were all a coverup. Maybe the social workers had had something to do with it too. And no one had seen Bob and Eve for two years; they hadn't even shown up for the hearings that took her away from them.

She was ashamed of all her worries, but something was terribly, terribly wrong with her new parents. She was convinced of it.

Her new father decided to begin a garden, something he had never done before, she was sure. He didn't know the first thing about it. Her father Bob had had a garden, his pride and joy. Barbara started watching her new father in his garden, anxiously seeking any clues. She sat out on a bench by the rows of new plants each day, Biff curled up in her lap. Mr. Winfield didn't seem to mind, in fact he generally looked at her every few minutes with a reassuring smile.

"Get that dog out of here!" he said one day.

"What . . . Daddy?" She shifted slightly away from him on the bench.

"I said get that dog out of here! He'll get into the garden!"

It was her first real argument with one of them. She didn't know what to do. "He won't bother anything; I'll hold on to him."

The man advancing toward her with the trowel in his hand was not her new father.

She decided to pretend that her new parents were not changing.

She found herself paying closer attention to the words they used. "Mystery," "Power," "Ice Cream," "Appropriate," "Pay off." Could her new parents have used any of those words? Could her old parents have?

"Sorry," "Terrible," "Nasty," "Disobedient." After awhile none of the words seemed right.

"Murder." Barbara wrote all the words down furiously into a large notebook. She began to cry when she could not record them quickly enough. Her parents simply talked too fast.

For a time Barbara thought that her new parents might have been changed into a third set of parents, not Bob and Eve, but a couple whose names she didn't even know, strangers who'd really wanted a little boy but had, at last, settled for her.

"What do you like to do on weekends? What is your favorite actor or actress? Where were you my last birthday?" She asked the Winfields many questions, but couldn't tell if they were giving her the right answers or not.

She has lost her way.

No matter where she turns, Bob and Eve are waiting for her. They've taken over the Winfields. They've killed her dog.

The clothes she wears are Eve's clothes. The words she says are Bob's. She's lost her way. She cannot find her way out of this house.

Bob and Eve. They'll always be there for her. Reminding her.

She's in the car with Bob and Eve driving up into the mountains. Years ago. Her stomach hurts with tension; she's doubled over in pain.

"Stop yer whinin'!" Bob reaches over and slaps her across the face.

"Straighten up!" Eve screams from the backseat, her fingers in Barbara's shoulders like claws.

"Don't know why we put up with your smartness and your complainin'!" Bob screams at her.

And suddenly it is too much. Barbara screams and leaps at the steering wheel. Bob shouts and pounds on her head, trying to make her let go. But she is determined; she will kill her parents. She will kill them all.

Suddenly the car is floating away from the cliff, and the last thing Barbara hears is Bob weeping, Eve screaming and begging as they begin to drop.

Only she survives. But Bob and Eve will always be there for her. Reminders. When she walks down the street the faces of all the passersby melt, become Bob's face, Eve's face.

"No one can be anyone else for me," she says into the mirror, and Bob and Eve and the Winfields all nod in agreement—the first time, she realizes, her parents have ever agreed with her.

Highwaymen

by W. Benson Dooling

Boyle slipped a long pistol from his boot, and drew the trigger back. Its sharp clack-click was mellowed by the soft swish of his cloak, as he drew it more closely about his shoulders and waist; for this was a chill night, one of the somber kind, and this a minute during such a night when sounds soften expectantly, when insects cease their drone, and seem to wait. Boyle pulled lower the sagging front of his featherless velvet hat, and slipped a mask of some dark stuff about his eyes. His horse neighed.

From below on the road by which he stood, straight and expectant on his mount—a road that twined and curled down the mountainside, a hard-packed road much used by the private carriages of the aristocracy, and hardly wide enough for a public coach—came the rattle of hoofs of a jogging pair, and the clank and turmoil of spinning wheels. The volume of sound increased, grew louder and more distinct as the vehicle approached, and Boyle heeled his beast to the road as a small coach wheeled into view.

"Stand and deliver, whelp!"

225

Boyle's voice was acid, with a sharpness that brooked no argument. A frightened coachman hauled in his pair.

A moon shone, but softly; it was not bright enough to illumine any sentiment on the driver's face, but it disclosed a gaunt, gray-mustached man, who alighted quickly from the coach—an elderly, dignified, green-coated man, who muttered, "Sire, I had heard your kind were more polite!"

"Politeness is the courtly gesture of honest hypocrites, Milord . . . but quick!—your valuables!" Boyle waved his weapon carelessly, and leant low in his saddle, peering quickly into the dark coach.

"My money? There; it's all I have with me, fortunately!" The gaunt man sneered, and passed a small leathern bag to Boyle's waiting hand.

Said Boyle, "No jewels?"

Came the answer, "When traveling? But no, no jewels."

"My thanks! Who's in there?"

"My daughter: she's but a child."

"Then . . . I leave you the most precious of your accouterments. . . ."

A pale, blond head leant from the open coach, with two pretty blue, curious, peering eyes, and a small hand grasped the gentleman's sleeve. "Father," asked a young, frightened voice, "is that man the ghost they talked about at the Inns, who haunts the hills—the bandit ghost, Father?"

"Peace, child! Well, Sire, may we go?"

"But soft!" To the child Boyle said kindly, "Filly, I am but a collector of revenues. I have never met the spook of whom you speak, though, in sooth, I've heard his name. But you'll cloud your pretty face, thinking too much on ghosts. Better forget them, like me, my pretty dear. . . . Sire, you are at liberty to go. . . . Quick, whelp!"

The blond head vanished, and the gentleman regained his seat and slammed shut the door; the coachman whipped his horses on, too glad to go to resent the sobriquet "whelp" applied by Boyle.

Boyle heeled his sable, then gave him free rein. He wished the child had not spoken of the ghost, for Boyle did not believe in ghosts. Far forward he leant, and low-hanging branches threatened his hat. Once his cloak caught in brambles, and roughly tore loose again. The sharp wind was pleasing, biting at his hollow cheeks. Boyle was horribly emaciated: he was a sportive man, who drank and loved too much.

Night resumed its somber sounds: the chirping of tiny nocturnal insects; from somewhere away the hungry bay of a wolf; above, a screech-owl voiced its curdling sound. Boyle's horse drew back, affrighted; then, at a reassuring word from Boyle, moved on.

226

Suddenly he drew him in. This was a clearing in the wood, and the moon seemed suddenly more bright. Boyle was perplexed, and lost; he did not know this place. Strange! his horse had led him astray, though the beast knew so well the way from the road, through almost imperceptible paths in the thick wood, to the cabin that Boyle at present occupied.

A formation of trees, beyond the clearing, fascinated him: the moon shone full upon it, making strange shadows in the grass below. Sparse near the trunk, two trees stretched out long arms—chill and bare arms that touched, and seemed one lengthened arm. It looked like a gibbet, and, through some monstrous fantasy—caused, perhaps, by branches and leaves of trees beyond—the shadow on the sward enhanced this effect, and added a shadow like a man's, which seemed gently to move, to swing.

Affrighted, Boyle's horse drew back, and chawed his bit, and pawed with his forefeet, and rolled his flank. Boyle held him in, and perspiration beaded his brow: he saw that the horse was innocent of the trees and their fantasmagoria; that the beast was alarmed at something more subtle, something Boyle had not yet sensed.

"Soft, Ned!"

The beast was still: he trusted Boyle's intelligence.

"Stand and deliver, Sire!" The command came from behind him—a soft modulation, in courteous, almost tender tones, but hollow, somber, chilling; they seemed the voice of another world; the sentence seemed to come unwillingly, as though its author spoke against inclination, did something repugnant that seemed expected of him.

Boyle wheeled his horse. Before him, in the full moonlight, another horseman stood. His mount was snow-white, and fleshy, but looked fleet. Its rider was cloaked and masked, yet under the mask was a mat-white skull—a skull that did not grin, but held its jaws tight-set. A wisp of mustache adhered to where the upper lip had been. Dark, burning, liquid points shone through the mask slits; and the velvet hat was drawn too low for a forehead to be seen. Straight in his saddle the specter stood, holding his pistol muzzle toward Boyle's breast. He pulled his cloak about his waist, as though those fleshless ribs were chill. Boyle knew the saga of this one; knew that he had been hanged a hundred years before.

Boyle moaned: "The Ghost! . . . the devil! . . . the Ghost!"

Instinctively his hand reached down—a nervous, shaking, groping hand—and drew the pistol from his boot. A chill crept along his spine; his jaw gaped; his tongue slid out, strangely parched, and back again. His teeth chattered.

227

Clack-click! his pistol hammer made an awesome sound that seemed very loud. He swung the muzzle toward the other's head, and touched the trigger. Ned plunged at the sharp report, but the white steed stood nonchalantly, unperturbed. A little whiff of smoke cleared in the wind. The specter wiped the back of a hand across his brow, then leveled his pistol at Boyle's head, but refrained from firing it. Boyle was an excellent shot; he knew, despite his nervousness, that his bullet had struck his adversary between the eyes. He shoved his pistol into his boot.

Spectral and cool came the lamenting command: "Stand and deliver, Sire!"

A hand of white, glaring bones stretched out, and grasped the little leathern bag proffered by Boyle's outstretched, quavering palm.

"Sire, you are at liberty to go: but quickly, Sire!"

There was no sound from the white steed's quick hoofs as he wheeled and hurried his ghastly rider away—a rider who seemed not to stoop before low-hanging limbs, but who stayed in his saddle as he rode. Boyle was alone.

How long he waited there, trembling, is problematical. Drawing his pistol, he reloaded it and played nervously with the hammer. Ned was still, but a cold sweat covered him. Boyle looked again toward the trees that had startled him: they seemed but trees.

Then he spoke softly to Ned, heeled him on, riding gently, his weapon across his chest.

Then he laughed harshly, as Ned swung into a trot, at last free of that spectral clearing and the things it had held: "Soft, Ned, good horse! . . . I hope Mag's in tender mood tonight . . . I hope she has some hot punch on . . . in sooth, we can hand her nothing that jingles tonight, old horse!"

The Honor of Don Pedro

by Wallace J. Knapp

Nothing appeared to be unusual about Major Stuart d'Aubigny as he stood in the plaza of Toledo, immaculate from the yellow collar of his blue uniform to where his trousers tucked into his cavalry boots, yet his three friends stared at him in bewilderment.

"You mean you were the—the guest last night of a Spanish *señora?*" Coarse-looking Captain Poiret of the artillery rubbed his tongue over his thick lips. "But where was her husband?"

"He did not interfere."

The hazel eyes of sleek Captain Jules Marteau, attached to the French staff, gleamed in amazement.

"Mais, mon ami," he burst forth, "I know these Spaniards, I. For three years I fight here to help Napoleon keep King Joseph on the throne, but never have I heard of a Spanish don willingly permitting another man to visit his wife. Is he, perhaps, a friend of your family?"

Until now, Major d'Aubigny might have been called handsome. In his face, as well as in his name, lurked evidence of the romance of a bygone Scotch soldier of fortune with a demoiselle of the d'Aubigny family. Fair-haired, taller than most of the Frenchmen in that army in Toledo making its final stand against Wellington's combined British, Portuguese and Spanish force, he had always been sure of a smile from even the black-eyed *señoritas* who hated the foreign intruders. But none of them would have dreamed romance, seeing the black look of hatred now on his face.

"Friend?" he exploded. "He's the worst enemy our family ever had, the treacherous beast! He stole the sweetheart of an ancestor of mine. He used her to get French military secrets which he and the Great Captain used to defeat my country. Indeed he is no friend."

"Yet he let you visit his wife," Marteau insisted.

Before Major d'Aubigny could explain, the fourth member of that little group in the Zocodover interrupted. Jesus-Marie Constans—the sort that could give grace and charm even to a misfit lieutenant's uniform—brought his gaze reluctantly back from the winding Tagus River, seen over the walls of the market place.

"But El Gran Capitán is of the Sixteenth Century," he pointed out.

"This happened in 1503," the major agreed calmly.

Captain Poiret's head came back with such a jerk that he almost displaced his eye-glasses.

"The husband of the *señora* alive in 1503!" he cried. "What is this, a joke? How old is your companion of last night?"

"What matters her age if she be beautiful?"

Lieutenant Constans nodded slightly. Rumor had it that while still a student in Paris he had published a remarkable volume of lyrics whose imaginative charm still stood in the way of his military advancement, blinding his superiors to his bravery in battle. His wide-set, baby blue eyes looked anything but war-like.

"Tell us about her," he begged.

"What can I tell?"

"How did you happen to meet her?" Captain Poiret showed his crooked teeth in a grin of anticipation.

"When we arrived last night, we found you early comers had all the good quarters. They billetted my cavalry in a church beyond the Alcazar, a gloomy old ruin. The moment I stepped inside, I had a queer feeling like—well, once sailing home from the Indies I had the same feeling just before a tornado struck our ship. I get these warnings sometimes."

"Perhaps you owe it to your ancestors. The Scotch have always been fey," Constans remarked, but Poiret glared through his glasses.

"Something exciting is sure to happen," the major went on. "That's why I couldn't sleep. I had a place between a couple of tombs in a little chapel, but I just tossed and turned. Then I was conscious of someone crouching in the shadows. I couldn't see clearly. There was a spear of moonlight on the floor between us. I thought it might be a rebel Spaniard waiting to kill me, and here I lay unarmed. Even my cavalry sword I'd left with the rest of our weapons near the door. I drew my legs stealthily up under me, but before I leaped, either some of the guard threw more fuel on the fire or my eyes grew accustomed to the darkness. Anyway, I suddenly realized it was a woman, kneeling in prayer. She seemed slim, and from the angle of her head, young."

"Young?" echoed Marteau. "Didn't you say her husband—Sixteenth Century—is this a ghost story?"

Poiret, polishing his glasses, growled.

"It better not be!"

"But what was she doing in the church?" asked Constans.

230

"That I couldn't imagine at first. Why would a Spanish *señora* visit a church full of billetted soldiers? Then I realized. This chapel was the shrine, probably, of her patron saint."

"And I suppose she was beautiful." Poiret, the artillery captain, licked his lips.

For a moment, that winter afternoon in 1812, the major remained silent, watching an ox-cart with wheels taller than his six feet of muscular perfection. After it had squeezed into one of the narrow streets opening off Toledo's main plaza, he nodded as though to himself.

"You would not believe my description," he announced. "I shall let you see her. Tonight we'll have a banquet at which she shall be the guest of honor. It will be my revenge."

All three of them echoed the last word.

"Yes, revenge. Her treacherous husband almost lost to my ancestor the patronage of Louis. I was going to put an end to his boasting about it. If you will be witnesses this evening, I agree. Among the regimental baggage I discovered a case or two of champagne, and if you like sherry—well, *messieurs,* shall we meet here in the Zocodover at eleven tonight and go to banquet with the *señora* Dorotea de Donoso?"

At their nod of agreement, he waved a casual salute and turned away.

His three friends watched him descend the sloping street past the inn where once Cervantes had lived. Marteau gave a characteristic shrug.

"Impossible!" he murmured. "She won't come tonight. The Spanish women are better guarded than Napoleon's diamonds."

Constans drew a long breath.

"Dorotea de Donoso," he repeated, rolling the syllables on his tongue like a savory morsel. "No wonder they call Spain the Land of Romance. Why, even the names of the people embody its poetry and imagination."

"Well, that story of the major's better not be imagination," Poiret growled. "If it's a joke, I'll call him out and shoot him."

"We'll all massacre him," Marteau agreed. "No matter how much champagne he gives me, I'll never forgive him if he makes a fool out of me. I almost believe his story."

"I do believe it." Constans' handsome face was serious. "Stuart met someone last night who made a tremendous impression. I noticed the change the first moment I saw him."

"I, too," Marteau agreed. "But I thought he was tired from the ride."

"And now we know it was insomnia," Poiret leered. "You know the Spanish proverb: 'Insomnia near a beautiful woman is the gift of Heaven.' I hope we see something worth while tonight."

"We shall," Constans promised, and there was a far-away look in his blue eyes.

II

Through the cobbled streets of Toledo, so narrow that cart hubs had worn ruts in the walls on either side, Major d'Aubigny guided his three guests about midnight, with a full moon trying to cast light into the canyons between the adobe houses. Of the *señoritas* leaning over the mantilla-draped balconies, few smiled and none spoke, since most of the inhabitants of Toledo sided with Wellington and hoped to throw off Napoleonic domination.

The officers still kept looking at him askance, half suspecting the whole thing was a joke. And when they reached the ruined church, it looked as though they had grounds for their suspicions. The sentinel, standing stiffly at the door, directed them into a gloomy place where canvas and blankets curtained off even those windows behind which the moon should be visible.

Their boots echoed hollowly as they clanked across the stone floor to a table set before the great altar. A few smoking lanterns and a half-dozen candles on the table let them barely make out the bottles and glasses. They sat on carved larchwood choir benches, the only wood that had escaped the bonfires.

"But where's the *señora?*" Captain Poiret demanded with a grin that revealed his disfiguring teeth. "Will she come?"

"She'll be here." The calm assurance of the major's voice fell upon them like a chill. "It is not time yet for you to meet her."

"But you weren't serious about her husband being a general back in the time of the Gran Capitán?" he persisted.

"When you have seen her, I'll explain."

"See?" grumbled the artillery officer. "How do you expect us to see her when I can't see my hand before my face?"

"When the time comes, there will be plenty of light, too," their host promised, but Marteau had already begun to feel creepy. Quite the opposite of the major in appearance, small and dark, for he claimed no Scotch ancestors, fiery and hot-tempered, he displayed his lack of orderliness in the bagginess of his trousers and the careless way his coat was buttoned. But he was no fool. He had begun to suspect that something was wrong in the ruined, gloomy church. He remembered the report of some Spanish rebels who had poisoned a roomful of French invaders, invited to a banquet, and had burned the dwelling. Could it be that d'Aubigny had gone crazy or had sold out to the rebels?

The popping of champagne corks brought him out of his revery. Even the feeble light let him admire the deft way their host thumbed out the stoppers and let the sparkling liquor cascade into their glasses. After one taste, Marteau felt that he would be willing to toast with such nectar the ugliest of Spanish matrons and at d'Aubigny's behest hail her as queen of love and beauty. Then he noticed that Constans was not emptying his goblet as frequently as the others did.

"Drink! Drink, *mon ami,*" he urged.

"I am waiting for *la doña* Dorotea," the lieutenant barely whispered, his blue eyes seeming to look into the future.

"All in time," the major promised. "Moonlight is the light for love. In the moonlight you shall see her, and after that, my revenge." He looked up at one of the curtained windows. "Time for one more glass," he calculated. "To the loveliest lady in the world."

"More beautiful because she is the wife of an enemy," Poiret cackled.

"Shut up!" Constans almost spit at him.

With meaningless laughter Marteau and the artillery officer arose unsteadily to drink the toast. Then Major d'Aubigny caught up one of the candles.

"And now, *messieurs,* to My Lady's sleeping-chambers."

The others, only slightly more sure of their footing, serpentined after him toward the little chapel. At the stone railing he stopped them with a gesture and went on alone. Stopping before the window, he reached up and with a single tug tore away the curtain stretched across the colored glass.

He had calculated well. Like a theatrical spotlight, the moonlight streamed in to pick out a lady kneeling on a tomb. From the other side of the railing came a burst of ribald laughter.

"A damned monument!" shouted Marteau.

"In love with a statue!" scoffed Poiret, showing his crooked teeth, but Lieutenant Constans caught his breath.

"Lovely!" he whispered. "Under the moonlight, she might be flesh and blood."

"So she's the woman who married the conqueror of your ancestor?" cackled Marteau. "What a pity she isn't alive! Plenty of ways you could have had a very enjoyable revenge.

"And under her husband's eyes at that," added the artillery officer.

"He looks as though he guarded her even in death," Constans mused. And indeed, as their eyes became accustomed to the light, they could see the armored figure on the tomb next to hers, his gauntletted hands resting on his sword and a strained, watchful look upon his face turned in her direction.

They chattered with liquor-loosened tongues.

"What do you think of my last night's companion?" the major finally demanded.

"He whose chisel created her was a genius," Constans declared. "I can understand why Pygmalion hoped to bring his statue to life with a kiss."

"A kiss," laughed d'Aubigny, and then more violently: "That's it, a kiss. A kiss with her husband, the grandee, looking on. Watch, you dullards. Learn how a beautiful Spanish *señora* should be loved."

He tottered toward her, but Constans, vaulting over the railing, was at his side, clutching his shoulder.

"Don't be a fool," he cried. "Don't insult the dead!"

"Insult? I wish I could. But my kisses are no insult to a lovely woman."

"Her husband was a Spanish grandee," the lieutenant insisted, "and you know how Spaniards worship family honor."

"Don't we French regard our family honor?" the major snarled. "Here. Look at this. You read Spanish, don't you?"

With a finger trembling with rage, he followed along the inscription on the tomb, picked out by the moonlight.

AQUI YACE DON PEDRO DONOSO
GUERRERO CABALLERO

"And see what else it says: 'Whose victory at the Garigliano in 1503 brought dominion to his king and honor to himself.' *Caballero*, is he, when he stole another man's sweetheart? And great warrior when he learned by treachery all his enemy's plans? When I saw his monument last night, I knew I was fated to avenge my ancestor. I made up my mind to despoil this boasting monument before I left, but you have shown me a better way. I hope that from wherever Spanish warriors go, he is looking down to see how I take my revenge."

"You're drunk, Stuart," Constans told him, "or you'd never so debase yourself. The man's dead. You're not insulting him. It's a crime against lovely womanhood to pollute that statue with your beastly caresses."

"*Vive la France!*" Marteau called out in a cracked voice. "Down with the dons!"

The major flung off Constans' restraining hand.

"Look down, don Pedro Donoso. The d'Aubigny are revenged." He took a step nearer that miracle in marble. "Come, *señora!* Forget your decrepit old Spanish husband. Show me how warm-blooded Spanish maidens love."

One more step he took, between the tombs, then half turned his head to mock the kneeling caballero behind him.

"Watch, cuckold!" he jeered. "My revenge is complete. Now boast your honor of a grandee, if you can."

He bent to kiss the kneeling woman.

Only Constans saw what happened next. The artillery officer had his glasses off and was polishing them. Marteau had turned for a goblet of wine to toast the occasion and the next he knew Major d'Aubigny lay dead on the floor of the chapel, his skull bashed in behind.

To the billetted cavalrymen who rushed up alarmed by the shouting, Constans explained that their leader had lost his footing and slipped. He realized the impossibility of making those uncouth soldiers believe what his eyes had seen, but even his reason refused to accept. Yet he knew no mere fall could so have crushed the major's head.

A queer, creepy feeling ran up and down his spine as he remembered that scowl darkening don Pedro's brow, and saw that gauntletted hand crash down upon the insulter of his honor. And wasn't there a changed expression in the features of that stone caballero? They had lost that strained, watchful look, and instead there appeared the proud, haughty gaze befitting an honorable grandee.

The House of Shadows

by Mary Elizabeth Counselman

The train pulled up with a noisy jerk and wheeze, and I peered out into the semi-gloom of dusk at the little depot. What was the place?—"Oak Grove." I could read dimly the sign on the station's roof. I sighed wearily. Three days on the train! Lord, I was tired of the lurching roll, the cinders, the scenery flying past my window! I came to a sudden decision and hurried down the aisle to where the conductor was helping an old lady off.

"How long do we stop here?" I asked him quickly.

"About ten minutes, ma'am," he said, and I stepped from the train to the smooth sand in front of the station. So pleasant to walk on firm ground again! I breathed deeply of the spicy winter air, and strolled to the far side of the station. A brisk little wind was whipping my skirts about my legs and blowing wisps of hair into my eyes. I looked idly about at what I could see of Oak Grove. It was a typical small town—a little sleepier than some, a little prettier than most. I wandered a block or two toward the business district, glancing nervously at my watch from time to time. My ten minutes threatened to be up, when I came upon two dogs trying to tear a small kitten to pieces.

I dived into the fray and rescued the kitten, not without a few bites and scratches in the way of service wounds, and put the little animal inside a store doorway. At that moment a long-drawn, it seemed to me derisive, whistle from my train rent the quiet, and as I tore back toward the station I heard it chugging away. I reached the tracks just in time to see the caboose rattling away into the night.

What should I do? Oh, why had I jumped off at this accursed little station? My luggage, everything I possessed except my purse, was on that vanished train, and here I was, marooned in a village I had never heard of before!

Or had I? "Oak Grove" . . . the name had a familiar ring. Oak Grove . . . ah! I had it! My roommate at college two years before had lived in a town called Oak Grove. I darted into the depot.

"Does a Miss Mary Allison live here?" I inquired of the station-master. "Mary Deane Allison?"

I wondered at the peculiar unfathomable look the old man gave me, and at his long silence before he answered my question. "Yes'm," he said slowly, with an odd hesitancy that was very noticeable. "You her kin?"

"No," I smiled. "I went to college with her. I . . . I thought perhaps she might put me up for the night. I've . . . well, I was idiot enough to let my train go off and leave me. Do you . . . is she fixed to put up an unexpected guest, do you know?"

"Well"—again that odd hesitancy—"we've a fair to middlin' hotel here," he evaded. "Maybe you'd rather stay there."

I frowned. Perhaps my old friend had incurred the disapproval of Oak Grove by indiscreet behavior—it seems a very easy thing to do in rural towns. I looked at him coldly.

"Perhaps you can direct me to her house," I said stiffly.

He did so, still with that strange reluctance.

I made my way to the big white house at the far end of town, where I was told Mary Allison lived. Vague memories flitted through my mind of my chum as I had seen her last, a vivacious cheerful girl whose home and family life meant more to her than college. I recalled hazy pictures she had given me of her house, of her parents and a brother whose picture had been on our dresser at school. I found myself hurrying forward with eagerness to see her again and meet that doting family of hers.

I found my way at last to the place, a beautiful old Colonial mansion with tall pillars. The grounds were overgrown with shrubbery and weeds, and the enormous white oaks completely screened the great house from the street, giving it an appearance of hiding from the world. The place was sadly in need of repairs and a gardener's care, but it must have been magnificent at one time.

I mounted the steps and rapped with the heavy brass knocker. At my third knock the massive door swung open a little way, and my college friend stood in the aperture, staring at me without a word. I held out my hand, smiling delightedly, and she took it in a slow incredulous grasp. She was unchanged, I noticed—except, perhaps, that her dancing bright-blue eyes had taken on a vague dreamy look. There was an unnatural quiet about her manner, too, which was not noticeable until she spoke. She stood in the doorway, staring at me with those misty blue eyes for a long moment without speech; then she said slowly, with more amazement than I thought natural, "Liz! Liz!" Her fingers tightened about my hand as though she were afraid I might suddenly vanish. "It's . . . it's good to see you! Gosh! How . . . why did you come here?" with a queer embarrassment.

"Well, to tell the truth, my train ran off and left me when I got off for a breath of air," I confessed sheepishly. "But I'm glad now that it did . . . remembered you lived here, so here I am!" She merely stared at me strangely, still clutching my hand. "There's no train to Atlanta till ten in the morning." I hesitated, then laughed, "Well, aren't you going to ask me in?"

"Why . . . why, of course," Mary said oddly, as if the idea was strange and had not occurred to her. "Come in!"

I stepped into the great hall, wondering at her queer manner. She had been one of my best friends at college, so why this odd constraint? Not quite as if she did not want me around—more as if it were queer that I should wish to enter her house, as if I were a total stranger, a creature from another planet! I tried to attribute it to the unexpectedness of my visit; yet inwardly I felt this explanation was not sufficient.

"What a beautiful old place!" I exclaimed, with an effort to put her at ease again. Then, as the complete silence of the place struck me, unthinkingly I added, "You don't live here alone, do you?"

She gave me the oddest look, one I could not fathom, and replied so softly that I could hardly catch the words, "Oh, no."

I laughed. "Of course! I'm crazy . . . but where is everybody?"

I took off my hat, looking about me at the Colonial furniture and the large candelabra on the walls with the clusters of lighted candles which gave the only light in the place—for there were no modern lighting fixtures of any kind, I noted. The dim candle-light threw deep shadows about the hall—shadows that flickered and moved, that seemed alive. It should have given me a sense of nervous fear; yet somehow there was peace, contentment, warmth about the old mansion. Yet, too, there was an incongruous air of mystery, of unseen things in the shadowy corners, of being watched by unseen eyes.

"Where is everybody? Gone to bed?" I repeated, as she seemed not to have heard my question.

"Here they are," Mary answered in that strange hushed voice I had noticed, as if some one were asleep whom she might waken.

I looked in the direction she indicated, and started slightly. I had not seen that little group when I entered! They were standing scarcely ten feet from me just beyond the aura of light from the candles, and they stared at me silently, huddled together and motionless.

I smiled and glanced at Mary, who said in a soft voice like the murmur of a light wind, "My mother . . ."

238

I stepped forward and held out my hand to the tall kind-faced woman who advanced a few steps from the half-seen group in the shadows. She seemed, without offense, not to see my hand, but merely gave me a beautiful smile and said, in that same hushed voice Mary used, "If you are my daughter's friend, you are welcome!"

I happened to glance at Mary from the corner of my eye as she spoke, and I saw my friend's unnatural constraint vanish, give place to a look, I thought wonderingly, that was unmistakably one of relief.

"My father," Mary's voice had a peculiar tone of happiness. A tall distinguished-looking man of about forty stepped toward me, smiling gently. He too seemed not to see my outthrust hand, but said in a quiet friendly voice, "I am glad to know you, my dear. Mary has spoken of you often."

I made some friendly answer to the old couple; then Mary said, "This is Lonny . . . remember his picture?"

The handsome young man whose photograph I remembered stepped forward, grinning engagingly.

"So this is Liz!" he said. "Always wanted to meet one girl who isn't afraid of a mouse . . . remember? Mary told us about the time you put one in the prof's desk." He too spoke in that near-whisper that went oddly with his cheery words, and I found myself unconsciously lowering my voice to match theirs. They were unusually quiet for such a merry friendly group, and I was especially puzzled at Mary's hushed voice and manner—she had always been a boisterous tomboy sort of person.

"This is Betty," Mary spoke again, a strange glow lighting her face.

A small girl about twelve stepped solemnly from the shadows and gave me a grave old-fashioned curtsey.

"And Bill," said Mary, as a chubby child peeped out at me from behind his sister's dress and broke into a soft gurgling laugh.

"What darling kids!" I burst out.

The baby toddled out from behind Betty and stood looking at me with big blue eyes, head on one side. I stepped forward to pat the curly head, but as I put out a hand to touch him, he seemed to draw away easily just out of reach. I could not feel rebuffed, however, with his bright eyes telling me plainly that I was liked. It was just a baby's natural shyness with strangers, I told myself, and made no other attempt to catch him.

After a moment's conversation, during which my liking for this charming family grew, Mary asked if I should like to go to my room and freshen up a bit before dinner. As I followed her up the stairs, it struck me forcibly—as it had before only vaguely—that this family, with the exception of Mary, were in very bad health. From father to baby, they were most pasty-white of complexion—not sallow, I mused, but a sort of translucent white like the glazed-glass doors of private offices. I attributed it to the uncertain light of the candles that they looked rather smoky, like figures in a movie when the film has become old and faded.

"Dinner at six," Mary told me, smiling, and left me to remove the travel-stains.

I came downstairs a little before the dinner hour, to find the hall deserted—and, woman-like, I stopped to parade before a large cheval-glass in the wall. It was a huge mirror, reflecting the whole hall behind me, mellowly illumined in the glow of the candles. Turning about for a back-view of myself, I saw the little baby, Bill, standing just beside me, big eyes twinkling merrily.

"Hello there, old fellow," I smiled at him. "Do I look all right?" I glanced back at the mirror . . . and what it reflected gave me a shock.

I could see myself clearly in the big glass, and most of the hall far behind me, stretching back into the shadows. But the baby was not reflected in the glass at all! I moved, with a little chill, just behind him . . . and I could see my own reflection clearly, but it was as if he was simply not there.

At that moment Mary called us to dinner, and I promptly forgot the disturbing optical illusion with the parting resolve to have my eyes examined. I held out my hand to lead little Bill into the dining-room, but he dodged by me with a mischievous gurgle of laughter, and tod-dled into the room ahead of me.

That was the pleasantest meal I can remember. The food was excel-lent and the conversation cheery and light, though I had to strain to catch words spoken at the far end of the table, as they still spoke in that queer hushed tone. My voice, breaking into the murmur of theirs, sounded loud and discordant, though I have a real Southern voice.

Mary served the dinner, hopping up and running back into the kitchen from time to time to fetch things. By this I gathered that they were in rather straitened circumstances and could not afford a servant. I chattered gayly to Lonny and Mary, while the baby and Betty lis-tened with obvious delight and Mary's parents put in a word occasion-ally when they could break into our chatter.

It was a merry informal dinner, not unusual except that the conver-sation was carried on in that near-whisper. I noticed vaguely that Mary and I were the only ones who ate anything at all. The others merely toyed with their food, cutting it up ready for eating but not tasting a bite, though several times they would raise a fork to their lips and put it down again, as though pretending to eat. Even the baby only splashed with his little fork in his rice and kept his eyes fixed on me, now and then breaking into that merry gurgling laugh.

We wandered into the library after the meal, where Mary and I chatted of old times. Mr. Allison and his wife read or gave ear to our prattling from time to time, smiling and winking at each other. Lonny, with the baby in his lap and Betty perched on the arm of his chair, laughed with us at some foolish tale of our freshman days.

At about eleven Mary caught me yawning covertly, and hustled me off to bed. I obediently retired, thankful for a bed that did not roll me from side to side all night, and crawled in bed in borrowed pajamas with a book, to read myself to sleep by the flickering candle on my bedside table.

I must have dropped off to sleep suddenly, for I awoke to find my candle still burning. I was about to blow it out and go back to sleep when a slight sound startled the last trace of drowsiness from me.

It was the gentle rattle of my doorknob being turned very quietly.

An impulse made me feign sleep, though my eyes were not quite closed and I watched the door through my eyelashes. It swung open slowly, and Mrs. Allison came into the room. She walked with absolute noiselessness up to my bed, and stood looking down at me intently. I shut my eyes tightly so my eyelids would not flutter, and when I opened them slightly in a moment, she was moving toward the door, apparently satisfied that I was fast asleep. I thought she was going out again, but she paused at the door and beckoned to some one outside in the hall.

Slowly and with incredible lack of sound, there tiptoed into my room Mr. Allison, Lonny, Betty, and the baby. They stood beside the bed looking down at me with such tender expressions that I was touched.

I conquered an impulse to open my eyes and ask them what they meant by this late visit, deciding to wait and watch. It did not occur to me to be frightened at this midnight intrusion. There swept over me instead a sense of unutterable peace and safety, a feeling of being watched over and guarded by some benevolent angel.

They stood for a long moment without speaking, and then the little girl, bending close to me, gently caressed my hand, which was lying on the coverlet. I controlled a start with great effort.

Her little hand was icy cold—not with the coldness of hands, but with a peculiar *windy* coldness. It was as if some one had merely blown a breath of icy air on me, for though her hand rested a moment on mine, it had no weight!

Then, still without speaking but with gentle affectionate smiles on all their faces, they tiptoed out in single file. Wondering at their actions, I dropped off at last into a serene sleep.

Mary brought my breakfast to my bed next morning, and sat chattering with me while I ate. I dressed leisurely and made ready to catch my ten o'clock train. When the time drew near, I asked Mary where her family was—they were nowhere in the house and I had seen none of them since the night before. I reiterated how charming they were, and how happy my visit had been. That little glow of happiness lighted my friend's face again, but at my next words it vanished into one that was certainly frightened pleading. I had merely asked to tell them good-bye.

That odd unfathomable expression flitted across her face once more. "They . . . they're gone," she said in a strained whisper. And as I stared at her perplexedly, she added in confusion, "I . . . I mean, they're away. They won't be back until . . . nightfall," the last word was so low it was almost unintelligible.

So I told her to give them my thanks and farewells. She did not seem to want to accompany me to the train, so I went alone. My train was late, and I wandered to the ticket window and chatted with the station-master.

"Miss Allison has a charming family, hasn't she?" I began conversationally. "They seem so devoted to each other."

Then I saw the station-master was staring at me as if I had suddenly gone mad. His wrinkled face had gone very pale.

"You stayed there last night?" His voice was almost a croak.

"Why, yes!" I replied, wondering at his behavior. "I did. Why not?"

"And . . . you saw . . . *them?*" his voice sank to a whisper.

"You mean Mary's family?" I asked, becoming a little annoyed at his foolish perturbation. "Certainly I saw them! What's so strange about that? What's wrong with them?"

My approaching train wailed in the distance, but I lingered to hear his reply. It came with that same reluctance, that same hesitancy, after a long moment.

"They died last year," he whispered, leaning forward toward me and fixing me with wide intent eyes. "Wiped out—every one of 'em exceptin' Mary—by smallpox."

How He Left the Hotel

by Louisa Baldwin

I used to work the passenger lift in the Empire Hotel, that big block of building in lines of red and white brick like streaky bacon, that stands at the corner of Bath Street. I'd served my time in the army and got my discharge with good conduct stripes, and how I got the job was in this way. The hotel was a big company affair, with a managing committee of retired officers and such like, gentlemen with a bit o' money in the concern and nothing to do but fidget about it, and my late Colonel was one of 'em. He was as good tempered a man as ever stepped when his will wasn't crossed, and when I asked him for a job, "Mole," says he, "you're the very man to work the lift at our big hotel. Soldiers are civil and business-like, and the public like 'em only second best to sailors. We've had to give our last man the sack, and you can take his place."

I liked my work well enough and my pay, and kept my place a year, and I should have been there still if it hadn't been for a circumstance— but more about that just now. Ours was a hydraulic lift. None o' them ricketty things swung up like a poll-parrot's cage in a well staircase, that I shouldn't care to trust my neck to. It ran as smooth as oil, a child might have worked it, and safe as standing on the ground. Instead of being stuck full of advertisements like a' omnibus, we'd mirrors in it, and the ladies would look at themselves, and pat their hair, and set their mouths when I was taking 'em downstairs dressed of an evening. It was a little sitting room with red velvet cushions to sit down on, and you'd nothing to do but get into it, and it 'ud float you up, or float you down, as light as a bird.

All the visitors used the lift one time or another, going up or coming down. Some of them was French, and they called the lift the "as-senser," and good enough for them in their language no doubt, but why the Americans, that can speak English when they choose, and are always finding out ways o' doing things quicker than other folks, should waste time and breath calling a lift an "elevator," I can't make out.

I was in charge of the lift from noon till midnight. By that time the theatre and dining-out folks had come in, and any one returning later walked upstairs, for my day's work was done. One of the porters worked the lift till I came on duty in the morning, but before twelve there was nothing particular going on, and not much till after two o'clock. Then it was pretty hot work with visitors going up and down constant, and the electric bell ringing you from one floor to another like a house on fire. Then came a quiet spell while dinner was on, and I'd sit down comfortable in the lift and read my paper, only I mightn't smoke. But nobody else might neither, and I had to ask furren gentlemen to please not to smoke in it, it was against the rule. I hadn't so often to tell English gentlemen. They're not like furreners, that seem as if their cigars was glued to their lips.

I always noticed faces as folks got into the lift, for I've sharp sight and a good memory, and none of the visitors needed to tell me twice where to take them. I knew them, and I knew their floor as well as they did themselves.

It was in November that Colonel Saxby came to the Empire Hotel. I noticed him particularly because you could see at once that he was a soldier. He was a tall, thin man about fifty, with a hawk nose, keen eyes, and a grey moustache, and walked stiff from a gunshot wound in the knee. But what I noticed most was the scar of a sabre cut across the right side of the face. As he got in the lift to go to his room on the fourth floor, I thought what a difference there is among officers. Colonel Saxby put me in mind of a telegraph post for height and thinness, and my old Colonel was like a barrel in uniform, but a brave soldier and a gentleman all the same. Colonel Saxby's room was number 210, just opposite the glass door leading to the lift, and every time I stopped on the fourth floor Number 210 stared me in the face.

The Colonel used to go up in the lift every day regular, though he never came down in it, till—but I'm coming to that presently. Sometimes, when we was alone in the lift, he'd speak to me. He asked me in what regiment I'd served, and said he knew the officers in it. But I can't say he was comfortable to talk to. There was something stand off about him, and he always seemed deep in his own thoughts. He never sat down in the lift. Whether it was empty or full he stood bolt upright, under the lamp, where the light fell on his pale face and scarred cheek.

One day in February I didn't take the Colonel up in the lift, and as he was regular as clockwork, I noticed it, but I supposed he'd gone away for a few days, and I thought no more about it. Whenever I stopped on the fourth floor the door of Number 210 was shut, and as he often left it open, I made sure the Colonel was away. At the end of a

244

week I heard a chambermaid say that Colonel Saxby was ill, so thinks I that's why he hadn't been in the lift lately.

It was a Tuesday night, and I'd had an uncommonly busy time of it. It was one stream of traffic up and down, and so it went on the whole evening. It was on the stroke of midnight, and I was about to put out the light in the lift, lock the door, and leave the key in the office for the man in the morning, when the electric bell rang out sharp. I looked at the dial, and saw I was wanted on the fourth floor. It struck twelve as I stept into the lift. As I past the second and third floors I wondered who it was that had rung so late, and thought it must be a stranger that didn't know the rule of the house. But when I stopped at the fourth floor and flung open the door of the lift, Colonel Saxby was standing there wrapped in his military cloak. His room door was shut behind him, for I read the number on it. I thought he was ill in his bed, and ill enough he looked, but he had his hat on, and what could a man that had been in bed ten days want with going out on a winter midnight? I don't think he saw me, but when I'd set the lift in motion, I looked at him standing under the lamp, with the shadow of his hat hiding his eyes, and the light full on the lower part of his face that was deadly pale, the scar on his cheek showing still paler.

"Glad to see you're better, sir," but he said nothing, and I didn't like to look at him again. He stood like a statue with his cloak about him, and I was downright glad when I opened the door for him to step out in the hall. I saluted as he got out, and he went past me towards the door.

"The Colonel wants to go out," I said to the porter who stood staring. He opened the front door and Colonel Saxby walked out into the snow.

"That's a queer go," said the porter.

"It is," said I. "I don't like the Colonel's looks; he doesn't seem himself at all. He's ill enough to be in his bed, and there he is, gone out on a night like this."

"Anyhow he's got a famous cloak to keep him warm. I say, supposing he's gone to a fancy ball and got that cloak on to hide his dress," said the porter, laughing uneasily. For we both felt queerer than we cared to say, and as we spoke there came a loud ring at the door bell.

"No more passengers for me," I said, and I was really putting the light out this time, when Joe opened the door and two gentlemen entered that I knew at a glance were doctors. One was tall and the other short and stout, and they both came to the lift.

"Sorry, gentlemen, but it's against the rule for the lift to go up after midnight."

"Nonsense!" said the stout gentleman, "it's only just past twelve, and it's a matter of life and death. Take us up at once to the fourth floor," and they were in the lift like a shot.

When I opened the door, they went straight to Number 210. A nurse came out to meet them, and the stout doctor said, "No change for the worse, I hope." And I heard her reply, "The patient died five minutes ago, sir."

Though I'd no business to speak, that was more than I could stand. I followed the doctors to the door and said, "There's some mistake here, gentlemen; I took the Colonel down in the lift since the clock struck twelve, and he went out."

The stout doctor said sharply, "A case of mistaken identity. It was someone else you took for the Colonel."

"Begging your pardon, gentlemen, it was the Colonel himself, and the night porter that opened the door for him knew him as well as me. He was dressed for a night like this, with his military cloak wrapped round him."

"Step in and see for yourself," said the nurse. I followed the doctors into the room, and there lay Colonel Saxby looking just as I'd seen him a few minutes before. There he lay, dead as his forefathers, and the great cloak spread over the bed to keep him warm that would feel heat and cold no more. I never slept that night. I sat up with Joe, expecting every minute to hear the Colonel ring the front door bell. Next day every time the bell for the lift rang sharp and sudden, the sweat broke out on me and I shook again. I felt as bad as I did the first time I was in action. Me and Joe told the manager all about it, and he said we'd been dreaming, but, said he, "Mind you, don't you talk about it, or the house'll be empty in a week."

The Colonel's coffin was smuggled into the house the next night. Me and the manager, and the undertaker's men, took it up in the lift, and it lay right across it, and not an inch to spare. They carried it into Number 210, and while I waited for them to come out again, a queer feeling came over me. Then the door opened softly, and six men carried out the long coffin straight across the passage, and set it down with its foot towards the door of the lift, and the manager looked round for me.

"I can't do it, sir," I said. "I can't take the Colonel down *again*, I took him down at midnight yesterday, and that was enough for me."

"Push it in!" said the manager, speaking short and sharp, and they ran the coffin into the lift without a sound. The manager got in last, and before he closed the door he said, "Mole, you've worked this lift

246

for the last time, it strikes me." And I had, for I wouldn't have stayed on at the Empire Hotel after what had happened, not if they'd doubled my wages, and me and the night porter left together.

Jerry Bundler

by W. W. Jacobs

It wanted a few nights to Christmas, a festival for which the small market-town of Torchester was making extensive preparations. The narrow streets which had been thronged with people were now almost deserted; the cheap-jack from London, with the remnant of breath left him after his evening's exertions, was making feeble attempts to blow out his naphtha lamp, and the last shops open were rapidly closing for the night.

In the comfortable coffee-room of the old "Boar's Head", half a dozen guests, principally commercial travellers, sat talking by the light of the fire. The talk had drifted from trade to politics, from politics to religion and so by easy stages to the supernatural. Three ghost stories, never known to fail before, had fallen flat; there was too much noise outside, too much light within. The fourth story was told by an old hand with more success; the streets were quiet, and he had turned the gas out. In the flickering light of the fire, as it shone on the glasses and danced with the shadows on the walls, the story proved so enthralling that George, the waiter, whose presence had been forgotten, created a very disagreeable sensation by suddenly starting up from a dark corner and gliding silently from the room.

"That's what I call a good story," said one of the men, sipping his hot whisky. "Of course it's an old idea that spirits like to get into the company of human beings. A man told me once that he travelled down the Great Western with a ghost, and hadn't the slightest suspicion of it until the inspector came for tickets. My friend said the way that ghost tried to keep up appearances by feeling for it in all its pockets and looking on the floor was quite touching. Ultimately it gave it up and with a faint groan vanished through the ventilator."

"That'll do, Hirst," said another man.

"It's not a subject for jesting," said a little old gentleman who had been an attentive listener. "I've never seen an apparition myself, but I know people who have, and I consider that they form a very interesting link between us and the after-life. There's a ghost story connected with this house, you know."

"Never heard of it," said another speaker, "and I've been here some years now."

"It dates back a long time now," said the old gentleman. "You've heard about Jerry Bundler, George?"

"Well, I've just 'eard odds and ends, sir," said the old waiter, "but I never put much count to 'em. There was one chap 'ere what said 'e saw it, and the gov'ner sacked 'im prompt."

"My father was a native of this town," said the old gentleman, "and knew the story well. He was a truthful man and a steady churchgoer, but I've heard him declare that once in his life he saw the appearance of Jerry Bundler in this house."

"And who was this Bundler?" inquired a voice.

"A London thief, pickpocket, highwayman—anything he could turn his dishonest hand to," replied the old gentleman; "and he was run to earth in this house one Christmas week some eighty years ago. He took his last supper in this very room, and after he had gone up to bed a couple of Bow Street runners, who had followed him from London but lost the scent a bit, went upstairs with the landlord and tried the door. It was stout oak, and fast, so one went into the yard, and by means of a short ladder got on to the window-sill, while the other stayed outside the door. Those below in the yard saw the man crouching on the sill, and then there was a sudden smash of glass, and with a cry he fell in a heap on the stones at their feet. Then in the moonlight they saw the white face of the pickpocket peeping over the sill, and while some stayed in the yard, others ran into the house and helped the other man to break the door in. It was difficult to obtain an entrance even then, for it was barred with heavy furniture, but they got in at last, and the first thing that met their eyes was the body of Jerry dangling from the top of the bed by his own handkerchief."

"Which bedroom was it?" asked two or three voices together.

The narrator shook his head. "That I can't tell you; but the story goes that Jerry still haunts this house, and my father used to declare positively that the last time he slept here the ghost of Jerry Bundler lowered itself from the top of his bed and tried to strangle him."

"That'll do," said an uneasy voice. "I wish you'd thought to ask your father which bedroom it was."

248

"What for?" inquired the old gentleman.

"Well, I should take care not to sleep in it, that's all," said the voice, shortly.

"There's nothing to fear," said the other. "I don't believe for a moment that ghosts could really hurt one. In fact my father used to confess that it was only the unpleasantness of the thing that upset him, and that for all practical purposes, Jerry's fingers might have been made of cotton-wool for all the harm they could do."

"That's all very fine," said the last speaker again; "a ghost story is a ghost story, sir; but when a gentleman tells a tale of a ghost in the house in which one is going to sleep, I call it most ungentlemanly!"

"Pooh! nonsense!" said the old gentleman, rising; "ghosts can't hurt you. For my own part, I should rather like to see one. Good night, gentlemen."

"Good night," said the others. "And I only hope Jerry'll pay you a visit," added the nervous man as the door closed.

"Bring some more whisky, George," said a stout commercial; "I want keeping up when the talk turns this way."

"Shall I light the gas, Mr. Malcolm?" said George.

"No; the fire's very comfortable," said the traveller. "Now, gentlemen, any of you know any more?"

"I think we've had enough," said the other man; "we shall be thinking we see spirits next, and we're not all like the old gentleman who's just gone."

"Old humbug!" said Hirst. "I should like to put him to the test. Suppose I dress up as Jerry Bundler and go and give him a chance of displaying his courage?"

"Bravo!" said Malcolm, huskily; drowning one or two faint "Noes." "Just for the joke, gentlemen."

"No, no! Drop it, Hirst," said another man.

"Only for the joke," said Hirst, somewhat eagerly. "I've got some things upstairs in which I am going to play in *The Rivals*—knee-breeches, buckles, and all that sort of thing. It's a rare chance. If you'll wait a bit I'll give you a full dress rehearsal, entitled 'Jerry Bundler; or The Nocturnal Strangler'."

"You won't frighten us," said the commercial, with a husky laugh.

"I don't know that," said Hirst sharply; "it's a question of acting, that's all. I'm pretty good, ain't I, Somers?"

"Oh, you're alright—for an amateur," said his friend, with a laugh.

"I'll bet a level sov. you don't frighten me," said the stout traveller.

"Done!" said Hirst. "I'll take the bet to frighten you first and the old gentleman afterwards. These gentlemen shall be the judges."

"You won't frighten us, sir," said another man, "because we're prepared for you; but you'd better leave the old man alone. It's dangerous play."

"Well, I'll try you first," said Hirst, springing up. "No gas, mind."

He ran lightly upstairs to his room, leaving the others, most of whom had been drinking somewhat freely, to wrangle about his proceedings. It ended in two of them going to bed.

"He's crazy on acting," said Somers, lighting his pipe. "Thinks he's the equal of anybody almost. It doesn't matter with us, but I won't let him go to the old man. And he won't mind so long as he gets an opportunity of acting to us."

"Well, I hope he'll hurry up," said Malcolm yawning; "it's nearly twelve now."

Nearly half an hour passed. Malcolm drew his watch from his pocket and was busy winding it, when George the waiter, who had been sent on an errand to the bar, burst suddenly into the room and rushed towards them.

" 'E's comin', gentlemen," he said breathlessly.

"Why, you're frightened, George," said the stout commercial, with a chuckle.

"It was the suddenness of it," said George, sheepishly; "and besides, I didn't look for seein' 'im in the bar. There's only a glimmer of light there, and 'e was sitting on the floor behind the bar. I nearly trod on 'im."

"Oh, you'll never make a man, George," said Malcolm.

"Well, it took me unawares," said the waiter. "Not that I'd have gone to the bar by myself if I'd known 'e was there, and I don't believe you would, either, sir."

"Nonsense," said Malcolm. "I'll go and fetch him in."

"You don't know what it's like, sir," said George, catching him by the sleeve. "It ain't fit to look at by yourself, it ain't, indeed. It's got the—*What's that?*"

They all started at the sound of a smothered cry from the staircase and the sound of somebody running hurriedly along the passage. Before anybody could speak, the door flew open and a figure bursting into the room flung itself gasping and shivering upon them.

"What is it? What's the matter?" demanded Malcolm. "Why, it's Mr. Hirst." He shook him roughly and then held some spirit to his lips. Hirst drank it greedily and with a sharp intake of his breath gripped him by the arm.

"Light the gas, George," said Malcolm.

The waiter obeyed hastily. Hirst, a ludicrous but pitiable figure in

250

knee-breeches and coat, a large wig all awry, and his face a mess of grease paint, clung to him, trembling.

"Now, what's the matter?" asked Malcolm.

"I've seen it," said Hirst, with a hysterical sob. "O Lord, I'll never play the fool again, never!"

"Seen what?" said the others.

"Him—it—the ghost—anything!" said Hirst, wildly.

"Rot!" said Malcolm, uneasily.

"I was coming down the stairs," said Hirst, "just capering down—as I thought—it ought to do. I felt a tap—"

He broke off suddenly and peered nervously through the open door into the passage.

"I thought I saw it again," he whispered. "Look—at the foot of the stairs. Can you see anything?"

"No, there's nothing there," said Malcolm, whose own voice shook a little. "Go on. You felt a tap on your shoulder—"

"I turned round and saw it—a little wicked head and a white dead face. Pah!"

"That's what I saw in the bar," said George. " 'Orrid it was—devilish!"

Hirst shuddered, and, still retaining his nervous grip of Malcolm's sleeve, dropped into a chair.

"Well, it's a most unaccountable thing," said the dumbfounded Malcolm, turning to the others. "It's the last time I come to this house."

"I leave tomorrow," said George. "I wouldn't go down to that bar again by myself, no, not for fifty pounds!"

"It's talking about the thing that's caused it, I expect," said one of the men; "we've all been talking about this and having it in our minds. Practically we've been forming a spiritualistic circle without knowing it."

"Hang the old gentleman!" said Malcolm, heartily. "Upon my soul, I'm half afraid to go to bed. It's odd they should both think they saw something."

"I saw it as plain as I see you, sir," said George, solemnly. "P'raps if you keep your eyes turned up the passage you'll see it for yourself."

They followed the direction of his finger, but saw nothing, although one of them fancied that a head peeped round the corner of the wall.

"Who'll come down to the bar?" said Malcolm, looking round.

"You can go, if you like," said one of the others, with a faint laugh; "we'll wait here for you."

The stout traveller walked towards the door and took a few steps up

251

the passage. Then he stopped. All was quite silent, and he walked slowly to the end and looked down fearfully towards the glass partition which shut off the bar. Three times he made as though to go to it; then he turned back, and, glancing over his shoulder, came hurriedly back to the room.

"Did you see it, sir?" whispered George.

"Don't know," said Malcolm softly. "I fancied I saw something, but it might have been fancy. I'm in the mood to see anything just now. How are you feeling now, sir?"

"Oh, I feel a bit better now," said Hirst, somewhat brusquely, as all eyes were turned upon him. "I dare say you think I'm easily scared, but you didn't see it."

"Not at all," said Malcolm, smiling faintly despite himself.

"I'm going to bed," said Hirst, noticing the smile and resenting it. "Will you share my room with me, Somers?"

"I will with pleasure," said his friend, "provided you don't mind sleeping with the gas on full all night."

He rose from his seat, and bidding the company a friendly good-night, left the room with his crestfallen friend. The others saw them to the foot of the stairs, and having heard their door close, returned to the coffee-room.

"Well, I suppose the bet's off?" said the stout commercial, poking the fire and then standing with his legs apart on the hearthrug: "though, as far as I can see, I won it. I never saw a man so scared in all my life. Sort of poetic justice about it, isn't there?"

"Never mind about poetry or justice," said one of his listeners; "who's going to sleep with me?"

"I will," said Malcolm affably.

"And I suppose we share a room together, Mr. Leek?" said the third man, turning to the fourth.

"No, thank you," said the other, briskly; "I don't believe in ghosts. If anything comes into my room I shall shoot it."

"That won't hurt a spirit, Leek," said Malcolm, decisively.

"Well, the noise'll be like company to me," said Leek, "and it'll wake the house too. But if you're nervous, sir," he added, with a grin, to the man who had suggested sharing his room, "George'll be only too pleased to sleep on the doormat inside your room, I know."

"That I will, sir," said George fervently; "and if you gentlemen would only come down with me to the bar to put the gas out, I could never be sufficiently grateful."

They went out in a body, with the exception of Leek, peering carefully before them as they went. George turned the light out in the bar

252

and they returned unmolested to the coffee-room, and, avoiding the sardonic smile of Leek, prepared to separate for the night.

"Give me the candle while you put the gas out, George," said the traveller.

The waiter handed it to him and extinguished the gas, and at the same moment all distinctly heard a step in the passage outside. It stopped at the door, and as they watched with bated breath, the door creaked and slowly opened. Malcolm fell back, open-mouthed, as a white, leering face, with sunken eyeballs and close-cropped bullet head, appeared at the opening.

For a few seconds the creature stood regarding them, blinking in a strange fashion at the candle. Then, with a sidling movement, it came a little way into the room and stood there as if bewildered.

Not a man spoke or moved, but all watched with a horrible fascination as the creature removed its dirty neckcloth and its head rolled on its shoulder. For a minute it paused, and then, holding the rag before it, moved towards Malcolm.

The candle went out suddenly with a flash and a bang. There was a smell of powder, and something writhing in the darkness on the floor. A faint, choking cough, and then silence. Malcolm was the first to speak. "Matches," he said, in a strange voice. George struck one. Then he leapt at the gas and a burner flamed from the match. Malcolm touched the thing on the floor with his foot and found it soft. He looked at his companions. They mouthed inquiries at him, but he shook his head. He lit the candle, and, kneeling down, examined the silent thing on the floor. Then he rose swiftly, and dipping his handkerchief in the water-jug, bent down again and grimly wiped the white face. Then he sprang back with a cry of incredulous horror, pointing at it. Leek's pistol fell to the floor and he shut out the sight with his hands, but the others crowding forward, gazed spellbound at the dead face of Hirst.

Before a word was spoken the door opened and Somers hastily entered the room. His eyes fell on the floor. "Good God!" he cried. "You didn't—"

Nobody spoke.

"I told him not to," he said, in a suffocating voice. "I told him not to. I told him—"

He leaned against the wall, deathly sick, put his arms out feebly, and fell fainting into the traveller's arms.

John Charrington's Wedding

by Edith Nesbit

No one ever thought that May Foster would marry John Charrington;
but he thought differently, and things which John Charrington intended should happen had a way of happening. He asked her to marry
him before he went up to Oxford. She laughed and refused him. He
asked her again next time he came home. Again she laughed, tossed
her blonde head, and again refused. A third time he asked her; she said
it was becoming a confirmed habit, and laughed at him more than
ever.

John was not the only man who wanted to marry her; she was the
belle of our village, and we were all in love with her more or less; it was
a sort of fashion, like heliotrope ties or Inverness capes. Therefore we
were as much annoyed as surprised when John Charrington walked
into our little local club—we held it in a loft over the saddler's, I
remember—and invited us all to his wedding.

'Your wedding?'

'You don't mean it?'

'Who's the happy fair? When's it to be?'

John Charrington filled his pipe and lighted it before he replied.
Then he said:

'I'm sorry to deprive you fellows of your only joke, but Miss Foster
and I are to be married in September.'

'You don't mean it?'

'He's got the mitten again, and it's turned his head.'

'No,' I said, rising, 'I see it's true. Lend me a pistol someone, or a
first-class fare to the other end of Nowhere. Charrington has bewitched the only pretty girl in our twenty mile radius. Was it mesmer-
ism, or a love-potion, Jack?'

'Neither, sir, but a gift you'll never have—perseverance—and the
best luck a man ever had in this world.'

There was something in his voice that silenced me, and all chaff of
the other fellows failed to draw him further.

The queer thing about it was that, when we congratulated Miss

Foster, she blushed, and smiled, and dimpled, for all the world as though she were in love with him and had been in love with him all the time. Upon my word, I think she had. Women are strange creatures.

We were all asked to the wedding. In Brixham, every one who was anybody knew everybody else who was anyone. My sisters were, I truly believe, more interested in the *trousseau* than the bride herself, and I was to be best man. The coming marriage was much canvassed at afternoon tea-tables, and at our little club over the saddler's; and the question was always asked: 'Does she care for him?'

I used to ask that question myself in the early days of their engagement, but after a certain evening in August I never asked it again. I was coming home from the club through the churchyard. Our church is on a thyme-grown hill, and the turf about it is so thick and soft that one's footsteps are noiseless.

I made no sound as I vaulted the low wall and threaded my way between the tombstones. It was at the same instant that I heard John Charrington's voice and saw her. May was sitting on a low, flat grave-stone, her face turned towards the full splendour of the setting sun. Its expression ended, at once and for ever, any question of love for him; it was transfigured to a beauty I should not have believed possible, even to that beautiful little face.

John lay at her feet, and it was his voice that broke the stillness of the golden August evening.

'My dear, I believe I should come back to you from the dead, if you wanted me!'

I coughed at once to indicate my presence, and passed on into the shadow fully enlightened.

The wedding was to be early in September. Two days before, I had to run up to town on business. The train was late, of course, for we were on the South-Eastern, and as I stood grumbling with my watch in my hand, whom should I see but John Charrington and May Foster. They were walking up and down the unfrequented end of the plat-form, arm-in-arm, looking into each other's eyes, careless of the sympathetic interest of the porters.

Of course I knew better than to hesitate a moment before burying myself in the booking-office, and it was not till the train drew up at the platform that I obtrusively passed the pair with my Gladstone, and took the corner in a first-class smoking-carriage. I did this with as good an air of not seeing them as I could assume. I pride myself on my discretion, but if John were travelling alone, I wanted his company. I had it.

'Hullo, old man,' came his cheery voice, as he swung his bag into my carriage, 'here's luck. I was expecting a dull journey.'

'Where are you off to?' I asked, discretion still bidding me turn my eyes away, though I saw, without looking, that hers were red-rimmed.

'To old Branbridge's,' he answered, shutting the door, and leaning out for a last word with his sweetheart.

'Oh, I wish you wouldn't go, John,' she was saying in a low, earnest voice. 'I feel certain something will happen.'

'Do you think I should let anything happen to keep me, and the day after tomorrow our wedding day?'

'Don't go,' she answered, with a pleading intensity that would have sent my Gladstone on to the platform, and me after it. But she wasn't speaking to me. John Charrington was made differently—he rarely changed his opinion, never his resolutions.

He just touched the ungloved hands that lay on the carriage door.

'I must, May. The old boy has been awfully good to me, and now he's dying I must go and see him, but I shall come home in time—' The rest of the parting was lost in a whisper and in the rattling lurch of the starting train.

'You're sure to come?' she spoke, as the train moved.

'Nothing shall keep me,' he answered, and we steamed out. After he had seen the last of the little figure on the platform, he leaned back in his corner and kept silence for a minute.

When he spoke it was to explain to me that his godfather, whose heir he was, lay dying at Peasemarsh Place, some fifty miles away, and he had sent for John, and John had felt bound to go.

'I shall be surely back tomorrow,' he said, 'or, if not, the day after, in heaps of time. Thank Heaven, one hasn't to get up in the middle of the night to get married nowadays.'

'And suppose Mr Branbridge dies?'

'Alive or dead, I mean to be married on Thursday!' John answered, lighting a cigar and unfolding the *Times*.

At Peasemarsh station we said 'good-bye', and he got out, and I saw him ride off. I went on to London, where I stayed the night.

When I got home the next afternoon, a very wet one, by the way, my sister greeted me with:

'Where's Mr Charrington?'

'Goodness knows,' I answered testily. Every man since Cain has resented that kind of question.

'I thought you might have heard from him,' she went on, 'as you give him away tomorrow.'

'Isn't he back?' I asked, for I had confidently expected to find him at home.

'No, Geoffrey'—my sister always had a way of jumping to conclusions, especially such conclusions as were least favourable to her fellow creatures—'he has not returned, and, what is more, you may depend upon it, he won't. You mark my words, there'll be no wedding tomorrow.'

My sister Fanny has a power of annoying me which no other human being possesses.

'You mark my words,' I retorted with asperity, 'you had better give up making such a thundering idiot of yourself. There'll be more wedding tomorrow than ever you'll take first part in.'

But though I could snarl confidently to my sister, I did not feel so comfortable when, late that night, I, standing on the doorstep of John's house, heard that he had not returned. I went home gloomily through the rain. Next morning brought a brilliant blue sky, gold sun, and all such softness of air and beauty of cloud as go to make a perfect day. I woke with a vague feeling of having gone to bed anxious, and of being rather averse from facing that anxiety in the light of full wakefulness.

With my shaving-water came a letter from John which relieved my mind, and sent me up to the Fosters with a light heart.

May was in the garden. I saw her blue gown among the hollyhocks as the lodge gates swung to behind me. So I did not go up to the house, but turned aside down the turfed path.

'He's written to you too,' she said, without preliminary greeting, when I reached her side.

'Yes, I'm to meet him at the station at three, and come straight on to the church.'

Her face looked pale, but there was a brightness in the eyes and a softness about the mouth that spoke of renewed happiness.

'Mr Branbridge begged him so to stay another night that he had not the heart to refuse,' she went on. 'He is so kind, but . . . I wish he hadn't stayed.'

I was at the station at half-past two. I felt rather annoyed with John. It seemed a sort of slight to the beautiful girl who loved him, that he should come, as it were out of breath, and with the dust of travel upon him, to take her hand, which some of us would have given the best years of our life to take.

But when the three o'clock train glided in and glided out again, having brought no passengers to our little station, I was more than annoyed. There was no other train for thirty-five minutes; I calculated that, with much hurry, we might just get to the church in time for the ceremony; but, oh, what a fool to miss that first train! What other man would have done it?

The thirty-five minutes seemed a year, as I wandered round the station reading the advertisements and the time-tables and the company's bye-laws, and getting more and more angry with John Charrington. This confidence in his own power of getting everything he wanted the minute he wanted it, was leading him too far.

I hate waiting. Everyone hates waiting, but I believe I hate it more than anyone else does. The three-thirty-five was late too, of course.

I ground my pipe between my teeth and stamped with impatience as I watched the signals. Click. The signal went down. Five minutes later I flung myself into the carriage that I had brought for John.

'Drive to the church!' I said, as some one shut the door. 'Mr Charrington hasn't come by this train.'

Anxiety now replaced anger. What had become of this man? Could he have been taken suddenly ill? I had never known him have a day's illness in his life. And even so he might have telegraphed. Some awful accident must have happened to him. The thought that he had played her false never, no, not for a moment, entered my head. Yes, something terrible had happened to him, and on me lay the task of telling his bride. I almost wished the carriage would upset and break my head, so that someone else might tell her.

It was five minutes to four as we drew up at the churchyard. A double row of eager onlookers lined the path from lych-gate to porch. I sprang from the carriage and passed up between them. Our gardener had a good front place near the door. I stopped.

'Are they still waiting, Byles?' I asked, simply to gain time, for of course I knew they were, by the waiting crowd's attentive attitude.

'Waiting, sir? No, no, sir; why it must be over by now.'

'Over! Then Mr Charrington's come?'

'To the minute, sir; must have missed you somehow, and I say, sir,' lowering his voice, 'I never see Mr John the least bit so afore, but my opinion is he's 'ad more than a drop; I wouldn't be going too far if I said he's been drinking pretty free. His clothes was all dusty and his face like a sheet. I tell you I didn't like the looks of him at all, and the folks inside are saying all sorts of things. You'll see, something's gone very wrong with Mr John, and he's tried liquor. He looked like a ghost, and he went in with his eyes straight before him, with never a look or a word for none of us; him that was always such a gentleman.'

I had never heard Byles make so long a speech. The crowd in the churchyard were talking in whispers, and getting ready rice and slippers to throw at the bride and bridegroom. The ringers were ready with their hands on the ropes, to ring out the merry peal as the bride and bridegroom should come out.

A murmur from the church announced them; out they came. Byles was right. John Charrington did not look himself. There was dust on his coat, his hair was disarranged. He seemed to have been in some row, for there was a black mark above his eyebrow. He was deathly pale. But his pallor was not greater than that of the bride, who might have been carved in ivory—dress, veil, orange-blossoms, face and all.

As they passed out, the ringers stooped—there were six of them—and then, on the ears expecting the gay wedding peal, came the slow tolling of the passing bell.

A thrill of horror at so foolish a jest from the ringers passed through us all. But the ringers themselves dropped the ropes and fled like rabbits out into the sunlight. The bride shuddered, and grey shadows came about her mouth, but the bridegroom led her on down the path where the people stood with handfuls of rice; but the handfuls were never thrown, and the wedding bells never rang. In vain the ringers were urged to remedy their mistake; they protested, with many whispered expletives, that they had not rung that bell; that they would see themselves further before they'd ring anything more that day.

In a hush, like the hush in a chamber of death, the bridal pair passed into their carriage and its door slammed behind them.

Then the tongues were loosed. A babel of anger, wonder, conjecture from the guests and the spectators.

'If I'd seen his condition, sir,' said old Foster to me as we drove off, 'I would have stretched him on the floor of the church, sir, by Heaven I would, before I'd have let him marry my daughter!'

Then he put his head out the window.

'Drive like hell,' he cried to the coachman; 'don't spare the horses.'

We passed the bride's carriage. I forebore to look at it, and old Foster turned his head away and swore.

We stood in the hall doorway, in the blazing afternoon sun, and in about half a minute we heard wheels crunching the gravel. When the carriage stopped in front of the steps, old Foster and I ran down.

'Great Heaven, the carriage is empty! And yet—'

I had the door open in a minute, and this is what I saw—

No sign of John Charrington; and of May, his wife, only a huddled heap of white satin, lying half on the floor of the carriage and half on the seat.

'I drove straight here, sir,' said the coachman, as the bride's father lifted her out, 'and I'll swear no one got out of the carriage.'

We carried her into the house in her bridal dress, and drew back her veil. I saw her face. Shall I ever forget it? White, white, and drawn with agony and horror, bearing such a look of terror as I have never seen since, except in dreams. And her hair, her radiant blonde hair, I tell you it was white like snow.

As we stood, her father and I, half mad with the horror and mystery of it, a boy came up the avenue—a telegraph boy. They brought the orange envelope to me. I tore it open.

'*John Charrington was thrown from the dog-cart on his way to the station at half-past one. Killed on the spot.*—BRANBRIDGE, Peasemarsh Place.'

And he was married to May Foster in our Parish Church at *half-past three*, in presence of half the parish!

'*I shall be married on Thursday dead or alive!*'

What had passed in that carriage on the homeward drive? No one knows—no one will ever know.

Before a week was over they laid her beside her husband in the churchyard where they had kept their love-trysts.

This is the true story of John Charrington's wedding.

Kharu Knows All

by Renier Wyers

Self-described as "The World's Greatest Medium," Tuan Kharu managed to eke out a fairly comfortable subsistence by swindling gullible people who sought communication with the dead. He lived in the hope that one day there would come to his murky, incense-laden séance-parlor an opulent victim from whom he could glean what he termed "important money."

Such a victim was waiting to see him now. Of this he felt certain as —with the trace of a leer on his swarthy and bewhiskered face—his beady black eyes read the name on the calling-card he held in his hand:

"Mrs. Victoria Sanderson."

He had seen that name before. He stroked his black Mefistofelian beard, nodded his turbaned head, and said in an affected oriental accent:

"Tell Madam that I am in meditation. I shall grant her a consultation as soon as I have finished. Begone!"

"Yes, sir." The youth who served as the man's only corporeal assistant, a combination office-boy and secretary, retreated from the parlor to the reception room, closing the door behind him.

The instructions, Kharu decided, would keep the woman in properly awesome suspense, while he prepared for the interview. He went about this preparation, humming a little tune. It was not, as one might have expected, an exotic strain from the mystic East, nor yet a spiritual hymn. It was *Happy Days Are Here Again,* a melody reminiscent of the days of his fraudulent stock and bond activities, when he was known as Tim Carewe, salesman of spurious securities.

He had, when stocketeering ceased to be profitable, applied his talents to his present fake mediumship. By changing his name and raising a mustache and beard, he had eluded his duped investors and outraged creditors. With the aid of a few books of occult lore, he became a sufficiently transformed personality to establish himself in his new business without leaving town.

"Happy days are here again, te-dum-tedum," he concluded as he studied the contents of his filing-cabinet. It contained, in alphabetical order, death notices clipped from the press. In a trice, he found what he wanted, a clipping only seven days old. He compared it with the calling-card and chuckled. The clipping bore the words:

"Sanderson—Joseph L. Sanderson, beloved husband of Victoria. Funeral from late residence, 1087 Astor Street, June 5th." This was pasted on an index card on which was penciled, "See General News File."

The swindler's beady eyes gleamed, for this notation meant that the deceased had been prominent enough to "rate" an obituary in the news columns. Yes, here it was, a brief biography of Joseph L. Sanderson, wealthy, retired lumber dealer. The item was illustrated with a one-column, half-tone reproduction of a photograph portraying a firm, leonine face, a broad forehead under a thick mane of snow-white hair.

Kharu studied the clippings a moment, then put them away and darkened the room by drawing the long window-drapes together. He turned a light switch. The effect of these maneuvers was a dim, eery light in which nothing was clearly discernible. The smoking incense-burners enhanced the mystery of the atmosphere. It was one in which susceptible people could easily delude themselves into believing that they were in the presence of the wraiths and souls of their departed loved ones summoned here by the self-acclaimed supernatural powers of the Great Kharu. He seated himself in a throne-like chair behind the massive table on which reposed a huge crystal globe. He adjusted his turban and pressed a buzzer.

Mrs. Victoria Sanderson, elderly and bent, was escorted in by the medium's assistant. He left her standing timidly in the center of the séance-parlor and backed out, closing the door softly. She peered about her and gasped, as from a deep shadow Kharu rose majestically to his feet. He was draped in a flowing robe of blood-red silk. He stepped from behind the table, swept forward, bowed low over the timid little woman's hand and said in soothing, sympathetic tones:

"My dear Madam Sanderson! I am honored. Pray be seated here before the crystal and compose yourself. Do not speak until you are ready. I feel with you, and deeply, the sorrow that grips your heart in these dark days of bereavement. But your sorrow will be lightened. I know, for Kharu knows all. Only yesterday, during my hour of meditation there appeared to my vision the face of a kindly man, a good man, with snow-white hair, who whispered to me, 'Victoria will come. Tell Victoria not to grieve too deeply, for death is merely one's passing through a door to a better world. I am happy here in the spirit realm and I want her to be happy, too.' Those, Madam, are the very words the spirit spoke to me."

The aged woman's face was lighted with hope. "That was Joseph!" she exclaimed excitedly. "It's true! The dead do live again! He always said so. His friends never knew it, but he was deeply interested in psychic phenomena. He often told me that if he died first he'd come back or send a message to me. I did not think of that until last night when I saw your advertisement in *The Neighborhood Observer* and decided to come here."

"He guided you, caused you to read my announcement," said the Great Kharu solemnly.

He was pleased to note that the woman was even more impressionable than she had at first appeared. Recently widowed, with no kin in whom she could confide, she was pathetically eager to believe that there could be a return of the soul of the man who had been everything to her. As she spoke, she unwittingly revealed things which, when repeated to her in a different phraseology a few minutes later by Kharu, filled her with reverent awe.

"You are a great man, Kharu," she said after the séance.

He modestly bowed in acknowledgment.

* * *

Within a few weeks, she was entirely under his influence. Gradually the control of the fortune her husband had bequeathed to her slipped into the greedy fingers of the faker. He had scores of devices for parting her from her money. At his word, she contributed to him sums of cash and checks, for non-existent "causes and uplifts". She donated fifty thousand dollars to help him found an "Institute of Psychic Research". Of this sum he actually spent a few dollars for blue-prints and a prospectus. The rest he banked under his own name.

He poisoned her mind against the counsel of well-meaning acquaintances who admonished her not to be so reckless with her inheritance. He succeeded in his designs by convincing her that all his suggestions as to her investments came from her dead husband. Several times he had caused the spirit of Joseph L. Sanderson to appear before her in the darkness of the séance-parlor. She did not know that what she saw was a stereopticon projection of a slide made from the newspaper picture of the deceased. Kharu so cleverly concealed the lantern and arranged the lighting effects that his own sheeted body, moving slightly under the drape on which the picture was projected, seemed part of the specter that bore a strong leonine head crowned with a thick shock of snow-white hair.

"I speak through the voice of Kharu," said the specter. "Kharu knows all. He is our friend. Give him power of attorney. Place all you possess in his care."

This message and others in a similar vein produced excellent results for Kharu. Within a year he had bled the woman penniless.

"What shall I do now, Kharu?" she asked tearfully. "I am facing eviction from the apartment in which Joseph and I spent so many happy years. The tradesmen are dunning me. And now you say that the money I entrusted to you is all gone!"

"Yes," said Kharu coldly. "Most of the investments recommended by the spirit of your departed husband are hopelessly lost." The faker knew from experience that the quickest way of getting rid of fleeced victims was to be "hard-boiled" about it.

"But I gave you—"

"You forced the money on me, Madam!" He glared hostilely.

"But can't you help me? Please! Ask Joseph—he would help me."

"I've been unable to get in communication with the spirit of Joseph L. Sanderson for some time. Perhaps he is angry that you have wasted your inheritance by living beyond your means. Whatever the cause, silence is the only effect of my recent attempts to evoke his spirit. It's strange, but"—he shrugged "—it's the way of the occult world." He glanced at his wrist-watch.

"I have another appointment," he lied. "Will you come to see me some other time? I shall be glad to give you another consultation—at the usual price."

She fumbled with her gloves, staring at him rheumy-eyed, apparently too dulled by the dread of bleak poverty to comprehend. "I said that I have another appointment," he rasped. "Please get out!"

The very next morning after this interview, Kharu dismissed his assistant and closed his office doors for ever. By evening he was ensconced in his new quarters in a penthouse thirty-eight stories above Lake Shore Drive. Gone were his mustache and beard. Gone were the turban and flowing robes. He was his old self again, Tim Carewe, sleeker, more dapper, and richer than ever before. Smoking a fifty-cent cigar, he strolled pridefully through the apartment, only half listening to the expensive radio in the ornate living-room. The radio voice, racing against time, rattled on:

"—the body of the suicide who leapt to her death in the Chicago River from the Michigan Avenue bridge last midnight was recovered today and identified as that of Mrs. Victoria Sanderson, widow of the late Joseph L. Sanderson, millionaire lumber dealer who died at almost the same hour, the same day, exactly a year ago. You have just heard 'News Flashes' from Station WLS. We return to our studios where Finney Briggs and his orchestra are playing—"

Carewe leapt to the instrument and switched off the current. "God!" he muttered. "I didn't think she'd do that."

But the shock was only momentary. He shook it off with a shrug of his shoulders. Too bad! She had been such a "lovely mooch". So easy to "take". With the cigar held at a cocky angle in his smug, oily face, he plunged his hands into his pockets and strolled leisurely out through the French doors onto the terrace. Ah, this was glorious!— this sense of being on top of the world, literally and figuratively. He leaned on the parapet, gazing out over the blackness of Lake Michigan and the stars overhead. Directly below him some four hundred feet down, two streams of autos flowed past each other, almost in silence; for at this great height the hum of motors and swish of rubber on concrete was barely audible.

This quietness, this remoteness from the mundane life below, however, instead of having a soothing effect, began—after a few moments —to give him a sensation of uneasiness, a tinge of scalp-tickling fear. The palms of his hands grew moist with sweat. He felt that he was being watched. He whirled about. What he saw caused him to cringe back against the parapet in terror.

There on the tiled terrace, between him and the French doors, stood an elderly pair. The woman was small and bent, the man stocky. From his broad shoulders protruded a short, stout neck above which was a firm leonine face under a thick shock of white hair.

Tim Carewe stared and stared but could not stare his visitors away.

His throat muscles tightened in fear. "Mrs. Sanderson," he barely managed to whisper huskily, "who—what—" He could not finish. He ran his hand over his face as though to brush away what he saw. It was a futile gesture. The pair was approaching him, drawing ever nearer. This thing could not be!

"Go away, go away!" he screamed. "You're dead, both of you! You can't come back like this! I know. I'm Kharu, the World's Greatest Spirit Medium. Kharu knows all. I know there are no ghosts. It's all a racket, I tell you. A racket!"

Still the bent little woman and the stocky old man approached him. They were not walking—yet they moved toward the cowering figure of the once dapper Tim Carewe.

A horrible obsession seized his brain; it was that if this pair touched him he would become as they, shadowy, unreal, not of this earth and flesh. The obsession drove reason from his mind, as inch by inch the figures wafted forward. He scrambled up onto the ledge of the parapet.

The pair was now directly before and below him. The short, stocky man's firm leonine face under the shock of white hair glared up at him, relentlessly and coldly. The little, bent woman shook her head sadly. From the tile, the figures rose upward, wavering slightly like smoke in a current of air. Only their staring, accusing eyes remained steady. They bored deep into the brain of Tim Carewe.

He gibbered wildly and leapt into space.

The Last
of Squire Ennismore

by Mrs. J. H. Riddell

"Did I see it myself? No, sir; I did not see it; and my father before me did not see it; nor his father before him, and he was Phil Regan, just the same as myself. But it is true, for all that; just as true as that you are looking at the very place where the whole thing happened. My great-grandfather (and he did not die till he was ninety-eight) used to tell, many and many's the time, how he met the stranger, night after night, walking lonesome-like about the sands where most of the wreckage came ashore."

"And the old house, then, stood behind that belt of Scotch firs?"

"Yes; and a fine house it was, too. Hearing so much talk about it when a boy, my father said, made him often feel as if he knew every room in the building, though it had all fallen to ruin before he was born. None of the family ever lived in it after the squire went away. Nobody else could be got to stop in the place. There used to be awful noises, as if something was being pitched from the top of the great staircase down in to the hall; and then there would be a sound as if a hundred people were clinking glasses and talking all together at once. And then it seemed as if barrels were rolling in the cellars; and there would be screeches, and howls, and laughing, fit to make your blood run cold. They say there is gold hid away in the cellars; but not one has ever ventured to find it. The very children won't come here to play; and when the men are plowing the field behind, nothing will make them stay in it, once the day begins to change. When the night is coming on, and the tide creeps in on the sand, more than one thinks he has seen mighty queer things on the shore."

"But what is it really they think they see? When I asked my landlord to tell me the story from beginning to end, he said he could not remember it; and, at any rate, the whole rigmarole was nonsense, put together to please strangers."

"And what is he but a stranger himself? And how should he know the doings of real quality like the Ennismores? For they were gentry, every one of them—good old stock; and as for wickedness, you might

266

have searched Ireland through and not found their match. It is a sure thing, though, that if Riley can't tell you the story, I can; for, as I said, my own people were in it, of a manner of speaking. So, if your honour will rest yourself off your feet, on that bit of a bank, I'll set down my creel and give you the whole pedigree of how Squire Ennismore went away from Ardwinsagh."

It was a lovely day, in the early part of June; and, as the Englishman cast himself on a low ridge of sand, he looked over Ardwinsagh Bay with a feeling of ineffable content. To his left lay the Purple Headland; to his right, a long range of breakers, that went straight out into the Atlantic till they were lost from sight; in front lay the Bay of Ardwinsagh, with its bluish-green water sparkling in the summer sunlight, and here and there breaking over some sunken rock, against which the waves spent themselves in foam.

"You see how the current's set, Sir? That is what makes it dangerous for them as doesn't know the coast, to bathe here at any time, or walk when the tide is flowing. Look how the sea is creeping in now, like a race-horse at the finish. It leaves that tongue of sand bars to the last, and then, before you could look round, it has you up to the middle. That is why I made bold to speak to you; for it is not alone on the account of Squire Ennismore the bay has a bad name. But it is about him and the old house you want to hear. The last mortal being that tried to live in it, my great-grandfather said, was a creature, by name Molly Leary; and she had neither kith nor kin, and begged for her bite and sup, sheltering herself at night in a turf cabin she had built at the back of a ditch. You may be sure she thought herself a made woman when the agent said, 'Yes: she might try if she could stop in the house; there was peat and bog-wood,' he told her, 'and half-a-crown a week for the winter, and a golden guinea once Easter came,' when the house was to be put in order for the family; and his wife gave Molly some warm clothes and a blanket or two; and she was well set up.

"You may be sure she didn't choose the worst room to sleep in; and for a while all went quiet, till one night she was wakened by feeling the bedstead lifted by the four corners and shaken like a carpet. It was a heavy four-post bedstead, with a solid top: and her life seemed to go out of her with the fear. If it had been a ship in a storm off the Headland, it couldn't have pitched worse and then, all of a sudden, it was dropped with such a bang as nearly drove the heart into her mouth.

"But that, she said, was nothing to the screaming and laughing, and hustling and rushing that filled the house. If a hundred people had been running hard along the passages and tumbling downstairs, they could not have made greater noise.

"Molly never was able to tell how she got clear of the place; but a man coming late home from Ballycloyne Fair found the creature crouched under the old thorn there, with very little on her—saving your honour's presence. She had a bad fever, and talked about strange things, and never was the same woman after."

"But what was the beginning of all this? When did the house first get the name of being haunted?"

"After the old Squire went away: that was what I purposed telling you. He did not come here to live regularly till he had got well on in years. He was near seventy at the time I am talking about; but he held himself as upright as ever, and rode as hard as the youngest; and could have drunk a whole roomful under the table, and walked up to bed as unconcerned as you please at the dead of the night.

"He was a terrible man. You couldn't lay your tongue to a wickedness he had not been in the forefront of—drinking, duelling, gambling,—all manner of sins had been meat and drink to him since he was a boy almost. But at last he did something in London so bad, so beyond the beyonds, that he thought he had best come home and live among people who did not know so much about his goings on as the English. It was said that he wanted to try and stay in this world for ever; and that he had got some secret drops that kept him well and hearty. There was something wonderful queer about him, anyhow.

"He could hold foot with the youngest; and he was strong, and had a fine fresh colour in his face; and his eyes were like a hawk's; and there was not a break in his voice—and him near upon threescore and ten!

"At last and at long last it came to be the March before he was seventy—the worst March ever known in all these parts—such blowing, sleeting, snowing, had not been experienced in the memory of man; when one blusterous night some foreign vessel went to bits on the Purple Headland. They say it was an awful sound to hear the deathcry that went up high above the noise of the wind; and it was as bad a sight to see the shore there strewed with corpses of all sorts and sizes, from the little cabin-boy to the grizzled seaman.

"They never knew who they were or where they came from, but some of the men had crosses, and beads, and such like, so the priest said they belonged to him, and they were all buried deeply and decently in the chapel graveyard.

"There was not much wreckage of value drifted on shore. Most of what is lost about the Head stays there; but one thing did come into the bay—a puncheon of brandy.

268

"The Squire claimed it; it was his right to have all that came on his land, and he owned this sea-shore from the Head to the breakers—every foot—so, in course, he had the brandy; and there was sore illwill because he gave his men nothing, not even a glass of whiskey.

"Well, to make a long story short, that was the most wonderful liquor anybody ever tasted. The gentry came from far and near to take share, and it was cards and dice, and drinking and story-telling night after night—week in, week out. Even on Sundays, God forgive them! The officers would drive over from Ballyclone, and sit emptying tumbler after tumbler till Monday morning came, for it made beautiful punch.

"But all at once people quit coming—a word went round that the liquor was not all it ought to be. Nobody could say what ailed it, but it got about that in some way men found it did not suit them.

"For one thing, they were losing money very fast.

"They could not make head against the Squire's luck, and a hint was dropped the puncheon ought to have been towed out to sea, and sunk in fifty fathoms of water.

"It was getting to the end of April, and fine, warm weather for the time of year, when first one and then another, and then another still, began to take notice of a stranger who walked the shore alone at night. He was a dark man, the same colour as the drowned crew lying in the chapel graveyard, and had rings in his ears, and wore a strange kind of hat, and cut wonderful antics as he walked, and had an ambling sort of gait, curious to look at. Many tried to talk to him, but he only shook his head; so, as nobody could make out where he came from or what he wanted, they made sure he was the spirit of some poor wretch who was tossing about the Head, longing for a snug corner in holy ground.

"The priest went and tried to get some sense out of him.

" 'Is it Christian burial you're wanting?' asked his reverence; but the creature only shook his head.

" 'Is it word sent to the wives and daughters you've left orphans and widows, you'd like?' But no; it wasn't that.

" 'Is it for sin committed you're doomed to walk this way? Would masses comfort ye? There's a heathen,' said his reverence; 'Did you ever hear tell of a Christian that shook his head when masses were mentioned?'

" 'Perhaps he doesn't understand English, Father,' says one of the officers who was there; 'Try him with Latin.'

"No sooner said than done. The priest started off with such a string of aves and paters that the stranger fairly took to his heels and ran.

" 'He is an evil spirit,' explained the priest, when he stopped, tired out, 'and I have exorcised him.'

"But next night my gentleman was back again, as unconcerned as ever.

" 'And he'll just have to stay,' said his reverence, 'For I've got lumbago in the small of my back, and pains in all my joints—never to speak of a hoarseness with standing there shouting; and I don't believe he understood a sentence I said.'

"Well, this went on for a while, and people got that frightened of the man, or appearance of a man, they would not go near the sand; till in the end, Squire Ennismore, who had always scoffed at the talk, took it into his head he would go down one night, and see into the rights of the matter. He, maybe, was feeling lonesome, because, as I told your honour before, people had left off coming to the house, and there was nobody for him to drink with.

"Out he goes, then, bold as brass; and there were a few followed him. The man came forward at sight of the Squire and took off his hat with a foreign flourish. Not to be behind in civility, the Squire lifted his.

" 'I have come, sir,' he said, speaking very loud, to try to make him understand, 'to know if you are looking for anything, and whether I can assist you to find it.'

"The man looked at the Squire as if he had taken the greatest liking to him, and took off his hat again.

" 'Is it the vessel that was wrecked you are distressed about?'

"There came no answer, only a mournful shake of the head.

" 'Well, *I* haven't your ship, you know; it went all to bits months ago; and, as for the sailors, they are snug and sound enough in consecrated ground.'

"The man stood and looked at the Squire with a queer sort of smile on his face.

" 'What *do* you want?' asked Mr. Ennismore in a bit of a passion. 'If anything belonging to you went down with the vessel, it's about the Head you ought to be looking for it, not here—unless, indeed, its after the brandy you're fretting!'

"Now, the Squire had tried him in English and French, and was now speaking a language you'd have thought nobody could understand; but, faith, it seemed natural as kissing to the stranger.

" 'Oh! That's where you are from, is it?' said the Squire. 'Why couldn't you have told me so at once? I can't give you the brandy, because it mostly is drunk; but come along, and you shall have as stiff a glass of punch as ever crossed your lips.' And without more to-do off they went, as sociable as you please, jabbering together in some out-landish tongue that made moderate folks' jaws ache to hear it.

"That was the first night they conversed together, but it wasn't the last. The stranger must have been the height of good company, for the Squire never tired of him. Every evening, regularly, he came up to the house, always dressed the same, always smiling and polite, and then the Squire called for brandy and hot water, and they drank and played cards till cock-crow, talking and laughing into the small hours.

"This went on for weeks and weeks, nobody knowing where the man came from, or where he went; only two things the old house-keeper did know—that the puncheon was nearly empty, and that the Squire's flesh was wasting off him; and she felt so uneasy she went to the priest, but he could give her no manner of comfort.

"She got so concerned at last that she felt bound to listen at the dining-room door; but they always talked in that foreign gibberish, and whether it was blessing or cursing they were at she couldn't tell.

"Well, the upshot of it came one night in July—on the eve of the Squire's birthday—there wasn't a drop of spirit left in the puncheon—no, not as much as would drown a fly. They had drunk the whole lot clean up—and the old woman stood trembling, expecting every min-ute to hear the bell ring for more brandy, for where was she to get more if they wanted any?

"All at once the Squire and the stranger came out into the hall. It was a full moon, and light as day.

" 'I'll go home with you to-night by way of a change,' says the Squire.

" 'Will you so?' asked the other.

" 'That I will,' answered the Squire.

" 'It is your own choice, you know.'

" 'Yes; it is my own choice; let us go.'

"So they went. And the housekeeper ran up to the window on the great staircase and watched the way they took. Her niece lived there as housemaid, and she came and watched, too; and, after a while, the butler as well. They all turned their faces this way, and looked after their master walking beside the strange man along these very sands. Well, they saw them walk on, and on, and on, and on, till the water took them to their knees, and then to their waists, and then to their arm-pits, and then to their throats and their heads; but long before that the women and the butler were running out on the shore as fast as they could, shouting for help."

"Well?" said the Englishman.

"Living or dead, Squire Ennismore never came back again. Next

271

morning, when the tides ebbed again, one walking over the sand saw the print of a cloven foot—that he tracked to the water's edge. Then everybody knew where the Squire had gone, and with whom."

"And no more search was made?"

"Where would have been the use searching?"

"Not much, I suppose. It's a strange story, anyhow."

"But true, your honour—every word of it."

"Oh! I have no doubt of that," was the satisfactory reply.

The Light Was Green

by John Rawson Speer

Sudden madness at seventy miles an hour! Alone in the cab of a locomotive with a madman. Will Bryant, the engineer of the Fire Flyer, was insane. But why?

What had suddenly turned this man I had worked with for over six years, and had known as a quiet, steady-going person, into the raving madman I now saw before me?

His eyes violent, his face contorted with fear, he was cowering there in the cab, pleading with some invisible presence. For a paralyzing instant I felt that presence. But there was no time to lose. As the fireman of the Fire Flyer, I would have to assume Will's responsibility. There was no time to ask questions. I had to get to the throttle of that locomotive.

As I rushed to him from my side of the cab, he suddenly seized a shovel and struck me over the head. Blood trickled into my eyes, blurring my vision, and then I slipped away into unconsciousness with only a fading but horrible picture of Will Bryant, insane.

What happened after that in the cab of that engine, pulling a trainload of passengers seventy miles an hour, terrifies me constantly.

When I regained my senses after the blow Will had given me, I found him staring at the steam gage, and gibbering like an idiot. The air was set on the brakes, and the Flyer was pulled in alongside the main track, waiting for Number 93 to pass her.

I must have been unconscious for fully fifteen minutes. During that time the Fire Flyer had thundered on her way with no one at the throttle—unless it was, as Will Bryant swears, the spirit of Nat Carson. Nat Carson had been dead for ten years!

There was nothing to do but turn Will over to the authorities, who committed him to an asylum.

Although I had been his closest friend, there were things in his life which he had never mentioned, even to me. The doctors, after much deliberation, decided remorse, coupled with a deep sense of guilt, had caused Will to have this intense belief in the return of the dead. I followed their theories with interest, and for some time believed that he would eventually realize that only his worry-ridden mind had produced the sight he claimed he saw in the cab that night.

But I know now that Will Bryant will never recover. The last visit I had with him made me see how hopeless it was. Some of the fear that comes to lock him in delirious madness now attaches itself to me.

I can still see him, the way he looked that last day I talked to him in Terrington Asylum; his eyes dull, a hopeless sorrow showing from within them as he said:

"Steve, I am sane, as sane as any man, but I can never take my place in normal society again. Don't you think I have tried to convince myself that there was nothing unnatural about that night? I've gone over every detail of the affair, but the result is always the same: Nat Carson, dead though he may have been, sat in the cab of our engine; he pulled that train, and I know what he intended to do. I know, Steve! He was there. I saw him, I tell you. I did! I did!"

"Will, please!" I gripped his shaking hands and held them tightly. "Don't talk or think about it if it disturbs you. I only want to help you. I want to see you well again so that you can leave this place."

Will shook his head sadly.

"I don't want to leave here now, Steve. I feel safer here where they can watch me at night. I have a room here, Steve, where there are no train whistles blasting in my ears.

"Steve, I'm going to tell you everything, just as I see it. They call me crazy, but that is because they have no other term for my affliction. It is not really insanity; 'haunted' is the word.

"You remember hearing about the train wreck I was in ten years ago? As you know, Nat Carson was the engineer who allowed his train to run by a signal supposed to be set against him. I was firing for him then. See these scars on my arms—all from that wreck. We crashed through the rear of a freight train, plowed through a chain of box-cars as if they had been mere cigar boxes. Both of us missed death for no other reason than that it wasn't our time to go.

"At the Board of Investigation, I told them what I believed I should. I told them that Nat had been drinking a little. He did take chances, unforgivable chances like that. I used to warn him that some day he would be caught. Nat could be drunk and still not show it. Of course the fact that I was in love with his girl and had never really liked him had something to do with my testimony.

"At the trial he claimed he saw the signal as green. He swore the red signal set against us was green, and that I was a liar. 'You're sending me to hell!' he cried. But I stuck to my testimony.

"You know the rest; two weeks later Nat Carson killed himself. I tried to believe like all the others that he had done it because he realized the crime he had committed in risking the lives of all those passengers.

"The years went on. I was promoted to engineer, a regular 'hog head' with my own train to pull. I seldom thought of Nat any more; only when stories of that wreck were recalled would I think of him. That was only natural.

"Not until one night in the yards, years later, did I come face to face with what has doomed me. I had checked my engine over to the round-house hostler and was walking across to the dispatcher's shack. The steam and smoke from the trains was all mixed up with the fog that was settling down over the yards. Brakemen's lanterns were bobbing in and out among the cars. You know how it is on foggy nights in the yards. I wasn't paying much attention to anything when, out of that fog, a face leered at me, then vanished. It was quick, so quick that, although I was frightened, I did not believe I had actually seen it. Surely I had only imagined that I saw Nat Carson.

" 'What am I thinking about?' I asked myself; even laughed a little. 'Must be seeing ghosts,' I said, and went on into the dispatcher's office.

"I didn't think any more about it. That's how much it meant to me then. People are often imagining that they see faces of those who are dead. They're like flashes, quick pictures from the subconscious mind.

"Two nights later, at the other end of the run, I saw a figure walking toward me. I noticed it particularly because it seemed intent upon walking right through me. It was under a street lamp on the corner near my home. This time it did not disappear, and there was no doubt in my mind as to who it was. He stood there sneering at me, Steve! I couldn't move or talk as he eyed me with contempt, moved around me, and finally walked on down the street.

"All that night I tried to tell myself that it was only my imagination playing tricks. But why should it?

"For weeks I would see Nat Carson, always at night, usually in the yards or around my home. It was then that I began thinking of the testimony I had given at the Board of Investigation.

"That Nat Carson was trying to communicate with me from beyond the borders of this life seemed the only conclusion to draw. That he was accusing me of his death, there was no doubt.

"The last night before the thing really happened, I was looking at a green switch-lantern. A voice whispered in my ear: 'It's green! Green like the night we crashed that freight. Green, I tell you!'

"I turned and saw Nat Carson's face. I called out to him, but he turned and ran. From then on I could feel his presence all around me.

"You remember how you looked at me when I climbed into the cab that last night I took the run, Steve? I felt that somewhere on that train Nat Carson was hiding, waiting to confront me. Just before we pulled out I was on the verge of getting out of the cab and leaving the train.

" 'A-b-o-a-r-d!' I heard the conductor drawl. From force of habit, I started my train.

"Slow at first (I never jerked the Flyer, you know that), easy, evenly we started. I dreaded to see the lights from the station moving by. Gradually faster, yard lights, crossings, twinkling stars—green signals—open country! The Fire Flyer was on its way.

"The headlight's gleaming spear of silver shot through the darkness; wheels clicked over track joints; a crossing whistled by. She was rolling smoothly, powerfully on.

" 'Green!' I called to you from my side of the cab when I saw the signal.

" 'Green!' you answered back to me when you saw it. And from somewhere I heard that damned voice: 'It's green, green like that night we crashed into that freight!'

"I tried to control myself, tried to throw out the thoughts that were crowding into my brain. But as we rolled along, I found myself thinking: 'This *is* like the night we went through those box-cars!'

"Again I felt that cold breath upon my neck, eyes peering into my back. I turned, but no one was there—only the swaying coaches, and you down on the bridge tending your fire.

"Pulling myself together again, I peered straight ahead at the glistening track. Another green signal! 'Nat! Nat!' Each clack of steel upon steel seemed to sing out, 'Nat! Nat!'

"Again that voice, the feeling of his presence behind me. I wanted to cry out, to stop the train, and search for that voice. Conscience? I tried to tell myself that it should not bother me. Why didn't he leave me alone to run my train? I wasn't fit to highball a fast locomotive over the road with such voices, such icy breaths upon my back.

"Gladly I welcomed the lights of a station, the first station on the run. I wanted to climb down out of the cab and remain there. Something horrible, I knew, lay ahead of me on that lone stretch of track. It was impossible to confess to you how I felt. Words would not come to me, Steve.

"Miles yet ahead, miles of torture. Would daylight never come? Perhaps that might drive away the awful fear.

"Speeding again in the country, only the lights from the interlocker towers five miles apart, only an occasional farmhouse with a lonely lamp lit. Shadows on the hills, creeping shadows, and that chilling breath, that voice: 'Green! It was green!'

"This time the voice seemed louder, much more real and certain. Only by sheer force of mind could I keep my back turned to it.

"It came again! I had to look. A grim, awful-looking face was staring at me from the tender. I swear it was Nat Carson, and he spoke to me. Somehow I mumbled the words: 'Nat, where in God's name did you come from?'

" 'From the blinds maybe,' he laughed. 'Maybe I been ridin' 'em all night waitin' for this little stretch of track. Ten years since we rode side by side in the cab of an engine, ain't it? Ten years ago tonight we were ridin' along this same old road, you an' me. Only difference was that I was settin' at the throttle and you was tossin' coal into the belly of the old hog.

" 'Watchin' your signals, pal? Crack train you're pullin' now. How's it feel to be settin' there watchin' the drivers go up and down?'

"He moved toward me. I screamed because I couldn't help it. I wanted to beat out the sight of that leering face. It must have been at that time that I struck you with the shovel, Steve, although I do not remember that. All I know is that Nat Carson, who was dead, who had been dead all those years, was now climbing onto my seat in the cab. Nothing I could do would make him go away.

"I saw him climb up onto the seat and take hold of the throttle. He said, 'I'm pullin' this train tonight. She's my train again!'

"I tried to push him away. 'Nat, you're crazy!' I cried.

" 'Crazy!' He laughed as his fingers pulled the throttle out, and the locomotive bellowed with the force of steam driving its wheels on to greater speed.

" 'Yes, crazy! I've been crazy ever since that night when I saw the signal green. Then those cars . . . remember how we piled into 'em? Remember how the old 789 looked when she bit through that "crumm," plowed off the track, and dug her pilot into the dirt? Remember!'

" 'Nat, watch those signals!' I begged. 'Let me up there, Nat. Take your punishment out on me, but don't risk the lives of others.'

"The Flyer hit a sharp curve, bounced uncertainly from side to side a moment, then fled madly down the track.

" 'Ten years ago,' Nat began slowly, 'ten years ago we both saw that signal green. But you lied! You lied to make me lose my job, to lose Lucille because you wanted her, and because you hated me. You told them about my drinking. In every way you put the blame of that wreck upon my soul. I thought I could escape it when I sought death, but it was still there. And now you're going to pay for every moment of doubt and torture. Tonight we celebrate the tenth anniversary of that wreck!'

" 'What are you going to do?' I asked hoarsely.

" 'What am I going to do? He gave the throttle another pull. 'I'm going to pull the Flyer tonight. Somewhere along this road there's a red signal set against us, and we're going by it, seventy miles an hour we're going by it!'

" 'No, Nat! No! You can't do this!'

" 'Seventy, eighty miles an hour we're going by it,' he chanted. 'And then, if you live, try to tell the Board of Investigation why you went by that danger signal. Try to tell them that a man who has been dead for ten years forced you to run by that signal. Listen to them laugh as you tell your crazy story. See the doubt on their faces as I saw it when I tried to tell them the signal was green.'

"Giving the throttle one final jerk, he sent the locomotive roaring like some wounded animal charging blindly to its own destruction.

"He sang out: 'The Flyer to Hell! No signals—clear track! Red means green, and green means nothing. A dead man at the throttle, pulling the fastest train that ever polished steel. We're on our way. We're highballing it to hell!'

"On we roared, with all those passengers slumbering in the Pullmans or chatting and talking. All of them innocently riding behind an engine headed for death—pulled by death itself!

"I closed my eyes and tried to pray. I don't know how long I stood there or what went on after that. The next thing I remember was hearing the scream of the whistle, the sound of the air being set on the brakes, the flanges biting into the wheels, and the train groaning to a stop.

"When I looked we were pulled onto a siding at Elva. Far ahead on the track beside us I could hear a train coming at full speed. It was Number 93. Before we left the last station there had been no orders to pull onto the siding to let 93 go by.

"All that time, Steve, our train had been out of our hands. You were unconscious; I was helpless. Someone pulled that train onto the siding! Who, Steve, who?"

Will was shaking now. Terror, relived, had made him a trembling, sobbing wreck.

"But, Will, if the spirit of Nat Carson intended to destroy that train, why did we find it safely side-tracked to permit another train to pass us as per changed-schedule?" I tried to reason with him, for my sake as well as his own, for now even I felt that perhaps it was true.

"There is only one answer," Will replied brokenly. "Nat Carson stopped at the last station before Elva and received orders side-tracking us. No matter what revenge he had planned for me, something would not let him kill the others. He took that train onto the siding, left it standing there, and went away; his revenge was realized. Just as I had sent him for ever from the cab of an engine, so he has sent me.

"Nat Carson pulled that train. Nat Carson's dead but he pulled that train. He still comes back to remind me that I sent him to hell! He'll come tonight, and tomorrow night, and every night of my life. Oh, God, help me!"

Will broke into uncontrollable sobbing. The attendants were rushing to him. Nothing I could say would calm him.

"Nat Carson's dead! I sent him to hell. He pulled that train. He came back to pull that train. Nat Carson returned from the dead!"

As I started to go, a thought came to me; a brilliant thought it seemed at the time. Those orders, received at the last station before the side-track at Elva, had to be signed! Will must have signed them. Surely he had only gone into a trance of terror and imagined all he told me. If those orders were signed with Will's name they would prove everything to him. I would be able to recognize his signature no matter how shaken he might have been when he signed it.

I hurried to the station dispatcher, and, running through his orders, I found the date of Will's last run.

My heart stopped, then began beating wildly.

The signature on those orders was Nat Carson's!

McGill's Appointment

by Elsie Ellis

"Flighty" McGill entered the warden's office and saluted him.

"McGill," said Warden Fowles, "you seem very anxious to get a parole this week."

"Yes, sir, I am," said McGill.

"You say you have an appointment to keep outside?" said the warden.

"Yes, sir."

"Will you tell me just what sort of appointment it is?"

"It's pretty—personal, sir."

"Hm. You wanted to get out so you could get to the city tonight, didn't you?"

"Yes, sir, I did."

"Hm. Well, I have an idea what you wanted to do when you got out," said the warden.

There was a touch of malignity in his voice. He reached for the telephone.

"You're not going to get parole today, or for twenty years, McGill," he said. "You can make up your mind to that."

"I had about done so, sir," said McGill. "You see, sir, we inside hear at least a little about what happens outside."

"Take that chair," ordered the warden roughly.

The clock said 9, and the moonlight that fell for honest people lay on the floor of the office like a lake. McGill looked at it and smiled faintly. Then a spasm crossed his face; his appointment was at 9. McGill gripped the arms of his chair tightly, seemed to pray for a moment, and then the warden saw him rest his forehead on his hands.

The connection the warden wanted was made.

"Here is District Attorney Downey," said the operator.

The warden heard the voice of his friend at the other end of the hundred-mile circuit.

"Hello, Jim." he said, "this is George."

"Hello!" The voice was nervous. "What's been done?"

"About your wedding anniversary, Jim?"

279

"Yes. Did he—did he get the parole?"

"Well, it came from the board all right; McGill's conduct reports have been perfect. But I fixed it up. We have our own little system here."

"Funny, George, but I feel as if he were on his way here now. You heard about the note I got?"

"No. Not from McGill?"

"Yes. It said that he was going to keep his appointment on time, but that he was coming to me instead of to Judith. I never could understand what she could see in that fellow, George. But if we hadn't arranged his little trip she'd have married *him,* not *me.* I'm a bit afraid of him. He swore that neither jail nor hell would keep him away. The five years are up tonight at 9, and it's just 9 now. I tell you I have a feeling . . . that he's coming back."

"Nonsense, Jim, old boy. I don't know how the devil he got that letter through, but there's not a bit of a chance of his getting there to —what was it, choke you? He's sitting right here now, not ten feet from me—"

"George!" The cry was one of more than human fright. "George! What's that you say? Who's sitting there—not ten feet—"

"Why, McGill, of course—"

"George! McGill. . . ."

There was a gasping sound.

"McGill's sitting right here, Jim, as quiet as a lamb. We've been working him pretty hard. Looks as if he'd gone to sleep. . . . Hello!! Hello! Hello, there, Jim! Hello, Jim! Operator! Hello! Hello! Hello!"

There was a strange silence at the other end of the line, and then there was the sound of someone breathing hard. Something struck the telephone instrument. There was a shriek, and the wire was quiet.

The warden was working the receiver hook wildly. Someone's voice came to his ear. There was a murmuring, and someone spoke into the telephone.

"Hello!" cried the warden. "This is Warden Fowles. What's the matter with Jim—Mr. Downey?"

"Don't know exactly, sir. We just found him lying here. He seems to have been choked to death, sir. We can't find anyone—"

Fowles sprang across the room. McGill's lifeless hand held a vial from the prison hospital labeled "laudanum."

The Man on B-17

by Stephen Grendon

O. k., I'll go over it again from the beginning.

The way it happened was like this. I was bringing Number Twelve down toward Hungerford; you highball from Rexford's Crossing—that's about thirty miles back—but you have to wheel in toward B-Seventeen sort of easy on account of that curve there. The trestle is on a curve, and the gorge below, with the river running deep and swift there. That night. . . .

No, that wasn't the night it happened. I'm telling you this because it began after that—quite a while. This was a night in the beginning of winter—maybe three months ago. Late November. Snow falling. Yes, the first night of snow. O. K.—then it was the eighteenth. I don't fix the date, but if you say that was the first night of snow, then that was it.

Well, that night I wheeled around toward B-Seventeen, and I saw this fella standing there. I thought it was Bart Hinch. Bart had a shack this side of the trestle; he walked it out of Hungerford regular about that time of night. But this guy wasn't Bart; he was a slim guy, not Bart's build much, and he was just standing there on the trestle—along about the middle. The headlight caught him, and I hit the whistle hard. I couldn't stop, and I didn't see how he was going to cut out in time. But he did it somehow. Never hit a thing, just went on smooth as you please. And then there at the other end, I could have sworn I saw a woman, just standing there, waiting—probably for that guy on B-Seventeen.

Well, sir, that was the beginning.

After that, I saw him again. I saw him fairly regular. And one night coming down toward town, I was wheeling in extra-slow—oh, that was around Christmas; we'd had a deep snow, and it was blowing some, white gusts of snow over the trestle, and I thought I'd better take her slow around the curve; that's a tricky one—and there he was again, but closer to the end of the trestle; so I leaned out of the cab and I hollered at him.

"Light-footed?" I yelled at him.

He looked at me. I thought he smiled.

No, I couldn't be sure. The snow was blowing, and there he was standing beside the track at the bank—not two feet from the trestle and I said to Carroll—he was in the cab with me that night—I said, "That guy's looking for trouble," I said, "and if he keeps up that way, he'll find it. Head on."

Carroll can tell you. Carroll said, "Who is he?" and I said, "Hanged if I know!"

Very next night we saw him again, Carroll and me both. This time he was square in the middle of the trestle, and I swear before God I thought we were going to hit him. I said to Carroll, "We're going to hit him!" I said, and I was bearing down on that whistle for all she had. He was there in the middle of the bridge, and the snow falling all around him. I didn't see him till just before we hit him.

We started slowing down at the other end of the trestle. No, I didn't feel a thing. Most of the time you can tell. I didn't know what to do, but then I figured it wasn't much use stopping; the snow was that thick you couldn't see anything anyway, and if we knocked him off the trestle, why, he'd be way down somewhere in the gorge, maybe swept along in the water, God knows where. There was no use in it; we could report it in Hungerford.

No, I didn't report it. Reason was when we stopped at Hungerford, Mr. Kenyon, the conductor, came up alongside from the last coach. "You see that fellow on B-Seventeen?" he asked. I started to explain that I couldn't stop, and then I began to wonder how *he'd* seen him. I said, yes, I'd seen him, and with this and that, it came out he saw him *after* we passed over the trestle. Saw the woman, too. She was on the other side that night. Carroll's side, but Carroll wasn't looking that way. I don't know how he did it. Light-footed is hardly the word. That bridge is narrow—narrower'n most. About the only way he could do it is to hang down off the side, and I don't know how he could do it that way at night, what with the snow and the ice underneath. Be bound to slip off and go right down. But Mr. Kenyon saw him right smack in the middle of the trestle; he must have bounced right back up from wherever he went.

"What was he doing?" I asked.

"Looked to be waiting for somebody," said Mr. Kenyon.

Well, that was the way I took it from the first. Maybe the woman. But then, the woman seemed to be waiting for someone, too. It didn't figure out right; it didn't add up. After that, I wasn't quite so nervous when I saw him again.

Sure, I saw him again. About a week later, that was. He was walking the trestle. Just walking. I saw him sort of rise up just behind the marker for the bridge, they're all numbered the way they should be and the last bridge before Hungerford is that one—B-Seventeen. He rose up and he started walking toward town. If I hadn't known better I'd have sworn that he climbed up out of the gorge along the wall there.

No, he couldn't have done it. Wall's almost sheer on that side for twenty feet or so down before it gets craggy enough to climb. Ain't a man alive could do it on a night like that one, a winter night with snow and ice. It was like glass along the side of the gorge, and I don't see that there was any way it could be done. But as I said, there he was. I turned to Carroll and I said, "There he is again."

"Damn his eyes!" said Carroll. "Old Twelve's going to get him one of these nights."

Those were his very words. I couldn't argue with him about that. I figured then it was just a matter of time before we hit him. I didn't care how good he was at ducking out of the way. I've seen 'em beat that game so long, and then they get caught. A train highballing along that way ain't something anybody in his right mind's going to take and fight. You can tell by the feeling you get in one of those steam-wagons, in your hands and all through you when you're pushing her down—and Number Twelve's no hay-burner, no, nor no tramp, either; Number Twelve's an old girl you can count on, a real battleship—and you get the feeling she wouldn't like it when a guy keeps daring her, and sooner or later she'd take him.

Well, it was the same that night. Saw him on the trestle, and then somehow he was on the other side; he must have run pretty fast. I opened the window and leaned out and hollered at him.

"Don't you believe in signs?" I hollered, meaning he should take notice where it says at both ends of B-Seventeen that trespassing is forbidden and so on. He didn't pay me no more attention than as if I'd been the wind. But that time I saw his face. Young fellow. Not like Bart at all. Had on a tassel-cap and a mackinaw. Looked fair—light-haired. Couldn't have weighed more'n a hundred seventy-five. O. K., I thought, I'll turn you in.

So I did. I waited till we hit Elroy and gave his description to the cinder-bull there, and the cinder-bull went out—it was clear that night, with a moon showing, and not cold; he went out right away. Number Twelve's the night owl through Hungerford and Elroy. He went out that night and the next night and the next. That guy was on the trestle every night. But the cinder-bull didn't see hide nor hair of him. Of the woman, either. And he was there at least two out of those three times. Because Carroll saw her once, and I saw her the second time, and we probably just missed her the other time. She was probably there, all right, just like the other times. So the cinder-bull gave up. He wouldn't argue. "I'm the Casey Jones," I said, "and Carroll's an old rawhider, and the ticket snatcher, Mr. Kenyon—all three of us saw him," I said. But I might as well have talked to the wind. So I ran in my report to the Super and let it go at that.

We kept on seeing him and the woman, sometimes regular, sometimes after a week or so when we didn't see either one. It went that way all through the winter. It went on that way until that night early this month, first week in March, when it happened—and since then neither of us has seen a thing, not a solitary thing.

Well, just like I said before, we bore down on B-Seventeen that night with the snow blowing thick as smoke all around us. Carroll saw him first—and he let out a yell. "There he is again!" And I looked, and sure enough—there he was, a-kneeling in the middle of the trestle. Kneeling—yes, sir! Right smack in the middle, and I knew we were going to get him, I knew the old girl was going to take and pitch him off into the gorge. I wanted to close my eyes, but I couldn't. And a good thing, maybe, I couldn't.

"Three of 'em!" Carroll hollered out.

And sure enough, there was three. That guy in the tassel-cap and the mackinaw was at this end, and the woman was at the other end. The headlight showed 'em all three just as plain. The guy in the mackinaw was braced, seemed like, to keep anyone coming from the bridge; and the woman on the other end. She looked—well, no, I wouldn't say *mean*, just *grim*—and he looked *terrible*, like as if he was angry and cold and set to kill. The one in the middle—that one—well, we saw him before we hit him, and we knew him; that one was Bart Hinch.

We hit him. There's no more to say about that. He was there and we couldn't stop, and whatfore in God's name he was kneeling there in the middle of the trestle, praying or whatever it was he was doing, nobody'll ever know. It wasn't our fault; we couldn't throw Number Twelve off the trestle just to save him. So we hit him, and I felt it when the old girl knocked him off into the gorge, and it near made me sick to know we'd done it.

We stopped at Hungerford. That was two miles away, maybe a little better. You could see where we hit him. There was nothing we could do but report it, and let them go back, come daylight, to find what they could.

284

Sure, I'd talked with Bart Hinch a good many times.

No, never heard him say anything about somebody waiting for him on B-Seventeen. I don't know what he said in his cups in town, and he never said anything to me about hating to walk home at night. Could be that's how come he didn't go out much after dark, but me—I wouldn't know.

No, I never knew Tod Benning. All I know about him is that he ran off somewhere before he was to marry Lois Malone and that it killed her or she killed herself or something like that. Never heard that Bart owed him money and that he set out to collect it and never came back. Talk's cheap.

What did it look like on the trestle that night? Well, it looked to me as if the fella in the mackinaw was holding down one end of the bridge and the woman was holding down the other so's Bart couldn't get off either way. I don't care how it sounds—you asked me, and I'm telling you. Carroll'll tell you the same thing. That's the way it looked. Sure, it was snowing. Sure, I might be mistaken. But the old girl's light cut right through that snow, and I saw those faces—and Bart Hinch's was mortal afraid, and it didn't look like he was seeing Number Twelve, either, but just those two, that fella in the mackinaw and the woman.

No, sir, we hit only once, only one thing. That was Bart Hinch. I saw it. I saw how the old girl just tossed him out of the way, out into the gorge. Then he was gone into the blackness and the snow underneath. I felt it where I sat. So did Carroll. He'll tell you the same. Only once.

How do I account for their being two bodies down there? I don't account for it. Bart was killed by Number Twelve. I said that. I saw it happen. The other one, the one you say is Tod Benning, you said yourself was dead a long time, two years or so, maybe more. I've been in Number Twelve seven years, and this is the first time we ever hit a man. Anyway, they say there's no bones broken—and the old girl would have broken him up some. So maybe he fell or was flung off the trestle—I can't say.

Yes, I can identify the man on B-Seventeen if you show him to me. Or his picture. The woman, too. It'll be the same as last time. You put those pictures down in front of me, and it'll be the same.

The man is number five, there, and the woman's number thirteen.

No mistake. At least, *I'm* not making the mistake, and Carroll's not making it. So it must be yours. If the woman's picture is one of Lois Malone—well, the woman on the trestle that night looked enough like her to be her twin sister, even if she never had one. But you don't fool me on that man, number five there. I saw him as plain as I see you, more than once. That's the man. And if you say that's a picture of Tod Benning, then that body you drug up out of the river isn't Tod Benning's no matter what the doctor and the dentist have to say, because that's the man Carroll and Mr. Kenyon and I saw on B-Seventeen.

That's the way it happened. Just like I've been telling you. Beginning with that night I was bringing Number Twelve around toward Hungerford and I saw this fella standing there on B-Seventeen.

𝔐𝔞𝔫𝔡𝔬𝔩𝔦𝔫

by Will Charles Oursler

"No, I can not do it. I break my contract, I know. But music is gone from me; I can no longer compose."

"But you can't do this to me, Rand. We're old friends. I've promised to have at least one piece by you in our next production. You can't let me down."

"I'm sorry, Wolfson. We are old friends, but I can't do the impossible. And it is impossible for me to compose anything now that sounds like music. I'm through."

"Perhaps you'll change your mind."

After Wolfson was gone, Gordon Rand leaned back in his chair, and in silence watched the butler clear the table. A quiet filled the room. Drunken shadows from the candle danced silently on the panelled walls; the corners were lost in leaden gloom.

"Squires!"

"Yes, sir."

"I'm going to sleep tonight in the bedroom."

"In the bedroom, sir? You mean the room that was—"

"The room I shared with my wife. I know it hasn't been used since —since last year. But to arrange the place won't take you long. I guess I'm just sentimental, Squires, but you see, it was a year ago tonight that my wife died. Nothing but sentiment, Squires."

"I know. I didn't remind you, sir. One doesn't always wish to be reminded of such things, if you'll pardon my saying so. Is there anything else?"

"Oh, yes, Squires. You remember my wife's mandolin?"

"Yes, sir. It's in its case, in a corner of the library."

"Now look. First of all, pack my suitcase for my trip tomorrow. Then bring the suitcase and mandolin to the bedroom. I'm taking both with me, and I must be all set to leave. And bring some wood to the bedroom, too; I may make a fire later."

"Very good, sir. Good-night, sir."

Alone, Mr. Rand rose from the table, walked to the mantel, and switched on a light. The shadowed portrait above him seemed to come to life. Lustrous eyes of a beautiful woman looked gravely down at him; one might almost have thought the soft lips were about to speak.

"It won't be long now, dear—not long." His words broke the stillness. "I'm coming to join you."

He could bear it no longer. One whole year of living without her; one wretched year of hell! The world needed him? Needed a composer whose music was dead, whose notes had become jarring and discordant? He had been a great composer once, perhaps; that time was over. He would never write music again; the world would be better off without him.

Tomorrow, he was going to Roaring Falls, for a rest and a change of scene. He laughed mirthlessly. At least, it would be a change; one could say no more. In the swirling torrent of the falls he would find swift and sure death; beyond that, he did not care.

"Tomorrow, Alice. Tomorrow."

The bedroom was a book, a diary of past hours; a book which Gordon Rand alone could read. Trivial, forgotten scenes re-enacted themselves before him. How many times he had built a fire for the two of them! He stood before the struggling flame and poked at the smoldering logs. Now he had the blaze crackling arrogantly in the grate; methodically, he put the smoking fire-irons back on their stand, and turned around, half expecting to find her there, her kind eyes upon him. How vain the hope!

He sat long before the fire; dreaming, wishing, wondering. Fate had taken from him the only thing in life that counted; there was no use going on. Music, too, was gone from his soul. It had been there when he had written their piece; her piece. The melody ran through his mind now, tormentingly. He had better go to bed.

He undressed slowly. By the time he finished his toilet, the red embers glowed only dully, sullenly, in the grate. The room was nearly dark. He opened the window wide and went to bed. Ordinarily he would have lain awake for some time; his mind was upset and excited. But it had been a long day, and his body needed rest. He was asleep in a few minutes. Outside, the wind howled wildly through the trees.

Music! He fought his way back to consciousness, and opened his eyes. The room was pitch-black. He had only been dreaming, of course. Dreaming that she played for him! The mandolin had sounded so real. Their piece!

A soft tinkle reached him, as if someone were really playing the instrument. What was that? His senses could not deceive him now; he was awake. Someone must be there; some madman, strumming tunelessly on the mandolin. He could hear the notes clearly now. This was real. Someone was in the room. Quickly he sprang from his bed, and switched on the lights.

The room was empty.

He shut the window, put on his dressing-robe, and went to examine the mandolin. It was safe in its case. Impossible! Yet no one could have put it away and escaped, without a sound.

He put out the light, opened the window and returned to bed. Wide awake now, he listened carefully. There it was, those notes. Music! Music from a mandolin shut in its case! A cold shiver ran through him, a shiver of delight, of wonder. It *was* real, and it could mean one thing only; a sign from her.

"I understand now." His voice was low, barely audible.

Squires woke him in the morning with breakfast.

"Good morning, sir. Mr. Wolfson is waiting to see you. You had better hurry, sir, or you'll miss the train."

"I'm not going to take it, Squires. Bring Mr. Wolfson up here; he won't mind if I'm still in bed. I want to talk to him."

The butler ushered Mr. Wolfson in, and stood at attention at the foot of the bed.

"Sit down, Wolfson."

"Well, how do you feel about it today?"

"I've changed my mind."

"Good! Wonderful! Grand! My Lord, what did it?"

"You're an old friend, Wolfson, and I'll tell you. I know you won't let it get out.—No, stay here, Squires. You've known me since I was a child. I want you to hear this, too."

He paused.

"I was going to commit suicide today, Wolfson. I was going to kill myself. Fed up with everything. I wanted something of my wife's near me when I died; I was taking her mandolin. But last night, in this room, I had a sign. Someone played that mandolin. I didn't dream it; I heard it with my own ears. Yet no one was here, and the instrument was in its case. I tell you, it was a voice from the beyond. That's what changed my mind, Wolfson."

"Sure, old man." The producer smiled indulgently. "I won't speak of it to anyone. Now, when are you going to start on my work?"

"Today—at once!"

He leapt from bed, threw on his robe, and hurried downstairs. Mr. Wolfson trailed after him.

Squires stayed behind. He opened the windows to air the place, and began to make the bed.

Suddenly he stopped. That tinkle! it was what Mr. Rand must have heard. But this came from the fireplace. In a second he realized; it was the pokers, the tongs, swinging in the wind from the window.

"But I shan't mention it to Mr. Rand," said Squires.

Downstairs, someone was at the piano. The butler heard swelling, rapturous music that filled the morning with its beauty.

The Metronome

by August W. Derleth

As she lay in bed, with the pleasant, concealing darkness all around her, her lips were half parted in a smile that was the only expression of her relief that the funeral was over at last. And no one had suspected that she and the boy had not fallen into the river accidentally, no one had guessed that she *could* have saved her step-child if she had wanted to. "Oh, poor Mrs. Farwell, how terrible she must feel!" She could hear their words ringing faint and far away in the close-pressing darkness of the night.

What remorse she had fleetingly felt when at last the child had gone down, when he had disappeared beneath the surface of the water for the last time, and when she herself lay exhausted on the shore, had

289

long since passed from her. She had ceased to think how she could have done it—she had even convinced herself that the river bank had caved in accidentally, that she had forgotten how weak it was there, and how deep the water below, and how swift the current.

In the next room her husband moved. He had suspected nothing. "Now I have only you," he had said to her, sorrow in the worn lines of his face. It had been difficult for her those first few days, but the definite consignment of Jimmy's body to the grave had lessened and finally dissipated the faint doubts that haunted her.

Still, thinking soberly, it was difficult for her to conceive how she could have done it. It was certainly impulsive, but irritation at the boy and hatred because of his resemblance to his mother had fostered her desire. And that metronome! At ten years a boy ought to have forgotten such childish things as a metronome. If he had played the piano and needed it to keep time—that might have been a different thing. But as it was, no, no—too much. Her nerves couldn't have stood it another day. And when she had hidden the metronome, how he had enraged her by singing that absurd little ditty which he had heard Walter Damrosch sing in explanation of the nickname *Metronome Symphony* for Beethoven's *Eighth* on one of the Friday morning children's hour programs! The words of it, those absurdly childish words which Beethoven had sent to the inventor of the metronome, ran through her mind, ringing irritatingly in the chambers of her memory.

> How d'you do,
> How d'you do,
> How d'you do,
> My dear, my dear
> Mis-ter Mel-zo!

Or something like that. She could not be sure of them. They rang insistently in her memory to the second movement of the symphony, beating like the metronome, tick-tick, tick-tick, endlessly. The metronome and the song had after all crystallized her feeling for the son of Farwell's first wife.

She thrust the song from her memory.

Then abruptly she began to wonder where she had hidden the metronome. It was rather a pretty thing, quite modern, with a heavy silver base, and a little hammer on a grooved steel rod extending upward against the background of a curved triangle of silver. She had not yielded to her first impulse to destroy it because she had thought that after the boy was gone it would make a lovely ornament, even though it had belonged to Jimmy's mother. For a moment she thought of Margot, who ought to be glad that she had sent Jimmy to his mother —provided there was a place beyond. She remembered that Margot had believed.

Could she have put the thing on one of the shelves in her closet? Perhaps. It was odd that she could not remember something which still stood out as one of her most important acts in the few days immediately preceding Jimmy's drowning. She lay thinking about it, thinking how attractive it would look on the grand piano, just that single ornament, silver against the piano's brownish black.

And then suddenly the ticking of the metronome broke into her ruminations. How odd, she thought, that it should sound just now, while her thoughts dwelt upon it! The sound came quite clearly, tick-tick, tick-tick, tick-tick. But when she tried to ascertain its direction, she could not do so. It seemed to swell, growing louder, and fading away again, which was most unusual. She reflected that she had never known it to do that before in all the time that Jimmy had plagued her with its ticking. She became more alert, listening more intently.

Abruptly she thought of something that sent an arresting thrill coursing through her. For a moment she held her breath, suspended her faculties. Didn't she hide the metronome after Jimmy had given it to her to wind? Unless her memory failed her, she did. Then it could not now be ticking, for it had been run down, and it had not been wound up again. For a fleeting moment she wondered whether Henry had found it and wound it for a joke and set it going at this hour. She glanced at her wristwatch. A quarter of one. It required a far stretch of the imagination to believe Henry capable of such a joke. More likely he would confront her with his find and say, "Look here, I thought you told me Jimmy'd lost this, and here I find it on your shelf; he couldn't possibly have reached there." The thought reminded her that she had hidden it somewhere above Jimmy's reach.

She listened.

Tick-tick, tick-tick, tick-tick. . . .

Did Henry hear that? she wondered. Probably not. He slept quite soundly always.

After a moment of hesitation, she got up, groped about in the dark for her electric candle, and went to the closet. She opened the door, thrust her hand and the candle into the yawning maw of dark, and listened. No, the metronome was not there. Yet she could not help pulling one or two hat-boxes aside to be sure. She almost always hid things there.

* * *

She withdrew from the closet and stood leaning against its closed door, her brow marred by a frown of irritation. Good heaven! was she destined to hear that infernal ticking even after Jimmy's death? She moved resolutely to the door of her room.

But suddenly a new sound struck into her consciousness.

Someone was walking about beyond the door somewhere, padding about on soft, muffled feet!

Her first thought was naturally enough of Henry, but even as the thought occurred to her she heard his bed creak. She wanted to imagine that for some reason the maid or the cook had returned to the house, but she could not accept the absurdity of the thought of their returning for anything at one o'clock in the morning. And burglars were out of the question.

Her hand hesitated on the knob. Then she opened the door almost angrily and looked into the hall, holding the electric candle high above her. There was nothing there. She recognized instantly that she would have preferred to see someone there. How too absurd! she thought, apprehensively irritated.

At the same moment she heard the footsteps again, slight and far away now, sounding faintly from downstairs. The ticking of the metronome had become more insistent; so loud it was that for a frantic instant she was afraid it might wake Henry.

And then came a sound that flooded her being with icy terror, the sound of a little boy's voice singing in a far place,

> How d'you do,
> How d'you do,
> How d'you do,
> My dear, my dear
> Mis-ter Mel-zo!

She fell back against the door-jamb, and clung there with her free hand. Her mind was in turmoil. But in a moment the voice faded and died away, and the ticking of the metronome sounded louder than ever. She felt only relief as she heard its sound superseding that other.

She stood for a few moments pulling herself together. Then she tightened her fingers about the electric candle and went slowly along the corridor, pressing herself close to the wall. As she approached the top of the stairs she clasped her other hand about the small tube of light, so that whatever was below might not see. She descended the stairs, apprehensive lest they creak and betray her presence.

* * *

292

There was nothing in the hall below, but there was a sound from the library. Gently she pushed the door open, and the ticking of the metronome welled out and engulfed her. She did not at once see beyond the threshold. Only after she had stepped into the room did her eyes catch sight of the vague little shadow against the opposite wall, an indistinct thing wandering along the line of the wall, peering behind furniture, looking upward at the bookcases, reaching phantom hands into corners—Jimmy, looking for his metronome!

She stood immobile, her very breath held within her by some impending horror. Jimmy, dead Jimmy, whom she had seen buried that morning—only the strength of her will saved her from pitching forward in a faint.

On came the spectral child. Toward her it came, and past her it went, searching, prying into every nook where the metronome might be hidden. Around again and again.

With a great effort she found her voice. "Go away," she whispered harshly. "Oh, go away."

But the child did not hear. It continued its phantom quest, futilely covering the same ground it had already covered many times. And the insistent tick-tick, tick-tick of the metronome continued to sound like the strokes of a hammer in the oppressive night-haunted room.

Her hand slipped nervelessly from the tube of light just as the child passed her. She saw its face, turned up toward her, its eyes, usually so kind, now malevolent, its mouth petulant and angry, its little hands clenched.

Frantically she turned to escape, but the door would not open.

After three futile attempts to wrench it open, she looked for some obstacle to its movement. The child was at her side, holding its hand lightly against the door, its touch enough to keep the door immovable. She tried once again. The knob turned in her hand, as before, but the door refused to budge. The expression on the child's face had become so malignant that she dropped the electric candle in sudden fright and fled toward the window directly opposite the door.

But the child was there before her.

She tried to raise the window, slipping the lock with her free hand. It would not move. Even before she looked, she felt the child's hand holding down the window. There it was, vaguely white, transparent, leaning lightly against the glass.

It was the same with the only other window the room contained. When she tried to raise her hand to break the glass, she found that the child had only to stand before the window and her hand could not even penetrate through the air to the glass.

Then she turned and slipped into the dark corner behind the grand piano, sobbing in terror.

Presently the child was at her side. She felt it emanating a ghastly cold that penetrated her thin night-clothes.

"Go away, go away," she sobbed.

She felt the child's face pressing close to her, its eyes seeking hers, its eyes accusing her, its phantom fingers reaching out to touch her.

With a wild cry of terror, she fled. Once more she made for the door, but the child was there before her hand fell upon the knob. And she knew without turning the knob that her effort was in vain. Then she tried to snap on the light, but the same influence that had prevented her from breaking the window was again at work.

Once more she sought the comparative safety of a dark corner, and again the child found her out and nuzzled close to her, like an animal seeking warmth.

Then suddenly the gates of her mind pressed inward and collapsed, and she felt a deeper, more maddening fear invading her reason. She began to beat at the enclosed walls with her clenched fists. Then she found her voice and screamed to release the malefic horror that hemmed her in.

The last thing she knew was the pulling of the child's spectral hands at her waist. Then she collapsed in a heap against the wall. Something struck her a sharp blow against the temple, and at the same instant the clammy frigidity of the child's phantom body pressed down upon her face. The waiting darkness advanced and engulfed her.

Henry Farwell found his wife lying against the wall near the grand piano. He came to his knees at her side. He had had enough medical training to suspect that his wife had been suffocated by something wet, for there was still a dampness on her features. He did not understand the strong smell of the river in the room. Looking upward, he saw an enormous landscape painting hanging awry above her body, but certainly this could not have made the wound in her temple.

Then abruptly he saw what had struck his wife in falling from behind the landscape, where it had been hidden. It was the metronome.

Miss Prue

by Fred Chappell

Miss Prue had received news that her faithful suitor, Mr. M., had died a suicide, but still she waited in full confidence for his knock. He had taken a drug, they said. It would certainly be in his character to float off to eternity in a numb sleep. Suicide was very naughty, of course, but she had to admire his taste; no loud noises or bad smells, no ugly ropes or machines. He had just drifted away, as their conversation had so languidly drifted every Thursday afternoon for the past twenty years.

Was all in good order for their accustomed tea? The rug was swept, the furniture dusted and oiled, the windows sparkling. Her gray-barred emasculated cat, Wisdom, lay fat and sleeping on the hearth where the low fire licked. The doilies were in place, starched stiff. She had made beaten biscuits, and there were boiled ham and strawberry preserves. She took pride in meticulous order, decorous behavior. If anything got upset, if her plans went awry, what might happen? But nothing ever went wrong; she was too careful. Mr. M. would be pleased, as he always was.

One. Two. Three.

There they were, his habitual raps. They sounded muffled, weak, in the dim and motionless air of her drawing room. Before answering she examined herself in the heavy gilt-framed mirror that hung above the dark mahogany table. Her hair was gray now, but she had applied a modicum of color to her cheeks. The high-necked dress, color of a fallen oak leaf, set her face off, she thought, sufficiently.

She opened, and it was Mr. M. indeed, but changed. Death had transfigured this gentle man; he was thinner than ever, and pale, pale as a cloud, pale as a glass curtain. His eyes were like cinders in the deep sockets. He seemed to belong more to the cool gray autumn wind than to the world of animal flesh.

"Punctual as usual," she said brightly. "Do come in, Mr. M. May I take your coat?"

She waited as he struggled wearily out of the long, weighty overcoat. She didn't help, not wanting to touch the dead man. Never had she touched him when alive. She took the coat carefully when he offered it and hung it with his black muffler in the closet.

"Won't you sit in the fireside chair?" she asked. "It's a raw, cold day. The tea will be ready soon, and that should warm you."

"Thank you," he said. His voice was windblown ash in a desert land.

She went into her gleaming little kitchen and set the pot off the heat and spooned in the Earl Grey and covered the pot with a blue knit cozy. She took it into the drawing room and placed it on the hearth, as company for Wisdom. Then they sat and waited for it to brew.

She tried not to stare. "Well, here you are," she said.

"Yes."

"I knew you'd come, no matter what. It's Thursday afternoon."

It seemed to require great effort for him to turn his eyes toward her. "It is the last time, Miss Prue."

She clucked her tongue. "Now don't be downhearted, Mr. M. Into every life some rain must fall. We have to bear up, you know."

"But I died, Miss Prue. I ought really to be in my grave, awaiting judgment."

"Yet you came to call on me. It's so like you, so thoughtful."

"No," he said. "It isn't manners. Not exactly."

"Let us take our tea," she said. She poured two steaming leafy cups. He supported his saucered cup with one hand on his bony knee. When she brought her proud tray of food, he declined it with an exhausted wave of his hand.

What a pity, she thought. Poor man. "But you did come to call," she said. "For see, here you are."

"I had to ask a question."

"What do you wish to ask?"

"Was there something, was there anything, I could have said that—"

"That what? Please speak clearly, Mr. M."

"That would have made it different between us?"

"How can you desire it to be different? We have been a fixed pair these last twenty years."

"We might have been closer," he said, and what a world of cold this latter word implied.

"How closer? How steadier? Few married couples are as close and steady as we have been."

"Might we not have gotten married?"

She flicked her hand at the question as if it were a tedious housefly.

"That is not in our personalities, I think. We are a different sort, you and I."

"So there was nothing I might have done?"

"Done? Oh yes, done. You might have swept me off my feet, Mr. M. You might have carried me away like an impetuous bandit or a dashing pirate."

His eyes dropped. But maybe he was not looking at the hooked rug, but through the crust of the earth to the shoals of mineral and the molten seas of fire. "That was not my style," he said at last.

"Oh no." She crowed her agreement. "Not *our* style. Not at all. We are well fitted, the two of us."

"That was the tragedy," he said.

"A melodramatic word, *tragedy*. Haven't we enjoyed our company together? Haven't we had our Thursdays, our tea and our talk?"

"There are other things." His voice was like the sound of wind in a ragged thornbush. "I know now that there are other things, though I don't quite know what they are."

"Then how do you know there are other things?"

"If there were not, I would be content in my death. I would be a long way from here, Miss Prue."

She rose abruptly. "You haven't touched your tea, and it is simply delicious. I shall take another cup, and some ham and preserves. I took the trouble, Mr. M., of beating biscuits."

Slowly he turned his head aside. "I'm sorry."

"Now now, don't fret." She poured her tea and returned to her seat. "I believe that you never learned to appreciate some very important things. We were never vulgar, but didn't you find our delicacy with one another actually . . . well, sensual? There were times when we positively *swilled* nuance. Was that lost upon you?"

"Lost?" It was the cry of the Arctic moon. "Everything is lost. There is nothing."

"Nonsense," she said firmly. "You have allowed this matter of your health to upset you unduly. I am going to brew a fresh pot, and you are to have some and see if it doesn't brace you up. I won't take no for an answer, Mr. M." When she lifted the pot from the hearth, Wisdom opened one yellow eye, then returned to his dream of Stilton cheese and scarab beetles.

In the kitchen she made tea afresh, humming an old sentimental song. She had seen him this way before, disheartened over one or another. But she'd brought him around. What the hapless man needed was a good talking-to, a pepping-up to stiffen his backbone. Men were

297

so easily discouraged. It was a bad thing, to let oneself get down like that, and something she never allowed herself.

When the kettle whistled, she thought for a moment it wailed her name. *Miss Prue Prue Prue.* She pursed her lips, set the kettle off.

When she returned to the drawing room, it was as still as an engraving in an old album. His cup and saucer were on the marble-topped coffee table, but Mr. M. was absent. She whispered, "Where are you?"

She looked in the closet. His overcoat and muffler were not there. "Oh, Mr. M.," she said.

The cat opened his eyes and closed them again.

She looked out the front door. The light was gray, the air cold. "I forgot to tell you about Wisdom," she said. "Last week he had a strange infection, but I'm sure he's all right now."

Mr. M. was not there; no one was there. A big crow settled in the top of the oak by her flagstone walk. It gave her one cool and careless regard, then flew off across the valley and over the mountain.

Monsieur De Guise

by Perley Poore Sheehan

That any one should live in the center of Cedar Swamp was in itself so singular as to set all sorts of queer ideas to running through my head.

A more sinister morass I had never seen. It was as beautiful and deadly as one of its own red mocassins, as treacherous and fascinating.

It was a tangle of cypress and cedar almost thirty miles square, most of it under water—a maze of jungle-covered islands and black bayous. There were alligators and panthers, bear and wild pig. There were groans and grunts and queer cries at night, and silence, dead silence by day.

That was Cedar Swamp as I knew it after a week of solitary hunting there. I no longer missed the sun. My eyes had become used to the perpetual twilight. My nerves no longer bothered me when I stepped into opaque water, or watched a section of gliding snake. But the silence was getting to be more than I could bear. It was too uncanny.

And now, just after I had noticed it, and wondered at it for the hundredth time, I heard a voice. It was low and clear—that of a woman who sings alto. There were four or five notes like the fragment of a strange song. And then, before I had recovered from the shock of it, there was silence again.

I was up to my knees in water at the time, wading a narrow branch between two islands. I must have stood there for a full minute waiting for the voice to resume, but the silence closed in on me deeper than ever. With a little shiver creeping over one part of my body after another, I stole ashore.

The island was one of the highest I had yet encountered. I had not taken a dozen steps up through the dank growth of its shelving shore before I found a deeply worn path.

This, I could see, ran down to the water-front on one direction, where I caught a glimpse of a boat-house masked by trees. I turned and followed the path in the other direction up a gentle slope.

As I advanced, the jungle around me thinned out and became almost park-like. There were open stretches of meadow and clumps of trees, suggesting a garden. But I was so intent on discovering the owner of the voice that the wonder of this did not at first impress me. I had, moreover, an eery, uneasy sensation of being watched.

I walked slowly. I carried my gun with affected carelessness. I looked around me as though I were a mere tourist dropped in to see the sights.

I had thus covered, perhaps, a quarter of a mile, when the path turned into an avenue of cabbage-palmetto, at the further end of which I saw a house.

It was large and white with a pillared porch, such as they used to build before the war. It was shaded by a magnificent grove of live-oak trees. There were beds of geranium and roses in front, and clusters of crepe-myrtle and flowering oleander on a well-clipped lawn.

It all gave an impression of infinite care, of painstaking up-keep, of neatness and wealth, yet, there was not a soul in sight. Not a servant was there. No dog barked, I saw no horses, no chickens, no pigeons, nor sheep; no familiar animate emblem whatever of the prosperous farm.

I stood in the presence of this silent and lonely magnificence with a feeling that was not exactly fear, but rather stupefaction. For a moment I was persuaded that I had emerged from the great swamp into some unknown plantation of its littoral.

But a moment was enough to convince me that this could not be. I was, without the slightest doubt, almost at the exact center of the morass. I was too familiar with its circumference and general contour to be wrong as to that. For a dozen miles at least, in every direction, Cedar Swamp surrounded this island of mystery with its own mysterious forests and bayous.

Once again I was acutely aware of being stared at. Almost at the same instant a man's voice addressed me from behind my back.

"Monsieur," it asked, "why do you hesitate?"

I might as well confess it right away—I believe in ghosts. I have seen too many things in my life that were not to be explained by the commonly accepted laws of nature. I have lived too much among the half-civilized and learned too much of their odd wisdom to recognize any hard and fast definition of what is real and what is not.

From the moment I heard that bit of song in the swamp, I felt that I was passing from the commonplace into the weird. My succeeding impressions had confirmed this feeling.

And now, when I heard the voice behind me: "Monsieur, why do you hesitate?"—I was not sure that it was the voice of a human being at all. I turned slowly, my mind telling me that I should see no one.

It was with a distinct feeling of relief, therefore, that I saw a small, pale, well-dressed old man smiling at me as though he had read my secret thoughts.

His face was cleanly shaven and bloodless. His head, partly covered by a black velvet skull-cap, was extremely large. His snow-white hair was silky and long. His eyes, which were deeply sunken, were large and dark. His appearance, as well as the question which he had just put to me suggested the foreigner. He was not alone un-American; he appeared to be of another century, as well.

I said something about intruding. He made a brusk gesture, almost of impatience, and, telling me to follow him, started for the house.

It was as though I was an expected guest. Only the absence of servants maintained that feeling of the bizarre, which never left me.

The interior of the house was in keeping with its outward appearance—sumptuous and immaculate. My host led me to the door of a vast chamber on the first floor, motioned me to enter, and, standing at the door, said:

"Monsieur, luncheon will be served when you reappear. Pray, make yourself at home."

Then he left me.

Two details of this room impressed me: the superlative richness of the toilet articles, all of which were engraved with a coat-of-arms, and the portrait of a woman, by Largilliére. All women were beautiful to Largilliére, but in the present instance he had surpassed himself.

300

The gentle, aristocratic face, with its tender, lustrous eyes, was the most alluring thing I had ever seen. At the bottom of the massive frame was the inscription: *"Anne-Marie, Duchesse de Guise. Anno 1733."*

I was still marveling at the miracle which had brought such an apparition to the heart of an American swamp when I heard a light step in the hallway, and I knew that my host was awaiting me.

The luncheon, which was served cold in a splendid dining-room, had been laid for two. I wondered at this, for still no servant appeared, and surely I could not have been expected. And my host added to my mystification rather than lessened it when he said: "Monsieur, I offer you the place usually reserved for my wife."

Apart from this simple statement, the meal was completed in silence. Now and then I thought I surprised him, nodding gravely, as though someone else were present.

I suspected him several times of speaking in an undertone. But, my mind was so preoccupied with the inexplicable happenings of the preceding hour that I was not in a condition to attack fresh mysteries now.

He scarcely touched his food. Indeed, his presence there seemed to be more in the nature of an act of courtesy than for the purpose of taking nourishment. As soon as I had finished he arose and invited me to follow him.

Across the hall was a music-room, with high French windows, opening on the porch. He paused at one of these windows now and plucked the flower from a potted heliotrope. The perfume of it seemed to stimulate him strangely. He at once became more animated. A slight trace of color mounted to his waxen cheeks. Turning to me, abruptly, he remarked:

"I mentioned just now my wife. Perhaps you noticed her portrait?"

As he spoke, a faint breath of the heliotrope came to me, and with it, by one of those odd associations of ideas, the portrait by Largilliére. I saw again the gentle face and the lustrous eyes, but the date—1733. Surely, this was not the portrait he referred to.

But he had seen the perplexity in my face, and he broke out in French: *"Oui, oui; c'est moi, monsieur de Guise."* And then, in English: "It was the portrait of my wife you saw, *madame la duchesse par monsieur Largilliere.*"

"But then, *madame,* your wife," I stammered, "is dead."

He was still smelling the heliotrope. He looked up at me with his somber eyes for a moment as though he had failed to grasp my meaning. Then he said:

"No, no. There is no such thing as death—only life. For, what is life?—the smile, the perfume, the voice. Ah, the voice! Will you hear her sing?"

For a brief instant my head turned giddily. The world I had always known, the world of tragedies, of sorrows, of physical joys and pains, the world of life and death, in short, was whirling away from beneath my feet.

And I began to recall certain old stories I had heard about the visible servants of the invisible, the earthly agents of the unearthly. Such things have been known to exist.

M. de Guise was walking up and down the room murmuring to himself in French. I could catch an occasional word of endearment. Once I saw him distinctly press the heliotrope to his lips. He had forgotten my presence, apparently. He was in the company of some one whom he alone could see. And then he seated himself at the piano.

I had a presentiment of what was coming. I dropped into a chair and closed my eyes.

Again the heliotrope perfumed the air around me. I saw the smooth brow, the sympathetic eyes, the magic smile of the Duchesse de Guise, and then a voice—that voice I had heard in the swamp—began to sing, so soft, so sweet, that a little spasm twitched at my throat and a chill crept down my back.

It was a love-song, such as they sang centuries ago. I know little French, but it told of love in life and death—*"Moi, je t'ai, vive et morte, incessament aimée."*

And when I opened my eyes again, all that I saw was the shrivelled black figure of Monsieur de Guise, his silvered head thrown back with the air of one who has seen a vision.

Subconsciously I had heard something else while listening to the song. It was the swift, muffled throb of an approaching motor-boat. M. de Guise had heard it, too, for now he left the piano and approached the window. Presently, I could see a dozen negroes approaching along the avenue of palms. They seemed strangely silent for their race.

"These are my people," said my host. "Once a week I send them to the village. They will carry you away."

The afternoon was far advanced when I bade M. de Guise farewell. As I looked back for the last time the sunset was rapidly dissolving the great white house and its gardens in a golden haze. His figure on the porch was all that linked it to the world of man.

Late that night I was landed at a corner of Cedar Swamp, adjacent to my home. My black boatman, who had spoken never a word immediately backed his barge away into the darkness, leaving me there alone.

And, although I have since made several efforts to repeat my visit to M. de Guise, I have never been successful. Once, indeed, I found again what I believed to be his island, but it was covered entirely with a dense, forbidding jungle. Which will doubtless discredit this story, as it has caused even me to reflect.

But grant that the story is true, and that M. de Guise was merely mad. Why, then in a certain event, which I need not mention, may God send me madness, too!

Mordecai's Pipe

by A. V. Milyer

"January 7—McNally sent the pipe today. I found it waiting when I returned home from the office this evening. Oh, it's quite an ordinary-looking pipe; a four-inch stem, badly chewed around the mouthpiece, and a large, round bowl, worn smooth and dark from constant handling. One would never think to look at it that it had had such a gruesome past.

"But McNally swears that it was the one cherished possession of old Peter Mordecai, the fellow they executed at the state prison last week. And what a malevolent old devil *he* must have been! Seems that all the other prisoners shunned him as they would a plague—but then who wouldn't shun a man who's killed four children and used their bodies for God-only-knows what crazy rites? Not that the absence of fellowship worried Mordecai, though; for they say that he even refused to speak to guards, silencing their attempts with that wolfish snarl that the newspapers made so much of.

"Oh, how plainly I can see him—smoking his pipe as he grins over the mangled bodies of his victims; smoking it throughout the endless days at the death-house; even smoking it as he takes that last, brief walk to the gallows. I can see him on the very scaffold, shoving his pipe at McNally with a muttered 'Here, Warden,' and a rotten, knowing leer as though he were in possession of some filthy secret.

"Is it any wonder that McNally didn't want it? Is it any wonder that, knowing of my bad taste for gruesome curios, he sent it along to me? I'm sure that no one, however morbid, could desire a more macabre souvenir than this, the pipe of Mordecai.

"It's odd how past events can cast a sinister light upon perfectly innocent objects. This pipe, now—just because of old Mordecai's devilish malevolence, his unearthly hate of all mankind—it repels and fascinates me at the same time. Oh, the power of the human mind is unlimited.

"But enough of this! First thing you know I'll be seeing old Mordecai himself in one of the shadowy corners of my little study here. Too much imagination is a bad thing. . . ."

Pettigrew laid down his pen, pushed back the voluminous diary that was his sole emotional outlet, and gazed fixedly at the battered old briar that lay on the desk before him. He quivered perceptibly as the odd little thought grew in his mind; the thought that told him to smoke the pipe.

With a wry half-smile at his own queerness he tried to dismiss the thought, but it persisted. Smoke the pipe—the pipe that a madman's lips had last caressed; the pipe that murdering fingers had last fondled. How novel it would be! How utterly fantastic! The normal element in Pettigrew's mind whispered "No!"; the morbid strain shouted "Yes!"

Pettigrew found himself reaching slowly for the humidor that rested at his left elbow. He picked up the battered briar and carefully packed the hard-coated interior of the bowl with his private mixture of fragrant tobaccos. Then, with an involuntary shudder of disgust at his audacity, he thrust the bitten mouthpiece into his mouth and carefully applied a match.

As he expelled the first blue smoke-cloud from his lungs, Pettigrew reflected with amusement upon the shocked amazement his friends would register if he told them of his rather ghastly experiment. He was suddenly brought back to the present by a momentary twinge of pain. He had, it seemed, pinched a portion of his soft mouth-tissue between stem and teeth so that it bled. With a grimace at his own nervousness, he replaced the pipe and again inhaled deeply. Odd that the pipe should seem so unwieldy, almost as if unseen fingers were tugging at it!

The blinding suddenness of the flash of red-hot agony brought Pettigrew to his feet in a mad leap that upset his chair with a crash.

Like a puppet on a string he caromed madly about the room, knocking over lamps and furniture in a sudden fight for breath. His throat was gripped by a constricting band of fire that filled it with hellish, strangling pain—a grip that made his brain spin and roar in an insane cacophony. His clawing fingers were tearing wildly at his contorted mouth when he finally crashed to the floor.

Doctor Clayton, from his crouched position over Pettigrew's sprawled body, beckoned to Sergeant McCullough.

"Of all the damn-fool ways to die!" growled the doctor, pointing to the gaping jaws that helped make a grotesque mockery of the empurpled thing that had once been a human face. "It's a pipe—you can barely see part of the bowl there at the top of his throat. But how in God's name could a fellow possibly swallow a pipe—stem first, at that? McCullough, if it weren't all so damned ridiculous I'd swear that someone *rammed* it down the poor devil's throat!"

The Murderer's Violin

by Erckmann–Chatrian

Karl Hâfitz had spent six years in mastering counterpoint. He had studied Haydn, Glück, Mozart, Beethoven, and Rossini; he enjoyed capital health, and was possessed of ample means which permitted him to indulge his artistic tastes—in a word, he possessed all that goes to make up the grand and beautiful in music, except that insignificant but very necessary thing—inspiration!

Every day, fired with a noble ardour, he carried to his worthy instructor, Albertus Kilian, long pieces harmonious enough, but of which every phrase was 'cribbed'. His master, Albertus, seated in his armchair, his feet on the fender, his elbow on a corner of the table, smoking his pipe all the time, set himself to erase, one after the other, the singular discoveries of his pupil. Karl cried with rage, he got very angry, and disputed the point; but the old master quietly opened one of his numerous music-books, and putting his finger on the passage, said:

'Look there, my boy.'

Then Karl bowed his head and despaired of the future.

But one fine morning, when he had presented to his master as his own composition a fantasia of Boccherini, varied with Viotti, the good man could no longer remain silent.

'Karl,' he exclaimed, 'do you take me for a fool? Do you think that I cannot detect your larcenies? This is really too bad!'

And then perceiving the consternation of his pupil, he added— 'Listen. I am willing to believe that your memory is to blame, and that you mistake recollection for originality, but you are growing too fat decidedly; you drink too generous a wine, and, above all, too much beer. That is what is shutting up the avenues of your intellect. You must get thinner!'

'Get thinner!'

'Yes, or give up music. You do not lack science, but ideas, and it is very simple; if you pass your whole life covering the strings of your violin with a coat of grease how can they vibrate?'

These words penetrated the depths of Hâfitz's soul.

'If it is necessary for me to get thin,' exclaimed he, 'I will not shrink from any sacrifice. Since matter oppresses the mind I will starve myself.'

His countenance wore such an expression of heroism at that moment that Albertus was touched; he embraced his pupil and wished him every success.

The very next day Karl Hâfitz, knapsack on his back and bâton in hand, left the hotel of the Three Pigeons and the brewery sacred to King Gambrinus, and set out upon his travels.

He proceeded towards Switzerland.

Unfortunately at the end of six weeks he was much thinner, but inspiration did not come any the more readily for that.

'Can any one be more unhappy than I am?' he said. 'Neither fasting nor good cheer, nor water, wine, or beer can bring me up to the necessary pitch; what have I done to deserve this? While a crowd of ignorant people produce remarkable works, I, with all my science, all my application, all my courage, cannot accomplish anything. Ah! Heaven is not good to me; it is unjust.'

Communing thus with himself, he took the road from Brück to Freibourg; night was coming on; he felt weary and footsore. Just then he perceived by the light of the moon an old ruined inn half-hidden in trees on the opposite side of the way; the door was off its hinges, the small window-panes were broken, the chimney was in ruins. Nettles and briars grew around it in wild luxuriance, and the garret window scarcely topped the heather, in which the wind blew hard enough to take the horns off a cow.

Karl could also perceive through the mist that a branch of a fir-tree waved above the door.

'Well,' he muttered, 'the inn is not prepossessing, it is rather ill-looking indeed, but we must not judge by appearances.'

So, without hesitation, he knocked at the door with his stick.

'Who is there? what do you want?' called out a rough voice within.

'Shelter and food,' replied the traveller.

'Ah ha! very good.'

The door opened suddenly, and Karl found himself confronted by a stout personage with square visage, grey eyes, his shoulders covered with a great-coat loosely thrown over them, and carrying an axe in his hand.

Behind this individual a fire was burning on the hearth, which lighted up the entrance to a small room and the wooden staircase, and close to the flame was crouched a pale young girl clad in a miserable brown dress with little white spots on it. She looked towards the door with an affrighted air; her black eyes had something sad and an indescribably wandering expression in them.

Karl took all this in at a glance, and instinctively grasped his stick tighter.

'Well, come in,' said the man; 'this is no time to keep people out of doors.'

Then Karl, thinking it bad form to appear alarmed, came into the room and sat down by the hearth.

'Give me your knapsack and stick,' said the man.

For the moment the pupil of Albertus trembled to his very marrow; but the knapsack was unbuckled and the stick placed in the corner, and the host was seated quietly before the fire ere he had recovered himself.

This circumstance gave him confidence.

'Landlord,' said he, smiling, 'I am greatly in want of my supper.'

'What would you like for supper, sir?' asked the landlord.

'An omelette, some wine and cheese.'

'Ha, ha! you have got an excellent appetite, but our provisions are exhausted.'

'You have no cheese, then?'

'No.'

'No butter, nor bread, nor milk?'

'No.'

'Well, good heavens! what *have* you got?'

'We can roast some potatoes in the embers.'

Just then Karl caught sight of a whole regiment of hens perched on the staircase in the gloom of all sorts, in all attitudes, some pluming themselves in the most nonchalant manner.

'But,' said Hâfitz, pointing at this troop of fowls, 'you must have some eggs surely?'

'We took them all to market this morning.'

'Well, if the worst comes to the worst you can roast a fowl for me.'

Scarcely had he spoken when the pale girl, with dishevelled hair, darted to the staircase, crying:

'No one shall touch the fowls! no one shall touch my fowls! Ho, ho, ho! God's creatures must be respected.'

Her appearance was so terrible that Hâfitz hastened to say:

'No, no, the fowls shall not be touched. Let us have the potatoes. I devote myself to eating potatoes henceforth. From this moment my object in life is determined. I shall remain here three months—six months—any time that may be necessary to make me as thin as a fakir.'

He expressed himself with such animation that the host cried out to the girl:

'Genovéva, Genovéva, look! The Spirit has taken possession of him; just as the other was—'

The north wind blew more fiercely outside; the fire blazed up on the hearth, and puffed great masses of grey smoke up to the ceiling. The hens appeared to dance in the reflection of the flame while the demented girl sang in a shrill voice a wild air, and the log of green wood, hissing in the midst of the fire, accompanied her with its plaintive sibilations.

Hâfitz began to fancy that he had fallen upon the den of the sorcerer Hecker; he devoured a dozen potatoes, and drank a great draught of cold water. Then he felt somewhat calmer; he noticed that the girl had left the chamber, and that only the man sat opposite to him by the hearth.

'Landlord,' he said, 'show me where I am to sleep.'

The host lit a lamp and slowly ascended the worm-eaten staircase; he opened a heavy trap-door with his grey head, and led Karl to a loft beneath the thatch.

'There is your bed,' he said, as he deposited the lamp on the floor; 'sleep well, and above all things beware of fire.'

He then descended, and Hâfitz was left alone, stooping beneath the low roof in front of a great mattress covered with a sack of feathers.

He considered for a few seconds whether it would be prudent to sleep in such a place, for the man's countenance did not appear very prepossessing, particularly as, recalling his cold grey eyes, his blue lips, his wide bony forehead, his yellow hue, he suddenly recalled to mind that on the Golzenberg he had encountered three men hanging in chains, and that one of them bore a striking resemblance to the landlord; that he had also those grave eyes, the bony elbows, and that the great toe of his left foot protruded from his shoe, cracked by the rain.

He also recollected that that unhappy man named Melchior had been a musician formerly, and that he had been hanged for having murdered the landlord of the Golden Sheep with his pitcher, because he had asked him to pay his scanty reckoning.

This poor fellow's music had affected him powerfully in former days. It was fantastic, and the pupil of Albertus had envied the Bohemian; but just now when he recalled the figure on the gibbet, his tatters agitated by the night wind, and the ravens wheeling around him with discordant screams, he trembled violently, and his fears augmented when he discovered, at the farther end of the loft against the wall, a violin decorated with two faded palm-leaves.

Then indeed he was anxious to escape, but at that moment he heard the rough voice of the landlord.

'Put out that light, will you?' he cried; 'go to bed. I told you particularly to be cautious about fire.'

These words froze Karl; he threw himself upon the mattress and extinguished the light. Silence fell on all the house.

Now, notwithstanding his determination not to close his eyes, Hâfitz, in consequence of hearing the sighing of the wind, the cries of the night-birds, the sound of the mice pattering over the floor, towards one o'clock fell asleep; but he was awakened by a bitter, deep, and most distressing sob. He started up, a cold perspiration standing on his forehead.

He looked up, and saw crouched up beneath the angle of the roof a man. It was Melchior, the executed criminal. His hair fell down to his emaciated ribs; his chest and neck were naked. One might compare him to a skeleton of an immense grasshopper, so thin was he; a ray of moonlight entering through the narrow window gave him a ghastly blue tint, and all around him hung the long webs of spiders.

Hâfitz, speechless, with staring eyes and gaping mouth, kept gazing at this weird object, as one might be expected to gaze at Death standing at one's bedside when the last hour has come!

Suddenly the skeleton extended its long bony hand and took the violin from the wall, placed it in position against its shoulder, and began to play.

309

There was in this ghostly music something of the cadence with which the earth falls upon the coffin of a dearly-loved friend—something solemn as the thunder of the waterfall echoed afar by the surrounding rocks, majestic as the wild blasts of the autumn tempest in the midst of the sonorous forest trees; sometimes it was sad—sad as never-ending despair. Then, in the midst of all this, he would strike into a lively measure, persuasive, silvery as the notes of a flock of gold-finches fluttering from twig to twig. These pleasing trills soared up with an ineffable tremolo of careless happiness, only to take flight all at once, frightened away by the waltz, foolish, palpitating, bewildering—love, joy, despair—all together singing, weeping, hurrying pell-mell over the quivering strings!

And Karl, notwithstanding his extreme terror, extended his arms and exclaimed:

'Oh, great, great artist! oh, sublime genius! oh, how I lament your sad fate, to be hanged for having murdered that brute of an innkeeper who did not know a note of music!—to wander through the forest by moonlight!—never to live in the world again—and with such talents! O Heaven!'

But as he thus cried out he was interrupted by the rough tones of his host.

'Hullo up there! will you be quiet? Are you ill, or is the house on fire?'

Heavy steps ascended the staircase, a bright light shone through the chinks of the door, which was opened by a thrust of the shoulder, and the landlord appeared.

'Oh!' exclaimed Hâfitz, 'what things happen here! First I am awakened by celestial music and entranced by heavenly strains; and then it all vanishes as if it were but a dream.'

The innkeeper's face assumed a thoughtful expression.

'Yes, yes,' he muttered, 'I might have thought as much. Melchior has come to disturb your rest. He will always come. Now we have lost our night's sleep; it is no use to think of rest any more. Come along, friend; get up and smoke a pipe with me.'

Karl waited no second bidding; he hastily left the room. But when he got downstairs, seeing that it was still dark night, he buried his head in his hands and remained for a long time plunged in melancholy meditation. The host relighted the fire, and taking up his position in the opposite corner of the hearth, smoked in silence.

At length the grey dawn appeared through the little diamond-shaped panes; then the cock crew, and the hens began to hop down from step to step of the staircase.

310

'How much do I owe you?' asked Karl, as he buckled on his knapsack and resumed his walking-staff.

'You owe us a prayer at the chapel of St Blaise,' said the man, with a curious emphasis—'one prayer for the soul of Melchior, who was hanged, and another for his *fiancée,* Genovéva, the poor idiot.'

'Is that all?'

'That is all.'

'Well, then, good-bye—I shall not forget.'

And, indeed, the first thing that Karl did on his arrival at Freibourg was to offer up a prayer for the poor man and for the girl he had loved, and then he went to the Grape Hotel, spread his sheet of paper upon the table, and, fortified by a bottle of 'rikevir', he wrote at the top of the page *The Murderer's Violin,* and then on the spot he traced the score of his first original composition.

The Night Caller

by G. L. Raisor

Sherry Elder's descent into madness began on a Thursday.

It was eight o'clock in the evening and she was stacking the dinner dishes. For Sherry and her daughter, Amy, there would be no escape.

It began, quite simply, when she answered the phone.

"Hello," she said, cupping the receiver to her ear as she examined a water-spotted glass. Dead silence greeted her. She pushed back hair that was beginning to show the first signs of gray and waited for the caller to speak. "Hello," she repeated, impatience in her voice.

A crackling came this time, and beneath that the faintest suggestion of breathing.

"Who is this?" she demanded.

The labored breathing grew louder and suddenly the connection was broken. Sherry replaced the phone and leaned her head against the wall. Unease settled in her stomach as she listened to the winter rain that whispered against the window. Outside, a car slowed and then drove on by.

311

"Was it a wrong number, Mommy?"

Startled, Sherry looked down at her daughter. "Yes it was." With a conscious effort she brightened. "Speaking of numbers, I think we should give your dad a call."

Amy glanced at the phone and then fixed her mother with an incredulous expression that only a five-year-old can muster. "You know we're not supposed to bother Daddy at work . . . less it's real important."

Sherry sighed and shadows filled her eyes.

Amy picked up on the fear in her mom's face. "Is Daddy coming home soon?"

"I don't know, sweetheart," Sherry answered distractedly, "Michael's got a lot of downed phone lines to fix."

"What's wrong, Mommy?"

"Nothing. Nothing at all. Hey! Don't you know too much worrying can cause wrinkles?" Without warning, she reached down and scooped up Amy. Laughing, Sherry began spinning around and around. Amy's long blond hair floated outward and her screams of mock-fear filled the room.

Amy threw her arms around Sherry's neck. "Mommy . . . I wish Daddy didn't work so much."

"You do, huh? Well, that makes two of us."

The little girl buried her face in the material of Sherry's sweater. "Is Daddy *really* going to read me a story before I go to bed?"

"Of course he is. Daddy said he would be home by nine and he would never lie to his favorite girl on her birthday."

As she put Amy on the couch, Sherry thought she heard the phone ring . . . once. But there was a storm coming, so she couldn't be sure of what she heard. Maybe it was only her imagination.

Later in the night, a sound awoke Sherry. It was faint, unidentifiable. She sat up in bed, wide awake, and looked around the darkened room. Something was out of kilter. When she had gone to sleep, all the lights were on. Now they were off. The storm had passed, but it had taken the electricity with it. She tried to identify what had pulled her awake. Whatever it was had come from inside the house. Her eyes darted to the clock and she saw it had stopped at 11:23.

The sounds came again. From the kitchen this time.

With a groan, she felt across the bed for Michael.

And found it empty.

Silently, she slipped from the bed and padded down the hallway to Amy's room.

And it too was empty.

The house was different tonight, quiet. Without electricity there was none of the background noises she had grown used to. The silence was oppressive. She leaned against the wall and listened as the scraping sound again drifted from the darkness. Something heavy was being dragged across the floor, and she felt a little trickle of fear.

Where was Amy?

Sherry groped her way into the kitchen, trying to control the shivering that seized her. Her eyes searched the room, trying to locate her daughter. And when she found Amy, it took her a moment to comprehend what she saw: Amy was perched on a chair with the phone pressed to her ear, eyes tightly closed.

The small voice was filled with happiness. "Daddy, that's my favorite."

At the sound of Amy's voice, Sherry felt relief so intense she thought her knees would buckle. What she had heard was Amy dragging a chair over to the phone so she could talk to her dad. Yet something felt wrong.

"My God, she's walking in her sleep," Sherry whispered to herself. Gently, ever so gently, she reached out and eased the phone from the tiny hand. "We've got to get you back to bed, young lady." Out of habit, Sherry placed the warm plastic against her own ear . . .

. . . and stiffened as the now familiar crackling bubbled up.

Then came the breathing, ragged and guttural. Revulsion and fear distorted her face as she tried to pull the receiver away. But she was too slow.

"—time—" crawled from out of the static, the faint words driving slivers of ice deep into her chest.

"Who is this?" Sherry asked in a fierce, low voice.

The phone went silent.

With nerveless fingers she hung up. *"Take it easy. Just stay calm."* But that wasn't so easy in the face of one simple fact; even though she had heard a voice speak on the phone, she didn't remember hearing the phone ring.

She was quite certain of that.

Pushing down the fright that threatened to overwhelm her, she carried Amy back to bed. She went to the kitchen, took a deep breath and reached for the phone.

It rang.

On the fourth ring she found the courage to pick it up and say hello.

"Mrs. Elder?" a sad-voiced man asked.

She made a noise that he took for affirmation.

"I'm afraid I've got some bad news . . ." The voice paused, and quite suddenly she could hear Michael and Amy talking to each other, their last conversation before Michael left for work. She knew the voices were only in her head, but each word was distinct and she could make them out quite clearly. Their voices bounced back and forth in a crazy counterpoint that was, somehow, more real than the words coming from the phone.

The anonymous man continued on, telling her things that couldn't possibly be true. Her life was shattering into fragments that she could never put back into any kind of order. She was helpless as the voices warred for her attention.

(". . . *Daddy'll read you a special story before bedtime, sweetheart.*")

"Michael Elder has been involved in an accident."

(*"You promise, Daddy?"*)

"He touched a power line."

(*"I promise, Amy."*)

"They're rushing him over to County. Do you want us to send someone around to take you?"

"No, I have a car," she heard herself say. When the voice finally went away, Sherry laid her face against the coolness of the kitchen table for a second and tried to blot out all thought. But her mind kept playing back the two words from Amy's phone call. Over and over. The words that had so painfully emerged from the static were beginning to make sense.

Sitting in the oasis of light that spilled through the window, she attempted one last time to convince herself that it was all some kind of mistake, and for a moment, she was almost able to believe.

Almost.

She clutched her car keys and rose to get Amy. At that instant the electricity came back on, filling the room with a sudden brightness that hurt her eyes. The television she had left on for company roared with static, but beneath that was another sound. A phone ringing. Sherry stared at it a long moment before she picked it up and listened. Her eyes filled with dull acceptance when the crackling came again, the crackling that sounded like what?

High voltage ripping through flesh?

Michael's flesh?

Haltingly a voice began, "Once . . ." then stronger, "upon . . . a time . . ."

"Michael, *stop it*," she begged as tears trickled down. "You don't have to read her any more bedtime stories. It's okay, you don't have to —" The static rose and fell.

314

". . . there were three bears," the voice continued on in an unrelenting monotone, as if it were a recording that would not—*could not* —stop until it reached its appointed end.

Sherry slammed the phone down and turned to find Amy staring at her with frightened eyes. "Who was that, Mommy?"

"Nobody, sweetheart," she said, dabbing at her tears. "It was just a wrong number."

As the sleepy pajama-clad form ran over and climbed up onto her lap, the phone began to ring again. Sherry sat frozen in the chair, staring straight ahead. Waiting for it to stop. Praying for it to stop.

But over and over, with unceasing regularity it jangled, the sound seemed to grow louder with each ring.

"Mommy, aren't you going to answer?"

"No, I've had enough of phones to last a lifetime." She ripped the plug from the wall. The silence was deafening. Releasing a painful breath that she had been unaware of holding, she pulled Amy close. "Come on, kiddo, let's get you dressed. We've got to get out of here, right now. Daddy's waiting for us."

Before she could move, the phone began to ring.

The Night Wire

by H. F. Arnold

"New York, September 30 CP Flash

"Ambassador Holliwell died here today. The end came suddenly as the ambassador was alone in his study. . . ."

There is something ungodly about these night wire jobs. You sit up here on the top floor of a skyscraper and listen in to the whispers of a civilization. New York, London, Calcutta, Bombay, Singapore— they're your next-door neighbors after the street lights go dim and the world has gone to sleep.

Along in the quiet hours between two and four, the receiving operators doze over their sounders and the news comes in. Fires and disasters and suicides. Murders, crowds, catastrophes. Sometimes an earth-

315

quake with a casualty list as long as your arm. The night wire man takes it down almost in his sleep, picking it off on his typewriter with one finger.

Once in a long time you prick up your ears and listen. You've heard of some one you knew in Singapore, Halifax or Paris, long ago. Maybe they've been promoted, but more probably they've been murdered or drowned. Perhaps they just decided to quit and took some bizarre way out. Made it interesting enough to get in the news.

But that doesn't happen often. Most of the time you sit and doze and tap, tap on your typewriter and wish you were home in bed.

Sometimes, though, queer things happen. One did the other night, and I haven't got over it yet. I wish I could.

You see, I handle the night manager's desk in a western seaport town; what the name is, doesn't matter.

There is, or rather was, only one night operator on my staff, a fellow named John Morgan, about forty years of age, I should say, and a sober, hard-working sort.

He was one of the best operators I ever knew, what is known as a "double" man. That means he could handle two instruments at once and type the stories on different typewriters at the same time. He was one of the three men I ever knew who could do it consistently, hour after hour, and never make a mistake.

Generally we used only one wire at night, but sometimes when it was late and the news was coming fast, the Chicago and Denver stations would open a second wire, and then Morgan would do his stuff. He was a wizard, a mechanical automatic wizard which functioned marvelously but was without imagination.

On the night of the sixteenth he complained of feeling tired. It was the first and last time I had ever heard him say a word about himself, and I had known him for three years.

It was just three o'clock and we were running only one wire. I was nodding over reports at my desk and not paying much attention to him, when he spoke.

"Jim," he said, "does it feel close in here to you?"

"Why, no, John," I answered, "but I'll open a window if you like."

"Never mind," he said. "I reckon I'm just a little tired."

That was all that was said, and I went on working. Every ten minutes or so I would walk over and take a pile of copy that had stacked up neatly beside the typewriter as the messages were printed out in triplicate.

It must have been twenty minutes after he spoke that I noticed he had opened up the other wire and was using both typewriters. I thought it was a little unusual, as there was nothing very "hot" coming in. On my next trip I picked up the copy from both machines and took it back to my desk to sort out the duplicates.

The first wire was running out the usual sort of stuff and I just looked over it hurriedly. Then I turned to the second pile of copy. I remembered it particularly because the story was from a town I had never heard of: "Xebico." Here is the dispatch. I saved a duplicate of it from our files:

"Xebico, Sept 16 CP BULLETIN

"The heaviest mist in the history of the city settled over the town at 4 o'clock yesterday afternoon. All traffic has stopped and the mist hangs like a pall over everything. Lights of ordinary intensity fail to pierce the fog, which is constantly growing heavier.

"Scientists here are unable to agree as to the cause, and the local weather bureau states that the like has never occurred before in the history of the city.

"At 7 p.m. last night municipal authorities—

(more)"

That was all there was. Nothing out of the ordinary at a bureau headquarters, but, as I say, I noticed the story because of the name of the town.

It must have been fifteen minutes later that I went over for another batch of copy. Morgan was slumped down in his chair and had switched his green electric light shade so that the gleam missed his eyes and hit only the top of the two typewriters.

Only the usual stuff was in the right-hand pile, but the left-hand batch carried another story from Xebico. All press dispatches come in "takes," meaning that parts of many different stories are strung along together, perhaps with but a few paragraphs of each coming through at a time. This second story was marked "add fog." Here is the copy:

"At 7 p.m. the fog had increased noticeably. All lights were now invisible and the town was shrouded in pitch darkness.

"As a peculiarity of the phenomenon, the fog is accompanied by a sickly odor, comparable to nothing yet experienced here."

Below that in customary press fashion was the hour, 3:27, and the initials of the operator, JM.

There was only one other story in the pile from the second wire. Here it is:

"2nd add Xebico Fog

"Accounts as to the origin of the mist differ greatly. Among the most unusual is that of the sexton of the local church, who groped his way to headquarters in a hysterical condition and declared that the fog originated in the village churchyard.

" 'It was first visible as a soft gray blanket clinging to the earth above the graves,' he stated. 'Then it began to rise, higher and higher. A subterranean breeze seemed to blow it in billows, which split up and then joined together again.

" 'Fog phantoms, writhing in anguish, twisted the mist into queer forms and figures. And then, in the very thick midst of the mass, something moved.

" 'I turned and ran from the accursed spot. Behind me I heard screams coming from the houses bordering on the graveyard.'

"Although the sexton's story is generally discredited, a party has left to investigate. Immediately after telling his story, the sexton collapsed and is now in a local hospital, unconscious."

Queer story, wasn't it? Not that we aren't used to it, for a lot of unusual stories come in over the wire. But for some reason or other, perhaps because it was so quiet that night, the report of the fog made a great impression on me.

It was almost with dread that I went over to the waiting piles of copy. Morgan did not move, and the only sound in the room was the tap-tap of the sounders. It was ominous, nerve-racking.

There was another story from Xebico in the pile of copy. I seized on it anxiously.

"New Lead Xebico Fog CP

"The rescue party which went out at 11 p.m. to investigate a weird story of the origin of a fog which, since late yesterday, has shrouded the city in darkness, has failed to return. Another and larger party has been dispatched.

"Meanwhile the fog has, if possible, grown heavier. It seeps through the cracks in the doors and fills the atmosphere with a depressing odor of decay. It is oppressive, terrifying, bearing with it a subtle impression of things long dead.

"Residents of the city have left their homes and gathered in the local church, where the priests are holding services of prayer. The scene is beyond description. Grown folk and children are alike terrified and many are almost beside themselves with fear.

"Amid the wisps of vapor which partly veil the church auditorium, an old priest is praying for the welfare of his flock. They alternately wail and cross themselves.

"From the outskirts of the city may be heard cries of unknown voices. They echo through the fog in queer uncadenced minor keys. The sounds resemble nothing so much as wind whistling through a gigantic tunnel. But the night is calm and there is no wind. The second rescue party— (more)"

I am a calm man and never in a dozen years spent with the wires have been known to become excited, but despite myself I rose from my chair and walked to the window.

Could I be mistaken, or far down in the canyons of the city beneath me did I see a faint trace of fog? Pshaw! It was all imagination.

In the pressroom the click of the sounders seemed to have raised the tempo of their tune. Morgan alone had not stirred from his chair. His head sunk between his shoulders, he tapped the dispatches out on the typewriters with one finger of each hand.

He looked asleep. Maybe he was—but no; endlessly, efficiently, the two machines rattled off line after line, as relentlessly and effortlessly as death itself. There was something about the monotonous movement of the typewriter keys that fascinated me. I walked over and stood behind his chair, reading over his shoulder the type as it came into being, word by word.

Ah, here was another:

"Flash Xebico CP

"There will be no more bulletins from this office. The impossible has happened. No messages have come into this room for twenty minutes. We are cut off from the outside and even the streets below us.

"I will stay with the wire until the end.

"It is the end, indeed. Since 4 p.m. yesterday the fog has hung over the city. Following reports from the sexton of the local church, two rescue parties were sent out to investigate conditions on the outskirts of the city. Neither party has ever returned nor was any word received from them. It is quite certain now that they will never return.

"From my instrument I can gaze down on the city beneath me. From the position of this room on the thirteenth floor, nearly the entire city can be seen. Now I can see only a thick blanket of blackness where customarily are lights and life.

"I fear greatly that the wailing cries heard constantly from the outskirts of the city are the death cries of the inhabitants. They are constantly increasing in volume and are approaching the center of the city.

"The fog yet hangs over everything. If possible, it is even heavier than before, but the conditions have changed. Instead of an opaque, impenetrable wall of odorous vapor, there now swirls and writhes a shapeless mass in contortions of almost human agony. Now and again the mass parts and I catch a brief glimpse of the streets below.

"People are running to and fro, screaming in despair. A vast bedlam of sound flies up to my window, and above all is the immense whistling of unseen and unfelt winds.

"The fog has again swept over the city and the whistling is coming closer and closer.

"It is now directly beneath me.

"God! An instant ago the mist opened and I caught a glimpse of the streets below.

"The fog is not simply vapor—it lives! By the side of each moaning and weeping human is a companion figure, an aura of strange and vari-colored hues. How the shapes cling! Each to a living thing!

"The men and women are down. Flat on their faces. The fog figures caress them lovingly. They are kneeling beside them. They are—but I dare not tell it.

"The prone and writhing bodies have been stripped of their cloth-ing. They are being consumed—piecemeal.

"A merciful wall of hot, steamy vapor has swept over the whole scene. I can see no more.

"Beneath me the wall of vapor is changing colors. It seems to be lighted by internal fires. No, it isn't. I have made a mistake. The colors are from above, reflections from the sky.

"Look up! Look up! The whole sky is in flames. Colors as yet unseen by man or demon. The flames are moving; they have started to intermix; the colors rearrange themselves. They are so brilliant that my eyes burn, yet they are a long way off.

"Now they have begun to swirl, to circle in and out, twisting in intricate designs and patterns. The lights are racing each with each, a kaleidoscope of unearthly brilliance.

"I have made a discovery. There is nothing harmful in the lights. They radiate force and friendliness, almost cheeriness. But by their very strength, they hurt.

"As I look, they are swinging closer and closer, a million miles at each jump. Millions of miles with the speed of light. Aye, it is light, the quintessence of all light. Beneath it the fog melts into a jeweled mist, radiant, rainbow-colored of a thousand varied spectra.

"I can see the streets. Why, they are filled with people! The lights are coming closer. They are all around me. I am enveloped. I—"

The message stopped abruptly. The wire to Xebico was dead. Be-neath my eyes in the narrow circle of light from under the green lamp-shade, the black printing no longer spun itself, letter by letter, across the page.

The room seemed filled with a solemn quiet, a silence vaguely impressive, powerful.

I looked down at Morgan. His hands had dropped nervelessly at his sides, while his body had hunched over peculiarly. I turned the lampshade back, throwing the light squarely in his face. His eyes were staring, fixed.

Filled with a sudden foreboding, I stepped beside him and called Chicago on the wire. After a second the sounder clicked its answer.

Why? But there was something wrong. Chicago was reporting that Wire Two had not been used throughout the evening.

"Morgan!" I shouted. "Morgan! Wake up, it isn't true. Some one has been hoaxing us. Why—" In my eagerness I grasped him by the shoulder.

His body was quite cold. Morgan had been dead for hours. Could it be that his sensitized brain and automatic fingers had continued to record impressions even after the end?

I shall never know, for I shall never again handle the night shift. Search in a world atlas discloses no town of Xebico. Whatever it was that killed John Morgan will for ever remain a mystery.

O Come Little Children . . .

by Chet Williamson

"It even *smells* like Christmas," the boy told his mother, as they strolled down the narrow aisles of the farmer's market. That it looked and sounded like that happiest of holidays went without saying. Carols blared everywhere, from the tiniest of the stand-holder's transistor radios to the brass choir booming from the market's PA system. Meat cases were framed with strings of lights, a myriad of small trees adorned a myriad of counters across which bills the color of holly were pushed and goods and coins returned, and red and green predominated above all other hues. But it was the odors that entranced: the pungency of gingerbread, the sweet olfactory sting of fresh Christmas cookies. There were mince pies and pumpkin pudding, and a concoction of cranberry sauce and dried fruit in syrup whose aroma made the boy pucker and salivate as though a fresh lemon had brushed his tongue. The owner of the sandwich stand was selling small, one-dollar, Styrofoam plates of turkey and stuffing to those too rabid to wait until Christmas, three long days away. The smell was intoxicating, and the line was long.

The boy's mother, smiling and full of the spirit, bought many things that would find their way to their own Christmas table, and the sights and sounds and smells kept the boy from being bored, as he usually was at the Great Tri-County Farmer's and Flea Market.

It was on the way out, as he and his mother walked through the large passage that divided the freshness of the food and produce stands from the dusty tawdriness of the flea market, that the boy saw the man dressed as Santa Claus. At first glance he did not seem a very *good* Santa Claus. He was too thin, and instead of a full, white, cottony, fake beard, his own wispy mass of facial hair had been halfheartedly lightened, as though he'd dipped a comb in white shoe polish and given it a few quick strokes. "There," the boy's mother remarked, "is one of Santa's *lesser* helpers."

The boy was way past the point where every Santa was the *real* Santa. In truth, he was just short of total disbelief. TV, comic books, and the remarks of older friends had all taken their toll, and he now thought that although the existence of the great man was conceivable, it was not likely, and to imagine that any of these kindly, red-suited men who smiled wearily in every department store and shopping mall was the genuine article was quite impossible.

Even if he had believed fully, he doubted if anyone under two would have accepted the legitimacy of the Santa he saw before him. Aside from the thinness of both beard and frame, the man's suit was threadbare in spots, the black vinyl boots scuffed and dull, and the white ruffs at collar and cuffs had yellowed to the color of old piano keys. His lap was empty. The only person nearby was a cowboy-hatted man sitting on a folding chair identical to that on which the Santa sat. A Polaroid Pronto hung from his neck, and next to him a card on an easel read YOUR PICTURE WITH SANTA—$3.00. The $3.00 part was printed much smaller than the words. The boy and his mother were nearly by the men when the one in the red suit looked at them.

The boy stopped. "Mom," he said, loud enough for only his mother to hear. "May I sit on his lap?"

She gave an impatient sigh. "Oh, Alan . . ."

"Please?"

"Honey, do you really *want* your picture taken with . . . ?"

"I don't want a picture. I just want to sit on his lap."

"No, sweetie," she said, looking at the man looking at the boy. "I don't think so."

They were in the parking lot by the time she looked at her son once more. To her amazement, huge tears were running down his face. "What's wrong, honey?"

"I wanted to sit on his *lap*," the boy choked out.

"Oh, Alan, he's not Santa, he's just a helper. And not a very good one either."

"Can't I? Please? Just for a minute . . ."

She sighed and smiled, thinking that it would do no harm, and that she was in no hurry. "All right. But no picture."

The boy shook his head, and they went back inside. The man in the red suit smiled as he saw the boy approach without hesitation, and patted his thigh in an unspoken invitation for the boy to sit. The man in the cowboy hat stood up, but before he could bring the camera to eye level, the boy said, "No picture, please," and the man, with a look of irritation directed at the boy's mother, sat down again.

The boy remained on the man's lap for less than a minute, talking so quietly that his mother could not hear. When he started to slide off, he stopped suddenly, as though caught, and his mother saw that the metal buckle of the boy's loose-hanging coat belt had become entangled in the white plush of the man's left cuff. The man tried unsuccessfully to extricate it with the fingers of his gloved right hand, then put the glove in his mouth and yanked his hand free. With his long, thin fingers he freed the boy, who hopped smiling onto the floor and waved a hand enclosed in his own varicolored mittens. When he rejoined his mother, he was surprised to find her scowling. "What's wrong?"

"Nothing," she answered. "Let's go."

But he knew something was wrong and found out later at dinner. "*I* think he must have been *on* something."

"Oh, come on," his father said, taking a second baked potato. "Why?"

His mother went on as though he were not there. "He just *looked* it. He had these real hollow eyes, like he hadn't slept in days. Really thin. The suit just hung on him. And, uh . . ." She looked at the boy, who pretended to be interested in pushing an unmelted piece of margarine around on his peas.

"What?"

"His hand. He took off his glove and his hand was all bruised, like he'd been shooting into it or something."

"Shooting what?" the boy asked.

"Drugs," his father said, before his mother could make something up.

"What's that? Like what?"

His mother smiled sardonically at his father. "Go ahead, Mr. Rogers. Explain."

"Well . . . *drugs*. Like your baby aspirin, only a lot stronger. People take some drugs just to make them feel good, but then later they feel real bad, so you shouldn't ever take them at all."

"What's the shooting part?"

"Like a shot, when the doctor gives you a shot."

"Like Mommy's diabetes."

"Yeah, like that. Only people who take too many *bad* drugs have their veins . . ." He saw the question on the boy's face. ". . . their little blood hoses inside their skin collapse on them. So they might stick the needles in their legs, or in the veins in the backs of their hands, or even their feet or the inside of their mouth, or . . ."

"That's fine, thank you," his mother said sharply. "I think we've learned enough tonight."

"He wouldn't do *that*," the boy said. "He was too *nice*."

His father shook his head. "Aw, honey, you never know. Nice people can have problems too." And then his mother changed the subject.

The next day the boy told his mother that he wished he could see Santa Claus again. "Santa Claus?" she asked.

"At the market. *You* know."

"Oh, Alan, *him*? Honey, you saw him yesterday. You told him what you wanted then, didn't you?"

"I don't want to tell him what I want. I just want to see him because he's *nice*. I *liked* him."

After the boy was in bed, his father and mother sat in the living room, neither of them paying attention to the movie on cable. "He say anything to you about Santa today?" he asked her.

She nodded. "Couple of times. You?"

"Yeah. He really went for this guy, huh?"

"I don't know why."

"Oh, Alan can be so compassionate—probably felt sorry for the guy."

She shook her head. "No, it wasn't like that. He really seemed drawn by him, almost as though . . . ." She paused.

"As though he really thought the guy was Santa Claus?" her husband finished.

"I don't know," she answered, looking at the car crash on the TV screen but not really seeing it. "Maybe."

She turned off the movie with no complaints from her husband, and began to go over the final list of ingredients for their Christmas dinner. "Uh-oh," she murmured, and went out to the kitchen. In a minute she returned, frowning lovingly at her husband. "Well, it's not that I don't appreciate your making dinner tonight, but I just realized your oyster stew used the oysters for the Christmas casserole."

"You're kidding."

"Nope." She was amused to see that there was actually panic in his face.

"What'll we *do?*"

"Do without."

"But . . . but oyster casserole's a tradition."

"Some tradition—just because we had it last year."

"I liked it."

"And where are we going to find oysters on a Sunday?"

"It's not the day, it's the month. And December has an *R* in it."

"Sure. But Sunday doesn't have *oysters* in it. The IGA's closed, Acme, Weis . . ."

His face brightened. "The farmer's market! They have a fish stand, and they're open tomorrow. You could run out and . . ."

"Me? I didn't cook the oyster stew."

"You ate it."

She put her left hand over his head and pounded it gently with her right. "Sometimes you are a real sleazoid."

"Now, Mrs. Scrooge," he said, pulling her onto his lap, "where's that Christmas spirit, that charity?"

"Good King Wenceslas I ain't."

"How about if I vacuum while you're gone so my mother doesn't realize what a slob you are?"

"How many pounds of oysters do you want?"

It started to snow heavily just before midnight and stopped at dawn. The snow was light and powdery, easy for the early morning trucks to push from the roads. The family went to church, then came home for a simple lunch, as if afraid to ingest even a jot too much on the day before the great Christmas feast. "Well," the boy's mother said after they'd finished cleaning up the dishes, "I'm off for oysters. Anyone want to come?"

"To the farm market?" asked the boy. His mother nodded. "Can I see Santa?"

His father and mother exchanged looks. "I don't think so," she replied. "Do you want to go anyway?"

He thought for a moment. "Okay."

The parking lot was still covered with snow, although the cars had mashed most of it down to a dirty gray film. Only the far end of the parking lot, where a small, gray trailer sat attached to an old, nondescript sedan, was pristine with whiteness. It was typical, the boy's mother thought, of the management not to pay to have the lot plowed —anyone who'd hire a bargain basement Santa like that one and then charge three bucks for a thirty-five cent picture with him.

The seafood stand was out of oysters, but its owner said that the small grocery shop at the market's other end might still have some. "Could I see Santa?" the boy asked as they walked.

"Alan, I told you no. Besides, he's probably gone by now. He's got a busy night tonight." She knew it sounded absurd even as she said it. If *that* Santa was going to be busy, it wouldn't be delivering toys—it would probably be looking for a fix. Repulsion crossed her face as she thought again of those hollow eyes, that pale skin, the telltale bruises on his bare hand, and she wondered what her son could possibly see in that haggard countenance.

She thought she would ask him, but when she looked down, he was gone. In a sharp, reflexive motion, she looked to the other side, then behind her, but the boy was not there. She strained to see him through the forest of people, then turned and retraced her steps, as her heart beat faster and beads of cold sweat touched her face. "Alan!" she called, softly but high, to pierce the low, murmuring din around her. "Alan!"

It took some time for the idea to occur that her son had disobeyed her and had set out to find the market's Santa Claus on his own. She had not thought him capable of such a thing, for he knew and understood the dangers that could face a small child alone in a public place, especially a place like a flea market that had more than its share of transients and lowlifes. She told herself that he would be all right, that nothing could happen to a little boy the day before Christmas, that someone she knew would see him and stop him and take care of him until she could find him, or that he would be there on Santa Claus's lap, smiling sheepishly and guiltily when he spotted her.

She was running now, jostling shoppers, their arms loaded with last-minute thoughts. Within a minute, she entered the large open area

326

between the markets. The chairs and the sign were there, the Santa and his photographer were not. Neither was her son.

For a long moment she stood, wondering what to do next, and finally decided to find the manager and ask him to make an announcement on the PA system. But first she called her husband, for she could no longer bear to be alone.

By the time he met her in the manager's office, the announcement had been made four times without a response. The boy's father held his mother, who was by this time crying quietly, very much afraid. "Where was he going?" the manager, a short, elderly man with a cigarette in one hand and a can of soda in the other, asked.

"I thought it was to see Santa, but he wasn't there when I got there."

The manager nodded. "Yeah, he quit at noon. I wanted him to work through five, but he wouldn't. Said he hadda meet somebody."

The boy's father looked at the manager intently over his wife's head. "Who is this guy?"

"Santa? Don't know his name. Just breezed in about a week ago and asked if I wanted a Santa cheap."

"What do you mean you don't know his name? You *pay* him, don't you?"

"Cash. Off the books. You'll keep that quiet now. And Riley, my helper, he got a Polaroid, so we made enough to pay him outta the pictures."

The boy's father took his arms from around his wife. "Where is this guy?"

"He's got a trailer the other side of the lot."

"All right," the father nodded. "We're going to talk to him. And if he can't give us any answers, we're calling the police."

The manager started to protest, but the couple walked out of the office and down the aisles, trying hard not to run and so admit their panic to themselves. "It'll be all right," the boy's father kept saying. "We'll find him. It'll be all right."

And they did. When they walked into the open area where Santa had been, their son was standing beside the gold aluminum Christmas tree. He smiled when he saw them, and waved.

They ran to him, and his mother scooped him up and hugged him, crying. His father placed a hand on his head as if to be certain he was really there, then tousled his hair, swallowing heavily to rid his throat of the cold lump that had been there since his wife's call.

"Where *were* you?" the boy's mother said, holding him ferociously. "Where did you *go*?"

"I wanted to see him," he said, as if that were all the explanation necessary.

"But I told you *no*. You know better, Alan. Anything could've happened. We were worried sick."

"I'm sorry, Mom. I just *had* to see him."

"But you didn't," his father said. "So where *were* you? Why didn't you answer the announcements?"

"Oh, I saw him, Dad. I was *with* him."

"You . . . *where?*"

"He was here. He said he was waiting for me, that he'd been hoping I'd come again. He looked really different, he didn't have on his red suit or anything."

His mother shook her head. "But . . . I *looked* here."

"Oh, I *found* him here okay. But then we went to his place."

"*What?*" they both asked at once.

"His trailer. It's sort of like the one Grandpa and Grandma have."

"Why . . . did you go out there?" his mother asked, remembering the trailer and the car at the end of the lot.

"He asked me to."

"Alan," his father said, "I've told you never, *never* to go with anyone for *any* reason."

"But it was all right with him, Dad. I knew I'd be safe with *him*. He told me when we were walking. Out to his trailer."

"Told you *what?*"

"How he always looks for somebody."

"Oh, my God. . . ."

"What's the matter, Mom?"

"Nothing. Nothing. What else did this . . . man say?"

"He just said he always comes back this time of year, just to see if people still believe in him. He said lots of people *say* they do, but they don't, not really. He said they just say so because they want their *kids* to believe in him. But if he finds one person who really believes, and knows who he really is, then it's all gonna be okay. 'Til next Christmas. He said it's almost always kids, like me, but that that's okay. As long as there's somebody who believes in him and trusts him enough to go with him."

The boy's father knelt beside him and put his big hands on the boy's thin shoulders. "Alan. Did he touch you? Touch you anywhere at all?"

"Just here." he held up his mitten-covered hands. "My hands."

"Alan, this man played a mean joke on you. He let you think that he's somebody that he really isn't."

328

"Oh no, Dad, you're wrong."

"Now listen. This man was *not* Santa Claus, Alan."

The boy laughed. *"I know *that*! I haven't believed in Santa Claus for almost a whole *month!"*

His mother barely got the words out. "Then who . . . ?"

"And you were wrong too, Mom. He didn't have any little needle holes in his hands. Just the big ones. Straight through. Just like he's supposed to."

Her eyes widened, and she put her fist to her mouth to hold in a scream. Her husband leaped to his feet, his face even paler than before. "Where's this trailer?" he asked in a voice whose coldness frightened the boy.

They strode out the door together into the late afternoon darkness. Street lights illuminated every part of the parking lot. "It . . . was there," she said, staring across at white emptiness.

"The *bastard*. Got out while the getting was good. He . . ." The father paused. "There?" he said, pointing.

"Yes. It was right over there." The boy nodded in agreement with his mother.

"It couldn't've been." He started to walk toward the open space, and his family followed. "There are no tracks. It hasn't snowed. And there's no wind." He looked at the unbroken plain of powdered snow.

"Hey! Hey, you folks!" They turned and saw the manager laboring toward them, puffs of condensation roaring from his mouth. "That your kid? He okay?"

The boy's father nodded. "Yeah. He seems to be. We were trying to find that man. Your Santa Claus. But he's . . . gone."

"Huh! You believe that? And I still owe him fourteen bucks." He turned back toward the warmth of the market, shaking his head. "Left without his money. Some people . . ."

"Never mind," his wife said. "He's all right. Let him believe." She touched her husband's shoulder. "Maybe we should all believe. It's almost easier that way."

When they got home, the boy took off his mittens, and his father and mother saw the pale red marks, one in each palm, where he said the man's fingers had touched him. They were suffused with a rosy glow, as if the blood pulsed more strongly there. "They'll go away," the boy's father said. "In time, they'll go away." But they did not.

On the Brighton Road

by Richard Middleton

Slowly the sun had climbed up the hard white downs, till it broke with little of the mysterious ritual of dawn upon a sparkling world of snow. There had been a hard frost during the night, and the birds, who hopped about here and there with scant tolerance of life, left no trace of their passage on the silver pavements. In places the sheltered caverns of the hedges broke the monotony of the whiteness that had fallen upon the coloured earth, and overhead the sky melted from orange to deep blue, from deep blue to a blue so pale that it suggested a thin paper screen rather than illimitable space. Across the level fields there came a cold, silent wind which blew a fine dust of snow from the trees, but hardly stirred the crested hedges. Once above the skyline, the sun seemed to climb more quickly, and as it rose higher it began to give out a heat that blended with the keenness of the wind.

It may have been this strange alternation of heat and cold that disturbed the tramp in his dreams, for he struggled for a moment with the snow that covered him, like a man who finds himself twisted uncomfortably in the bed-clothes, and then sat up with staring, questioning eyes. 'Lord! I thought I was in bed,' he said to himself as he took in the vacant landscape, 'and all the while I was out here.' He stretched his limbs, and, rising carefully to his feet, shook the snow off his body. As he did so the wind set him shivering, and he knew that his bed had been warm.

'Come, I feel pretty fit,' he thought. 'I suppose I am lucky to wake at all in this. Or unlucky—it isn't much of a business to come back to.' He looked up and saw the downs shining against the blue like the Alps on a picture-postcard. 'That means another forty miles or so, I suppose,' he continued grimly. 'Lord knows what I did yesterday. Walked till I was done, and now I'm only about twelve miles from Brighton. Damn the snow, damn Brighton, damn everything!' The sun crept higher and higher, and he started walking patiently along the road with his back turned to the hills.

'Am I glad or sorry that it was only sleep that took me, glad or sorry, glad or sorry?' His thoughts seemed to arrange themselves in a metrical accompaniment to the steady thud of his footsteps, and he hardly sought an answer to his question. It was good enough to walk to.

Presently, when three milestones had loitered past, he overtook a boy who was stooping to light a cigarette. He wore no overcoat, and looked unspeakably fragile against the snow. 'Are you on the road, guv'nor?' asked the boy huskily as he passed.

'I think I am,' the tramp said.

'Oh! then I'll come a bit of the way with you if you don't walk too fast. It's a bit lonesome walking this time of day.' The tramp nodded his head, and the boy started limping along by his side.

'I'm eighteen,' he said casually. 'I bet you thought I was younger.'

'Fifteen, I'd have said.'

'You'd have backed a loser. Eighteen last August, and I've been on the road six years. I ran away from home five times when I was a little 'un, and the police took me back each time. Very good to me, the police was. Now I haven't got a home to run away from.'

'Nor have I,' the tramp said calmly.

'Oh, I can see what you are,' the boy panted; 'you're a gentleman come down. It's harder for you than for me.' The tramp glanced at the limping, feeble figure and lessened his pace.

'I haven't been at it as long as you have,' he admitted.

'No, I could tell that by the way you walk. You haven't got tired yet. Perhaps you expect something the other end?'

The tramp reflected for a moment. 'I don't know,' he said bitterly, 'I'm always expecting things.'

'You'll grow out of that,' the boy commented. 'It's warmer in London, but it's harder to come by grub. There isn't much in it really.'

'Still, there's the chance of meeting somebody there who will understand—'

'Country people are better,' the boy interrupted. 'Last night I took a lease of a barn for nothing and slept with the cows, and this morning the farmer routed me out and gave me tea and toke because I was so little. Of course, I score there; but in London, soup on the Embankment at night, and all the rest of the time coppers moving you on.'

'I dropped by the roadside last night and slept where I fell. It's a wonder I didn't die,' the tramp said. The boy looked at him sharply.

'How do you know you didn't?' he said.

'I don't see it,' the tramp said, after a pause.

'I tell you,' the boy said hoarsely, 'people like us can't get away from this sort of thing if we want to. Always hungry and thirsty and dog-tired and walking all the time. And yet if anyone offers me a nice home and work my stomach feels sick. Do I look strong? I know I'm little for

331

my age, but I've been knocking about like this for six years, and do you think I'm not dead? I was drowned bathing at Margate, and I was killed by a gypsy with a spike; he knocked my head right in, and twice I was froze like you last night, and a motor cut me down on this very road, and yet I'm walking along here now, walking to London to walk away from it again, because I can't help it. Dead! I tell you we can't get away if we want to.'

The boy broke off in a fit of coughing, and the tramp paused while he recovered.

'You'd better borrow my coat for a bit, Tommy,' he said, 'your cough's pretty bad.'

'You go to hell!' the boy said fiercely, puffing at his cigarette; 'I'm all right. I was telling you about the road. You haven't got down to it yet, but you'll find out presently. We're all dead, all of us who're on it, and we're all tired, yet somehow we can't leave it. There's nice smells in the summer, dust and hay and the wind smack in your face on a hot day; and it's nice waking up in the wet grass on a fine morning. I don't know, I don't know—' he lurched forward suddenly, and the tramp caught him in his arms.

'I'm sick,' the boy whispered—'sick.'

The tramp looked up and down the road, but he could see no houses or any sign of help. Yet even as he supported the boy doubtfully in the middle of the road a motor car suddenly flashed in the middle distance, and came smoothly through the snow.

'What's the trouble?' said the driver quietly as he pulled up. 'I'm a doctor.' He looked at the boy keenly and listened to his strained breathing.

'Pneumonia,' he commented. 'I'll give him a lift to the infirmary, and you, too, if you like.'

The tramp thought of the workhouse and shook his head 'I'd rather walk,' he said.

The boy winked faintly as they lifted him into the car.

'I'll meet you beyond Reigate,' he murmured to the tramp. 'You'll see.' And the car vanished along the white road.

All the morning the tramp splashed through the thawing snow, but at midday he begged some bread at a cottage door and crept into a lonely barn to eat it. It was warm in there, and after his meal he fell asleep among the hay. It was dark when he woke, and started trudging once more through the slushy roads.

Two miles beyond Reigate a figure, a fragile figure, slipped out of the darkness to meet him.

'On the road, guv'nor?' said a husky voice. 'Then I'll come a bit of the way with you if you don't walk too fast. It's a bit lonesome walking this time of day.'

'But the pneumonia!' cried the tramp, aghast.

'I died at Crawley this morning,' said the boy.

Our Late Visitor

by Marvin Kaye

Hearing an ascending tread upon the stairs leading to my workroom door, I peered out and saw Albert mounting the steps. I confess my first thoughts were completely selfish: *How the devil did he find us out here in the middle of the woods?*—and then, since he is often garrulous, *Now I shall never finish writing my chapter tonight!* But then my natural hospitality surfaced, and my conscience smote me fiercely for wishing away my closest friend. I resolutely set aside my petty problems—for, after all, I recollected, what were they compared to *his,* considering that he had died the previous week?

Of course, Jan and I only had the news second-hand, and we never put much faith in the *Times.* According to the obituary, rites were held in Albert's ancestral New England home, while a memorial ceremony was conducted in the city. But my own precarious health forbade me from attending it.

As he crossed the threshold of my den, I greeted Albert heartily and complimented him on the ruddiness of his complexion. He really looked the picture of health, and this made me something doubt the reliability of the newspaper accounts of his dissolution. I settled him in my easy chair, put a bottle of Majorska on the table by his side, and heartily pumped his cold hand. Despite the inconvenience of his visit (it was well past midnight), I was really quite pleased to see him, the more I thought of it. For several days, my spirits had been at their lowest ebb, and Albert's infectious *joie de vivre* seemed the fittest prescription for exorcising my *acedia.*

For several minutes, we exchanged hearty banalities. Naturally I was curious to learn the details of his interment, but I shrank from broaching the subject. I could not be sure whether it was proper etiquette to discuss so personal a topic, and besides, it was far too lugubrious when gaiety was what I craved!

We had scarce emptied the fifth when a sharp rap from the floor beneath quelled our festivities. Albert's voice is a big one that makes walls quake and furniture tremble. I feared its deep timbre had penetrated to the nursery below. Excusing myself, I descended the stairs and found Jan in our child's room, singing her back to sleep.

"You woke her!" she accused me, and I sheepishly explained that Albert had paid an unexpected call.

"How *dare* he?" she demanded. "He's supposed to be dead!"

"Hush! He'll hear you!"

"I don't care if he does. What right has he to intrude at this time of night and disturb the entire house? *Is he dead or not?*"

"Please," I implored, trying to quell her ire with a gesture, "what does it matter? After all, he *is* our friend!"

"He's your friend, not mine," Jan objected. "If he is *not* dead, it's too late for a social visit, and if he *is,* then he certainly has no business here! Hasn't he any sense of propriety?"

I did what I could to calm her, but to no avail. Her tenacity resembles nothing so much as a decapitated gila monster whose severed head still clings to the victim it has bitten. She positively insisted that I return to the attic and determine the precise state of Albert's health. I was reluctant to insult my guest, and told her so, but Jan would not be gainsaid.

"And while you're talking to him," she added, "see that he keeps quiet and doesn't waken Elania again. I had to sing her back to sleep, and you know how I hate music!"

"But isn't her musical turtle working?" I asked.

"*No.* It's broken! And it's not a turtle, as you know very well! It's a beetle—no matter *what* you tell Elania!"

The turtle was a long-standing toy of contention between Jan and me. It *was,* of course, a stuffed beetle with a music-box inside, but I detest crawling things, so I divested it of a few of its cloth legs and christened it "turtle," with which nomenclature our daughter heartily concurred.

"What harm is it," I repeatedly asked, "if Elania thinks of it as a turtle?"

"*Because,*" Jan insisted, "*it is a beetle!* A beetle is a beetle and a turtle is a turtle!"

I have often tried to reason with my wife. I have said again and again that if we *think* something is so, then it *is,* and have referred her to Pirandello for confirmation of my argument. But Jan's frame of reality is unshakably objective, and no internalization upon the mystery of things touches her. *I am,* she would have it, *therefore I think.*

I returned to the attic, and found Albert puffing on his clay pipe. A second fifth of vodka, half depleted, was at his elbow, and a merry smile played upon his thick lips.

"And now," he proclaimed as soon as I had shut the door, "I do believe it is time for a song!"

In vain, I tried to suppress his urge to carol forth, but I might as soon have harnessed the whirlwind. He has a well-trained voice. Once he carried spears at the Met, but in his maturer days, had graduated to the enviable role of torturer in "Samson and Delilah" and frequently had the privilege of burning out the strongman's eyes. Thus my friend was amply qualified to break into the refrain of "La Calunnia" at three o'clock in the morning. My half-hearted protests forgotten, I sat at my work-table and listened, entranced.

He had scarce gotten halfway through the coda when a loud double-rap at the door of my den stopped him smack upon the final repetition of the word "flagello."

I had no opportunity to bid the knocker enter. Before the words could clear the roof of my mouth, the door slammed wide open and Jan strode in, fury in her eyes.

Albert rose and respectfully bowed to her. Then he drank her health and swallowed the rest of the vodka in his glass.

"I asked you to quiet him down!" she barked at me, then rounded on my friend. "And *you!!* What right have you to be here at this time of morning? Don't you know this is the only chance my husband has to work undisturbed?"

"I beg your pardon," Albert murmured, taking her hand in his and pressing her fingers to his lips, "but I so wished to see you all once more, and there simply was no opportunity to consider the niceties of timing."

She snatched back her hand, scarcely mollified. "That's the way you always *were,* Albert!" she accused. "My husband's welfare never concerned you, it's always been your convenience that has determined the scope of friendship—"

"Jan!" I pleaded, "you're insulting our guest!"

"I don't care, it's true! You're only an article of furniture to him. Whenever he wants to relax, he puts his feet up on you."

The situation was clearly impossible, and I turned to Albert with a shrug. My lips were sealed, but he knew what my pantomime meant right enough: *"We know what women are!"*

"Well, well," said Albert, walking to the door, "it is clear to me I have not timed my visit as conveniently as I might have, and so, I will say goodnight." He bowed, and turned to depart, but Jan, crossing her arms, fixed him with a stare.

"Not so fast, Albert!" she snapped. "You are *not* leaving until you answer one question!"

"Janice!" I begged, "Albert has come such a long way to visit us. Is it necessary to be so rude as—" but I got no further. She turned her baleful stare upon me, and my heart sank in a morass of cowardice.

"Well?" she asked in a threatening voice, glowering at me. Her foot tapped impatiently. "Will *you* ask him or shall I?"

I forestalled her with a resigned gesture and turned to Albert. His pudgy face wore his customary good-humored grin and he spread his hands apart in a gesture of amused bewilderment.

"What can you possibly ask," he inquired, "that would offend me? Despite what this good woman says, you are my dearest friend and I willingly open the secrets of my heart to your inspection. 'Speak, demand, I'll answer.' "

His words cheered me. After all, what wrong *could* my curiosity commit? It was neither a subject of embarrassment nor shame. I cleared my throat and resolved to hesitate no longer.

"Albert, *mon vieux,*" I said, smiling to prove that the matter was really of trifling consequence, "the fact is that Janice and I read some disturbing news in last Tuesday's *Times* . . ."

I paused, expecting him to catch my meaning. But he merely stared at me with a blank expression on his face.

"I am at a complete loss," he said at last, "to discover to what you allude. I do not recall any distressing articles in last week's papers—but perhaps you were not aware that I subscribe to the *Post?*"

"Well, then you see," I replied, flustered, "the *Times* . . . you know . . . that is . . . the fact is . . ." The words stuck in my throat, but Jan, grown weary of my dilatory approach, blurted out what I had tried to gently insinuate.

"The newspaper," she told Albert, *"positively stated you were dead."*

He stared at her amazed. Then he looked at me, and I cannot adequately describe the anguished expression that filled his eyes. Sorrow was the principal emotion, and pain, too. Yet there was something worse—a keen disappointment that exceeded the normal bounds of that mundane humor. All of Albert's inextinguishable zest for life had been suddenly, impossibly, but irrevocably quelled.

"I wish," he moaned in a daunted, mournful voice such as I have never heard him use before, "I wish most mightily that you *had never told me!*" And even as he spoke, the arch of his balding scalp caved inwards and his round skull turned into a hollow concavity. The lights within his eyes guttered and died, and the smile upon his lips flickered like a death's-head grin before the *labia* sucked in and disappeared. His arms and legs and trunk deflated, collapsed, as if they had been filled with Jell-O subjected to a bath of scalding water.

Where my friend had stood, there was nothing but a damp stain which oozed out of one of my daughter's oldest, most cruelly ravaged rag dolls that lay crumpled on the floor. Its face, half-obliterated by the devouring tooth of Time, soaked up the spreading liquid that poured from its body. I knelt beside the pool and, upon tasting it, identified it as Majorska vodka.

"For once," said Jan as she stripped off her nightdress and clambered into bed an hour later, "it appears as if the *Times* got its facts straight."

"Yes," I murmured sullenly, "but why did *we* have to bring it to his attention?"

"After all," she said, lightly caressing my cheek with her fingertips, "he *had* to be told, sooner or later. Would you rather he'd heard it from a stranger instead of from his closest friends?"

I tried to argue about the necessity of telling him *at all*, but I could not make her see my point. Besides, her hands were busy beneath the covers, and soon I found myself preoccupied with other, more immediate concerns.

But before Janice permitted me to finish the business at hand, I had to promise her to tell Elania that her turtle was really a beetle.

Out of Copyright

by Ramsey Campbell

The widow gazed wistfully at the pile of books. "I thought they might be worth something."

"Oh, some are," Tharne said. "That one, for instance, will fetch a few pence. But I'm afraid your husband collected books indiscriminately. Much of this stuff isn't worth the paper it's printed on. Look, I'll tell you what I'll do—I'll take the whole lot off your hands and give you the best price I can."

When he'd counted out the notes, the wad over his heart was scarcely reduced. He carried the bulging cartons of books to his van, down three gloomy flights of stairs, along the stone path which hid beneath lolling grass, between gateposts whose stone globes grew continents of moss. By the third descent he was panting. Nevertheless he grinned as he kicked grass aside; the visit had been worthwhile, certainly.

He drove out of the cracked and overgrown streets, past rusty cars laid open for surgery, old men propped on front steps to wither in the sun, prams left outside houses as though in the hope that a thief might adopt the baby. Sunlight leaping from windows and broken glass lanced his eyes. Heat made the streets and his perceptions waver. Glimpsed in the mirror or sensed looming at his back, the cartons resembled someone crouching behind him. They smelled more dusty than the streets.

Soon he reached the crescent. The tall Georgian houses shone white. Beneath them the van looked cheap, a tin toy littering the street. Still, it wasn't advisable to seem too wealthy when buying books.

He dumped the cartons in his hall, beside the elegant curve of the staircase. His secretary came to the door of her office. "Any luck?"

"Yes indeed. Some first editions and a lot of rare material. The man knew what he was collecting."

"Your mail came," she said in a tone which might have announced the police. This annoyed him: he prided himself on his legal knowledge, he observed the law scrupulously. "Well, well," he demanded, "who's saying what?"

"It's that American agent again. He says you have a moral obligation to pay Lewis' widow for those three stories. Otherwise, he says— let's see—'I shall have to seriously consider recommending to my clients that they boycott your anthologies.' "

"He says that, does he? The bastard. They'd be better off boycotting him." Tharne's face grew hot and swollen; he could hardly control his grin. "He's better at splitting infinitives than he is at looking after his people's affairs. He never renewed the copyright on those stories. We don't owe anyone a penny. And by God, you show me an author who needs the money. Rolling in it, all of them. Living off their royalties." A final injustice struck him; he smote his forehead. "Anyway, what the devil's it got to do with the widow? She didn't write the stories."

To burn up some of his rage, he struggled down to the cellar with the cartons. His blood drummed wildly. As he unpacked the cartons, dust smoked up to the light bulbs. The cellar, already dim with its crowd of bookshelves, grew dimmer.

He piled the books neatly, sometimes shifting a book from one pile to another, as though playing Patience. When he reached the ace, he stopped. *Tales Beyond Life,* by Damien Damon. It was practically a legend; the book had never been reprinted in its entirety. The find could hardly have been more opportune. The book contained "The Dunning of Diavolo"—exactly what he needed to complete the new Tharne anthology, *Justice from Beyond the Grave.* He knocked lumps of dust from the top of the book, and turned to the story.

Even in death he would be recompensed. Might the resurrectionists have his corpse for a toy? Of a certainty—but only once those organs had been removed which his spirit would need, and the Rituals performed. This stipulation he had willed on his death-bed to his son. Unless his corpse was pacified, his curse would rise.

Undeed, had the father's estate been more readily available to clear the son's debts, this might have been an edifying tale of filial piety. Still, on a night when the moon gleamed like a sepulture, the father was plucked tuber-pallid from the earth.

Rather than sow superstitious scruples in the resurrectionists, the son had told them naught. Even so, the burrowers felt that they had mined an uncommon seam. Voiceless it might be, but the corpse had its forms of protest. Only by seizing its wrists could the corpse-miners elude the cold touch of its hands. Could they have closed its stiff lids, they might have borne its grin. On the contrary, neither would touch the gelatinous pebbles which bulged from its face . . .

Tharne knew how the tale continued: Diavolo, the father, was dissected, but his limbs went snaking round the town in search of those who had betrayed him, and crawled down the throats of the victims to drag out the twins of those organs of which the corpse had been robbed. All good Gothic stuff—gory and satisfying, but not to be taken too seriously. They couldn't write like that nowadays; they'd lost the knack of proper Gothic writing. And yet they whined that they weren't paid enough!

Only one thing about the tale annoyed him: the misprint "undeed" for "indeed." Amusingly, it resembled "undead"—but that was no excuse for perpetrating it. The one reprint of the tale, in the twenties,

339

had swarmed with literals. Well, this time the text would be perfect. Nothing appeared in a Tharne anthology until it satisfied him.

He checked the remaining text, then gave it to his secretary to retype. His timing was exact: a minute later the doorbell announced a book collector, who was as punctual as Tharne. They spent a mutually beneficial half hour. "These I bought only this morning," Tharne said proudly. "They're yours for twenty pounds apiece."

The day seemed satisfactory until the phone rang. He heard the girl's startled squeak. She rang through to his office, sounding flustered. "Ronald Main wants to speak to you."

"Oh, God. Tell him to write, if he still knows how. I've no time to waste in chatting, even if he has." But her cry had disturbed him; it sounded like a threat of inefficiency. Let Main see that someone round here wasn't to be shaken! "No, wait—put him on."

Main's orotund voice came rolling down the wire. "It has come to my notice that you have anthologized a story of mine without informing me."

Trust a writer to use as many words as he could! "There was no need to get in touch with you," Tharne said. "The story's out of copyright."

"That is hardly the issue. Aside from the matter of payment, which we shall certainly discuss, I want to take up with you the question of the text itself. Are you aware that whole sentences have been rewritten?"

"Yes, of course. That's part of my job. I am the editor, you know." Irritably Tharne restrained a sneeze; the smell of dust was very strong. "After all, it's an early story of yours. Objectively, don't you think I've improved it?" He oughtn't to sound as if he was weakening. "Anyway, I'm afraid that legally you've no rights."

Did that render Main speechless, or was he preparing a stronger attack? It scarcely mattered, for Tharne put down the phone. Then he strode down the hall to check his secretary's work. Was her typing as flustered as her voice had been?

Her office was hazy with floating dust. No wonder she was peering closely at the book—though she looked engrossed, almost entranced. As his shadow fell on the page she started; the typewriter carriage sprang to its limit, ringing. She demanded, "Was that you before?"

"What do you mean?"

"Oh, nothing. Don't let it bother you." She seemed nervously annoyed—whether with him or with herself he couldn't tell.

At least her typing was accurate, though he could see where letters had had to be retyped. He might as well write the introduction to the story. He went down to fetch *Who's Who in Horror and Fantasy Fiction*. Dust teemed around the cellar lights and chafed his throat.

Here was Damien Damon, real name Sidney Drew: b. Chelsea, 30 April 1876; d.? 1911? "His life was even more bizarre and outrageous than his fiction. Some critics say that that is the only reason for his fame . . ."

A small dry sound made Tharne glance up. Somewhere among the shelved books, a face peered at him through a gap. Of course it could be nothing of the sort, but it took him a while to locate a cover which had fallen open in a gap, and which must have resembled a face.

Upstairs he wrote the introduction. ". . . Without the help of an agent, and with no desire to make money from his writing, Damon became one of the most discussed in whispers writers of his day. Critics claim that it was scandals that he practiced magic which gained him fame. But his posthumously published *Tales Beyond Life* shows that he was probably the last really first-class writer in the tradition of Poe . . ." Glancing up, Tharne caught sight of himself, pen in hand, at the desk in the mirror. So much for any nonsense that he didn't understand writers' problems. Why, he was a writer himself!

Only when he'd finished writing did he notice how quiet the house had become. It had the strained unnatural silence of a library. As he padded down the hall to deliver the text to his secretary his sounds felt muffled, detached from him.

His secretary was poring over the typescript of Damon's tale. She looked less efficient than anxious—searching for something she would rather not find? Dust hung about her in the amber light, and made her resemble a waxwork or a faded painting. Her arms dangled, forgotten. Her gaze was fixed on the page.

Before he could speak, the phone rang. That startled her so badly that he thought his presence might dismay her more. He retreated into the hall, and a dark shape stepped back behind him—his shadow, of course. He entered her office once more, making sure he was audible.

"It's Mr. Main again," she said, almost wailing.

"Tell him to put it in writing."

"Mr. Tharne says would you please send him a letter." Her training allowed her to regain control, yet she seemed unable to put down the phone until instructed. Tharne enjoyed the abrupt cessation of the outraged squeaking. "Now I think you'd better go home and get some rest," he said.

When she'd left he sat at her desk and read the typescript. Yes, she had corrected the original; "undeed" was righted. The text seemed perfect, ready for the printer. Why then did he feel that something was wrong? Had she omitted a passage or otherwise changed the wording?

He'd compare the texts in his office, where he was more comfortable. As he rose, he noticed a few faint dusty marks on the carpet. They approached behind his secretary's chair, then veered away. He must have tracked dust from the cellar, which clearly needed sweeping. What did his housekeeper think she was paid for?

Again his footsteps sounded muted. Perhaps his ears were clogged with dust; there was certainly enough of it about. He had never noticed how strongly the house smelled of old books, nor how unpleasant the smell could be. His skin felt dry, itchy.

In his office he poured himself a large Scotch. It was late enough, he needn't feel guilty—indeed, twilight seemed unusually swift tonight, unless it was an effect of the swarms of dust. He didn't spend all day drinking, unlike some writers he could name.

He knocked clumps of dust from the book; it seemed almost to grow there, like gray fungus. Airborne dust whirled away from him and drifted back. He compared the texts, line by line. Surely they were identical, except for her single correction. Yet he felt there was some aspect of the typescript which he needed urgently to decipher. This frustration, and its irrationality, unnerved him.

He was still frowning at the pages, having refilled his glass to loosen up his thoughts, when the phone rang once. He grabbed it irritably, but the earpiece was as hushed as the house. Or was there, amid the electric hissing vague as a cascade of dust, a whisper? It was beyond the grasp of his hearing, except for a syllable or two which sounded like Latin—if it was there at all.

He jerked to his feet and hurried down the hall. Now that he thought about it, perhaps he'd heard his secretary's extension lifted as his phone had rung. Yes, her receiver was off the hook. It must have fallen off. As he replaced it, dust sifted out of the mouthpiece.

Was a piece of paper rustling in the hall? No, the hall was bare. Perhaps it was the typescript, stirred on his desk by a draft. He closed the door behind him, to exclude any draft—as well as the odor of something very old and dusty.

But the smell was stronger in his room. He sniffed gingerly at *Tales Beyond Life*. Why, there it was: the book reeked of dust. He shoved open the French windows, then he sat and stared at the typescript. He was beginning to regard it with positive dislike. He felt as though he had been given a code to crack; it was nerve-racking as an examination. Why was it only the typescript that bothered him, and not the original?

He flapped the typed pages, for they looked thinly coated with gray.

Perhaps it was only the twilight, which seemed composed of dust. Even his Scotch tasted clogged. Just let him see what was wrong with this damned story, then he'd leave the room to its dust—and have a few well-chosen words for his housekeeper tomorrow.

There was only one difference between the texts: the capital *I*. Or had he missed another letter? Compulsively and irritably, refusing to glance at the gray lump which hovered at the edge of his vision, he checked the first few capitals. *E, M, O, R, T* . . . Suddenly he stopped, parched mouth open. Seizing his pen, he began to transcribe the capitals alone.

E mortuis revoco.

From the dead I summon thee.

Oh, it must be a joke, a mistake, a coincidence. But the next few capitals dashed his doubts. *From the dead I summon thee, from the dust I recreate thee . . .* The entire story concealed a Latin invocation. It had been Damien Damon's last story and also, apparently, his last attempt at magic.

And it was Tharne's discovery. He must rewrite his introduction. Publicized correctly, the secret of the tale could help the book's sales a great deal. Why then was he unwilling to look up? Why was he tense as a trapped animal, ears straining painfully? Because of the thick smell of dust, the stealthy dry noises that his choked ears were unable to locate, the gray mass that hovered in front of him?

When at last he managed to look up, the jerk of his head twinged his neck. But his gasp was of relief. The gray blotch was only a chunk of dust, clinging to the mirror. Admittedly it was unpleasant; it resembled a face masked with dust, which also spilled from the face's dismayingly numerous openings. Really, he could live without it, much as he resented having to do his housekeeper's job for her.

When he rose, it took him a moment to realize that his reflection had partly blotted out the gray mass. In the further moment before he understood, two more reflected gray lumps rose beside it, behind him. Were they hands, or wads of dust? Perhaps they were composed of both. It was impossible to tell, even when they closed over his face.

343

Pacific 421

by August W. Derleth

"Just to be on the safe side, I wouldn't spend too much time over the hill at the far end of your property," said the agent with an apologetic smile.

Colley took the keys and pocketed them. "That's an odd thing to say. Why not?"

"Around mid-evening especially," continued the agent.

"Oh, come—why not?"

"That's just what I've been told. Something strange there, I'd guess. Give yourself time to become used to the place first."

Albert Colley had every intention of doing that. He had not bought a place in the country just out of a village on the Pacific line without the determination to become used to it before he invited his stepfather down—if he could screw up courage enough to have the old curmudgeon around for a week or so. If it were not for the old man's money—well, if it were not for that, and the fact that Albert Colley was his only legal heir, he would have been free of the old man long before this. Even as it was, Philander Colley was a trial that made itself felt in the remotest atom of Albert's being.

Of course, the agent's off-hand reference had been a mistake. Few people, in any case, are qualified to judge just how any given man will act, especially on such short acquaintance as there had been between Colley and the agent for the Parth house two miles out of that Missouri town. Colley was a cool customer, cooler than the agent guessed him to be. Colley apprehended at once that there was something a little strange about the far end of the property he had bought—a good forty-acre piece, with the house right up next to the road in a little clump of trees there, and, as he understood it from that old map in the county surveyor's office, a portion of the Pacific line cutting across the far edge of his property, over a little gully there. From the road and the house, his property stretched through a garden, then through a dense belt of woods to an open place beyond which there was a little knoll, politely called "the hill," and past this, the railroad and the termination of Colley's newly acquired property at the foot of a steeper slope, likewise for the most part wooded.

And, being a cool customer, Colley went that first evening for a tour of exploration, half expecting some denizened beast to spring at him out of the woods, but not afraid, for all that. He walked down to the point where the railroad crossed the trestle over the gully and then turned to look down the tracks, this way and that; the railroad came around a curve, crossed the trestle and the edge of his property, and disappeared around a further curve to westward. He stood for a while on the trestle, smoking a cigar, and taking pleasure in the sound of night-hawks swooping and sky-coasting in the evening sky. He looked at his watch. Almost nine o'clock. Well, that was as close to mid-evening as a man would want, he thought.

He left the trestle and was beginning to walk leisurely back to the house when he heard the whistle and rumble of an approaching loco-motive. He turned there on the edge of his woods to look. Yes, it was coming, brightly lit; so he stood and watched the powerful, surging force of the train thunder across the trestle, eight passenger cars streaming speedily along behind the locomotive—*Pacific 421*—on the way to the west coast. Like most men, he had always had a kind of affinity for trains; he liked to see them, ride on them, hear them. He watched this one out of sight and turned.

But at that moment there fell upon his ears the most frightful explo-sion of sound—a screaming of steel on steel, a splintering of wood, a great rush of steam, the roar of flames crackling, and the shrill, horrible screaming of people in agony. For a moment he was paralyzed with shock; then he realized that the train must have leaped the tracks or crashed into an eastbound train, and, without stopping to think that he ought to telephone for help, he sped back to the tracks and raced down as fast as he could to round the curve of the hill there to west-ward.

It was just as well that he did not summon help first.

There was nothing, nothing at all on the tracks beyond the curve!

For a moment Colley thought that the train must be found farther along, over the horizon; but that was impossible, for the tracks stretched away under the stars to join a greater network of railroads beyond, and there was nothing whatever on them. The evening train had gone through, and he—well, he had undoubtedly suffered a kind of auditory hallucination. But it jarred him still; for an hallucination, the experience had been shakingly convincing, and it was a somewhat subdued Albert Colley who made his way back along the tracks and into his property once more.

He thought about it all night.

In the morning he might have forgotten it but for the fact that he took a look at the village weekly he had had delivered to his house by the rural postman and his eye caught sight of train schedules; trains leaving for the west on the Pacific line were scheduled at 6:07 and at 11:23. There numbers were different, too—there was no *Pacific 421* among them.

Colley was sharp. He had not been engaged in dubious business practices for some years without becoming shrewd about little matters. It did not take much to figure out that something was very much wrong. He read the railroad schedule over carefully and deliberately, and then got up and took a quick walk down through the garden, through the woods, to the railroad tracks.

Their appearance under the sun was puzzling, to put it mildly. They were rusted and gave every evidence of deterioration under disuse. Wild roses, fox grass, evening primroses, weeds grew between the ties, and bushes climbed the embankment. The ties and the trestle were in good shape, but the fact remained that the railroad did not have the look of being in use. He crossed the trestle and walked for over a mile until he came to the double track which was certainly the main line. Then he walked back until he came to the tracks of the main line far around the slope of the hill on the other side. The cut-off spur across his property was not more than five miles in length, all told.

It was well past noon when he returned to the house. He made himself a light lunch and sat down to think the matter over.

Very peculiar. Then there had been the agent's half-hearted warning. A faint prickling made itself felt at the roots of his scalp, but something turning over in his scheming mind was stronger.

It was Saturday afternoon, or he would have made it a point to drive into the village and call on the agent; but the agent would be out of his office; the trip would be futile. What he could and would do, however, was to walk down through the garden and the woods, over the hill to the railroad embankment in mid-evening and keep an eye out for the *Pacific 421.*

It was not without some trepidation that he made his way through the woods to the railroad that night. He was filled with a certain uneasy anticipation, but he would not yield to his inner promptings to return to the house and forget what he had seen. He took up his stand at the foot of an old cottonwood tree and lit a cigar, the aromatic smoke of which mingled with the pleasant, sweet foliage fragrance to make a pleasant cloud of perfume around him.

As nine o'clock drew near, he grew restive. He looked at his watch several times, but the time passed with execrable slowness. The train was manifestly late.

Nine-fifteen, nine-thirty, nine-forty-five—and at last ten. No train.

Colley was more mystified than ever, and he returned to the house that night determined to repeat his experiment on the morrow.

But on Sunday night he saw no more than he had seen the previous day. No locomotive whistled and roared across the trestle and away around the curve of the hill, drawing its passenger cars, brilliantly alight after it—nothing at all. Only the wind sighed and whispered at the trestle, and a persistent owl hooted from the hillside beyond the ravine bridged by the trestle. Colley was puzzled, and, yes, a little annoyed.

He went into the village on Monday and paid a call on the agent.

"Tell me," he said affably, "doesn't the old *Pacific 421* run out of here any more?"

The agent gave him an odd glance. "Not since the accident. I think even the number's been discontinued. Let me see—the accident took place about seven years ago, when that spur across your land was still part of the main line."

"Oh, it's no longer in use, then?"

"No, it hasn't been for years—ever since the accident." He coughed. "You haven't seen anything, have you?"

It was at this point that Colley made his fatal mistake. He was too clever for his own good. Because his thoughts were several leaps and bounds ahead of the agent's, he said gravely, "No. Why?"

The agent sighed his relief. "Well, some people have laid claim to seeing a ghost there." He laughed. "A ghost train, if you can believe it!"

"Interesting," said Colley dryly, his skin at the back of his neck chilling.

"That wreck occurred on a Friday evening, and it's usually on Friday that the so-called apparition is seen. And then it seems to have its limitations; I've never seen it myself; nor have very many people. I did have the experience of being with someone who claimed to be seeing it. But I never heard of a ghost, man or train, which could be seen and heard by one person and not by someone standing beside him, did you?"

"Never," agreed Colley gravely.

"Well, there you are. I was afraid you, too, might have seen something. I was just a little nervous about it."

"I suppose that's what you meant."

"Yes. Maybe I shouldn't have said anything."

"No harm done," said Colley, smiling good-naturedly.

He was really not paying much attention to what the agent was saying, for he was busy with his own thoughts. His own thoughts would have been of considerable interest to his stepfather, for they concerned him very much indeed. Philander Colley had a weak heart, and it had occurred to Albert Colley that with a careful build-up and the sudden exposure of the old man to that ghost train some Friday night, the old man's heart might give out on him, and that would leave Albert, as the old man's only heir, in sound financial shape.

He had expected the agent to put the matter more or less as he did. Incredible as it seemed, the idea of a phantom train was not entirely beyond the bounds of possibility. Of course, curiously, Colley did not actually believe in the phantom train as anything supernatural—doubtless there was some kind of scientific explanation for it, he felt, thus betraying a juvenile faith in one kind of superstition as opposed to another. But as long as *something* came rushing along there and wrecked itself, repeating the catastrophe of that Friday evening seven years ago, it might as well be put to his own use. After all, that train, whatever its status, *did* cross his land, and he had a certain proprietary right in it.

Forthwith he wired his stepfather that he had got settled, and the old man might like to come down from his place in Wisconsin and take a look around Colley's place in the Missouri country.

The old man came, with dispatch.

If Albert Colley had his dark side, the old man was cantankerous enough to match his stepson any day, any time, any place. He was the sort of crotchety old devil who would argue about anything under the sun, at scarcely the shadow of a provocation. Small wonder Colley wanted to get rid of him!

Colley lost no time in setting the stage. He told the old man that it was his regular habit to walk down to the end of his property every evening, and would like the old man to accompany him.

Bitterly complaining, the old man went along.

As they approached the railroad tracks—it was Wednesday night, and nothing was likely to happen—Colley coughed unctuously and said that the stretch of abandoned tracks before them had the reputation of being haunted.

"Haunted?" repeated the old man, with a sarcastic laugh. "By what?"

"A train that was wrecked here about seven years ago. *Pacific 421.*"

"Cock and bull story," snapped Philander.

"There *are* people who claim to have seen it."

"Out of their minds. Or drunk. You ought to know what you can see when you're drunk, Albert. I remember that time you saw alligators all over your room."

"Still, you know," said Albert, trying his best to be patient, "one ought not to dismiss such stories too casually. After all, things happen, and science cannot always explain them satisfactorily."

"Things! What things? Optical illusions, hallucinations—such like. No, my boy, you never were very bright in school, but I never thought it would come to this—a belief in ghosts. And what a ghost, to be specific!" He turned on him almost fiercely. "Have you seen it yourself?"

"N-no," faltered Albert.

"Well, then!" snorted the old man.

That ended the conversation about the phantom train for that evening. Albert was just a little disappointed, but not too badly; after all, he must go slowly; the groundwork for Friday night's hoped-for fatal apparition must be laid carefully. What he could not accomplish on Wednesday, he might well be able to do on the following evening. And then, on Friday. . . . Ah, but Friday was still two days away!

So, on Thursday evening they walked down to the tracks again. The old man wanted to go out on to the trestle, and there he stood, talking about trestles in Wisconsin from which he had fished as a boy—quite a long time before he had married Albert's mother. Albert had a hard time bringing the conversation around to the phantom train, and he had hardly mentioned it before the old man cut him off with his customary rudeness.

"Still going on about that ghost train, eh?"

"The fact is, there seems to be some question about the story both ways."

"I should think there would be!" He snorted. "I can't figure out how a sane, normal, healthy young man would want to even think of such drivel, let alone go on about it the way you do."

"Keep an open mind, Philander," said Albert with ill-concealed asperity.

"My mind's been open all my life," retorted the old man. "But not to a lot of silly superstitions and womanish fears."

"I can't recall having expressed fear of any kind," said Albert frigidly.

"No, but you sound like it."

"I'm not in the habit of being afraid of something I've never seen," said Albert.

"Oh, most people are afraid of the dark." He strove to peer through the gloom into the gully. "Tell me—sand or rock on the sides down there?"

"Rock for the most part. The sand's been washed away."

"Look to be some trees growing down there."

"Young ones—just a few."

Poor Albert! He lost ten minutes talking about rocks, trees, declivities, angles, degrees, and erosion of wind as against that of water, and by that time he was almost too exhausted to bring up the subject of the phantom train again. But he strove manfully and came up with a weak question.

"Tell me, Philander—what *would* you do if you saw that train coming at us?"

"That ghost train?"

"Yes, the one some people believe in."

"Why, close my eyes till she went past," said the old man promptly.

"Then you *would* be afraid of it," charged Albert.

"If there were any such thing, you're darn tootin' I would!"

That was something in the way of a hopeful sign, at least, thought Albert, walking slowly back at his stepfather's side. Well, tomorrow night would tell the story. And if somehow it failed, there was always Friday night a week hence. Patience and fortitude, Albert, my boy! he told himself, meanwhile contemplating with pleasure his acquisition of his stepfather's material possessions. He resolved to time their visit with the utmost care tomorrow night.

All that day he went out of his way to be nice to the old man, on the theory that those who are about to die deserve such little pleasures as it is possible to give; and he was unnaturally ready to forgive the old man his cantankerousness and irritability—which startled Philander because it was an attitude for which Albert never won any medals. If the old man had not been so selfish himself, he might have thought about this change in his stepson; but he opined that perhaps Albert was in need of money and was about to make a touch, and took pleasure for hours thinking up ways in which to rebuff Albert.

As for Albert, he grew hourly more elated as that fateful Friday passed on its way. Time went heavy-footed, but Albert could be patient. After all, Philander's money drew closer moment by moment, and it was of proportions worth waiting for, even if the old man were not exactly what a man might call "rich."

For some reason, all the signs were auspicious. That is to say, along about mid-afternoon, the old man began to recall tales of hauntings he had heard in his youth, and waxed quite garrulous. Albert considered this virtually a sign from—well, not heaven, of course; heaven would hardly be giving him a green light. Anyway, it was a sign, a kind of portent that all was destined to happen as Albert planned it.

So that evening he gave Philander one of his best cigars, lit it for him jovially, and set out with him for the railroad tracks. He had had a few moments of ghastly fear that the old man might not accompany him, but there was no stopping him. He had in fact taken over Albert's little walk, and called it his "constitutional."

"This is the night, you know, that ghost train is said to appear," said Albert cautiously.

"Friday, eh?"

"Yes, it was on Friday that the accident took place."

"Funny thing—how methodical ghosts and suchlike can be, eh?"

Albert agreed, and then very subtly, according to plan, discredited the entire narrative, from beginning to end. It would not do to appear too gullible, when the old man knew very well he was not.

He had hoped they might be able to take up a stand at the edge of the woods, so that Philander might get the best possible view and the maximum shock at sight of that speeding spectre, but the old man insisted upon walking further. Indeed, he ventured out upon the embankment, he walked along the tracks, he even crossed the trestle. This was not quite in accordance with Albert's plans, but he had to yield to it; he followed his stepfather across the trestle, observing in some dismay that the hour must be close to nine.

Even as he thought this, the sound of a thin, wailing whistle burst upon his ears, and almost immediately thereafter came the rumble of the approaching train. Ahead of them the light of the locomotive swung around and bore down on them; it was the ghost train, rushing at them with the speed of light, it seemed, with kind of demoniac violence wholly in keeping with the shattering end to which it was destined to come.

Even in the sudden paroxysm of fright that struck him, Albert did not forget to act natural; this was as he had planned it—to pretend he saw nothing; all he did was to step off the tracks to one side. Then he turned to look at his stepfather. What he saw filled him with complete dismay.

The old man stood in the middle of the right-of-way relighting his cigar. Not a hair of his head had turned, and his eyes were not closed.

Yet he appeared to be gazing directly at the approaching train. Albert remembered with sickening chagrin that the agent had said many people could not see the train.

But if Philander Colley could not see the spectral train, he was nevertheless not immune. For at the moment that the phantom locomotive came into contact with the material person of the old man, Philander was knocked up and catapulted into the gully with terrific force, while the agent of his disaster went on its destined way, its lighted coaches streaming by, vanishing around the hill, and ending up, as before in a horrific din of wreckage.

Albert had to take a minute or two to collect himself. Then he ran as best he could down the slope to where his stepfather lay.

Philander Colley was very thoroughly dead. He had been crushed and broken—just as if he had been struck by a locomotive! Albert did not give him a second thought; however it had been done, Philander's end had been accomplished. He set off at a rapid trot for the car to run into the village and summon help.

Unfortunately for Albert Colley, the villagers were wholly devoid of imagination. A ghost train, indeed! There was plenty of evidence from Wisconsin that Albert Colley and his stepfather had not got along at all well. And Albert was the old man's only heir, too! An open and shut matter, in the opinion of the officials.

If there were any such thing as a phantom train, why hadn't Albert Colley said something about it before? The agent could testify he had not. It was plain as a pikestaff that Albert had beaten up the old man and probably pushed him off the trestle. With commendable dispatch Albert Colley was arrested, tried, and hanged.

The Pedicab

by Donald R. Burleson

Jerry slammed the door, hard enough to rattle the bay window in its frame.

Snow had been falling for most of the day, and now that the evening had settled over the town like a blind gray shroud, the growing gloom was a fit setting for his own mood. Trudging away from the house in his parka and boots and gloves, with the snow pelting heavily against the fur-lined hood covering his head, he could hear and feel the echoes of his exchange with Carol, reverberant in his mind, and when he left the projection of warm light from the front window and headed into the darkness of the storm, he felt as if he were moving out of the light in more ways than one, leaving life behind, entering a cavernous shadow-realm that seemed to spell all that was left to him. Glancing back once at the house with its living room window aglow in the night, he pulled the hood tighter and walked on, leaning into the biting wind, moving his feet through drifts of snow.

For just one moment there, one priceless moment, he could have done it; he could have said the right words, could have taken her close to him, could have ended the trouble.

But he hadn't. A strange, cold recalcitrance had swept over him, and he hadn't said those right words, even though he had been able to hear them stirring somewhere in his mind. No, he had gone to the closet for his parka, and with a surge of fresh resentment had simply walked out.

Jerry, please. Her face, her brimming eyes had asked what her voice seemed not quite able to ask. She was asking him to forgive her, and the eyes, the face loomed up in a vision before him now, stark and imploring. But the winter-brittle trees overhead creaked with their mounting burden of gray-white, and in this reality the face vanished in an uncompromising moil of snow. The wind sent the falling flakes swirling in mad kaleidoscopic patterns before him, around him. He walked on.

He had confronted her last night—God, was it only twenty-four hours ago?—with his knowledge of her little affair with his one-time business partner Tom Burgess. They had spent the night together the previous Saturday while he had been down to Boston for a conference, and he had found out, and finally last night had no longer been able to be silent. He told her that he knew.

It had been nasty then. She had turned on him, defiant.

"Well, sure, it's all right for *you*, though, isn't it, Jerry? House Eleven was just fine for you!"

So there it was, out in the open again, ringing in the air around them—between them. After all this time, she had thrown that up to him.

Blinking against the fugitive flakes that found their way into the shelter of the hood and stung his eyes, he halted a moment to see where he was. He had come to the end of Darien Street, where it made a T with Kalb Lane, which led toward town to the right and, to the left, led up a slight incline to wind lazily among further residential sections dotted with split-entry houses like his own. The snow was drifting so high over the curbs that only the positions of familiar fences and houses and trees told him approximately where the pavement was. Wriggling his fingers inside his gloves to revive the circulation, he moved off onto Kalb Lane to the left, up the hill.

After all this time. To bring it out of hiding and throw it in his face, after all this time.

He made his way slowly up the hill, a gentle enough incline in good walking weather, a treacherous path now, his boots slipping from time to time on the hard ice beneath the snow. The houses on each side were powdery ghosts turning their wan eyes indifferently upon him as he passed. The single streetlamp now overhead looked pathetic, unconvincing. Momentarily, he thought he could hear some odd, distant sound enmeshed somewhere in the raging of the wind, but he didn't feel like thinking about such things. He made himself go on.

For eight years nothing had been said about it. He realized that it had always been lurking just beneath the surface of their marriage, a crusty old wound covered over with layers of new flesh but never really healed.

They had had some kind of foolish newlywed spat that time eight years ago, when he was in the Air Force and they were overseas, in Taiwan, renting a little apartment in town a few miles from the military base. He had had a few beers that night, and the argument with Carol —over what? he didn't even remember now—had assumed a seriousness out of all proportion, and he had stormed melodramatically out the door, into the street, and had flagged down the first pedicab that came by.

Pedicabs. In those days in Taiwan they were everywhere you looked. The streets bristled with them, those curious but eminently practical little vehicles that raised a constant jangling din in the air, night and day. Pedicab, *noun:* the front half of a bicycle, with a two-wheeled canopied seat in the back, canopy up if it was raining, usually down otherwise. For a few cents the driver would pedal you clear across town, and more quickly and maneuverably and reliably than a taxi, which would cost more.

Shuffling through the blinding snow now, he could still remember the way the pedicab boy had looked, thin but muscular, dressed in the usual khaki pants and ragged T-shirt and bowl-like hat, the eager and enterprising young Chinese face peering out at him from beneath the brim. "You want pedicab!" More a statement of probable fact than a question, this, and delivered with a big smile.

Jerry had climbed into the seat, where the dilapidated cloth canopy was folded down, and he had handed a ragged bill to the boy. "House Eleven." And the pedicab had started off. The rickety vehicle must almost have known its own way there, because House Eleven, on a grimy back street, was one of the most popular of the sordid little "houses" in the city, off-limits to military personnel and constantly being raided by the military police and local police alike, but thriving still.

Some little distance along, the boy had stopped the pedicab beside a warehouse and looked back at him. "I take you go home."

Jerry had gaped, uncomprehending. "What?"

The boy looked nervous, but persevered. "I see you all time in Hsi Men Ding, shop with pretty wife. House Eleven trouble, you no wanna go. *Hwei jya ba.* Go home wife."

"Look, kid," Jerry had hissed at him, "when I want a lecture on how to live my life, it won't be from you. Now get moving. House Eleven!"

The boy, evidently understanding enough of this for the purpose, looked resigned, and turned back around and pedaled them away through the noisy streets.

On his way out the door of House Eleven, Jerry had already essentially forgotten the tiny-waisted and ludicrously painted girl he had just been with, and was already sober and penitent, thinking of Carol. But on his way out that door the wife of someone from work had spotted him, and with the military social grapevine it wasn't long before Carol knew.

Reaching the top of the windswept incline now, he shook some of the heavy snow off his parka and veered down some nameless street off to the right, its outline only vaguely discernible in the shifting, undulating blanket of numbing white. Here, too, the houses huddling in the storm gazed out of compassionless square eyes of pale light as he passed, and he felt very, very alone.

Their relationship had survived. They had talked about it; Carol at first had cried and talked of leaving him, but he had been truly sorry for what he had done, and she seemed in time to forgive him, at least enough to keep them together. After his leaving the Air Force and returning part-time to school and settling into a career in southern New Hampshire, Elsie was born, and then Danny, and things seemed okay. But always, dimly stirring under the surface like unnameable shapes at the bottom of a pond—the memory, the hurt, the guilt. With never a word spoken about any of it.

Until now, until last night.

Overhead, the wind sang an eerie night-song, whipping and crackling through the ancient oaks and scattering snow in a crazy profusion of storm. He passed the last of the lighted houses and pushed on toward the lightless edge of a wood that crept almost to the white-muffled border of the street. He stopped and peered into the black maw beneath the trees, where the snow was gradually filtering down to line the gnarled roots in cryptic hieroglyphs of shadowed whiteness on the frozen ground. "The woods are lovely, dark and deep"—the words of the poem came to him unbidden, and he wondered if he had actually spoken them aloud, beneath the howl of the wind. Wasn't the poem supposed to conceal a Freudian death-wish? English 201, eons ago when he and Carol were—

Were what? Pretending that it was all forgotten?

They had argued bitterly last night, exchanging mindless accusations, finally subsiding into a kind of sullen truce that amounted to a tacit agreement not to speak to each other at all. Then tonight, tonight. It had all broken open again.

Blinking, he squinted myopically into the sable depths of the wood and didn't even try now to shake off the snow that was accumulating on the parka and making a crusty ring of white around the fur-lined face-opening in the hood. Did she really think that that was fair, now after all these years, when he was working hard to be a good husband and father, to dally with another man and then fling his own long-ago lapse into his face as if to square things, tit for tat? Was that fair?

He took a crunching step onto the snow bordering the wood.

Yet the worst of it was tonight, that poignant little moment afterward, after his own bitter words, when she wordlessly asked him, with those sad eyes searching his face, to forgive her and to believe that now, finally, she had fully forgiven him. Something in him had yearned to say yes, yes, it's all right, I know the thing with Tom was meaningless, yes, now we can be closer than we ever were before, we can start here, now, fresh, and everything will be okay. But stubbornness had washed over him and overruled all that, and in the moment when he could have said it, he didn't.

And the woods did look lovely, dark and deep, because the moment had passed and it was too late now, wasn't it? Not too late to forgive her, but too late to say it—too late for her to forgive him for not saying it.

Trudging another step toward the trees, he thought: I can't believe how tired I am, how nice it would be just to lie down in there, lie down and let the thoughts stop coming. He took another step.

And stopped. And listened.

Something, some sound hidden in the cacophony of the wind. Some high, half-remembered sound. But no, there was nothing, nothing but the storm. He shifted one foot, ready to continue.

No, wait. Again. The sound again, out of the ruffling curtains of snow. Almost like a—

From far off down the snow-covered street, dimly emerging from the crazed maelstrom of white—a shape.

He blinked and rubbed his watery eyes with white-crusted gloves. The thing drew closer but not much clearer, still obscure in the storm. Closer now, and the outlines just beginning to clear. And the sounds— the creaking of cold wood, the high keening of a bell.

The pedicab, its raised canopy torn and flapping noisily in the wind, pulled to a clattering stop beside him. The driver, hunched angularly over his handlebars, wore—incongrously, in this biting cold—khaki pants and a torn and soiled T-shirt; only a dim suggestion of a distantly familiar young face showed from under the hat.

They regarded each other wordlessly. Neither moved. Jerry felt numb in the brain, frozen and unable even to question what he was seeing. The world was congealed into one icy moment that seemed to draw out, to become endless. At length, without thinking, he dragged his heavy boots out of the enveloping snow and climbed into the rickety seat, ducking his head beneath the flapping cloth, and the pedi- cab began to move.

His mind only vaguely registered that the vehicle, its wheels cutting through the mounting snow, its bicycle bell ratcheting and chirping into the wind, clattered its way back to Kalb Lane, past rows of houses, back down the hill, back onto Darien Street in the bewildering white drifts, stopping at the edge of a mellow shaft of light cast across the snow from a window.

He climbed down, stood in the street, and looked at the thin but muscular driver.

The boy, already turning the pedicab around to leave, gave him a glimpse of a shy but determined smile.

"*Jei-tzu wo dai ni hwei jya le*. This time I take you go home."

The wind whipped up a frenzy of snow, and by the time his vision cleared, there was only the lighted window, where Carol waited.

The Phantom Express

by H. Thompson Rich

Once, twice, three times the station-clock's thin steel minute-hand had traced its monotonous circuit. Over in a corner of the big room several tired itinerants sat half-asleep. From behind the barred ticket window a telegraph instrument talked fitfully. Elsewhere silence, save when the main door swung narrowly to admit an occasional overcoated, sleeted figure—and a squall of zero air. The Transcontinental was late.

Boom! Out of the dark came a dull epic of sound. *Boom!* It spread through the air like fog. *Boom!* Twelve times, till the night was saturated with muffled reverberations.

Hardly had the last lifeless echo faded, when a series of piercing shrieks announced the long-awaited Transcontinental. A moment later she rolled into the shed, steaming and sheathed in ice.

Engineer Hadden stepped wearily from the cab and swung off up the platform, chafing his chilled hands together. The stationmaster ambled out to meet him, throwing shadowy circles from his swinging lantern.

"Open track ahead, Hadden. Orders to hit 'er up!"

Behind them the passengers were piling aboard. Hadden half turned.

"Dangerous business, hitting her up this sort of weather," he muttered, "but orders are orders!"

He climbed back into the cab. When the signal came, he opened the throttle. Swiftly the Transcontinental slid out of the shed.

Then he looked at his watch. It read 12:05.

"A straight stretch for eighty miles!" he exclaimed, and let her out.

The locomotive rocked and leapt ahead—now forty, now fifty, now sixty miles an hour.

"Mike!" he yelled, and the wash of air whipped the words back into the fireman's ear like pistol shots. "Mike, we make Mansford by 1."

"An hour?" screamed the latter. *"An hour?* Eighty miles? Man, yer dr-reaming!"

"Maybe I am," said Hadden grimly, giving her another notch.

* * *

On into the night they rushed, faster and faster, till it was all O'Connell could do to keep that dancing devil of a steam-gage needle up to where it belonged. Stripped to his red flannel shirt, he stood in the lurid glow of the fire-box stoking like a madman, while the ground reeled and swayed beneath him and the sky hissed dizzily over his head.

Firm on the little cab seat sat the chief, gazing fixedly ahead. He was tired and cold, and he thought how comfortable his little home would be, at the end of the run. He pictured Mary, his wife, waiting for him at the door—then the steaming supper—then sleep.

He yawned. He nodded.

On and on they roared, up grades, down inclines, over trestles, leaving behind them a long unbroken ribbon of echoes.

Suddenly Hadden jumped and rubbed his eyes. Then he stiffened and peered into the dark ahead—and saw a long, straight line of racing lights.

"Another express, not a mile away!"

"Mike! for the love of God, look!"

"Look where?"

O'Connell looked.

"I see nothin'!" he shouted back.

"You see what?"

"I see nothin'!"

"Then look again!"

O'Connell looked again.

"I see nothin', I say—nothin' at all!"

"Michael O'Connell," muttered the engineer, "you're a liar!"

They pulled into Mansford on the stroke of 1. Hadden watched the other express disappear into the dark ahead, and climbed angrily from his cab. He had been assured an open track. He would see what they meant by blocking the Transcontinental.

But the stationmaster knew of no train ahead.

"I tell you, your track is clear," he repeated, "open and clear to the end of the run!"

"You can tell me and be damned!" swore Hadden. "I tell you it's not!"

Suddenly he climbed back into his seat. It was 1:05.

"We'll make it by 2," he said, opening her up. "God, I'm tired!"

Soon they were roaring on into the dark again—and suddenly the other express loomed up ahead, a ghostly vanguard.

"Mike!" yelled Hadden; "for the last time, look ahead!"

O'Connell looked once more.

"I see nothin'—nothin'!" he exclaimed. "Ferget it!"

"All right. Shut up!" sighed the chief, and was silent.

Now they entered Cleft Forest Valley and went thundering down a steep incline, filling the precipitous places with their clamor. And all at once, following with haggard eye the phantom express, Hadden saw it dive over a dizzy trestle, saw it shudder—saw it leave the rails and hurtle down, down, into abysmal darkness and utter destruction.

Then, like a man suddenly roused from a trance, he awoke to the horror of the situation. In an instant he did a dozen things, and O'Connell clung desperately to a stanchion while the swaying locomotive steadied itself to a grinding, jolting stop—just twenty feet from the yawning brink of the bridgeless chasm.

"The trestle must have been swept away by the storm—we're right at the edge of the gulch—it's a miracle—the engineer is all that saved us," came from the breathless crowd that poured out of the cars and collected about the scene.

Later, when Hadden and O'Connell were brought before an investigating committee they had nothing to say, and took their reward in silence.

And there the matter rested.

The Piper from Bhutan

by David Bernard

I regret, gentlemen, the trouble I have caused; but I'm deeply grateful for this chance to tell my side of the story. And I believe I can show you that, despite the bitter remarks by Professor Du Bois, my action does not warrant my expulsion from this college.

I've studied psychology under Professor Du Bois for four years; my record and the testimony of my classmates will prove that, prior to the experiment the other night, my relationship with Professor Du Bois was mutually satisfactory. I say now, as I've said, that he's intellectually dishonest and untrue to the spirit of experimental science. The truth, gentlemen, is no insult.

It started with the wizened old man from Bhutan. He came to the college with delegates from some mystic society. He could play music, so they told Professor Du Bois, that could restore vitality to the recently dead, keeping them alive until he stopped playing on his pipe. I was working in the laboratory with Professor Du Bois; he told the delegates he was busy.

"Besides," he said, "I have tested at least a dozen individuals with similar claims in the past and unfailingly showed them up as frauds or clever hypnotists. The thing is just physiologically impossible; when you're dead, as the old saying goes. . . . Good day, my friends."

Well, I won't repeat what the mystics said, but they left in a huff, taking the shriveled little man, in his outlandish costume, with them. And soon after we were again disturbed by a visit. It was the professor's brother-in-law, Detective-Lieutenant Crane, and he had bad news about Richford Mason, a friend of Professor Du Bois.

"Mason died early this morning," Lieutenant Crane said, "snuffed out by an overdose of morphine given to him as medicine." Then he went on to tell the shocked professor that Mason's partner, Rumster, was being held. "We know he's guilty as hell, but he's got enough of an alibi to beat conviction if we bring him to trial—unless we can break him."

And that, gentlemen, is how the experiment started: Professor Du Bois to demonstrate the power of suggestion, his special field in psychology; Lieutenant Crane to "break" a confession.

The professor called the mystic society, saying he had decided to give the old Bhutanese piper a scientific test. They apologized for calling him a closed-minded bigot, and other choice epithets, and said they'd give him all the space he wanted in the next issue of their magazine to report his findings. They, of course, had already "proven" the piper's magical ability to their complete satisfaction. They were disappointed when the professor said they couldn't have representation at the experiment, but after all, scientific recognition is scientific recognition.

Well, gentlemen, I accompanied the professor, Lieutenant Crane, and the little old piper to the home of a radio impersonator, who had known the late Richford Mason. Professor Du Bois planned everything. He spoke to the radio artist, with the latter imitating Richford Mason's voice, while the Bhutanese played away on his pipe and Lieutenant Crane and I worked with a phonographic machine, making records.

The piper took it all deadly seriously, though he kept jabbering in his Tibetan or Chinese dialect, asking, I'm sure, where the dead body was. His music, well—you can't hear it now, for which I'm terribly sorry—but what music!

It wailed, seemed to be talking, pleading, in a weird melancholy voice that somehow seemed to beat right through you. No melody, as we know the term, just a haunting, lilting strain, like nothing I've ever heard before—or hope again to hear!

At Professor Du Bois' direction, we made two excellent recordings, and in a few hours everything was ready.

In a secluded house at the end of town, the accused Rumster was made the subject of the experiment. We had the corpse of Richford Mason in one room; in another, the Bhutanese piper. In the room where the lieutenant, the professor and I sat with Rumster were the two records.

One was on a phonograph on the table. The other was on a phonograph hidden behind the sofa. This hidden machine had a catch protruding just a sixteenth of an inch from the corner of the rug. A tug with your shoe-tip would set off the record.

Well, first Lieutenant Crane gave Rumster the third degree; but no use. He looked guilty, his voice sounded guilty, and his story had a few frayed edges—but he denied the crime while admitting he had the best motive for it.

Then Professor Du Bois, introduced to the accused as a friend of the late Richford Mason, went to work. It made me laugh sardonically to hear the professor build up a case for "the subtle revivifying effects of music, that is, the vibrations we call music."

In his book, *Backgrounds of Psychology*, Professor Du Bois calls the ancients "misguided and misguiding interpreters of natural phenomena, with no just claim whatsoever to science." But to Rumster he said:

"The wise men of the ancient world, Asclepiades and Pythagoras, taught and demonstrated the profound effect of music upon the body. The sages of Egypt, indeed, went so far as to bring life to the dead, so it is reliably reported." He went on and on, citing the reports of travelers in the orient, and after that sank in, he mentioned the Bhutanese piper.

"One wise old man, who has astounded observers by his ability to infuse life into the recently dead with the magical music of his pipe, has been brought to this country." And he showed Rumster clippings

362

from the sensational press, which of course had been inspired by the unscientific "experiments" of the mystic society.

Well, as the professor kept on, Rumster scoffed, but he was getting uneasy, perspiring, wondering. Then Professor Du Bois said, "Last night, after hearing of the marvelous success of this piper from Bhutan, we brought him to the bier of Richford Mason—to try him out—"

"And it worked!" Lieutenant Crane cut in.

"It worked?" Rumster yelled, and Lieutenant Crane growled:

"Yeah! That's what I said, and we got his word that you did it, murdered him!"

While Rumster chafed and squirmed, the lieutenant calmly fished a typed confession from his pocket and gave it to Rumster to sign. But Rumster whimpered, "You can't f-fool me like that."

"This is no joke, Rumster," Professor Du Bois said very gravely. "We made a phonographic recording of what happened last night, when the strange music of the Bhutanese piper lured the soul of Richford Mason, your late partner, back to his dead body. I know, Rumster, I spoke to Mason!"

One thing I can't take away from Professor Du Bois; he is a master of suggestion, and he demonstrated it that night. Rumster forced a laugh, but fooled nobody. He was scared; still he would not sign the confession.

At Professor Du Bois' signal, I walked to the phonograph on the table; and after a few more questions, the professor said, "Go ahead."

You should have seen Rumster's eyes pop as the record started. The music started faintly, the piping gaining strength and abruptly breaking into a wild interblending of notes and octaves utterly bewildering in its harmony. Over and over the haunting music repeated, sad, wailing, mysteriously appealing—and then a new note lilted into it, and the music faded off a bit and suddenly there sounded—a voice!

Hollow, throaty, the groan of one awakening uneasily from deep slumber. Sonorously it spoke:

"Who calls me? Why do you wake me? What do you want?"

"M-Mason!" Rumster wheezed. And from the phonograph came the voice of Professor Du Bois, quivering:

"It is I, John Du Bois."

"Oh," came the monotonously dull voice, "why am I called back?"

"A matter of justice, Richford. A question to ask."

Then silence, save for the weird wail of the pipe.

Again the voice of Du Bois:

"Please, Richford, do not sleep, just for a while. Please. Do you hear me?"

"I do. I hear you. But this pains. . . . What do you want?"

"Tell me—who killed you?"

"I am not dead."

"I know—"

"You do not know. Not until you are where I now am will you know. Now I know the meaning of what men fear. Merely the body—"

"Yes, Richford, who killed your body?"

"Him I pity, not hate. What a fool! Did he know what I now know, what I now see, never would he have done it. But here all things are clear; into the innermost heart and thoughts of those left behind does one see, and I know the anguish and torture that possess his guilt-burdened soul—"

"Who, Richford, who was it?"

"Rumster, Marvin Rumster. The moment I took that medicine he mixed for me, I knew. For my cough, he said. That terrible choking cough; but now, of all that I am now free—"

The record ended abruptly. I halted the machine, and Lieutenant Crane pushed the confession into Rumster's lap. I got a wink from Professor Du Bois because it was certain that Rumster couldn't stand much more. He sighed and gulped and played with the confession, but at length he stiffened and started denying all over again.

"I didn't, I didn't, I didn't, I tell you!"

Lieutenant Crane came back at him: "All right, then, you tell that to *him*. We didn't want to hurt him, but I see we got to do it."

That was the cue for Professor Du Bois' ace. The lieutenant and I wheeled the cadaver into the room, right next to the gaping Rumster. That worked on him for several minutes, and after we gave him smelling-salts, and he still weakly refused to sign, Professor Du Bois brought the Bhutanese piper into the room.

The wizened old man's eyes lit up when he saw the corpse; he tuned up his pipe with several sharp squeaks and waited eagerly for the signal from Professor Du Bois.

"Ready?" the lieutenant rapped at Rumster, gripping him by the collar to keep him from turning away from the corpse.

That was my cue. I sidled over to the corner, so that catch just barely protruding from the rug would be in easy reach of my toe, to set the second record going.

"Ready?" repeated the lieutenant, shaking Rumster.

"Wh-what f-for?"

"To talk to Mason, as soon as he comes back. To tell him—"

Rumster cried that he couldn't, wouldn't.

"All right, then, sign that confession!"

I had the idea that Rumster sobbed out "Yes!" But Lieutenant Crane nodded to the professor and the professor signaled to the Bhutanese, who proceeded to fill the room with his eery music. Low, weirdly wailing, precisely as on the first record, it gained strength slowly, somehow beating through you, gripping you. Fascinated, I stared at Rumster's blood-drained, open-mouthed face. I saw him gain control of himself abruptly, leaping a full yard off the sofa, bolting madly for the door.

Screaming, "Let me out!" he was collared at the door by Lieutenant Crane. And he signed the confession there, scribbling his name as if his life depended on it, and was pushed out, into the arms of a waiting detective.

I saw Professor Du Bois walk toward the grinning lieutenant, while the Bhutanese wailed away—and with startling suddenness, there broke into the weird strain—a voice!

The voice of Richford Mason, groaning ghastlily! Horrified, I whirled on the corpse. And as God is my judge, gentlemen—the explanations and skeptical remarks of Professor Du Bois to the contrary—I swear I saw those thin blue lips part, the eyelids of that yellowish waxy face flutter.

Maybe I did go temporarily berserk, but, what I saw—and heard—I rushed headlong for that piper, bore him into the sofa, ripping the pipe away from his mouth and smashing it over my knee.

The professor and the lieutenant grabbed me, crying out if I had gone stark crazy. I yelled out what had happened.

"Why," the professor said, while the lieutenant guffawed, "you yourself set the record going."

I fell back when he said that, for the second record was designed just that way; but then I fairly leaped at him, telling him the truth, gentlemen:

"In my excitement, I completely forgot to tug the catch!"

Professor Du Bois' face went pale at that. He stooped behind the sofa, examining the phonograph. He emerged with the record in his hand.

"You're wrong, dead wrong," he said slowly, huskily. A look a little bit like fright was on his face. "You *did* set this record off. That voice we . . . you heard was from the record."

"Why sure," Lieutenant Crane put in, "only a guy as guilty as Rumster would believe this music humbug. When you're dead—"

But I looked down at the catch protruding from the rug. Not a centimeter more than the sixteenth of an inch at which it had originally been fixed was it protruding.

The professor laughed when I showed that to him; and he laughed again when I asked him why he hadn't shown the record to me to prove I was wrong instead of so hurriedly taking it from the hidden phonograph. Then I asked him why the ghastly groaning had stopped precisely when I ripped that pipe from the Bhutanese; and he called me a gullible, sophomoric fool.

"When you threw the old man into the sofa the impact jarred the phonograph, halting the record."

That forced upon me how the mind of a scientist, no less than the zealous religionist's, can become grooved and open only to orthodoxy. But as I turned angrily to leave, I saw one more thing. And what I saw, coupled with the furious outburst I got from Professor Du Bois when I mentioned it, made me fly off the handle and tell the professor the strong but true words for which he now would have me expelled.

I saw the arms of Richford Mason, the lifeless arms which had been folded across his chest in a posture of serene repose—I saw them hanging limply, almost trailing to the floor from the sides of the table bed.

Rats

by M. R. James

"And if you was to walk through the bedrooms now, you'd see the ragged, mouldy bedclothes a-heaving and a-heaving like seas." "And a-heaving and a-heaving with what?" he says. "Why, with the rats under 'em."

But was it with the rats? I ask, because in another case it was not. I cannot put a date to the story, but I was young when I heard it, and the teller was old. It is an ill-proportioned tale, but that is my fault, not his.

It happened in Suffolk, near the coast. In a place where the road makes a sudden dip and then a sudden rise; as you go northward, at the top of that rise, stands a house on the left of the road. It is a tall red-brick house, narrow for its height; perhaps it was built about 1770. The top of the front has a low triangular pediment with a round window in the centre. Behind it are stables and offices, and such garden as it has is behind them. Scraggy Scotch firs are near it: an expanse of gorse-covered land stretches away from it. It commands a view of the distant sea from the upper windows of the front. A sign on a post stands before the door; or did so stand, for though it was an inn of repute once, I believe it is so no longer.

To this inn came my acquaintance, Mr. Thomson, when he was a young man, on a fine spring day, coming from the University of Cambridge, and desirous of solitude in tolerable quarters and time for reading. These he found, for the landlord and his wife had been in service and could make a visitor comfortable, and there was no one else staying in the inn. He had a large room on the first floor commanding the road and the view, and if it faced east, why, that could not be helped; the house was well built and warm.

He spent very tranquil and uneventful days: work all the morning, an afternoon perambulation of the country round, a little conversation with country company or the people of the inn in the evening over the then fashionable drink of brandy and water, a little more reading and writing, and bed; and he would have been content that this should continue for the full month he had at disposal, so well was his work progressing, and so fine was the April of that year—which I have reason to believe was that which Orlando Whistlecraft chronicles in his weather record as the "Charming Year."

One of his walks took him along the northern road, which stands high and traverses a wide common, called a heath. On the bright afternoon when he first chose this direction his eye caught a white object some hundreds of yards to the left of the road, and he felt it necessary to make sure what this might be. It was not long before he was standing by it, and found himself looking at a square block of white stone fashioned somewhat like the base of a pillar, with a square hole in the upper surface. Just such another you may see at this day on Thetford Heath. After taking stock of it he contemplated for a few minutes the view, which offered a church tower or two, some red roofs of cottages and windows winking in the sun, and the expanse of sea—also with an occasional wink and gleam upon it—and so pursued his way.

In the desultory evening talk in the bar, he asked why the white stone was there on the common.

"A old-fashioned thing, that is," said the landlord (Mr. Betts), "we was none of us alive when that was put there." "That's right," said another. "It stands pretty high," said Mr. Thomson, "I dare say a sea-mark was on it some time back." "Ah! yes," Mr. Betts agreed, "I 'ave 'eard they could see it from the boats; but whatever there was, it's fell to bits this long time." "Good job too," said a third, " 'twarn't a lucky mark, by what the old men used to say; not lucky for the fishin', I mean to say." "Why ever not?" said Thomson. "Well, I never see it myself," was the answer, "but they 'ad some funny ideas, what I mean, peculiar, them old chaps, and I shouldn't wonder but what they made away with it theirselves."

It was impossible to get anything clearer than this: the company, never very voluble, fell silent, and when next someone spoke it was of village affairs and crops. Mr. Betts was the speaker.

Not every day did Thomson consult his health by taking a country walk. One very fine afternoon found him busily writing at three o'clock. Then he stretched himself and rose, and walked out of his room into the passage. Facing him was another room, then the stair-head, then two more rooms, one looking out to the back, the other to the south. At the south end of the passage was a window, to which he went, considering with himself that it was rather a shame to waste such a fine afternoon. However, work was paramount just at the moment; he thought he would just take five minutes off and go back to it; and those five minutes he would employ—the Bettses could not possibly object—to looking at the other rooms in the passage, which he had never seen. Nobody at all, it seemed, was indoors; probably, as it was market day, they were all gone to the town, except perhaps a maid in the bar. Very still the house was, and the sun shone really hot; early flies buzzed in the window-panes. So he explored. The room facing his own was undistinguished except for an old print of Bury St. Edmunds; the two next him on his side of the passage were gay and clean, with one window apiece, whereas his had two. Remained the south-west room, opposite to the last which he had entered. This was locked; but Thomson was in a mood of quite indefensible curiosity, and feeling confident that there could be no damaging secrets in a place so easily got at, he proceeded to fetch the key of his own room, and when that did not answer, to collect the keys of the other three. One of them fitted, and he opened the door. The room had two windows looking south and west, so it was as bright and the sun as hot upon it as could be. Here there was no carpet, but bare boards; no pictures, no wash-ing-stand, only a bed, in the farther corner: an iron bed, with mattress and bolster, covered with a bluish check counterpane. As featureless a room as you can well imagine, and yet there was something that made

Thomson close the door very quickly and yet quietly behind him and lean against the window-sill in the passage, actually quivering all over. It was this, that under the counterpane someone lay, and not only lay, but stirred. That it was some *one* and not some *thing* was certain, because the shape of a head was unmistakable on the bolster; and yet it was all covered, and no one lies with covered head but a dead person; and this was not dead, not truly dead, for it heaved and shivered. If he had seen these things in dusk or by the light of a flickering candle, Thomson could have comforted himself and talked of fancy. On this bright day that was impossible. What was to be done? First, lock the door at all costs. Very gingerly he approached it and bending down listened, holding his breath; perhaps there might be a sound of heavy breathing, and a prosaic explanation. There was absolute silence. But as, with a rather tremulous hand, he put the key into its hole and turned it, it rattled, and on the instant a stumbling padding tread was heard coming towards the door. Thomson fled like a rabbit to his room and locked himself in: futile enough, he knew it was; would doors and locks be any obstacle to what he suspected? but it was all he could think of at the moment, and in fact nothing happened; only there was a time of acute suspense—followed by a misery of doubt as to what to do. The impulse, of course, was to slip away as soon as possible from a house which contained such an inmate. But only the day before he had said he should be staying for at least a week more, and how if he changed plans could he avoid the suspicion of having pried into places where he certainly had no business? Moreover, either the Bettses knew all about the inmate, and yet did not leave the house, or knew nothing, which equally meant that there was nothing to be afraid of, or knew just enough to make them shut up the room, but not enough to weigh on their spirits: in any of these cases it seemed that not much was to be feared, and certainly so far he had had no sort of ugly experience. On the whole the line of least resistance was to stay.

Well, he stayed out his week. Nothing took him past that door, and, often as he would pause in a quiet hour of day or night in the passage and listen, and listen, no sound whatever issued from that direction. You might have thought that Thomson would have made some attempt at ferreting out stories connected with the inn—hardly perhaps from Betts, but from the parson of the parish, or old people in the village; but no, the reticence which commonly falls on people who have had strange experiences, and believe in them, was upon him. Nevertheless, as the end of his stay drew near, his yearning after some kind of explanation grew more and more acute. On his solitary walks he persisted in planning out some way, the least obtrusive, of getting another daylight glimpse into that room, and eventually arrived at this scheme. He would leave by an afternoon train—about four o'clock. When his fly was waiting, and his luggage on it, he would make one last expedition upstairs to look round his own room and see if anything was left unpacked, and then, with that key, which he had contrived to oil (as if that made any difference!), the door should once more be opened, for a moment, and shut.

So it worked out. The bill was paid, the consequent small talk gone through while the fly was loaded: "pleasant part of the country—been very comfortable, thanks to you and Mrs. Betts—hope to come back some time," on one side: on the other, "very glad you've found satisfaction, sir, done our best—always glad to 'ave your good word—very much favoured we've been with the weather, to be sure." Then, "I'll just take a look upstairs in case I've left a book or something out—no, don't trouble, I'll be back in a minute." And as noiselessly as possible he stole to the door and opened it. The shattering of the illusion! He almost laughed aloud. Propped, or you might say sitting, on the edge of the bed was—nothing in the round world but a scarecrow! A scarecrow out of the garden, of course, dumped into the deserted room. . . . Yes; but here amusement ceased. Have scarecrows bare bony feet? Do their heads loll on to their shoulders? Have they iron collars and links of chain about their necks? Can they get up and move, if never so stiffly, across a floor, with wagging head and arms close at their sides? and shiver?

The slam of the door, the dash to the stair-head, the leap downstairs, were followed by a faint. Awaking, Thomson saw Betts standing over him with the brandy bottle and a very reproachful face. "You shouldn't a done so, sir, really you shouldn't. It ain't a kind way to act by persons as done the best they could for you." Thomson heard words of this kind, but what he said in reply he did not know. Mr. Betts, and perhaps even more Mrs. Betts, found it hard to accept his apologies and his assurances that he would say no word that could damage the good name of the house. However, they *were* accepted. Since the train could not now be caught, it was arranged that Thomson should be driven to the town to sleep there. Before he went the Bettses told him what little they knew. "They says he was landlord 'ere a long time back, and was in with the 'ighwaymen that 'ad their beat about the 'eath. That's how he come by his end: 'ung in chains, they say, up where you see that stone what the gallus stood in. Yes, the fishermen made away with that, I believe, because they see it out at sea and it kep' the fish off, according to their idea. Yes, we 'ad the account from the people that 'ad the 'ouse before we come. 'You keep that room shut up,' they says, 'but don't move the bed out, and you'll find there won't be no trouble.' And no more there 'as been; not once he haven't come out into the 'ouse, though what he may do now there ain't no sayin'. Anyway, you're the first I know on that's seen him since we've been 'ere: I never set eyes on him myself, nor don't want. And ever since we've made the servants' rooms in the stablin', we ain't 'ad no difficulty that way. Only I do 'ope, sir, as you'll keep a close tongue, considerin' 'ow an 'ouse do get talked about'": with more to this effect.

The promise of silence was kept for many years. The occasion of my hearing the story at last was this: that when Mr. Thomson came to stay with my father it fell to me to show him to his room, and instead of letting me open the door for him, he stepped forward and threw it open himself, and then for some moments stood in the doorway holding up his candle and looking narrowly into the interior. Then he seemed to recollect himself and said: "I beg your pardon. Very absurd, but I can't help doing that, for a particular reason." What that reason was I heard some days afterwards, and you have heard now.

The Readjustment

by Mary Austin

Emma Jossylin had been dead and buried three days. The sister who had come to the funeral had taken Emma's child away with her, and the house was swept and aired, then, when it seemed there was least occasion for it, Emma came back. The neighbor woman who had nursed her was the first to know it. It was about seven of the evening, in a mellow gloom: the neighbor woman was sitting on her own stoop with her arms wrapped in her apron, and all at once she found herself going along the street under an urgent sense that Emma needed her. She was half-way down the block before she recollected that this was impossible, for Mrs. Jossylin was dead and buried, but as soon as she came opposite the house she was aware of what had happened. It was all open to the summer air; except that it was a little neater, not other-

371

wise than the rest of the street. It was quite dark; but the presence of Emma Jossylin streamed from it and betrayed it more than a candle. It streamed out steadily across the garden, and even as it reached her, mixed with the smell of the damp mignonette, the neighbor woman owned to herself that she had always known Emma would come back.

"A sight stranger if she wouldn't," thought the woman who had nursed her. "She wasn't ever one to throw off things easily."

Emma Jossylin had taken death, as she had taken everything in life, hard. She had met it with the same hard, bright, surface competency that she had presented to the squalor of the encompassing desertness, to the insuperable commonness of Sim Jossylin, to the affliction of her crippled child; and the intensity of her wordless struggle against it had caught the attention of the townspeople and held it in a shocked, curious awe. She was so long a-dying, lying there in the little low house, hearing the abhorred footsteps going about her house and the vulgar procedure of the community encroach upon her like the advances of the sand wastes on an unwatered field. For Emma had always wanted things different, wanted them with a fury of intentness that implied offensiveness in things as they were. And the townspeople had taken offence, the more so because she was not to be surprised in any inaptitude for their own kind of success. Do what you could, you could never catch Emma Jossylin in a wrapper after three o'clock in the afternoon. And she would never talk about the child—in a country where so little ever happened that even trouble was a godsend if it gave you something to talk about. It was reported that she did not even talk to Sim. But there the common resentment got back at her. If she had thought to effect anything with Sim Jossylin against the benumbing spirit of the place, the evasive hopefulness, the large sense of leisure that ungirt the loins, if she still hoped somehow to get away with him to some place for which by her dress, by her manner, she seemed forever and unassailably fit, it was foregone that nothing would come of it. They knew Sim Jossylin better than that. Yet so vivid had been the force of her wordless dissatisfaction that when the fever took her and she went down like a pasteboard figure in the damp, the wonder was that nothing toppled with her. And as if she too had felt herself indispensable, Emma Jossylin had come back.

The neighbor woman crossed the street, and as she passed the far corner of the gate, Jossylin spoke to her. He had been standing, she did not know how long a time, behind the syringa bush, and moved even with her along the fence until they came to the gate. She could see in the dusk that before speaking he wet his lips with his tongue.

"She's in there," he said at last.

"Emma?"

He nodded. "I been sleeping at the store since—but I thought I'd be more comfortable—as soon as I opened the door, there she was."

"Did you see her?"

"No."

"How do you know, then?"

"Don't you know?"

The neighbor felt there was nothing to say to that.

"Come in," he whispered, huskily. They slipped by the rose tree and the wistaria and sat down on the porch at the side. A door swung inward behind them. They felt the Presence in the dusk beating like a pulse.

"What do you think she wants?" said Jossylin. "Do you reckon it's the boy?"

"Like enough."

"He's better off with his aunt. There was no one here to take care of him, like his mother wanted." He raised his voice unconsciously with a note of justification, addressing the room behind.

"I am sending fifty dollars a month," he said; "he can go with the best of them." He went on at length to explain all the advantage that was to come to the boy from living at Pasadena, and the neighbor woman bore him out in it.

"He was glad to go," urged Jossylin to the room. "He said it was what his mother would have wanted."

They were silent then a long time, while the Presence seemed to swell upon them and encroached upon the garden. Finally, "I gave Zeigler the order for the monument yesterday," Jossylin threw out, appeasingly. "It's to cost three hundred and fifty." The Presence stirred. The neighbor thought she could fairly see the controlled tolerance with which Emma Jossylin threw off the evidence of Sim's ineptitude.

They sat on helplessly without talking after that, until the woman's husband came to the fence and called her.

"Don't go," begged Jossylin.

"Hush!" she said. "Do you want all the town to know? You had naught but good from Emma living, and no call to expect harm from her now. It's natural she should come back—if—if she was lonesome like—in—the place where she's gone to."

"Emma wouldn't come back to this place," Jossylin protested, "without she wanted something."

"Well, then, you've got to find out," said the neighbor woman.

All the next day she saw, whenever she passed the house, that Emma was still there. It was shut and barred, but the Presence lurked behind the folded blinds and fumbled at the doors. When it was night and the moths began in the columbine under the window, It went out and walked in the garden.

Jossylin was waiting at the gate when the neighbor woman came. He sweated with helplessness in the warm dusk, and the Presence brooded upon them like an apprehension that grows by being entertained.

"She wants something," he appealed, "but I can't make out what. Emma knows she is welcome to everything I've got. Everybody knows I've been a good provider."

The neighbor woman remembered suddenly the only time she had ever drawn close to Emma Jossylin touching the child. They had sat up with it together all one night in some childish ailment, and she had ventured a question: "What does his father think?" And Emma had turned her a white, hard face of surpassing dreariness. "I don't know," she admitted; "he never says."

"There's more than providing," suggested the neighbor woman.

"Yes. There's feeling . . . but she had enough to do to put up with me. I had no call to be troubling her with such." He left off to mop his forehead, and began again.

"Feelings," he said; "there's times a man gets so wore out with feelings, he doesn't have them any more."

He talked, and presently it grew clear to the woman that he was voiding all the stuff of his life, as if he had sickened on it and was now done. It was a little soul knowing itself and not good to see. What was singular was that the Presence left off walking in the garden, came and caught like a gossamer on the ivy tree, swayed by the breath of his broken sentences. He talked, and the neighbor woman saw him for once as he saw himself and Emma, snared and floundering in an inexplicable unhappiness. He had been disappointed too. She had never relished the man he was, and it made him ashamed. That was why he had never gone away, lest he should make her ashamed among her own kind. He was her husband; he could not help that, though he was sorry for it. But he could keep the offence where least was made of it. And there was a child—she had wanted a child, but even then he had blundered—begotten a cripple upon her. He blamed himself utterly, searched out the roots of his youth for the answer to that, until the neighbor woman flinched to hear him. But the Presence stayed.

He had never talked to his wife about the child. How should he? There was the fact—the advertisement of his incompetence. And she had never talked to him. That was the one blessed and unassailable memory, that she had spread silence like a balm over his hurt. In return for it he had never gone away. He had resisted her that he might save her from showing among her own kind how poor a man he was. With every word of this ran the fact of his love for her—as he had loved her with all the stripes of clean and uncleanness. He bared himself as a child without knowing; and the Presence stayed. The talk trailed off at last to the commonplaces of consolation between the retchings of his spirit. The Presence lessened and streamed toward them on the wind of the garden. When it touched them like the warm air of noon that lies sometimes in hollow places after nightfall, the neighbor woman rose and went away.

The next night she did not wait for him. When a rod outside the town—it was a very little one—the burrowing owls *whoowhooed,* she hung up her apron and went to talk with Emma Jossylin. The Presence was there, drawn in, lying close. She found the key between the wistaria and the first pillar of the porch; but as soon as she opened the door she felt the chill that might be expected by one intruding on Emma Jossylin in her own house.

" 'The Lord is my shepherd!' " said the neighbor woman; it was the first religious phrase that occurred to her; then she said the whole of the psalm, and after that a hymn. She had come in through the door, and stood with her back to it and her hand upon the knob. Everything was just as Mrs. Jossylin had left it, with the waiting air of a room kept for company.

"Em," she said, boldly, when the chill had abated a little before the sacred words—"Em Jossylin, I've got something to say to you. And you've got to hear," she added with firmness as the white curtains stirred duskily at the window. "You wouldn't be talked to about your troubles when . . . you were here before, and we humored you. But now there is Sim to be thought of. I guess you heard what you came for last night, and got good of it. Maybe it would have been better if Sim had said things all along instead of hoarding them in his heart, but, anyway, he has said them now. And what I want to say is, if you was staying on with the hope of hearing it again, you'd be making a mistake. You was an uncommon woman, Emma Jossylin, and there didn't none of us understand you very well, nor do you justice, maybe; but Sim is only a common man, and I understand him because I'm that way myself. And if you think he'll be opening his heart to you every night, or be any different from what he's always been on account of what's happened, that's a mistake, too . . . and in a little while, if you stay, it will be as bad as it always was . . . men are like that . . . you'd better go now while there's understanding between you." She

375

stood staring into the darkling room that seemed suddenly full of turbulence and denial. It seemed to beat upon her and take her breath, but she held on.

"You've got to go . . . Em . . . and I'm going to stay until you do," she said with finality; and then began again:

" 'The Lord is nigh unto them that are of a broken heart,' " and repeated the passage to the end. Then, as the Presence sank before it, "You better go, Emma," persuasively: and again, after an interval:

" 'He shall deliver thee in six troubles.

" 'Yea, in seven there shall no evil touch thee.' " The Presence gathered itself and was still; she could make out that it stood over against the opposite corner by the gilt easel with the crayon portrait of the child.

" 'For thou shalt forget thy misery. Thou shalt remember it as waters that are past,' " concluded the neighbor woman, as she heard Jossylin on the gravel outside. What the Presence had wrought upon him in the night was visible in his altered mien. He looked, more than anything else, to be in need of sleep. He had eaten his sorrow, and that was the end of it—as it is with men.

"I came to see if there was anything I could do for you," said the woman, neighborly, with her hand upon the door.

"I don't know as there is," said he. "I'm much obliged, but I don't know as there is."

"You see," whispered the woman, over her shoulder, "not even to me." She felt the tug of her heart as the Presence swept past her. The neighbor went out after that and walked in the ragged street, past the schoolhouse, across the creek below the town, out by the fields, over the headgate, and back by the town again. It was full nine of the clock when she passed the Jossylin house. It looked, except for being a little neater, not other than the rest of the street. The door was open and the lamp was lit; she saw Jossylin black against it. He sat reading in a book like a man at ease in his own house.

Rebels' Rest

by Seabury Quinn

Eileen walked faster as she neared the cemetery. It was not like an Irish graveyard, this little Pennsylvania burying ground, not like the little acres planted to God's harvest which she had known at home. There was no church to send the music of its bells across the low green billows of its mounded graves, no yews and holly-trees in which the kind winds whispered slumber-songs, no lich gate at its entrance underneath whose gable the tired living and the peaceful dead might pause a moment in eternity ere they went diverse ways. Like most things in this strange new land it seemed to be entirely functional. Just as no one ever thought of dropping into the cool, whisper-haunted shadows of the church for rest and prayer and meditation on a summer's afternoon, so no one ever thought of going to the cemetery save when friends or relatives were buried. No one ever thought of stopping there to kneel beside the grave of some loved one and whisper, "God give you rest and caring, dear soul!"

They seemed to dread the dead in America. At home it had been different. Kinfolk and friends and neighbors did not change essentially when they moved from their cottages to the churchyard. But . . .

She drew her hooded cape more closely round her and walked faster as she reached the cemetery wall. Perhaps the dead were unfriendly in America. So many of the living were.

It was in 1918 that Chris Huncke met Sheilah Maclintock. He was a Pennsylvania Dutchman, big, blond, rather stolid, unimaginative, and very handsome in his American uniform. Sheilah was his opposite, small, black-haired, blue-eyed, as typically Irish as a sprig of shamrock. She was a member of the Women's Motor Corps, and piloted an antique Daimler with the expertness of a racing driver, making mock of London fogs, policemen, two-star generals and even second lieutenants with sharpwitted Hibernian impartiality. Christian fell in love with her at first sight, Sheilah needed several looks before she gave her heart and unswerving devotion to the big, inarticulate American.

He brought her back in 1919, rushed her round New York in a deliriously ecstatic honeymoon, then took her to his farm near Chambersburg, where he shed his uniform and the never-quite-convincing air of gay insouciance he had worn with it, and reverted to type.

His father and his father's great-grandfather had been farmers, sturdy folk who held their land by grant from Governor Penn and later stubbornly against both redskins and redcoats. Their ways were right and all their judgments true.

Sheilah stood it for as long as she could, which was not quite a year. The atmosphere of the old house, the seldom-opened "best room" with its horsehair furniture, waxed flowers and shell ornaments spread like a miasma over the entire place, stifling her. Who could sing songs of the mountainy men of Donegal or the leprechaun or the *gean canach,* the love-talker, with a picture of *Grosvater* Huncke, dressed in broadcloth and starched linen and bearded like a billy-goat, scowling disapprovingly down at her? Who could stand the dour, uncompromising religiosity of the neighbors?

She loved the out of doors, did Sheilah Maclintock, the soft, sweet rain, the limpid sunshine, the springiness of fresh green turf. One day as she walked home from the village the urge to feel the caress of the roadside grass against her feet was more than she could withstand, and so she dropped down on a wayside boulder to peel off shoes and stockings when who should drive by in his Stutz Bearcat but Emil Herbst, son of Max Herbst, the president of the savings bank.

Prohibition had not yet come to America, but foregleamings of its high morality had reached the county, which had voted dry at the last election. Consequently nearly every second shop in the village was a speakeasy, and when Emil gathered with other village *jeunes dorés* behind Gus Schwing's pool parlor that evening he had provocative things to say concerning Sheilah's pretty feet and legs and Sheilah's deportment on the public highway. The story of her escapade spread with fissionable swiftness through the village and surrounding country, and next morning Mrs. Friedrich Eichelburg was early on the telephone.

As she took up the receiver Sheilah heard the sequenced clickings of a dozen others being lifted. Everyone on the line was indulging in a little morning's eavesdropping.

"Good morning, Mrs. Huncke," her self-appointed mentor greeted. "I feel it is my Christian duty to tell you—" then for the next half hour she discoursed upon the differences between American morality and the loose-reined mores of decadent Europe.

"Ochone!" exploded Sheilah when she could wedge a word in. "Your Christian duty is it, ye *sthronsuch*? Faith, 'tis meself that's after thinkin' ye'd be servin' both your God and neighbors better if ye kept your sharp nose out o' other people's business!"

* * *

The ladies of the congregation didn't quite draw their skirts aside as she passed after that, but she was not invited to their *kaffee klatches*, nor to help with the church suppers, nor serve on their committees. Perhaps it would not be quite accurate to say that they sent her to Coventry, but certainly they consigned her to Birmingham.

And so, before a year had passed she packed her scanty wardrobe, for she'd take nothing Christian's money bought, and set out for the home she'd left six years before when she went off to do her bit in the Great War.

She hitch-hiked as far as Harrisburg, and there she found employment as a waitress and saved every spare penny till she had enough to pay her steerage passage back to Galway. She left no note of farewell, and if Christian made an effort to find her it was not apparent. The ostracism which the neighbors had visited on his wife had extended to him; he was a gregarious soul, and life had not been pleasant on the farm since Sheilah came. When the days stretched into weeks, and the weeks to months, and still no word of her, he gradually accepted the verdict that she was "no better than she should be," and found contentment if not happiness in a second marriage.

Sheilah shared a cottage with her aged Uncle Brian, cooked his meals and washed his clothes and worked his patch of garden, for he was infirm with rheumatism, and also something of a *sleiveen,* which is to say he was a man who'd rather take his ease than not, and didn't worry overmuch if the weeds grew waist-high. It was a bleak, bare spot on which the cottage stood, all day and night they heard the angry surges of the Atlantic, in summer there was salt spray in the air, in winter there were bitter winds and storms. Before she'd been home two months Sheilah gave birth to Christian's child, a daughter whom she named Eileen.

She had small traffic with the country folk, and they in turn were reticent, respecting her privacy. If on occasion neighbor women speculated over a pleasant scandal-flavored dish of tea that she was neither wife nor widow, they kept their speculations to themselves and caused her no embarrassment.

Each night when Sheilah knelt to pray she begged, "God keep and prosper him," and when she rose from her knees it was with that sick, awful feeling of emptiness which one who has not lost the thing that she most loves cannot know. *"Ullagone, avourneen,"* she would whisper, "we loved each other so! Where did all the beautiful, sweet love go? Why did you ever let 'em take you from me—and me from you?"

Then one night when she had reached thirty-eight and looked at least fifteen years older, Sheilah heard the Woman of the Shee sing underneath her window, and knew her time was come. "I'm goin', pulse o' me heart," she told Eileen, "and it's precious little I can leave ye. In the ginger jar fornenst the clock's a hoard o' twenty pounds. 'Twill care for my buryin' and pay your passage to your father in America, and for the love he bore me when we two were wed he'll take ye in and look after ye. Bid him a kindly greetin', child, and tell him that I loved him to the last."

It seemed to Christian time flowed backward for him when Eileen arrived. She had blue-black Irish hair and intensely blue eyes; her skin was like damask, glowing, warm; even the dimple in her pointed chin and the soft-lipped, tender smile of her were reminiscent of her mother. He felt as if Sheilah had come back to him, and the old love woke and stirred the spiced embalmings in its tomb. She was his daughter, yes, but she was something more, she was the reincarnation of the first and only real love of his life.

And because he loved her he was harsh with her. Her every little fault was magnified because it seemed to detract from the ideal of perfection he imagined her to be, and he was heavy-tongued in his scoldings.

But if Christian lashed his daughter with scourges his wife Beulah scourged her with scorpions. If Beulah Huncke had once been pretty nothing in her makeup testified to it. Everything about her was sharp with cutting sharpness. Her thin shoulders, her small, bright, vindictive eyes, her narrow profile, her thin, long hands and feet revealed her as a woman of edges, not curves. She wore her hair in a small knot at the back of her head, and drew it back so tightly that it seemed to make her eyeballs pop; her voice rasped like a file on steel, as if there were a grit of malice in her throat. Heaven had denied her offspring, and this frustration added gall and wormwood to the acid of her nature. In Eileen she found someone on whom she could vent her spite against life.

That afternoon she had been more than usually unbearable. "I s'pose you figger on settin' 'round and waiting for your pap to die and leave the farm to you?" she asked Eileen. "Well, leave me tell you, Missie, you'll never get an inch o' *this* land. I'll see to it that he cuts you out o' his will. And meantime there'll be no idle hands around here. I need some things at Eberhardt's. Go get 'em for me. Right away, not next week." She handed Eileen a small shopping list— thread, needles, pins, little, unconsidered trifles that could be packed in a pocket—and, "Now, off you go," she ordered, "and see that you get back by supper time. No traipsing off with men, the way your mother—"

"Leave my mother out o' this, ye *collich*," Eileen broke in with a wrathful sob. " 'Tis a thing you're not fit to soil her name with your foul tongue!"

They said that ghosts walked in the little cemetery after sunset. Ghosts of the men who lay in Rebels' Rest.

Eileen had heard a dozen different versions of the story, yet all were substantially the same. How John McCausland's men had ridden into Chambersburg that morning in July of '64, levied a tribute of a hundred thousand dollars on the town, then burnt it to the ground and rode away with shouts of laughter. By God, their cause might be a lost one, but they, at least, had singed old Grant's whiskers! And then the tale went on to tell how the militia and the enraged farmers poured a spilth of lead on them as they rode pellmell to rejoin Jubal Early, how saddle after saddle had been emptied, so that where six hundred laughing, roistering bully boys had ridden into Chambersburg that morning a scant five hundred reached McConnellsburg.

Death had wiped out animosities, so when the rebels had retreated the farmers gathered up their dead and laid them side by side with demurely folded hands on their breasts and caps pulled down upon their faces, and when a plot had been marked off for them in the graveyard old Pastor Brubaker had read his office over them.

They had been buried properly, those wild Virginia lads, with prayer and Scripture reading, aye, and a word of forgiveness from the pastor, but still men said they could not rest. Some said they found the cold earth of this northern country a hard bed; some—and these were the majority—declared they hungered for revenge.

The whispering night wind chased the clouds that clawed with ghostly fingers at the newly risen moon as Eileen reached the cemetery gate, and for an instant everything was almost bright as noon, then a black cloud wrack slid over the moon's disc, and shadows obscured everything.

She felt everything inside her coming loose, and had no notion what to do about it as the cloud-curtain moved away and she saw a form by the grilled gate of the graveyard.

It was a man—or shaped like one—a slim and neatly built young man with sunburned cheeks and a thin line of dark mustache across his upper lip. He wore a gray suit and long boots, a yellow kerchief looped about his neck, and a little yellow cap with a black leather visor was set jauntily upon his curling hair.

381

"*Ovoch!*" Eileen felt the hot breath churn in her throat. "If you're a natural man, God save ye, sir; but if you're a Thing o' the Darkness, Christ's agony between us!"

"Faith, 'tis a long time I've been waitin' for a civil word!" The young man smiled and raised a hand to his cap in semi-military salute. "Thank ye kindly for your courtesy, me dear. I could not spake till I was spoken to, an' though I've waited more nor eighty year before this selfsame gate the only greetin' I've received until jist now has been a frightening squeal."

"God save us all," Eileen quavered, "you're Irish!"

"As Irish as they come, me jewel. I'm Teig McCarthy—Teig O'Shane McCarthy, late—too late, God knows!—o' th' parish o' Clondevaddock in th' County o' Galway."

Fear slipped from Eileen as a wave slides off the beach: "And whatever are ye doin' here, poor creature?" she asked.

"*Ochone,* 'tis a long story, so it is, yet not so long as I could wish for," answered he with an infectious grin. " 'Teig, *avick,*' me father—may th' turf lie lightly on him!—says to me, 'there's naught but mortgages to be raised on th' ould place, an' precious few o' them. Ye'd best be goin' to Ameriky to seek your fortune, as your Cousin Dion did.'

"So off I goes like any silly goose o' Westmeath, an' presently I comes to rest on Misther Dabney Fortesque's plantation in Virginny. There's war abrewin' in th' States, an' presently they're callin' ivery able-bodied man to th' colors. You know how 'tis, pulse o' me heart; a fight's a fight to an Irishman, an' divil a bit cared I which side I fought on, so long as they were givin' me a horse to ride an' three meals ivery day an' now an' then a spot o' pay.

"Then off we rides, an' presently we comes to Chambersburg where we scares th' Yankees out o' siven years fine growth before we sets th' town ablaze about their ears. But as we rides away one of 'em gets me in th' chist wid his bullet and drops me deader nor a herring! Ah, well, I don't know as I should complain. 'Twas war, an' if he hadn't shot me 'tis altogether likely I'd ha' shot him. At any rate, they gave me dacent buryin', an' here I've been for more nor eighty year—"

"But why is it you're walkin' now?" Eileen demanded. "Is it that ye have a debt unpaid, or sins upon your soul—"

"Whist, dear one, don't be talkin'!" he broke in. "We're a queer lot, an' a lonesome lot, we dead folk from th' *Innis Fodhla*. Were you yersilf in some strange land for eighty year an' more, an' niver able to go back, there'd be a hunger on your soul for news o' home. Isn't it so?"

"It is!" Eileen agreed fervently. "And ghost or man, 'tis glad I am I've found ye, Teig McCarthy, for 'tis meself that comes from County Galway, with the heart o' me a-breakin' to go home."

Impulsively she put her hands out to him. *"Och,* Teig McCarthy, can't you see me heart is hollow with homesickness?"

"Hold hard, Eileen *alannah!*" he warned. "I'm yearnin' for ye like a drunkard for his draught, but if ye put your lips to mine ye join me. Mind ye, girl, th' quick an' dead can't mingle, an' th' dead may not come back!"

"No matter, Teig *avourneen,"* she breathed softly. "No—matter—" Her voice sank to a muted whisper and her eyes closed as she leant toward him with parted lips. "Ah, Teig, Teig McCarthy, ye jewel o' the world!"

Slowly, deliberately, he drew her to him, put his arms about her, kissed her on the mouth. He kissed her slowly, bending her head back against his arm till she felt weak and helpless, and glad to be that way at last. A cloud-veil crept across the moon like a blind being drawn, and darkness spread over the landscape. All about them was the scent of pine trees and the stillness of the night.

Supper time came at the Huncke farm, but no Eileen. Night passed and morning dawned, cool, clear and lovely, with limpid, bright pellucid air and sunlight sparkling over everything. But no sign of Eileen.

With dogs borrowed from the sheriff's office they traced her from the village to the cemetery, and at the gate the hounds gave little frightened whimpers and cringed against the deputy.

There was a susurrus of gossip at the next meeting of the Ladies' Sewing Circle. "The cemetery, eh?" Mrs. Thea Hauptmann shook her head like one who fears—and hopes for—the worst. "The cemetery. H'mm. A nice, secluded, woodsy place. Like mother like daughter, I always say. You listen to me once. That girl went off with someone!"

Which was unquestionably so.

Relationships

by Robert Sampson

A few days after his forty-eighth birthday, Hadley Jackson learned that he could materialize the women from his past. Only think a little at an angle and there they sat, sassy as life, talking as if time were nothing. As if their lives had continued to touch his. The ability to call them upset him considerably. Not fearfully though; he never felt fear.

To that time, he had been spending ever larger chunks of the evening burrowed in his apartment. He lived with two cats, Gloria and Bill. He had developed the habit of reading aloud to them: selections from news magazines, the poems of Emily Dickinson. The cats were unconcerned by his choices. Reading aloud gave him the feeling that his life still retained both direction and a trace of high white fire.

One Monday he thought of Mildred Campbell. At one time he had cared a good deal for her. They had never reached what, in the contemporary tongue, was called a relationship. Between them, something essential had been omitted. She didn't, or couldn't, return his feelings. Eventually they allowed each other to drift away amid a sort of wan regret.

All of a sudden, there she sat in a chair by his table. She wore a blue dress of some slinky material and dark hose and dark blue heels. The tip of her left shoe vibrated against the carpet, as it did when she wanted to go home and was about to tell him so.

He knew at once that she was not real. Apparently she did, too. It did not seem to bother her.

"This won't do you any good," she said. Her voice, quick and pleasant as ever, was tinted with dark impatience. Sooner or later that emotion marred all their meetings.

"I was just thinking about you."

"Well, I'm far away. To tell the truth, I haven't thought about you for years."

"You never did. Not much," he said.

She laughed at that, and a cat stuck its head through her left shoulder and looked out at him. It made him feel a little sick, then irritated, since it established so clearly that Mildred was some kind of cloud.

"Let's not bother with this," she said. "I liked you for about ten minutes once. But, Lord God, you can't stretch ten minutes forever."

"I liked you longer than that."

"Don't kid yourself," she said. And was gone. The cat still looked at him. It jumped down and slipped under the table.

He touched the chair she had sat in and sniffed the air. No trace of her fragrance remained. It occurred to him that if Mildred came, others might follow. So he sat down again and thought of Ruth. He couldn't angle his thoughts properly; the correct mind set eluded him. Later he wandered slowly around the block, smelling night leaves, wondering if it were possible to leave Creative Chemicals and set up a consulting business.

The following night, he thought of Ruth again. This time she appeared promptly. She wore a long white formal-looking dress with gold at ears and neck. Her hair was paler blond than he had remembered. She was a little tight; that, too, was familiar. Sprawling back on the davenport, she grinned at him and crossed her ankles.

"Old friends meet again." Her lips were bright red. Only something was wrong with her eyes. A whitish film covered them.

"Twenty-odd years," he said. "Pretty long between visits. Where you living now?"

"I'm dead," she replied. "Years and years ago."

"I'm sorry. I thought about you a lot. But I didn't know where you'd moved to."

"That's the way of it," she said. "You get separated and the space between just keeps getting bigger. You never know where a person gets to or what they do when they get there."

He was shocked at her eyes and could think of nothing to say. Her voice was low and amused. As she turned her head, gold flashed.

"Just because I'm dead, there's nothing wrong with me. I mean, I'm not about to tear out your throat or any dumb thing like that."

"What's it like being dead?"

"I don't know. It isn't anything you can describe. You hear all this foolishness . . ."

Her fingers minutely adjusted her skirt. "I guess I better go," she said. "The damn whiskey's dying in me."

As she rose, he said with sudden regret: "I'm sorry you died."

"It was quick. I remember that."

After she was gone, he sat silently, thinking. A cat nudged his dangling hand. Her eyes had been very terrible. He realized that he had forgotten to ask where she had lived or how her life had been. Shame leaped in him. Or perhaps guilt. The emotion tasted metallic, gray, the taste of nails.

She had recognized him, he thought. After all these years.

He slept in his chair. When he woke, it was still dark outside but the light was on and the cats had crowded between his leg and the chair arm.

The following evening, his daughter, Janet, called from Phoenix. Her voice was enthusiastic, warm, and slipped over certain subjects quickly, as if a question from him would drop them both through a fragile crust. The combination of effusiveness and reticence annoyed him.

"I'm fine," she told him. "Everybody's fine."

"I mean, how are you, really?"

"Just fine, Dad." Her voice took on a note of remote querulousness. His ex-wife, Helen, Janet's mother, another man's wife, had banged up her car on the way to a class in stained glass. Helen wanted to know, Janet said, if he'd like a suncatcher for his window—a glass cactus or sleeping Mexican. He refused. Helen constantly offered him small gifts through his daughter, never directly talking with him. The effect was of receiving messages relayed from another planet. Perhaps, he thought, it's Janet trying to keep us in touch. A cat rubbed its neck against his calf.

"Goodbye," she said. The telephone droned hollowly against his ear.

Later he drove slowly across town to the theater at the Mall. Bright clouds streaked the sky like strips of stained glass, rose and green, whitish-gray.

In the theater, the lights faded down, and an endless succession of commercial messages shouted across the screen. No one in them was older than twenty-five.

As the sales messages jittered past, Hadley thought suddenly of Rosemary Chalson. Years ago, they had met accidentally at a showing of "South Pacific." For nearly the entire picture, he agonized whether to take her hand. As he finally decided to reach out, laughter stirred through the audience. Rosemary clapped both hands under her chin and leaned back, laughing, exposing her gums. This he found disagreeable. Before he decided what to do about her hand, the film ended.

Thinking of her now, and the long tortures of adolescence, he glanced right. Rosemary sat in the next seat, a tub of popcorn in her lap. As ferocious youth bounced across the screen, she lifted a single kernel to her lips.

He blurted: "It's been years . . ."

He saw the startled white flicker in her eyes. Her body angled infinitesimally from him.

Immediately he saw that she was not Rosemary. Dull horror ran through him. He blurted: "Excuse me. Excuse me."

Rising, he struggled past a succession of knees to the aisle. People stared irritably past him, intent on the yelling screen.

Outside the theater, he felt the icy crawl of his back. She looked exactly like Rosemary, he thought. The error frightened him. His mind felt full of dangerous potential, like a cocked gun.

He drove from the Mall, passing beneath apricot lights mounted on high silver poles. The street angled through rows of beige apartments. Nothing moved. The smooth dark sky was unmarred by star or moon. In the hollow street, in the dull light, the apartments seemed images painted on air. Behind them hung featureless nothing, waiting to be shaped.

Some basic similarity existed, he thought, between the street and his laboratory where, for the past week, the complex process of installing a computer system was underway. Behind ranks of cabinets and boxes dangled a wilderness of black cords. The tips of each glittered silver, waiting for connection.

In his life, he thought, there had been too much disconnection. Too many dangling cords. Only past connections remained. He seemed hardly linked to the present.

The woman beside him bent to adjust her seat. When she straightened, he recognized Helen Wycott—Wrycott. He was sharply disturbed. He had not seen her since college. Nor had he thought of her since.

Now they come without being called, he thought.

She eyed him disdainfully. "You always acted too good for everybody."

"I didn't feel that way," he said.

"That's not what it looked like."

They turned into a dark street with dark houses behind strips of yard. Mailboxes shone dully along the curb. He could think of no reason why she came. Over the years, she had put on much weight, and her remembered features floated within a cruel expanse of cheek.

He said: "You always were so clever and quick. I never knew what to say to you."

"You spent too much time thinking about yourself."

"That isn't true," he said, trying to remember.

"It's true, all right. You do it now."

They rode in silence for several blocks. She looked steadily at him, shaking her head.

"You better give this up," she told him. "There's more to life than people you used to know."

"Listen," he said, "I didn't call you here."

"I want off here," she said.

He stopped the car. When he opened her door, she was gone. Night air smelled moistly cool and his hands trembled faintly. Aggravation, he thought.

On going back over their conversation, it struck him that he had, however slightly, won an advantage over her. He drove home briskly, humming to himself and tapping time to himself on the steering wheel. Objectively, of course, he was showing all the signs of dementia. He considered the possible collapse of his mind cheerfully. Perhaps he had now entered a mania phase. How interesting that the symptoms of his detachment from reality expressed themselves as women. That seemed distantly amusing.

When he opened the door of the apartment, the cats ran toward him uttering sharp cries of greeting. Above their noise he heard the light flutter of feminine voices.

In the living room, two women smiled at him. One was Ruth, this evening wearing neatly tailored black with pearls. She lulled effusively on the davenport, clearly having had a great deal to drink. The other woman, wearing a ragged blue cardigan and jeans, sat primly in a straight chair, knees together. He did not recognize her.

Ruth waved breezily at him. "You come sit right down here. We've been deciding what to do with you."

The other woman said: "I bet you don't remember me."

When she smiled, sweetness suffused her bony face. A former friend of his ex-wife. He recalled the smile. Nothing else.

"I remember," he said tentatively.

"Virginia Cox," she said. "Virginia Ames now. I have four grand-children now."

"That's nice," he said. Ruth tittered. Her fingers floated over his hand, and she leaned toward him.

"It's just been ages," Virginia said. "I thought you were so hand-some. Of course, you were married, so I didn't tell you that."

"It's different now," Ruth said.

"Same as it always was," Virginia said. "Just more open."

Ruth slumped back, laughing loudly. "She's right, Hadley. More open."

"I suppose so," he said, still unable to look at her eyes.

"We're shocking him," Virginia said.

"That's a man," Ruth said. She patted his knee, her bright-tipped fingers vanishing and reappearing in the material of his trousers. "Weren't you in love with me once. Hadley?"

He looked from the floor to the amused faces of the women. "I guess once I was."

"He guesses," Ruth purred. "He doesn't know. He guesses."

"Well, the point is, you can't hang in the past forever," Virginia said. The quick smile illuminated her face.

"The past was fun," Ruth added.

"But it's gone now, you know," Virginia said. "You can't keep raking it up. So Ruth and I, we've decided to help you out."

She stood up, not looking at all like a grandmother. "What a pretty cat. What's his name?"

"Bill," he said.

As he glanced toward the cat, Virginia was gone.

"Wait a minute," he cried, turning quickly to Ruth.

"That's all we wanted to tell you," she said.

Her figure wavered and her arms and body slipped sideways, separating from her shoulders and head. She said, "Don't think for a minute we weren't here. Mania, my foot."

"I wanted to say . . ."

"You're sweet," she said. "Can you be home at five tomorrow night?"

Her figure came to pieces, flowing across the room in translucent strands. It was after ten o'clock. Dropping onto the davenport, he ground his face against the flowered cushions.

At five the following evening, the door bell rang once, briefly. As if it had been touched in embarrassment, as a duty, and once was going to be all. When he opened the door, Bill attempted to dart out and had to be captured and held. Facing him in the doorway was a tall, lean-faced woman with heavy dark hair. She smiled tentatively at him and dropped her eyes, which were dark gray. Embarrassment rose in waves from her. In a low voice, she asked:

"Are you Mr. Jackson? Hadley Jackson?"

"Yes, m'am."

"Did you know Ruth Payne once?"

"Ruth? Oh, yes."

Her lips thinned and she looked so uneasy, he felt a pulse of sympathy.

"This probably sounds awful funny," she said, not looking at him. "She wanted me—she kept telling me to see you."

"I see," he said.

She looked directly at him then and their eyes touched. As she examined him some of the tension left her. She seemed intelligent and wary.

"You know about Ruth?" she asked.

"She died."

"Yes, she died."

He thought that she would say more but she did not.

After a moment, he said, "Reconnection," not loudly.

Faint color touched her face; she looked away.

He said swiftly before she could recover herself and flee: "I was just going down the street for a cup of coffee. Would you like one?"

She regarded the air between them as if it were imprinted with complex instructions. "Yes. I think so. That would be nice."

"I'll just get my coat. Come in."

Still holding the cat, he stepped aside. Head lifted, smiling faintly, she entered his apartment for the first time.

Rendezvous

by Richard H. Hart

"Tell Marcel I said to hang on—that if he lets go I'll kick the daylights out of him! I'll be there as soon as possible."

Doctor Dumont spoke earnestly, although his words were light; they were meant to encourage the sufferer, to stiffen the will-power which alone could whip on the flagging heart until his arrival.

The doctor hung up the receiver with fingers slightly trembling and snatched his medicine case from a chair. He opened the little bag and glanced within it to make sure that his needle-set and a plentiful supply of digitalis were in their places. Then he seized his hat and rushed from the house; a moment's delay might mean victory for his ancient enemy, Death.

390

A plan of action—the only plan that might succeed—had popped into his head at old Etienne's first words. Etienne had said: "Mist' Favret is tak' bad, Mist' Doct'! T'ink pro*babl'* you bette' come quick!" Etienne was only an unschooled Cajun, who "cou'n' read one w'd, if he's big as box-ca'"—but he loved Marcel Favret even as Doctor Dumont loved him, and there had been an agony of fear in his voice. The doctor had decided instantly that he must catch the westbound train.

The difficulty was that the train had already left New Orleans. It was at that very moment aboard the huge iron ferry-barge being shoved across the Mississippi by a puffing tug. Doctor Dumont would have to catch it, if at all, somewhere along the opposite bank.

As ill-luck would have it, he had chosen that particular week to have his car overhauled. He could telephone for a taxi, of course, but at that evening rush-hour too many precious minutes might elapse before it arrived. The street-cars were reasonably fast and dependable, and he knew that he could afford to run no risks. He would take one.

An up-river Magazine car rumbled to a stop just as he reached the corner, and he swung thankfully aboard. The decision as to which ferry to choose had been made for him; he would cross the river at Walnut Street, and try to catch the train at Westwego.

Unconsciously, he seated himself at the extreme front of the car, as if to be that much closer to his goal. Marcel Favret was his life-long companion and dearest friend, and his patient only incidentally. Favret, suffering an unexpected relapse, needed the administration of digitalis most acutely, and only Doctor Dumont might ascertain from his symptoms the exact dosage which would save him.

There was not the slightest use in looking at his watch, but the doctor found himself doing so constantly. At each single tap of the conductor's bell, demanding a stop, he ground his teeth impatiently. Each double tap, signaling renewed progress, caused him a sigh of relief. He must—he *must*—arrive in time.

Then, only five minutes' ride from Walnut Street, Disaster showed its ugly face. The street-car's bell emitted a shower of angry *clangs;* the motorman whirled back the controller and threw on the brakes. The car ground to a stop.

Doctor Dumont was on his feet instantly, trying to beat down a great surge of despair.

There was no need to ask questions. Squarely across the track sprawled a huge tank-truck with one wheel missing and a rear axle gouged into the pavement. The street-car was effectively blocked.

* * *

Acting without volition, the doctor leaped down from the car and started walking rapidly along the street. The outraged passengers behind him might expostulate with motorman and truck-driver until they were tired; it would do them no good. As for him, he must catch the west-bound train across the river.

He had covered nearly two blocks at a furious pace when he realized the futility of his course. He couldn't walk to Walnut Street in less than twenty minutes, and he knew that his old legs would carry him less than half the distance if he attempted to run. He must find some other way.

At the corner, he turned abruptly to the left and made his way toward the Mississippi. He would have to find a boatman to ferry him across; surely there were motorboats in plenty along the levee. A motorboat he must have, for the river was high and its rushing current would carry a skiff too far downstream in the crossing. Even now, he could hear in the still night air the whistle of the train as it left Gretna. And he must catch that train.

The thought galvanized his tired legs; he crossed Water Street at a trot. He dashed between rows of mean shanties and found himself upon a crumbling wharf. As he paused for breath, his gaze automatically wandered out across the swirling water.

Abruptly, he dashed a hand across his eyes as if to brush away an impossible sight. He had exerted himself too much, he thought. Otherwise how could be be seeing a steam ferry-boat at this point? Surely he wasn't as ignorant of New Orleans as all that!

But the sight remained, and to his ears came the confirmatory *pow-pow-pow* of the stern-wheeler. In eager amazement he heard the jangling of the pilot's bell and watched the boat glide smoothly up to the landing-stage. A moment more and he had sprung aboard.

The ferry-boat remained at the landing-stage for a minute or so, its huge paddle-wheel turning over at half speed. But no other passenger came aboard, and presently the bell jangled again and the boat swung out into the current. The paddle-wheel churned with an accelerating rhythm as the black water swirled past and the crumbling wharf fell farther and farther back into the darkness.

As suspense and excitement subsided within him, Doctor Dumont realized that the air off the river was something more than chilly. He turned up his coat-collar and stepped through the door of the engine-room in search of warmth. He recognized the possibility that this was against the rules, but the fact that there were no other passengers aboard emboldened him. The little infraction would surely be overlooked.

"Pretty cool, tonight," he remarked to the engineer.

The engineer nodded without speaking. He was a big-framed man with an immense red nose. One of his legs had been cut off just below the knee and the missing portion had been replaced with an old-fashioned, hand-carved wooden peg. It struck the deck with a dull thump whenever he moved about.

Doctor Dumont's feeling of relief impelled him to be sociable. He drew out his emergency flask.

"Prescription liquor—twelve years old," he said. "Have a drink with me."

He was wholly unprepared for the change which came suddenly over the engineer. The fellow's eyes opened wide, his nostrils dilated, and his lips drew back from yellow teeth in a grimace of frightful rage. He took two steps forward and raised a ham-like fist. Doctor Dumont backed prudently through the door without stopping to argue; he had seen madness often enough to recognize the gleam from those wild eyes.

At that moment came a fortunate diversion. The bell overhead clattered loudly, and the engineer sullenly allowed his arm to fall, then went back to his levers. Doctor Dumont replaced his flask and hastened around to the opposite side of the deck. The crossing was at an end.

A narrow lane bordered with tall weeds diverged from the levee, and the doctor made his way along it at a brisk walk. A hundred yards farther along, he found himself at the highway. Roaring up the pavement came a westbound bus; frantically the doctor flagged it down. Only when he was safely aboard did he realize that he had not paid his ferry-fee: in his haste he must somehow have missed the ticket office. He made a mental note to drop by sometime and pay the delinquent fare; notwithstanding the mad engineer, that had been one trip which was certainly worth the money.

He caught the train at Westwego with only seconds to spare. An hour later he was descending from it at the little town where he had practised for so many years, and where his patient awaited him. He hoped fervently that he would be in time.

Etienne met him at the station with a little automobile; it seemed to the doctor that the wheezy motor quivered with impatience.

"How's Marcel?" he demanded as he climbed in.

"Wo'se," said Etienne. "I promise *le bon Saint* can'le long's my a'm if he's get bette'—but he's wo'se." He fed more gasoline to the now roaring motor.

The little car shot forward along the dark road and began a nerve-torturing race. It turned unbanked curves on slithering tires and missed trees, fence-posts and culverts by inches. At last Etienne threw his weight on the brakes and racked it to a stop.

Both men were out of the car before it had ceased to vibrate, and Etienne led the way into the house. They found Marcel Favret unconscious, and the old Cajun went down on his knees beside the bed as the doctor fumbled with the latch of his medicine case.

"I'm just in time," the doctor muttered, fitting needle to syringe with practised speed. "Thirty minutes more—perhaps even fifteen—and Marcel would have been done for. That ferry-boat came like a dispensation."

It was a long, tense fight, and although Doctor Dumont prided himself on his freedom from superstition he more than once seemed to feel the air about him stirred by unseen wings as he labored and watched over his patient. There was an acrid taste in his mouth, and it was as if restraining hands tugged at his every muscle. Never had his enemy appeared so loth to relinquish a victim.

But skill and devotion triumphed at last, and the presence of Death was no longer felt in the room. The patient was breathing quietly and regularly when Doctor Dumont signed to Etienne to accompany him from the bedchamber.

"He needs nothing but sleep, now," said the doctor as he closed the door behind them. "And, while he's getting it, maybe you could scrape me up a sandwich. I've eaten nothing since noon."

"You bet," Etienne said, his brown old face aglow with gratitude and admiration. "I fix you somet'ing bette'. I fix you nice om'lette an' drip you pot *café*. Good *souper* fo' good doct'."

They went out into the kitchen, and while he skilfully cracked eggs and dropped them from their shells into an earthenware bowl Etienne asked the doctor how he had managed to catch the train. Doctor Dumont settled himself comfortably at the table, then recounted his difficulties and told of how they had been overcome.

Etienne shredded a clove of garlic and added it to the eggs. "You say you catch de fe*rie* somew'ere aroun' State Street o' Jeffe'son Av'nue?" he asked. "You *certain* it not Napole*on* o' Walnut?"

"Absolutely," the doctor assured him. "I didn't notice the name of the street, but there was a box-factory alongside the wharf where I caught the boat, and there's no such factory at either Walnut Street or Napoleon Avenue. I know that much about the city."

"Hoh—de box-fact'ry fe*rie!*" exclaimed Etienne. He thoughtfully

394

added salt, pepper, tabasco and fresh basil leaves to the mixture in the bowl. "You say de enginee' had a wooden leg?"

"Yes. And, if you ask me, the old devil's crazy as a bat."

"Hmmm. Maybe. Hmmm." Etienne whisked the omelette to a creamy froth, then turned it into a skillet under which a low fire burned. "You want I should tell you 'bout one-leg' enginee' w'ich wo'k on box-fact'ry fe*rie?*"

"Go ahead," said Doctor Dumont, his eyes on the omelette.

Etienne chuckled. "A hom'lette mus' cook slow," he said.

He put a lid on the skillet and took up a small coffee-pot.

"It all happen' w'ile I living in Nyawlins," he began. "I living on Magazine Street, an' wo'king ove' at *sirop* fact'ry. I have to cross rive' two time eve'y day on box-fact'ry fe*rie.* Enginee' on boat name' Leblanc. Big man wit' red head."

"The engineer on the boat tonight had red hair," put in Doctor Dumont, looking up momentarily.

"Yeah?" The old Cajun poured boiling water over the dark-roasted coffee and chicory and set the pot on the back of the stove to drip. He resumed:

"Enginee' Leblanc like w'isky too much. All time he have bottle in's pocket. Drink, drink, drink; all day long. Not get so ve'y dronk, but drink too much. One day he's not pay 'tention to pilot's bell, an' not reverse hengine quick 'nough—bump landing float ha'd. Ca*bam!* Leblanc' own brothe' is was standing on float, waiting fo' fe*rie;* bump make him fall off an' drown."

"You mean that he caused his own brother to drown?" demanded the doctor.

"Yeah. He's brothe' is can swim, but bump head on piling, is knock out. Neve' come up. Dey is not find him fo' two hou's."

"Did that stop the engineer's drinking?"

"*Non!*" snorted Etienne. "Not'ing is stop him drinking. Two week afte' he's brothe' drown, he drinking some mo' an' put's foot unde' connecting-rod. *Bam!* Mash foot *comme ça!*" He crushed one of the egg-shells in his brown fist.

"I see," said the doctor. "Gangrene—and amputation. That is how he acquired his wooden leg. What happened then?"

"One night w'ile he's in *l'hôpital* he's brothe' come to him an' tell him—"

"You mean another brother?" interrupted the doctor.

Etienne folded the omelette dexterously and transferred it to a platter. He poured out a cup of coffee and set platter and cup before the doctor before he spoke.

"*Non.* Same brothe'. Brothe' tell him if he's not stop drinking so much w'isky he's going be sorry. Going be sorry long's he's live—an' lots longe'.'"

"Wait a minute!" exclaimed the doctor, pausing in the act of putting his fork into the savory omelette. "You're getting all mixed up. First you say his brother was drowned, and then you say his brother came to him while he was in the hospital. I don't understand what you mean."

"Maybe you un'e'stan' mo' bette' w'en I'm finish'," Etienne returned. "W'en Leblanc get out of *l'hôpital,* wit' he's wooden leg, de fe*rie* comp'ny is not want him to wo'k fo' dem some mo'. But he's tell 'em he's going get lawye'—bigges' lawye' in Nyawlins—an' sue 'em fo' big *dommage* fo' lose's leg in acci*dent.* Den fe*rie* comp'ny is say he can go back to wo'k if he's not sue 'em.

"He's not drink much fo' one-two week afte' he's go back to wo'k. Den one day he's got he's bottle again, an' a big crowd of people is going ove' rive' to ball-game. Mus' be dey is hund'ed men an' women on fe*rie*-boat. Leblanc is drink too much, an' not watch he's wate'-gage. Steam-gage go all way round. Den Leblanc is tu'n mo' wate' into boile'—an' she's blow up. Ca-*bam!* People dat's not kill' is drown'. Eve'y one. Leblanc too."

"Another kind of drunken driver," commented Doctor Dumont, turning from Etienne and attacking the omelette with vast appetite. "It was a good story, all right, but you got mixed up about the brother who was drowned coming to the hospital. The way you told it, it seemed as if he came to the hospital after he was drowned."

"He *did* come afte' he's drown'."

The doctor swallowed a huge draft of the black Louisiana coffee, wiped his mouth, and set down the cup with an air of satisfaction. Then he said reproachfully:

"I'm surprised at you, Etienne: telling me a story like that. What did I ever do to deserve it?"

"Do?" echoed the old Cajun, shrilly. "W'at you do? You tell me you cross de rive' tonight on box-fact'ry fe*rie,* between Walnut an' Napole*on*—di'n't you? It's twenty-fi' yea's, dis ve'y mont', dat En-ginee' Leblanc is blow up boat wit' hund'ed people on him—an' dey ain' been no steam-fe*rie* on dat pa't of de rive' since!"

396

The Return

by R. Murray Gilchrist

Five minutes ago I drew the window curtain aside and let the mellow sunset light contend with the glare from the girandoles. Below lay the orchard of Vernon Garth, rich in heavily flowered fruit-trees—yonder a medlar, here a pear, next a quince. As my eyes, unaccustomed to the day, blinked rapidly, the recollection came of a scene forty-five years past, and once more beneath the oldest tree stood the girl I loved, mischievously plucking yarrow, and, despite its evil omen, twining the snowy clusters in her black hair. Again her coquettish words rang in my ears: 'Make me thy lady! Make me the richest woman in England, and I promise thee, Brian, we shall be the happiest of God's creatures.' And I remembered how the mad thirst for gold filled me: how I trusted in her fidelity, and without reasoning or even telling her that I would conquer fortune for her sake, I kissed her sadly and passed into the world. Then followed a complete silence until the *Star of Europe,* the greatest diamond discovered in modern times, lay in my hand—a rough unpolished stone not unlike the lumps of spar I had often seen lying on the sandy lanes of my native county. This should be Rose's own, and all the others that clanked so melodiously in their leather bulse should go towards fulfilling her ambition. Rich and happy I should be soon, and should I not marry an untitled gentlewoman, sweet in her prime? The twenty years' interval of work and sleep was like a fading dream, for I was going home. The knowledge thrilled me so that my nerves were strung tight as iron ropes and I laughed like a young boy. And it was all because my home was to be in Rose Pascal's arms.

I crossed the sea and posted straight for Halkton village. The old hostelry was crowded. Jane Hopgarth, whom I remembered a ruddy-faced child, stood on the box-edged terrace, courtesying in matronly fashion to the departing mail-coach. A change in the sign-board drew my eye: the white lilies had been painted over with a mitre, and the name changed from the Pascal Arms to the Lord Bishop. Angrily aghast at this disloyalty, I cross-questioned the ostlers, who hurried to and fro, but failing to obtain any coherent reply I was fain to content myself with a mental denunciation of the times.

At last I saw Bow-Legged Jeffries, now bent double with age, sunning himself at his favourite place, the side of the horse-trough. As of old he was chewing a straw. No sign of recognition came over his face as he gazed at me, and I was shocked, because I wished to impart some of my gladness to a fellow-creature. I went to him, and after trying in vain to make him speak, held forth a gold coin. He rose instantly, grasped it with palsied fingers, and, muttering that the hounds were starting, hurried from my presence. Feeling half sad I crossed to the churchyard and gazed through the grated window of the Pascal burial chapel at the recumbent and undisturbed effigies of Geoffrey Pascal, gentleman, of Bretton Hall; and Margot Maltrevor his wife, with their quaint epitaph about a perfect marriage enduring for ever. Then, after noting the rankness of the docks and nettles, I crossed the worn stile and with footsteps surprising fleet passed towards the stretch of moorland at whose further end stands Bretton Hall.

Twilight had fallen ere I reached the cottage at the entrance of the park. This was in a ruinous condition: here and there sheaves in the thatched roof had parted and formed crevices through which smoke filtered. Some of the tiny windows had been walled up, and even where the glass remained snake-like ivy hindered any light from falling into their thick recesses.

The door stood open, although the evening was chill. As I approached, the heavy autumnal dew shook down from the firs and fell upon my shoulders. A bat, swooping in an undulation, struck between my eyes and fell to the grass, moaning querulously. I entered. A withered woman sat beside the peat fire. She held a pair of steel knitting-needles which she moved without cessation. There was no thread upon them, and when they clicked her lips twitched as if she had counted. Some time passed before I recognised Rose's foster-mother, Elizabeth Carless. The russet colour of her cheeks had faded and left a sickly grey; those sunken, dimmed eyes were utterly unlike the bright black orbs that had danced so mirthfully. Her stature, too, had shrunk. I was struck with wonder. Elizabeth could not be more than fifty-six years old. I had been away twenty years; Rose was fifteen when I left her, and I had heard Elizabeth say that she was only twenty-one at the time of her darling's weaning. But what a change! She had such an air of weary grief that my heart grew sick.

Advancing to her side I touched her arm. She turned, but neither spoke nor seemed aware of my presence. Soon, however, she rose, and helping herself along by grasping the scanty furniture, tottered to a window and peered out. Her right hand crept to her throat; she untied the string of her gown and took from her bosom a pomander set in a battered silver case. I cried out; Rose had loved that toy in her childhood; thousands of times we played ball with it. . . . Elizabeth held it to her mouth and mumbled it, as if it were a baby's hand. Maddened with impatience, I caught her shoulder and roughly bade her say where I should find Rose. But something awoke in her eyes, and she shrank away to the other side of the house-place: I followed; she cowered on the floor, looking at me with a strange horror. Her lips began to move, but they made no sound. Only when I crossed to the threshold did she rise; and then her head moved wildly from side to side, and her hands pressed close to her breast, as if the pain there were too great to endure.

I ran from the place, not daring to look back. In a few minutes I reached the balustraded wall of the Hall garden. The vegetation there was wonderfully luxuriant. As of old, the great blue and white Canterbury bells grew thickly, and those curious flowers to which tradition has given the name of 'Marie's Heart' still spread their creamy tendrils and blood-coloured bloom on every hand. But 'Pascal's Dribble', the tiny spring whose water pulsed so fiercely as it emerged from the earth, had long since burst its bounds, and converted the winter garden into a swamp, where a miniature forest of queen-of-the-meadow filled the air with melancholy sweetness. The house looked as if no careful hand had touched it for years. The elements had played havoc with its oriels, and many of the latticed frames hung on single hinges. The curtain of the blue parlour hung outside, draggled and faded, and half hidden by a thick growth of bindweed.

With an almost savage force I raised my arm high above my head and brought my fist down upon the central panel of the door. There was no need for such violence, for the decayed fastenings made no resistance, and some of the rotten boards fell to the ground. As I entered the hall and saw the ancient furniture, once so fondly kept, now mildewed and crumbling to dust, quick sobs burst from my throat. Rose's spinet stood beside the door of the withdrawing-room. How many carols had we sung to its music! As I passed my foot struck one of the legs and the rickety structure groaned as if it were coming to pieces. I thrust out my hand to steady it, but at my touch the velvet covering of the lid came off and the tiny gilt ornaments rattled downwards. The moon was just rising and only half her disc was visible over the distant edge of the Hell Garden. The light in the room was very uncertain, yet I could see the keys of the instrument were stained brown, and bound together with thick cobwebs.

Whilst I stood beside it I felt an overpowering desire to play a country ballad with an over-word of 'Willow browbound'. The words in strict accordance with the melody are merry and sad by turns: at one time filled with light happiness, at another bitter as the voice of one bereaved for ever of joy. So I cleared off the spiders and began to strike the keys with my forefinger. Many were dumb, and when I struck them gave forth no sound save a peculiar sigh; but still the melody rhythmed as distinctly as if a low voice crooned it out of the darkness. Wearied with the bitterness, I turned away.

By now the full moonlight pierced the window and quivered on the floor. As I gazed on the tremulous pattern it changed into quaint devices of hearts, daggers, rings, and a thousand tokens more. All suddenly another object glided amongst them so quickly that I wondered whether my eyes had been at fault—a tiny satin shoe, stained crimson across the lappets. A revulsion of feeling came to my soul and drove away all my fear. I had seen that selfsame shoe white and unsoiled twenty years before, when vain, vain Rose danced amongst her reapers at the harvest-home. And my voice cried out in ecstasy, 'Rose, heart of mine! Delight of all the world's delights!'

She stood before me, wondering, amazed. Alas, so changed! The red-and-yellow silk shawl still covered her shoulders; her hair still hung in those eldritch curls. But the beautiful face had grown wan and tired, and across the forehead lines were drawn like silver threads. She threw her arms round my neck and, pressing her bosom heavily on mine, sobbed so piteously that I grew afraid for her, and drew back the long masses of hair which had fallen forward, and kissed again and again those lips that were too lovely for simile. Never came a word of chiding from them. 'Love,' she said, when she had regained her breath, 'the past struggle was sharp and torturing—the future struggle will be crueller still. What a great love yours was, to wait and trust for so long! Would that mine had been as powerful! Poor, weak heart that could not endure!'

The tones of a wild fear throbbed through all her speech, strongly, yet with insufficient power to prevent her feeling the tenderness of those moments. Often, timorously raising her head from my shoulder, she looked about and then turned with a soft, inarticulate, and glad murmur to hide her face on my bosom. I spoke fervently; told of the years spent away from her; how, when working in the diamond-fields she had ever been present in my fancy; how at night her name had fallen from my lips in my only prayer; how I had dreamed of her amongst the greatest in the land—the richest, and, I dare swear, the loveliest woman in the world. I grew warmer still: all the gladness which had been constrained for so long now burst wildly from my lips: a myriad of rich ideas resolved into words, which, being spoken, wove

400

one long and delicious fit of passion. As we stood together, the moon brightened and filled the chamber with a light like the day's. The ridges of the surrounding moorland stood out in sharp relief.

Rose drank in my declarations thirstily, but soon interrupted me with a heavy sigh. 'Come away,' she said softly. 'I no longer live in this house. You must stay with me to-night. This place is so wretched now; for time, that in you and me has only strengthened love, has wrought much ruin here.'

Half leaning on me, she led me from the precincts of Bretton Hall. We walked in silence over the waste that crowns the valley of the Whitelands and, being near the verge of the rocks, saw the great pine-wood sloping downwards, lighted near us by the moon, but soon lost in density. Along the mysterious line where the light changed into gloom, intricate shadows of withered summer bracken struck and re-ceded in a mimic battle. Before us lay the Priests' Cliff. The moon was veiled by a grove of elms, whose ever-swaying branches alternately increased and lessened her brightness. This was a place of notoriety—a veritable Golgotha—a haunt fit only for demons. Murder and theft had been punished here; and to this day fireside stories are told of evil women dancing round that Druids' circle, carrying hearts plucked from gibbeted bodies.

'Rose,' I whispered, 'why have you brought me here?'

She made no reply, but pressed her head more closely to my shoul-der. Scarce had my lips closed ere a sound like the hiss of a half-strangled snake vibrated amongst the trees. It grew louder and louder. A monstrous shadow hovered above.

Rose from my bosom murmured. 'Love is strong as Death! Love is strong as Death!'

I locked her in my arms, so tightly that she grew breathless. 'Hold me,' she panted. 'You are strong.'

A cold hand touched our foreheads so that, benumbed, we sank together to the ground, to fall instantly into a dreamless slumber.

When I awoke the clear grey light of the early morning had spread over the country. Beyond the Hell Garden the sun was just bursting through the clouds, and had already spread a long golden haze along the horizon. The babbling of the streamlet that runs down to Halkton was so distinct that it seemed almost at my side. How sweetly the wild thyme smelt! Filled with the tender recollections of the night, without turning, I called Rose Pascal from her sleep.

'Sweetheart, sweetheart, waken! waken! waken! See how glad the world looks—see the omens of a happy future.'

No answer came. I sat up, and looking round me saw that I was alone. A square stone lay near. When the sun was high I crept to read the inscription carved thereon:—'*Here, at four cross-paths, lieth, with a stake through the bosom, the body of Rose Pascal, who in her sixteenth year wilfully cast away the life God gave.*'

The Return

by G. G. Pendarves

"H-m-m! Might spend a night in many worse places than this!" said Arnold Drysdale to himself, as his host disappeared; leaving him alone in the great vaulted room, lit by the dancing flicker of a log-fire.

The portraits on the paneled walls were veiled by the shadowy darkness, but beyond the circle of radiance within which Drysdale sat could be seen the dim outline of the Bechstein grand, the huddle of chairs at the far end of the music room, the pale glimmer of flowers in tall vases, and the clouded splendor of the gold brocade curtains drawn across the windows.

"Yes! It's a very easy way of earning five pounds!" went on Drysdale reflectively, lounging back in his chair and lighting a cigarette. "And what's more—I believe it's done the trick with Millicent," he chuckled complacently; "she thinks I'm no end of a hero to take on the wager and spend a night in the haunted room!" His lazy brown eyes half closed as he thought of Millicent Fayne—her youth, her loveliness, her dawning love for himself, and above all her wealth. "Nothing like a misspent youth for teaching a man the sort of woman he ought to marry," he concluded; "discrimination is better than innocence, and experience than much fine love!"

He looked round sharply as the far door of the room opened, and a man's tall figure showed for an instant against the lighted corridor without, before the door was closed again and the intruder approached.

"That you, Holbrook?" said Drysdale, thinking his host had returned to add a word of warning or advice. "Come back to see me hobnobbing with your spectral friend—eh?"

"It's not Holbrook! It's I. . . . Jim McCurdie!"

"Wha-a-a-t?" Drysdale sprang to his feet. "Why, where . . . how?"

"I wasn't sure if I could get here tonight, so I did not let Holbrook know I was coming—thought I'd just give you a surprise!"

"Surprize!" echoed Drysdale faintly, his hands clenched so that the knuckles gleamed, his cigarette dropping from suddenly relaxed lips to the rug at his feet.

Jim McCurdie sat down at the table, and looked across at his companion with a grin. "I heard you were at your old game of playing hero," he said, "and I thought it was a good opportunity of finding you alone. I've wanted this little chat with you for the last eight years!"

"Then you weren't. . . . you didn't. . . . you came back after all from that expedition?"

"Yes—I came back after all. We're pretty tough—we McCurdies—and there were several good reasons for my getting back. It's a bit too late for doing all I meant to do—but there's still one thing!"

A silence fell. The shadows in the big room seemed to thrust forward to peer and listen, as Drysdale sank into his chair and looked at his old rival opposite him—incredibly aged and altered from the gay, carefree youth whom Drysdale had sent on that deadly mission eight years ago.

"Then the ambush—?" Drysdale bit back the words too late; against his will the fatal question had shaped itself into words.

"Ah yes—the ambush! You knew all about the ambush, didn't you? You urged me and my men to take that particular route across the desert, knowing that Ibn Said and his ruffians waited by the Well of Tiz for us! You cowardly—lying—thief!"

The last deliberately spoken words hit like ice into Drysdale's consciousness, and partly steadied his whirling thoughts.

"Thief!" he stuttered; "thief!"

"Thief—one who steals what belongs to another man," explained McCurdie, leaning forward until his eyes blazed like points of blue flame into those of his companion. Drysdale's gaze fell before them and he half rose from his seat.

"Sit still," ordered McCurdie. "I've come a long way for the pleasure of meeting you once more; and now you're going to listen!"

"Don't make a fool of yourself," sneered Drysdale, his confidence returning as he began to adjust himself to the situation. "Thief—you call me!" He shrugged his shoulders. "Jean Kennedy was quite ready to be stolen, if that's what you mean."

"You tricked her and lied to her and deceived her! You left her to die miserably—as you left me."

"That's your own rotten imagination at work," answered Drysdale. "She went abroad the year after you—er—disappeared; no one ever heard what became of her."

"She went to Bruges—she lived at a mean little inn called *Le Chat Gris*—and died there when her son—and yours—was born!"

Drysdale started back, his nonchalance again stripped from him. "How the devil did you—?"

McCurdie's lean brown hands toyed with the match box on the table. "I know where she lies buried in the paupers' graveyard down by the river—she and her nameless son. I know that you stopped her allowance when her reproaches annoyed you; and that she became a wretched, half-starved slave to the innkeeper, Père Grossart, and his drunken wife."

"Damn you—you paid them to tell you this fairy-tale!" blustered Drysdale.

"I have never spoken to them in my life," was the answer.

"Liar! No one else in the world could know that she—that I—"

"So—you corroborate the story."

"No, curse you, I don't!" shouted Drysdale, getting to his feet. "You've found them out by accident and concocted this tale to try to ruin me."

"Before you ruin Millicent Fayne—as a climax to your varied career."

Drysdale's angry face changed, the red faded, and ugly unexpected lines appeared round his mouth. His brown eyes were suddenly hard and calculating.

"So *that's* your little game!" he said at last. "We're rivals once more! I did not know you had ever met Millicent," he went on. "You're going to try to use my 'guilty past' as a weapon! Very neat—I see—I see!" And turning to the whisky and soda which stood on the table, he began to fill his glass.

For a moment the other man sat very still, looking steadily at Drysdale; then, pushing back his chair, he got up and stood with his back to the glowing fire, his thin brown hands clasped behind him.

"I thought that even you would see such an obvious thing," McCurdie rejoined at last. "You'll leave here tonight—now, in fact!"

All the baffling, violent emotions that had possessed Drysdale during the last few minutes boiled up suddenly within him, his interlocutor's words of easy command setting a match to his fury. With a swift,

404

uncontrolled movement he hurled the glass he held, striking McCurdie full in the face.

There was a sharp hissing sound as the liquid splashed on the hot tiles of the hearth, and the glass shivered against the mantelpiece a few feet behind McCurdie's head.

"Good God!" Drysdale's voice was a mere thread of sound, as the eyes of the other man continued to look stedfastly into his own. "Who —what are you?"

"I am Jim McCurdie, whom you sent to death eight years ago in the Desert of Tlat."

Drysdale gasped and held on to the back of a chair, while the familiar surroundings of the music room receded to vast distances and a swimming darkness enveloped him. Then, slowly, reason asserted itself. How absurd of him to think, even for a moment, that the glass had passed *through* McCurdie's head! It was merely an effect of the firelight and his own jangled nerves.

"It appears you did not die—in spite of my efforts," he answered, with a barely perceptible tremor in his voice.

"I was buried by the Well of Tiz, with six spear-wounds through my body."

Drysdale looked stunned for a moment, but a lifelong habit of disbelieving what he did not understand conquered his rising fear.

"Either you're Jim McCurdie or his double! In any case you're making a nuisance of yourself," he said finally, and drawing an automatic from his pocket he leveled it at his companion, who had moved until he stood with his back to the paneled wall at the right of the fireplace. "I am going to shoot you. If you did not die in the desert, you'll die here and now! I shall say I thought you were the ghost that haunts this room!"

"I *am* the ghost!" replied McCurdie. "I have waited eight years to get back again; and tonight gave me my entrance to the world of humans once more. In this room there is power I could adapt to my needs—power to materialize—to borrow for a brief time a visible human garment for my soul."

"Splendid!" answered Drysdale, with a sneering laugh. "You always had a powerful imagination, McCurdie. Well, I am going to deprive you of your garment once and for all."

He raised his arm and a shot rang out—but the tall figure stood motionless before him, the blue eyes steady on his own.

"Curse it!" muttered Drysdale, "This light—" he fired again and yet again. "Die, can't you!" he shrieked, stumbling up close to that quiet figure, and putting the muzzle of his weapon to its breast he fired

405

one shot after another in rapid succession; then fell with a wild yell of laughter to the ground, the smoking revolver clenched in his fingers.

Holbrook was the first to find him lying there, and hastily dropped his handkerchief over that agonized, grinning face, before the startled guests and servants poured into the room.

The paneled wall to the right of the fireplace was riddled with bullets; but no sign of blood—no foot nor fingerprint of any assailant did the keenest man from Scotland Yard ever discover.

What or *whom* Drysdale had tried to shoot was never known—for the dead can not speak; or if they do, they are not believed.

Rose Rose

by Barry Pain

Sefton stepped back from his picture. 'Rest now, please,' he said.

Miss Rose Rose, his model, threw the striped blanket around her, stepped down from the throne, and crossed the studio. She seated herself on the floor near the big stove. For a few moments Sefton stood motionless, looking critically at his work. Then he laid down his palette and brushes and began to roll a cigarette. He was a man of forty, thick-set, round-faced, with a reddish moustache turned fiercely upwards. He flung himself down in an easy-chair, and smoked in silence till silence seemed ungracious.

'Well,' he said, 'I've got the place hot enough for you today, Miss Rose.'

'You 'ave indeed,' said Miss Rose.

'I bet it's nearer eighty than seventy.'

The cigarette-smoke made a blue haze in the hot, heavy air. He watched it undulating, curving, melting.

As he watched it Miss Rose continued her observations. The trouble with these studios was the draughts. With a strong east wind, same as yesterday, you might have the stove red-hot, and yet never get the place, so to speak, warm. It is possible to talk commonly without talking like a coster, and Miss Rose achieved it. She did not always neglect the aspirate. She never quite substituted the third vowel for the first. She rather enjoyed long words.

She was beautiful from the crown of her head to the sole of her foot; and few models have good feet. Every pose she took was graceful. She was the daughter of a model, and had been herself a model from childhood. In consequence, she knew her work well and did it well. On one occasion, when sitting for the great Merion, she had kept the same pose, without a rest, for three consecutive hours. She was proud of that. Naturally she stood in the first rank among models, was most in demand, and made the most money. Her fault was that she was slightly capricious; you could not absolutely depend upon her. On a wintry morning when every hour of daylight was precious, she might keep her appointment, she might be an hour or two late, or she might stay away altogether. Merion himself had suffered from her, had sworn never to employ her again, and had gone back to her.

Sefton, as he watched the blue smoke, found that her common accent jarred on him. It even seemed to make it more difficult for him to get the right presentation of the 'Aphrodite' that she was helping him to paint. One seemed to demand a poetical and cultured soul in so beautiful a body. Rose Rose was not poetical nor cultured; she was not even business-like and educated.

Half an hour of silent and strenuous work followed. Then Sefton growled that he could not see any longer.

'We'll stop for today,' he said. Miss Rose Rose retired behind the screen. Sefton opened a window and both ventilators, and rolled another cigarette. The studio became rapidly cooler.

'Tomorrow, at nine?' he called out.

'I've got some way to come,' came the voice of Miss Rose from behind the screen. 'I could be here by a quarter past.'

'Right,' said Sefton, as he slipped on his coat.

When Rose Rose emerged from the screen she was dressed in a blue serge costume, with a picture-hat. As it was her business in life to be beautiful, she never wore corsets, high heels, nor pointed toes. Such abnegation is rare among models.

'I say, Mr Sefton,' said Rose, 'you were to settle at the end of the sittings, but—'

'Oh, you don't want any money, Miss Rose. You're known to be rich.'

'Well, what I've got is in the Post Office, and I don't want to touch it. And I've got some shopping I must do before I go home.'

Sefton pulled out his sovereign-case hesitatingly.

'This is all very well, you know,' he said.

'I know what you are thinking, Mr Sefton. You think I don't mean to come tomorrow. That's all Mr Merion, now, isn't it? He's always saying things about me. I'm not going to stick it. I'm going to 'ave it out with 'im.'

'He recommended you to me. And I'll tell you what he said, if you won't repeat it. He said that I should be lucky if I got you, and that I'd better chain you to the studio.'

'And all because I was once late—with a good reason for it, too. Besides, what's once? I suppose he didn't 'appen to tell you how often he's kept me waiting.'

'Well, here you are, Miss Rose. But you'll really be here in time tomorrow, won't you? Otherwise the thing will have got too tacky to work into.'

'You needn't worry about that,' said Miss Rose, eagerly. 'I'll be here, whatever happens, by a quarter past nine. I'll be here if I die first! There, is that good enough for you? Good afternoon, and thank you, Mr Sefton.'

'Good afternoon, Miss Rose. Let me manage that door for you— the key goes a bit stiffly.'

Sefton came back to his picture. In spite of Miss Rose's vehement assurances he felt by no means sure of her, but it was difficult for him to refuse any woman anything, and impossible for him to refuse to pay her what he really owed. He scrawled in charcoal some directions to the charwoman who would come in the morning. She was, from his point of view, a prize charwoman—one who could, and did, wash brushes properly, one who understood the stove, and would, when required, refrain from sweeping. He picked up his hat and went out. He walked the short distance from his studio to his bachelor flat, looked over an evening paper as he drank his tea, and then changed his clothes and took a cab to the club for dinner. He played one game of billiards after dinner, and then went home. His picture was very much in his mind. He wanted to be up fairly early in the morning, and he went to bed early.

He was at his studio by half-past eight. The stove was lighted, and he piled more coke on it. His 'Aphrodite' seemed to have a somewhat mocking expression. It was a little, technical thing, to be corrected easily. He set his palette and selected his brushes. An attempt to roll a cigarette revealed the fact that his pouch was empty. It still wanted a few minutes to nine. He would have time to go up to the tobacconist at the corner. In case Rose Rose arrived while he was away, he left the studio door open. The tobacconist was also a newsagent, and he bought a morning paper. Rose would probably be twenty minutes late at the least, and this would be something to occupy him.

But on his return he found his model already stepping on to the throne.

'Good morning, Miss Rose. You're a lady of your word.' He hardly heeded the murmur which came to him as a reply. He threw his cigarette into the stove, picked up his palette, and got on excellently. The work was absorbing. For some time he thought of nothing else. There was no relaxing on the part of the model—no sign of fatigue. He had been working for over an hour, when his conscience smote him. 'We'll have a rest now, Miss Rose,' he said cheerily. At the same moment he felt human fingers drawn lightly across the back of his neck, just above the collar. He turned round with a sudden start. There was nobody there. He turned back again to the throne. Rose Rose had vanished.

With the utmost care and deliberation he put down his palette and brushes. He said in a loud voice, 'Where are you, Miss Rose?' For a moment or two silence hung in the hot air of the studio.

He repeated his question and got no answer. Then he stepped behind the screen, and suddenly the most terrible thing in his life happened to him. He knew that his model had never been there at all.

There was only one door out to the back street in which his studio was placed, and that door was now locked. He unlocked it, put on his hat, and went out. For a minute or two he paced the street, but he had got to go back to the studio.

He went back, sat down in the easy-chair, lit a cigarette, and tried for a plausible explanation. Undoubtedly he had been working very hard lately. When he had come back from the tobacconist's to the studio he had been in the state of expectant attention, and he was enough of a psychologist to know that in that state you are especially likely to see what you expect to see. He was not conscious of anything abnormal in himself. He did not feel ill, or even nervous. Nothing of the kind had ever happened to him before. The more he considered the matter, the more definite became his state. He was thoroughly frightened. With a great effort he pulled himself together and picked up the newspaper. It was certain that he could do no more work for that day, anyhow. An ordinary, commonplace newspaper would restore him. Yes, that was it. He had been too much wrapped up in the picture. He had simply supposed the model to be there.

He was quite unconvinced, of course, and merely trying to convince himself. As an artist, he knew that for the last hour or more he had been getting the most delicate modelling right from the living form before him. But he did his best, and read the newspaper assiduously.

He read of tariff, protection, and of a new music-hall star. Then his eye fell on a paragraph headed 'Motor Fatalities'.

He read that Miss Rose, an artist's model, had been knocked down by a car in the Fulham Road about seven o'clock on the previous evening; that the owner of the car had stopped and taken her to the hospital, and that she had expired within a few minutes of admission.

He rose from his place and opened a large pocket-knife. There was a strong impulse upon him, and he felt it to be a mad impulse, to slash the canvas to rags. He stopped before the picture. The face smiled at him with a sweetness that was scarcely earthly.

He went back to his chair again. 'I'm not used to this kind of thing,' he said aloud. A board creaked at the far end of the studio. He jumped up with a start of horror. A few minutes later he had left the studio, and locked the door behind him. His common sense was still with him. He ought to go to a specialist. But the picture—

'What's the matter with Sefton?' said Devigne one night at the club after dinner.

'Don't know that anything's the matter with him,' said Merion. 'He hasn't been here lately.'

'I saw him the last time he was here, and he seemed pretty queer. Wanted to let me his studio.'

'It's not a bad studio,' said Merion, dispassionately.

'He's got rid of it now, anyhow. He's got a studio out at Richmond, and the deuce of a lot of time he must waste getting there and back. Besides, what does he do about models?'

'That's a point I've been wondering about myself,' said Merion. 'He'd got Rose Rose for his "Aphrodite," and it looked as if it might be a pretty good thing when I saw it. But, as you know, she died. She was troublesome in some ways, but, taking her all round, I don't know where to find anybody as good today. What's Sefton doing about it?'

'He hasn't got a model at all at present. I know that for a fact, because I asked him.'

'Well,' said Merion, 'he may have got the thing on further than I thought he would in the time. Some chaps can work from memory all right, though I can't do it myself. He's not chucked the picture, I suppose?'

'No; he's not done that. In fact, the picture's his excuse now, if you want him to go anywhere and do anything. But that's not it: the chap's altogether changed. He used to be a genial sort of bounder—bit tyrannical in his manner, perhaps—thought he knew everything. Still, you could talk to him. He was sociable. As a matter of fact, he did know a good deal. Now it's quite different. If you ever do see him—and that's not often—he's got nothing to say to you. He's just going back to his work. That sort of thing.'

'You're too imaginative,' said Merion. 'I never knew a man who varied less than Sefton. Give me his address, will you? I mean his studio. I'll go and look him up one morning. I should like to see how that "Aphrodite's" getting on. I tell you it was promising; no nonsense about it.'

One sunny morning Merion knocked at the door of the studio at Richmond. He heard the sound of footsteps crossing the studio, then Sefton's voice rang out.

'Who's there?'

'Merion. I've travelled miles to see the thing you call a picture.'

'I've got a model.'

'And what does that matter?' asked Merion.

'Well, I'd be awfully glad if you'd come back in an hour. We'd have lunch together somewhere.'

'Right,' said Merion, sardonically. 'I'll come back in about seven million hours. Wait for me.'

He went back to London and his own studio in a state of fury. Sefton had never been a man to pose. He had never put on side about his work. He was always willing to show it to old and intimate friends whose judgment he could trust; and now, when the oldest of his friends had travelled down to Richmond to see him, he was told to come back in an hour, and that they might then lunch together!

'This lets me out,' said Merion, savagely.

But he always speaks well of Sefton nowadays. He maintains that Sefton's 'Aphrodite' would have been a success anyhow. The suicide made a good deal of talk at the time, and a special attendant was necessary to regulate the crowds round it, when, as directed by his will, the picture was exhibited at the Royal Academy. He was found in his studio many hours after his death; and he had scrawled on a blank canvas, much as he left his directions to his charwoman: 'I have finished it, but I can't stand any more.'

Safety Zone

by Barry N. Malzberg

The view that human relations exist only as engulfment is a serious limitation on a narrative artist. Toward the end of his life, Lovecraft seems to have been unhappily aware of this.

—Joanna Russ

On the singles circuit in Providence, every night a new night. The most densely populated state, of course. Every night a new disaster, I should have said. Some are tall and some are short, some are thin and some are rich (but never those who come on to you) but there is, as they say, a common denominator. That common denominator is not sex, however, it is craziness. Why do I partake? This is a question for the tombstone. In the meantime, I move around. It keeps me interested.

On the left, that night, two guys were arguing about craft. Love craft, they said, he would have been a hundred years old this year. Can you imagine that guy being a hundred? They giggled. Love craft, I want to respond, love craft is not a hundred years old, love craft has not been *born* in this place. But I deduced from the conversation that the subject was some writer, not sex. Supernatural writer. Love craft is the most supernatural thing around, I wanted to say, but starting a conversation is always risky. They went on to talk about dogs and then colors in space. It takes all kinds.

Engulfment, this guy on my right said, a strange-looking dude with big eyeballs and hands, the hands floundering into one another. He leaned forward. That's what I wanted, don't you see? But of course that was the mistake.

What mistake? I said, not to be encouraging, just to give him a place to hang his hat.

Just one of them, he said. To embrace one another, it is necessary that we give, not merely entrap. What's your name?

Not a terrific night at Dancer's Lounge. The two on my left were already getting ready to split, maybe to try out some love craft on each other, a few of the bowling machine boys behind me pounding on each other, giving high signs, another cluster at the machine itself.

Nowhere really to hide then and all of them had hit on me and knew enough to stay away.

Well, I should quit weekday nights, sure. I really should, go to community college, improve my mind, but what is the point? What is the point, really? Community college is full of guys like this too and nothing to drink and the other way is to stay in the apartment and look at George and look at George and look at George until I want to throw an ashtray or worse. It is best to get out. Before his agoraphobia stopped him cold as George put it, he felt the same way. Now he feels the other way. He is into chapters of his autobiography.

What's it to you? I said to the guy with the eyeballs. What's your name?

Howard Phillips, he said. I'm forty-seven years old. He put a hand on my arm, ran his fingers up and down. It's not engulfment, he said. I was looking for a little tenderness, that was all. You still haven't told me—

I'm Donna, I said. Just Donna. Do you have to touch my arm?

Well, no, he said. He raised his hand, shrugged his shoulders, moved back on the stool. I don't have to do anything. You're pretty, he said. Do you want to go for a walk?

A walk? I said, you have to be kidding. In the faint light he seemed to have a certain charm, maybe an intensity, but he was an old guy and no way around it. On the other hand, this was the first time at Dancer's in months that I had been offered anything but a drink or the chance to have a heavenly experience. No, I said, I don't want to walk. I just got here. I want to sit a while, make the scene. I haven't seen you here before.

I live in the neighborhood, he said. I just haven't been around for a while. I kind of keep to myself.

Right, I say, there's a lot of that around. People are keeping to themselves a lot these days. It has to do with the times.

But you're pretty, Donna, he said. I look at you and I wish I had come here a long time ago. Engulfment, that was all wrong. I should have been trying to get out of myself, to really give. You know what I mean?

Is your first name Howard and your last name Phillips? I said. Or are you Howard Phillips something else?

Oh, he said. I'm just Howard Phillips. He shook his head, thought of leaning forward, then seemed to consider it too dangerous and half turned. Tell me about yourself, he said. I want to get to know you, Donna.

There's nothing to know. I come and sit on stools and listen to the music. What is this about engulfment?

Oh, never mind, he said. That's something else. I shouldn't have brought it up. He reached out, touched my hand. You have nice hands, he said.

Let it go, I said. I might have said it a little loudly. He dropped my hand fast, picked up his glass, seemed to shudder. You don't start touching someone you don't know, I said.

One of the guys behind me said, This guy bothering you, Donna? You want us to talk to him? Richie will straighten him right out.

Leave him out of it, I said. I need help, I'll tell you.

Because we're always ready to serve, Donna. We're here to help you. You're our mascot.

I listened to them laugh. I heard that laugh a lot without ever wanting to go anywhere with it. Hey, guy, what's your name? Richie said, looking at Howard Phillips, you got an agenda? You got business? They all laughed again.

I waved at Richie. Go away. I said. I can handle this. Howard Phillips just wants to talk, isn't that right?

Howard Phillips nodded, both hands flat on the bar. Talk, he said, that's right. Nothing else. He hunched over as if under attack. I don't want to hurt anyone, he said. I just wanted to talk to you, that's all, see what I was missing. See what was going on here.

That's all right, Richie, I said. You hear him now? He just wants conversation.

Well, you're the girl, Richie said. Donna's the conversation girl.

Providence has sure changed, Howard Phillips said. It's changed a lot.

Since when? I said. Since last night?

Oh, something like that, he said. He stood suddenly, loomed over me. I wonder what Sonia would have made of this, he said. I wonder what would have happened to her here.

Sonia? A girlfriend of yours?

My wife, Howard Phillips said. I mean, she used to be my wife. I've been divorced for years and years. You don't think that I'd dishonor her by coming out to drink alone and talking to a young lady if I were still married, do you? Come on, he said, with a sudden change of expression, that kind of shift I had already come to understand. A very peculiar guy. Let me take you outside. I just want to walk with you. I can't take too much of being inside places. I have to move around. And I write too many letters. I won't hurt you, he said. I'll pay for your drink, here. He reached into his pocket, put a twenty on the bar.

I have plenty of money, he said. Money was never a problem for me, Donna. Can we walk?

It was all too much for me. One minute you are sitting in a dark place, trying to make a little open channel for yourself and the next some strange tall guy is all over you, making demands. You ought to meet George, I said. You and he should really get together.

George?

The guy I live with, I said. He can't stand to go outdoors. *You* say you can't stand being in small spaces. Maybe the two of you could trade off, strike a happy medium. I don't mind, I said, I'll go for a walk with you. It's all the same to me. It's Tuesday night and I don't want to go anywhere.

You live with someone? Howard Phillips said.

Last time I looked, I said. I stood, moved toward the door. You want to walk or something then? It's up to you. I waved to the guys clumped around the machine, two of them waved back. Up to her old tricks, they were thinking. They should only know, I thought. They should know what I got here.

Howard Phillips waited at the door, opened it for me, gently eased me into the parking lot. A nice night, he said, looking up and then at the ground, cobblestones and stars, splitting the difference, looking at me. But it's changed all right, Providence. It's not what it was.

You said that before, I said. You didn't tell me how it's changed. Since when?

Actually I've been away for a long time, he said. I've been out of the city for years. I don't live here any more. I came to have a look at it, that was all. He took my wrist, led me through the parking lot, past my car, onto the path, then we went through the fence. It wasn't like this when I was here before, he said. All that light. The cars.

Looking for Sonia? I said.

What's that?

Is that another reason you came back? To look for Sonia?

Oh, he said. That seemed to stop him flat for a minute. Cobblestones and stars. We walked down the sidewalk, his hand on my wrist curiously delicate but old, *old*. There is something about a guy past forty, his touch, that I really cannot stand. I'm not looking for Sonia, he said. That's all behind me. I lost interest in that a long, long time ago, even when she was still around.

You and George, I said. It was a mistake to go walking with Howard Phillips, I decided and stopped on the sidewalk, then turned him around. I've had enough air, I said. Let's go back inside.

We're barely *out,* Howard Phillips said, and you want to go back. Are you afraid of me? You shouldn't be, you know.

I'm not afraid of anyone, I said.

His hands were on my shoulders. There's nothing to be afraid of, he said. Not engulfment, not the hounds, not the creatures. Nothing at all. It's all gone, don't you understand? I've checked it out here and back and there's just nothing. That's all I wanted to say.

Well, you said it.

I had big ideas, he said. I thought that there was something else. But there really isn't, you know. Which is what I wanted to tell you.

You told me, I said. I began to pull him back toward the bar. We've had our walk and our night on the stars and you've told me about that and about engulfment and about Sonia, too. Now why don't you go home and sleep it off? It was a hard thing to say but that was the only way to put it. I was thinking of the night, another night with George come back to the apartment to watch him staring at the miniseries and making little cutouts of his life on the table. Come and go, try to stay out of it, but you always had to come back, just like Howard Phillips. Engulfment, maybe that was a good word for it.

I've been sleeping, he said. I've slept and I've slept. I can't sleep any more. His grasp was huge and sudden upon me. I could feel his big hands pressing me into him and then the smell of him rising in the crushed space between us, a smell which might have been sex, might have been dank, like nothing I had ever known. Can't you hear the hounds? he said. Can't you hear them beyond the horizon?

I can't hear anything, I said. Let me go. You're starting to hurt me now and you're scaring me. Sometimes it is best to take the direct approach. Let me go, I said, or I'll scream.

He dropped his hands right away, backed away from me. You too, he said, you're another. You're like the rest of them.

I've had enough, I said. One yell and all of the boys would have been at the door, then in the parking lot, fighting for me regardless of the hard times I had given some of them, but I could tell that this was not necessary. You can sense when they are broken and aren't going to give you trouble any more. That's all right, I said. Just go home. It will feel better later on.

It will never feel better, he said. It is better to give than to receive.

Well, sure, I said. Sure, absolutely. Now that he was standing there sniveling I could even feel a little pity for him. It comes and it goes. Take care, I said. I'll see you around sometime.

I could come back in with you.

That wouldn't be a good idea, I said. That definitely would not be a good idea. There are some people there who don't want to see you, who wouldn't be so glad to see you, I think, if I told them.

All right, he said. You don't hear the hounds, he said. You don't hear the dogs, the sound beyond the horizon? You're too young yet, he said. You'll hear them.

Pal, I said, I don't hear a fucking thing and turned and went away from him, walked the walk into the place and went up to the bar and waited for Sam to drop the napkin around. The guys looked at me, shrugged, went back to the machine. That was fast, Richie said. Faster than your regular.

Yeah, I said, well go shove it, you and your foul mouth and went on to say some other stuff, the kind of stuff I can say to Richie, thinking about this and that and nothing at all and the strange guy in the parking lot who found that Providence had changed. Oh, it's changed, Howard Phillips, I said, it's changed all right. But not enough for you, I think, not the way you wanted it to. It's *never* going to change the way you want it. What you want, I think, is a fucking ASPCA.

Later, some drinks later, I went out to my car, no sign of Howard Phillips of course and drove back to the place, found George passed out, his mouth an open *O,* stretched next to his half-done puzzle, the Carson show bouncing and flickering along on the network. I would like to say I got engulfed but that was not my fate. It is no fate for a serious person, say I, but lying down in the other room, listening to George breathe, thinking of my life and all of the sounds and spaces of it, I thought I heard, for the first time, the sound of the dogs in the distance.

Strange. A strange guy. I wonder what happened to Sonia.

Shadows Cast Behind

by Otto E. A. Schmidt

Humdrum, indeed, must have been the existence of that man who, having reached middle age, can look back on no episode or occurrence in his past life that was either uncanny, outré, or inexplicable by the ordinary laws of physics. When a man has been blessed, or otherwise, by being the chief actor in such incidents, he has food for speculation for the rest of his natural life, and perhaps beyond. Let skeptics scoff—who can blame them, not having taken part in the happenings themselves?—but I, having seen, sensed and felt what I have find it impossible to "laugh off."

It was back in the 80's, in the early days of my novitiate as a United States customs guard, that I was assigned the offshore detail on the passenger steamship *Glory of the West* as she lay tied up at the Broadway dock in San Francisco one winter's night. Well do I remember it.

To the uninitiated I may explain that the duty of the offshore or deck detail of the customs guarding force consists in preventing the smuggling of goods by boat or otherwise off the vessel by way of the offshore or waterward side.

Brrr, what a disagreeable night! Despite my heavy overcoat and muffler, I shivered. A fine drizzle, driven by a cold, gusty wind, seemed to penetrate to my very marrow as I tramped up and down the deck with feet heavy and chill as two chunks of ice.

I heard quick footsteps approaching—ah, the lieutenant of the watch.

"Hello," said a cheery voice.

"Hello, lieutenant," I returned.

"How's everything?" he asked, gazing round and taking in the general surroundings.

"Oh, everything's all right," I replied, "at least as right as it can be when you're cold and wet and miserable. This job of guarding-officer is no snap. If every night were like this one I'd chuck it up and go to heaving coal."

"It's a pretty nasty night, that's a fact," said Wood, sympathetically,

418

"especially for the offshore detail. But this is only one night. Cheer up, Stallard, there'll be other nights, fine nights that you'll enjoy and that'll make you feel glad to be one of Uncle Sam's boys. You'd better go below," he continued, "and have the ship's watchman fix you up a cup of coffee. I'll relieve you for a few minutes."

A fine chap, that John Wood, a man with a heart freighted deep with sympathy and thoughtfulness for his fellow-man. No wonder he had the love and respect of the whole watch.

I hastened down to the deck below by way of the port gangplank and soon was enjoying the warmth and cheer of the snug little galley. Presently I rejoined the lieutenant, feeling greatly invigorated and refreshed. After a few more words he left me to resume my solitary vigil.

The wind hummed in the rigging and the rain swished down on the slippery deck glistening in the glow of the distant dock-lights. The winches alternately hissed and purred over the main hatch, like great cats crouched in the shadow of the forward cabins waiting for their prey. I tarried often before them, for their slight warmth was grateful; it was good to clasp the steam pipes and thaw out the griping cold from my numbed fingers.

Seven bells, half-past 3, chimed from some "lime juicer" anchored near—four long hours before my relief would start from the distant mail dock at the other end of San Francisco's waterfront! I thought ruefully of my warm bed at home. Why the devil should there be such a thing as night work? Why couldn't everybody sleep at night like white folks, as the good Lord intended?

I walked aft and looked over the dreary expanse of the bay, overhung with the misty curtains of the night. The faint light on Yerba Buena Island vaguely blinked a sleepy warning to the mariner venturesome enough to risk his craft in the jaws of the storm, and ever and anon the hoarse murmur of the fog signal on Alcatraz boomed across the heaving space like a deep sonorous snore.

I stood close by the door of the smoking saloon. It was unlocked, I knew, for I had tried it before. I turned the handle and peered into the gloom within. A soft, delicious warmth enfolded me, for it was the sailing day of the *Glory of the West* and her steam pipes were full. I stepped inside and sat down on the end of the richly upholstered settee that ran along the wall framing the doorway, leaving the door slightly open so that I could see almost the whole length of the deck forward and a wide stretch of waters alongside. Surely, I thought, from this point I should be able to detect and prevent any attempt at smuggling overboard; at least, nothing could be pulled off in the short time it would take to thaw some of the chill out of my bones. But would I be performing my strict duty?

While still debating this conflict between desire and duty, I heard a light step ascending the heavily carpeted stairs leading from the dining saloon. I turned and beheld a mess-boy lighting the two lamps in the smoking room in which I sat. I was still wondering at this proceeding, which was unusual at this time of the morning, when I heard voices and more footsteps. Three men came up from below.

I was fairly caught, and, though ashamed to be found in this equivocal position, pride would not permit me to seem to run away; so I assumed a look of indifference and kept my seat. I wondered how it happened that passengers were already on board, for, although the vessel was to sail that day, it was not customary to allow them to come aboard so long before the sailing hour. I judged that they were passengers because they did not look like seafaring men. They wore no uniforms, nor any of the habiliments of seamen.

One of them said something I did not catch to the messboy, who nodded and softly retired below. No one noticed me, nor, indeed, even seemed aware of my presence.

Of the last comers one was a big, broad-shouldered man, with ruddy, bearded face and enormous hands; the second, small and dark-skinned with glistening black eyes and long mustachios; while the third was tall and slender, blond and smooth-shaven—evidently an Englishman from his speech and appearance.

The big man offered a cigar to each of his companions, and they all seated themselves at the starboard table near the opposite wall; the big man to the right, the dark man to the left, and the Englishman facing me where I sat on my settee shrinking against the wall near the door.

"Well, Mottingly," began the big man in a deep, booming voice which he tried to make low and subdued, "I hope that bite we've just had will change our luck. It's a new one on me. I generally sit through a game till I've had enough. A gambler would think it unlucky; but we ain't superstitious, are we? Anyhow, we can't have no worse luck than we been having. Garcia," turning to the dark man, "what're you goin' t'do with all your winnings? Lemme sell you a mine. Put your money back in the groun' where it come from, an' let her grow." He laughed; but the Englishman only frowned—the look on his face was stern, the muscles tensely drawn.

The man addressed as Garcia smiled, showing a set of very white teeth. Instinctively I disliked him.

"What, me?" he said, with a shrug. "Oh, I no can count my ween-

420

ings till she be hatch; ha, ha, ha," he laughed at his own attempted witticism.

The big man laughed back. "Don't you try to hatch nothin' now, Garcia, 'cause you ain't no farmer."

Their pleasantry was here interrupted by the return of the messboy with a tray containing a bottle, three glasses and two packs of cards, which he set upon the table. The Englishman seized the bottle and poured a drink for each. I could see his hand tremble slightly as he drank. A gleam came into his eyes as he cried: "Now for our revenge, eh, Thompson? Let us be at it."

He shuffled a pack of cards and they cut for the deal. The big man dealt and I saw that the game was to be poker. No chips were used, only the hard coin, with which all appeared to be plentifully supplied.

They played steadily for a half-hour or more, the big man losing slightly, for he played very cautiously, the Englishman losing heavily; while the bright, yellow gold rose in ever-growing, glittering piles at Garcia's right hand.

The strained look in the Englishman's eyes grew more tense, the frown on his brow deeper. He drank often, and I could see that he was gradually losing his nerve.

At last the big man said: "Say, Mott, I think we've had enough, let's quit."

"No," exclaimed Mottingly testily, "you drop out if you want to. Luck is bound to turn for me sometime. Damme, I'll make it or break the blasted bank!"

"Verry well, *Señor,*" spoke Garcia, yawning, "eef you weesh we queet, I queet. I am the so tire', I sleepy."

"No," said Thompson quietly, with a sharp glance at the last speaker, "I'll stay in."

The game went on again, but much more silently, with an undercurrent of something sinister, some force not apparent on the surface of play and conversation.

I was becoming aware of a feeling I could not explain. A message—I could not yet comprehend what—was being telegraphed to me by my subconscious mind. Once, I thought—but no, I must be mistaken, else the others would have noticed it. Yes, there it was again. I was sure I could not be wrong this time. I was indignant, shocked. In my excitement I had almost risen to my feet and was pointing to Garcia, the words ready to shout on my tongue, when something in the Englishman's attitude held me spellbound. The blue tinge had faded from his face, it was now white as snow; his jaws were set, the lines deep-drawn, while the flesh seemed to have receded from the bones of his cheeks. But he was cool, ah, so cool! His hands were steady as a rock as he laid down his cards. So, then, someone else had seen it, too! His actions and appearance seemed silently to call a halt in the play. All waited for him to proceed. It was his move!

He coolly struck a match and lighted a fresh cigar. "I say, Garcia," he commenced, "I have no more money with me, you've cleaned me out. But here's the deed to the Lone Pine mine that I just paid Mr. Thompson $10,000 for. I'll stake the mine against your pile there and what you won from us last night, which ought to make it about even, as near as I can figure it—"

"Hell, no!" broke in Thompson; "don't do it, Mottingly. Let the stuff go, you can't buck against such a streak of bad luck as you've uncovered. But the mine is a good one and will pay it all back to you in a short time."

Mottingly raised his hand as if to command silence.

Garcia played thoughtfully with a stack of coins, letting them fall to the table with a rippling sound. "Ah," he observed softly, "I deed not think Meester Motting-a-ly she shall need one—ha—nurse."

Thompson flushed redly. Mottingly's jaw set more firmly, but he went on evenly, as though there had been no interruption: "Provided," he spoke slowly and distinctly, almost hissingly, "provided Mr. Thompson deals the cards—"

"What-a for that?" cried Garcia quickly, his teeth showing in an evil snarl, his eyes flashing luridly from the ghastly greenish yellow of his face.

All three were leaning forward in a crouching attitude and were, unconsciously, slowly rising. The light of understanding had broken on the face of Thompson, now livid with fury.

"Otherwise," went on the tense, slow, almost monotonous voice of Mottingly, "otherwise you will refund to him and to me every cent you have won from us."

There was an instant's pause. The situation was tense. The adversaries—now such in earnest—were keenly eyeing one another, each studying the situation and calculating chances. The sword of fate hung by a hair.

Garcia spoke coolly now, almost contemptuously; but there was a furtive, hunted look in the eyes that glanced rapidly from one to the other of his opponents and over and beside and beyond them. "For why you ask-a that, Meester Motting-a-ly, you spick verry—ha—strange—what-a for shall I to geeve to you the money I have win?"

They were now all on their feet.

422

"Because," thundered Mottingly, raking the spreading pile of gold toward himself with one hand and making a quick backward movement with the other, "you've been dealing from the bottom of the pack. You're a damned cheat! I saw—"

There were three blinding flashes of light even before Garcia's hissed "You lie" was fairly uttered, followed by a crash.

"Hello," said a voice, "ain't you afraid of the ghosts?"

The ship's watchman was holding a lantern up to my face with one hand, while the other was on the handle of the door, which evidently had just banked shut.

"What ghosts?" I gasped.

"Why, the ghosts of three men that killed one another over a game of cards in here about twenty years ago. I heard it from the mate that was on her at the time."

"Were they all killed?" I inquired regretfully.

"Yep, there was an Englishman, an American and a Chileno. There were two empty shells in the Chileno's gun an' one in the American's. The Englisher didn't fire a shot—wasn't quick enough on the draw, I guess. That Chileno was a bad one. Professional gambler. Had six notches on his gun already. They say their ghosts come back every once in a while, so you wanta look out for 'em."

"Say," I said, quite irrelevantly, "are there any passengers aboard?"

He gave me a strange, inquiring look as he answered, "No, not yet. Nobody aboard 'cept me an' you an' some o' the crew. Why?"

"Phew," I said, without answering his question, "it's close in here. Guess I'll go out and get some fresh air."

How grateful the damp coolness of the outside felt! I looked at my watch; it showed 3:45. Only five minutes since I had consulted it last! I could not credit it. I held it to my ear—yes, it was still running. I seemed to have spent hours in that accursed smoking saloon, and yet in reality it had been only five minutes.

The rest of that interminable watch I passed in deep thought, wondering, speculating, doubting. Up and down, up and down the melting deck I tramped, well forward, though; not venturing abaft the main saloon amidships. I shivered, but not from the cold alone.

I told no one of my adventures, but made cautious and veiled inquiries at the steamship offices. The personnel of the company, naturally, had undergone many changes in the last twenty years and I could find no one who remembered any tragedy connected with the *Glory of the West*.

At last I bethought me of that treasury of pioneer Californian history, *The Daily Alta-California*, one of the first San Francisco newspapers. I spent many of my spare hours poring over its back files and eventually my industry was rewarded by the finding of an account of the death of three men, passengers on the American steamship *Glory of the West*, in a gambling row substantially as related by the ship's watchman.

In the cases of the American and the Chilean the coroner's jury had rendered a verdict of death by gunshot wounds each at the hands of the other. In the case of the Englishman, however, they had allowed that grim and perverted sense of humor, common in those days, even touching the most sacred and solemn subjects, to move them to bring in a verdict "that the deceased had come to his death by suicide consequent on paralysis of the dexter digits." The victim proved to be a remittance man, the second son of Lord C——, and the remains were turned over to the British consul.

I was so profoundly impressed that I determined to follow the matter up in an effort to learn just how accurate the details of my dream, or vision, might prove.

By inquiring at the consulate I learned that the father of the murdered Mottingly was still alive. Thereupon I addressed a long and carefully worded letter to Lord C—— in which I related my vision in detail, and added a copy of the newspaper account of the tragedy and of the coroner's distorted findings. I wound up my recital with a request for a photograph of his deceased son to identify and verify my dream picture.

So long a time passed that I had begun to believe my communication had gone astray when I received a reply as follows:

London, Engl. C. B.
March 2d, 188—.

John D. Stallard, Esq.,
Ahlborn House,
San Francisco, California, U. S. A.

Honoured Sir:

In behalf of my client, Lord C——, let me premise with a statement of his gratitude and appreciation of the great service you have rendered him and his family at such pains and labour to yourself.

Some twenty years ago the body of the unfortunate young man, the second son of his Lordship, arrived here accompanied by a copy of the death certificate containing a statement of the verdict of the coroner's jury as to the cause of death.

I may here state, en passant, *that father and son had parted in anger several years previously after a stormy interview over the subject of the young man's drinking and gambling habits. His Lordship thereupon disowned him, denied him the use of the family residences, and dismissed him with a lump sum and the injunction never again to enter his presence until he had proven his manhood.*

But, unfortunately, his failings had too strong a hold on him to be shaken off here, surrounded by his old associates, and he emigrated to the States, where he drifted about until his means were exhausted. His father turned a deaf ear to his appeals for further assistance but Lady C——, his mother, kept him liberally supplied with funds, as I happen to know, it being my province to attend to the remittances.

These circumstances, together with strong religious scruples and his stern, judicial temperament as a magistrate of the Queen's bench, caused his Lordship to refuse permission to place the body in the family vault. (No doubt you are aware that an ancient law of England, now obsolete, required that a suicide should be buried at a crossroads with a stake driven through his middle.)

The remains, perforce, were consigned to unconsecrated ground. From that time forward the suite in the C—— mansion formerly occupied by the deceased was, according to the servants, haunted by the spirit of the young master wailing and crying to be gathered to his ancestors.

Your experience, while it would be inadmissible in court as legal testimony, in conjunction with your interpretation and explanation of the grotesque and frivolous verdict of the coroner's jury and the mute evidence of the two guns, so strongly impressed his Lordship and the lay and ecclesiastical authorities that the body has been exhumed and placed in the family crypt with appropriate ceremonies.

His Lordship was also greatly moved by your graphic description of his son's manly stand in the last act of his life drama.

It may interest you to know that since the disinterment and reburial the servants assert all ghostly manifestations by the young man's alleged spirit have ceased.

I have written you, by his Lordship's direction, thus fully and frankly in consideration of your kind and conscientious services which entitle you to every confidence.

I am posting, under separate cover, a photograph of young Mottingly, and if it be not too great a further trespass on your time and patience my client would greatly appreciate a report from you as to how it compares with the picturization of his son that appeared to you in your vision.

> *Assuring you again of his Lordship's deep appreciation and cordial acknowledgement of your distinguished favour, I am, with the highest personal respect,*
> *Your most obedient servant,*
> *John N. D. ——, Q. C.*

I opened the packet containing the photograph with mingled emotions, but surprize was not one of them when I beheld in the shadowy likeness an exact replica of the face of the man who had appeared in my vision as young Mottingly.

Shadows in the Grass

by Steve Rasnic Tem

Mark had read about the accident in the paper a week ago, a terrible thing, how the young boy had been killed on the road that wound around the park while his mother watched from the grassy bend, still eating their picnic lunch, still stretched out beneath the tree even as her son was struck by the car.

The boy had been riding his brand new bicycle, the paper said. The way Mark remembered it, it had been the first time. He was showing off for his mother.

It was easy for Mark to become obsessed with that kind of story. After finding out about such a tragic incident he felt compelled to read everything he could about the accident—buying up all editions of the city's three newspapers for the next several weeks, watching every TV newscast he could—seeking any additional information. He needed to know the woman's reaction, the feelings of relatives and schoolmates, the driver's reaction and those of his neighbors. He usually took the time to visit the scene, map it out, figure how it would look from every angle. He needed to visualize the incident in his own mind, in every detail, then take it apart and analyze it.

He was not a voyeur, although he had been accused of it, first by his ex-wife and then by a few police officers who caught him taking photographs one day. It was, simply, that Mark Simms was an unhappy man, but with no tragic memories of his own to account for such unhappiness. There was no sad past, no ghosts to haunt him.

Mark Simms was a reasonable man, and that lack of sad memory to explain his depressions was terribly, unacceptably unreasonable.

He had collected his first sad memory when he had gone into the hospital to have his appendix removed. In the next bed there was an old man dying of cancer, a *father* dying of cancer he soon discovered, as men and women of varying ages came to visit the old man in his last days. Mark got to know the family very well on their visits, and questioned them thoroughly concerning their father—what it had been like growing up in his house, where he had taken them on vacations, if he had been understanding, if he had been a strict disciplinarian.

And slowly Mark acquired their memories of the old man. Their past became his own, and when the father died, it was his own father dying. He had acquired their grief.

He had been thunderstruck when the old man died, weeping for hours, and what had followed had been a week-long depression. But for the first time in Mark's life, there seemed to be a *reason* for the depression.

He parked his car at the side of the park road, a hundred yards or so away from the bend where the boy had been killed. He began walking swiftly, anxious to get to the spot at about the same time of day the accident had occurred, hoping to see the same shadows, the same mixture of light and dark on asphalt, grass and trees the little boy's mother had seen. Mark had never lost a child.

As he came around the bend he saw that there was a woman already on the grass beside the road, stretched out beneath the tree, apparently having a picnic. He felt profoundly let down, and was rapidly plotting some way to scare the woman off when he recognized her from her picture in the paper. It was the boy's mother.

He approached her slowly. She was an older woman, gray streaks in her light brown hair, although Mark wondered if that were a change since the accident. Silver-blue eyes that seemed to fade a bit when she looked up at him. She continued to hum to herself, as if she didn't know he was there. She sat on a bright purple quilt, a wicker basket by her side, and a young boy's red jacket with white-striped sleeves beside that.

Mark took off his hat. "Ma'am, I'm sorry about your son."

She turned her head slightly, her eyes turning a darker blue. "You mean Bobby? Yes . . . he's gone off playing on his bicycle now, missed his lunch. But he'll be back . . . he gets hungry, you know."

Mark stared at her, not knowing what to say. He'd never encountered this before. He lowered himself to the ground and sat beside her, touching her arm gently. "Lady . . . your boy . . . he's dead . . ." He held his breath, wondering if telling her might be a mistake.

"He gets hungry . . ." she said more quietly than before. "He'll be back real soon now."

Mark leaned back on his elbows. He wasn't sure what he should do now, but was tempted to forget the whole thing and leave. He felt sorry for the woman, but she was obviously in no condition to discuss grief with him—she wasn't feeling any grief. The selfishness of the thought made him feel bad about himself, and made it difficult for him to leave just yet.

He gazed at the green and brown area around them. Long, thin shadows left by their forms seemed to ripple through the uneven grass. A darker shadow where the sun had fixed the trunk of the tree. Round shadows left by nothing Mark could figure. Round shadows moving . . .

Mark turned quickly to the road, but something shiny and metallic reflected the sun back into his eyes so that he couldn't see. He rubbed his eyes painfully, and then there was nothing in the road. He thought of a passing car, but he would have heard it.

"That boy . . ." The woman sighed. "Wouldn't even stop when I waved. Guess he's gonna go round just one more time."

Mark stared down the road, but could see nothing. He rubbed his hands together nervously, then turned to the woman. "Lady . . . maybe you better let me take you home. It's getting late and you shouldn't . . ."

"I've gotta wait for Bobby, mister. Can't leave him out here by himself. He'll be afraid . . ."

It seemed to be getting colder, the wind beginning to chill. Mark stood up and walked away from the woman, toward the interior of the park, wondering if he could find a police officer on patrol, or a phone box where he could call one. He felt sure the woman would stay out all night if he didn't get help.

About thirty feet away he stopped, hearing voices behind him. He turned around and looked at the woman. She was speaking softly, and the shadows seemed lighter somehow next to her. Like a silhouette the light had begun to erase. A round shadow against the rough tree trunk, a glimmer of reflecting metal, shadowed branches gesturing excitedly like a little boy's arms . . .

428

Mark ran to the woman. She turned and smiled. "I let him go round with his new bike just one more time, but he'll be coming back for lunch real soon. Bobby's a good son, mister."

"Lady . . ." He stopped. There was nothing he could do for her. He began to walk slowly down the road toward his car. He intended to call the authorities when he got home. He had some responsibility.

The sun was lower in the sky now, lower than the leafy branches that had blocked it so well, down behind the trunks and lower boughs —and the shadows in the grass had multiplied.

He had no poignant memories of his own, so he borrowed them from others. He'd had no tragic past.

The shadows rippled through the grass beside him, just off the narrow roadway, as the wind picked up. Legs and arms, hands and fingers, long thin fingers like greedy snakes . . . Mark imagined if he threw food there, picnic food, the gray hands would gobble it up.

He walked more swiftly as it began to rain, a drop at a time. He'd only wanted something to remember, some image to justify his sadness. The shadows ran. He could hear the crackle of raindrops on the fallen leaves, steadily increasing their pace until they sounded to him like roaring flames. He could see his car just ahead.

He could not remember hearing anything, but for some reason he turned his head, and the reflection off the chrome handlebars blinded him.

He screamed, and suddenly the loose, bent wheel was spinning past him. He started running toward his car, trying to outrun the wheel.

When he reached the door the bent wheel fell on its side. Mark looked down.

Underneath the blur of turning spokes there lay a shadow. Small and frantically pressing at the pedal. Almost like a small foot.

He opened the door and slipped into the car, starting the engine immediately. But then he found he couldn't leave. It was raining outside.

He wanted to take their grief and make it his own; he stole their memories. But he would not take responsibility for their ghosts. He would not. He began to move the car forward.

Then stopped. It was raining outside. He couldn't just leave.

He reached back and unlocked the door. Then he pushed it open into the rain.

He could barely see it in his rearview mirror. The stormy afternoon was almost too dark for shadows. But there was a slightly darker grayness suddenly at the edge of the door, then a new scent of wetness in the back seat. He closed the door and picked up speed.

Mark filled his nostrils with the smell of wet hair and jeans, soggy tennis shoes. He had never lost a child. He didn't want to miss any detail.

The Sixth Tree

by Edith Lichty Stewart

Police Headquarters,
Los Angeles, California.

Gentlemen:
The coroner's inquest held over the mutilated body of Professor Carhart to account for the baffling circumstances surrounding his death gave the verdict: "Met death at the claws and teeth of some wild beast, presumably a mountain lion."

Considering the prominent and honorary position held by the professor in some of our foremost universities, I felt justified in suppressing the astounding diary, herewith enclosed, found by me in the dead man's room after the inquest.

I submit the diary without comment. Any conclusion derived from its perusal can be only too ghastly and unbelievable.

Respectfully,
J. Donohue, Operative.

As we entered the canyon, that dreaded sensation of oppression and suffocation surged upon me and I tore away my collar and lifted the hat from my throbbing head.

There are hypocrites who prate vapidly of the exaltation and exhilaration inspired in the human by these same mountains. Liars! Who should know more of mountains than I, who for thirty years have studied them, chipped away at their exteriors, articulated every rock and stratum in their towering frames, explored and explained their very entrails? Why, I have even proved to myself that they possess a soul, or souls—personality—malignant human emotions. God! What I have suffered!

Is it in revenge for my exhaustive knowledge of them that they torture me so? When night comes—it is night now—they shake from their torpor and become monstrosities crowding closer and closer, stooping to compress the air about my fevered head, crushing into my brain. It is only by ignoring them that I gain relief; so I am writing now in a frenzy to escape them.

As I said, we had entered the canyon. There were only the stage-driver and I. I had been dismissed from the university with only the explanation that my course of study was becoming erratic. Why had I selected the little lodge at the source of this rugged ravine for my retreat? It should have been the last place in the world for me to seek rest; yet I was here. The gray road twisted its dusty way into the gathering dusk of the mountains. The stage-driver essayed a few conversational stupidities, but I soon silenced his chatter. He looked at me askance and whipped up the horses. The trail turned abruptly. The door behind was closed. Mountains reared about me on either side and a feeling of panic assailed me. I was indeed in the enemy's territory.

An hour passed in silence. Suddenly a bend in the road interrupted the monotony of the scene. With what emotions I beheld a cabin—an adobe cabin crouched back from the road against the hill! Five—no, six—gaunt trees, that might once have been willows, stood in a ghostly row before it. Its windows, glassless and shadeless like the lidless eyes of a skull, leered and peered down at us. A glance had seared it on my mind—and then we had passed it.

"What place was that?"

The driver lashed his horses to greater speed.

"A good place to keep away from after dark."

I waited impatiently for him to volunteer further information, but the fool was evidently sulky. I would wheedle.

"My good man, your reply only arouses my curiosity."

He slowed down. The road lay straight. Turning, I could see the haggard eyes of the house as it watched for the effect the driver's tale would have upon me.

It seems that some years before, after a heavy rain, some hikers had found in front of the deserted cabin five shallow graves, one beneath each tree. Each grave had contained a man. Investigation had identified them as a group of sheep-herders—rough customers at the best. They had evidently spent the night in the cabin, for the place was littered with empty bottles, cards and poker chips.

Who had committed the wholesale murder and buried the bodies was never discovered. Rumor had it that the five sheep-herders had located a mine back in the mountains and had hired a geologist to go

431

with them to assay the ore, but this was never substantiated. There was no one who had actually seen the geologist or knew much about the mine.

"Where are the bodies now?"

The driver shrugged. "Nobody claimed them, so they were thrown back into their graves, the dirt shoveled on again, and left till Judgment Day."

"Well, if they are dead and disposed of till the Day of Judgment, why are you afraid of this place?" I asked with some scorn.

He shook his head darkly. "There's six trees and only five graves under 'em."

"Well?"

"They say there's a curse on this place until the sixth tree has a dead man, too."

"Bah!" I cried. "Nursery tales!"

But I must have spoken strangely, for his long whip curled out over the horses' heads and we swung around the last bend. No longer was the cabin visible, but I knew I would return.

It must have been midnight as I approached the cabin, a midnight that held its breath and waited for something. A hush of expectancy had stilled every sound of the night. I stepped over the graves—one, two, three, four, five. There was no wind, and yet I am sure I heard a rustle, or better, a faint creaking in the naked branches of the sixth tree as I passed beneath it.

Suddenly I halted. My heart swelled and burst into a volley of stifled beatings. There could be no illusion; a wan, lurid glow slowly grew from the surrounding darkness. There was a light within the cabin. Someone was there. I lashed my cowering senses to action and noiselessly approached the window.

Staggering, I clutched the windowledge for support. The uneven light from a guttering candle secured in an empty bottle disclosed what I had (God help me!) expected to see. They—one, two, three, four, five of them—they were there, the same and yet how horrible! Lifelessly, yet with terrible relentlessness, they played at their everlasting cards. Their dank hair hung in wisps over sunken eyes. The leathery skin of their faces sagged loosely over fleshless skulls. Their clothes hung in tatters, slimed with earth and mud.

And their hands! Fascinated, in terror, I watched those lean, blackened claws deal the mildewed and ragged cards. Their nails, long and broken, scratched over the rough table as they clutched at the chips. They were intent on their game, unaware of my presence. But even as I gratefully assured myself of this their eyes were on me. There was no hate, no fury, no fiendish glee in their expression, rather a blankness, a patient waiting. They had ceased to play. All the waiting in the universe concentrated about me. There was a vacant place beside the dealer. When I could resist no longer, I went within.

The dawn lay pallid on the hills when I flung away from the cabin. There was no sound or motion from the sixth tree as I shrank from its reaching fingers. When clear of it, I ran—ran in the madness of terror to the hotel, locked my door and fell sobbing in wrath and exhaustion on the bed.

I had lost! There was no depth to the agony of my soul. We had played for no obvious stakes, but only too well I knew the prize for which we fought. There would be two more nights of play with two more chances to win. I arose, bathed my scorching brow, and all day I sat figuring, figuring. As a man of science I had often scoffed at the thing called luck, for any game of cards must be reducible to some science or system. Night found me triumphant. Scarcely could I wait for the darkness that I might hasten to their humiliation.

And that night I won! I won, I say! They were waiting for me as before. The cards were dealt, and then I proved that all things are explained by science. A man so learned can hold the world in his hand, immune from the uncertainties of chance and accident!

My triumph grew as the dawn approached. I grew reckless. I chuckled. I laughed. I taunted them in their ghastly dead faces. They sat immobile, playing, playing. Their silence infuriated me. I tried to sting them to retort, but my words found answer only in the angry mutterings of the echo from the hollow room. When, as before, the candle choked and expired like a dying man and their wasted forms faded into the shadows of the cabin, I hurled the cards after them and went stumbling and laughing into the morning, drunk with my triumph. As I passed beneath the accursed tree it dared to trail clinging, warmthless fingers across my cheek. I jerked away in loathing and derision. I still can feel the iciness of its touch.

They have asked me, these curious ignorant fools here, where I spend the nights. They talk and whisper about me in little groups that grow silent and disperse when I approach. Well, tonight is the last night, and then I shall be free and far away. If I had not been a man of science and evolved a system, then I might have known defeat; and these gaping fools might have something to fill their empty brains and furnish them with silly chatter. They would find my mutilated body, clawed as though by a mountain lion flung into a shallow grave—beneath the sixth tree.

But I shall not lose! When this night curdles into dawn I shall stuff their filthy graves, stamping the dirt upon them until it fills their mouths and blinds their staring eyes. And the tree? I shall leave it to wring its bony hands for ever in impotent chagrin.

But why am I lingering here? It is time for the game to begin and—they are waiting.

The Soul of Laploshka

by Saki

Laploshka was one of the meanest men I have ever met, and quite one of the most entertaining. He said horrid things about other people in such a charming way that one forgave him for the equally horrid things he said about oneself behind one's back. Hating anything in the way of ill-natured gossip ourselves, we are always grateful to those who do it for us and do it well. And Laploshka did it really well.

Naturally Laploshka had a large circle of acquaintances, and as he exercised some care in their selection it followed that an appreciable proportion were men whose bank balances enabled them to acquiesce indulgently in his rather one-sided views on hospitality. Thus, although possessed of only moderate means, he was able to live comfortably within his income, and still more comfortably within those of various tolerantly disposed associates.

But towards the poor or to those of the same limited resources as himself his attitude was one of watchful anxiety; he seemed to be haunted by a besetting fear lest some fraction of a shilling or franc, or whatever the prevailing coinage might be, should be diverted from his pocket or service into that of a hard-up companion. A two-franc cigar would be cheerfully offered to a wealthy patron, on the principle of doing evil that good may come, but I have known him indulge in agonies of perjury rather than admit the incriminating possession of a copper coin when change was needed to tip a waiter. The coin would have been duly returned at the earliest opportunity—he would have taken means to ensure against forgetfulness on the part of the borrower—but accidents might happen, and even the temporary estrangement from his penny or sou was a calamity to be avoided.

The knowledge of this amiable weakness offered a perpetual temptation to play upon Laploshka's fears of involuntary generosity. To offer him a lift in a cab and pretend not to have enough money to pay the fare, to fluster him with a request for sixpence when his hand was full of silver just received in change, these were a few of the petty torments that ingenuity prompted as occasion afforded. To do justice to Laploshka's resourcefulness it must be admitted that he always emerged somehow or other from the most embarrassing dilemma without in any way compromising his reputation for saying "No". But the gods send opportunities at some time to most men, and mine came one evening when Laploshka and I were supping together in a cheap boulevard restaurant. (Except when he was the bidden guest of some one with an irreproachable income, Laploshka was wont to curb his appetite for high living; on such fortunate occasions he let it go on an easy snaffle.) At the conclusion of the meal a somewhat urgent message called me away, and without heeding my companion's agitated protest, I called back cruelly, "Pay my share; I'll settle with you tomorrow." Early on the morrow Laploshka hunted me down by instinct as I walked along a side street that I hardly ever frequented. He had the air of a man who had not slept.

"You owe me two francs from last night," was his breathless greeting.

I spoke evasively of the situation in Portugal, where more trouble seemed brewing. But Laploshka listened with the abstraction of the deaf adder, and quickly returned to the subject of the two francs.

"I'm afraid I must owe it to you," I said lightly and brutally. "I haven't a sou in the world," and I added mendaciously, "I'm going away for six months or perhaps longer."

Laploshka said nothing, but his eyes bulged a little and his cheeks took on the mottled hues of an ethnographical map of the Balkan Peninsula. That same day, at sundown, he died. "Failure of the heart's action" was the doctor's verdict; but I, who knew better, knew that he had died of grief.

There arose the problem of what to do with his two francs. To have killed Laploshka was one thing; to have kept his beloved money would have argued a callousness of feeling of which I am not capable. The ordinary solution, of giving it to the poor, would by no means fit the present situation, for nothing would have distressed the dead man more than such a misuse of his property. On the other hand, the bestowal of two francs on the rich was an operation which called for some tact. An easy way out of the difficulty seemed, however, to present itself the following Sunday, as I was wedged into the cosmopolitan crowd which filled the side-aisle of one of the most popular Paris churches. A collecting-bag, for "the poor of Monsieur le Curé," was buffeting its tortuous way across the seemingly impenetrable human sea, and a German in front of me, who evidently did not wish his appreciation of the magnificent music to be marred by a suggestion of payment, made audible criticisms to his companion on the claims of the said charity.

"They do not want money," he said; "they have too much money. They have no poor. They are all pampered."

If that were really the case my way seemed clear. I dropped Laploshka's two francs into the bag with a murmured blessing on the rich of Monsieur le Curé.

Some three weeks later chance had taken me to Vienna, and I sat one evening regaling myself in a humble but excellent little Gasthaus up in the Währinger quarter. The appointments were primitive, but the Schnitzel, the beer, and the cheese could not have been improved on. Good cheer brought good custom, and with the exception of one small table near the door every place was occupied. Half-way through my meal I happened to glance in the direction of that empty seat, and saw that it was no longer empty. Poring over the bill of fare with the absorbed scrutiny of one who seeks the cheapest among the cheap was Laploshka. Once he looked across at me, with a comprehensive glance at my repast, as though to say, "It is my two francs you are eating," and then looked swiftly away. Evidently the poor of Monsieur le Curé had been genuine poor. The Schnitzel turned to leather in my mouth, the beer seemed tepid; I left the Emmenthaler untasted. My one idea was to get away from the room, away from the table where *that* was seated; and as I fled I felt Laploshka's reproachful eyes watching the amount that I gave to the piccolo—out of his two francs. I lunched next day at an expensive restaurant which I felt sure that the living Laploshka would never have entered on his own account, and I hoped that the dead Laploshka would observe the same barriers. I was not mistaken, but as I came out I found him miserably studying the bill of fare stuck up on the portals. Then he slowly made his way over to a milk-hall. For the first time in my experience I missed the charm and gaiety of Vienna life.

After that, in Paris or London or wherever I happened to be, I continued to see a good deal of Laploshka. If I had a seat in a box at a theatre I was always conscious of his eyes furtively watching me from the dim recesses of the gallery. As I turned into my club on a rainy afternoon I would see him taking inadequate shelter in a doorway opposite. Even if I indulged in the modest luxury of a penny chair in the Park he generally confronted me from one of the free benches, never staring at me, but always elaborately conscious of my presence. My friends began to comment on my changed looks, and advised me to leave off heaps of things. I should have liked to have left off Laploshka.

On a certain Sunday—it was probably Easter, for the crush was worse than ever—I was again wedged into the crowd listening to the music in the fashionable Paris church, and again the collection-bag was buffeting its way across the human sea. An English lady behind me was making ineffectual efforts to convey a coin into the still distant bag, so I took the money at her request and helped it forward to its destination. It was a two-franc piece. A swift inspiration came to me, and I merely dropped my own sou into the bag and slid the silver coin into my pocket. I had withdrawn Laploshka's two francs from the poor, who should never have had that legacy. As I backed away from the crowd I heard a woman's voice say, "I don't believe he put my money in the bag. There are swarms of people in Paris like that!" But my mind was lighter than it had been for a long time.

The delicate mission of bestowing the retrieved sum on the deserving rich still confronted me. Again I trusted to the inspiration of accident, and again fortune favoured me. A shower drove me, two days later, into one of the historic churches on the left bank of the Seine, and there I found, peering at the old wood-carvings, the Baron R., one of the wealthiest and most shabbily dressed men in Paris. It was now or never. Putting a strong American inflection into the French which I usually talked with an unmistakable British accent, I catechized the Baron as to the date of the church's building, its dimensions, and other details which an American tourist would be certain to want to know. Having acquired such information as the Baron was able to impart on short notice, I solemnly placed the two-franc piece in his hand, with the hearty assurance that it was "pour vous," and turned to go. The Baron was slightly taken aback, but accepted the situation with a good grace. Walking over to a small box fixed in the wall, he dropped Laploshka's two francs into the slot. Over the box was the inscription, "Pour les pauvres de M. le Curé."

That evening, at the crowded corner by the Café de la Paix, I caught a fleeting glimpse of Laploshka. He smiled, slightly raised his hat, and vanished. I never saw him again. After all, the money had been *given* to the deserving rich, and the soul of Laploshka was at peace.

The Sphinx
Without a Secret

by Oscar Wilde

One afternoon I was sitting outside the Café de la Paix, watching the splendour and shabbiness of Parisian life, and wondering over my vermouth at the strange panorama of pride and poverty that was passing before me, when I heard someone call my name. I turned round, and saw Lord Murchison. We had not met since we had been at college together, nearly ten years before, so I was delighted to come across him again, and we shook hands warmly. At Oxford we had been great friends. I had liked him immensely, he was so handsome, so high-spirited, and so honourable. We used to say of him that he would be the best of fellows, if he did not always speak the truth, but I think we really admired him all the more for his frankness. I found him a good deal changed. He looked anxious and puzzled, and seemed to be in doubt about something. I felt it could not be modern scepticism, for Murchison was the stoutest of Tories, and believed in the Pentateuch as firmly as he believed in the House of Peers; so I concluded that it was a woman, and asked him if he was married yet.

"I don't understand women well enough," he answered.

"My dear Gerald," I said, "women are meant to be loved, not to be understood."

"I cannot love where I cannot trust," he replied.

"I believe you have a mystery in your life, Gerald," I exclaimed; "tell me about it."

"Let us go for a drive," he answered, "it is too crowded here. No, not a yellow carriage, any other colour—there, that dark green one will

438

do"; and in a few moments we were trotting down the boulevard in the direction of the Madeleine.

"Where shall we go to?" I said.

"Oh, anywhere you like!" he answered—"to the restaurant in the Bois; we will dine there, and you shall tell me all about yourself."

"I want to hear about you first," I said. "Tell me your mystery."

He took from his pocket a little silver-clasped morocco case, and handed it to me. I opened it. Inside there was the photograph of a woman. She was tall and slight, and strangely picturesque with her large vague eyes and loosened hair. She looked like a clairvoyante, and was wrapped in rich furs.

"What do you think of that face?" he said; "is it truthful?"

I examined it carefully. It seemed to me the face of someone who had a secret, but whether that secret was good or evil I could not say. Its beauty was a beauty moulded out of many mysteries—the beauty, in fact, which is psychological, not plastic—and the faint smile that just played across the lips was far too subtle to be really sweet.

"Well," he cried impatiently, "what do you say?"

"She is the Gioconda in sables," I answered. "Let me know all about her."

"Not now," he said; "after dinner," and began to talk of other things.

When the waiter brought us our coffee and cigarettes I reminded Gerald of his promise. He rose from his seat, walked two or three times up and down the room, and, sinking into an arm-chair, told me the following story:—

"One evening," he said, "I was walking down Bond Street about five o'clock. There was a terrific crush of carriages, and the traffic was almost stopped. Close to the pavement was standing a little yellow brougham, which, for some reason or other, attracted my attention. As I passed by there looked out from it the face I showed you this afternoon. It fascinated me immediately. All that night I kept thinking of it, and all the next day. I wandered up and down that wretched Row, peering into every carriage, and waiting for the yellow brougham; but I could not find *ma belle inconnue*, and at last I began to think she was merely a dream. About a week afterwards I was dining with Madame de Rastail. Dinner was for eight o'clock; but at half past eight we were still waiting in the drawing-room. Finally the servant threw open the door, and announced Lady Alroy. It was the woman I had been looking for. She came in very slowly, looking like a moonbeam in grey lace, and, to my intense delight, I was asked to take her into dinner. After we had sat down, I remarked quite innocently, 'I think I caught sight of you in Bond Street some time ago, Lady Alroy.' She grew very pale, and said to me in a low voice, 'Pray do not talk so loud; you may be overheard.' I felt miserable at having made such a bad beginning, and plunged recklessly into the subject of the French plays. She spoke very little, always in the same low musical voice, and seemed as if she was afraid of someone listening. I fell passionately, stupidly in love, and the indefinable atmosphere of mystery that surrounded her excited my most ardent curiosity. When she was going away, which she did very soon after dinner, I asked her if I might call and see her. She hesitated for a moment, glanced round to see if anyone was near us, and then said, 'Yes; to-morrow at a quarter to five.' I begged Madame de Rastail to tell me about her; but all that I could learn was that she was a widow with a beautiful house in Park Lane, and as some scientific bore began a dissertation on widows, as exemplifying the survival of the matrimonially fittest, I left and went home.

"The next day I arrived at Park Lane punctual to the moment, but was told by the butler that Lady Alroy had just gone out. I went down to the club quite unhappy and very much puzzled, and after long consideration wrote her a letter, asking if I might be allowed to try my chance some other afternoon. I had no answer for several days, but at last I got a little note saying she would be at home on Sunday at four and with this extraordinary postscript: 'Please do not write to me here again; I will explain when I see you.' On Sunday she received me, and was perfectly charming; but when I was going away she begged of me, if I ever had occasion to write to her again, to address my letter to 'Mrs. Knox, care of Whittaker's Library, Green Street.' 'There are reasons,' she said, 'why I cannot receive letters in my own house.'

"All through the season I saw a great deal of her, and the atmosphere of mystery never left her. Sometimes I thought that she was in the power of some man, but she looked so unapproachable that I could not believe it. It was really very difficult for me to come to any conclusion, for she was like one of those strange crystals that one sees in museums, which are at one moment clear, and at another clouded. At last I determined to ask her to be my wife: I was sick and tired of the incessant secrecy that she imposed on all my visits, and on the few letters I sent her. I wrote to her at the library to ask her if she could see me the following Monday at six. She answered yes, and I was in the seventh heaven of delight. I was infatuated with her: in spite of the mystery, I thought then—in consequence of it, I see now. No; it was the woman herself I loved. The mystery troubled me, maddened me. Why did chance put me in its track?"

"You discovered it, then?" I cried.

"I fear so," he answered. "You can judge for yourself."

"When Monday came round I went to lunch with my uncle, and about four o'clock found myself in the Marylebone Road. My uncle, you know, lives in Regent's Park. I wanted to get to Piccadilly, and took a short cut through a lot of shabby little streets. Suddenly I saw in front of me Lady Alroy, deeply veiled and walking very fast. On coming to the last house in the street, she went up the steps, took out a latch-key, and let herself in. 'Here is the mystery,' I said to myself; and I hurried on and examined the house. It seemed a sort of place for letting lodgings. On the doorstep lay her handkerchief, which she had dropped. I picked it up and put it in my pocket. Then I began to consider what I should do. I came to the conclusion that I had no right to spy on her, and I drove to the club. At six I called to see her. She was lying on a sofa, in a tea-gown of silver tissue looped up by some strange moonstones that she always wore. She was looking quite lovely. 'I am so glad to see you,' she said; 'I have not been out all day.' I stared at her in amazement, and pulling the handkerchief out of my pocket, handed it to her. 'You dropped this in Cumnor Street this afternoon, Lady Alroy,' I said very calmly. She looked at me in terror, but made no attempt to take the handkerchief. 'What were you doing there?' I asked. 'What right have you to question me?' she answered. 'The right of a man who loves you,' I replied; 'I came here to ask you to be my wife.' She hid her face in her hands, and burst into floods of tears. 'You must tell me,' I continued. She stood up, and, looking me straight in the face, said, 'Lord Murchison, there is nothing to tell you.' . . . 'You went to meet someone,' I cried; 'this is your mystery.' She grew dreadfully white, and said, 'I went to meet no one.' . . . 'Can't you tell the truth?' I exclaimed. 'I have told it,' she replied. I was mad, frantic; I don't know what I said, but I said terrible things to her. Finally I rushed out of the house. She wrote me a letter the next day; I sent it back unopened, and started for Norway with Alan Colville. After a month I came back, and the first thing I saw in the *Morning Post* was the death of Lady Alroy. She had caught a chill at the Opera, and had died in five days of congestion of the lungs. I shut myself up and saw no one. I had loved her so much, I had loved her so madly. Good God! how I had loved that woman!"

"You went to the street, to the house in it?" I said.

"Yes," he answered.

"One day I went to Cumnor Street. I could not help it; I was tortured with doubt. I knocked at the door, and a respectable-looking woman opened it to me. I asked her if she had any rooms to let. 'Well, sir,' she replied, 'the drawing-rooms are supposed to be let; but I have not seen the lady for three months, and as rent is owing on them, you can have them.' . . . 'Is this the lady?' I said, showing the photograph. 'That's her, sure enough,' she exclaimed; 'and when is she coming back, sir?' . . . 'The lady is dead,' I replied. 'Oh, sir, I hope not!' said the woman; 'she was my best lodger. She paid me three guineas a week merely to sit in my drawing-room now and then.' . . . 'She met someone here?' I said; but the woman assured me that it was not so, that she always came alone, and saw no one. 'What on earth did she do here?' I cried. 'She simply sat in the drawing-room, sir, reading books, and sometimes had tea,' the woman answered. I did not know what to say, so I gave her a sovereign and went away. Now, what do you think it all meant? You don't believe the woman was telling the truth?"

"I do."

"Then why did Lady Alroy go there?"

"My dear Gerald," I answered, "Lady Alroy was simply a woman with a mania for mystery. She took these rooms for the pleasure of going there with her veil down, and imagining she was a heroine. She had a passion for secrecy, but she herself was merely a Sphinx without a secret."

"Do you really think so?"

"I am sure of it," I replied.

He took out the morocco case, opened it, and looked at the photograph. "I wonder?" he said at last.

The Splendid Lie

by S. B. H. Hurst

A quiet night in a valley of the Cotswold Hills in England, in December, 1917. A night like a Christmas card. Stars, snow on the ground and an old brick house that had seen a hundred thousand nights.

In the library of the house two elderly men sat at a desk. One was a famous classical scholar, professor in a university, the other, the owner of the house, Lord Daywater, a member of the War Cabinet.

"The guns in Flanders seem very far from this peaceful place," said the professor. "It's good to know that your boy will be home on leave in a few days!"

Lord Daywater smiled. Then he said, somewhat dryly, "Yes! And that reminds me! Two old fools—you and I—had better attend to a small matter of signing our names to a certain document! My boy insists upon it, and you can't blame him. Shall we do it now?"

The professor smiled.

"We have been a couple of fools," he answered. "To be brutally frank, we have been a couple of liars. We meant well, of course, but, all the same—liars! It did not matter so much about me. My folly did not seem so far out of place. I am only a university professor. But you! Only your unusual ability saved you from being asked to resign from the government. The opposition papers even said you ought to. I remember certain remarks about 'a ghost-hunter is hardly a man to expect sensible work from, especially in time of war!' . . . Yes, get out that document, and let's sign it!"

Lord Daywater opened a drawer and took out a typewritten document.

"It's only fair to the boy," he said. "You can't blame him for wishing to have proof of his father's sanity. He will have children some day. So he begged us to sign this. This admission that we lied to bring comfort to broken hearts! It will not be published until after we are dead. But, Dick, we did mean well. Couple of liars, but we have given comfort to thousands. Because all men crave knowledge of life beyond the grave—if there is any. You and I do not believe there is. It's just a harmless superstition. Yet all the world thinks we are ardent spiritualists, and thousands of poor women, wives, mothers and sweethearts have taken comfort because we have appeared in public and said that we *know* men live after death, *because we have proof of spirit communication!* Don't blame my level-headed boy for asking us to sign this admission. After our deaths he will publish it, in the interest of truth, in an effort to curb the superstition we have publicly endorsed. We were fools, and liars, too, but we have brought happiness to thousands! And I don't regret having lied. If I have helped to dry a tear I am rewarded!"

The professor nodded.

"Your boy was always such a logical little chap. Playful always, but sternly matter of fact under the playfulness—even when quite a little chap and I used to carry him around on my back. Do you remember how he loved to climb up to the high window there—and knock on the pane and grin at us when we were in here playing chess? That window over there. . . . Great Scott!"

Tapping on the pane and smiling at the two old men was a young man in a torn and muddy uniform.

"He startled me," shouted the professor.

"He always loved to startle us!" the father shouted joyfully.

They rushed to the library door, into the hall, to the front door of the house. Lord Daywater flung it open, shouting.

"He must have got earlier leave than he expected. And he wanted to surprize us as he did when he was little—tapping on the window! Bet you a quid he is hiding from us, in his old way!"

He shouted into the night.

"Bob! Bob! Come in, you young rascal!"

The light wind of a winter night murmured over the snow.

"Come on!" shouted Daywater joyfully to the professor. "We'll catch him and roll him in the snow as we used to do! The young tease. You run around the house that way, and I will run this—just as we used to do! Playful young rascal, but we two old men will catch him and roll him in the snow!"

The professor ran one way, Daywater panted the other. They met at the back of the house.

"Did you see him?" shouted the father.

"No!" puffed the classical scholar. "He dodged us, as he always did! Bet he's sitting in the library laughing at us. Come on back, Day!"

The two old men plowed through the snow, back to the front door. They heard the telephone in the library ringing violently.

"Damn that phone!" panted Daywater as they rushed in. "But where's the boy?"

"Hiding some place," laughed the professor. "Answer that phone, old man."

Lord Daywater lifted the receiver.

"Yes!" he said. "Oh, a telegram for me. Yes, read it!"

He turned to the professor.

"A wire for me down at the village. I told the operator to read it to me. While he is doing it—it may be important, you know—go and find that boy of mine, will you? Tell him he'll get spanked for playing tricks on two staid and distinguished gentlemen!"

The operator in the village began to read the message. Lord Daywater listened.

"We regret to report that your son, Captain the Honorable Robert Daywater, was killed in action three days ago. We would have advised you earlier, but the heavy bombardment made communication difficult. The war council extends its sympathy."

A Sprig
of Rosemary

by H. Warner Munn

When I was a boy in the little village of Pequoig, which is hidden away in a fold of northwestern Massachusetts' hilly country, I remember distinctly an old man with a long white beard seen often on the streets and side lanes, always alone.

Stump, stump, stump, would go his peg-leg on the plank sidewalks as he strode along, with occasionally a sharp rattle of his cane along the pickets of the bordering fences.

We boys would cry to each other, "Watch out, here comes old Uncle Moses!" as he came in sight; then it was "Good day to you, Mr. Crockett!" to his face.

"Humph!" was his invariable reply, while his beard twitched as though about to throw off sparks and the gnarled hand clenched on his stout stick. Crack! Down it would come on the boards and off he would march, as though mightily insulted by our greeting. Stump, stump, stump, down the street; the hollow sound from the boarding coming back long after he was out of sight.

There was a tale in the village, that old Uncle Moses had not always been so morose, but his leg and his temper left him together, shot away by a cannon ball during the War of 1812.

He came home, hurt body and soul, eager for sympathy, limping straight to the door of the girl who had promised to be his bride when the war was over. For would he not be covered with glory and resplendent with glittering buttons and braid?

She took one long horrified look at him, standing there on her stoop, haggard, worn and crippled, leaning on his crutches, and she threw up her hands in dismay.

"Oh, Moses!" she cried, "I'd rather see you dead than coming home this way!" and slammed the door in his face.

Hurt and bewildered, his heart became like ice. From that day on, he had a kind word for no one; scowling, friendless, solitary, he stumped the streets of Pequoig and grew old alone.

The avuncular appellation came not from any kin of his, for he had no relatives. People called him Uncle because of his pawnbroker habits, and the name stuck. He loaned money at exorbitant interest and only upon excellent security. No tale of hard times could induce him to part with a penny due him, and many a curse was heaped upon his head from some poor soul thrust out into the wide world, sans house, property or hope.

Little by little, his fingers poked into every pie in Pequoig. Hardly an individual but was somehow in his debt, and one in debt to Uncle Moses rarely threw off his bonds.

The Civil War came and found many that took advantage of his pocketbook. Was the man with a family drafted? To old Uncle Moses then, for the hundred dollars to pay some single man to take his place.

Long after the war was over, some found their paid interest had totalled many times the principal, but the original sum loaned had not been abated a penny and they still owed old Uncle Moses one hundred dollars.

Mortgages, civic funds, rents, all came eventually to his eager clutching hands and there was a specter behind every man's bed as he tossed sleepless at night; for there was no pity in old Uncle Moses' stony heart for any living being.

By some he was looked upon with disgust and repulsion, by others with scorn, but underneath there was fear and hatred. And so time wore on.

As he grew older, the familiar stumping was heard less frequently, but the village dogs avoided him still, for there was power in his arm and a bite in his stick even in these late days when I came to know him.

At that time the pleasant custom of decorating graves on Memorial Day had recently come into fashion and was received with great enthusiasm and interest in Pequoig.

How well I remember seeing old Uncle Moses, standing with his weight on his peg-leg, looking on at the exercises in Highland Cemetery, mentally reckoning up the cost in good hard cash of all the flowers and wreaths laid out for the rains to destroy!

"Humph!" he grunted loudly. "Pagan superstition! Criminal waste of money!" and stumped away home.

This spread through the village on indignant tongues, and feeling ran high, so that there was talk of hooded men and tar and feathers. Nothing probably would have come of it in the end, for the fear of his power was too great, but there was no time given to decide the question.

* * *

The very next morning, a debtor calling to pay money due, found old Uncle Moses dead in his chair, with his jaw dropped down and with his stick clutched firmly in his hand.

All over town there was silent rejoicing and if ever there was talk of a judgment sent straight from heaven, it was then, with Moses Crockett as a horrible example.

He had made no will, so even before his burial, a special town meeting was called to settle the question of his money. Almost unanimously it was voted to cancel all debts owing to his estate, bring back and settle again all townspeople who had been evicted through him, and use the remainder of his wealth in civic improvements.

It might be thought that this would have caused old Uncle Moses to turn over in his coffin, but calm and peaceful he lay, and was lowered into the grave. The ground leveled, a simple headstone placed and the sexton went away and left him alone as he would have chosen to be.

And while the town was glad, in a furtive shamefaced way, to see the last of him, a family living near the river were made happy for another reason.

Almost at the very instant that the spades patted down the last heap of loose earth in the Crockett lot, a girl baby was born to the Keltons.

She did not cry at first, like most babies, quickly afterward to fall asleep, but the beginning of her life was one of smiles.

"What shall we call her, Patience?" said Abner, stroking his wife's hair with a horny, work-gnarled hand.

"We will call her Rosemary, dear," she answered weakly. "Rosemary. Rosemary Kelton. Isn't it lovely, Abner? She likes it, see how she smiles! Rosemary—that's for remembrance."

Then mother and daughter fell fast asleep and the great day was over.

The Keltons were one of the expatriated families brought back to better times by the death of old Uncle Moses. Soon they left the little shack by the river and returned into the village again to their old home.

One day Abner, his wife, and Rosemary, still in arms, went through the cemetery. They paused beside the grave of Moses Crockett for a moment. There were none of the usual eulogies of the dead upon his stone, merely a record of the dates of birth and death and his name; that was all.

"Poor old man!" said Mrs. Kelton. "I'm sorry for him. Nobody ever had a good word for him."

"Why should they?" flared up Abner. "He never did anything decent for anybody while he lived. In fact, the only good thing he ever did was die and get out of the way. Why, in a few more years, nobody in Pequoig would have been able to breathe unless they asked old Crockett's permission! Why, what's the matter with the child?"

For little Rosemary, whether frightened by her father's violent and angry tone, or for another reason, had commenced to cry bitterly and would not be comforted. Nor did she ever after that show such a liking for her father as had been her wont.

Another year crept by. Little Rosemary became "free, goin' on four," as she would proudly announce to all who begged to be informed.

Again on Memorial Day, the family went to Highland Cemetery to lay tributes upon ancestral resting-places.

Here in Pequoig, it has always been a custom that a thing worth doing at all is worth doing well, and the graves were loaded with flowers. This made it all the more noticeable, when they passed, as they were obliged to do, old Moses Crockett's grave.

It was bare and untended. The grass grew upon it uncut and in stiff clumps. The headstone had tipped drunkenly askew. The whole effect was that of desolation and neglect.

Rosemary looked at this depressing sight and hung back on her mother's hand.

"Mama! Why hasn't he got some flowers, too? Everybody else has got lots. Couldn't they give him a few?"

Mrs. Kelton looked at the grave and at her earnest-faced little girl. It did seem petty and spiteful to neglect this hard, unloved man, now that he was dead and gone.

"Give him this if you like, little daughter," she smiled, and broke off a little sweet-smelling sprig of blue flowers from the bouquet she carried. "It's rosemary, the pretty little shrub that we named you after. Put it there, dear. Now come, we will be late for the exercises."

"Why didn't he have any flowers, Mama?"

"Nobody loved him, darling. He didn't have any little girl like you to think about him and bring him flowers. He was all alone, you see."

"Poor old man! I'll be his little girl, Mama. I'll love him too and bring him flowers. Can't I be your little girl and his too, Mama?"

Tears sprang to her mother's eyes. She knelt and hugged her baby.

"Mother's thoughtful little daughter! Of course you can. We will come here together, whenever you wish."

And there the matter ended for a while.

On Sundays Mrs. Kelton and Rosemary came to be regular visitors to the grave. It took on a different aspect.

448

The headstone was straightened, the grass neatly clipped, with seed sown to fill in the bare spots. Flowers were brought, fresh every week, whatever was in season at the time. A little bush had sprung up of itself upon the grave and one day Mrs. Kelton noticed that the spot it occupied must be directly over the old man's heart. It was rosemary.

The year wore away to early fall. Goldenrod and fringed gentians appeared upon the grave and the little girl had formed the habit of going to the cemetery alone.

At first, she had wandered off and had been sought anxiously and with much concern, only to be found coming home with the calm explanation that having nothing else to do she had gone to the cemetery with flowers for old Uncle Moses.

Entering into the spirit of the play, Abner asked teasingly, "How did he like 'em? Did he thank ye for 'em, now?"

" 'Deed he did, Papa. He walked all the way here with me, too, but when he saw you he went back."

Abner's eyes almost popped from his head. He looked at his wife. She paled.

"Are you sure it was him, dear? How was he dressed?"

"Course 'twas him. He wore the same clothes he always wears. A black suit, big wide floppy hat, and his shoes are square at the toe.

"Poor man," she interrupted herself. "I mean 'shoe,' of course, because he's only got one foot. But he gets along real good with his peg-leg and his cane with the silver on the handle."

Over the child's head, the parents exchanged an awed look. She had described his garb to the life, and there was not a picture of Moses Crockett in the entire village of Pequoig!

"You have seen him before, then?" queried Abner.

"Course. Lots of times. We talk together every time I go up there."

"What about?"

"Oh, things," she replied, evasively. "He talks like he's glad to have me for a little girl."

Home again, the parents held a long colloquy, and arrived at the opinion that for the sake of her future sanity she must be kept away from the grave.

So, for a month, Highland Cemetery went unvisited by any Kelton, and grass grew up in clumps upon the grave and turned brown and sere in the chill nights of autumn.

Rosemary wept, but parental orders were stern. Then one day she was missing again and was found this time in the cemetery itself, radiant and happy. She was sitting by the headstone, talking rapidly, and appeared to be enjoying herself so much that Mrs. Kelton had not the heart to drag her away, but withdrew unobserved.

She came home in wild excitement. Old Uncle Moses, it appeared, had hit a big dog with his cane, when it jumped out at her as she was passing by Asa Higgins' house.

Abner Kelton put on his hat and coat and went out without saying a word. In front of the Higgins house lay a dog. He did not remember ever having seen it about the village. Its back had been broken by a heavy blow and it was dead.

He went to Highland Cemetery in the gathering dark. Standing before the grave he took off his hat.

"I'm much obliged, Mr. Crockett," he said, in a steady voice. "We think the world of that little girl."

Off in the depths of the wooded cemetery a whippoorwill sounded its plaintive, half-human cry. It came like a distant, sardonic laugh.

Abner started and put on his hat. "You poor, dumb fool!" he said to himself and strode home.

There is little more to tell.

Scarlet fever came to Pequoig before the first snow fell, and among the early victims was Rosemary Kelton. Parched and hot, she threw herself about upon her little bed in the agonies of delirium and nothing the anguished parents could do would bring her ease.

"I want Uncle Moses. Why don't Uncle Moses come to me?" she kept continually calling, and in desperation Abner Kelton went to Highland Cemetery with grief in his heart.

He knelt beside the grave.

"God," he said, very simply, "I ain't much on praying, but if you can let Moses Crockett come home with me for a spell, I'll be much obliged."

He paused; he felt there should be something more, but nothing would come to his mind. There was no sound to be heard but the wind dolefully whining through the leafless branches of the weeping willows, and soughing in the pines.

"Amen," he said, and stood up.

He walked out of the cemetery on the gravel path. He stopped and looked back; there was nothing to be seen, but he thought that he heard an irregular step on the gravel behind him.

He went on, down into the village. Far behind came a hollow stump, stump, stump, on the board walk, and faint but clear, a long rattle such as might be made by a stick dragged along the white-painted pickets of a fence.

Abner Kelton hurried home.

Stump, stump, stump, on the other side of the street.

Abner Kelton raised the latch of his gate and went into his house.

Lying on her bed, Rosemary smiled at him. "You sent him, didn't you, Papa? He loves you too now, Papa, because you came for him. He said he came before, but your hearts were against him and he couldn't get in. How good his cool hands feel on my forehead!"

She fell off into easy slumber, and that night the fever broke.

The parents spoke little of what had happened, but lying awake, they heard in the nights of sickness that followed, little noises that sounded like the slight tapping of a wooden leg set softly as might be in the taking of steps. And there was talking from below stairs. Sometimes they could swear they heard another voice besides that of their daughter, but so often as they went down to see, the other voice stopped and they found Rosemary muttering in her sleep.

So they gave up and left her with her unseen companion, for that she was in loving care could not be doubted.

But, although the fever was gone, Rosemary did not get well. Day by day she became more thin and pale, daily more feeble, until in spite of all their efforts she whispered one evening with a tired little sigh: "I love my Mama and Papa, and my Uncle Moses," and closed her eyes for ever, with the setting of the sun.

That was a night of sleepless sorrow. The grief-stricken mother sat by the bedside of her first-born and mourned, dry-eyed and heartbroken.

Along toward morning, outraged nature had her way, and she dropped off to sleep in her rocker. People afterward thought she dreamed what followed, but she always swore that a sudden noise brought her eyes open.

Rosemary was sitting up in the bed, holding out her arms to some one behind her mother. She was unable to turn, but she heard a deep, hearty, happy laugh, no more like the surly tones that she remembered from Moses Crockett than anything in the world.

"I knew you would come back for me, Uncle Moses," crowed the little girl, with a lovely smile. "I waited for you. I just couldn't go by myself. It was so far and so dark."

The person behind Mrs. Kelton laughed again.

"Come," said the hearty, good-humored tones. "Come, darling, we will go together. Did you think I would let the only one in the whole wide world who ever loved old Uncle Moses go alone?"

Then she saw that there were two Rosemarys, for one jumped out of bed and left the other lying there. The first Rosemary ran past the rocker.

"Here," said the happy voice, "put on your shoes. We are going to have a long journey, you know. So! There we are. Now, put this on the bed, then when your mother wakes up, she will know that everything is all right, and you will be waiting for her to follow us by and by."

The first Rosemary ran back to the bed and tucked something into the clasped fingers of the second.

"Now then, here we go. Come on. Up! You shall have a ride."

The door opened and closed again. At once Mrs. Kelton sprang up. She darted to the bed and took a tiny twig from between the fingers of the little girl who lay smiling there.

At last, tears blinded her eyes, but she heard a sound in the room and dashed them away. Abner stood at the foot of the stairs, looking sadly at her. She walked toward him.

"Oh, Abner," she began and paused, listening.

Stump, stump, stump, far away on the board sidewalk, and faint but clear, the sharp rattle of a stick on a picket fence.

She held up the sweet-smelling sprig before his face.

"Rosemary," she said unsteadily. "Rosemary. That's for remembrance."

The Stone Coffin

by "B"

I

The year was 1754, the month October. The Chapel at Magdalene had been undergoing renovation all the summer, at the hands of the ingenious Mr Collins, of Clare Hall—indeed, since the beginning of the Easter Term the College services had been held in St Giles' Church adjacent.

452

Mr Dobree the Bursar, a big bluff man, was pacing in the Court in the Autumn sunshine. Some workmen were carrying planks and poles out of the doorway of the Chapel staircase. The Bursar's companion, a little meagre figure in rusty black, peering about him through big horn spectacles, was Mr Janeway, the President of the College. Presently they went in at the Chapel door, and stood regarding the building. 'Dear now!' said Mr Janeway, staring about him, 'I hardly see where I am! A great change, no doubt! But it is a chaste design!'

It certainly was a change! but out of a Gothic building with an open roof, much as we see it now, the ingenious Mr Collins had made a place more like, one would have said, the dining-hall of a Roman consul than a Christian Church. The roof was cut off by a flat plaster ceiling, heavily ornamented. A classical arch spanned the sanctuary, and the East window was obliterated by a columned piece of statuary. The floor was elegantly paved with black and white marble.

Mr Dobree looked complacently about him. 'It is not such a change to my eyes,' he said, 'Because I have watched the work from the beginning. It seems to me a very respectable place!'

'And pray what does the Master think of it all?' said Mr Janeway.

'That I cannot tell,' said Mr Dobree rather curtly. 'Has he seen the progress of the work?' said Mr Janeway.

'The Master,' said Mr Dobree, 'Has been, to my knowledge, twice in the chapel since the work began. He ran in once without his wig, in a greasy cassock, and spoke rudely to the workmen about the noise they made—as if such work could be done in silence! He was disturbed at his accounts, he said. Once again he met Mr Collins in the chapel, when the carved piece over the table was up. He said to Mr Collins that he was given to understand that the figures were those of saints and angels, but that they appeared to him to be something much more indelicate. Then he laughed, and said he supposed it was the effect of the plaster work, at which Mr Collins was greatly mortified. But so long as he can find fault and has nothing to pay, the College may go hang for him. He has gotten a Prebend of Durham, they say, by interest, this last week, and that is all he cares for.'

'Tut, tut,' said Mr Janeway soothingly.

'Now,' said Mr Dobree, striding up the chapel, 'Come hither with me, and I will relate to you a curiosity. About six weeks ago the workmen were laying the floor, and one came to me and said they had found somewhat. It was hereabouts, by this step.' He stamped on the pavement, and then continued, 'When I came in, they had uncovered and broken in pieces the lid of a stone coffin just here, and I bade them take the bits out. I tell you it was a strange sight beneath! There lay a man, his head in a niche made for it in the stone, robed from head to foot in an embroidered robe, of the colour of a butterfly—one of the orange-brown ones that you may see sitting on summer flowers—with figures and patterns inwrought. The flesh was all perished, and the skull, with its dark eye-holes, stared very dismally out, with something like hair atop of it. I doubt he had lain there since monkish days, and it displeased me very much. I stooped down and picked at the robe, and it all came away in my hands, falling to dust, leaving but a few coloured threads. The bones had mouldered too, all but the thigh-bones, and they were brittle. 'Come,' said I, 'the less we look on this the better!' So I took a besom in my hand and swept the whole carcase, bones and dust and robe and all, to one end of the coffin; and it made but a little heap there. I prodded the skull out of its niche, and that all came to dust too. But while I brushed, I heard a tinkling, and I picked out of the mess a little cup and platter of some metal, very dark, and a big ring with a blue stone—all very Popish and disgraceful to my eyes. I have them in my chamber, and I shall send them to Mr Gray, at Pembroke Hall, who cares about such oddities. Then I had the coffin broken up, and carried to the stonemasons' yard, and dropt all the dust into the hole thus made, saw that they put soil on the place and battered it well down. A good riddance, I think!'

'Dear now!' said Mr Janeway, musing, 'That is a strange story—a very strange story! But, Mr Dobree, if you will pardon me, I do not like your action very well. It seems to me that the man, whoever he was, was piously bestowed here, and had a right to his rest—so it appears to me, but I speak under correction!'

'Pish!' said Mr Dobree, 'Here's a pother about a parcel of old Popish bones! I am one who hold by the glorious Reformation, and I would cleanse the temple of all such recusants, if I had my choice. Why, the thought of that ugly figure, under my feet, would have made me very squeamish at my prayers. I wonder at you, Mr Janeway, indeed I do!'

'Well, well,' said Mr Janeway, 'There are many opinions; but I cannot like the business. May be he was a holy man, even if he died in sad error. I doubt if he could have known better.'

'A sincere study of the Word would have shown him his abominations,' said Mr Dobree. 'I am a Protestant, born and bred, and I have no patience with old mummeries.'

Mr Janeway sighed and said no more, and presently they went away.

It might have been a week later that Mr Dobree awoke suddenly at night in his room, which was in the right-hand corner of the first Court, as you come in by the gate, on the ground floor. He awoke half in terror and half in anger, troubled by a dream, and thought that he heard someone moving very softly about his room; which was lighted only by a little high window in a deep recess that looked out towards the river, on to what was then a little street or lane of houses, running parallel to the College. The window was bare of any curtain, and Mr Dobree thought that he saw a very faint figure cross the glimmering panes, it being bright moonlight without.

Mr Dobree was as bold as a lion. He sate up in bed and shouted out in his great voice, EH, WHAT? HOLLA-HO! WHO IS THAT? EH, WHAT DID YOU SAY? WHAT DO YOU THERE, SIRRAH?

His voice reverberated in the little bare room, and died away, leaving a shocking silence. Nothing moved or spoke. He felt for his tinderbox and made a light, and then jumping out of bed, in nightcap and nightgown, looked about everywhere, first in his bedroom, then through his two keeping-rooms, and even in his cupboards, but he saw no sign of anything living. After some time he went back to bed, but not to sleep. He was angry with himself for being afraid, and half suspected a trick; but his door was firmly latched, and no one seemed to have come in that way, while the windows into the court were safely shuttered.

In the morning, after a draught of small beer, which he used for his breakfast, and when he had made his toilet, he felt better; but for all that he wished for company, and made his way to Mr Janeway's rooms in the second Court as soon as might be. He found Mr Janeway reading in a book, with coffee beside him, and sitting down he told him his adventure rather shamefacedly. Mr Janeway nodded his head and said very little, save this, that he too, when his stomach was at all disordered, suffered from disturbing dreams. 'A little sick fancy, no doubt!' he added comfortably.

'It may be!' said Mr Dobree moodily; 'But I think there was someone with me in the room. Yet what sticks even more in my mind was a dream I had dreamed, which I cannot fully recall.'

'What was it like?' said Mr Janeway.

'What was it?' said Mr Dobree; 'That I cannot quite tell—but it was an ill dream. I was in a dull place, methought between buildings. They were buildings, I believe; and a dark sort of thing poked its head out in front of me in an ugly way. It seems to me now that it had on a parti-coloured robe, of black or white, or both—like a gown, and like a surplice. There was something drawn over the head of it; and the face was very white; now, as I think of it, I believe it had no eyes; it said something to me, which still sounds in my ears like Latin, in a very low voice; and it seemed to be angry—Yes, Sir, it was angry, was that person!'

'Dear now!' said Mr Janeway, looking over his glasses at Mr Dobree, 'That's a bad story and a confused story! Is it your way to dream like that, Mr Dobree? It seems to me a dark affair.'

'Why, Sir!' said Mr Dobree with a sudden anger, 'It appears to me that you are but very poor company this morning! I come to my old friend to be made cheer with, and you can only shake your head and look dismal. This is not friendly, Sir! You are not speaking your mind!'

'Nay, Sir,' said Mr Janeway, 'Be not so peevish! There is something that presses upon my spirits, since you spoke your dream, and I am grown very heavy. You must think no more of it, Sir. It was but a touch of vapours, such as comes to us lonely men, as we get older and more solitary.'

Mr Dobree got up, shaking his head and looking very sullen, and marched off without a word. He went about his business as usual, but he found himself day by day in a disordered mood. He ate little and spoke not at all, though he had been ever ready with his tongue. He slept brokenly; and presently as he sate alone in his room, he began to hear whispers in his ear, or he would think that he was called; and his brother Fellows began to be concerned about him, wondering why he peered so often into the corners of the room, and why he wheeled round so sharply in the street to look behind him as he walked alone.

IV

It was a very wet and dull afternoon at the end of November, and Mr Dobree had sate all day indoors. Just about dusk he remembered that he had a word to say to the stonemason who worked for the College about some tiling on the roof. He went out of his rooms and found the whole place very still, with a light rain falling. He walked out of the gate, and turned to the left at once, down the lane that ran close by the College, the stonemason's yard being at the end of it, by the water's edge.

When he got there he found the mason with a lantern in his hand looking about among some piled-up stones in the yard. Mr Dobree went to speak to him, and broke off in the middle. He felt very much displeased to see what was evidently the head-piece of the old stone coffin lying on the ground. 'How comes that there?' he said with a sudden sharpness. 'Why, Sir' said the mason 'You ordered me to take it and break it all up, and it has lain there ever since.' 'What is that which lies inside it?' said Mr Dobree in a loud voice. The mason turned his lantern on the piece. It was roughly worked, the strokes of the chisel being visible where the head had lain, and it was pierced with a hole, the use of which Mr Dobree did not like to guess. 'There is nothing here!' said the mason. 'No,' said Mr Dobree, 'There is not—I see plainly now. I was dazzled—It was but the shadow. Yet I certainly thought . . .' He broke off, turned on his heel and went away, the business being still unsettled. The mason stood, lantern in hand, watching him as he marched out of the yard. Then he shook his head, and went into the house.

A moment later Mr Dobree was hurrying up the lane. It was very dark, and the rain kept all men at home. On his right, the wall of the College towered up in the misty air, and he could see a few lighted windows, very high above. The houses on his left seemed all dark and comfortless. He went on until he was close outside his own rooms, which lay next the street.

Suddenly out of the window of his own bedroom, just above him, not a yard away, there came with a silent haste the head and shoulders of a man, wrapped up, it seemed to Mr Dobree, in a parti-coloured robe, black and white, with a hood over the face, but the face itself was visible, a dead yellow-white, like baked clay, with holes for eyes. There came a faint, thin voice upon the air, and words that sounded in Mr Dobree's agonised ears like '*Quare inquiestasti me ut suscitarer?*' But Mr Dobree heard no more. He fell all his length in the wet road, and presently turned over on his back, where they afterwards found him, still looking upwards.

A Strange Goldfield

by Guy Boothby

Of course nine out of every ten intelligent persons will refuse to believe that there could be a grain of truth in the story I am now going to tell you. The tenth may have some small faith in my veracity, but what I think of his intelligence I am going to keep to myself.

In a certain portion of a certain Australian Colony two miners, when out prospecting in what was then, as now, one of the dreariest parts of the Island Continent, chanced upon a rich find. They applied to Government for the usual reward, and in less than a month three thousand people were settled on the Field. What privations they had to go through to get there, and the miseries they had to endure when the *did* reach their journey's end, have only a remote bearing on this story, but they would make a big book.

I should explain that between Railhead and the Field was a stretch of country some three hundred miles in extent. It was badly watered, vilely grassed, and execrably timbered. What was even worse, a considerable portion of it was made up of red sand, and everybody who has been compelled to travel over that knows what it means. Yet these enthusiastic seekers after wealth pushed on, some on horseback, some in bullock waggons, but the majority travelled on foot; the graves, and the skeletons of cattle belonging to those who had preceded them punctuating the route, and telling them what they might expect as they advanced.

That the Field did not prove a success is now a matter of history, but that same history, if you read between the lines, gives one some notion of what the life must have been like while it lasted. The water supply was entirely insufficient, provisions were bad and ruinously expensive; the men themselves were, as a rule, the roughest of the rough, while the less said about the majority of the women the better. Then typhoid stepped in and stalked like the Destroying Angel through the camp. Its inhabitants went down like sheep in a drought, and for the most part rose no more. Where there had been a lust of gold there was now panic, terror—every man feared that he might be the next to be attacked, and it was only the knowledge of those terrible three hundred miles that separated them from civilisation that kept many of them on the Field. The most thickly populated part was now the cemetery. Drink was the only solace, and under its influence such scenes were enacted as I dare not describe. As they heard of fresh deaths, men shook their fists at Heaven, and cursed the day when they first saw pick or shovel. Some, bolder than the rest, cleared out just as they stood; a few eventually reached civilisation, others perished in the desert. At last the Field was declared abandoned, and the dead were left to take their last long sleep, undisturbed by the clank of windlass or the blow of pick.

It would take too long to tell all the different reasons that combined to draw me out into that 'most distressful country'. Let it suffice that our party consisted of a young Englishman named Spicer, a wily old Australian bushman named Matthews, and myself. We were better off than the unfortunate miners, inasmuch as we were travelling with camels, and our outfits were as perfect as money and experience could make them. The man who travels in any other fashion in that country is neither more nor less than a madman. For a month past we had been having a fairly rough time of it, and were then on our way south, where we had reason to believe rain had fallen, and, in consequence, grass was plentiful. It was towards evening when we came out of a gully in the ranges and had our first view of the deserted camp. We had no idea of its existence, and for this reason we pulled up our animals and stared at it in complete surprise. Then we pushed on again, wondering what on earth place we had chanced upon.

'This is all right,' said Spicer, with a chuckle. 'We're in luck. Grog shanties and stores, a bath, and perhaps girls.'

I shook my head.

'I can't make it out,' I said. 'What's it doing out here?'

Matthews was looking at it under his hand, and, as I knew that he had been out in this direction on a previous occasion, I asked his opinion.

'It beats me,' he replied; 'but if you ask me what I think I should say it's Gurunya, the Field that was deserted some four or five years back.'

'Look here,' cried Spicer, who was riding a bit on our left, 'what are all these things—graves, as I'm a living man. Here, let's get out of this. There are hundreds of them and before I know where I am old Polyphemus here will be on his nose.'

What he said was correct—the ground over which we were riding was literally bestrewn with graves, some of which had rough, tumbledown head boards, others being destitute of all adornment. We turned away and moved on over safer ground in the direction of the Field itself. Such a pitiful sight I never want to see again. The tents and huts, in numerous cases, were still standing, while the claims gaped at us on every side like new-made graves. A bullock dray, weather-worn but still in excellent condition, stood in the main street outside a grog shanty whose sign-board, strange incongruity, bore the name of 'The Killarney Hotel'. Nothing would suit Spicer but that he must dismount and go in to explore. He was not long away, and when he returned it was with a face as white as a sheet of paper.

'You never saw such a place,' he almost whispered. 'All I want to do is to get out of it. There's a skeleton on the floor in the back room with an empty rum bottle alongside it.'

He mounted, and, when his beast was on its feet once more, we went on our way. Not one of us was sorry when we had left the last claim behind us.

Half a mile or so from the Field the country begins to rise again. There is also a curious cliff away to the left, and, as it looked like being a likely place to find water, we resolved to camp there. We were within a hundred yards or so of this cliff when an exclamation from Spicer attracted my attention.

'Look!' he cried. 'What's that?'

I followed the direction in which he was pointing, and, to my surprise, saw the figure of a man running as if for his life among the rocks. I have said the figure of a man, but, as a matter of fact, had there been baboons in the Australian bush, I should have been inclined to have taken him for one.

'This is a day of surprises,' I said. 'Who can the fellow be? And what makes him act like that?'

We still continued to watch him as he proceeded on his erratic course along the base of the cliff—then he suddenly disappeared.

'Let's get on to camp,' I said, 'and then we'll go after him and endeavour to settle matters a bit.'

Having selected a place we offsaddled and prepared our camp. By this time it was nearly dark, and it was very evident that, if we wanted to discover the man we had seen, it would be wise not to postpone the search too long. We accordingly strolled off in the direction he had taken, keeping a sharp look-out for any sign of him. Our search, however, was not successful. The fellow had disappeared without leaving a trace of his whereabouts behind him, and yet we were all certain that we *had* seen him. At length we returned to our camp for supper, completely mystified. As we ate our meal we discussed the problem and vowed that, on the morrow, we would renew the search. Then the full moon rose over the cliff, and the plain immediately became wellnigh as bright as day. I had lit my pipe and was stretching myself out

460

upon my blankets when something induced me to look across at a big rock, some half-dozen paces from the fire. Peering round it, and evidently taking an absorbing interest in our doings, was the most extraordinary figure I have ever beheld. Shouting something to my companions, I sprang to my feet and dashed across at him. He saw me and fled. Old as he apparently was, he could run like a jack-rabbit, and, though I have the reputation of being fairly quick on my feet, I found that I had all my work cut out to catch him. Indeed, I am rather doubtful as to whether I should have done so at all had he not tripped and measured his length on the ground. Before he could get up I was on him.

'I've got you at last, my friend,' I said. 'Now you just come along back to the camp, and let us have a look at you.'

In reply he snarled like a dog and I believe would have bitten me had I not held him off. My word, he was a creature, more animal than man, and the reek of him was worse than that of our camels. From what I could tell he must have been about sixty years of age—was below the middle height, had white eyebrows, white hair and a white beard. He was dressed partly in rags and partly in skins, and went barefooted like a black fellow. While I was overhauling him the others came up—whereupon we escorted him back to the camp.

'What wouldn't Barnum give for him?' said Spicer. 'You're a beauty, my friend, and no mistake. What's your name?'

The fellow only grunted in reply—then, seeing the pipes in our mouths, a curious change came over him, and he muttered something that resembled 'Give me.'

'Wants a smoke,' interrupted Matthews. 'Poor beggar's been without for a long time, I reckon. Well, I've got an old pipe, so he can have a draw.'

He procured one from his pack saddle, filled it and handed it to the man, who snatched it greedily and began to puff away at it.

'How long have you been out here?' I asked, when he had squatted himself down alongside the fire.

'Don't know,' he answered, this time plainly enough.

'Can't you get back?' continued Matthews, who knew the nature of the country on the other side.

'Don't want to,' was the other's laconic reply. 'Stay here.'

I heard Spicer mutter, 'Mad—mad as a March hare.'

We then tried to get out of him where he hailed from, but he had either forgotten or did not understand. Next we inquired how he managed to live. To this he answered readily enough, 'Carnies.'

Now the carny is a lizard of the iguana type, and eaten raw would be

461

by no means an appetizing dish. Then came the question that gives me my reason for telling this story. It was Spicer who put it.

'You must have a lonely time of it out here,' said the latter. 'How do you manage for company?'

'There is the Field,' he said, 'as sociable a Field as you'd find.'

'But the Field's deserted, man,' I put in. 'And has been for years.'

The old fellow shook his head.

'As sociable a Field as ever you saw,' he repeated. 'There's Sailor Dick and 'Frisco, Dick Johnson, Cockney Jim, and half a hundred of them. They're taking it out powerful rich on the Golden South, so I heard when I was down at "The Killarney", a while back.'

It was plain to us all that the old man was, as Spicer had said, as mad as a hatter. For some minutes he rambled on about the Field, talking rationally enough, I must confess—that is to say, it would have seemed rational enough if we hadn't known the true facts of the case. At last he got on to his feet, saying, 'Well, I must be going—they'll be expecting me. It's my shift on with Cockney Jim.'

'But you don't work at night,' growled Matthews, from the other side of the fire.

'We work always,' the other replied. 'If you don't believe me, come and see for yourselves.'

'I wouldn't go back to that place for anything,' said Spicer.

But I must confess that my curiosity had been aroused, and I determined to go, if only to see what this strange creature did when he got there. Matthews decided to accompany me, and, not wishing to be left alone, Spicer at length agreed to do the same. Without looking round, the old fellow led the way across the plain towards the Field. Of all the nocturnal excursions I have made in my life, that was certainly the most uncanny. Not once did our guide turn his head, but pushed on at a pace that gave us some trouble to keep up with him. It was only when we came to the first claim that he paused.

'Listen,' he said, 'and you can hear the camp at work. Then you'll believe me.'

We *did* listen, and as I live we could distinctly hear the rattling of sluice-boxes and cradles, the groaning of windlasses—in fact, the noise you hear on a goldfield at the busiest hour of the day. We moved a little closer, and, believe me or not, I swear to you I could see, or thought I could see, the shadowy forms of men moving about in that ghostly moonlight. Meanwhile the wind sighed across the plain, flapping what remained of the old tents and giving an additional touch of horror to the general desolation. I could hear Spicer's teeth chattering behind me, and, for my own part, I felt as if my blood were turning to ice.

'That's the claim, the Golden South, away to the right there,' said the old man, 'and if you will come along with me, I'll introduce you to my mates.'

But this was an honour we declined, and without hesitation. I wouldn't have gone any further among those tents for the wealth of all the Indies.

'I've had enough of this,' said Spicer, and I can tell you I hardly recognised his voice. 'Let's get back to camp.'

By this time our guide had left us, and was making his way in the direction he had indicated. We could plainly hear him addressing imaginary people as he marched along. As for ourselves, we turned about and hurried back to our camp as fast as we could go.

Once there, the grog bottle was produced, and never did three men stand more in need of stimulants. Then we set to work to find some explanation of what we had seen, or had fancied we saw. But it was impossible. The wind might have rattled the old windlasses, but it could not be held accountable for those shadowy grey forms that had moved about among the claims.

'I give it up,' said Spicer, at last. 'I know that I never want to see it again. What's more, I vote that we clear out of here to-morrow morning.'

We all agreed, and then retired to our blankets, but for my part I do not mind confessing I scarcely slept a wink all night. The thought that that hideous old man might be hanging about the camp would alone be sufficient for that.

Next morning, as soon as it was light, we breakfasted, but, before we broke camp, Matthews and I set off along the cliff in an attempt to discover our acquaintance of the previous evening. Though, however, we searched high and low for upwards of an hour, no success rewarded us. By mutual consent we resolved not to look for him on the Field. When we returned to Spicer we placed such tobacco and stores as we could spare under the shadow of the big rock, where the Mystery would be likely to see them, then mounted our camels and resumed our journey, heartily glad to be on our way once more.

Gurunya Goldfield is a place I never desire to visit again. I don't like its population.

The Stranger

by Ambrose Bierce

A man stepped out of the darkness into the little illuminated circle about our failing campfire and seated himself upon a rock.

"You are not the first to explore this region," he said, gravely.

Nobody controverted his statement; he was himself proof of its truth, for he was not of our party and must have been somewhere near when we camped. Moreover, he must have companions not far away; it was not a place where one would be living or traveling alone. For more than a week we had seen, besides ourselves and our animals, only such living things as rattlesnakes and horned toads. In an Arizona desert one does not long coexist with only such creatures as these: one must have pack animals, supplies, arms—"an outfit." And all these imply comrades. It was perhaps a doubt as to what manner of men this unceremonious stranger's comrades might be, together with something in his words interpretable as a challenge, that caused every man of our half-dozen "gentlemen adventurers" to rise to a sitting posture and lay his hand upon a weapon—an act signifying, in that time and place, a policy of expectation. The stranger gave the matter no attention and began again to speak in the same deliberate, uninflected monotone in which he had delivered his first sentence:

"Thirty years ago Ramon Gallegos, William Shaw, George W. Kent and Berry Davis, all of Tucson, crossed the Santa Catalina mountains and traveled due west, as nearly as the configuration of the country permitted. We were prospecting and it was our intention, if we found nothing, to push through to the Gila river at some point near Big Bend, where we understood there was a settlement. We had a good outfit but no guide—just Ramon Gallegos, William Shaw, George W. Kent and Berry Davis.

The man repeated the names slowly and distinctly, as if to fix them in the memories of his audience, every member of which was now attentively observing him, but with a slackened apprehension regarding his possible companions somewhere in the darkness that seemed to enclose us like a black wall; in the manner of this volunteer historian was no suggestion of an unfriendly purpose. His act was rather that of a harmless lunatic than an enemy. We were not so new to the country as not to know that the solitary life of many a plainsman had a tendency to develop eccentricities of conduct and character not always easily distinguishable from mental aberration. A man is like a tree: in a forest of his fellows he will grow as straight as his generic and individual nature permits; alone in the open, he yields to the deforming stresses and tortions that environ him. Some such thoughts were in my mind as I watched the man from the shadow of my hat, pulled low to shut out the firelight. A witless fellow, no doubt, but what could he be doing there in the heart of a desert?

Having undertaken to tell this story, I wish that I could describe the man's appearance; that would be a natural thing to do. Unfortunately, and somewhat strangely, I find myself unable to do so with any degree of confidence, for afterward no two of us agreed as to what he wore and how he looked; and when I try to set down my own impressions they elude me. Anyone can tell some kind of story; narration is one of the elemental powers of the race. But the talent for description is a gift.

Nobody having broken silence the visitor went on to say:

"This country was not then what it is now. There was not a ranch between the Gila and the Gulf. There was a little game here and there in the mountains, and near the infrequent water-holes grass enough to keep our animals from starvation. If we should be so fortunate as to encounter no Indians we might get through. But within a week the purpose of the expedition had altered from discovery of wealth to preservation of life. We had gone too far to go back, for what was ahead could be no worse than what was behind; so we pushed on, riding by night to avoid Indians and the intolerable heat, and concealing ourselves by day as best we could. Sometimes, having exhausted our supply of wild meat and emptied our casks, we were days without food or drink; then a water-hole or a shallow pool in the bottom of an arroyo so restored our strength and sanity that we were able to shoot some of the wild animals that sought it also. Sometimes it was a bear, sometimes an antelope, a coyote, a cougar—that was as God pleased; all were food.

"One morning as we skirted a mountain range, seeking a practicable pass, we were attacked by a band of Apaches who had followed our trail up a gulch—it is not far from here. Knowing that they outnumbered us ten to one, they took none of their usual cowardly precautions, but dashed upon us at a gallop, firing and yelling. Fighting was out of the question: we urged our feeble animals up the gulch as far as there was footing for a hoof, then threw ourselves out of our saddles and took to the chaparral on one of the slopes, abandoning our entire outfit to the enemy. But we retained our rifles, every man—Ramon Gallegos, William Shaw, George W. Kent and Berry Davis."

"Same old crowd," said the humorist of our party. He was an Eastern man, unfamiliar with the decent observances of social intercourse. A gesture of disapproval from our leader silenced him and the stranger proceeded with his tale:

"The savages dismounted also, and some of them ran up the gulch beyond the point at which we had left it, cutting off further retreat in that direction and forcing us on up the side. Unfortunately the chaparral extended only a short distance up the slope, and as we came into the open ground above we took the fire of a dozen rifles; but Apaches shoot badly when in a hurry, and God so willed it that none of us fell. Twenty yards up the slope, beyond the edge of the brush, were vertical cliffs, in which, directly in front of us, was a narrow opening. Into that we ran, finding ourselves in a cavern about as large as an ordinary room in a house. Here for a time we were safe: a single man with a repeating rifle could defend the entrance against all the Apaches in the land. But against hunger and thirst we had no defense. Courage we still had, but hope was a memory.

"Not one of those Indians did we afterward see, but by the smoke and glare of their fires in the gulch we knew that by day and by night they watched with ready rifles in the edge of the bush—knew that if we made a sortie not a man of us would live to take three steps into the open. For three days, watching in turn, we held out before our suffering became insupportable. Then—it was the morning of the fourth day—Ramon Gallegos said:

" 'Senores, I know not well of the good God and what please him. I have live without religion, and I am not acquaint with that of you. Pardon, senores, if I shock you, but for me the time is come to beat the game of the Apache.'

"He knelt upon the rock floor of the cave and pressed his pistol against his temple. 'Madre de Dios,' he said, 'comes now the soul of Ramon Gallegos.'

"And so he left us—William Shaw, George W. Kent and Berry Davis.

"I was the leader: it was for me to speak.

" 'He was a brave man,' I said—'he knew when to die, and how. It is foolish to go mad from thirst and fall by Apache bullets, or be skinned alive—it is in bad taste. Let us join Ramon Gallegos.'

" 'That is right,' said William Shaw.

" 'That is right,' said George W. Kent.

"I straightened the limbs of Ramon Gallegos and put a handkerchief over his face. Then William Shaw said: 'I should like to look like that—a little while.'

"And George W. Kent said that he felt that way, too.

" 'It shall be so,' I said: 'the red devils will wait a week. William Shaw and George W. Kent, draw and kneel.'

"They did so and I stood before them.

" 'Almighty God, our Father,' said I.

" 'Almighty God, our Father,' said William Shaw.

" 'Almighty God, our Father,' said George W. Kent.

" 'Forgive us our sins,' said I.

" 'Forgive us our sins,' said they.

" 'And receive our souls.'

" 'And receive our souls.'

" 'Amen!'

" 'Amen!'

"I laid them beside Ramon Gallegos and covered their faces."

There was a quick commotion on the opposite side of the campfire: one of our party had sprung to his feet, pistol in hand.

"And you!" he shouted—"*you* dared to escape?—you dare to be alive? You cowardly hound, I'll send you to join them if I hang for it!"

But with the leap of a panther the captain was upon him, grasping his wrist. "Hold it in, Sam Yountsey, hold it in!"

We were now all upon our feet—except the stranger, who sat motionless and apparently inattentive. Some one seized Yountsey's other arm.

"Captain," I said, "there is something wrong here. This fellow is either a lunatic or merely a liar—just a plain, everyday liar whom Yountsey has no call to kill. If this man was of that party it had five members, one of whom—probably himself—he has not named."

"Yes," said the captain, releasing the insurgent, who sat down, "there is something—unusual. Years ago four dead bodies of white men, scalped and shamefully mutilated, were found about the mouth of that cave. They are buried there; I have seen the graves—we shall all see them to-morrow."

The stranger rose, standing tall in the light of the expiring fire, which in our breathless attention to his story we had neglected to keep going.

"There were four," he said—"Ramon Gallegos, William Shaw, George W. Kent and Berry Davis."

With this reiterated roll-call of the dead he walked into the darkness and we saw him no more.

At that moment one of our party, who had been on guard, strode in among us, rifle in hand and somewhat excited.

"Captain," he said, "for the last half-hour three men have been standing out there on the mesa." He pointed in the direction taken by the stranger. "I could see them distinctly, for the moon is up, but as they had no guns and I had them covered with mine I thought it was their move. They have made none, but, damn it! they have got on to my nerves."

"Go back to your post, and stay till you see them again," said the captain. "The rest of you lie down again, or I'll kick you all into the fire."

The sentinel obediently withdrew, swearing, and did not return. As we were arranging our blankets the fiery Yountsey said: "I beg your pardon, Captain, but who the devil do you take them to be?"

"Ramon Gallegos, William Shaw and George W. Kent."

"But how about Berry Davis? I ought to have shot him."

"Quite needless; you couldn't have made him any deader. Go to sleep."

Summerland

by Avram Davidson

Mary King said—and I'm sure it was true—that she couldn't remember a thing about the séance at Mrs. Porteous's. Of course no one tried to refresh her memory. Mary is a large woman, with a handsome, ruddy face, and the sound of that heavy body hitting the floor and the sight of her face at that moment—it was gray and loose-mouthed and flaccid—so unnerved me that I am ashamed to say I just sat there, numb. Others scurried around and cried for water or thrust cushions under her head or waved vials of ammoniated lavender in front of her, but I just sat frozen, looking at her, looking at Mrs. Porteous lolling back in the armchair, Charley King's voice still ringing in my ears, and my heart thudding with shock.

I would not have thought, nor would anyone else, at first impression, that the Kings were the séance type. My natural tendency is to associate that sort of thing with wheat germ and vegeburgers and complete syndromes of psychosomatic illnesses, but Charley and his wife were beef-eaters all the way and they shone with health and cheer and never reported a sniffle. Be exceedingly wary of categories, I told myself; despise no man's madness. Their hearty goodwill, if it palled upon me, was certainly better for my mother than another neighbor's whining or gossip would have been. The Kings, who were her best friends, devoted to her about 500 percent of the time I myself was willing to give. For years I had lived away from home, our interests and activities were too different, there seemed little either of us could do when long silences fell upon us as we sat alone. It was much better to join the Kings.

"Funny thing happened down at the office today—" Charley often began like that. Ordinarily this opening would have shaken me into thoughts of a quick escape. Somehow, though, as Charley told it, his fingers rippling the thick, iron-gray hair, his ruddy face quivering not to release a smile or laugh before the point of the story was revealed— somehow, it *did* seem funny when Charley told it. To me, the Kings were old people, but they were younger than my mother, and I am sure they helped keep her from growing old too fast. It was worth it to me to eat vast helpings of butter-pecan ice cream when the Real Me hungered and slavered for a glass of beer with pretzel sticks on the side.

If tarot cards, Rosicrucian literature, séances, and milder non-contortionistic exercises made an incongruous note in the middle-class, middle-aged atmosphere the Kings trailed with them like "rays of lambent dullness"—why, it was harmless. It was better to lap up pyramidology than lunatic-fringe politics. Rather let Mother join hands on the ouija board than start cruising the Great Circle of quack doctors to find a cure for imaginary backaches. So I ate baked alaska and discussed the I Am and astral projection, and said "Be still, my soul" to inner yearnings for highballs and carnal conversation. After all, it was only once a week. And I never saw any signs that my mother took any of it more seriously than the parchesi game which followed the pistachio or peanut-crunch.

I am an architect. Charley was In The Real Estate Game. A good chance, you might think, for one hand to wash the other, but it hardly ever happened that our commercial paths crossed. Lanais, kidney-shaped swimming pools, picture windows, copper-hooded fireplaces, hi-fi sets in the walls—that was my sort of thing. "Income property"—

that was Charley's. And a nice income it was, too. Much better than mine.

How does that go?—Evil communications corrupt good manners? —Charley might have said something of that sort if I'd ever told him what Ed Hokinson told me. Hoke is on the planning commission, so what with this and that, we see each other fairly often. Coincidence's arm didn't stretch too long before Charley King's name came up between us. Idly talking, I repeated to Hoke a typical Charleyism. Charley had been having tenant trouble.

"Of course there are always what you might call the Inescapable Workings of Fate, which all of us are subject to, just as we are to, oh, say, the law of Supply and Demand," said Charley, getting outside some dessert. "But by and large whatever troubles people of that sort" —meaning the tenants—"think they have, it's due to their own improvidence, for they won't save, and each week or month the rent comes as a fresh surprise. And then you have certain politicians stirring them up and making them think they're badly off when really they're just the victims of Maya, or Illusion." Little flecks of whipped cream were on his ruddy jowels. Mary nodded solemnly, two hundred pounds of well-fed, well-dressed, well-housed approbation.

"Maya," said Hoke. "That what he calls it? Like to come with me and see for yourself? *I* know Charley King," Hoke said. In the end I did go. Interesting, in its own way, what I saw, but not my kind of thing at all. And the next day was the day Charley died. He was interred with much ceremony and expense in a fabulous City of the Dead, which has been too well described by British novelists for me to try. Big, jolly, handsome, life-loving Mr. Charley King. In a way, I missed him. And after that, of course, Mary and my mother were together even more. After that there was even less of the Akashic Documents or Anthroposophism or Vedanta, and more and more of séances.

"*I* know I have no cause to grieve," Mary said. "*I* know that Charley is happy. I just want *him* to *tell* me so. That's not asking too much, is it?"

How should I know? What is "too much?" I never do any asking, myself, or any answering for that matter.

So off they went, my mother and Mrs. Mary King, and—if I couldn't beg off—I. Mrs. Victory's, Mrs. Reverend Ella Maybelle Snyder's, Madame Sophia's, Mother Honeywell's—every spirit-trumpet in the city must have been on time-and-a-half those days. They got little-girl angels and old-lady angels. They got doctors, lawyers, Indian chiefs, and young boy-babies—they must even have gotten Radio Andorra—but they didn't get Charley. There were slate-messages and automatic writings and ectoplasm enough to reach from here to Punxatawney, P. A., but if it reached to Charley he didn't reach back. All the mediums and all their customers had the same line: There is no grief in Summerland, there is no pain in Summerland—Summerland being the choice real estate development Upstairs, at least in the Spiritualist hep-talk. They all *believed* it, but somehow they all wanted to be assured. And after the séance, when all the spooks had gone back to Summerland, *what* a consumption of coffee, cupcakes, and cold cuts.

Some of the places were fancy: you bought "subscription" for the season's performance and discussed parapsychology over canapés and sherry. Mrs. Porteous's place, however, was right out of the 1920s, red velveteen por*teers* on wooden rings, and all. I almost fancied I could feel the ectoplasm when we came in, but it was just a heavy condensation of boiled cabbage steam and hamburger smoke.

Mrs. Porteous looked like a caricature of herself—down-at-hem evening gown, gaudy but clumsy cosmetic job, huge rings on each finger, and, *oh,* that *voice.* Mrs. Porteous was the phoniest-looking, phoniest-sounding, phoniest-*acting* medium I have ever come across. She had a lady-in-waiting: sagging cheeks, jet-black page-boy bob or bangs or whatever you call it, velvet tunic, so on.

"Dear friends," says the gentlewoman, striking a Woolworth gong, "might I have your attention please. I shall now request that there be no further smoking or talking whilst the séance is going on. We guarantee—*nothing.* We shall attempt—*all.* If there is doubt—if there is discord—the spirits may not come. For there is no doubt, no discord, there is no grief nor pain, in Summerland." So on. Let us join our hands . . . let us bow our heads . . . I, of course, peeked. The Duchess was sitting on the starboard side of the incense, next to Mrs. Porteous, who was rolling her eyes and muttering. Then Charley King screamed.

It was Mrs. Porteous's mouth that it came from, it was her chest that heaved, but it was Charley King's voice—I know his voice, don't you think I know his voice? He screamed. My mother's hand jerked away from mine.

"The fire! The fire! Oh, Mary, how it burns, how—"

Then Mary fell forward from her seat, the lights went on, went off, then on again, everyone scurried around except me—I was frozen to my seat—and Mrs. Porteous—she lay back in her arm chair. Finally I got to my feet and somehow we managed to lift Mary onto a couch. The color came back to her face and she opened her eyes.

"That's all right, dear," my mother said.

"Oh my goodness!" said Mary. "What happened? Did I faint? Isn't that silly. No, no, let me get up; we must start the séance."

Someone tugged at my sleeve. It was the Duchess.

"Who was that?" she asked, looking at me shrewdly. "It was her husband, wasn't it? Oh-yes-it-twas! He was burned to death, wasn't he? And he hasn't yet freed himself from his earthly ties so he can enter Summerland. He must of been a skeptic."

"He didn't burn to death," I said. "He fell and broke his neck. And he wasn't a skeptic."

(Hoke had said to me: "Of course the board was rotten; the whole house was rotten. All his property was like that. It should have been condemned years ago. No repairs, a family in each room, and the rent sky-high—he must have been making a fortune. You saw those rats, didn't you?" Hoke had asked. "Do you know what the death rate is in those buildings?")

The Duchess shook her head. Her face was puzzled.

"Then it couldn't of been her husband," she said. "There is no pain," she pointed out reasonably, "in Summerland."

"No," I said to her. "No, I'm sure there isn't. I know that."

But I knew Charley King. And I know his voice.

The Terrible Old Man

by H. P. Lovecraft

It was the design of Angelo Ricci and Joe Czanek and Manuel Silva to call on the Terrible Old Man. This old man dwells all alone in a very ancient house in Water Street near the sea, and is reputed to be both exceedingly rich and exceedingly feeble; which forms a situation very attractive to men of the profession of Messrs. Ricci, Czanek and Silva, for that profession was nothing less dignified than robbery.

The inhabitants of Kingsport say and think many things about the Terrible Old Man which generally keep him safe from the attentions of gentlemen like Mr. Ricci and his colleagues, despite the almost certain fact that he hides a fortune of indefinite magnitude somewhere about his musty and venerable abode. He is, in truth, a very strange person, believed to have been a captain of East India clipper ships in his day; so old that no one can remember when he was young, and so taciturn that few know his real name. Among the gnarled trees in the front yard of his aged and neglected place he maintains a strange collection of large stones, oddly grouped and painted so that they resemble the idols in some obscure Eastern temple. This collection frightens away most of the small boys who love to taunt the Terrible Old Man about his long white hair and beard, or to break the small-paned windows of his dwelling with wicked missiles; but there are other things which frighten the older and more curious folk who sometimes steal up to the house to peer in through the dusty panes. These folk say that on a table in a bare room on the ground floor are many peculiar bottles, in each a small piece of lead suspended pendulum-wise from a string. And they say that the Terrible Old Man talks to these bottles, addressing them by such names as Jack, Scar-Face, Long Tom, Spanish Joe, Peters and Mate Ellis, and that whenever he speaks to a bottle the little lead pendulum within makes certain definite vibrations as if in answer. Those who have watched the tall, lean, Terrible Old Man in these peculiar conversations do not watch him again. But Angelo Ricci and Joe Czanek and Manuel Silva were not of Kingsport blood; they were of that new and heterogeneous alien stock which lies outside the charmed circle of New England life and traditions, and they saw in the Terrible Old Man merely a tottering, almost helpless grey-beard, who could not walk without the aid of his knotted cane and whose thin, weak hands shook pitifully. They were really quite sorry in their way for the lonely, unpopular old fellow, whom everybody shunned, and at whom all the dogs barked singularly. But business is business, and to a robber whose soul is in his profession, there is a lure and a challenge about a very old and very feeble man who has no account at the bank, and who pays for his few necessities at the village store with Spanish gold and silver minted two centuries ago.

Messrs. Ricci, Czaneck and Silva selected the night of April eleventh for their call. Mr. Ricci and Mr. Silva were to interview the poor old gentleman, whilst Mr. Czanek waited for them and their presumably metallic burden with a covered motor car in Ship Street, by the gate in the tall rear wall of their host's grounds. Desire to avoid needless explanations in case of unexpected police intrusions prompted these plans for a quiet and unostentatious departure.

As prearranged, the three adventurers started out separately in order to prevent any evil-minded suspicions afterward. Messrs. Ricci and Silva met in Water Street by the old man's front gate, and although they did not like the way the moon shone down upon the painted stones through the budding branches of the gnarled trees, they had more important things to think about than mere idle superstition. They feared it might be unpleasant work making the Terrible Old Man loquacious concerning his hoarded gold and silver, for aged sea-captains are notably stubborn and perverse. Still, he was very old and very feeble, and there were two visitors. Messrs. Ricci and Silva were experienced in the art of making unwilling persons voluble, and the screams of a weak and exceptionally venerable man can be easily muffled. So they moved up to the one lighted window and heard the Terrible Old Man talking childishly to his bottles with pendulums. Then they donned masks and knocked politely at the weather-stained oaken door.

Waiting seemed very long to Mr. Czanek as he fidgeted restlessly in the covered motor car by the Terrible Old Man's back gate in Ship Street. He was more than ordinarily tender-hearted, and he did not like the hideous screams he had heard in the ancient house just after the hour appointed for the deed. Had he not told his colleagues to be as gentle as possible with the pathetic old sea-captain? Very nervously he watched that narrow oaken gate in the high and ivy-clad stone wall. Frequently he consulted his watch, and wondered at the delay. Had the old man died before revealing where his treasure was hidden, and had a thorough search become necessary? Mr. Czanek did not like to wait so long in the dark in such a place. Then he sensed a soft tread or tapping on the walk inside the gate, heard a gentle fumbling at the rusty latch, and saw the narrow, heavy door swing inward. And in the pallid glow of the single dim street lamp he strained his eyes to see what his colleagues had brought out of that sinister house which loomed so close behind. But when he looked, he did not see what he had expected; for his colleagues were not there at all, but only the Terrible Old Man leaning quietly on his knotted cane and smiling hideously. Mr. Czanek had never before noticed the color of that man's eyes; now he saw that they were yellow.

Little things make considerable excitement in little towns, which is the reason that Kingsport people talked all that spring and summer about the three unidentifiable bodies, horribly slashed as with many cutlasses, and horribly mangled as by the tread of many cruel boot-heels, which the tide washed in. And some people even spoke of things as trivial as the deserted motor car found in Ship Street, or certain especially inhuman cries, probably of a stray animal or migratory bird, heard in the night by wakeful citizens. But in this idle village gossip the Terrible Old Man took no interest at all. He was by nature reserved, and when one is aged and feeble one's reserve is doubly strong. Besides, so ancient a sea-captain must have witnessed scores of things much more stirring in the far-off days of his unremembered youth.

The Terror by Night

by E. F. Benson

The transference of emotion is a phenomenon so common, so constantly witnessed, that mankind in general have long ceased to be conscious of its existence, as a thing worth our wonder or consideration, regarding it as being as natural and commonplace as the transference of things that act by the ascertained laws of matter. Nobody, for instance, is surprised, if when the room is too hot, the opening of a window causes the cold fresh air of outside to be transferred into the room, and in the same way no one is surprised when into the same room, perhaps, which we will imagine as being peopled with dull and gloomy persons, there enters some one of fresh and sunny mind, who instantly brings into the stuffy mental atmosphere a change analogous to that of the opened windows. Exactly how this infection is conveyed we do not know; considering the wireless wonders (that act by material laws) which are already beginning to lose their wonder now that we have our newspaper brought as a matter of course every morning in mid-Atlantic, it would not perhaps be rash to conjecture that in some subtle and occult way the transference of emotion is in reality material too. Certainly (to take another instance) the sight of definitely material things, like writing on a page, conveys emotion apparently direct to our minds, as when our pleasure or pity is stirred by a book, and it is therefore possible that mind may act on mind by means as material as that.

Occasionally, however, we come across phenomena which, though they may easily be as material as any of these things, are rarer, and therefore more astounding. Some people call them ghosts, some conjuring tricks, and some nonsense. It seems simpler to group them under the head of transferred emotions, and they may appeal to any of the senses. Some ghosts are seen, some heard, some felt, and though I know of no instance of a ghost being tasted, yet it will seem in the following pages that these occult phenomena may appeal at any rate to the senses that perceive heat, cold, or smell. For, to take the analogy of wireless telegraphy, we are all of us probably "receivers" to some extent, and catch now and then a message or part of a message that the eternal waves of emotion are ceaselessly shouting aloud to those who have ears to hear, and materialising themselves for those who have eyes to see. Not being, as a rule, perfectly tuned, we grasp but pieces and fragments of such messages, a few coherent words it may be, or a few words which seem to have no sense. The following story, however, to my mind, is interesting, because it shows how different pieces of what no doubt was one message were received and recorded by several different people simultaneously. Ten years have elapsed since the events recorded took place, but they were written down at the time.

Jack Lorimer and I were very old friends before he married, and his marriage to a first cousin of mine did not make, as so often happens, a slackening in our intimacy. Within a few months after, it was found out that his wife had consumption, and, without any loss of time, she was sent off to Davos, with her sister to look after her. The disease had evidently been detected at a very early stage, and there was excellent ground for hoping that with proper care and strict regime she would be cured by the life-giving frosts of that wonderful valley.

The two had gone out in the November of which I am speaking, and Jack and I joined them for a month at Christmas, and found that week after week she was steadily and quickly gaining ground. We had to be back in town by the end of January, but it was settled that Ida should remain out with her sister for a week or two more. They both, I remember, came down to the station to see us off, and I am not likely to forget the last words that passed:

"Oh, don't look so woebegone, Jack," his wife had said; "you'll see me again before long."

Then the fussy little mountain engine squeaked, as a puppy squeaks when its toe is trodden on, and we puffed our way up the pass.

London was in its usual desperate February plight when we got back, full of fogs and still-born frosts that seemed to produce a cold far more bitter than the piercing temperature of those sunny altitudes from which we had come. We both, I think, felt rather lonely, and even before we had got to our journey's end we had settled that for the present it was ridiculous that we should keep open two houses when one would suffice, and would also be far more cheerful for us both. So, as we both lived in almost identical houses in the same street in Chelsea, we decided to "toss," live in the house which the coin indicated (heads mine, tails his), share expenses, attempt to let the other house, and, if successful, share the proceeds. A French five-franc piece of the Second Empire told us it was "heads."

We had been back some ten days, receiving every day the most excellent accounts from Davos, when, first on him, then on me, there descended, like some tropical storm, a feeling of indefinable fear. Very possibly this sense of apprehension (for there is nothing in the world so virulently infectious) reached me through him: on the other hand both these attacks of vague foreboding may have come from the same source. But it is true that it did not attack me till he spoke of it, so the possibility perhaps inclines to my having caught it from him. He spoke of it first, I remember, one evening when we had met for a good-night talk, after having come back from separate houses where we had dined.

"I have felt most awfully down all day," he said; "and just after receiving this splendid account from Daisy, I can't think what is the matter."

He poured himself out some whisky and soda as he spoke.

"Oh, touch of liver," I said. "I shouldn't drink that if I were you. Give it me instead."

"I was never better in my life," he said.

I was opening letters, as we talked, and came across one from the house agent, which, with trembling eagerness, I read.

"Hurrah," I cried, "offer of five gu^{as}—why can't he write it in proper English—five guineas a week till Easter for number 31. We shall roll in guineas!"

"Oh, but I can't stop here till Easter," he said.

"I don't see why not. Nor by the way does Daisy. I heard from her this morning, and she told me to persuade you to stop. That's to say, if you like. It really is more cheerful for you here. I forgot, you were telling me something."

The glorious news about the weekly guineas did not cheer him up in the least.

"Thanks awfully. Of course I'll stop."

He moved up and down the room once or twice.

"No, it's not me that is wrong," he said, "it's It, whatever It is. The terror by night."

"Which you are commanded not to be afraid of," I remarked.

"I know; it's easy commanding. I'm frightened: something's coming."

"Five guineas a week are coming," I said. "I shan't sit up and be infected by your fears. All that matters, Davos, is going as well as it can. What was the last report? Incredibly better. Take that to bed with you."

The infection—if infection it was—did not take hold of me then, for I remember going to sleep feeling quite cheerful, but I awoke in some dark still house and It, the terror by night, had come while I slept. Fear and misgiving, blind, unreasonable, and paralysing, had taken and gripped me. What was it? Just as by an aneroid we can foretell the approach of storm, so by this sinking of the spirit, unlike anything I had ever felt before, I felt sure that disaster of some sort was presaged.

Jack saw it at once when we met at breakfast next morning, in the brown haggard light of a foggy day, not dark enough for candles, but dismal beyond all telling.

"So it has come to you too," he said.

And I had not even the fighting-power left to tell him that I was merely slightly unwell. Besides, never in my life had I felt better.

All next day, all the day after that fear lay like a black cloak over my mind; I did not know what I dreaded, but it was something very acute, something that was very near. It was coming nearer every moment, spreading like a pall of clouds over the sky; but on the third day, after miserably cowering under it, I suppose some sort of courage came back to me: either this was pure imagination, some trick of disordered nerves or what not, in which case we were both "disquieting ourselves in vain," or from the immeasurable waves of emotion that beat upon the minds of men, something within both of us had caught a current, a pressure. In either case it was infinitely better to try, however ineffectively, to stand up against it. For these two days I had neither worked nor played; I had only shrunk and shuddered; I planned for myself a busy day, with diversion for us both in the evening.

"We will dine early," I said, "and go to the 'Man from Blankley's.' I have already asked Philip to come, and he is coming, and I have telephoned for tickets. Dinner at seven."

Philip, I may remark, is an old friend of ours, neighbour in this street, and by profession a much-respected doctor.

Jack laid down his paper.

"Yes, I expect you're right," he said. "It's no use doing nothing, it doesn't help things. Did you sleep well?"

"Yes, beautifully," I said rather snappishly, for I was all on edge with the added burden of an almost sleepless night.

"I wish I had," said he.

This would not do at all.

"We have got to play up!" I said. "Here are we two strong and stalwart persons, with as much cause for satisfaction with life as any you can mention, letting ourselves behave like worms. Our fear may be over things imaginary or over things that are real, but it is the fact of being afraid that is so despicable. There is nothing in the world to fear except fear. You know that as well as I do. Now let's read our papers with interest. Which do you back, Mr. Druce, or the Duke of Portland, or the Times Book Club?"

That day, therefore, passed very busily for me; and there were enough events moving in front of that black background, which I was conscious was there all the time, to enable me to keep my eyes away from it, and I was detained rather late at the office, and had to drive back to Chelsea, in order to be in time to dress for dinner instead of walking back as I had intended.

Then the message, which for these three days had been twittering in our minds, the receivers, just making them quiver and rattle, came through.

I found Jack already dressed, since it was within a minute or two of seven when I got in, and sitting in the drawing-room. The day had been warm and muggy, but when I looked in on the way up to my room, it seemed to me to have grown suddenly and bitterly cold, not with the dampness of English frost, but with the clear and stinging exhilaration of such days as we had recently spent in Switzerland. Fire was laid in the grate but not lit, and I went down on my knees on the hearth-rug to light it.

"Why, it's freezing in here," I said. "What donkeys servants are! It never occurs to them that you want fires in cold weather, and no fires in hot weather."

"Oh, for heaven's sake don't light the fire," said he, "it's the warmest muggiest evening I ever remember."

I stared at him in astonishment. My hands were shaking with the cold. He saw this.

"Why, you are shivering!" he said. "Have you caught a chill? But as to the room being cold let us look at the thermometer."

There was one on the writing-table.

"Sixty-five," he said.

There was no disputing that, nor did I want to, for at that moment it suddenly struck us, dimly and distantly, that It was "coming through." I felt it like some curious internal vibration.

"Hot or cold, I must go and dress," I said.

Still shivering, but feeling as if I was breathing some rarefied exhilarating air, I went up to my room. My clothes were already laid out, but, by an oversight, no hot water had been brought up, and I rang for my man. He came up almost at once, but he looked scared, or, to my already-startled senses, he appeared so.

"What's the matter?" I said.

"Nothing, sir," he said, and he could hardly articulate the words. "I thought you rang."

"Yes. Hot water. But what's the matter?"

He shifted from one foot to the other.

"I thought I saw a lady on the stairs," he said, "coming up close behind me. And the front door bell hadn't rung that I heard."

"Where did you think you saw her?" I asked.

"On the stairs. Then on the landing outside the drawing-room door, sir," he said. "She stood there as if she didn't know whether to go in or not."

"One—one of the servants," I said. But again I felt that It was coming through.

"No, sir. It was none of the servants," he said.

"Who was it then?"

"Couldn't see distinctly, sir, it was dim-like. But I thought it was Mrs. Lorimer."

"Oh, go and get me some hot water," I said.

But he lingered; he was quite clearly frightened.

At this moment the front-door bell rang. It was just seven, and already Philip had come with brutal punctuality while I was not yet half dressed.

"That's Dr. Enderly," I said. "Perhaps if he is on the stairs you may be able to pass the place where you saw the lady."

Then quite suddenly there rang through the house a scream, so terrible, so appalling in its agony and supreme terror, that I simply stood still and shuddered, unable to move. Then by an effort so violent that I felt as if something must break, I recalled the power of motion, and ran downstairs, my man at my heels, to meet Philip who was running up from the ground floor. He had heard it too.

"What's the matter?" he said. "What was that?"

Together we went into the drawing-room. Jack was lying in front of the fireplace, with the chair in which he had been sitting a few minutes before overturned. Philip went straight to him and bent over him, tearing open his white shirt.

"Open all the windows," he said, "the place reeks."

We flung open the windows, and there poured in so it seemed to me, a stream of hot air into the bitter cold. Eventually Philip got up.

"He is dead," he said. "Keep the windows open. The place is still thick with chloroform."

Gradually to my sense the room got warmer, to Philip's the drug-laden atmosphere dispersed. But neither my servant nor I had smelt anything at all.

A couple of hours later there came a telegram from Davos for me. It was to tell me to break the news of Daisy's death to Jack, and was sent by her sister. She supposed he would come out immediately. But he had been gone two hours now.

I left for Davos next day, and learned what had happened. Daisy had been suffering for three days from a little abscess which had to be opened, and, though the operation was of the slightest, she had been so nervous about it that the doctor gave her chloroform. She made a good recovery from the anaesthetic, but an hour later had a sudden attack of syncope, and had died that night at a few minutes before eight, by Central European time, corresponding to seven in English time. She had insisted that Jack should be told nothing about this little operation till it was over, since the matter was quite unconnected with her general health, and she did not wish to cause him needless anxiety.

And there the story ends. To my servant there came the sight of a woman outside the drawing-room door, where Jack was, hesitating about her entrance, at the moment when Daisy's soul hovered between the two worlds; to me there came—I do not think it is fanciful to suppose this—the keen exhilarating cold of Davos; to Philip there came the fumes of chloroform. And to Jack, I must suppose, came his wife. So he joined her.

The Theater Upstairs

by Manly Wade Wellman

"Look, a picture theater—who'd expect one here?"

Luther caught my arm and dragged me to a halt. We'd been out on a directionless walk through lower Manhattan that evening—"flitting" was Luther's word, cribbed, I think, from Robert W. Chambers. The old narrow street where we now paused had an old English name and was somewhere south and east of Chinatown. Its line of dingy shops had foreign words on their dim windows, and lights and threadbare curtains up above where their proprietors lodged. And right before us, where Luther had stopped to gaze, was a narrow wooden door that bore a white card. CINEMA, it said in bold, plain capitals. And, in smaller letters below: Georgia Wattell.

I was prepared to be embarrassed by that name. Everyone suspected, and a few claimed to know positively, that Georgia Wattell had committed suicide at the height of her Hollywood career because Luther had deserted her. But my companion did not flinch, only drew up that thick body of his. A smile wrinkled his handsome features, features that still meant box-office to any picture, even though they were softening from too much food and drink and so forth.

"Wonder which of Georgia's things it is," Luther mused, with a gayety slightly forced. "Come on, I'll stand you a show."

I didn't like it, but refusal would seem accusation. So I let him draw me through the door.

We had stairs to walk up—creaky old stairs. They were so narrow that we had to mount in single file, our shoulders brushing first one wall, then the other. I was mystified, for doesn't a New York ordinance provide that theaters cannot be on upper floors? There was no light on those stairs, as I remember, only a sort of grayness filtering from above. At any rate, we saw better when we came to the little foyer at the top. A shabby man stood there, with lead-colored eyes in his square face and a great shock of coarse gray hair.

"Admission a quarter," he mumbled in a soft, hoarse voice, and accepted the half-dollar Luther produced. "Go on in."

With one hand he pocketed the coin and with the other drew back a dark, heavy curtain. We entered a long hall, groped our way to seats— we were the only patrons, so far as I could tell—and almost at once the screen lit up with the title: THE HORLA, by Guy de Maupassant.

"Creepy stuff—good!" muttered Luther with relish, then added some other comment on the grisly classic. What with trying to hear him and read the cast of players at the same moment, I failed in both efforts. The shimmering words on the screen dissolved into a pictured landscape, smitten by rain which the sound apparatus mimicked drearily. In the middle distance appeared a cottage, squat and ancient, with a droopy, soft-seeming roof like the cap of a toadstool. The camera viewpoint sailed down and upon it, in what Luther called a "dolly shot." We saw at close quarters the front porch.

482

Two women sat on the top step, exchanging the inconsequential opening dialog. Georgia Wattell seated at center with her sad, dark face turned front, was first recognizable. Her companion, to one side and in profile, offered to our view a flash of silver-blond hair and a handsome, feline countenance.

"It's Lilyan Tashman," grunted Luther, and shut up his mouth with a snap. He might have said more about this uneasy vision of two dead actresses talking and moving, but he did not. A third figure was coming into view at the left, shedding a glistening waterproof and a soaked slouch hat. My first glimpse of his smooth black hair and close-set ears, seen from behind, struck a chord of memory in me. Then his face swiveled around into view, and I spoke aloud.

"This can't be!" I protested. "Why, Rudolph Valentino died before anybody even dreamed of sound pic—"

But it was Valentino nevertheless, and he had been about to speak to the two women. However, just as I exclaimed in my unbelieving amazement, he paused and faced front. His gaze seemed to meet mine, and suddenly I realized how big he was on the screen, eight or ten feet high at the least. Those brilliant eyes withered me, his lip twitched over his dazzling teeth—the contemptuous rebuke-expression of an actor to a noisy audience.

So devastatingly real was that shadowy snub that I almost fell from my seat. I know that Luther swore, and that I felt sweaty all over. When I recovered enough to assure myself that my imagination was too lively, Valentino had turned back to deliver his interrupted entrance line. The show went on.

So far there was nothing to remind me of de Maupassant's story as I had read it. But with Valentino's first speech and Georgia Wattell's answer the familiar plot began. Of course, it was freely modified, like most film versions of the classics. For one thing, the victim of the invisible monster was not a man but a woman—Georgia, to be exact—and it seemed to me at the time that this change heightened the atmosphere of helpless horror. Valentino might have done something vigorous, either spiritual or physical, against de Maupassant's Horla. Georgia Wattell, with her sorrowfully lovely face and frail little body, seemed inescapably foredoomed.

The remainder of the action on the porch was occupied by Georgia's description of the barely-understood woes she was beginning to suffer at the Horla's hands. Miss Tashman as her friend and Valentino as her lover urged her to treat everything as a fancy and to tell herself that all would be well. She promised—but how vividly she acted the part of an unbeliever in her own assurance! Then the image of the

483

porch, with those three shadows of dead players posed upon it in attitudes of life, faded away.

The next scene was a French country bedroom—curtained bed, *prie-dieu* and so on. Georgia Wattell entered it, unfastening her clothing.

"Ho!" exploded Luther somewhat lasciviously, but I did not stop to be disgusted with him. My mind was wrestling with the situation, how items so familiar in themselves—lower New York, the motion picture business, the performers, de Maupassant's story—could be so creepy in combination.

Well, Georgia took off her dress. I saw, as often before, that she had a lovely bosom and shoulders, for all her fragility. Over her underthings she drew an ample white robe, on the collar of which fell her loosened dark hair. Kneeling for a moment at the *prie-dieu,* she murmured a half-audible prayer, then turned toward the bed. At that moment there entered—just where, I cannot say—the Horla.

It was quite the finest and weirdest film device I have ever seen. No effect in the picture versions of *Frankenstein* or *Dracula* remotely approached it. Without outline or opacity, less tangible than a shimmer of hot air, yet it gave the impression of living malevolence. I felt aware of its presence upon the screen without actually seeing it; but how could it have been suggested without being visible? I should like to discuss this point with someone else who saw the picture, but I have never yet found such a person.

It was there, anyway. Georgia registered sudden and uneasy knowledge of it. Her body shuddered a trifle inside the robe and she paused as if in indecision, then moved toward the bed. A moment later she moaned wildly and staggered a bit. The thing, whatever triumph of photo-dramatic trickery it was, enveloped her.

She went all blurred and indistinct, as though seen through water. Doesn't de Maupassant himself use that figure of speech? Then the attacking entity seemed to pop out into a faint approach to human shape. I could see shadowy arms winding around the shrinking girl, a round, featureless head bowed as if its maw sought her throat. She screamed loudly and began to struggle. Then Valentino and Miss Tashman burst into the room.

With their appearance the Horla released her and seemed to retire into its half-intangible condition. I, who had utterly forgotten that I saw only a film, sighed my inexpressible relief at the thing's momentary defeat, then whispered to Luther.

"I don't like this," I said. "Let's get out, or I won't sleep tonight."

"We stay right here," he mumbled back, his eyes bright and fascinated as they kept focussed on the screen.

Valentino was holding Georgia close, caressing her to quiet her hysterics and speaking reassuringly in his accented English. Lilyan Tashman said something apparently meant for comedy relief, which was badly needed at this point. But neither Luther nor I laughed.

Georgia suddenly cried out in fresh fear.

"It's there in the corner!" she wailed, turning toward the spot where the Horla must be lurking.

Both her companions followed her gaze, apparently seeing nothing. For that matter I saw nothing myself, though I well knew the thing was there.

Valentino made another effort to calm her.

"I'll put a bullet into it, darling," he offered, with an air of falling in with her morbid humor. "In the corner, you say?"

From his pocket he drew a revolver. But Georgia, suddenly calming her shudders, snatched the weapon from his hand.

"Don't!" she begged. "How can a bullet harm something that has no life like ours?"

"Here, don't point that gun at me!" begged Miss Tashman, retreating in comic fright.

Georgia moved forward in the picture, looming larger than her companions. "You can't kill spirits," she went on, tonelessly and quite undramatically. "Bullets are for *living* enemies."

She gazed out upon us.

Right here is where the whole business stopped being real and became nightmare. Georgia moved again, closer and closer, until her head and shoulders, with the gun hand lifted beside them, filled the screen. She looked as big as the Sphinx by then, but grim and merciless as no Sphinx ever was. And her enormous, accusing eyes weren't fixed upon me, but upon Luther.

My inner self began arguing silently. "That's odd," it said plaintively. "A gaze from the screen seems to meet that of each member of the audience. How can she be looking *past* me at—"

Georgia spoke, between immense, hardened lips, in a voice that rolled out to fill the whole theater:

"Jan Luther!"

And she swelled bigger, bigger beyond all reason, too big for the screen to contain. Suddenly there were only the hand and the gun, turned toward us like a cannon aimed point-blank.

Luther was on his feet, screaming.

"You can't!" he challenged wildly. "You—why, you're only a shadow!"

But the screen exploded in white light, that made the whole hall bright as day for just the hundredth part of a second. After that I was trying to hold Luther erect. He sagged and slumped back into his seat in spite of all I could do. Blood purled gently down his face from a neat round hole in his forehead.

I glanced wildly at the screen. The picture had shrunk back to ordinary dimensions now, showing again the bedroom, the three performers and everything else exactly as it had been.

Georgia was offering Valentino his pistol again. "Thanks, Rudy," she said.

I suppose I must have run crazily out of there, for my next memory is of panting the story in broken sentences to a big blue-coated policeman. He frowned as I tried to tell everything at once, then came back with me to the street with the foreign-labeled shops. When I couldn't find the door and its lettered card he laughed, not very good-naturedly, and accused me of being drunk. When I tried to argue he ordered me to move along or go to jail and sleep it off.

I haven't seen Luther since, nor heard from him. There has been plenty in the papers about his disappearance, though several editors have put it down as a publicity stunt. Three times recently I have gone into the part of town where I lost him, and each time I have seen, at a little distance along a sidewalk or across a street, the white-haired, leaden-eyed man who admitted us to the theater. But, though I always tried to hail him, he lost himself among the passers-by before I reached him.

At length I have decided to stay away from there altogether. I wish I could stop thinking about the affair as well.

Thirteen Phantasms

by Clark Ashton Smith

"I have been faithful to thee, Cynara, in my fashion."

John Alvington tried to raise himself on the pillow as he murmured in his thoughts the long-familiar refrain of Dowson's lyric. But his head and shoulders fell back in an overflooding helplessness, and there trickled through his brain, like a thread of icy water, the realization that perhaps the doctor had been right—perhaps the end was indeed imminent. He thought briefly of embalming fluids, immortelles, coffin nails and falling sods; but such ideas were quite alien to his trend of mind, and he preferred to think of Elspeth. He dismissed his mortuary musings with an appropriate shudder.

He often thought of Elspeth, these days. But of course he had never really forgotten her at any time. Many people called him a rake; but he knew, and had always known, that they were wrong. It was said that he had broken, or materially dented, the hearts of twelve women, including those of his two wives; and strangely enough, in view of the exaggerations commonly characteristic of gossip, the number was correct. Yet he, John Alvington, knew to a certainty that only one woman, who no one reckoned among the twelve, had ever really mattered in his life.

He had loved Elspeth and no one else; he had lost her through a boyish quarrel which was never made up, and she had died a year later. The other women were all mistakes, mirages: they had attracted him only because he fancied, for varying periods, that he had found in them something of Elspeth. He had been cruel to them perhaps, and most certainly he had not been faithful. But in forsaking them, had he not been all the truer to Elspeth?

Somehow his mental image of her was more distinct today than in years. As if a gathering dust had been wiped away from a portrait, he saw with strange clearness the elfin teasing of her eyes and the light tossing of brown curls that always accompanied her puckish laughter. She was tall—unexpectedly tall for so fairy-like a person, but all the more admirable thereby; and he had never liked any but tall women.

How often he had been startled, as if by a ghost, in meeting some women with a similar mannerism, a similar figure or expression of eyes or cadence of voice; and how complete had been his disillusionment when he came to see the unreality and fallaciousness of the resemblance. How irreparably she, the true love, had come sooner or later between him and all the others.

He began to recall things that he had almost forgotten, such as the carnelian cameo brooch she had worn on the day of their first meeting, and a tiny mole on her left shoulder, of which he had once had a glimpse when she was wearing a dress unusually low-necked for that period. He remembered too the plain gown of pale green that clung so deliciously to her slender form on that morning when he had flung away with a curt good-bye, never to see her again. . . .

Never, he thought to himself, had his memory been so good: surely the doctor was mistaken, for there was no failing of his faculties. It was quite impossible that he should be mortally ill, when he could summon all his recollections of Elspeth with such ease and clarity.

Now he went over all the days of their seven months' engagement, which might have ended in a felicitous marriage if it had not been for her propensity to take unreasonable offense, and for his own answering flash of temper and want of conciliatory tactics in the crucial quarrel. How near, how poignant it all seemed. He wondered what malign presidence had ordered their parting and had sent him on a vain quest from face to illusory face for the remainder of his life.

He did not, could not remember the other women—only that he had somehow dreamed for a little while that they resembled Elspeth. Others might consider him a Don Juan: but he knew himself for a hopeless sentimentalist, if there ever had been one.

What was that sound? he wondered. Had someone opened the door of the room? It must be the nurse, for no one else ever came at that hour in the evening. The nurse was a nice girl, though not at all like Elspeth. He tried to turn a little so that he could see her, and somehow succeeded, by a titanic effort altogether disproportionate to the feeble movement.

It was not the nurse after all, for she was always dressed in immaculate white befitting her profession. This woman wore a dress of cool, delectable green, pale as the green of shoaling sea-water. He could not see her face, for she stood with back turned to the bed; but there was something oddly familiar in that dress, something that he could not quite remember at first. Then, with a distinct shock, he knew that it resembled the dress worn by Elspeth on the day of their quarrel, the same dress he had been picturing to himself a little while before. No one ever wore a gown of that length and style nowadays. Who on earth could it be? There was a queer familiarity about her figure, too, for she was quite tall and slender.

The woman turned, and John Alvington saw that it was Elspeth—the very Elspeth from whom he had parted with a bitter farewell, and who had died without ever permitting him to see her again. Yet how could it be but Elspeth, when she had been dead so long? Then, by a swift transition of logic, how could she have ever died, since she was here before him now? It seemed so infinitely preferable to believe that she still lived, and he wanted so much to speak to her, but his voice failed him when he tried to utter her name.

Now he thought that he heard the door open again, and became aware that another woman stood in the shadows behind Elspeth. She came forward, and he observed that she wore a green dress identical in every detail with that worn by his beloved. She lifted her head—and the face was that of Elspeth, with the same teasing eyes and whimsical mouth! But how could there be two Elspeths?

In profound bewilderment, he tried to accustom himself to the bizarre idea; and even as he wrestled with a problem so unaccountable, a third figure in pale green, followed by a fourth and a fifth came in and stood beside the first two. Nor were these the last, for others entered one by one, till the room was filled with woman, all of whom wore the raiment and the semblance of his dead sweetheart. None of them uttered a word, but all looked at Alvington with a gaze in which he now seemed to discern a deeper mockery than the elfin tantalizing he had once found in the eyes of Elspeth.

He lay very still, fighting with a dark, terrible perplexity. How could there be such a multitude of Elspeths, when he could remember knowing only one? And how many were there, anyway? Something prompted him to count them, and he found that there were thirteen of the specters in green. And having ascertained this fact, he was struck by something familiar about the number. Didn't people say that he had broken the hearts of thirteen women? Or was the total only twelve? Anyway, if you counted Elspeth herself, who had really broken his heart, there would be thirteen.

Now all the woman began to toss their curly heads, in a manner he recalled so well, and all of them laughed with a light and puckish laughter. Could they be laughing at him? Elspeth had often done that but he had loved her devotedly nevertheless. . . .

All at once, he began to feel uncertain about the precise number of figures that filled his room; it seemed to him at one moment that there were more than he had counted, and then that there were fewer. He wondered which one among them was the true Elspeth, for after all he felt sure that there had never been a second—only a series of women apparently resembling her, who were not really like her at all when you came to know them.

Finally, as he tried to count them and scrutinize the thronging faces, all of them grew dim and confused and indistinct, and he half forgot what he was trying to do. . . . Which one was Elspeth? Or had there ever been a real Elspeth? He was not sure of anything at the last, when oblivion came, and he passed to that realm in which there are neither women nor phantoms nor love nor numerical problems.

Three Gentlemen in Black
by August W. Derleth

It was odd, after the way he had been dissatisfied with everything he had so far looked at, that this house should appeal to him so much. An out of the way place, certainly. He would be safe enough there from any manner of pursuit: the police especially, if it came to that. He need see no one day in, day out; he could grow a beard, if necessary, in addition to the straggly mustache.

The house at the end of the country lane had something compellingly familiar about it: a dream place, with aspects emerging as from a distant past, indistinct and vague. He did not pause to analyze this, apart from thinking it strange. He had thought his search for a suitable house in the country would never end, but here it was: the perfect place. Snug as a bug in a rug, as Uncle Alexander might say. And safe, really *safe:* well away from London, well away from anyone who knew him. And here he could stay until Uncle Alexander was dead; then he could come forward as the modest heir, and, incidentally, the *only* heir.

So far, of course, Uncle Alexander was not dead. He had not thought he might be. He had been, in fact, far too careful. The poisoned capsule had been put well in the center of the second layer in the case of veronal capsules Uncle Alexander carried. So the old man would die sometime, somewhere, within the next month or two. There was really no hurry; Orto Harper could afford to wait, and the thought of what an inheritance he would come into made waiting easy, the memory of how his Uncle Alexander had beaten him years ago—the big, ugly hands striking blindly at his young body; this memory made waiting a pleasure. To know that yours was the hand of Death, to know that sometime, somewhere, within the next two months, Uncle Alexander would die, that everybody he had known would testify about the old man's constant worry about his heart, that Uncle Alexander's considerable estate would shortly be yours!—Orto Harper felt a physical pleasure quite apart from intellectual pride in his work.

So he took the house and moved in—alone; he wanted no one around to say that he had acted queerly when news of his uncle's death reached him; and he set himself to planning a garden, thinking with amusement of the picture it made—a murderer busying himself among flowers. Not the first time, doubtless. But in the back of his mind, in the well of his thoughts, this thought stirred and rankled: this place was familiar, familiar from a distant past.

But try as he would, he could not place his finger on that familiarity. Sometimes certain aspects of the place struck him forcibly; he would come upon them—a brief vision of a distant valley among the trees, a corner in the house itself, the sunlight falling upon a stair—and know he had seen them before, know without question that these things had passed before his eyes at some distant time. Then again, he would feel all the freshness of something utterly new at certain other aspects of the rambling old country estate. Yet—there was something about the lake, dimly seen to eastward, that kept bothering him subconsciously.

Naturally enough, this feeling of vague familiarity irritated him; he had little enough to do—the garden and the press were his chief interests: the garden because it gave his hands something to do and took his mind off waiting; the press, to watch for the notice of his uncle's death. He held the headline he would see already in mind: *Death of Alexander Harper*—and the story of how he died in London or Paris or perhaps somewhere in the country: preferably the latter, for a hurried provincial physician would be far more likely to snap at a diagnosis of heart failure. So he pondered this odd familiarity, he dwelt upon it in his leisure; it began to annoy him with each new-found familiar thing, and presently he began to recognize a nebulous uneasiness; he experienced the conviction that there was something he should know, something he should remember.

But all he could think about at first was his life with Uncle Alexander. A dog's existence! He remembered how, not long after his father had killed himself, he had got into a little trouble, and Uncle Alexander had called him a "nasty wretch, likely to take after his father." And again, that first time his uncle had caught him abstracting an old book from his library with a view to pawning it, how the old man had stood looking balefully at him, his bushy brows pushed down in a grave frown over his eyes, and explained to the man-servant over his head, "He comes by it naturally, I suppose. Unless he's handled right, he'll turn out a bad egg." And then had come the ceaseless, painful beatings, the eternal punishment, the cruel humiliations.

For that, Orto Harper would shortly be repaid. Uncle Alexander took a veronal capsule every night, or almost every night, and one of these nights he would take the poisoned capsule so carefully prepared by his nephew. There was a savage, unholy joy in the thought.

Thinking thus, Orto Harper began to meditate suddenly upon the strange thrill he always got out of doing wrong, the unholy fascination of evil itself. Always, as long as he could remember, he had enjoyed wrongdoing: the first petty things—cruelty to others, bad temper, pilfering—the adolescent thefts, and now: *murder!* Ah, but he was sharp, he was a cute one! This was the burden of his thought, the theme that lay under it always. And he believed in himself.

He had been a week in the house before he noticed anything wrong. And then he thought only that it was a matter of digestion, perhaps some physical disturbance, painless, but still capable of arousing in him a nervousness which was translated into apprehension. For he *was* apprehensive. He noticed, for one thing, the curious absence of visitors. True, the house was well down the lane from the road, and the lane itself, as well as the house, was overhung with old trees. But people did not come near the place. He found his groceries at the end of the lane next the road, and any protest he made over the telephone to the grocer in Willomead was met with an obstinate and aggravating silence.

This made him furious until the night on which he saw the two gentlemen in black. It was just at the last of the dusk hour, at the boundary of night. He sat in the kitchen of the house, looking down the lane toward the road, when the two gentlemen in black appeared in the lane and came down toward him, walking briskly. Indeed, one of them seemed to be carrying an umbrella. Visitors, thought Orto. He sat still, watching. They came on to the small veranda. Momentarily, Orto expected their knock. It did not come. He peered out, mystified, but there was no one there.

He got up and went around to the front of the house, and almost walked into them. They were standing in the hall, and their aspects froze Orto Harper with terror. In the dim light there, he could see their lips move, but he heard no sound. He could see the bulk of them: fat, heavy men, the acme of British country respectability: but he could also see the outlines of window and door through them. And the door was still locked, as he had left it, his key hanging undisturbed in the lock!

Orto Harper may have been vain, but he was no fool. A man might say what he liked about the supernatural, but Orto Harper knew when he saw a ghost. At this moment, he saw two of them.

But it was not the fact that they were ghosts that frightened him; it was this: *their faces were familiar!* The same maddening familiarity reaching into the present from a distant past, too intangible to grasp, yet there. Somewhere, sometime, he had known these men; he had known them when they still lived. Indeed, he could swear to this: that at one time one of them at least—the one with the sideburns—had jostled him on his knee! Even so, he could not place them, though he racked his memory, standing there, the edge of fright still impinging upon his thought. As he sought to find a clue to their identity, the two of them parted, one to walk soundlessly up the long stairs, the other to enter the study.

Orto waited a moment; then silently he crossed the hall and looked into the study. There was no one there.

He began to feel a cold horror mushrooming up inside him, but above this, he became aware of an intense, insatiable curiosity. Who were these men? Where was this place? Obviously, it was not enough to think of it as a house in the country outside Willomead. For him, at least, there was something more. He resisted an impulse to go upstairs and look for the other one, feeling certain that he, too, would have vanished in the growing darkness.

Whatever fresh questions their appearance may have brought into his mind, at least one thing was explained: the curious reticence of the near-by villagers. Orto felt that he had somehow accomplished something, and, thinking thus, the fear in him began to ebb away, slowly at first, and then with increasing swiftness, until only the odd, rankling sense of something forgotten, some misplaced memory, something he ought to know remained. He resolved to investigate the ghosts of this old house at the first opportunity, making of it a chore to be done at his convenience.

He was still a little nervous and upset when he went to bed that night, and he dreamed. He dreamed about his father, saw the thin, sharp-eyed man with his long predatory fingers he had known in his early years. He saw him in a boat with two gentlemen in black, and he heard him speak to them, calling one "Uncle Robert," the other,

"Uncle Henry." Out on the lake they went, despite wind and choppy water, with his father smiling an evil smile, and the clouds darkening, and the wind rising. "My boy, be careful; your uncle and I can't swim." So fast it happened that even as the old one spoke, the boat went over, and the sly face of the young man, his father, was under water, swimming swiftly toward shore, and the two older men were floundering helplessly, calling vainly, sinking, drowning.

When he woke, Orto knew the men in his dream, the men whose spectral visit had been paid him the evening before; they were his great-uncles, Robert and Henry. And of his dream he dared not think; he pressed himself with query after query: where was this place? Where had he sought the sanctuary he fancied he would need after his crime? As if he did not know! He did. He had been here as a very small child, two years or so. The Harperson place in the country. *Harperson:* that was his grandfather's name, shortened by the old man's sons. And the place? Sold before the old man's death because of some obscure reason no one dared name.

He got up in the dark and looked out. A waning moon had risen and was shedding its pale orange glow over the landscape. Venus had preceded the sun into the eastern sky. Away off along the eastern horizon shimmered the lake. That would be the place, Orto thought, the place where it had happened. He wondered idly whether the two gentlemen in black were still waiting.

That was the first time he thought of them as *waiting.*

In the morning he went into the village, pausing at a pub that looked more aged than anything else to be seen along the hamlet's principal street. *Pelham's Place.* He bought himself some ale and sat down where he could talk. Wisely, he waited for the bluff, hearty, John-Bullish man behind the bar to say the first word. This he did presently.

"You at the old Harperson place?" A bit of curiosity in his question.

"Yes, I am," replied Orto.

A grunt was his reply. He waited.

Presently Pelham said, "Quiet place, by the look of it."

"Ah, you've seen it?" said Orto dryly. "Judging by the number of people thereabouts, I'd think nobody'd know the place was there."

Pelham rubbed industriously at a spot on the bar. "Yus," he said, "a quiet place. Not many people go there. Stories about."

"Won't frighten me."

Pelham looked more interested. "Nor me, neither," he maintained stoutly, "But I got a house and no need to go out there. You seen anything?"

"Two men in black, if that's what you mean."

Pelham grinned and nodded. "That's them. That's the Harperson's, all right. You seen 'em, then."

"What's the story?" asked Orto briskly.

Pelham leaned toward him confidentially. "You see, I ain't sayin' anything, I'm not. You got that? It's this way. They was drowned, them two, in the lake over eastward. You see? Couldn't swim; went out in a boat with a nephew of theirs. Windy day, lake choppy, rough. Boat tipped. Nephew couldn't save them. There you have it. But the nephew knew they couldn't swim, and like as not he didn't try to save 'em."

Orto looked at him with a faint feeling of violent illness not un-mixed with an equally faint awareness of the same unholy joy that always marked his own evil deeds. "You mean they were deliberately upset?"

Pelham nodded. "Everything above-board," he said. "Everything clear. No doubt. Coroner's jury said accident. Maybe it was. But a deliberate accident. You see? The two men were worth good plenty, yus indeed they were. Never married, but one of 'em was going to. That was the reason. That way his brother got it all—Newman Harperson; that was the man. The nephew's father."

"And I suppose the nephew inherited after his father, is that it?" He asked, but he knew what the answer would be.

"Nah! not a bit of it. Reckon the old man guessed. At least, he wasn't sure himself. He gave it all to his other son, Alexander; every shilling of it. Sold the place right after, too, and changed the family name." He began to chuckle.

"And the nephew?"

"Ah, that was the joke of it, yus. He hung himself. He did it in his brother's house in London. Gone there to beg a bit, I'd no doubt. But the brother was a shrewd one, and the other was going out of his mind, he was. Said they was after him, those two, his uncles—two men in black, he said. That was his story."

Orto looked at him in alarmed surprise. "Was it in the papers?" he asked.

"Not much. My sister got it from a woman whose niece worked in Alexander Harper's place."

Orto left the pub remembering all he knew he should have remembered when first he had seen the old place. And above all his knowledge of why its familiarity should have struck him, he remembered how his Uncle Alexander had stood over him and said, "He comes by it naturally!"

He understood many things, but he was not afraid, stilling the small voice inside. Even if his plans in regard to Uncle Alexander went wrong, he was confident that he could outwit the police. Still, he felt oddly cheated, as if this evil in him in which he had so long gloried was not, after all, entirely of his own doing.

Going down the lane, he began to think of what Pelham had said—that the two Harpersons had hounded his father, had driven him to suicide. Certainly he had made away with himself; there was no doubt whatever about that. Orto could remember that without difficulty. Now that his doubts about the house had been settled, he began to think more about his spectral visitors of the preceding night. Why had he not seen them before? Would he see them again? He waited for night with a curious kind of apprehension, a breathless tension which he could recognize as if he were somewhere outside himself watching.

As before, they came down the lane that night: the two of them, talking, gesticulating: two gentlemen in black with the outlines of trees and shrubs seen through them. He sat where he was, in the kitchen, and waited. Presently they were there, in the room with him, their soundless talking constant, and he watched, fascinated. Once or twice they looked at him with a strange, speculative air; they knew him, but for some reason, they were waiting. He could not escape the conviction that they were waiting for something that concerned him.

It seemed to him several times as if he could hear them speak, but he knew he could not; he knew that words formed in his mind alone; but he knew also that somehow those words came from the two long-dead great-uncles Harperson. They were talking about his father, about him, about Uncle Alexander; it was as if he could feel their animated thoughts in the room with him. He began therefore, because he could not help it, to think of his father, how they had found him with his own hands about his neck in addition to the rope, how his father's fingers and thumbs had been sunk into the flesh of his neck. And he shuddered, looking at the great, spectral hands before him, hands so much like Uncle Alexander's.

For the first time he thought of flight.

But he could not flee. Not while Uncle Alexander was alive and he was secure here, could always be secure from prying eyes, until the time came to reply to advertisements for his whereabouts and he could come modestly forward to claim his uncle's estate—he, a countryman then, isolated and unaware of his uncle's death. He was too smart to do anything rash—not Orto Harper! And even if the police began to make inquiries!

But he need not have feared the police.

The next night he found it in the paper, the small dark head: *Death of Alexander Harper,* and the story: *A body, identified as that of the late Alexander Harper, K. C. B., was found last night in a first-class compartment in the Orient Express. Mr. Harper, it was asserted by several companions, had been complaining constantly of heart trouble, and had had two attacks within the preceding twenty-four hours. Death was attributed to failure of the heart, pending further examination. At the time of his death, Mr. Alexander Harper was engaged on a delicate mission for the Foreign Office. . . .*

Orto read the story through once and again, and he felt flowering in him that same deep-seated physical sense of evil power, the same thrill he had always known. He folded the paper almost reverently and hurried up the lane to the house. Now he need only wait. A few weeks, a month—and he could come forward, be rich, have all his uncle's money. Now at last, at long last he was avenged for all the beatings, the cruel humiliations, the endless insults he had endured at the bestial hands of Uncle Alexander.

He came toward the porch in the evening halflight and saw them: two middle-aged gentlemen in black, the acme of British country respectability. They stood on the back porch waiting for him, and when he paused, apprehensive, began to move toward him, slowly, patiently, like two great animals with all the time in the world. But this time there was no innocuousness about them; there was the sharp, clear aura of terror and death.

They did not take trouble to conceal their hatred and contempt, did not disguise their intentions, and Orto's courage drained out of him. He stood for a frozen moment, conscious of the horrible fear beating up within him. He knew now how his father had died. He knew how those great spectral hands would catch hold of his own and fix them around his throat, force his own fingers and thumbs into the flesh of his neck. But in a second, his old confidence briefly rose. He could escape, he could run; they would not follow him into the road beyond the lane.

He dropped the paper and turned. He ran down the lane with a kind of fierce exultation pulsing through him, a last insane uprushing of his abnormal vanity, the thrill of working evil and evading punishment.

Looking ahead, he saw someone turn into the lane. He felt safer, even though the two behind him had lost no distance. He was tempted to raise his voice and shout, but in a moment he saw that he would be quite close enough to make shouting superfluous.

At that moment he saw that the figure ahead was a third gentleman in black, nebulous as those other two, with the white line of the road clearly visible through his fragile substance.

He stopped, half turned, and saw his great-uncles waiting, grim, inexorable. He was frozen where he stood, but he felt his legs give, felt himself sinking to his knees, the ground rising to meet him. Slowly, slowly he turned his head and looked at the oncoming third.

It was his Uncle Alexander, grave, grim, determined; his Uncle Alexander coming at him as at the boy he had flogged in the library so often, flexing his great hands!

The Tree-Man Ghost

by Percy B. Prior

The day was hot, as the July sun filled Strathspey with pulsing heat, which danced and waved along the ground. Colin Kerr and Alan Maclure trudged along on their way to Abernesby, longing for a breath of cool air or the welcome shade of a tree.

"When we reach yon tree," Colin said, "I'm going to rest awhile."

He pointed to a solitary-looking tree which grew beside a little brook—a brook which, by and by, made its way into the River Spey. The grass all round was beautifully green, but the tree looked strange. At some time it must have been struck by lightning, which had blasted its head, and left it withered and white, and given the trunk a curious tilt, so that it seemed to stoop forward as if peering at something on the ground. Two out-flung branches, looking exactly like arms, grew on either side of it, and heightened its likeness to a human being.

One could imagine an owl making its home in it, or bats, but certainly not little singing birds. Still there was shelter under its branches, and the two weary travelers sank down thankfully on the grass.

There was an ancient ruin on the other side of the burn. An old legend told that treasure had been buried somewhere near. Colin Kerr, who was an old man and knew many ancient stories, told Alan the tale as they sat and rested. Robbers had plundered an old church and had hidden their booty somewhere among the ruins. They had been caught and hanged, and the secret of these hidden treasures had never been revealed.

Alan's eyes gleamed as he listened. "I wish we could find it," he said. "We could live like gentlemen, Colin, and do no more work."

Colin, stretched on the grass, laughed drowsily. "There would be no blessing on it," he said. "It was stolen from the Church."

He lay on his right side as he slept, and because he was left-handed, as are all the Kerrs, his dagger hung over his right hip. Alan's eyes were attracted by the sunlight gleam on its hilt, then his eyes wandered to the face of the sleeping man. How old he looked as he slept! His bare throat almost scraggy—it would not take much to—why on earth was he thinking such things?

Colin's mouth was slightly open and he snored as he slept; he was an old man—he couldn't have many years to live—and again Alan tried to shake off the evil suggestions which were creeping like serpents into his mind. He would go to sleep, too. But it was no use. His brain was in a whirl.

Unwillingly he looked again at his companion's face. How soundly he slept! The sun was still glittering on the hilt of his dagger. Moved by an irresistible impulse, Alan put forth his hand and drew the weapon out of its sheath. But next moment he was dreadfully alarmed, for the sleeper began to moan and mutter and toss his hands about, and then Alan saw coming out of his mouth a strange, indistinct form, scarce bigger than a bumble-bee, but without wings.

It crawled along the sleeper's clothes down on the sod till it came to the brook, which it would neither fly over nor swim. It turned back and back and tried again. It did this so often that Alan stretched the dagger over the brook, and allowed the strange insect to creep over to the other side. Alan's attention was now fixed on this strange sight. He followed it, and saw it disappear right into a part of the old ruin, which was thickly overgrown with heather and moss. It did not stay long in this place, but, crawling out again, it made its way back to the sleeper, and re-entered his mouth. Alan was so amazed he could not keep silent any longer. He gave a cry which awakened Colin.

"What is wrong with you?" Colin asked, sitting up and yawning.

"You have wakened me from a beautiful dream. I dreamed I was walking through a fine, rich country, and came at length to the shores of a noble river; and just where the clear water went thundering down a precipice there was a bridge all of silver, which I crossed; and then, entering a noble palace on the opposite side, I saw great heaps of gold and jewels, and I was just going to load myself with the treasure when you rudely awoke me, and I lost all. I am going to dig in the ruins—perhaps I'll find the treasure; and if I do I'll restore it to the Church," Colin Kerr said.

"I'll help you," said Alan; but his face was evil as he said the words, and when Colin was not looking he hid the stolen dagger in his belt.

They had no proper tools, but they set to work with their hands, and, sure enough, they found, just at the place where the strange insect had entered, a hoard of gold and silver, and silver vessels, and armpieces and jewels.

"Colin," Alan whispered, "could we not keep this to ourselves? No one knows about it, and we found it."

Colin turned on him in rage. "The things belong to the Bishopric of Dornoch," he said. "Often and often have I heard my father tell the story. Remember what happened to the man in the Bible that took the garment and the wedge of silver, and the bar of gold."

"Old wives' tales," Alan cried.

Colin, his face white with rage, turned on him with angry words. Then, like a flash, Alan had his dagger out—it flashed through the air, there was a queer choking sound, a sobbing breath, and Colin sank on his knees, fighting, with a stream of blood flowing from his throat.

"I—call—that—tree—to witness," he gasped, "that—I—have—been—foully murdered."

But Alan heeded not. He was mad with excitement, and scarcely gave a thought to the murdered man.

In frantic haste he tore up the stones, and found more buried treasure—there were gold and silver church vessels, coins far more than he could carry. He gloated over his hoard—it was all his—all his! He threw a triumphant look at the figure of the dead man—and then suddenly, for the first time, he noticed how strange the tree looked. It was almost as though it were standing peering down at him, lifting up its arms in horror. Its blasted top seemed to peep out at him from the leaves like a face.

He felt a momentary chill, but next minute he had turned to his find again—he was filling his pockets and his knapsack with the treasure.

* * *

Late that evening he returned with a spade and buried his companion at the foot of the tree. It was not a pleasant task, and he knew that if he would stop to think he would be miserable. So in frantic haste he hid his crime, filled a sack with money, and hurried away.

It is said he went to the town of Perth to live, and that he became a wealthy man. No one knew how he had come by his money, and no one wished to make friends with him. He lived alone, and by and by people began to notice that this unhappy-looking rich young man was always followed by a shadow. It was not his own shadow either, but that of a tree with a blasted head and strange outspread branches. One man, Harry Murray by name, went the length of saying that one evening he had seen this shadow tree, and that from its top a white and terrible face had looked out.

Alan himself pretended to be unconscious of this strange shadow, but often as he walked on the road he would stop suddenly, and so would the tree shadow. Once, impelled by some unknown force, he journeyed back to Speyside and found the actual tree just as he had first seen it. No one had ever inquired about Colin Kerr. His secret was safe. The tree with the dead man buried beneath it could not do him any harm.

That night the tree kept step with him, walking beside him, peering forward as if to look into his face, watching him, threatening him, filling him with nameless and numberless terrors.

This went on for years, so say the records, which also relate that "for all his gear, he never got a friend to bide wi' him, nor a lass to marry him. At last he was weary of it all, and went to the priest and told him the way of it." The priest listened to the strange tale.

It is said that Alan sought to enter the monastery to make reparation. All the wealth which had brought him so little happiness he restored to the Church, but the tree overshadowed him till his dying day, which came very soon after his confession.

The Reverend Dr. Forsyth, minister of Abernesby, tells that the queer tree has long since rotted away; but the Tree-Man is still to be seen, flitting—a ghost, with a tree shadow—along Strathspey.

The True History
of Anthony Ffryar

by Arthur Gray

The world, it is said, knows nothing of its greatest men. In our Cambridge microcosm it may be doubted whether we are better informed concerning some of the departed great ones who once walked the confines of our Colleges. Which of us has heard of Anthony Ffryar of Jesus? History is dumb respecting him. Yet but for the unhappy event recorded in this unadorned chronicle his fame might have stood with that of Bacon of Trinity, or Harvey of Caius. *They* lived to be old men: Ffryar died before he was thirty—his work unfinished, his fame unknown even to his contemporaries.

So meagre is the record of his life's work that it is contained in a few bare notices in the College Bursar's Books, in the Grace Books which date his matriculation and degrees, and in the entry of his burial in the register of All Saints' Parish. These simple annals I have ventured to supplement with details of a more or less hypothetical character which will serve to show what humanity lost by his early death. Readers will be able to judge for themselves the degree of care which I have taken not to import into the story anything which may savour of the improbable or romantic.

Anthony Ffryar matriculated in the year 1541–2, his age being then probably fifteen or sixteen. He took his BA degree in 1545, his MA in 1548. He became a Fellow about the end of 1547, and died in the summer of 1551. Such are the documentary facts relating to him. Dr Reston was Master of the College during the whole of his tenure of a Fellowship and died in the same year as Ffryar. The chamber which Ffryar occupied as a Fellow was on the first floor of the staircase at the west end of the Chapel. The staircase has since been absorbed in the Master's Lodge, but the doorway through which it was approached from the cloister may still be seen. At the time when Ffryar lived there the nave of the Chapel was used as a parish church, and his windows overlooked the graveyard, then called 'Jesus churchyard', which is now a part of the Master's garden.

Ffryar was of course a priest, as were nearly all the Fellows in his day. But I do not gather that he was a theologian, or complied more than formally with the obligation of his orders. He came to Cambridge when the Six Articles and the suppression of the monasteries were of fresh and burning import: he became a Fellow in the harsh Protestant days of Protector Somerset: and in all his time the Master and the Fellows were in scarcely disavowed sympathy with the rites and beliefs of the Old Religion. Yet in the battle of creeds I imagine that he took no part and no interest. I should suppose that he was a somewhat solitary man, an insatiable student of Nature, and that his sympathies with humanity were starved by his absorption in the New Science which dawned on Cambridge at the Reformation.

When I say that he was an alchemist do not suppose that in the middle of the sixteenth century the name of alchemy carried with it any associations with credulity or imposture. It was a real science and a subject of University study then, as its god-children, Physics and Chemistry, are now. If the aims of its professors were transcendental its methods were genuinely based on research. Ffryar was no visionary, but a man of sense, hard and practical. To the study of alchemy he was drawn by no hopes of gain, not even of fame, and still less by any desire to benefit mankind. He was actuated solely by an unquenchable passion for enquiry, a passion sterilizing to all other feeling. To the somnambulisms of the less scientific disciples of his school, such as the philosopher's stone and the elixir of life, he showed himself a chill agnostic. All his thought and energies were concentrated on the discovery of the *magisterium*, the master-cure of all human ailments.

For four years in his laboratory in the cloister he had toiled at this pursuit. More than once, when it had seemed most near, it had eluded his grasp; more than once he had been tempted to abandon it as a mystery insoluble. In the summer of 1551 the discovery waited at his door. He was sure, certain of success, which only experiment could prove. And with the certainty arose a new passion in his heart—to make the name of Ffryar glorious in the healing profession as that of Galen or Hippocrates. In a few days, even within a few hours, the fame of his discovery would go out into all the world.

The summer of 1551 was a sad time in Cambridge. It was marked by a more than usually fatal outbreak of the epidemic called 'the sweat', when, as Fuller says, 'patients ended or mended in twenty-four hours.' It had smouldered some time in the town before it appeared with sudden and dreadful violence in Jesus College. The first to go was little Gregory Graunge, schoolboy and chorister, who was lodged in the College school in the outer court. He was barely thirteen years old, and known by sight to Anthony Ffryar. He died on July 31, and was

503

buried the same day in Jesus churchyard. The service for his burial was held in the Chapel and at night, as was customary in those days. Funerals in College were no uncommon events in the sixteenth century. But in the death of the poor child, among strangers, there was something to move even the cold heart of Ffryar. And not the pity of it only impressed him. The dim Chapel, the Master and Fellows obscurely ranged in their stalls and shrouded in their hoods, the long-drawn miserable chanting and the childish trebles of the boys who had been Gregory's fellows struck a chill into him which was not to be shaken off.

Three days passed and another chorister died. The College gates were barred and guarded, and, except by a selected messenger, communication with the town was cut off. The precaution was unavailing, and the boys' usher, Mr Stevenson, died on August 5. One of the junior Fellows, sir Stayner—'sir' being the equivalent of BA—followed on August 7. The Master, Dr Reston, died the next day. A gaunt, severe man was Dr Reston, whom his Fellows feared. The death of a Master of Arts on August 9 for a time completed the melancholy list.

Before this the frightened Fellows had taken action. The scholars were dismissed to their homes on August 6. Some of the Fellows abandoned the College at the same time. The rest—a terrified conclave—met on August 8 and decreed that the College should be closed until the pestilence should have abated. Until that time it was to be occupied by a certain Robert Laycock, who was a College servant, and his only communication with the outside world was to be through his son, who lived in Jesus Lane. The decree was perhaps the result of the Master's death, for he was not present at the meeting.

Goodman Laycock, as he was commonly called, might have been the sole tenant of the College but for the unalterable decision of Ffryar to remain there. At all hazards his research, now on the eve of realisation, must proceed; without the aid of his laboratory in College it would miserably hang fire. Besides, he had an absolute assurance of his own immunity if the experiment answered his confident expectations, and his fancy was elated with the thought of standing, like another Aaron, between the living and the dead, and staying the pestilence with the potent *magisterium*. Until then he would bar his door even against Laycock, and his supplies of food should be left on the staircase landing. Solitude for him was neither unfamiliar nor terrible.

So for three days Ffryar and Laycock inhabited the cloister, solitary and separate. For three days, in the absorption of his research, Ffryar forgot fear, forgot the pestilence-stricken world beyond the gate, almost forgot to consume the daily dole of food laid outside his door.

504

August 12 was the day, so fateful to humanity, when his labours were to be crowned with victory: before midnight the secret of the *magisterium* would be solved.

Evening began to close in before he could begin the experiment which was to be his last. It must of necessity be a labour of some hours, and, before it began, he bethought him that he had not tasted food since early morning. He unbarred his door and looked for the expected portion. It was not there. Vexed at the remissness of Laycock he waited for a while and listened for his approaching footsteps. At last he took courage and descended to the cloister. He called for Laycock, but heard no response. He resolved to go as far as the Buttery door and knock. Laycock lived and slept in the Buttery.

At the Buttery door he beat and cried on Laycock; but in answer he heard only the sound of scurrying rats. He went to the window, by the hatch, where he knew that the old man's bed lay, and called to him again. Still there was silence. At last he resolved to force himself through the unglazed window and take what food he could find. In the deep gloom within he stumbled and almost fell over a low object, which he made out to be a truckle-bed. There was light enough from the window to distinguish, stretched upon it, the form of Goodman Laycock, stark and dead.

Sickened and alarmed Ffryar hurried back to his chamber. More than ever he must hasten the great experiment. When it was ended his danger would be past, and he could go out into the town to call the buryers for the old man. With trembling hands he lit the brazier which he used for his experiments, laid it on his hearth and placed thereon the alembic which was to distil the *magisterium.*

Then he sat down to wait. Gradually the darkness thickened and the sole illuminant of the chamber was the wavering flame of the brazier. He felt feverish and possessed with a nameless uneasiness which, for all his assurance, he was glad to construe as fear: better that than sickness. In the College and the town without was a deathly silence, stirred only by the sweltering of the distilment, and, as the hours struck, by the beating of the Chapel clock, last wound by Laycock. It was as though the dead man spoke. But the repetition of the hours told him that the time of his emancipation was drawing close.

Whether he slept I do not know. He was aroused to vivid consciousness by the clock sounding *one.* The time when his experiment should have ended was ten, and he started up with a horrible fear that it had been ruined by his neglect. But it was not so. The fire burnt, the liquid simmered quietly, and so far all was well.

Again the College bell boomed a solitary stroke: then a pause and another. He opened, or seemed to open, his door and listened. Again the knell was repeated. His mind went back to the night when he had attended the obsequies of the boy-chorister. This must be a funeral tolling. For whom? He thought with a shudder of the dead man in the Buttery.

He groped his way cautiously down the stairs. It was a still, windless night, and the cloister was dark as death. Arrived at the further side of the court he turned towards the Chapel. Its panes were faintly lighted from within. The door stood open and he entered.

In the place familiar to him at the chancel door one candle flickered on a bracket. Close to it—his face cast in deep shade by the light from behind—stood the ringer, in a gown of black, silent and absorbed in his melancholy task. Fear had almost given way to wonder in the heart of Ffryar, and, as he passed the sombre figure on his way to the chancel door, he looked him resolutely in the face. The ringer was Goodman Laycock.

Ffryar passed into the choir and quietly made his way to his accustomed stall. Four candles burnt in the central walk about a figure laid on trestles and draped in a pall of black. Two choristers—one on either side—stood by it. In the dimness he could distinguish four figures, erect in the stalls on either side of the Chapel. Their faces were concealed by their hoods, but in the tall form which occupied the Master's seat it was not difficult to recognise Dr Reston.

The bell ceased and the service began. With some faint wonder Ffryar noted that it was the proscribed Roman Mass for the Dead. The solemn introit was uttered in the tones of Reston, and in the deep responses of the nearest cowled figure he recognised the voice of Stevenson, the usher. None of the mourners seemed to notice Ffryar's presence.

The dreary ceremony drew to a close. The four occupants of the stalls descended and gathered round the palled figure in the aisle. With a mechanical impulse, devoid of fear or curiosity, and with a half-prescience of what he should see, Anthony Ffryar drew near and uncovered the dead man's face. He saw—himself.

At the same moment the last wailing notes of the office for the dead broke from the band of mourners, and, one by one, the choristers extinguished the four tapers.

'Requiem aeternam dona ei, Domine,' chanted the hooded four: and one candle went out.

'Et lux perpetua luceat ei,' was the shrill response of the two choristers: and a second was extinguished.

506

'Cum sanctis tuis in aeternum,' answered the four: and one taper only remained.

The Master threw back his hood, and turned his dreadful eyes straight upon the living Anthony Ffryar: he threw his hand across the bier and held him tight. 'Cras tu eris mecum,' he muttered, as if in antiphonal reply to the dirge-chanters.

With a hiss and a sputter the last candle expired.

The hiss and the sputter and a sudden sense of gloom recalled Ffryar to the waking world. Alas for labouring science, alas for the fame of Ffryar, alas for humanity, dying and doomed to die! The vessel containing the wonderful brew which should have redeemed the world had fallen over and dislodged its contents on the fire below. An accident reparable, surely, within a few hours; but not by Anthony Ffryar. How the night passed with him no mortal can tell. All that is known further of him is written in the register of All Saints' Parish. If you can discover the ancient volume containing the records of the year 1551— and I am not positive that it now exists—you will find it written:

> Die Augusti xiii
>> Buryalls in Jhesus churchyarde
>>> Goodman Laycock ⎫
>>> Anthony Ffryar ⎭ of yᵉ sicknesse

Whether he really died of 'the sweat' I cannot say. But that the living man was sung to his grave by the dead, who were his sole companions in Jesus College, on the night of August 12, 1551, is as certain and indisputable as any other of the facts which are here set forth in the history of Anthony Ffryar.

Two

by Al Sarrantonio

Sometimes now, when a cup fell from a cupboard, or a book fell from its shelf, or a spoon hit a pan or the television snapped on loud, she suddenly heard the scream of brakes.

"Mom?"

He placed his knife on his fork, ever so gently, but the sound went through her like a fingernail down a blackboard.

"Yes, Tanny?" The voice was a practiced voice, not really her own. The practiced voice was calm; her own voice wanted to scream and scream like those brakes.

"My birthday—"

"I know, Tanny," and the practiced voice spoke a little too quickly, a little too loud.

He came close, a mop of dark amber hair over darkly serious eyes, and carefully opened a paper, putting it by her plate. *A boy without a father.* She wanted to touch him, but she was afraid that if she touched him, if she lay her hand on his head, he would fall to pieces and that when the pieces hit the floor she would hear the wail of locked brakes forever.

Oh Carl, why can't you be here for him again!

And then Tanny was gone, with the door to his room clicking gently shut (*scream!*) and the house grew winter cold around her.

That night, each night, she dreamed a dream. Sometimes it began with Tanny and Carl fishing on the short dock that jutted crookedly into the blue lake as she looked on. Sometimes she sat in a wooden-slatted beach chair and watched while Tanny and Carl flew a kite in the small meadow by the cabin, or while they rowed in aimless circles at the exact center of the lake while their laughs, high and low and crystal clear over the water, reached her content ears. Sometimes Carl and Tanny were sitting at dinner in the cabin while she served them, a single candle orangely illuminating their faces for her. This is how it had been in life: she the happy spectator as her son and husband lived their happy lives before her. After one of these scenes, the rest of the dream was always the same. They were in their bright yellow station wagon—Carl and Tanny in matching short-sleeved red and white checked sport shirts and she in a light blue dress. Carl drove, and they moved down the brown and green mountain like a drop of white wine down an upheld corkscrew. There was laughter in the car, Tanny's high laugh mixing with the low laughs of she and Carl. Tanny hit a camp pan with a spoon and he and Carl sang for her in the back seat. And then suddenly there was the scream of locked brakes, and then all the bright colors, green and brown and yellow and blue, turned bright red—

Oh Carl! she cried out, awakening; and his name, his face and his deep laugh were all mingled with the sound of locked and screaming brakes.

In the day she looked at her son and wanted to cry because his father was not there for him.

It was snowing when Tanny's birthday present came. It was unloaded by two men, tall, in coveralls and parkas, but they were gone nearly before they were there. The big box was opened and suddenly the truck was gone and Tanny was gone, leaving her stranded outside his closed bedroom door.

"Tanny?" her practiced voice said.

"Thanks, Mom." The voice was distant.

She began to speak again but then she went away.

Dinner sat and cooled, and after the time for patience came and went she knocked softly on his door. She heard a shuffling, the flick of a switch (*scream!*). She reached for the knob but suddenly he was there.

"Sorry," he said, and he rushed past to the dinner table, closing the bedroom door behind him.

There was a candle-flame in his eyes, a warmth that hadn't been there for a long time. It warmed something in her, and for the first time in a long time the screaming went away.

"Tanny?"

He looked up, a startled deer.

Suddenly she didn't need the practiced voice.

"I . . . know how hard it's been on you since . . . the summer," she said, and as she said this the screaming tried to start again, way down at the bottom of her mind. "I . . . I know how much you miss your father, how much fun you two had together. I know you miss all those places he used to bring you and the things he did for you. I know you miss the things he used to make, the puppets and the toys he brought home as a surprise, and the popcorn he made, and the surprises he always had. I . . . wanted you . . . to know that I . . ."

She couldn't go on, and then her body was trembling all over and in her ears the sound, the high, tearing, locking sound . . .

Beyond the screams that filled her ears she heard the soft click of a bedroom door.

In the night, after the dream came and was gone and with it all its horrid sounds, as she lay breathing quietly again in the center of her large, sweat-soaked bed, she heard laughter. Tanny's voice was there, and another one, lower-pitched.

She held her breath and closed her eyes, and the voice didn't go away.

"And then we'll build a campfire," Tanny's voice said.

Muffled laughter.

"And then can we go to the movies?"

The other voice said something she couldn't hear, and then the two voices laughed again.

In bare cold feet she made her way to his room. Under the door were colors, red and green. As she threw open the door she suddenly remembered waking up in the hospital to see that Tanny was there but Carl wasn't. *I don't know how any of you got out alive, there was nothing we could do for your husband, we think the other driver was drunk, poor boy, growing up now with no father* . . . She remembered the red and white checked sport shirt Tanny still had on, the torn sleeve on one arm, the v-shaped rip showing his bruised skin underneath, the blank, struck-animal look of loss in his eyes . . .

"Tanny . . ."

"Mom."

On the screen before him, as he hit a button, something red moved away into the distance, becoming haze.

"I was just playing a little bit."

She looked at the screen, at her son.

He held up a fat book of instruction meekly for her inspection. "You program in numbers and stuff and it . . ." He looked down. "It makes someone for you to talk to."

She reached down to touch him and suddenly she was lost again, powerless, trembling.

"No, Tanny, it's . . . all right. Go back to bed."

Oh, Carl!

All through the night she dreamed of Tanny and Carl together

510

again, and in her wakeful moments the laughter and voices from Tanny's room came and went . . .

In the morning, after Tanny's cocoa cup was drained and his snow-boots were buckled and his mittens dry and secure and his hood and books in place, after the yellow bus had gobbled him up (she always closed her eyes when this happened, listening for the snap of the closing door that would start the screaming in her ears), she went into his room.

She went in there to dust, she told herself. She went in to straighten up, to take all the empty boxes and string and paper stuffing from his birthday present away. She did all this, and more. She straightened the comic books and dusted his reading lamp; put his running sneakers and hiking boots back in the closet. She did all this, and then she stood before the machine.

It looked more of a mystery to her than it had the night before. Now, with its buttons unlit and cold, with its screen a cold green eye, it looked dead and yet somehow *alive*.

She touched a button and nothing happened.

She touched a green button, way off to the right, and winced at the sound of a flicking switch.

The screen went bright and something, a red shadow, was there, moving across the screen and then gone.

A boy without a father.

"Carl?" she whispered, and then she quickly touched the green button again, watching the screen turn dark, dead green, and hurried from the room.

The days and nights passed, and the voices and laughter continued.

"Tanny, we have to talk."

"I'll be late for school, Mom."

"I'll drive you."

Over his oatmeal, he looked up. "You never drive," he said, and it was an accusation.

She said, very slowly and carefully, "I've heard you every night with your machine."

"Oh," Tanny said in a low voice.

"I want you to know it's all right as long as you don't carry it too far."

He looked as though he wanted to find a place in his oatmeal to hide. "Thanks."

"Tanny—" she started to say, wanting to tell him as her shivering began how much she wanted more than anything in the world to have his father back again so that she could watch the two of them and be happy, but he pushed away from the table, and was into his coat and out the door just as the bright yellow bus stopped to swallow him up.

In the long morning, at each tick of the hall clock and each creaking sigh of the big empty house settling around her, she sat in her chair and heard the imaginary screaming of brakes.

The world went round. White snow melted into gray slush, which melted into silver water, which melted into the warming earth. Green shoots, tender things with strong roots, shot up, along with white dandelions that waved in the wind and then exploded, sending themselves away. The sun burned warm yellow again. School boys grew thin, as winter mittens were packed into mothball boxes and hooded snowsuits turned, like midnight pumpkins, into canvas jackets with thin zippers.

The spring didn't warm or launch her, but found her wrapped all the more tightly in her cocoon. By day she wandered the house restlessly, straightening and then straightening again; by night she lay awake staring at a spot grown hers in the center of the darkened ceiling and listening to the laughter from Tanny's room. She tried to think of Tanny and Carl together, but this only brought a chill to her bones. She never went into his room now; but sometimes, when the door lay open a crack or when he ran out to his bus, leaving it open, she would walk slowly past, as though in awe, and steal a look at the icy blank screen within. *Carl*. She and Tanny hardly spoke; their meals were silent eating times with only the setting out of plates beforehand and the cleaning of dishes afterwards to frame them. When the yellow bus disgorged him after school he went to his room, and when he finished his supper he went to his room again. On Sunday he stayed in his room all day. It finally came to her, through the thick, gauzy layers of her isolation, that his bond with the machine was becoming too strong.

"School will be over soon, Tanny," she said one Sunday, when the sunlight was so warm and close it seemed to heat the food on their plates.

He nodded distractedly.

"Would you like to go away for the summer, just you and me?"

He looked up, as if seeing her for the first time in a long while. "Where?" he said. There was discomfort in his voice, as if he wasn't sure he was really speaking with her.

She took a long slow breath, fighting the demons within her.

512

"We could go to the mountains." Again a measured, practiced breath. "To the cabin."

He looked at her so hard her composure began to crumble, but then she realized that he was trying to comprehend what she had said.

"You mean it?"

Fighting the paralysis that wanted to overtake her, she nodded, and tried to smile. "I thought we could fish, get the old boat out—though we might have to work on it a bit to get it in shape."

"Really?" There was a trace of excitement in his voice; but it disappeared as he saw the suddenly terrified look on her face which she was unable to hide any longer.

"I guess not, Mom." Again he looked down at his plate, getting ready to dismiss her from his thoughts.

With great effort she froze a smile on her face.

"I really mean it, Tanny. Just like old times. I can watch while the two of you—"

She was unable to control herself then. The trembling began in her hands and soon her whole body was shaking. Then she was sobbing into her hands. She couldn't stop shaking, and the tears wouldn't stop. *"The . . . two . . . of . . . you . . ."* she sobbed.

When she did stop crying, and looked up to see that it was dark in the house and that the warm May sun had gone away leaving only night, leaving her alone in a pool of darkness, she heard, down the hall from behind the closed door the sound of laughing voices, and she knew that now there really were two of them again.

May bloomed into June. The yellow bus drove quicker these days, hurrying toward the end of school and summer rest. The bus seemed almost angry, impatient for these last few school-days, these days of tests and short-sleeve shirts and the abrupt and rude opening of windows by shouting girls and boys calling to friends on the sidewalk, to be over.

She passed these mornings in the kitchen, at the table before her cold cup, or in the livingroom, sunk deep in a chair in the one dark corner where even spring and coming-summer had not penetrated. She felt as if she were wasting away; as if, within her cocoon, the time for blooming had passed and now all that was left was slow and inevitable decay. Each day the cold chair swallowed more of her; and in her mind, as if she were chained to a seat in a movie theater, or strapped before Tanny's machine, she endlessly reviewed scenes of Tanny and Carl doing things together while she watched. Her nightmare became a constant day and night visitation which always ended with the same scene of blood and loss. She thought of Tanny recreating these same scenes with his father in front of his machine, and these thoughts made her even more helpless in the face of the mounting dread and weakness she felt.

Tanny avoided her. He walked from the room if he stumbled on her quiet, shade-like figure. They ate their meals at the same table but there might well have been a wall of brick down its center; and, when he took to leaving his meals uneaten, to go back to his room, putting a more material wall between them, she said nothing. Only her body spoke then, and the shuddering and the sobs it gave her filled her with nothing.

As the month wore on the noises from Tanny's room grew strangely quieter. Suddenly there was little of laughter from behind the closed door, only great frightening silences punctuated by sullen words of assent and approval. She wanted to move from her clinging bed when this happened, but her body would not let her.

When he came down to eat his silent breakfast on the last day of school something moved deep within her. There was something there, a small and violent flame that burned still in a place where there was no grief or fear, and it suddenly kindled and pushed her to action.

"Tanny," she said weakly, and she had to rise in painful stages from her living room chair. She could hear him in the kitchen, hurrying to finish, hurrying to be gone before she could face him.

"Tanny," she cried, and as she stumbled to the hallway he was past her and out the front door, slamming it (*scream!*) behind him. She rushed to the window and as he stepped on the bright yellow bus he looked fleetingly back at her. There was an odd look, of surprise, almost, on his face, and something else strange about him . . . And then the bus was gone.

For hours she hovered around his room like a lost bird. She tidied the room next to it; the room behind it. The rugs in the hallway she brushed and then vacuumed and then brushed again. The laundry closet across the way she cleaned from top to bottom. The chair in the living room beckoned but she blocked it from her mind, knowing that by what she was doing that tiny flame within her was pushing her toward the place she had to be.

Finally, late in the afternoon, she pushed open the door to Tanny's room.

The flame within her almost died at that moment. She fought to control the shivering that began with her hands, the thing that would destroy her and make her unable to go on. The room was . . . different. There was no laughter left. There was a sense of defeat—of death

514

—in the air. Suddenly she knew the worst that would happen, what the dread and chill and weakness of the past months had been leading her toward.

Please Carl, no.

She now saw that the machine was on.

As she closed the door behind her and turned, she saw its blinking Christmas-color display and her heart gave a skip as that *something,* that red formless shadow, moved back and away from her on the screen.

She moved closer, and the screen remained perfectly flat to her, glowing soft ruby.

Again the shadow moved toward her, away.

"Carl?" she said, barely controlling her voice. "Carl, can you speak to me?"

That shadow again, an outline with a dark nebulous center, there and gone.

"You have to talk with me!"

Leaning over, she hit a gem-like button.

Nothing happened, and she hit another and another.

The screen abruptly changed, showing an out-of-focus outline of a figure that wavered and then broke up into static.

"Carl, talk to me!"

The ruby screen returned. The shadow moved across from right leisurely to left, then disappeared.

Suddenly in her mind she saw Tanny get on the bright bus that morning again and she knew what had been strange about him: He was wearing his red and white checkered sport shirt, the one he had been wearing the day of the accident; in her mind's eyes she saw the torn fabric on the arm falling open as he stepped up into the bus, looking back at her with that odd look . . .

She knew what Tanny was going to do. *A boy without a father.*

"Carl!"

She hit the gem-filled console with her fists.

The screen went gray, and then green, and then a shadow, as from down a long tunnel, moved closer to her and became large and then became defined. The edges filled in, replacing green with the hardness of bones. Around the bones wrapped muscle, and then the fine lines of vessels carrying pumping red blood, and then a fine taut layer of skin and clothing and fine features.

The figure began to laugh, a fine, low, melodious sound impregnated with sadness and sharing.

It was her own laugh, her own face.

"Well, Tanny," her own image said to her from the screen, the face she used to wear in the summer, the clothes the blue and yellow summer clothes she used to wear, the hair the fine fresh-washed and perfume smelling hair she used to have. "Have you thought any more about it? Do you still think this is what you have to do?" The figure gave out a warmth and an understanding that bathed the room.

The figure waited for an answer that didn't come.

"We'll talk about whatever you want," it went on, after a moment. "I know how lonely you feel. You know I try to help as much as I can. Though I may not know how to fix a bicycle very well, or how to make a puppet or put on a magic show, you know I'll try to help you with whatever you need." The figure brightened. "After all, now that your father is gone and there's only the two of us, we're all we've got, right?" Again the figure waited for an answer and then went on in a more soothing, infinitely sad tone. "Are you really sure you have to go back to your father? Aren't the two of us enough?"

Out in the street there was a sound, the stopping of a bus and then the unmistakable scream of locked brakes. She fell across the machine, her thin hands caressing it as though it was a child. She knew that someday someone would come, opening the door very quietly so as not to make the screaming start in her ears, not knowing that it was there always now, to find the two of them.

Under the Eaves

by Helen M. Reid

Thump—thump—thump.

Spasmodically, above the wailing of the wind and the dismal battering of the rain against the windows, the ominous sound was repeated.

Thump—thump—thump.

Something was hitting against the side of the house—something heavy. Hannah rose uneasily and laid down her sewing. Susan would be coming for the dress in the morning, but she could not keep her mind on the stitches.

She thought resentfully of Judy. The ingrate! That was the thanks you got for twenty years of slaving. To be left alone with nothing to listen to but the wind and the rain and that hideous thumping.

For perhaps the twentieth time that night she pulled the shade back from one of the windows and stared out into the darkness. Thump—thump. The sound was close now, but beyond the window was an abyss of blackness in which she could see nothing. Shivering, she sat down once more in front of the grate, where a fire struggled fitfully against the fury of the storm without and the semi-darkness of the room within. In its wavering circle of light she sat erect and defiant, the flames outlining her sharp features and thin knot of graying hair.

It wasn't because she was getting old, she told herself sternly. A night like this would get on anybody's nerves. If Nate hadn't cleared out as he did—She frowned impatiently.

"Where'd they a been without me, I'd like to know," she muttered. "And now they don't care what becomes o' me. Neither one o' them."

Anyway, thank goodness, the thumping had stopped. But what was that? Someone knocking? Who on earth would be venturing out in such a storm? But the knocking was repeated.

Resolutely she threw the door open. A rush of rain and wind blurred her vision for an instant, and in that instant a man pushed past her, a tall man, thin and somewhat stooped, with straggling gray hair that hung dripping about his seamed face; for in spite of the roughness of the night he wore no hat.

Hannah turned to face him; then abruptly she slammed the door shut and locked it.

"So you've come back to the old woman, have you?" She confronted him scornfully. "Found out nobody else would put up with you, I suppose."

He made no reply but settled himself in his favorite chair by the grate.

"That's right," she went on bitingly. "Make yourself comfortable. How you've got nerve to come back after walking out on me like you did I don't know."

"Seems to me you told me to walk out." His words were pleasant but disturbingly sarcastic. She noticed that his usual docility of manner was entirely gone.

"Better get on some dry clothes," she snapped. "You'll catch your death of cold."

A faintly sarcastic smile was his only reply. He made no movement, and for once she was at a loss what to say. She felt baffled and confused.

"You told me to go," he repeated, "and I went. Why do you blame me?"

She felt her face growing hot at the quiet rebuff.

"Blame you?" she retorted. "I blame you for being a shiftless, good-for-nothing fool, that's what. Look at Clem Hanks. You don't find him dilly-dallying his time away, and what's the result? He makes more money in a day than you'll ever make in a month. And if there's anything more useless than a man that can't make a decent living, I don't know what it is."

"You convinced me of that."

Something in his voice made her look at him intently. "Nate," she said slowly, "you know I don't mean things half as bad as I say them. If I'd a thought you had spunk enough to get out I'd a never told you to and that's God's truth."

She pointed to the sewing that lay where she had left it. "If it wasn't for the work Susan Hanks gives me to do I don't know how I'd keep body and soul together. Now you're back, maybe—"

"Won't Judy help?"

She fidgeted under the gaze of his steady eyes. "That girl—" She checked herself.

"Well?"

"She left after you did."

"Because—"

"Because she turned against her own mother, that's why. Didn't I do everything for her with my own hands? and now she takes sides with you. I'm sure I don't know why."

"Maybe I *was* of some use," he suggested.

"Land knows I'm glad enough you came back. I don't know what's come over me, but what with you gone and Judy gone, this place is like a tomb."

Thump—thump—thump. There it was again!

"I wish you'd see what that is," she said. "It gave me quite a turn when I was alone, but now you're here—"

The fire had burned low. Nate's chair seemed to have drawn back into the shadows.

"You won't mind, will you?" She was not in the habit of asking that question, but tonight seemed different.

Thump—thump—thump.

"Nate!"

518

A sudden flare from the dying fire illuminated the room. Nate's chair was empty!

"Nate! Nate!" she called wildly.

The wind shrieked around the house in a paroxysm of fury. The rain lashed against the windows. There was no other answer.

Thump—thump.

A cold trembling seized her. She ran to the window and threw it open. Thump—thump. The thing was almost close enough for her to touch. She reached out. Her hand closed on a sodden sleeve, a man's arm. She screamed. The next instant she had swayed and fallen.

When she opened her eyes she was stretched out in bed with Susan Hanks bending over her.

"Clem heard you scream and came and got me to look after you," she explained.

"Is he—dead?"

Susan looked away. "Yes," she said.

"Can't they do—something?" There was a note of pleading in Hannah's harsh voice. "He was in here," she said. "I was talkin' to him just before I found him—out there."

Susan left the room quickly. Hannah heard her speaking to someone in a low voice. Then the words of Clem's reply came to her distinctly.

"Better send for Judy," he said. "She is delirious. Nate was hanging from those eaves all evening. The doctor says he's been dead for hours."

A Visitor from Far Away

by Loretta Burrough

The wind was scooping great whining hollows in the air, whirling the snow against windowpanes and frosted roof of Laurel House, piling it deep upon projecting cornices, rolling it into soft white drifts on the

519

unprinted path to the front door. It was very still within the house; the hinges of a loose shutter squealed, groaned, worked up to a terrific bang against the wooden walls, squealed again.

It was so silent that to the woman lying quiet and nervous in the bed, the page she was turning seemed to shout hoarsely as it slipped back against its fellows, although she knew it had only whispered beneath her thumb. She was reading a book on astronomy, but as time passed she found it harder and harder to think about stars, harder to remember that they were shining somewhere beyond this blizzard in all the veiled brightness of their galaxies.

It was the knowledge that she was alone in the house, completely solitary, that frightened her. There were too many rooms beyond whose empty lighted windows (lighted by her as darkness fell, to cheat that dark) the pale white storm dipped and swayed. Ever since the Occurrence—that was how she phrased it to herself, as though it had been an eclipse, or an earthquake—she had taken good care not to be without a friend or servant in her house at night. Solitude was an invitation to those dreadful and oppressive thoughts that would sometimes descend upon her like a dark hawk even in the midst of a crowd's gayety; but more apt to happen—oh much more!—in solitude. And although the source of those thoughts lay twenty years back, and Mrs. Bowen at forty-five did not look in any way like Mrs. Bowen at twenty-five, they were one and the same and therefore subject to bad dreams and a strange horror of being left alone.

Mrs. Bowen closed her book and threw it aside, lay there a moment listening to the high-pitched voice of the storm, and then turned to look at the pink enameled face of the French clock on her dresser. Since she had last looked, time had crept on, turning the soft ticking into minutes, into half an hour; the small fragile hands pointed to a quarter of twelve. Her heart seemed to sink with depression. What was the matter with those intolerable servants! They knew the way she felt about being left alone. "Sure, ma'am," Nora had said, the rosy Irish brogue thick in her voice, "we'll be back quick as ever. If 'tweren't Mother was so sick—" And she had taken her sister in tow behind her, repeating, "We'll be back by ten-thirty, sure." An hour and fifteen minutes late, and not one word from them!

The doctor said this fright of hers, this horror of being alone, was all nonsense. Well, perhaps so, but it was not toward the doctor that Roger's reptilian head had turned that day in the dark shining courtroom, with the rain falling in thunderous torrents outside the windows. It was not to the doctor that Roger had said, in the moment of silence after the judge's voice sentencing him to life imprisonment for killing his wife's lover had ended, "I'll get even with you. I'll never stop thinking of how to do it. I'll never forget you—or forgive you." No, it had been to her, his wife, that Roger had pointed his long hand that always made her think of a spider, and spoken his ugly words.

Her dark brows contracting, Mrs. Bowen, forgetting now that it was all over long ago, put her hands to her throat with a curious look of terror. She was thinking of Roger and *that* night, months before his trial, when, the smoking empty gun flung away from him, he came at her, his fingers crooked for her throat, filthy names pouring from his lips.

And then, exhaling a deep relaxing sigh, she got out of bed and went to the window. She had been near, that time twenty years back! It had been touch and go for days after their man-servant had broken in and pulled Roger's fingers from her neck. She had testified at the trial gladly, eager to weave a thick strong rope for Roger's death. But they had only given him life imprisonment.

The curtains pulled behind her, she looked out at the blizzard. The snow seemed very deep, swirling into queer high shapes along the roof edge, like punch-bowls and cardinals' hats. In the light from the windows downstairs the flakes shone like sugar, rising and dipping; she had an oppressive feeling of the vastness of this billowing frozen movement that filled the night. Could it possibly—she sucked in her breath at the thought—be bad enough to keep the servants in the village? And even as she wondered, one hand pressed against the cold pane, the telephone rang in the room behind her.

The sound of the bell was like a gleam of light brightening her dreary thoughts; it suddenly made her again the middle-aged Mrs. Bowen whom everybody imagined a respectable widow, retired, occasionally taking a quiet part in the life of the near-by town, of whom nobody would have believed a connection with murder. Her steps quick across the thick rug, she hastened to answer.

"Ma'am?" That was Nora, her rich Irish voice coming faintly across the crackling wires; the connection was poor. "I'm terribly sorry, ma'am, but we can't get out tonight. The snow's that deep! I tried the garage and Haley's taxi stand, everywhere—nobody'd take us—they said 'twas suicide."

Mrs. Bowen was silent for a dark moment before she burst out, "But you girls can't, *can't* leave me alone here all night. It'd be different if George was home." George was her chauffeur, away on a two-weeks' vacation; it would be days before George even bought the return ticket that would bring him ultimately to Laurel House again.

Behind her back, she felt the empty place listening as though it were sardonically amused, the wind drawing away and returning to batter at the walls with a vigorous shout of renewal, the shutter at its unending cycle of squeal and bang. From the corner of her eye, she could see the white face of the snow peering in at her.

"You've got to come," she said, her voice rising. "You've got to come! Walk, if it's necessary."

"Ma'am!" Nora's voice was exasperated beneath its coating of servility. "We couldn't get two feet, ma'am. If you'll just look out the winder—the drifts is terrible. There ain't a car on the roads. Sure God himself couldn't walk it! Maybe tomorrow morning—we'll try hard then."

"Oh, Nora—" she said, despising herself for pleading, yet unable to stop. She had never been alone all night since *it* had happened twenty years ago; deep in her was this fixation, black with pain—not to be alone with the darkness and the unforgotten past. "Nora," she stumbled on, "I'll double your wages, if you start now and get out here!"

"Ma'am, we couldn't. We couldn't for a million dollars." The voice at the other end sounded protesting and cold. "Nobody can get out of town tonight, ma'am. Why don't you just turn on the radio nice and loud, fix up a little snack to eat, and then go to bed?"

"Oh!" said Mrs. Bowen, dropping the receiver back on the hook with a choked groan. It seemed to her that in the few moments she had been talking, the storm had grown worse. The wild sleety rattle of the snow against the windows sounded like unhappy voices complaining of something strange and terrible, beginning to speak of it far away in the white hills, and coming closer and closer until they shouted it against the shingled walls of Laurel House.

"Now," she suddenly said aloud, standing in the middle of the room with her fingers pressed against her forehead, "I'm not going to be an idiot. There's nothing to harm me here; certainly *he* can't harm me here, and that's all I'm afraid of, isn't it?" Disliking the foolish sound of her voice speaking in the emptiness, she stopped. What had Nora said? Turn on the radio, fix herself something to eat, go to bed. But—

The lights flickered; for a moment, the small glowing filaments in the bulbs failed and faded before they burned brightly again; somewhere, distant in the storm, a line had gone down, there had been some trouble.

Mrs. Bowen looked, her mouth quivering, at the room now bright again. That wouldn't do, would it? It wouldn't be very nice if the lights, all the lights, should go out; that would leave her alone in the dark. But there was, she was sure, a candle wrapped in the lower drawer of her dresser. She had it out in a moment, a bright yellow candle, set it in a holder on her dresser and lighted it. *Now* if the current went off—She saw that her hands trembled.

I'm a fool, she thought, looking at herself in the mirror; it showed a middle-aged woman with a fair, quiet face. It was all because Roger was not, somehow, an ordinary man. The threats of an ordinary man you could meet with laughter, but Roger's threats—his narrow gray eyes, with the look one moment so drowsy, the next so intense, the sharp cruel curving lines of his mouth, the long narrow hands that had always reminded her, because they were dark, crooked, brown and covered with hair, of two spiders crawling—all of Roger made it seem too sure that he had the power to make *his* threats come true.

It gave her pain to remember his face or his words or anything about him; memory of him was like a hand at her throat. She picked up the small French clock from her dresser and began to wind its delicate key, telling herself that when the hands touched twelve again it would be tomorrow and the sun would be shining.

And just as the slight little clicking sounds ceased within the mechanism and she set the clock back in its place, she heard a door open, and close, in the house.

For a moment she stood there, an imperceptible flash of time while her heart did not beat or air move in her lungs, and then she said suddenly, very loud, "Who's that? Is that you, Nora? Katie?" But of course it could not be Nora or Katie because she had been speaking to Nora only a few minutes ago, and she had said they could not come out. Besides, they could not have reached here from the village in so short a time; even on a fair night in an automobile they could not have made it. Nevertheless—her fingernails dug sharply into her palms, and her head turned slowly, listening—she was no longer alone in the house.

It had not been the wind that had opened and shut that door; although she was hungry to believe it, she knew it had not been the wind. The house was too sound, too solid. No, there was someone else within these walls and she must be sure at once whether it was friend or enemy. Her mouth was a little open; she could hear her breath coming between her lips with a small whistling sound—she could not help thinking that in the intervals when the wind outside sprang up blasting snow against the ringing windows, someone, anyone, could be coming slowly nearer and nearer to her while she could not hear him.

Spasms of cold seemed to sweep over her body as she moved to the dresser, jerked open the top drawer and took up the small revolver she always kept there. With it in her hand, she went to the bedroom door and paused with her fingers on the knob. Suddenly, a feeling of relief came hot and strong into her heart. Of course, of *course!* That was it. In the letter she had received from her chauffeur this morning, he had said he would be back Thursday, and this was only Monday—but he must have changed his plans. This was good sensible George who had come in downstairs, probably half numb with the bitter cold. She would give him the key to the cellaret in the library, and tell him to take some whisky to prevent his getting a chill. She twisted the door-knob.

Puzzled, she stared at the complete darkness beyond the door. Why had he turned out all the lights that she had left so brightly burning downstairs? The sound of sleety snow rattling on the long windows of the hall landing came up to her out of the blackness; an apprehension, formless and vague, seized her heart.

"Is that you, George?" she called. "Did you just come in a moment ago? Answer me, please!"

She waited, breathing quickly, listening to the noise of the storm and the silence of the dark lower house that seemed to be listening too, and then slammed the door shut and locked it quickly. She had just realized that if there were no cars on the road, no foot travelers, because of the blizzard, neither could there have been a George. A few words turned slowly in her mind as she looked at the blank panels: *But it was not the wind! There is someone here; yes, there is someone here.*

And there was nowhere to look for help. Outside the house was nothing but the whirling wastes of drifted snow and the wind that came rushing from the hills. Her eyes, turning here, there, and back again, touched the telephone. The police! They would surely try to come, to one in need.

She hurried across the room, the pearl-handled revolver clutched in her fingers, her ears intent, listening behind her. As she stooped to pick up the instrument, it rang with a sharp jangle beneath her hand.

"Hello, hello!" she cried into the mouthpiece. "Please, will you get the police for me? I want the police—I am all alone in my house and someone has broken in. This is Mrs. Bowen, Mrs. Bowen—Laurel House—please—"

A small voice, distinct and cool, came back. "I'm sorry, the connection is very bad—they are having trouble with the line. I cannot hear you. I want Mrs. Bowen, I have a telegram for her. Is this Mrs. Bowen? Will you speak louder, please?"

"Yes, yes," she groaned. "But please, I want—"

"I will read your telegram now," the voice went on. " 'Mrs. Roger Bowen, Laurel House, Galeville, Connecticut. Regret to inform you Roger Bowen died suddenly here today. Please wire disposition of body.' Signed Henry Adams, Warden San Marco Penitentiary. This connection is so poor, I'm afraid—there it goes!"

A series of sharp, sputtering clicks and the line went dead, as though it had suddenly frozen under the long piling weight of the snow. And almost as the telephone connection went, the electric lights faded, brightened, dimmed out at last to dark bulbs, and slowly the lighted candle on her dresser seemed to grow stronger in the dimness.

But Mrs. Roger Bowen was not aware of the telephone or the lights. She was watching the candle from the corners of her eyes. It seemed to her that two thin crooked brown hands were slowly descending out of the darkness toward the flaring flame.

The hands made her think—yes, they made her think of two spiders.

Waiter Number 34

by Paul Ernst

Chatham Kearns and Pierce Harkness walked leisurely toward the two chairs in the center of the Fifth Avenue window of the Console Club.

They were two choice chairs, but no one ever took them save Kearns and Harkness. Since the two had joined the club a dozen years ago, they had taken an unwritten lien on those chairs. No one ever disputed the lien: Harkness was worth nearly six hundred million dollars, and Kearns was cautiously rated at four hundred and fifty millions, though everyone knew his actual holdings totaled more than that.

The two men sat down—Kearns spare and small, like an undersized chicken hawk with frosty gray eyes and lank gray plumage; Harkness tall and corpulent, with small blue eyes like diamond points in a round, good-natured face.

"The same, Kearns?" said Harkness.

"The same," Kearns nodded, his voice dry and precise.

Harkness' big laugh boomed through the vaulted room of the Console Club.

"Vermouth! Is that a drink for a luncheon appetite? A martini would be more to the point."

"Not with my blood-pressure," said Kearns. "And not when I discuss matters of the importance of those to be decided in your board room this afternoon."

Harkness merely laughed again and flicked his gaze toward a figure in the wine-red livery of the club service near by.

The figure came toward their chairs, head inclined deferentially, face pleasant but blank. The man had an extraordinary face. It was very pale, and emaciated. His body was very thin, too, with a thinness which was exaggerated by the fact that he was nearly six feet tall.

Kearns gave the order, frowning a little as he did so.

"A vermouth and a martini. Serve them here, please. And tell the chef we'll lunch, a little later, on the fish I had shipped up here from my Florida place."

"Very good, sir," the man murmured, bowing a little. His voice was dull, pitched in a monotone.

He started toward the club bar.

"Just a minute," Kearns' dry voice rasped.

The man came back.

"You're new here, aren't you?"

"Yes, sir," the man said. "That is, I am new to most of the members, sir. I worked here many years ago—till 1917, when I left the club service to enlist."

He stood there, thin pale face impassive under Kearns' deepening frown. "Anything else, sir?" he said finally.

"No. I—" Kearns waved his hand irritably. "No. That's all."

The man left. Harkness stared at the irascible line between Kearns' frowning brows.

"What's the matter?" he asked carelessly.

"That man!" snapped Kearns. "That waiter! Number 34, I think his shield said. I don't like him."

"What's wrong with him?" said Harkness, smiling jovially.

"He has a face like a death's-head. Didn't you notice? He made me feel positively cold while he stood here."

"Kind of skinny," boomed Harkness in agreement. "What of it?"

"I just don't like him. The club should have cheerful-looking servants. I think I'll speak to the steward—"

"Oh, don't do that," said Harkness, who was a humane and kindly

526

man. "These are rather hard times. Why throw a man out of a job just because you don't like his face?"

Kearns drew his spare shoulders up, then relaxed them. He lit the cigar Harkness passed him.

"I'll have someone else serve us in the future. . . . About this afternoon's meeting, Harkness—"

He drew at the cigar, emitting small, precise puffs of smoke.

"The decision will probably go as you and I want it to go. And just between us two—I think the time is highly propitious."

"So do I," nodded Harkness, modulating his heavy voice so that it would not carry so far. "Did you read this fellow What's-his-name's report in yesterday's *Times*? Nearly two million young fellows just out of schools and can't find jobs. Those kids would go for a good war, Kearns."

Kearns nodded.

"And the rest of the country," Harkness went on, "has more or less got over the jitters of the last war. After all, nearly a generation has passed now."

"Some of the veterans talk pretty strongly," Kearns said cautiously.

"A small minority," Harkness shrugged. "No factor to be considered, when you remember the publicity channels we control. Radio, newspapers, politicians."

Their waiter came toward them with their drinks on a small tray. He inclined his head—he was the acme of subservience—and set the vermouth on the stand beside Kearns and the martini on the one next to Harkness.

"I'll sign the check," said Kearns, reaching for the pad and pencil on the tray.

"No, I'll sign it," boomed Harkness.

Kearns allowed his hand to be beaten by Harkness'.

"Anything else, sir?" said the waiter, taking back the signed check with long, very white fingers.

"That's all. . . . Wait." Harkness looked in his cigar-case. "Bring me half a dozen cigars. The man at the counter knows my brand."

"Very good, sir," murmured waiter number 34.

Harkness stared after the man with a small frown on his own face. Then he looked at Kearns.

"He *is* a peculiar kind of fellow, at that, though I can't put my finger on it. He's just—peculiar. Well, no matter. As I was saying, the human material for war exists in abundance—in these young people who have nothing on earth to do with themselves. And we have our propaganda machine in perfect shape—and now we have a lighted fuse to start war with."

"Precisely," nodded Kearns, sipping at his drink. "The *All Alone* incident is made to order."

"The United States and Great Britain are trying to settle the matter peacefully, though," said Harkness, pursing his lips.

"They can't if we bring enough pressure to bear on the two governments," said Kearns, his frosty eyes colder even than their wont. "Think of the points:

"The *All Alone,* an Australian ship, is suspected of bringing dope into our country. It turns out that suspicions were based on fact, but that's neither here nor there. Our Coast Guard cutters sink the boat when it refuses to stop at a shot across her bows. You see? A ship owned by a citizen of the British Empire is sunk, and the lives of British subjects jeopardized by our Coast Guard service! A thousand wars have been started for less reason than that."

"But the British don't want to make anything of the incident," grunted Harkness. "They agree the boat had no business trying to smuggle dope into the United States—"

"They'll talk differently when our British Export branches get busy. And a protest note from them can be magnified into an ugly thing. You know that, Harkness."

"I know," said Harkness, his amiable smile beginning to make its appearance on his good-natured face. "I'm just bringing up, in advance, the objections a few of our directors may bring up this afternoon."

"Those objections will be quickly disposed of," said Kearns, lips thinning masterfully under his hawk nose. "It's war—whenever we want it—and you and I know that if no one else does!"

"Yes," nodded Kearns. "War—"

He stopped. Waiter number 34 had appeared suddenly beside them with the ordered cigars on his little tray. Harkness stared at him keenly with his little, diamond-point blue eyes. The man's emaciated white face showed no sign that he had overheard anything.

"Will that be all, sir?"

"That's all," Harkness said.

"Damn the fellow," Kearns snapped peevishly, when waiter number 34 had left. "He moves like a shadow!"

Harkness grunted, and settled down in his great leather chair a little deeper. He crossed his legs and stared out the window at the shifting human patterns on the Fifth Avenue sidewalk.

528

"War, Kearns! You know what that means. You remember the last one."

Kearns' commanding gray eyes narrowed almost dreamily.

"Yes. Day and night shifts in your steel mills and chemical plants. All my marginal copper mines, now closed because there isn't enough market to run them profitably, opened again. All my coal mines humming. Metal and industrial stocks up a thousand per cent."

Precise small puffs came from his lips, from a cigar which burned with microscopic evenness around the ash-edge.

"But the country as a whole profits as well, Harkness. We mustn't forget that. Jobs for thousands, renewed spirit, young men taken into the service instead of rusting in idleness—all this will happen."

"Unless the war ends too quickly," remarked Harkness.

"Again, you only anticipate some of our objecting directors in pessimism, I think," Kearns smiled. "You know we can keep war flaming for months past its normal stopping-point. . . ."

His breath hissed between his teeth. Outright anger appeared on his spare, dominant face. Waiter number 34 had materialized beside their chairs again as though out of nowhere.

"Well? Well?" he snapped to the man.

"Pardon me, sir," the waiter murmured, voice deprecating, "the chef desires to know what salad he shall prepare—"

"Tell Louis to use his own initiative. We'll leave the rest of the luncheon to him. He ought to know what we like by now, and what will go well with the fish."

"Very good, sir."

The man glided away, his tall, thin figure seeming to melt into the shadows of the huge clubroom rather than disappear normally through the end doorway.

Kearns' eyes were icy as he gazed after him.

"Did it ever occur to you," he said to Harkness, "what a lot of things can be overheard by servants?"

"It's occurred to me many times," said Harkness dryly. "And for that reason I try to keep servants loyal to me. You know—jolly 'em along a bit. But there's no real danger in them if you avoid quoting actual figures and facts in their hearing. . . . Say, it's confoundedly cold in here, today, isn't it?"

"It is rather chilly," Kearns acquiesced, still glaring in the direction of the door through which waiter number 34 had gone.

Harkness finished his martini and chewed at the olive in the bottom.

"No use mincing words, Kearns. We and the interests we control can make a war out of the *All Alone* incident. We shall do so, in effect, this afternoon at the board meeting. Then we can phone our brokers to buy the right stocks, and begin buying raw materials for our factories at the present peace prices. We'll need some ships of our own, too. We can buy back a lot of the bottoms we sawed off at armistice terms seventeen years ago."

Kearns' thin lips parted a little in one of his rare smiles. Small, even teeth showed for a moment.

"War, Harkness," he said slowly. "Wartime orders, wartime profits. . . . Why, I remember a statistician of mine once figured up the profits I made from the battle of Verdun alone—"

Once more a shadow fell across the two men as waiter number 34 appeared beside their chairs.

Into Kearns' frosty eyes crept an expression that would have made any of his employees tremble. But waiter number 34 seemed not to notice.

"Beg pardon, sir," he murmured in his flat, dull voice, "but I thought I heard you gentlemen mention war. Is it your opinion there will be war again soon?"

Dull red surged in Kearns' gray cheek at such colossal impudence. But Harkness shot him a glance that commanded caution.

"There are always wars, my man," he said coolly. "There has never in history been a time when war was not being waged on some portion of the earth's surface."

"But I mean war such as the last big one, sir," said the waiter deferentially. "The World War. Are we facing another such catastrophe?"

"Who can tell?" Harkness said stiffly.

"You can take these glasses away," snapped Kearns.

"Certainly, sir." Waiter number 34 inclined his head. But he moved slowly as he put the empty glasses on his little club tray, and he did not move off at once.

"And I thought I heard one of you mention the battle of Verdun. Were either of you in Verdun, might I inquire?"

Kearns' eyes were icy lightnings. But Harkness, whose rough diplomacy had been a large factor in his enormous financial success, said:

"Hardly! Do you think we're the type to make good bayonet manipulators? I think I can say that our value to our country in time of war is far greater as industrial executives than it would be as soldiers in a trench."

"Of course, sir! I can realize that. But, begging your pardon, you are both in excellent physical shape, and you are both under sixty—I thought perhaps you had been officers during the war."

"That will be all—" Kearns began in a brittle tone.

But waiter number 34 went on.

"Quite a battle, Verdun," he said, gently, abstractedly. "I was in it. I was just a kid at the time. Nineteen. And as raw as any recruit that ever was shipped to fight another man's battles for him."

"Your reminiscences are not at all—" said Kearns in a strangled tone.

"I remember one hour particularly," waiter number 34 said almost dreamily. "But then, it is only natural that I should remember that particular hour."

Kearns' angry gaze ranged the clubroom for the steward or the assistant steward.

"It was a crowded hour, sir. I was in a sector where the shelling was hardest. The Germans had got our exact range an hour and ten minutes before, and were shelling us out of existence. And we were taking it pretty hard. Most of us in the division were youngsters, and most were as raw as myself.

"There'd been an attempt to go over the top that morning. No-man's land was littered with evidence of our failure.

"Right in front of our trench there was a pile of legs and arms, where a shell had exploded in a freakish kind of way that had somehow blown bodies out of existence but left the limbs—piled 'em like an untidy little pile of cordwood. Shells do funny things sometimes, sir.

"Beside the pile was a body without a head. That had been our second lieutenant. His uniform was immaculate except for the underside of him that lay in the mud and blood. His body had been untouched. Only his head had been taken off, clean as a whistle, leaving a bit of the neck-bone sticking up.

"But we didn't mind those things so much, sir. You get sort of used to them when you fight to save your country's honor. It was something else we minded more.

"Hanging in the barbed wire was a thing almost as ripped up as any of the dead youngsters that littered the ground. This was a buddy of mine by the name of Carrigan. He'd got caught in the wire and had had his spine notched by a machine-gun bullet so that he'd been paralyzed and unable to free himself. He'd hung there ever since, still alive."

Kearns' eyes flashed into Harkness'. But Harkness shook his head almost imperceptibly, though his own face was stony with anger.

"You'd laugh, sir, if I told you all the freakish tricks I saw war play. And one of them was the way Carrigan kept on living while he hung in the barbed wire.

"The air was crowded with shrapnel pieces and bullets—actually choked with flying metal. But only a little of it hit Carrigan, and then not mortally. He seemed to hang in a charmed spot. But Carrigan didn't want to be in a charmed spot. He wanted the end to come.

"You see, first he'd had his foot taken off at the ankle, as he hung there, and the mud his legs were dragging in had somehow kept him from bleeding to death. Then he'd had half his face shot away. And finally, toward the end, a bit of shrapnel had raked across his abdomen in such a way as to slice it half open, so that he—he kept spilling his vitals, if you understand me, sir.

"It was then that he'd stopped screaming for death to take him and began—just screaming. He didn't seem to stop for breath at all. He just yelled, on and on, staring at the part of him trailing through the rip. And it was that screaming that affected us in the trench so much.

"As I say, we were just a bunch of kids, fresh out of school when we enlisted. And our minds didn't seem tough enough to stand that screaming.

"We tried to kill Carrigan, because we all had loved him. But our fingers shook a little so that none of us could hit him, any more than the bullets from the other side could. He just hung there with a broken spine, and with his foot shot off and his body sliced open like a melon, screaming on and on out of his half of a face.

"The barbed wire held him up solidly. It was fine, strong wire. I think it had been made by one of your factories, Mr. Harkness, sir.

"You'd never believe what a body can go through before it dies. You'd have to see with your own eyes something like the drawn-out death of Carrigan. But it's hard to see a thing like that and stay sane. At least it was hard for us, his friends.

"All of us were going a little crazy, with the screaming and all, before that hour that sticks in my mind was over. And all of us were showing it in the way kids do in the trenches.

"The boy next to me—seventeen, he was, he'd lied about his age— had bitten through his lips so that I saw the white of his teeth through the red of a gash that was like a second mouth. Beyond him a farm lad a year older than myself was laughing. His laughing mingled with Carrigan's screaming, when both weren't drowned out by artillery fire, and I don't know which was worse. As he laughed he fired at Carrigan, loaded and fired, loaded and fired, and couldn't hit him.

"Down the line a youngster had finally stood up with a yell and climbed over the top to go and bayonet Carrigan. Of course he hadn't lasted very long. Three or four steps, he took, and he went down with something besides blood filling his helmet from a dozen holes in his head.

"That's all, sir. It was right after that that we started to yell as loud as we could, in a kind of chorus. And that drowned out the sound of Carrigan's yelling. It must have been a funny sight—all of us in that trench shouting, anything we could think of from prayers to blasphemy, with the farm lad's crazy laughing sounding above the rest. But then you see funny things in a war."

Waiter number 34 took a step away with his little tray on which the glasses reflected with crystal sleekness the sunlight pouring in the window of the Console Club.

"I hope you didn't mind my telling you these things, sir. I didn't mean to bore you—I just had the picture brought back to me, by your mention of war, of that hour when we yelled and stuffed our fingers in our ears to keep from hearing the screaming of the thing hanging in Mr. Harkness' barbed wire. Just an hour, seen by one man. It means little, of course. . . .

"It was just after we all started our yelling that a big one hit squarely in our trench and exploded."

He nodded subserviently, apologetically, and went off.

Behind him, Kearns sat rigid in his big chair, too angry for a moment to speak. Harkness' full face was apoplectic in hue.

"I'll have the steward fire him if it's the last thing I ever do!" Kearns said at last. "And I'll see to it that he's blacklisted everywhere in town! Such infernal insolence—"

"Fire him, yes," agreed Harkness, whose face had begun to get back some of its normal good-nature. "But let's not have him blacklisted, Kearns. Give the man a chance to find another job, if he can."

For Harkness was a humane and kindly man. . . .

Waiter number 34 went in through the swinging doors of the kitchen and set his tray and the empty glasses on the big dishwasher's rack. Then he moved slowly, wearily, toward the service door that opened onto narrow Eighty-fourth Street.

At the dishwashing machine a man with an artificial hand suddenly clutched the shoulder of the young fellow who assisted him. His fingers bit with a force that made the lad exclaim aloud.

"The man that just went out the door!" the dishwasher gasped. "That waiter! Who is he?"

"Number 34," growled the youngster, rubbing his shoulder.

"But his name! What's his name?"

"I don't know. He just started working here this morning—"

The man with the artificial hand ran toward the service door, opened it and looked up and down the street.

There was no sign of the figure in the wine-red club livery.

The dishwasher went back to his big machine, eyes cloudy and troubled.

"What's eating you?" said the younger man.

"That waiter—number 34," replied the dishwasher slowly. "His face looked familiar. Looked like a friend of mine that used to be a waiter here—same number, 34, too—back in 1916 when you were still a baby. But it couldn't have been him."

"Why not?" shrugged his assistant. "Guys do come back, sometimes, to work at places they worked in a long time ago."

"Not this man," said the dishwasher. "He died at Verdun in 1918."

The Woman in Gray

by Walker G. Everett

Bill was at a dinner party at the Carters when the subject first came up —a dinner to which he would never have gone if he could have thought of a single plausible excuse. Sarah Carter had a girl visiting her from the East; her school roommate or something, Bill thought vaguely. Bill was her dinner partner. They were talking about some people she didn't like.

"And they told it all over town," she said, "that I was the girl that was caught in the roadhouse, and that I had a red wig on so nobody would know me. Oh, how I wish I could get even with them—the most hateful people! Haven't you any suggestions?"

Bill looked pensive. Many Martinis had set up a pleasant buzzing in his brain, and everything in life se   very easy.

"You might tell everybody they have a crazy locked-up daughter nobody ever sees, and that's why they don't like young girls."

"Too easy. They have *three* daughters, all crazy, only not locked up. That is, yet."

"In that case, I don't know," said Bill. "Why don't you just leave it to me?"

She looked at him. "What do you mean? Do you make little wax images and stick pins in them?"

Ah! there she had stolen a march on him—because that was just what he had been going to say. So he took a piece of celery, applied his mental spurs to himself and came out in an inspiration.

"Haven't I ever told you about the lady in gray?"

"No! Who is she?"

"Just a lady in gray."

"Well, where is she?"

"She's right here beside me now!"

"Where?"—startled.

"Oh," said Bill, confidentially, getting into his stride, "you can't see her. I'm the only one that can see her, but she's right here by me all the time. I've known her for years."

"Goodness gracious!" exclaimed his partner. "Aren't you scared? Doesn't she haunt you?"

"Oh, no. She *likes* me. That's why she stays here.—Isn't it, Lady?" He turned and nodded to the imaginary figure beside him. "Of course, she's very modest, and goes out of the room when I'm undressed, but all the rest of the time she's here. Even her face is gray."

"Well," said the girl, making a violent effort to keep the conversation going, "doesn't she do anything at all?"

"Certainly. She gets after people I don't like."

"How terrible! Well, sic her on the Quarrys in Hartford, then. Tell her to do her worst."

"I will, right now. —Did you hear that, Lady? Hartford, Connecticut; Quarry's the name."

"The third house from the corner on the left," said the girl. "I don't want any mistake."

"She never makes a mistake," said Bill; "and now, I think dinner's over and we can get down to the serious part of the evening."

And that was the last Bill thought about it for two weeks, until Sarah Carter plowed across the room at a cocktail party, and said, "What's this about some Lady in Gray?"

"I don't know," said Bill. "What do you mean?"

"I had a letter from Elsa. She said to tell you your Lady in Gray did the work a little too well, and that you'd better be careful."

Bill looked thoughtful. "What else did she say?"

"Something about a family named Quarry. That had an automobile accident, and all died—five, I think."

"What a coincidence!" said Bill. "And what a story!"

He lost no time in telling it around, of course. It was a good story, with enough of pleasant actual horror in it, but not too much, the Quarrys remaining mythical; so that it was worth a chill and a laugh any place.

Two weeks later he was at a dinner at Corinne Gorman's house—a fine, old-fashioned dinner with old-fashioned cocktails before, new-fashioned highballs after, and good old-fashioned screaming all the way through. Bill sat by Corinne; her short boyish hair was circled with a gold band, and she had on a red velvet dress. She turned to him and pointed to two empty seats.

"I could kill those people," said Corinne. "They're always hours late anyway, and finally they phone from Winnetka that they've broken down." She tamped out a nice long two and one-half inch cigarette butt until it was twisted and grub-like. "Why don't you sic your Lady in Gray on them for me?"

"I would, but I don't hate them. *I* don't want them to turn over like the Quarrys," Bill answered.

"How well do you know them?" asked Corinne.

"Not very well."

"Well, I can tell you some things. They've named their children 'Peggy Jean' and 'Michael Peter'; they have some name for their car; they go to the circus every year, and laugh and laugh and eat cracker-jack and peanuts—that's the kind of people they are."

"Oh, well," said Bill, "I'd just as soon hate them myself. Sure, I'll send the Gray Lady after them—only they'd better look out."

That was the last they thought about it until dinner was nearly over, and Corinne was called to the telephone. She came back white.

"It was they," she whispered. "Terrible accident; a taxi hit them. Don't tell anybody for a minute."

"Were they badly hurt?" Bill asked.

"Yes."

He wondered suddenly if he ought to say anything about the absurd conversation regarding the Gray Lady. He decided not. Two coincidences were just a little too much. He knew there was nothing in it —hadn't he made her up out of a clear sky, just to amuse a guest of Sarah Carter? But, just the same, he felt it would be a little smart-alecky to allude to it. However, Corinne soon saved him the trouble.

536

"Never mention that Gray Woman again," she said. "Never, never, never, never."

"Oh, that didn't have anything at all to do with it," said Bill. "You know that."

"Well, I do. But it's a little too strange, that's all—as if Santa Claus should suddenly come down the chimney."

"Or you'd find a baby in a cabbage."

"I think that would be a great improvement," said Corinne. "But this isn't any time to be funny. I'll tell them now, and start the shrieks."

So Bill's Lady in Gray story became even more famous. "It's the funniest thing," people said; "somebody ought to send it in to the *New Yorker*. And you know, Bill is such a scream about it—he's afraid to hate anybody, he says, for fear she'll get after them—and he's going to rent her to the Government in the next war."

But Bill didn't think he was funny. He thought this, while not exactly playing with fire, was at least in bad taste. He didn't think he was in very good taste, anyway, for about this time he had a bad week; seven nights of drinking and running around town, cashing checks, all the time with a low wormish feeling of approaching reckoning under the talking, talking, talking of nightly parties to get over yesterday's hangover. And every day down at the office getting blearier, going to the water-cooler with the aspirin bottle in his hand and standing blindly in the window when the terrible eleven-thirty nausea swept over him in waves. But he didn't know what to do, because life didn't have much meaning, anyway, and he was having a better time than most people.

One warm night—it was the next Monday—he sat in his room, alone. The window was open, on blackness, soft and flecked with gold. The curtains were limp; his electric fan turned its flat face wearily from side to side, stirring up an ineffectual commotion in the air. A bell rang; he answered.

"Mr. Jacobson to see you."

"Tell him to come up."

What could he want, Jacobson from the office, whom he hardly knew, unctuous and self-righteous?

The door-bell buzzed.

"Come in. Good evening, good evening."

Jacobson came in and sat down. "Warm, isn't it?"

"Terribly."

"You probably wonder why I am here." Jacobson's mouse-like eyes took in the empty highball glass; the bowl of melted ice.

"Well," said Bill, "I do. Want a drink?"

"Thanks, no. Never touch it."

"Oh. O.K."

"What I wanted to see you about is this—Mr. Selfridge asked me to have a little talk with you—a friendly chat, merely, between friends," he purred.

Bill looked at him. "What a smack!" he thought. "Yes?"

"It's about your work—a word to the wise, as it were."

"Oh. Have I been lying down on the job? Am I going to get the gate?"

"Oh, no, not that. But the first, perhaps, a trifle. A little too many parties—eh? And Mr. Selfridge thought that just a quiet tip from a friend—"

Bill was reminded of the smile of a snake. "I see," he said. "Thank you."

"Oh, not at all—not at all. It's a pleasure."

"I don't doubt it."

"Oh, I didn't mean that! Well, I'll be running along." Jacobson got up. "Nice little place you've got here."

"Yes," said Bill. "I like it." (How he hated the man! Why didn't he go?)

"Well, I'd better go. I've got a new Chevy downstairs, and I have to go so slow it'll take me a while. I live in the suburbs, you know."

"Oh, you do? You have? How do you like it?"

"It's a fine little bus. You can see it from the window."

"I'll look out. Good-night. See you tomorrow."

"Good-night." And Jacobson was gone.

"That ass and his Chevy," thought Bill. "I wish—"

He went to the window, looked out. Presently Jacobson came out, climbed into a little yellow car with a black patch on the top, started out, and drove straight into the side of a big truck that had swung around the corner, with a horrible ripping and glassy noise.

"Good God!" said Bill.

He waited until he saw people, like sudden ants, flocking; then he came back, mixed himself a highball, and sat down on the couch. It had happened again. And just after being told all that about his job. Everything he did seemed to be wrong. And it was all his own fault. He gulped down his drink and made another, stronger. The light seemed so bright, and made the room look so empty, with only those

538

two black holes of windows, that he turned them out, and sat in the single ray that came from the bathroom.

When the lights were out, the room changed; the black windows became, gradually, a soft warm blue, like a promise of day to come. It was the room that was dark. But Bill just sat there, tapping his foot to some radio music that drifted in. Then he spoke out loud, "God! I hate myself!"

Then the door opened, and in came the Lady in Gray. Now, it wasn't anyone dressed up to frighten him, or his sister come to call. It was the Lady in Gray, and Bill knew it. He looked at her steadily as she came nearer, quietly, delicately. He felt his brains run down the inside of his skull like melting drug-store ice; the room started to rock, and then to swirl faster and faster. Finally she was halfway across the floor. He threw his glass at her. It smashed against the opposite wall.

Bill stood up and whirled around—the whole room was swinging in a grayish haze. He turned to the window.

They found him next morning, on the second-floor fire escape— one of those horizontal ones, with a weight on the end. He had landed almost in the middle, and was doing a ghastly little teeter-totter.

The Word of Bentley

by E. Hoffmann Price

The morning had been foggy. And now the whole world was one vast fog to John Bentley. The mist was becoming thicker, writhing and twisting, rolling in great banks to overwhelm him. He could just distinguish the faces of the train crew, whose strong hands had extricated him from the wreckage of his car. With a final effort he had waved them aside, so that they desisted from their attempt to move him. John Bentley's iron soul dominated those about him, even as it tottered perilously close to the Border. He knew that his daughter, Janet, kneeling at his side, would not step into the mists with him. For this he was glad, and glad also that an annuity that he had purchased in his day of power would provide for Janet and her mother.

But Bentley had one problem, and little time in which to solve it. He stared grimly into the fog that gathered, ever denser and yet more dense. He sought in his remaining moments to devise some way of keeping his word to Jim Woodford. To march alone into that engulfing grayness was nothing to Bentley, for he was weary, that morning early in 1930, and had been mortally weary ever since those fatal last days of 1929, when with a few other valorous, foolhardy souls he had sought to stem the rushing destruction that was overwhelming the market.

Some of those who had survived had faith in Bentley, and they had taken his unsecured word and given him a fresh start. But that terrible hammering had burned some of the iron out of his soul, so that the circling mists at the railroad crossing were a cool, quiet refuge undisturbed by the clack-clack of the teletype, and the flickering quotations of the tape.

He was only concerned with his word to Jim Woodford, who was now in the jungles of Yucatan, with his fortune in Bentley's hands.

"I'll watch 'em for you, Jim," he had said, as he grasped Woodford's hand, "till hell's no bigger than a cook-stove!"

And Woodford, knowing that John Bentley's word was his god, went on to the interior of Yucatan, far beyond any cable, or letter, or messenger.

The mists were crowding in closely, and John Bentley's word was becoming more tenuous than the shifting grayness. He knew that he could not keep it. And then, with one foot across the Border, that dying man whose dimmed eyes had seen only the failure of his one remaining purpose, grasped suddenly at a final hope. With an effort, he spoke, and put command into his voice.

"Janet, get my brief-case out of the wreck. Show these men where I kept it."

He could still distinguish those men he had forbidden to move him. He knew now why he had ordered them to desist.

Janet returned with the brief-case, and opened it.

"Pick out an irrevocable power-of-attorney form," he said, "and give me my pen."

The pen was broken, but enough ink clung to its point to enable him to sign his name, and have it witnessed.

"Janet, this gives you absolute authority over every share of stock I hold. I can't keep my promise to Woodford, but you'll do it for me. We can't fall down on Uncle Jim. So don't fail me."

And before his daughter could answer, the mists closed in on the speculator. She saw that he had gone smiling into the grayness, knowing that his word would be kept.

The weight of that trust bore down more heavily on Janet Bentley than the earth they had dropped into John Bentley's grave.

"Six feet of dirt is enough to keep any man in place," he had once said. "My old man couldn't afford a tomb, and I won't!"

Janet Bentley, with the appalling burden of that irrevocable power of attorney, wondered if any six feet of earth could bear down a man who had for so many years carried the load symbolized by that sheet of paper. She tried to explain it to her mother, who, though thirty years married to a speculator, still thought that preferred stocks were so called because of an unusual demand for them.

"Uncle Jim," she said, "has a strongbox full of securities up in Hartford. And the night he stopped to tell us good-bye, he developed a fidgety streak about leaving them to the mercy of whatever the market might do."

She paused, knowing the futility of explaining a "put" to her mother.

"So Daddy agreed to buy all of his holdings at a price lower than the recent quotations, but high enough so Uncle Jim wouldn't lose if the market broke badly. That way, he could go to Yucatan and not worry about returning and finding himself wiped out."

"But that was terribly foolish," protested Mrs. Bentley, "offering to buy them all at a certain figure, no matter how low they might drop. And I certainly don't think that you should worry about such a ridiculous promise. We've lost your father, and Jim Woodford will only lose some money."

"That's not the point," explained Janet, patiently. "Daddy wasn't taking any risk. He watched the tape every hour of the day. The moment things looked risky, all he would have to do would be to borrow some shares just like Uncle Jim had in his deposit box, and sell them before they dropped to the agreed price. And when Uncle Jim returned from Yucatan, he'd turn over his shares to the brokers that loaned shares to Daddy, and receive the price of those that were borrowed and sold. It's all very simple, isn't it, Mother?"

Mrs. Bentley admitted that it was quite clear. This paved the way for another objection.

"Why don't you turn that agreement over to Bennett & Keene? They could handle it."

"There is no record," replied Janet. "It was just a gentleman's agreement. And anyway, Uncle Jim may be gone so long that no house in town would sell a 'put' for that length of time. So I'm going to keep his word for him."

Mrs. Bentley sighed wearily. Gentlemen's agreements were such idiotic things.

"Mother, I've got to!" reiterated Janet. "Or he'd come out of his grave and do it himself. That's why his word was good when he was alive. That's why his friends staked him, last fall, so he could get a fresh start. If it came to the worst, I'd sell every share he's got, to protect his word to Uncle Jim."

"Janet, you'll do nothing that silly!" exclaimed Mrs. Bentley. "We'd have nothing left but that little annuity, we can barely live on."

"Try and stop me. I've got an irrevocable power of attorney. I can sell those stocks and buy bird seed if I want to!"

And Mrs. Bentley knew that she was beaten.

Janet consulted Charles Bennett, of Bennett & Keene.

"Miss Bentley," he assured her, "you have no cause for fear. We are rapidly recovering from the disturbance of 1929. Right now, they are betting that Steel will touch 200 within the next few days, and it's at 196 now. And if you sold short to protect Mr. Woodford's interests, you would run the grave risk of not being able to cover if the market advanced sharply. Very hazardous, Miss Bentley, very hazardous."

"Will you sell me a 'put' for Mr. Woodford's holdings, good until his return?" she demanded.

Mr. Bennett promptly declined, saying that Mr. Woodford might never return.

Janet did not know that even as Mr. Bennett spoke, there were underground mutterings in the Street. No one dared mention by name the giant who was rigging the market, so that he could dispose at a substantial profit of the many hundreds of thousands of shares he had bought during November to check the panic. One house did state in a bulletin that the "Old Man Across the Street" was doing a masterly job of making the market boom. That house suddenly collapsed. The others promptly issued optimistic reports, and recommended Steel at 195, and Telephone at 250. They dared not voice their suspicions about the sudden, unwarranted stock boom early in 1930.

Janet attributed her uneasiness to intuition, to the memory of John Bentley's last words, and the calm smile that had followed his iron-faced, grim peering through the mists.

"He's depending on me. Oh, Lord, if I could just look far enough ahead! They don't know, and those that do, won't tell the truth."

All that Janet could do was watch, and think. Think painfully, despairingly. John Bentley's word must be protected. That intangible gentleman's agreement had become a crushing burden. She went to

542

her father's office, of which she had the keys. It had not yet been subleased. She would sit in its emptiness, and make her decision.

"If I failed he'd turn over in his grave. I can't fail him. But I don't know what it's all about. They got an old veteran like him last fall. What can I do, now? Just sit and wait, and sell everything at the first sign of trouble, if it doesn't come so fast that I won't have time to sell."

Those terrible days of November, 1929, were still fresh in her mind. She knew with what deadly swiftness a market could drop.

As she sat there, Janet became acutely conscious of her father's personality in that office overlooking the street which had been his battlefield. At that battered desk he had fought his way up from nowhere. He had wrested a fortune from the tape that the ticker in the corner spewed forth by the yard. He had lost it, only to regain, and lose once more. And then, as he sought to recoup, Death had called him for more margin. And through all the vicissitudes of his career, he had clung to that dingy office, instead of moving to more ornate quarters during his prosperous days. The grimy plaster and the scarred woodwork had almost become a part of that old gray wolf who held fast to his word, until, as he had often said, "Hell was no bigger than a cook-stove."

Had his car been as far from the railroad crossing as his mind was that fatal morning, he would be at his desk, and in the chair that Janet occupied, keeping his pledge to Woodford, who was far in the jungles of Yucatan, unworried, and secure in the promise of John Bentley, who had never failed a friend.

The gray mists of that morning were surrounding Janet, now, as they had enveloped her father. The weariness of her mind had summoned them as a barrier to shut out the tumult from the outside. She could think better, sitting in his chair, and at his desk. There was a spot worn bare of varnish, where his elbow and forearm had rested; and there, neglected cigars had burned into the wood. That was the telephone into whose transmitter he had issued orders that had shaken the Street, and whipped the idly lagging tape to a frenzied gallop. And at that telephone he had sought to stem the debacle of November just past. If he were now at that desk, he would know how to protect Uncle Jim; he would know whether the Old Man Across the Street was rigging a rotten market to make it display unnatural optimism. He would know the meaning behind those symbols the ticker was printing on the narrow, white tape that was stronger than massive bars of steel, and more devastating than marauding armies. She could only read that so many shares of Steel had changed hands at such and such a price;

but he would know why, and what to do next, what order to snap into the transmitter.

A premonition of peril was shaking Janet as she stared at the ticker. Despite Mr. Bennett's suave optimism, a vague dread was gnawing at her. She was trembling, and knew not why, save that something was urging her to action. She sought to control herself, but in vain. John Bentley's presence now permeated the unaccountable wisps and veils of mist that swirled about the room, twining into columns like small waterspouts, and marching toward the ticker. Uncle Jim was in danger. If John Bentley were at the desk, he would know what to do.

Janet assured herself that the grayish mists were but the protests of nerves and eyes strained by worry. But she was no longer certain that John Bentley was not there.

She picked up the tape, blinked incredulously, regarded it again, then froze in horror. Steel couldn't be that low! She looked for the next quotation. It was lower. And the transactions were heavier. The tape was moving faster, now. That narrow strip of paper had the dreadful vitality of a charged wire. She was as sensitive to its menace as though she had been on the floor of the Exchange. Uncle Jim was ruined beyond redemption, wiped out as she sat there, in her father's chair. No wonder she had felt his presence. She had failed him, but he had not returned soon enough. She could not keep John Bentley's agreement to take Jim Woodford's stock at the agreed figure. It was too late. It was incredible that the market could have broken during the few minutes between Bennett & Keene's and her father's office, but the tape told the story. In despair she watched the prices drop, drop, drop, recover a fraction, and drop again.

Then she lifted the receiver from its hook, and spoke as John Bentley would have spoken: except that he would have been in time.

"Sell every last share. At the market. Immediately!" she directed, as she was connected with Bennett & Keene's office. "I'm not mistaken, and I mean what I say!"

Then she sank back in her father's chair, limp and faint from the ruin that had emerged from the ticker. The mists were thinning, and the grayness was no longer blocking the sunlight that filtered cheerlessly through the window-panes.

She left the office, and called on Bennett & Keene.

Mr. Bennett handed her the memorandum of the orders he had executed. She glanced at the first slip, gasped, looked at the ground glass screen on which the marching figures, greatly enlarged, were projected from the narrow tape.

"Why, what's the matter, Miss Bentley?" asked Mr. Bennett, solicitously, as he supported her by the arm.

She recovered from the dizziness that had for a moment clouded her senses. She looked again, and saw that Steel was at 197. The market had not crashed!

"Nothing, Mr. Bennett, thank you," she replied. "I've just been terribly worried lately." She knew better than to tell him who had urged her to look at that tape in her father's office. She scarcely dared tell herself the truth until after the clerk had written the check, and it had been signed, and countersigned.

Then Janet returned to her father's office, clipped the tangled mass of tape that lay at the foot of the ticker pedestal, and carefully put it into her handbag.

The market broke the following week. Janet called at Bennett & Keene's office regarding a minor detail of the transaction that had liquidated her father's holdings in time to protect his pledge to Woodford.

"Miss Bentley," demanded the broker, "what on earth made you sell that day? At the very top! Who tipped you off?"

She opened her handbag, and gave him a yard of tape, with its printed quotations.

"This," she said. "I read the tape in my father's office. Fortunately, the phone had not yet been disconnected. So I gave you a selling order, right away, before I could change my mind."

Mr. Bennett stared at the tape. Then he stared at her.

"Even now, they're not that low. Not yet," he contrived to say, as he frowned, perplexedly. "Where did you get this tape?"

She repeated her statement.

"Miss Bentley," he resumed, after another long, intent stare, "the ticker in your father's office was cut off the service cable the day after his death. It couldn't have been working and even in November, stocks weren't as low as it shows them. Haven't been for years! And this is new tape."

"Oh, well, let's not argue about it, Mr. Bennett," she replied, knowing the futility of discussion. "Just call it feminine intuition."

Whereupon Mr. Bennett attended to the business which had brought Janet to his office. Upon its completion, a few minutes later, she entered the customer's room again, where she paused to glance once more at the ground glass screen. Then she took the yard of tape from her handbag.

"Mr. Bennett," she said, "they've been dropping during our absence. Very rapidly. Now they are as low as they are shown on this tape which puzzles you so much. Look!"

He looked at the piece of tape, then glanced up, and saw moving across the ground glass those very figures, in the same sequence that was printed on the ribbon Janet had handed him. He stared blankly, and shook his head as if to deny his eyes. But as he recovered his speech, a frantic customer accosted him, and begged assurance that the bottom had been reached.

"Funny thing," said Janet to herself, as she left the customer's room. "I *did* notice that the ticker was dead when I stepped into Daddy's office. But somehow, I wasn't a bit surprised when it began printing quotations on the tape."

Janet did not pause for further words with Mr. Bennett. She knew that no sane broker could believe that a gray mist had set a dead ticker into motion so that John Bentley could keep his word.